BERNIE KOLENBERG/TIMES UNION

Debunking Vietnam myths

By JOHN OMICINSKI
Gannett News Service

WASHINGTON — Myths about the Vietnam War have persisted for decades, and may always be part of the folklore of the U.S. experience in Indochina.

A few, with attempts to set the record straight:

MYTH: Blacks died in the war out of proportion to their share of the U.S. population or in the U.S. military.

FACT: Caucasians made up 86 percent of Vietnam's 58,219 deaths, and 12.5 percent were African American, roughly their share of the U.S. total and well below their share of the

Vietnam infantryman saw 240 days of combat in a year because of fast-moving helicopters. In WWII, Pacific soldiers saw 40 days of combat over four years. The rate of amputations and crippling wounds in Vietnam was 300 percent higher than in WWII. Deaths would have been much higher were it not for the helicopter, which shuttled the wounded to hospitals in less than an hour on average. Those statistics come from the Vietnam Helicopter Pilots Association databases.

MYTH: Vietnam veterans' suicide rate was much higher than normal.

Sand in the Wind

Sand in the Wind

by Robert Roth

AN ATLANTIC MONTHLY PRESS BOOK

Little, Brown and Company — Boston — Toronto

FIRST EDITION

Portions of the lyric from "Someday Soon," by Ian Tyson, on page 478, © 1963 M. WIT-
MARK & SONS. All Rights Reserved. Used by permission of Warner Bros. Music.

Lines fom "If I Had a Hammer" (The Hammer Song), on page 284, Words & Music by
Lee Hays and Pete Seeger. TRO — © Copyright 1958 & 1962 LUDLOW MUSIC, INC., New
York, N.Y. Used by permission.

Library of Congress Cataloging in Publication Data

Roth, Robert, 1945-
  Sand in the wind.

  "An Atlantic Monthly Press book."
  I. Title.
PZ4.R84543San [PS3568.0856]   813'.5'4   73-8768
ISBN 0-316-75765-9

ATLANTIC-LITTLE, BROWN BOOKS
ARE PUBLISHED BY
LITTLE, BROWN AND COMPANY
IN ASSOCIATION WITH
THE ATLANTIC MONTHLY PRESS

Published simultaneously in Canada
by Little, Brown & Company (Canada) Limited

PRINTED IN THE UNITED STATES OF AMERICA

For all the numbers,
but especially the 0311's

Though the author served as a rifleman with the Fifth Marine Regiment in Vietnam, this book is fiction — neither personal account nor history — and its characters are fictional.

Then, returning to himself, let man consider his own being compared with all that is; let him regard himself as wandering in this remote province of nature; and from this little dungeon in which he finds himself lodged, I mean the universe, let him learn to set a true value on the earth, on its kingdoms, its cities, and on himself.

BLAISE PASCAL, circa 1650

BOOK ONE

1. Da Nang, July, 1967

The two groups of men studied each other — one group in a fenced-off area, the other passing by it. Each face searched the faces of those in the other group, seeking clues to what they themselves had looked like thirteen months past or what they would look like thirteen months hence — one group uneasy and alert, just off a plane from Okinawa; the other group laughing, joking, confident, ready to board it after waiting since before dawn for four or five of the longest, happiest hours they had ever experienced, now seeing the plane that would take them home, at last sure of something so long in doubt — their own survival.

The newly debarked group, some of them still glancing backwards, was led to the rear of the nearest building. They milled around nervously while waiting for their seabags. Beyond the barbwire fence less than twenty yards away, they could see a vast, shimmering plain of rice paddies stretching to the dark mountains miles in the distance. Dikes of gray-brown mud cut the plain into thousands of perfect squares, each a different shade of green. A few peasants and their water buffaloes moved slowly through the knee-deep water working these rice paddies.

An asphalt walkway ran along the near side of the fence, and every few minutes a young Vietnamese girl or two would pass by. The soldiers' eyes would follow these delicately beautiful girls. Their loose fitting black or white slacks ruffled beneath long, brightly colored silk dresses slit to the waist on both sides. Occasionally the girls would be carrying white parasols which accented the shiny black hair that fell gracefully down the hollows of their backs. Among the soldiers walked other, older, Vietnamese women in black slacks and dingy white blouses. Straw, cone-shaped hats blocked the sun from their lined faces. Many of them had crudely shaped cigars gripped between their yellow-stained teeth. These older women moved about with their heads down and their eyes scanning the ground for cigarette butts and pieces of paper to be swept into the dustpans they carried.

Occasionally a soldier would walk by holding a rifle balanced upside down on his shoulder, his hand on the front end of the barrel and a tag dangling from the stock. These weren't the M-14's or M-16's they had carried in the bush, but SKS's, formerly carried by Viet Cong or NVA soldiers. The newly arrived men stared at these rifles with envy, sometimes saying to themselves or to a friend, "When I leave Nam, I'll have one of them too."

A truck pulled up and the seabags in it were quickly tossed to the pavement. The men milled among them until, finding their own, they'd heave it on their shoulders and carry it towards the building. They would hesitate at the entrance until their eyes adjusted to the dim interior, then split up and join the appropriate lines to receive their orders. Rows of huge timbers supported the flat, corrugated roof and dwarfed the men standing near them. At one end of the building, a harsh artificial light glared down upon a few battered desks. A high counter separated this small area from the rest of the interior. Long lines of men stretched from the counter to the opposite end of the building. Other men sat or lay upon hard wooden benches. The atmosphere was similar to the gloom of a large, run-down train terminal.

In one of the shorter lines reserved for officers, there were only seven men. A major was talking to three of the others, all second lieutenants. This would be his second tour and he was enjoying the role of the old salt letting the boots know what they were in for. Behind these four, two more second lieutenants talked about a drunk they'd had in Okinawa. The last man in line, also a second lieutenant, faced away from the counter. His dark hair, though short, was cut somewhat longer than the "skin jobs" of the officers in front of him. He had the patient yet annoyed expression of someone accustomed, but never adjusted to standing in line. A half-smoked cigarette hung insolently from the corner of his mouth. He removed it and turned towards the counter. The line slowly shortened as he studied the spit-shined boots of those ahead of him. When he reached the counter, the clerk looked up with relief seeing that he was the last man to be processed. The lieutenant handed the clerk his orders.

"Lieutenant Kramer?"

"Yes."

"You'll be going to the Fifth Marine Regiment in An Hoa. Know anything about the Fifth?"

"No."

"The Arizona?"

Kramer shook his head.

"I wouldn't be in too much of a hurry to learn, sir. There'll be a truck by in about twenty minutes to take you to Ninth Motors. You'll be able to get a chopper from there. Wait right out front, somebody'll call your name."

4

Kramer nodded, lifted his seabag, and carried it to the entrance. Shading his eyes with his free hand, he looked for a place to set it down. The area was covered with prone bodies. Stepping over and between them, he made his way to an empty spot and jerked the seabag off his shoulder. He glanced at his watch, then stretched out on the ground using the bag as a pillow. After lying there a few minutes, he changed his mind and sat up, not wanting 'some lifer' to bother him about being unofficerlike. He glanced around with aloof curiosity, surprised at how calm and relieved he felt — glad to have all the training over with and not too concerned about what was to follow. What was there to be concerned about? Since his arrival everything he'd seen, every step he'd taken, had been expected, as if he'd done it a hundred times before. It was all a cliché. How simply he'd entered it, been caught within its slow momentum. Nothing remained but to follow it through — passively.

Kramer sat waiting. He became slightly more anxious and tried to keep from staring at his watch. Doing so always seemed to make time pass more slowly. The harder he tried to avoid it, the more he wanted to look. The watch was a Seiko, 'a good make,' he'd been told; but with an American's typical distrust for anything Japanese, he was always a little surprised to see it had the right time. He'd picked it up in Okinawa for thirty dollars and mailed his Rolex to his brother — 'No point in having some VC running around the rice paddies with a two hundred dollar souvenir.'

Kramer waited forty minutes, then decided to lie down again. It was over an hour before a corporal called out his name. The corporal told the men around him to get their seabags and board the six-by, an open troop-transport vehicle. The truck rambled over dirt roads for twenty minutes before reaching Ninth Motors. Kramer walked over to the company office to check in. A clerk glanced at his papers and spoke without looking up, "Fifth Marines." As he handed the orders back, he smiled and added, "The Arizona." The clerk then pointed across the road towards the helicopter landing zone. "The LZ's about a quarter mile that way, sir. When you get there, ask for a manifest slip and tell them you want to go to An Hoa."

More than forty Marines were waiting at the landing zone. Most of them had on jungle fatigues and boots worn free of polish. They lay around casually in small groups, taking advantage of what little shade was available. A confused-looking replacement walked towards Kramer to ask him a question; but upon seeing the officer's insignia on his collar, the replacement hesitated, then walked away. After an hour a helicopter circled. Practically everyone got up and started getting their gear ready. A member of the ground crew announced "An Hoa," and half the men sat down again while the others lined up at the edge of the landing pad. As soon as the chopper touched down, some men hurried off and those waiting to board rushed single file up the loading ramp.

Two benches ran laterally along the bulkheads. Kramer and about ten others got seats; the rest sat on the deck. Most of those on board were looking around smiling, enjoying the idea of getting from one place to another by a means other than their feet. Relaxed, Kramer leaned back against the bulkhead. He'd ridden on copters a few times before and had liked them. The chopper flew low and parallel to a ridge of mountains. Kramer looked over his shoulder out the window. Small streams billowed white down the mountains before reaching the rice paddies and becoming twisting ribbons of mercury. Tiny, barely moving human shapes dotted the various-shaded fields. The bright colors seemed alive and freshly painted. Scattered against the green background were numerous, perfectly shaped orange circles. Kramer mused about what they could be. 'Wells? No, too many. . . . Circular; man-made. . . . *Bomb craters!*' he finally realized, astonished at not having known this immediately.

The helicopter tilted to the opposite side leaving nothing but sky visible from his window. Kramer turned his head away and scanned the inside of the chopper. His eye caught a nervous face and he studied it until the copter started to descend. Again looking out the window, he noticed they were headed for a sprawling orange blotch in the corner of a large valley.

As soon as the helicopter landed, the passengers ran single file to the edge of the LZ. From there they headed off in different directions. Kramer picked out a corporal who looked as if he knew his way around. "Where do you check in at?"

"Follow me. I'm going by there."

An Hoa appeared to be a vast, orderless collection of huge bunkers. They were all rectangular, about six feet high, and constructed of large timbers packed with sandbags. Alleys of reddish orange dirt ran between the bunkers. Everything and everybody seemed to be coated with dust of this same color. It hung heavy in the air and Kramer could actually taste it in his mouth. He felt the sun upon his neck, and his eyes squinted from its glare. Carrying a seventy-pound seabag didn't make him any the more comfortable. In a few minutes, dark blotches of sweat had soaked through his clothing.

The corporal pointed to a large bunker, identifying it as Regimental Headquarters. Kramer dumped his seabag against its wall. A long line of enlisted men led through the entrance. He ducked beneath the low crossbeam and squeezed past them. The inside was dim and cavernous despite a number of fluorescent light fixtures hung crudely from the ceiling. Rough timbers stood at regular intervals supporting the roof. A wooden counter

6

ran the front length of the bunker, and behind it were a number of desks, only a few of them occupied. Kramer leaned against the counter, holding his orders in front of him. He was ignored by the first two clerks that walked by. A sergeant looked up from one of the nearer desks. Seeing Kramer, he slowly got to his feet and walked over. "Checking in, sir?"

"Yes."

"It'll take about a half hour to get your papers processed, sir. If you want, you can still probably get some chow at the officers' mess in the mean time."

"All right."

"Make a left as you go out the door. It's about six bunkers down. You'll see the sign."

"Thanks."

"You're welcome, sir."

The bunker was fronted by a fairly wide road. Marines walked along both sides of it. Jeep drivers, tearing around corners seeing how close they could come to splattering somebody on their windshields, yelled to friends they spotted along the road. Soldiers were hanging out of the backs of trucks shooting peace signs at everyone in sight. An occasional tank rumbled by with its driver looking straight ahead, daring anybody to get in his way. Anything that didn't move on two feet was followed by huge billows of orange dust.

Kramer noticed a group of shabbily dressed Vietnamese foraging through some garbage cans — 'The mess hall.' It was a small building of unpainted plywood walls with screens circling it just below the tin roof. He pushed the door open and saw that the messmen were starting to clean up. No one was eating, but a cook behind the chow line nodded so he went over and got a plate of what was left. Not liking milk, Kramer filled a canteen cup from a large thermos jug he thought contained water — only afterwards noticing the sickening green color of Kool-Aid. The food turned out to be just slightly worse than the stateside Marine Corps chow he had given up hope of ever getting used to. But he hadn't eaten since early that morning, so he forced the food down.

When Kramer got back to Regimental Headquarters, he was approached by the same sergeant. "Sir?"

"My orders."

"Your orders?"

"Yes, I'm checking in. You told me to come back in a half hour."

"Oh! Yes sir, they should be ready by now. I'll take a look." The sergeant returned to the counter reading the orders. "You've been assigned to Second Battalion, sir. It's outside the gate and about half a mile down the road. I'll get you a jeep."

When the jeep drove up, Kramer turned around to get his seabag. "Thought it was green," he mumbled to himself.

"What was that, sir?" the driver asked.

"Nothing, I just said my seabag used to be green, now it's brown," he answered while heaving it into the back of the jeep.

"The dust, sir?"

"Yeah, I guess you get used to it." The jeep lurched forward and headed down the road.

"No sir, not a chance. Around here it's either mud or dust — when you've got one, you pray for the other — but you never get used to either."

"Mud?"

"Yes sir, in the rainy season this whole fucking dump is covered with two feet of mud."

Kramer noticed a huge concrete superstructure just off the road. "What's that?"

"An Hoa's one of the few places in South Vietnam that has coal. The West Germans were building a big industrial complex here, but the war started and they had to pull out. Never finished the buildings, just the concrete frames. The only thing left is a hospital down the road, treats the villagers. They say sometimes a wounded VC walks in and they treat him too."

The jeep stopped in front of a wooden buliding. Kramer got out and entered it. A staff sergeant sat behind a desk and a first lieutenant leaned against it while talking to him. Kramer addressed both of them, "I just flew in from Da Nang. I'm checking in."

The staff sergeant stood up. "Yes, sir."

The first lieutenant offered his hand. "I'm Lieutenant Forest."

"Lieutenant Kramer."

"Glad to meet you, Kramer."

He turned and shook hands with the staff sergeant. "Staff Sergeant Allen. . . . Since the colonel's in the rear today, he'll probably want to talk to you. I'll take your orders and record book now."

Forest was about to address Kramer when a short, stocky man walked quickly through the door. "Good afternoon, sir. Lieutenant Kramer here has just been assigned to our battalion. Lieutenant Kramer, Lieutenant Colonel Nash."

They shook hands. "Glad to have you, Kramer. I'm sure we can use you."

'You won't be the first,' thought Kramer, nodding his head.

"Lieutenant Forest, if you're not too busy, why don't you show him around. Kramer, I'd appreciate it if you come back in ten minutes so I can talk to you."

8

"Yes, sir."

The colonel went into his office and Forest led Kramer out the door. "I guess the first thing you'd be interested in seeing is the officers' quarters so you can get rid of that seabag."

"Sounds like a good idea."

Kramer studied Forest as he led him between the plywood and canvas buildings. Though he was only slightly overweight, Forest's arms and face lacked muscle tone, making him appear fatter than he actually was. His close-cropped hair receded an inch or two at the corners of his forehead. He spoke with an almost feminine drawl. "Where you from, Kramer?"

"Florida, Miami, Florida."

"Hey, I've been there. Wild town."

"There're a lot wilder towns."

"I'm from Birmingham. Where'd you get your degree?"

"Gainesville, University of Florida," answered Kramer the way he always did when he thought the person he was talking to might otherwise say, "Oh, that's in Miami, isn't it?"

"That's in Miami, isn't it?" asked Forest.

"No, Gainesville."

"That's right, you said Gainesville, didn't you?"

Kramer nodded. "What'd you get your degree in, Forest?"

"Phys. Ed."

"Gonna teach Phys. Ed.?"

"No, I'm gonna make the Marine Corps my career. I just needed a degree to get my commission. It was real interesting though."

"I imagine it was." — 'A lifer. I knew it.'

"Did you see that Gook that just walked by?"

"Yeah."

"His name is Binh. He's a Kit Carson Scout. You know what they are, don't you — " Kramer did, but Forest continued without waiting for a reply. " — They're former VC or NVA who were captured or *chieu hoied*. We use them a lot. I make it a point never to trust a Gook, but he seems to be all right — brought up around here, knows the whole area like the back of his hand."

"Do you get many *chieu hois?*"

"Not around here. They usually fight to the death, but every once in a while we corner a few Gooks and they jump up yelling *"chieu hoi"* just to cheat my platoon out of some confirmed kills. The government gives the slant-eyed bastards a piece of land and more money than they've ever had in their lives."

"How long have you been here, Forest?"

"Call me Maynard."

Kramer waited a few seconds before asking again, "How long you been here, Maynard?"

Forest stopped in front of a plywood building. "Four months. This is our hootch." He grabbed Kramer's seabag. "I'll take it inside, and you can go see Nash."

"I've been looking at your record book, Kramer. The test scores in it indicate you're quite a bit more intelligent than most of the infantry officers we get here. This could make things a lot easier for you. Chances are it'll make them harder. Do you have any idea why you got infantry instead of finance . . . even though you have a degree in acounting?"

"I requested infantry, sir."

The colonel waited for more of an explanation but, when he saw none coming, went on. "I had a feeling you did. . . . As I was saying, you're going to see a lot of things done here you won't like. You're also going to see men get killed following orders you question. It's important, in fact it's your job, to see that there's as little of this as possible. You notice I say *possible*, because in most cases you won't be able to do a damn thing about it. This war's been going on for a long time. There's about as much chance of you changing the way it's fought as there is of you winning it single-handed. Your job is to make decisions within the boundaries set by your superiors, *and no more*. Otherwise you'll be risking your own neck and maybe the lives of your men. This war is just like any other — things are done in certain ways, not because they're best, but because they're judged best by those that make the decisions. Don't try and change things that can't be changed. You'll only end up doing more harm than good. Any questions so far?"

"No sir." While Nash spoke, Kramer concentrated more on him than on what he was saying. Kramer had expected a talk on how great the Corps was, what a good job it was doing, and how he was now a part of it and had a chance to add to its glory. He had also expected a lecture on the importance of the United States being in Vietnam. Kramer *hadn't* expected what he was now hearing. So far, Nash had refused to make a fool of himself, refused to give Kramer anything to scoff at. Kramer's chair seemed suddenly uncomfortable. Nash's eyes upon him, he remained motionless.

"I guess now you're mainly interested in what you'll be doing the next few days. First you'll stay here for five days of Induction School, then you'll join one of our rifle companies as a platoon commander. Anything else you need to know, you'll find out soon enough. I'm not going to waste your time. Any questions?"

"No sir."

As Kramer left the colonel's office, he wondered whether this had been the same speech all the boot lieutenants received. He doubted it. Kramer had been prepared to dislike Nash from the start, but so far he hadn't been able to find a good enough reason.

He was still thinking about Nash when he reached the officers' quarters — a rectangular, plywood building, fifty feet in length and a few feet off the ground. The interior was a single room, dark except where thin wedges of dust clouded light knifed in from the outside. At first the room seemed empty, but then Kramer noticed someone sleeping on a cot at the far end. Against the walls, a few stacks of modified ammo boxes served as shelves. In the center of the room stood a makeshift table made of some more ammo boxes with a poncho liner draped over them. A portable television and some magazines lay on top of it. Kramer fingered through the magazines while mumbling to himself, "*Playboy, Sports Illustrated, Leatherneck, Playboy, Leatherneck, Time* — how'd that get in there?"

Looking up, he noticed an M-16 lying on one of the cots. He walked over and picked it up, then sat down on the cot. Kramer pulled the bolt back and pushed his finger into the chamber. He examined his finger for carbon and nodded — 'Clean. Rule Number One: your rifle is your best friend, keep it clean.' He placed the rifle on his lap and leaned back against the wall.

'No surprises so far. . . . The way I wanted it.' And it was. He didn't have to be in Vietnam. 'Haven't regretted it yet,' he thought, but then remembered, 'Maybe . . . just that one time' — the time in the plane. He'd finished a month's leave and was headed for Camp Pendleton on the way to Vietnam. The plane took off into a bank of clouds. He felt relieved, free of decisions. All he could see were clouds swirling by his window — then, suddenly, no clouds. He glanced down, unthinkingly, immediately sorry that he had. The coast of South Florida lay beneath him, and off it the reefs. A thin white band sparkled between them like a ribbon of glass particles — the beach. But it was the reefs he stared at — light patches beneath the crystal blue water — wondering how many of them he had dived on. He saw them as if from a boat, remembering how the color of the water changed from light green, to blue, and finally to the rich dark blue of the Gulf Stream. The water was as he had seen it rarely — level, barely undulating, the only mark upon it being the wake of his boat. Staring down, fifty feet below him, he could see the coral heads — various shades of brown spotted with purple, slowly wavering sea fans and orange patches of fire coral — everything as distinct and clear as if it lay at the bottom of a glass paperweight. Dolphins swam near the surface, their prismed sides mirroring the sun's light back at him, changing it to flashes of blue and gold and green. The dark shapes of turtles and stingrays moved slowly along the bottom.

Only a glasslike surface separated him from this quieter, simpler, more beautiful world. He entered that world, floated slowly towards the bottom. The colors sharpened. A school of parrot fish swam by him unafraid — some of them royal blue, others mottled with patches of red and yellow and green. Closer to the rocks, a queen angelfish swam in small, unhurried circles. Thousands of colors changed and blended around him as if he were floating weightless within a barely moving kaleidoscope. Water was the silence that surrounded him. He'd escaped. Time itself seemed slowed, almost suspended. He saw it as within a dream — then and now.

'Ended it,' Kramer thought to himself, 'ended it for good.' Everything that had happened since he'd signed his enlistment papers made him surer. Never had he regretted what he was doing — except once, when he looked down and saw the reefs, knowing it was for the last time, forced to think, to remember. Now, once more, he remembered; but told himself, 'Never have to see them again. . . . No more second thoughts.'

Kramer drew the rifle up to his chest and let the bolt fly home with a loud, metallic crack. The cot across the room scraped the floor as the motionless figure bolted to a sitting position. Startled, Kramer also sat up. He had forgotten someone else was there. The figure turned its head, quickly scanning the room. At first its glance passed over Kramer, then slowly returned to him. It pivoted its body until its legs were over the edge of the cot and its feet fell to the floor. It nodded at him; then, in a sleepy voice, asked, "Who are you?"

He answered hesitantly, "Lieutenant Kramer. I've just been assigned here."

The figure lowered its face into its hands and spoke with muffled words. "I'm Lieutenant Hyatt. Just finished my tour. Came out of the bush last week." After a long pause, Hyatt continued. His voice seemed tired, but from something more than just being awakened. "Seemed like a long time while I was waiting for it to end, now it seems like I just got off the plane from Okinawa. . . . Probably be the same way for you."

"I guess so." Kramer waited for Hyatt to speak, but he just sat there with his head in his hands massaging his face. Kramer started to ask, "How was it?" but checked himself and asked instead, "Was it bad?"

"Some of it, some of it was real bad. The rest was all right. . . . Seems most of the time I remember the bad parts." Hyatt dropped his hands from his face and slowly raised his head. The room was too dark for them to make out each other's features, but their eyes stood out against their silhouettes, each pair focusing on the other. "I made a mistake once, about two months ago. I've been thinking about it a lot lately."

12

Hyatt got up and walked to the door. He placed one hand against the jamb and leaned his weight upon it. Kramer studied his dark outline — a blot against the deep pink evening clouds. Hyatt turned his head halfway back towards Kramer, seemingly looking in both directions at the same time. "It was in those mountains." He paused, as if wondering whether to continue.

Kramer sensed that he would, and asked himself uneasily, 'What's he want from me?'

"My platoon was up there alone. Just before sunset we got a few rounds of sniper fire from above us. Probably from about four hundred yards — too far away to be accurate, just harassment. I should have ignored it. But I wanted to take some sort of action instead of just sitting there. I called in mortars. The rounds fell two hundred yards above us. I adjusted the fire two hundred yards higher up, or at least I thought I did, so did my radioman. Mortars thought I said 'Come down two hundred,' all three of them said that's what it sounded like. A round fell near one of my squads — I should have made sure they were more spread out. . . . Two men were killed instantly, we couldn't even tell what parts belonged to who. Three more were wounded seriously, and two others slightly. The medivac chopper couldn't get in because it got dark too fast. Another man died just before dawn. Maybe he was luckier than the two amputees that lived . . . one of them had his balls blown off."

Kramer said to himself, 'At least it was short.' But suddenly Hyatt began speaking again. Kramer wanted to leave or say something to stop him, knowing that he couldn't do either, asking himself, 'Why the hell did he pick *me?*'

"I'll never forget that night," Hyatt continued, and it was his change of tone that most unnerved Kramer. He was no longer talking, or even speaking. It was as if he were reading lines, lines he had read a thousand times before, each word imperatively following from the one that preceded it. His emotions seemed to stem as much from the words themselves as from their meaning — as if their meaning were lost to him, and could only be found by repeating them again and again. "There wasn't any moon; you couldn't see a thing. You wanted to reach out and touch someone. Even if there was somebody right next to you, you were all alone. Two choppers circled right over us for an hour trying to find a place to land. The noise was scaring us shitless. . . . I guess everybody felt better when they gave up and left. I can't ever remember a time as silent as when those choppers left. We knew those men had to be medivacked, but I know damn well we were all relieved.

"The silence didn't last long though, maybe not more than a few seconds. One of the wounded moaned real loud — no words, just a moan.

13

That fucking sound cut through me like a razor. Then I heard some garbled words from the same direction. All three of them started mumbling, crying, moaning — one or two of them begging to die. I said to myself — maybe out loud — 'God, please, please let them die. Don't torture them.' They were filled with morphine, but it didn't do any good. They went on all night.

"The Gooks must have heard them. I guess it gave 'em pleasure — God knows they've suffered enough — because they started yelling and laughing at us. I don't think there was more than four of 'em, but they came in close, maybe twenty-five yards and from different sides. They were yelling and laughing like a bunch of jackals — never fired a shot. We could hear the brush move as they changed positions. It was the *only* time I've actually hated them. I'd lost men to them before, good men, but I never hated them.

"A few of my men lost their cool. *What cool?* Nobody had their cool that night. The idea that it was our own mortars that did the damage, that's what made it worse. You don't expect to lose men to your own mortars. Some of my men fired at the sounds, giving away their positions by the muzzle flashes, knowing they didn't have a chance to hit anything. If there had been more than a few Gooks out there, we would have been in real trouble. . . . They didn't leave till an hour before dawn. All night they kept it up, all fucking night."

Hyatt paused, and when he began speaking again, it was in a calm, deliberate tone. "It seemed like the sun was never gonna come up. Even when it did, it came real slow. All we could see were shadows, then bushes, . . . trees, rocks, . . . each other's silhouettes. Nobody even felt like chasing them. We were beaten. We didn't want revenge, we just wanted to get out of there. When it got barely light enough, we started to clear an LZ for the chopper. Nobody gave any orders — not me, not my squad leaders. Everybody knew what to do. They all moved slowly, with their heads down. We couldn't look at each other's faces. Each one of us was alone, trying to figure things out . . . because if what happened that night was real, *God*, what the fuck could be unreal?

"Nobody looked up when we first heard the choppers. Then, very slowly as we directed it in, everyone's eyes locked on the medivac chopper. The gun ships that came with it didn't prep-fire the area. I think we were all glad of that. As the medivac landed, we stared at it as if it was some sort of useless miracle. The men carrying the wounded and dead didn't run towards it. I never saw that before. Always, when a chopper landed, they ran to it. One of the crewmen motioned for them to hurry up, but they ignored him, walking real slow with the stretchers.

14

"After the medivac took off, I gave the order to move-out — back down to the lowlands and the rest of our company. It took us four hours to get there and my orders were the last words I heard. We marched slowly, and with our heads down — even the point man, and I didn't tell him to do otherwise. When we got back, nobody from the other platoons came up to us, they knew better. Usually my men would break up into groups. Not this time. Everyone just went his own way."

Hyatt took his arm from the door jamb, lowered one foot to the top step, hesitated, and then walked out the door without looking back.

Kramer's eyes followed him. He was still staring out the door when Forest came through it shaking his head. Upon seeing Kramer, he mumbled, "That Hyatt's a weird one. Can't get as much as a nod out of him." Kramer made no reply, still wondering why Hyatt had chosen to tell the story to him. "You wanna go to chow?"

Kramer looked up, for the first time seeming to notice Forest. "In a few minutes." He slowly pulled out a cigarette and leaned back on the cot, feet still touching the floor.

2. Hill 65

The convoy left An Hoa for Da Nang at eight in the morning. An hour and a half later a jeep, a six-by carrying troops, and two more six-bys carrying supplies, separated from the main body of the convoy as it passed Hill 65. The four vehicles proceeded up a steep dirt road that ran the length of one side of the hill. Just before it reached the top, the road hairpinned to the left and was bordered by a row of six 105-millimeter guns set under large sheets of camouflage netting. A cliff of sand rose fifteen feet above the opposite side of the road. The backs of five wood-and-screen barracks were visible atop it. The vehicles followed the curve to the left and passed in front of the barracks. Twenty yards farther down the road, a long line of Marines passed sandbags to the edge of a barbwire fence where other Marines were building bunkers and gun emplacements. At the crest of a sharp rise, two six-inch guns sat upon their tanklike vehicles. The crews of both guns lethargically uncrated huge shells and piled them in pyramids against a dirt embankment. The newly arrived vehicles proceeded another fifty yards before stopping at the center of the hill where wooden buildings clustered along both sides of the road.

As soon as the six-by stopped, the Marines in it jumped down and plodded off in various directions. A jeep sped by honking its horn at a lanky Marine with a bushy mustache. He waved to the driver and called out, "Delaney," then turned around to the two men walking behind him. "That's Delaney. He used to be in Third Platoon, but after his second Purple Heart he got pulled out of the bush and they made him a jeep driver. It's a skating job. . . . We've got to go back to the hootches we passed on the way up here. I'll show you the gunny's hootch when we get there."

The taller of the two men in back of him nodded, and the other said, "Corporal Harmon, I better get my knee checked. It's killing me."

Harmon turned around thinking, 'Hope I don't get this worthless motherfucker in my squad.' "Listen Graham, the first thing you and Chalice got to do is check in with the company gunnery sergeant, *then* you can start worrying about your knee."

16

When the three of them reached the hootches at the far end of the hill, Harmon pointed to the second one and told Chalice and Graham they would find the gunny inside. He then walked over to a powerfully built soldier sitting on the steps of the next hootch cleaning his rifle. "Sarge, did you miss me?"

The sergeant glanced up, and answered gruffly, "It's about fucking time you got back." As he stared at Harmon he began to smile and his eyes took on a slightly Asiatic cast.

Harmon reached down and started playing with the sergeant's light brown hair. "Did you really miss me that much, Hunky?"

The sergeant looked up sneering, "If I can't fuck it, I don't miss it. But I'll tell you right now, if you don't get your goddamn paw off my head, you'll be beating-off left-handed for the rest of your life."

Harmon snickered as he sat down. "What's been going on since I left?"

"Nothing much. We've still got the same fucked-up captain, the same fucked-up gunny, and the word is we're gonna get a new lieutenant; and chances are he'll be just as fucked-up as the rest of them."

"When?"

"I don't know. How was Japan?"

"Great. If I hadn't run outa coins, I woulda went AWOL and stayed another week."

"Yeah, I was gonna go there on my second R and R — went to Australia on my first — but I'm getting so short now I don't wanna waste the money. Anything I don't spend on whores, I'll spend on a car when I get back to the world."

"I know what you mean. The first day I was there I went ape-shit trying to fuck everything in sight — blew about two hundred dollars. But I finally found one I dug, so I stayed with her the rest of the time. Did a lot of sightseeing."

"Catch the siff?"

"Don't know yet. We'll see in a couple of days." Harmon rose to his feet. "I'm gonna ditch this pack and crash for a while. Don't let anybody wake me up."

"Yeah. . . . Hey listen, if you don't have lines tonight, I know where we can hear some records and drink a few beers."

"Sounds good. I'll see you later."

The sergeant started to put his rifle back together when he saw two pairs of new boots walking towards the steps. Not looking up, he thought, 'Here comes some more boot motherfuckers wantin' a chance to get their heads blown off.'

The two new men stopped in front of him and Graham asked, "Do you know where we can find Sergeant Hunky?"

"Sergeant Hunky, my ass, you *dumb* cocksucker." Graham took a step backward and started to speak. Before he could get a word out, the sergeant asked through a set of tightly clenched teeth, "Who told you to say that, that sonofabitch Martin?"

"The company gunnery sergeant, sir," Graham stammered.

"That's Martin, stupid. Let me tell you something right off the bat, pal. Anytime you do something that bastard tells you, you got a damn good chance of getting your ass blown away; and around here your chances of going home in a box are pretty good regardless."

"Yes, sir."

"Since when do you say '*sir*' to a sergeant? You're not in boot camp any more. My name is Kovacs, Sergeant Kovacs. . . . You both grunts, riflemen?"

Chalice nodded his head and Graham answered, "Yes, sir."

"You aren't too bright, are you? What's your name?"

"Private Graham."

"And yours?"

"Lance Corporal Chalice."

"Chalice, you'll be in Alpha Squad. Find Corporal Harmon, but don't wake him up if he's asleep. Graham, you'll be in Bravo. Sugar Bear's your squad leader. He's around somewhere. You can drop your gear in the hootch. It belongs to our platoon. I guess that wino told you you're in Second Platoon."

Chalice and Graham walked up the steps and into the hootch. A narrow aisle ran down its center. The rest of the room was taken up by two rows of cots covered with packs, rifles, and other equipment. As Graham stopped to take his pack off, he said, "That guy's a real bastard. I'm staying away from him."

Chalice kept walking towards the far end of the hootch where Harmon was sitting. "I'm in your squad."

"Glad to have you. Make room on one of the racks to drop your shit."

Chalice hesitated, saying, "I don't want anybody to get pissed off because I've got my gear on their rack. Where can I get my own?"

An amused look ran across Harmon's face. "Nobody sleeps on these racks. We've got to sleep in the bunkers where we stand watch. . . . How old are you?"

"Twenty-three."

"How'd you keep out of the service so long?"

"I was in college."

"That's what I thought. Where'd you go?"

"Duke."

"Good school. You didn't graduate, did you?"

18

"Yeah, I managed to."

"No shit, you'll be the only guy in the platoon with a degree. I've got three years at the University of Texas. We've got quite a few guys with some college in the platoon, a lot more than most platoons. What was your major?"

"English. What was yours?"

"Engineering."

"How come you didn't finish?" Chalice asked.

"I dunno — got bored, had some girl trouble, a lotta reasons. I guess I'll go back when I get out. . . . Did they ask you to be an officer?"

"Yeah, a couple a times. That's not for me."

"Same here."

"They asked you too, eh? It meant another year on my hitch, one more year of bullshit, giving dumb orders instead of taking them."

"That's the same fucking reason I didn't go. Hamilton had a chance to be an officer, too. He didn't want the bullshit either. You'll meet him later."

"They kept on telling me I'd be sorry I didn't go to OCS. Is it true?"

"Naw, you go through a lot more bullshit as an enlisted man; but when *you're* a civilian, the Marine Corps will still be fucking with them. I guess you've got a better chance of getting killed though."

"What's the story on Sergeant Kovacs?"

"He's damn straight. If he tells you to do something, do it. He don't fuck with you unless he has to. A lot of guys around here'd be dead if it wasn't for him. . . . He's roughstreet. You can tell by looking at him. If him and ten other guys went out on a patrol and only one came back, he'd be the one. . . . You know you're lucky to be in my squad. By some miracle, we've got the most intelligent squad in the company. You'd go batshit in some of the other squads just looking for someone to talk to. Our platoon ain't bad either."

"Do the lifers fuck with you much?"

"Yeah. I guess as long as you're in the Marine Corps you're gonna get fucked with. It's a little better here than stateside, but not as much as everybody expects. They can't harass you too much, it's too easy to get even. The company commander, Captain Trippitt, and Martin, the gunnery sergeant, are both bastards. You'll find out. . . . What rank are you?"

"Lance Corporal."

"How'd you make lance?"

"At language school."

"Monterey?"

"Yeah."

"No shit, I was supposed to go there, but they fucked up my orders. How was it?"

"Man, it was a beautiful scene. I couldn't believe the Marine Corps had anything to do with it. On weekends we used to go to San Francisco, or Big Sur, or Carmel."

"Yeah, I was really pissed off I didn't get to go. . . . I'm putting you in Tony 5's fire team. He doesn't talk much, but when he does, pay attention. It might save your life. He knows what he's doing, and besides he's got a bad temper. You *don't* wanna piss him off."

While they were talking, four men walked in the front door and sat down on the first few cots. They were getting up a card game when Harmon called out, "Hamilton, come here a minute."

Hamilton got up and walked towards them. "Hey man, how was your R and R?"

"Great. . . . I want you to meet Chalice, here. He's gonna be in our squad. I'm putting him in Tony 5's fire team."

"Glad to meet you. I'm Harmon's other fire team leader, Doug Hamilton."

"I'm Mark Chalice."

As they were shaking hands, another person walked over. He was short and slight, with straight black hair hanging over his dark forehead. "Harmon, you motherfucker, when'd you get back?" he asked in a fast talking, high pitched voice.

"A few minutes ago. This is a new guy in our squad, Mark Chalice. Chalice, this is Al Payne. He'll tell you anything you want to know. The sooner you forget what he tells you, the better off you'll be."

"Hey man, what kinda thing is that to say?"

"The truth, that's what. . . . Chalice here is a regular professor, a college graduate."

Payne looked at Chalice with a sly grin on his face. "A college degree ain't worth much if it can't keep you out of Nam, Professor. I'll — "

Harmon broke in, "You guys seen Tony 5 around?"

"I saw him walking towards the LZ a few minutes ago," Hamilton answered.

"Why don't you take Chalice down there and see if you can find him."

"Okay. C'mon, let's go." They went out the front door and started back down the road. "The LZ's all the way on the other end of the hill. Where you from?"

"Silver Springs, Maryland. Where you from?"

"St. Louis. I went to the University of Nebraska for a year and a half. Where'd you get your degree?"

"Duke." — 'Looks like a jock.' — "Play any sports?"

"Yeah, I played football for two years, but I stopped growing so they red shirted me and I quit."

"You *look* big enough."

"Nah. I'm five eleven now, but I grew two inches right after I joined the Crotch, *really* pissed me off. I was stupid to go there in the first place. You gotta be an elephant before they even look at you. . . . You know Harmon was right about Payne. He's not a bad guy, but he's a real shitbird. Don't pay much attention to what he tells you. . . . Did they fuck with you much in An Hoa?"

"No, not at all."

"They seemed friendly because you're new in-country. When you go back there from the bush, they really give you the business. I'd rather be on Hill 65 than in An Hoa any day."

"I thought you guys were always trying to get back to the rear."

"An Hoa ain't much of a rear. It gets hit by ground troops just as often as 65, and they get hit by rockets a lot more. See there's three kinds of bush. Hill 65 is the regular bush. The lowlands around here are the bad bush. And the Arizona is the big bad bush."

"That's all anybody talks about, the Arizona. Is it really that bad?"

"It's worse. No matter how bad you think it's going to be, it's always worse. Remember all those guys you've met that kept on telling you they couldn't wait to get to Nam and see some action. Well you never hear anybody say he wants to go back to the Arizona. It's just like fighting your way out of Red China."

Chalice and Hamilton passed the place where the six-by had unloaded the replacements. Walking along the same and only road, they approached a large tower with a tank on top of it. "What's that?"

"It's supposed to be a water tower, but since there's no well up here it's never had anything in it but air. Childs says some half-assed colonel must have decided he wanted a water tower because some other half-assed colonel he went to Annapolis with had one on his hill. He says he won't be surprised if one of these days they line up our whole company from the tower to the river and have us pass canteens up to fill it. It only holds about a hundred thousand gallons, so it wouldn't take more than a week."

"Who's Childs?"

"Just the skatingest motherfucker in the Marine Corps. He spends more time in the rear than the office poags. You'll meet him later. Come to think of it, maybe you won't. I haven't seen him in two months myself."

The road started a gradual upward grade; and now there were ammunition and supply bunkers lining both sides of it. When Chalice and Hamilton reached the top of the grade, they could see the helicopter landing zone below them. Set in a place where the top of the hill widened into a bubble, the LZ was just a square of corrugated steel plates, thirty yards across, with a bunker beside it. When they reached the bunker, Hamilton leaned over its wall and asked someone lying on the floor if he'd seen Tony 5. A Marine wearing a yellow T-shirt identifying him as a member of the ground crew sat up and told them Tony might be over at 106's. "You mean we've got to go all the way back to the other end of the hill?" Chalice asked.

"No, he meant the guns on the point. Those were 105's."

They followed the road to its end at the very edge of the hill. A large tower stood between two low bunkers with 106-millimeter guns mounted on top of them. The soldier in the tower was looking across the valley through a small telescope. Hamilton called up to him, "Have you seen Tony 5?"

"Yeah. He left for chow ten minutes ago."

"That's fucking great," Hamilton mumbled as he started to leave.

Chalice continued to stare across the valley. "Wait a minute. Let me get a good look at this."

"Sure. . . . Hey, you wanna go up in the tower?"

"Yeah."

When they reached the top, Hamilton told the lookout that Chalice was new, so they both started pointing things out to him. Chalice could see the entire An Hoa Valley, and no more. Dark green mountains defined the horizon on all sides. The road to An Hoa touched the base of Hill 65 at an angle. It paralleled a broad, smooth river. Both river and road ran the length of the valley. A half mile from the base of the hill, the orange road bisected a cluster of thatched roofed huts — the village. An isolated part of the village lay within the hollow of the kidney-shaped base of the hill. The cool, dark green color of the shade trees interspersed among the hootches stood out against the light green glare emanating from the surrounding rice paddies. At the far edge of the village, the river forked and the right branch passed under a large wooden bridge. The road was just as wide on the other side of the bridge, but the few buildings that lined it appeared deserted. Almost all the land on the near side of the river was either covered with huts or squared off into rice paddies. The far side was also squared off, but much of the land lay fallow and orange bomb craters dotted the entire area. Hamilton pointed towards it. "See that? That's the Arizona Territory."

Hamilton led Chalice back up the road. When they reached the center of the hill, he turned off into a maze of plywood buildings that sloped down its side. A long line of Marines ran along the valley side of the largest building. The air around it smelled of food and garbage. Payne stood in the middle of the line, talking in a loud voice to some men in back of him. As Hamilton and Chalice approached from his rear, he happened to glance back and spot them. "Hamilton, over here." They walked towards him, and Payne asked, "Professor, how you doing?"

"All right."

Payne started to say something else, but Hamilton interrupted him by addressing the dark, broad-shouldered Marine in back of Payne. "It's about time we caught up with you. We've been following you all over the fucking hill. I got a new man for your fire team." He turned his head back towards Chalice. "Professor, Tony 5; Tony 5, Professor."

As they shook hands, Tony 5 said indifferently, "Glad to have you in Alpha Squad." He turned away immediately and began talking to Hamilton.

Payne tried for a while to regain his audience, but finally turned to Chalice. Backing up, he motioned for him to get in line. Chalice looked at the long line in back of them and hesitated. Not catching this, Payne motioned again. Chalice saw that nobody was paying much attention, so he stepped into the line. Payne looked him over as if he were seeing him for the first time. "You're lucky to be in Alpha, you know?"

"What do you mean?"

Payne glanced around before whispering, "We've only got one nigger." Chalice made no reply and Payne added, "You may not hate 'em now, but you will after you've been here awhile. Look up there." He pointed to the front of the line. "Those cocksuckers are too good to wait like everybody else."

A few yards from the mess hall door, the line diffused into a large group of blacks. Chalice looked at the faces of the men standing behind him, only a few of them black. As other blacks approached, they joined the group at the door instead of going to the end of the line. Each new man was greeted with extended hands before melting into the crowd. Disgusted by the thought of having to wait in line for an hour, Chalice watched the black power handshakes that greeted the newcomers. Each man received extended hands and a phrase like, "Gimme some of that black power, brother." The type of handshake being used started like a regular one, then the two men would open their hands and grasp each other's thumbs to shake again. This was followed by each in turn adding another hand to the one extended, leaning down, and blowing into the three hands. They'd then grasp each other's wrists. The ceremony ended with each man at the same time tapping the other on both sides of the chest with a clenched fist. Chalice stood thinking, 'If that's what it takes to give them self-respect, it's all right with me.'

As he continued to watch, he heard a series of four distant but loud explosions, then the scream of a jet engine. A few of the Marines standing in line yelled, *"Get some!"*

Hamilton tapped Chalice on the shoulder and pointed out four clouds of smoke rising from the valley floor on the Arizona side of the river. "Phantom jets. Look, there's two of them coming in from the left."

Chalice's eyes caught a small silver speck as it dived towards the ground, then leveled off. When it reached the place where the first bombs had fallen, it banked sharply and four more clouds of smoke rose beneath it. The sound of exploding bombs was again followed by numerous cries of, *"Get some!"*

"How come some of the smoke's black and some of it's white?" Chalice asked Hamilton.

Hamilton started to answer, but Payne cut in, his voice jokingly diabolical. "Dark gray is from the HE, high intensity regular bombs. When they hit, arms and legs start flying all over the place. The white's from willie peter, white phophorous. When a hunk of it lands on a Gook, his body temperature starts it burning. It bubbles and burns right down to the bone. Even if Charlie knows enough to pack it with mud, he has to walk around looking for somebody to cut the phosphorous out before the mud dries." At first amused, Chalice now found little humor in Payne's graphic descriptions. "The real black clouds are napalm. If Charlie's lucky he gets caught right in the middle of it and suffocates, otherwise he runs around in circles with that hot jelly sticking to him. When we find him he looks like a burnt turkey."

The jets made their last bomb run, then streaked deafeningly low over the hill to be greeted by raised fists and more cries of, *"Get some!"*

The line had been slowly moving into the mess hall. The men filled their trays and sat down at a table near the long screen window overlooking the valley. While they were eating, Chalice didn't pay much attention to the conversation. He just stared out the window, struck by the beauty of the cool, green valley below, finding it hard to believe that there were people wandering around in it intent upon killing him and those around him, and that for the next thirteen months his whole life would center upon killing them first.

When they returned to the platoon hootch, Payne tried to talk Tony into playing some cards, but Tony said he wanted to check out Chalice first. He asked Chalice where his pack was and they walked over to it. "I'm not gonna waste my time trying to convince you because you won't be able to imagine how bad it is, but just for the record, the humping around here is murder. It'll really knock you on your ass. It makes anything you did at Parris Island or infantry training look like kid's stuff."

"Humping?" Chalice asked.

"Yeah, marching with packs on," Tony answered, his expression indicating that Chalice should have at least known that. "Let's see what you've got in your pack." Chalice emptied it onto the cot. Tony 5 shook his head in disbelief. "You shitting me, man?" Pointing to an air mattress, he asked, "Who told you to bring this rubber bitch out to the bush?"

"They issued them to all of us."

"I *know* they issue them to everybody, but that don't mean you have to carry them around. Only the office poags are lucky enough to get to sleep on these things. Too much extra weight; get rid of it."

"It only weighs about four pounds."

Tony looked him in the eye. "Don't you think I know how much it weighs? Look, Professor, when it comes to things like this, I give advice not orders, and I don't waste my time saying things just to hear myself talk. Now you're talking about carrying an extra four pounds. A week from now you won't wanna carry an extra pencil. There ain't one guy in this platoon that sleeps on a rubber bitch. Not because they don't want to, but because they don't wanna hump them. My advice is to shit-can it." Chalice flipped the air mattress off to one side. Tony pointed to a couple of pairs of underpants. "Didn't they tell you that it's too hot out here to wear skivvies? You wear 'em for five days and I'll guarantee you a terminal case of heat rash."

"Yeah, they told me, but I had room in my pack so I put them in."

"Don't worry about your pack. We won't have any trouble filling it up. Shit-can 'em."

"Okay."

Tony pointed to five paperbacks. "You don't plan on humping all those books, do you?"

"I had some more, but I left them in An Hoa."

"You shoulda left these too. You don't need to hump books. The guys get all kinds sent from home; comic books, fuck books, science fiction, mysteries, everything."

"I wanted to read these four books in particular."

"There's five here."

"One's a dictionary."

"Man, I thought I'd seen just about everything, but you're the first grunt I've ever met that carried a dictionary. I ain't never been to college, but if you're not sure about any of the words you come across out here, just ask me. I'll be glad to tell you what they mean." Chalice stood silently while Tony sifted through the rest of his gear. "Now we come to the fun part. How many grenades you got?"

"Four."

"Better pick up another one somewhere. When you're in a hole at night and you hear movement, you'll want all you can get. How many magazines you have?"

"Eight, that's all they issued me."

"You'll need at least twenty. Most of the guys carry twenty-five. You can get some more when somebody gets medivacked or goes to the rear. They take twenty rounds; but if you don't want your rifle to jam, just put in eighteen. We're one of the first battalions to get M-16's and they jam a lot easier than 14's. Don't *ever* let me catch you with a dirty rifle. Clean it every chance you get. The last time Golf Company hit the shit, we had to recover the bodies. I saw three guys with bullets in their heads and their M-16's lying next to them, half taken apart. When them rice-propelled motherfuckers come at you and your rifle jams, you ain't gonna have time to take it apart and clean it. . . . How many canteens you got?"

"Four."

"That's good. If you get thirsty easy, you might wanna pick up another one. There's three things you never wanna run out of in the bush: rounds, water, and shit paper. Shit paper's really a luxury, but it's a nice one. You can start putting your pack back together. One more thing, you'll be wantin' another type pack. These Marine Corps ones ain't worth a shit. When we run into some Arvins, buy a Gook pack off of 'em. They hold more and they're a lot more comfortable. Wait here. I'll be back with some presents for you in a minute."

Tony returned with an ammo can, a "law" (lightweight bazooka), and some other equipment. "Here," he said, dumping everything onto the cot. "The two newest guys in each fire team have to carry a can of machine gun ammo. They weigh about eighteen pounds and are a motherfucker to hump. Everybody in the squad has to carry either a law or a claymore mine. You'll carry a law. Here's a gas grenade. Chances are we'll never use it, but somebody's got to carry it. Do you know what *this* is?"

"A trip flare, isn't it?"

"Yeah, when we dig in at night, we set a few of these around our perimeter so Charlie can introduce himself before he falls into somebody's foxhole. Be careful with it. It can burn the hell out of you." Chalice nodded his head. "That's about it. We usually got working parties all day, but Gunny Martin's so drunk we'll probably skate for the afternoon."

26

A half hour before dusk, Second Platoon's hootch was alive with men getting ready to go on watch. Tony was walking around asking everybody if they'd seen Forsythe. When he reached Chalice, he asked, "You got all your gear ready?"

"What do I need besides my rifle and magazines?"

"Bring your grenades — just the frags, not the gas. Wear your flak jacket." Turning to Payne, he yelled, "C'mon, put the radio on and let's go."

"Forsythe ain't even here yet," Payne complained.

"Let *me* worry about Forsythe."

The bunker was at the other end of the hill and well off the road. Its floor was ten by twenty feet and dug out a few feet below ground level. Sandbags protected the plywood walls. There was a large gap between the walls and the corrugated steel roof on all but the rear side. The front wall supported a heavy wooden shooting counter.

Tony dropped his gear and looked towards Chalice. "Okay Professor, we all stay up till nine, then we each take a two hour fifteen minute watch. You've got to call in sid rats, situation reports, every fifteen minutes. Payne'll show you how to work the radio. If you hear anything, and I mean anything, wake somebody up. Only fire your rifle as a last resort. The muzzle flash'll give every Gook in sight your address. If you're sure you've got movement out there, the best thing to do is throw a frag. Since it's your first night, we'll let you have your choice of watch, but from now on we'll rotate."

"I'll take first then."

"Okay, what do you want, Payne?"

"Second."

"Good, I'll take last. I'm gonna find Forsythe now. I'll be back before dusk. Payne'll tell you anything you want to know and then some. See you later."

After Tony left the bunker, Payne said, "They're always kidding me. Don't pay attention to 'em." He then started repeating all the advice Tony had given Chalice. While he was going over everything for the second time, Chalice noticed someone in fighting gear approaching the bunker taking long, bounding strides. As he entered, he gave a friendly nod to Chalice and flung down his equipment by the door.

"Well no shit. Look who's here. Glad you could make it, Forsythe."

Forsythe answered with a grin, "You didn't think I'd leave you alone with a new man, did you? One shitbird in our fire team is enough." He offered his hand to Chalice. "You must be the Professor. Tony 5 told me about you. Glad to have you in our fire team."

"Thanks."

"Tony says you graduated college. Where'd you go?"

"Duke."

"No shit? I was accepted there and all ready to go — never quite made it. I'm from Raleigh."

"I'm from Silver Springs, Maryland. How come you didn't go?"

"It's a long story. I ended up heading for California."

"You went to school out there?"

"No, I just bummed around. Had a wild time. Maybe I'll go to Berkeley when I get out of the Crotch. I get my discharge as soon as I finish my tour."

"Berkeley's a cool place. I wouldn't have minded going there."

"You've been there?" Forsythe asked with interest.

"Quite a few times. When I was in language school at Monterey, we used to go up on weekends to watch the riots. Ever see any of them?"

Forsythe grinned with pride. "See 'em, I was in 'em."

"What'd the rest of the guys in the platoon say when they found out you used to run around with all the screaming freaks?"

"Not much. They figure anybody that hates the military can't be all bad. . . . A lot of the guys in the platoon are wise to how fucked up this war is, practically anybody with any college."

"That's good news. I was afraid I might end up in some gung ho outfit."

Forsythe tilted his head sideways and started grinning. "Are you fucking serious, man? The only gung ho bastards are the lifers. A lot of guys hate the Gooks, but they hate being in Nam worse."

Forsythe took the frags out of his grenade pouch and laid them on the shooting support. He then walked to the rear of the bunker to get his magazines and rifle. Payne, who had been unusually quiet, approached him and whispered, "You been partying?"

Chalice heard Forsythe whisper back, "A little."

Payne, still whispering, asked in an irritated voice. "How come you didn't let me in on it?"

"You weren't around. Besides, it wasn't my stuff." This ended the conversation, and Chalice didn't think much of it except that Forsythe didn't look as if he'd been drinking.

A few minutes later Tony 5 returned. He and Chalice stood watch while Forsythe and Payne sat down in the rear. Tony told him to memorize the terrain so he would know his fields of fire, and also to remember the location of each upright object. "When it gets dark, the bushes and fence posts start moving. I don't want you killing any of 'em."

Chalice tried to concentrate on the positions of different objects, but the peaceful beauty of the valley lulled his mind. The setting sun colored the

28

sky with a soft red glow, its oblique rays casting long shadows along the darkening rice paddies. The green trees interspersed among the native huts seemed almost black. Some children who had been playing against the slope of the hill started heading towards the village. Two of them rode a water buffalo, their short legs barely reaching a third of the way down its broad sides. It plodded slowly home, head hanging down. Three kids in white shirts and khaki shorts followed behind it, their bare feet kicking up water as they ran. Just as they reached the village, the red glow faded into the mountains and night spread towards them from the east like drifting smoke.

"It's nine o'clock," Tony said. "Professor, your watch lasts till eleven fifteen, then wake Payne. Forsythe, you've got third watch."

"How the hell did I luck out?"

"Why don't you try getting your sweet ass to the bunker the same time as everybody else? Your luck might change. . . . Besides, you had second watch last night."

"So I did. How 'bout that."

Tony turned to Chalice. "I'll be sleeping right in back of the bunker. If you see or hear anything, and I mean anything, wake me up. I'm gonna crash now."

"Me too," Payne said, following Tony out the door.

Forsythe got up and walked towards Chalice. "I'm not tired yet. I think I'll see some of the light show."

"Light show? You mean the illumination flares?"

"That's just part of it. You ain't seen nothing yet."

Chalice was thinking, 'This guy has to be a head,' when he heard a sharp pop, followed by a green burst of light above the bunker. "What was the pop before the illume went off?"

"That's the parachute. They fire them out of mortar tubes, and when they get high enough a little chute pops open so they float down slowly."

"Isn't there enough time between the pop and the flare lighting for a Gook to hit the deck?"

"Yeah, there's almost enough time for him to dig a foxhole. I guess if he were riding in a tank, we'd have him dead to rights. Too bad they don't have many tanks. . . . The guys in mortars usually keep a few around with the chutes cut off. They drop real fast, but they don't telephone ahead. When you want to use a hand illume and you don't want the pop, use a star cluster. They shoot five small flares that drop without a chute, still make a swoosh though."

"You'd think they'd be able to develop one that wouldn't give any warning."

"Sure they could, but some retired general's probably got the patent on this type."

While Forsythe was talking, Chalice heard a sharp, grating sound in the distance. "What was that?"

"Oh, that's Puff the Magic Dragon." Forsythe leaned across the counter and pointed to their left. "Look over there. See those four big illumes? They're the four corners of his grid square. He drops them and then fills the square with rounds."

"Puff the Magic Dragon?"

"It's some old prop plane they stripped down and filled with fifty-caliber machine guns. They say he can put a round in every square foot of a football field in less than a minute. Keep watching over there. Every fifth round is a tracer. It's a beautiful show."

Chalice was still leaning across the counter. "Is that the Arizona Territory?"

"Yeah, he works out over the Arizona practically every night."

Chalice saw a bright red dotted line dart down to the ground. "*Wow!* I've never seen anything like that. Looks like a mile-high neon sign. This *is* quite a show."

"Yeah, and just —" Forsythe stopped talking as the grating sound reached them again. "Did you hear it?"

"Yeah, it's hard to believe he's so far away."

"Just think, a new and different show every night. Did you see that?"

"Yeah, he did it again."

"No, I mean in the mountains." Forsythe pointed straight in front of the bunker. "There it is again."

Chalice saw it this time. Within a few seconds there had been about twenty bright white flashes on the mountainside across the valley. "Is that what you meant?"

"Yeah, those are mortars. They probably came from up there." He pointed back to the right side of the hill.

"How do you know they were ours? I didn't hear anything."

"I didn't either, but we probably could have if we'd been listening. They're ours because there were so many in such a short time. The Gooks are more careful — they don't have enough to waste. See what I mean about the show?"

"Yeah, it's outa sight. . . . Were you drinking this afternoon?"

"No," Forsythe laughed. "I don't drink much. Where'd you get that idea?"

"I heard you say something to Payne about partying."

Forsythe became suspicious. "We were just kidding around. . . . I better crash." He walked towards the threshold.

"Wait a minute. Which of these hand illumes are star clusters?"

Forsythe turned around and walked over to the ammo crate. "I can't see the labels now. Wait till an illume goes off."

While they stood waiting, Chalice spotted four purple and orange balls of fire shoot across the valley. "What was that?"

"What was what?"

"Looked like four big tracer rounds."

"Flying level?"

"Yeah."

"Rockets then."

"There it is again."

"Yeah, rockets, incoming at An Hoa."

"What do you mean?"

"They were VC rockets heading for An Hoa, could of hit our company area. Maybe one landed on top of the rack you were sleeping in last night."

"Nice thought."

"You'll have nicer ones before you get out of here." As Forsythe was talking, an illumination flare popped over the bunker. "Here," he said, handing Chalice a foot-long aluminum tube about an inch in diameter. "Star cluster."

"Can we shoot it off now for the hell of it?"

"Naw, you're not supposed to unless you've got a reason. . . . Ah, okay, why not?" Forsythe took the top off the tube and placed it on the bottom. He then raised his forearm and brought the bottom of the tube down sharply on the counter. Startled by the loud swooshing sound, Chalice stepped backwards. Five green balls of light burst above the bunker. They fell quickly towards the valley floor, casting an eerie glow upon the closest huts before disappearing. "That was cool. I wouldn't mind sending a few of those home. They'd be great for parties."

"I've already sent about ten, really about fifteen; but some of them must have got intercepted. Here comes somebody. *Halt!* Who is there?"

"Harmon."

"Okay."

"Did you guys shoot off a star cluster?"

"No, I think it came from behind us," Forsythe answered.

"Yeah, I'll bet. How 'bout cuttin' the shit? The Captain of the Guard tonight is a real asshole. . . . How's Chalice doing?"

"All right, we've been keeping him away from Payne."

"That's good. What watch does Payne have tonight?"

"Second."

"Good. I'm gonna stay up just to see if I can catch him crashing again. If I do, I'm gonna beat the shit out of him."

"Good idea. Wake me up first if you do. I wanna watch."

"Okay, I'll see you guys tomorrow. Don't fuck around anymore."

As Harmon walked back up the slope, Chalice asked, "What type of guy is he?"

"Damn straight. Him and Hunky — that's Kovacs — don't kiss any-body's ass. Watch out for Preston though."

"Who's he?"

"The right guide. Don't ever trust him. He's fairly harmless though. Any-time he starts his shit, Harmon gets Hunky to get him off our backs. If he pulls anything with you, just tell Harmon. . . . I'm gonna crash. See you tomorrow."

At daybreak Tony 5 woke his fire team. Chalice was collecting his gear when Forsythe stopped him. "Just leave it in the bunker. We'll pick it up after chow. . . . Did you bring a soft cover?"

"No. You mean we have to wear covers even in the bush?"

"Yeah. You wouldn't get ten feet before some lifer'd stop you. Take the liner out of your helmet and wear it."

"Where can I get a bush cover?" Chalice asked, referring to the broad-brimmed camouflage hats.

"Our battalion doesn't issue them. You can't wear them on the hill anyway. C'mon, let's go to chow."

"Man, this is as bad as stateside. What do we do after chow?"

"They'll split us up into different working parties."

"What type of working parties?"

"Everything you can think of — building bunkers, unloading supplies, burning shitters, policing the area, you name it."

"You really make it sound great."

"Oh yeah, I can't help but get enthused when I talk about it. See the sign?" Forsythe pointed to a reenlistment poster nailed on the side of a building.

Chalice read it aloud. " 'Mac Marine says, It's a great career, stick with it.' Well, you know a million Marines can't be wrong."

"Oh, they're not wrong now all right, but that's because they know how wrong they were when they signed that little white paper." Forsythe changed the subject. "Did the 105's bother you much?"

"Those big guns *were* 105's. They didn't start fucking with 'em till I got halfway asleep, then *boom*. I didn't know what the hell happened, so I grabbed my rifle and headed for the bunker. Tony was sleeping right in back of it and when I ran by he asked me where the fuck I was going. He said he didn't hear anything, but that it was probably the 105's. I can't believe he heard me walking by, but didn't hear those guns."

"You'll get like that too. You usually hear everything whether you're asleep or not. If it means danger, then you'll wake up; but sometimes when you should, you don't. There're a lot of dead Marines that'd tell you that if they could."

When they reached the mess hall, Forsythe walked over to two men, Chalice following behind him. "Professor, no platoon in the Corps is complete unless it's got a Polack everybody calls Ski, a Mexican named Ramirez or Gonzales, and an Indian called Chief. Here's Ski and Ramirez. You'll meet Chief later."

The darker one stuck out his hand first. He was about five feet two and slender, with a swarthy, exuberant face and large white teeth. "Glad to meet you, Prof. I'm Julio Ramirez from Charlie Squad. This is Ski." He pointed to a light-haired Marine next to him.

"I'm Dan Ojusinski. Ski's good enough. I'm in Bravo. . . . Where you from?"

"Silver Springs, Maryland. Where you guys from?"

"Pittsburgh," Ski answered. "You can guess where Ramirez is from."

"Laredo," Chalice guessed.

"There it is," Ski laughed.

After chow everybody headed back to the platoon hootch. When working parties were assigned, Forsythe saw to it that Chalice got the same party as he and Hamilton. The three of them and two others, Roads from Hamilton's fire team and Hemrick from Bravo Squad, were sent to a corporal in one of the offices at the center of the hill. He loaded them on a six-by and directed it towards the LZ. The choppers hadn't arrived yet, so they sprawled out in the sand near one of the bunkers and waited.

Chalice found himself staring at Roads, a tall, dark black with Caucasian features. His back propped up against the bunker, Roads ignored the rest of the men, the expression on his face too aloof to be belligerent. Chalice had noticed him in the platoon hootch and guessed he was some type of athlete, probably a basketball player. He moved about with effortless power, seemingly in control of every muscle in his body. No one had bothered to introduce Roads to him, and Chalice could see why. Roads was the only member of the platoon that had given him the impression of outward coldness. Though Roads had only been in the bush two

33

months his self-assurance belied this, as it had on his first day in-country. One of his long slender hands held a cigarette. A stiff breeze kept the ash glowing red. He slowly drew the cigarette towards his lips and inhaled. Chalice sat staring, waiting for the stream of smoke to emerge. Just as Roads seemed ready to exhale, his half-closed eyes opened as if he sensed something — the wind had stopped. Effortlessly, he blew a large smoke ring that traveled over a foot in front of him before the wind picked up again and blew it away. Roads half smiled as he let the rest of the smoke flow from the corner of his closed lips.

A conversation among the others drew Chalice's attention away from Roads. Hemrick, a skinny kid with large ears, had remarked that he'd rather be in the bush than on the hill. The corporal in charge of the working party asked him what he thought Hill 65 was. Hemrick replied testily, "I mean the *bad* bush. I'm tired of getting fucked with. You've always got to have a cover, but you can't wear a bush cover. You can't take your shirt off even though it smells like a jockstrap because they never get you clean ones. These working parties are a real pain. The food in the mess hall is as bad as C-rats. Shit, it is C-rats only it comes in larger cans. The only thing better about it is that you get a cold drink to wash the taste out of your mouth. The office poags up here have their own showers, and we aren't even allowed to use them. At least in the bush you come across a stream every once in a while that you can take a bath in, and — "

Hamilton interrupted, "Yeah, I can't stand the cheap shit either, but sometimes the bush ain't no bargain. Since you've been here, we've never been camped with the whole company for more than a few days, and it's even worse when you're set-in with the captain and the gunny. You get all the disadvantages and none of the advantages.

"I'll still take the bush."

"I will too," said Forsythe, "but it's not the bargain you make it out to be. When you're in the bush, you want Hill 65. When you're on Hill 65, you want the bush. That's the way the Marine Corps works. They get you to eat their shit because you're so tired of eating it one way you jump at the chance to eat it dished up some other way."

Hemrick started to say something, but the corporal called out, "Here's the choppers." One was circling the LZ while the other approached it, both with huge nets dangling from their fuselages. As the first chopper neared the ground, the men in the working party turned their backs to the LZ, protecting themselves from the sand whipped up by the copter blades. Chalice looked over his shoulder and watched the ground crew unhook the cargo-laden nets. After the second copter's net was detached, the working party moved onto the LZ and loaded the cargo, mostly

C-rations, into the truck. It drove back down the road, stopping in front of a bunker. The men jumped down and formed a line between it and the truck. After a few minutes, the whole operation became one big joke. They were throwing the heavy cartons to each other as fast as they could. When somebody would drop one, the others yelled at him in mock anger. Two hours later, the men unloaded the last carton and sat down exhausted. Forsythe had the only pack of cigarettes. He passed it around. Whoever took one made some sort of derogatory remark about the brand.

"Hey Corporal, can we get out of here?" Hamilton asked.

"Not yet."

"What do you mean?" Hemrick cut in. "We're done unloading the truck."

"Yeah, I know, but I'm supposed to drop you off at the S-2 office."

Hemrick cried out, "Are you shittin' me? We worked our asses off to get through with this in a hurry."

"Yeah, why didn't you tell us that before?" Forsythe added.

"Look man, don't blame me. C'mon, let's get in the six-by."

They took their time getting on the truck, complaining as they did so. When it reached the S-2 hootch, another corporal led them to some brooms and told them they had to field day the office. It was ten o'clock when they finished, and they again asked to leave. The corporal said the area had to be policed first. That took five minutes. Hamilton again asked if they could leave.

"No man, I'm sorry. I can't let you go to chow till eleven. Just wait till then." They sat around doing nothing for almost an hour. At eleven o'clock, as they walked away, the corporal called out, "Don't forget to be back at twelve. You've got some more stuff to do."

"Did you hear anything, Forsythe?"

"Not a thing, Hamilton. Did you?"

The platoon hootch grew noisier as the men straggled back from the mess hall. It was too much trouble to clear off the cots, so most of them lay down on the floor. Payne held up a deck of cards and yelled across the room, "Hey Professor, you wanna play?"

"Okay, poker?"

"No, backalley."

A tall, slender black lying on the floor a few yards away from Payne sat up and said, "We'll play." He nudged a short, pudgy youth with curly blond hair. The blond youth got up and they both walked over to Payne's cot.

"How's it going, Prof?"

Chalice turned around to see Forsythe standing behind him. "Hey, who are those guys playing cards with Payne and Hemrick?"

"They're Skip and Flip, the Bobbsey Twins. They're in guns."

"Funny, they don't look like twins."

"Most of the guys think they're identical, but they're really only Siamese. The tall black one's name is Skip. He's been in-country about six months, and he's a damn good machine gunner. The short, fat one is Flip, his assistant gunner, only been in-country two months. I forget what his real name is. We call him Flip because you never see one without the other."

"Hey listen, I've been meaning to ask you, do you do much reading?"

"I'd like to, but if comic and fuck books aren't your bag, you're pretty much out of luck around here."

"Here's the story: I've got some good books, but I don't wanna hump them all. If you're interested in reading some of them, we can each hump a few and trade off when we're done."

"Sounds good. What do you have?"

"*Absalom, Absalom!, Invisible Man, The Trial,* and *The Stranger.*"

"I've already read *The Stranger.* Let me have the one by Faulkner." Forsythe picked up the book and walked away.

Roads had overheard the conversation. He walked over to Chalice's cot and stood looking at the books for a few seconds. "All right if I read *The Trial* when you're done with it?"

Surprised by the first words he had heard Roads speak to anybody, Chalice said, "I've just finished it. You might think it's a little dry though. I've got a book here by Ralph Ellison you might be more interested in."

Roads's expression changed just enough to let Chalice know he'd made a mistake. He spoke slowly, with no emotion. "I've read both of them. I'd like to read *The Trial* again."

Chalice awkwardly handed the book to Roads, who nodded and immediately turned and left. When he was a few feet away, Chalice called out, "Wait." Roads turned around without saying anything. "Look, I'm having some more books sent to me and I don't want to hump them all. Forsythe is gonna hump a few. Maybe you want to also? That way we can have some good stuff to read." Roads nodded and walked away.

By twelve fifteen, only a few men were left in the barracks, the rest having gone to their working parties. Forsythe walked over to Chalice's cot. "We better get out of here, Prof, or somebody'll find something for us to do."

Hamilton and Payne followed them out the door. They walked over to

36

a lookout bunker on the edge of the barbwire. Two soldiers with flame throwers stood to their left. One of them was helping the other put the fuel pack on his back. Payne walked towards them. "Hey, what are you guys doing?"

"Getting some practice with the flames."

"What for? We never use the worthless things." They ignored Payne as they continued to struggle with the fuel pack. "Hey, the straps are too tight."

Forsythe remarked to Hamilton and Chalice, "The minute I saw that jerk walk over there, I knew he was going to tell them how to use their own flame throwers."

Hamilton said, "Yeah, everytime we get in a chopper I think he's gonna go up to the pilot and start telling him how to fly the thing."

"What are they gonna do, shoot them out in that field?" Chalice asked.

"Yeah," Hamilton answered, "it must be a hundred and ten degrees now, and it'll be a hundred and fifty when *they* start fucking around. Let's get outa here."

They walked over to get Payne who was trying to talk the two into letting him try one of the flames. Hamilton tapped him on the shoulder. "C'mon, let's go."

"Wait a minute. I wanna see 'em shoot these things."

Forsythe said to the one ready to shoot his flame thrower, "You know that's an old French mine field out there?"

Payne had been irritating him, and he snapped back, "So what? I'm just gonna shoot the flame thrower."

Forsythe stood silently for a moment, seemingly pondering the reply. "Oooooh, I thought you were gonna mow the lawn." He grabbed Payne's shirt collar. "Let's get out of here. We want these guys to be able to concentrate." After receiving a couple of dirty looks, they walked up the slope towards the road.

The swooshing sound of the flames was suddenly cut short by a loud explosion. Hamilton and Forsythe dove to the ground. Chalice followed their example; but Payne, who had been the only one looking back, just stood there and said, "Holy shit! Those guys must have got knocked twenty feet." Chalice looked back in time to see a dark cloud of smoke envelop the area where they had been. Hamilton ran towards it and the others followed. One of the men sat up, covered with soot. He checked himself for wounds, which to his amazement he couldn't find. The other man merely lay on his back repeating, "Sonofabitch! Sonofabitch!"

"Are you all right?" Payne asked.

"Yeah."

"I think so."

As they got to their feet, Forsythe said, "I thought you were just gonna use your flame throwers."

They ignored him as they checked their equipment. By this time about ten more people had come over to find out what had happened. Hamilton and Chalice started walking back up to the road and Forsythe followed. Before they had gotten twenty yards, Hamilton said, "Walk faster, here comes Preston."

"What a down," Forsythe moaned.

"Hey, wait up," Preston called.

"Too late."

A skinny, awkward-looking corporal approached. Chalice was struck by the dark brown color of his buck teeth as they protruded from a large, sarcastic grin. "Well, just who I wanted to see." Hamilton and Forsythe looked at each other with disgusted expressions. "C'mon back to the hootch with me. The gunny wants a working party."

"How 'bout it, Preston? Why don't you find somebody else?" Hamilton asked.

"I've got somebody else. They'll help you. C'mon, let's go."

They followed him back to the company area without speaking except for the times Forsythe repeated, "What a fucking bummer."

While they waited outside, Preston got eight men from inside the hootch. "The gunny wants these moved up there," he said, pointing from a stack of seventy or eighty ammo boxes to some higher ground on the edge of the barbwire.

Hamilton protested, "We just moved the fucking things down from there two days ago."

"The gunny changed his mind," Preston replied with a self-satisfied look on his face.

"*Jesus Christ!* Tell him to move them himself."

"I'm telling you to do it. If you wanna tell him something, that's your business, Hamilton."

"Thanks, pal."

The boxes were full of sand and rocks, and it took two men to carry each box. Plodding through the softer earth near the top of the knoll, they would often stumble to their knees or chests, then struggle to their feet again with a new coating of dry sand against their sweaty skin. The heat alone was enough to make just sitting in the sun exhausting. Before the job was finished, over three hours later, the rest of the platoon had straggled back from their working parties.

Chalice trudged down from the knoll towards the platoon hootch, hands

38

rubbed raw and dirt completely covering his face except where sweat had etched it away. After a few minutes of rest in the hootch, the men headed for the mess hall. The food was overcooked and bland. All Chalice could taste was the dirt that covered his hands and face. Right after chow, he trudged to his bunker. He was still exhausted when his watch started. Though he could hardly stand, the soreness of his body helped him to stay awake.

Chalice had lost track of the days and was surprised when somebody mentioned it was Sunday. "At least we don't have to go on any working parties today," he remarked at breakfast. Everyone stopped eating and stared at him until Forsythe finally droned, "In the bush, Sunday's like any other day, except you get a little present." Nobody mentioned what the present was, and he figured he'd find out soon enough so he didn't ask.

After chow there was a company formation. The four platoons lined up separately and in order. Sergeant Kovacs, the platoon sergeant, and Preston, the right guide, stood in front of Second Platoon. Each platoon was divided into four ranks; the three rifle squads in front and the guns and rocket squad in the rear. Being in Alpha, Chalice stood in the front rank. Kovacs yelled for everybody to cover down and shut up. Hearing a lot of laughter and talking behind him, Chalice looked over his shoulder. A few of the men were shoving each other, somebody in Charlie Squad was trying to get his hat back while it was being tossed from man to man, and Ski, oblivious to everything else going on around him, was playing with a Yo-Yo.

"KNOCK IT OFF!" Kovacs shouted, and shouted again until everybody quieted down. He continued to glare at his men, sure that someone was missing. "*Hemrick?*"

"Here."

"Get in the right rank. . . . *Ramirez?*"

"Here."

"*Payne?*"

No one answered until Ski said, "I saw him sleeping behind the air tower a half hour ago."

"JESUS CHRIST!"

"*Here,*" Forsythe answered, sending off a new round of laughter and shoving.

Kovacs stood glaring at him, teeth clenched and eyes appearing even more slanted than usual, finally yelling, "*Forsythe,* you motherfucker, why do you always have to be the biggest shitbird in the platoon?"

Forsythe returned the stare, and said in a serious, determined tone, "It's a dirty job, Sarge; but somebody's got to do it." Kovacs spun around before it became too obvious that he was about to laugh.

A stocky, ruggedly built man came out of the company office and walked briskly toward the front of the formation. He appeared to be about thirty-five and his ruddy face was the scowling type that can be found brooding over a glass of beer in practically any rundown bar. He held a large brown bottle in the stubby finger of his right hand.

Forsythe nudged Chalice. "Here comes your Sunday Surprise."

"I've noticed you men have been getting a little slack," Gunny Martin shouted in a whiskey tenor. "Yesterday I caught two of you walking around without covers. Not only don't I like to see men ignoring a Marine Corps tradition like keeping covered at all times, but I also don't like to see anybody with hair longer than mine." He took off his cover, exposing a red scalp with just enough hair on it to keep it from shining. "And as long as we're on this fucking hill, you will *not* wear bush covers or rain hats. If you don't have a utility cover, wear your helmet liner. Another goddamn thing: no one, except squad leaders and above, can have mustaches; and you *will* shave everyday as long as there's water.

"It seems we can't trust you men to take your malaria tabs every week, so we're starting a new system. From now on we'll all take our tabs together. I don't care if they do give you the shits. Which would you rather have, the shits or malaria?" There were numerous mumblings of "malaria" from the ranks. Martin ignored them and continued, "Now you know why you were told to bring canteens to this formation. Platoon Sergeants, come up here and get the tabs for your men."

When each man had been given a tablet, the gunny continued, "All right, I want everybody to hold their tabs in their right hands and their canteens in their left." Chalice did so, but noticed that both Payne and Forsythe had theirs in the opposite hands. He started to switch before realizing that they were just fooling around. "Okay, now swallow them." Chalice did so in time to see Forsythe flip his past his ear. Somebody behind them said in an irritated voice, "Goddamn you, Forsythe. That hit me right in the face. How 'bout droppin' 'em on the ground like everybody else?"

"All right," the Gunny shouted, "church call goes in fifteen minutes. I wanna see most of you there. A little religion never hurt anybody. . . . *DISmissed!*"

"Never did 'em much good," somebody in the back mumbled.

The members of the company broke formation and milled around the area. The ground was sprinkled with orange malaria tablets. Harmon walked around pressing them into the dirt with the toe of his boot.

40

Chalice grabbed Forsythe's arm, "Hey, how come nobody takes the malaria tabs?" Before Forsythe could reply, a knowing look came across Chalice's face and he answered his own question. "Oh, I get it. Malaria's a ticket outa this place."

"You shittin' me? You can't get outa here with malaria, not unless you get it for the third time."

"Then how come no —"

"Cause they don't do any fucking good. Just give ya the shits. There's one type of malaria they don't prevent. It just so happens that's the type everybody gets around here."

"Can't they fix the pill up?"

"They got another one, a white one."

"When do we get it?"

"We don't."

"Why not?"

Forsythe shrugged his shoulders. "I dunno. The captain and the rest of of the CP get it." He looked past Chalice and yelled, "*Childs, you mother-fucker.*"

Tony 5 added, "Well, *no* shit, look who's here."

They were referring to a skinny Marine approaching them wearing a pack, helmet, and the rest of his fighting gear. He had obviously just gotten off a convoy or a helicopter. Childs shook hands with a few of the men while Chalice stood ignored off to the side. His skinny neck tilted forward, making him appear slightly hunchbacked, and his eyes squinted from behind a pair of thick, dirty glasses. He removed them, exposing two large, blanched circles, spat on the lenses, and wiped them on his shirt.

Forsythe reached out and jabbed Childs's shoulder. "You sonofabitch, are you just visiting or do you plan to stay a while?"

"I haven't made up my mind yet. I was getting kind of bored in the rear. Let's go inside so I can drop this gear." They followed him into the hootch and sat down around him.

Forsythe asked, "How long were you in the rear? It must of been two months."

"No, ten weeks. Anything happen while I was gone?"

"Not much," Tony 5 answered. "We still haven't gotten a new lieutenant."

"Good!"

"How'd you manage to skate that long?" Forsythe asked.

"Well, my R and R in Japan was two weeks. I brought the clap back so that was another week. Then I lost my glasses and it took about ten days to get a new pair. I was really in bad shape; couldn't go on working parties, couldn't stand lines, just about the only thing I could do was fuck around. Then the heel fell off one of my boots. They didn't have my size so I had to walk around in Gook sandals. By the time they got my boots in, I got this thing." He pointed to a lump on his forearm the size of half a golf ball.

Forsythe leaned closer. "Hey man, that's a real work of art. How'd you grow it?"

"I don't know. It grew by itself."

"What do you feed it when it gets hungry?"

"Oh, it's not picky. It eats anything I do. Anyway, they sent me to Da Nang. I felt kinda important because I thought I was making medical history, but the doctors there acted like it wasn't much — like some post-puberty thing that happens to everybody. They'd come around, look at it, say 'Very interesting,' then walk away. They weren't sure what it was, but they all agreed I wasn't pregnant.

"Anyway, they got tired of looking at it, so they medivacked me to a hospital ship to get it removed. What an abortion that was. After waitin' around about a week, I asked when they were going to operate. They said they'd do it when they got a chance. 'A chance for what?' I asked. They said, 'When we get the time.' I told them that that was a real load off my mind, and that I'd originally thought they were gonna do it when they didn't have the time.

"Anyway, the hospital got to be a real drag. We had to eat after the crew did, and they never left anything good. We couldn't buy anything in the PX except cigarettes — we were Marines and the PX was for the crew, they said. And we had these ass-busting working parties *every fucking day*."

"Are you shittin' us?"

"That's where the trouble started. We were doing the squid's work. One day me and a guy named Simpson were swabbing the squid's recreation room. Here we were mopping their floor while these lazy sailors were playing Ping-Pong, shooting pool, and watching TV —"

"War is hell," Forsythe commented.

"— Simpson had one arm in a cast and was having a heck of a time with the mop. When he was doing the floor in front of the TV set, some fat sailor said, 'How 'bout hurrying up so we can watch the program?' Simpson answered real friendlylike, 'How 'bout kissin' my ass?' Well anyway, this squid forgot he didn't have any guts and told Simpson he was lucky his arm was in a cast or he'd get his ass kicked. Naturally I didn't want to see any trouble start so, quick thinker that I am, I tried to cool things off by sticking the end of my mop in the squid's face. I told him there was a fly on his nose, but he didn't believe it and came charging at me. I'm not saying this guy was big, but when he got up, the ship started to rock. Before he reached me, Simpson came on like Tarzan and flung his mop between the fat slob's legs. The big turd hit the deck so hard he slid ten yards on the water from the bucket he knocked over on the way down —"

Hamilton nodded his head while saying, "Served the fucking squid right."

"— Five of his friends started after me. Luckily, Simpson was an all-state pitcher in high school, because by this time he was over at one of the pool tables flinging billiard balls. Only the United States Navy would be stupid enough to put pool tables on a ship —"

"That's 'cause the Marine Corps doesn't have any ships," Forsythe pointed out.

"Anyway, I saw one of the squids look towards the other pool table. Realizing the tactical danger of such weapons in the hands of the enemy, I hauled ass to the table and jumped on top of it. Luckily, the last slob to use it hadn't put his cue back in the rack. I'm not bragging, but I put on a display of swordsmanship that would have made Errol Flynn drool. The only guy able to touch a ball was the first guy that tried. I caught him reaching for the five ball. His wrist'll never be the same. I don't wanna give you the idea that I was fightin' 'em off single-handed, Simpson was really on target. Boy, did he have a fast ball. One of those guys is gonna have an earache for the rest of his life. Anyway, Simpson got two lying on the floor at the same time, so the others ran. You shoulda seen the faces of the two on the floor when they realized the others had hauled ass. It didn't take 'em long to follow. In the meantime, Fatboy, who started the whole thing, finally got up. He decided to leave also. He could really run, considering he was dragging one leg behind him. Didn't run quite fast enough though. Simpson bounced a cue ball off his head just before he got out the door.

"So here was me and Simpson all alone in the rec room. We had to decide whether we were going to hold the ground we'd taken, or retreat to a more strategic position."

"You shoulda taken over the whole ship," Hamilton suggested.

"We were pretty fagged out, so we decided to hold what we had. We stuck a Ping-Pong table in front of the hatch and sat with our backs up against it. After resting a minute, I left Simpson at the hatch and started collecting the pool balls in my empty bucket. It wasn't ten minutes before some guy starts banging on the table like a maniac, saying he's an officer and to let him in. We didn't know whether it was a trick or not, so Simpson moved a card table near the door, put the bucket of pool balls on it,

43

then climbed on himself. When I got the Ping-Pong table moved back far enough, Simpson, who was standin' on the card table with his arm cocked, said it was okay, the guy *was* an officer. Anyway, we let the funny-looking fag in, and he was *really* pissed. Not only because of what had happened, but also because Simpson couldn't stop laughin' because of the look on the weirdo's face when I pulled the table away and he saw Simpson ready to let go with the billiard ball.

"Anyway, they kept me around for another week trying to figure out what to do with me. My attitude was gettin' bad and I wasn't gettin' along too well with the doctors because they kept on tellin' me I had a bad attitude —"

"How long did it take them to come up with that diagnosis?" Tony 5 asked.

"They must have worked overtime," Forsythe added.

"— They finally decided the reason I was givin' them so much trouble was that I didn't wanna go back to the bush. I guess they figured it was the worst thing they could do to me, so they sent me back here. They said they were doing it because I was a bad influence on the other patients and the growth on my arm was full grown now and it wouldn't get any bigger."

The men sat around nodding their heads until Hamilton asked, "How you gonna get it cut off?"

"They said I can have it done when I rotate back to the States. To tell the truth, I kinda like it — it's grown on me."

"Yeah, it sure looks that way," Forsythe commented. "Tell me, did anything interesting happen to you while you were gone?"

"A lot of things, but you guys probably wouldn't believe me if I told you."

Forsythe looked at Childs with admiration. "I gotta admit it, that was some fancy skating. Anyway you can get out of it, do it. You owe it to yourself."

Tony 5 nodded agreement and stood up. "There it is: You owe it to yourself. . . . C'mon, let's go to the chapel."

"Wait a minute," Childs said. "I gotta get somethin' outa my pack." While he was digging in his pack, a pool ball rolled out on the cot. He ignored it, and continued to rummage through his gear.

Forsythe picked it up. "What's this?"

Childs found what he was looking for and put it in his pocket. "Oh, just a souvenir. It had some blood on it, but it rubbed off." They tossed it around as they walked to the door.

Hamilton looked back and noticed Chalice still sitting down. "C'mon, aren't you going to chapel?"

44

"Naw, I'm not interested."

Forsythe cut in, "You think we are? It's better than working parties. C'mon." Chalice got up and followed them out the door.

The chapel was a converted field barracks. Except for crude benches in place of cots and the presence of an altar, it looked exactly like the platoon hootch. There were empty seats towards the front, but they sat in the last row. Tony 5 was on the aisle with Childs next to him. Forsythe sat next to Childs, and Chalice was between Forsythe and Hamilton. Forsythe began juggling the cue ball from hand to hand. Hamilton reached across Chalice and tried to grab it. He ended up with Forsythe's wrist instead. They were struggling over it as the chaplain walked in. Well over six feet tall, he was extremely broad and powerful looking. His thin black hair, cut skin close on the sides, was squared off into a crew cut on top. It had obviously been waxed in front to make it stand up. He walked towards the altar smiling and shaking hands with a few of the men on the way. His boots and the holster to his .45 were polished to a mirrored finish.

Forsythe and Hamilton were still struggling over the cue ball when the chaplain started speaking in a folksy, good-natured voice. "I'm glad to see all of you here today. I notice a lot of new faces so I'll introduce myself. I'm Captain Hindman, your battalion chaplain." There was a loud thud as Hamilton got yanked across Chalice's knees and onto the floor. Forsythe grinned as he held the cue ball between two fingers right in front of Hamilton's face. Hamilton grabbed for it and missed.

A dark Marine turned around and scowled, "How about showing a little respect?"

Hamilton looked up with a big, friendly grin on his face. "Sure, man." He got up off the floor and sat back down on the bench.

The chaplain hadn't noticed what had happened and was starting his sermon. "Men, today I want to talk to you about victory. Not the type of victory your company commanders usually talk about, but a type of victory related to it. I want to tell you about Jesus' victory over Satan. Jesus had fasted in the wilderness for forty days and forty nights. Imagine that. We complain when the choppers don't supply us and we have to go without C-rations for a day or two. Jesus didn't have any C-rations. Satan came to him and said, 'If thou be the Son of God, command that these stones be made bread.' Jesus answered him by saying, 'Man shall not live by bread alone, but by every word that proceedeth out of the mouth of God.'"

Chalice noticed Hamilton looking across him towards Forsythe, eyes focused on the cue ball as Forsythe rubbed it in his hands. Childs sat with his head down, kneading the lump on his forearm. Tony 5's huge body was leaning forward, arms dangling between his knees. His eyes slowly closed and his chin fell against his chest, causing his head to bob up and down as his lungs expanded and contracted. As he fell into a deeper sleep, his breathing became louder. Chalice heard a change in the chaplain's tone indicating he was about to make a point.

"You men are probably asking yourselves what this sermon has to do with you. Satan never came up to you and asked you to change stones to bread or offered you all the kingdoms of the world. No, he hasn't, but he tempts you in other ways with other things — *like marijuana.*"

Forsythe stared disgustedly at Hindman. Childs stopped playing with his lump long enough to raise his head and mumble audibly, "Are you shittin' me, Fred?" Hamilton was still looking at the cue ball, and Tony 5 continued to sleep.

The chaplain went on, "You start out smoking marijuana, then you get hooked on other narcotics. Pretty soon you're stealing and doing other works of the Devil just so you can buy more narcotics. Think about it: You start out smoking a little marijuana to get high and before you know it you're a full-time employee of the Devil. All you wanted to do was get high. I'll tell you a better way to get high, the way I do it. *I* get high on Jesus."

There was a sharp crack. Chalice shot a glance towards Forsythe in time to see the cue ball bouncing between his feet. Tony 5 woke up with a jolt, his eyes nervously shifting from side to side. Hamilton watched the ball as it rolled into the aisle before Forsythe could pick it up. Practically everybody in front of them had turned around to see what had happened. The dark Marine gave Forsythe a hard stare. Forsythe, sitting with a big, guilty grin on his face, said to him in a childlike voice, "I dropped it." The dark Marine turned back towards the front with a less than satisfied look on his face. Childs strolled nonchalantly into the aisle to pick up the cue ball. Distracted, Chaplain Hindman lost his train of thought. He stood silent for a few moments before continuing the sermon. "As I was saying, I get high when I think about the wonderful things He does, when I think about how much He loves us all, when I think how He loves our country. . . ."

When the services were over, most of those present stayed around to talk to the chaplain. Childs quickly got up and left, followed by Hamilton, Forsythe, Tony 5, and Chalice. Tony 5 said he wanted to see somebody

46

and headed off in a different direction. Childs and Hamilton walked in front. Forsythe, flipping the cue ball from hand to hand, and Chalice followed. Childs whispered to Hamilton so the others couldn't hear, "Is he all right?"

"Yeah, I think so."

"Maybe we better ditch him."

"Naw, he's okay."

"He parties?"

"If he doesn't, we'll turn him on."

"Okay."

Childs turned off the road and led them on a twisting path between a series of ammo bunkers. Chalice had been walking with his head down and hadn't been paying much attention to where they were going. Suddenly he found himself standing in front of a small Buddhist shrine. The others were already inside. The shrine was surrounded on three sides by the sandbagged walls of the three bunkers built around it. The side free of obstructions looked out over the valley. 'God! What's this doing here?' Ignoring those inside, Chalice slowly circled it. The shrine was only about fifteen feet square. Deep hues of orange and blue seeped through the coat of dust that covered its once brightly painted walls. Centered on a field of orange, a blue and white surreal, fire-breathing dragon dominated the frescos. There were intricately painted Chinese characters to each side of it. The four triangular sections of the roof rose to a pyramidlike apex. Atop this apex was a large ball of smooth, shiny marble banded by different shades of orange and white. Along the four ridges of the roof and facing up towards the marble ball were four convoluted dragons.

Hamilton called Chalice into the shrine, where he found the others standing around looking at each other. "Hey, what's going on?"

"We're trying something," Childs answered. "All right, are you guys ready?"

"I'm always ready," Forsythe answered.

Childs continued, "All right, everybody think about Jesus."

They stood silently until Chalice again asked, "What's going on?"

"We're trying to get high on Jesus," Childs answered.

"Yeah, man," Hamilton added, "let's give it a chance."

After standing around for a minute, Childs asked, "Is anybody high?"

"Not me," Hamilton replied, shaking his head.

Forsythe had a confused look on his face. "I don't understand it. Maybe we're doing it wrong."

"I doubt it," Childs said. "Why don't we try something else in the mean time?"

"Good idea."

Childs reached in his pocket. "I thought you'd like it, Hamilton." He pulled out a cellophane pack containing ten cigarettes. They were a little shorter than Pall Malls. He lit one and took a big drag. Chalice began to grin: there was no mistaking the aroma.

Childs handed the joint to Chalice who studied it for a while. "Man, I've never seen one this size before." He took a big drag and held it in. They passed it around until there was only half an inch left and Childs flicked the butt in the corner. "What'd you do that for?" Chalice asked in a surprised voice.

"It was getting hot."

"But the roach is the best part."

"I know, but we've got plenty more. It's easier on the throat this way."

Hamilton cut in, "Saving roaches is great back in the world, but it's a waste of time out here. We get all the grass we want for ten cents a joint."

"*Ten cents*, for a joint that size!"

"Yeah, and they're not junk either. This stuff is opium-cured. Hit you yet?"

"Wow, has it ever. I gotta sit down." He sat with his legs crossed and the others joined him in a close circle. They started smiling because the change of position had made them dizzy. "Would Tony 5 be pissed-off if he knew we were blowing grass?"

They all started laughing. Forsythe became hysterical and fell over backwards. Childs stopped long enough to ask, "Did you think his last name was 5?"

"*No*, I knew it was a nickname."

"Wait . . . wait and I'll tell you how he got it. . . . He's got a real short temper and when they made him a fire team leader he almost went batshit. There's usually at least one moron in each fire team. Tony had the Eighth Wonder of the World in his, a guy named Craig. This guy couldn't open a can of C-rats. If he hadn'ta sent home for one of those big can openers your mother uses, he'd a starved to death. We were so scared he was gonna shoot one of us, we made him keep his rifle on safe all the time. That didn't stop Old Craig though. One time he had an accidental discharge and the round went right by Tony's ear. You shoulda seen the look on Tony's face. We knew it was all over for Craig. Just as he started to go after him, I grabbed him around the waist. I didn't want Tony to kill him, not in front of all those people anyway. Next thing I remember, I was on the ground and a few other guys were trying to hold Tony back. He threw 'em off like flies. He finally gets to Craig — there he is standing over him panting like a water buffalo while Craig is lying on the ground trembling, rolled up in a little ball, ready to die. Tony bends down and

48

kisses him right on top of the head. Then he says, 'Thanks, Craig. Thanks for being the worst shot in the world. You can't even hit what you don't aim at.' Craig looks up and says, 'Thanks, Tony.' Anyway, we had a conference and decided to take the firing pin out of his rifle while he was sleeping. The dumb sonofabitch walked around the bush for three weeks without a firing pin.

"Anyway, we had some new guys in the squad that made all kinds of mistakes. We'd go on a night ambush and they'd make enough noise to tell every VC within ten miles where we were. To keep from losing his temper and killing someone, Tony stayed stoned practically all the time. A lot of us had been smoking, but never when we thought we were gonna hit the shit.

"We got the word one day that the whole battalion was going into the Arizona and we'd be there a couple of months. This meant we'd have to put Craig's firing pin back in. The Arizona's the only place you can't get grass, and if he ran out, Tony knew he'd go nuts, so he bought five hundred joints to take with him. Half his pack was filled with grass. A week after we went in, we got a new guy in our squad, also named Tony. It was kinda confusing so we started calling Tony 5, Tony 5. He was stoned the day we went into the Arizona, the day we came out, and all the days in between."

"He was *nice* all the time," Forsythe added.

"Didn't you guys have a better chance of getting killed with him stoned?"

"Naw, he was used to it. He's about the only guy we'd trust stoned."

"Did you smoke much in the Arizona?"

"Naw, unless you're like Tony 5, it's too dangerous."

"What happened to the other Tony?"

Childs's expression turned serious. "We were marching outa the Arizona, it was the last day, and Plain Tony was walking point. All we had to do was cross the river and we'd be outa there. It had been raining heavy and there was only one place for a couple a miles where we could cross. Everybody had a feeling it would be booby-trapped, so Tony 5 took the point and Plain Tony walked behind him. Just as we got to the river, Tony 5 tripped a booby trap. If those fucking things are put in right, you can never see 'em. Tony 5 only got a little scratch, a cheap Heart, but Plain Tony really got messed up. He died in a few minutes. . . . A good kid."

"That's a bust. . . . What happened to Craig?" Forsythe and Hamilton started laughing again.

"Oh him." Childs paused to light another joint. "The second day out we found some small bunkers and were fragging them to make sure no VC were inside. Craig was with me. I was ready to frag this one bunker and

49

he was on the other side of it. I told him to watch out. Then I threw the grenade in, yelled 'Fire in the hole' like I'm supposed to, and hit the deck. As soon as it blew, Craig started yelling 'I'm hit, I'm hit.' The idiot had stuck his head in the other opening of the bunker when I threw the frag in. He didn't know it was just another entrance. He thought he'd tripped a booby trap. . . . The lucky sonofabitch didn't get hit too bad, just bad enough to get sent back to the world."

The three brightly colored frescos on the wall opposite Chalice drew his attention. Each one was a different geometric design in orange, blue, and white. Their soft, curving configurations had an almost hypnotic effect on him. Childs waved an unlit joint in front of his face to ask whether he should light it. Chalice made no response and heard, as if from a distance, Hamilton's voice, "Go ahead"; then Forsythe's, "Run it."

Childs lit the joint and held it out to Chalice, who just stared at it for a while. Finally, he took it and said, "I can always tell when I'm stoned — it gets to be too much of a hassle to reach for the joint."

He passed it to Forsythe who added, "I always know I'm stoned when I'm halfway through an answer and I realize there wasn't any question." As he took a deep drag, the others burst out laughing. He tried to keep from laughing himself, but couldn't and started to cough.

Hamilton took the joint away from him and, before taking a drag, said, "The first time I realized how great grass is, was when I was driving around wrecked and stopped for a red light. Usually nothing pisses me off like a red light, but I just stared at it and smiled. It looked like the prettiest thing I'd ever seen."

"Did I ever tell you guys what it was like the time I was wrecked and got hit by a truck?" Childs asked.

"No."

"Uh, uh."

"It was kinda nice."

They sat grinning at each other until Hamilton awkwardly rose to his feet. "C'mon, we gotta get back to the hootch. I can't wait to find out the working party the gunny's got ready for us." The others stumbled to their feet and followed him out the passageway. As Chalice emerged from between the ammo bunkers, a surprisingly strong breeze brushed against his face, bringing with it the smell of rain. This was the first time he'd been high in a couple of weeks, and he had forgotten how pleasant it could be. Somehow he'd ended up with the cue ball, and was rubbing its smooth surface between his hands. The valley below had never looked so green, or so peaceful. It was hard for him to believe there were people down there with guns, just waiting for him.

3. The Bad Bush

The days passed with recurrent monotony, differentiated only by the various types of working parties that filled them. Chalice again found himself standing in the company formation waiting to be assigned another tedious working party. The corporal at the front of the formation was arbitrarily picking out men to be sent to different places on the hill. He pointed to Chalice. "You, you'll ride around on the Gook truck."

'Not bad,' thought Chalice. He had been wanting to get the job ever since he'd been on the hill. All it involved was riding on the Vietnamese garbage truck and seeing that they didn't pick up live ammunition or anything else that could be used as a weapon or booby trap. His interest stemmed from more than the lack of work involved. A pretty Vietnamese girl rode on the truck. He wanted to meet her, thinking that at the very least he would be able to get some practice speaking Vietnamese.

The truck was an old bus with the seats taken out and garbage piled ceiling high in their place. The driver, a young Vietnamese, owned the truck and gave the orders. The girl was one of his relatives. An older Vietnamese man rode along and did the dirty work. Before putting the garbage on the truck, he would sort it. All food waste was put aside to be sold as hog feed. Any wood, metal, or heavy cardboard was sold to the villagers to repair their huts. What little garbage remained was thrown away.

The girl was quite friendly and talkative until the driver made his resentment obvious to both her and Chalice. When he handed her a few cookies, she slipped one to Chalice. It tasted good, until Chalice realized it must have come from the garbage. When no one was looking, he flipped the rest of the cookie out the window. Noticing some members of his platoon heading back towards the company area, he waved. One of them yelled, "Didn't you get word? We're moving out." Chalice jumped off the truck and caught up with them, thinking, 'I should have known it, finally had a decent working party.'

The company area was alive with men filling canteens and adjusting packs. Chalice quickly got his equipment together. Sergeant Kovacs yelled for everybody to stage their gear in front of the hootch, and the packs were quickly arranged in four neat rows. Tony 5 handed Chalice a bar of C-4 plastic explosive to carry in his pack. Kovacs yelled, "SQUAD LEADERS, *pick up your C-rats*, six meals per man." When Chalice received his C-rations, he realized why only a few members of the platoon still had Marine Corps packs. Aside from their being more uncomfortable, they didn't hold as much as Vietnamese packs.

Chalice found himself caught up in, and awed by, the activity around him — the ordered chaos of well over a hundred men getting ready to do something they had known they would have to do, relieved and excited at the same time, glad enough about the coming change, as they would have been about any change, to be heedless of its consequences. The inertia of the hot, heavy air was broken by hurried footsteps, shouted orders, and the cracks of rifle bolts going home on now loaded chambers. As he looked around him, he realized that something different was happening; that his senses, mind, and reflexes had sharpened to a point that, in the drudgery of his days on the hill, he had forgotten was possible. It was as if, without knowing it, he had stepped over a line, one that separated irrevocably twenty-three years of past from whatever was to be his future. For the first time he sensed something that had been so absent as to throw doubt upon its existence, something that can only be myth until it becomes experience, a rare, demanding kind of excitement — the excitement of men at war.

Sergeant Kovacs called Second Platoon together. "All right, Fourth Platoon has the point. First Platoon follows them with the captain and the rest of the CP. We go next, and Third Platoon plays Tail-End Charlie."

Fourth Platoon had just put on their packs when the order was given to "Move-out." As Fourth Platoon started down the road, First Platoon put their packs on. The company was moving out in two columns, one on each side of the road. The gunny walked by Chalice, heading for First Platoon. He was followed by another man about thirty years old. Although he had never seen this man before, Chalice knew he had to be Captain Trippitt, the company commander. Their eyes met for a second, Chalice drawing his away first. Trippitt's ruddy face looked capable of only two expressions — dissatisfaction and rage; yet he still seemed far more human than given credit for in any of the descriptions that Chalice had heard. First Platoon started to move out, and Kovacs yelled, "Saddle-up." The squad leaders repeated his command, and everybody put on their packs. When Chalice got his on, Payne walked up to him. "Well Professor, now you're gonna see the *bad* bush. How's your pack feel?"

"It's killing me."

"Be glad you don't have to hump a radio, like me. This thing would really kick your ass. Hey, why don't you put your magazine pouch and law on after your pack? That way, when you wanna take off your pack, you can take them off first and they don't get in your way. Here, I'll give you a hand." The law had a strap attached at each end, and Chalice wore it across his chest like a bandoleer. He took it off and handed it to Payne, who said, "I don't know why we need these things when we've got 3.5's. They're more accurate and have a longer range." Chalice handed Payne his magazine pouch, then put his pack back on. He took the law from Payne and put his head and arm through the strap, adjusting it until it hung at his side. Chalice put on the magazine pouch in the same manner, except on the opposite shoulder. "Ain't that a lot better?" Payne asked with a look of satisfaction.

Tony 5 came over and Payne walked away. "Hey Prof, what happens if we get hit and you have to ditch your pack?"

"Whata you mean?"

"If you wanna get your pack off in a hurry, you'll have to take your magazines off first, then you'll have to put your magazines back on. You might even forget and leave them with your pack. You better switch 'em now. Hurry up, we're moving out in a minute."

Chalice dumped his gear again, thinking, 'I should have known it.' While putting it back on, he pointed to the two bazookas Guns Squad was carrying. "How come we need laws when we've got two 3.5 rocket launchers?"

"How'd you like to carry one of those big motherfuckers on a squad-size patrol? Besides, practically every other round for those things is a dud. Listen, we're gonna pull out in a minute and our squad leads off. I want you to be the first man in back of me. That means you'll be on the opposite side of the road and ten yards behind me. That's *twenty yards* behind the man in front of you. I don't wanna have to tell you to keep it spread out. If Charlie decides to lob a mortar or do any other type a damage, he'll do it when and where he can get the most men. You're just asking for it if you're on the ass of the guy in front of you."

Harmon yelled to Tony 5, "Start moving; keep it spread out."

They followed the road as it curved back around the barracks and sloped down the length of the hill. As each man went by the guard bunker, word was passed back for him to put a round in his chamber and take his weapon off safe. Chalice could see that the front of the column had already reached the low ground and was winding to the right along the road that would lead it through the ville. At the base of the hill the earth became softer and his boots sunk in up to his ankles. The ammo can strap started digging through his flak jacket into his shoulder. The slight breeze which had given them some comfort at the top of the hill had long since deserted them, and the air took on substance, becoming heavier and more oppressive. Sweat streamed down his face, blurring his vision and burning his eyes.

As he neared the edge of the village, his nostrils caught the pungent, squalid odor of decay. Though there had been very little rain for the last few days, a thin layer of orange mud covered the road. People walked outside of and between the two columns. They took little notice of the soldiers and even seemed to be purposely avoiding their glances. Most of them wore black pajamalike pants, and blouses ranging from dingy white to burgundy. The marketplace was two rows of adjoining shacks that bordered the road for a third of a mile. Bamboo poles supported roofs of thatch or tin, and the walls were either thatch or cardboard. Some of the shacks contained stacks of black-marketed C-rations. Others displayed piles of brightly colored yard goods. Old women squatted in front of the shacks with bowls of colorful and exotic-looking vegetables at their feet. A little boy stood behind three stacks of straw, cone-shaped hats. Chalice's eyes were caught by a beautiful girl sitting behind a hand-operated sewing machine. She looked up, but seeing his stare, quickly lowered her head. One of the last hootches contained a primitive, hand-operated grindstone. People were carrying grain towards it. In front of the mill lay several round, flat baskets over six feet in diameter filled with grain drying in the sun. A little boy stood beside them chasing away some small dogs with a stick. Chalice looked ahead to the end of the marketplace hoping that a breeze would meet him when he reached it. None did.

The column crossed a sturdy wooden bridge over a fork in the river that ran behind the ville. An old man stood in the middle of the bridge trying to calm a badly spooked water buffalo. The powerfully built beast's pink and gray nostrils pulsated as it eyed the troops passing by on both sides of it. Chalice remembered being warned to stay away from these animals — being told that the Vietnamese kids could pull their tails and climb all over them as if they were half-ton puppy dogs; but a Caucasian, because of his different body odor, couldn't get within twenty feet of them without risking his life.

On the other side of the bridge, two fairly large concrete buildings came into view. The near one had an orange shingled roof and an empty flag pole standing in front of it. The far one had a tin roof topped with a large cross. As he approached them, Chalice could see that both were pockmarked with bullet holes. The far one had had a rear corner blown away. The front of the shingled building was lettered with the Vietnamese words for school. Both buildings were abandoned.

54

Peasants walked along the edges of the road. Some carried large bundles of bamboo balanced on their shoulders. Others carried long poles projecting in front and in back of them. On both ends of these poles hung baskets of rice, vegetables, or firewood. Their bare feet took short, quick steps towards the marketplace.

Chalice's left arm was numb from the weight of the ammo can, so he switched it to his other shoulder. Although they hadn't been marching for more than an hour, he was already exhausted. He looked around at the other members of his platoon. They didn't seem as tired. He unsnapped his canteen for the third time. Finding it almost empty, he gulped down the remainder.

Forsythe called forward, "Hey Prof, take it easy on the water. We might not get any more for a day or two."

"Okay," Chalice yelled back, surprised at the effort it had taken to speak that one word. Up ahead, in the middle of the road, a little Vietnamese kid sat astride a bike with a Styrofoam cooler tied to the back of it. He talked to the soldiers as they passed by. One of the soldiers held out some money. The kid caught up with him, gave the Marine a Coke from the cooler, and took the money. Chalice, exhausted and having little control over the thoughts flashing through his mind, began to laugh without really knowing why. His mind finally connected the two ironic segments of the scene — soldiers walking along a road with loaded rifles, afraid of being ambushed or of stepping on a mine; and a little Vietnamese kid riding a bike right along with them, worried only about selling Cokes.

The columns stopped and the men sat down, at the same time passing the word back to "Take ten." Chalice dropped to his knees. The kid selling sodas approached him. "Hey Marine, you want bucoo cold soda?"

"Yeah." Chalice struggled to get his pocket open.

"Fifty cents."

He handed him the money and took the soda. It wasn't "bucoo" cold, but it was a lot colder than what he'd been drinking out of his canteen. He guzzled it down in two gulps. Forsythe called out from behind him, "Take it easy, don't drink so fast." Chalice pivoted towards him, amazed at how tired he felt. He scanned the other men, relieved to see that everybody else looked pretty beat also. Forsythe said to him, "This humping's a motherfucker, isn't it?"

"Yeah, I can't believe how dead I am."

"Don't sweat it. Everybody's bushed. We've been skating too long. . . . It's hot today, but it gets hotter."

"How hot do you think it is?"

" 'Bout a hundred and ten. Must be getting to the Skipper, too. We usually don't stop this soon. You can bet Trippitt isn't stopping to do us any favor."

"*Chalice*," Tony 5 called out gruffly, "face outboard and keep your eyes open."

Just as Chalice pivoted his body towards the river, the men in front of him began getting up and word was passed back to "Move-out." He rose to his feet awkwardly, at the same time mumbling, "Can't have been ten minutes. We just sat down." He remembered estimating the weight of his equipment when it lay staged in a neat pile in front of the platoon hootch — seventy pounds. But this had been no more than a number. Now it was a burden, a trial. Seventy pounds — it seemed unfair that the torture he was enduring could be measured, no *minimized*, by something as abstract and meaningless as a simple measure of weight.

Within a few minutes, Chalice was more exhausted than before they had taken the break. He looked over the other members of his squad — 'Guess I'm not any more beat than they are.' His eyes dropped to the ground and he stared at his dust- and mud-covered boots as they moved, as if by themselves, one in front of the other.

Tony 5 yelled back at him in an irritated voice, "*Get your head up!* What the fuck you looking at? Watch the flanks."

He raised his head and looked off the side of the road towards the river — 'God, wouldn't mind splashing around in that thing for a while.'

They marched for another two hours before word was passed from the rear to hold up the column. He turned around to see Graham sprawled on his back with a corpsman looking over him. Everybody started to sit down, Chalice being one of the first and nearly losing his balance.

Harmon called out in a voice loud enough for everybody in the squad to hear, "Hey Tony, I told you he was a shitbird." Chalice felt relieved that he hadn't been the one to quit. He sat looking towards the river. A young boy, up to his knees in water, led a water buffalo with two smaller children on its back. Chalice moved over a few feet in order to balance his pack on a rock. This took the weight off of his shoulders. His left arm had fallen asleep soon after the first break. He now massaged it and brought the feeling back, reminding himself to buy an Arvin pack the first chance he got. They sat for fifteen minutes before Trippitt ordered the point to start moving again. Harmon and the corpsman pulled Graham to his feet.

An amtrack, a large tanklike vehicle used to transport troops and supplies, lay on its side just off the road. A mine had ripped a large hole in its armor-plated bottom directly under the driver's seat. 'Bet they had to scrape that guy off the roof.' After another hour of marching, Chalice turned around to see how Graham was doing. 'Hope he falls on his face

56

pretty soon. Could use another break.' The sweat dripping from his fore-head seemed to be burning his eyes raw. Constantly blinking them didn't help. Shimmering waves of thick, humid air rose up from the road. Chalice glanced at the sun. It looked about four hours from setting. 'Doubt we'll march after dark. Hour to set in. Three, three more hours of humping . . . Can make that.' An hour later he was walking in a daze, his thoughts jumping from subject to subject, putting one foot in front of the other as if it were the natural thing to do. As tired as he was, Chalice knew that if he could keep on his feet, he'd keep moving. The column trudged on for another hour before the word to hold up was passed from the rear. He turned to see Graham lying on his back again. 'Thank God, thought he'd never drop.' Chalice sat down, careful to face outward. 'Lucky in my platoon. He'll come in handy.'

Tony 5 walked over to check on Graham. On his way back he stopped to talk to Chalice. "That's one gutless motherfucker."

Chalice looked up. "Man, I'm dead myself."

"Everybody is. You get better at it, but you never get used to it."

"How much farther we got?"

"Ain't sure. We were supposed to stop about two klicks back. The Skipper must of changed his mind. About another hour I guess."

"I can make that all right."

"You better be able to."

Graham finally got back on his feet, and the columns started moving again. Knowing they'd be stopping pretty soon, Chalice felt a lot stronger. In less than an hour they reached the remains of a burned-down pagoda. The columns peeled off the road and circled it.

Harmon went around to his men, telling them the company would sit tight until an hour before dusk, then cross the road and set-in between it and the river. Chalice looked around and saw everyone taking off their packs. As soon as he got his own pack off, a feeling of weightlessness ran through his body and he felt as if he were going to float off the ground. He moved his arms to get the circulation going again. Seeing the other men opening cans of C-rations, Chalice pulled a can of pears out of his pack. He fumbled to open it, his tongue sticking to the top of his mouth. Saving the syrup for last, he spooned out the pears, surprised at how delicious they tasted. The can was a third full of syrup. He lifted it up and let the thick liquid flow down his raw throat. Never had anything tasted so sweet.

Only a tip of the sun remained above the mountains when Hotel Company crossed the road to set-in. The company perimeter bordered the road on one edge and the river on the opposite edge. Second Platoon had the quarter of the circle adjacent to the river. Harmon stood talking to Tony 5 near the lip of a foxhole Chalice was digging. Sergeant Kovacs walked up and tapped Harmon on the shoulder. "The Skipper wants us to send out an ambush."

"Let me guess who's got it," Harmon said disgustedly.

"Alpha."

"That's what I thought."

Tony 5 cut in. "We won't have enough men to stand guard if we send out an ambush."

"That's what I told him, but he said to put three men in each foxhole instead of four. He said we've been getting too much sleep anyway." Kovacs looked across the river and added nonchalantly, "If you want to, you can sandbag."

Harmon nodded.

As Kovacs walked away, Tony 5 said to Chalice, "We're gonna sandbag this ambush. That means we're all gonna stay inside the perimeter. Don't make any mistakes over the radio or the shit'll hit the fan. You've got second watch, two hours and fifteen minutes again."

"Professor," Tony 5 whispered.

Chalice sat up. The cool night air quickly cleared his head. "My watch?"

"Yeah. I'm gonna sleep right in back of the hole. Remember, we're supposed to be on an ambush, so be careful with the radio. If you have to say anything, use your head; but try to wake me first."

Chalice picked up his rifle and slid into the hole. He felt different than he had while standing watch on Hill 65 — more alone. But he wasn't scared. There was something peaceful and reassuring about the black silence that surrounded him. It was soon broken by quiet, cautious footsteps from within the perimeter. Chalice turned, unable to see the silhouette until it was two steps from him.

The figure squatted and whispered, "Professor, everything okay?"

"Yeah. Kovacs?"

"Yeah. Don't make any mistakes with the radio."

"I won't."

"If you see some cat walking around in black PJ's, don't wish him good night, just blow him away."

"Haven't seen anything like that yet."

"Don't worry, he's there. It ain't often you see Charlie, but he sees you every day."

Kovacs remained silent for a few seconds, and Chalice finally asked, "Sarge, you ever kill any of them?"

"Quite a — What the fuck kinda question is that? Whata you think we're doing with these Gooks, playing tag?"

"I just wanted —"

"I know what you wanted — to know what it's like. Well it ain't no big thing. It's one of the rules. . . . Listen Professor, you seem all right most of the time, but I ain't sure. I'll give you some dope you won't find in those books you're humpin'. I've done some movin'. Every place I hit, the rules are different. The trick is to learn the rules before they learn you. Nam ain't no bargain, but the rules are a snap. There ain't but one: Kill them before they kill you. And there's a catch, too: The cocksucker who breaks the rule don't always pay the price. Don't *ever* let me think there's a chance I'll have to pay it for you." As Kovacs stood up, he grabbed Chalice's shoulder to show he wasn't angry. "I'm gonna crash. Take it easy . . . and be careful with the radio."

The company was ready to move out a few minutes after dawn. Kovacs called Second Platoon together. "Here's the story. We're gonna move down the road one kilometer, then turn off to the left and head for the base of the mountains. That's about three more klicks. We'll move along the mountains until the whole column is parallel to the road, then we sweep back on-line. The last tree line is about one klick from the road. We'll probably set-in there for a couple of hours."

Chalice said to Forsythe. "That doesn't sound too bad, only six kilometers. We did about ten yesterday."

"Yeah, but those ten klicks were on a road. Today we move through rice paddies and brush. That's no picnic. We'll be moving on-line, and when you do that you don't go around heavy brush, you go through it."

Kovacs called for everybody to form up. The company again moved out in two columns. Chalice's leg and shoulder muscles felt ready to tear away from his bones, but he was glad they had started early so as to take advantage of the early morning chill. It seemed only a few minutes had passed before they turned off the road towards the mountains. As Chalice stared at them, he felt more confident, telling himself that three kilometers didn't seem too far.

The rice paddies began about fifty yards from the road. The first dike was only a few feet high. Chalice put one foot on it and hopped over. The water came halfway up his thighs. Not used to the weight of his pack, he stumbled and almost lost his balance. Moving through that much water was hard enough in itself, but the foot of soft mud underneath it made matters worse. Before he'd gone ten yards, he knew what Forsythe had meant. He felt as if he were walking on a huge piece of flypaper.

When he stepped up on the next dike his pants legs bulged with water.

Hamilton yelled to him, "Unblouse your trousers and roll up the cuffs."

"What about the leeches?"

"Fuck the leeches. You can't carry around ten gallons of water."

The dikes were only twenty yards apart. When Chalice reached the next one, he unbloused his pants legs. The man in front of him had already crossed the next dike. Chalice hurried to catch up. He could now move more easily, but by the time he caught up he was out of breath. After traveling through a kilometer of rice paddies, they came to a hundred yards of high ground. Chalice took a few steps on it and found the difference hard to believe. 'If only I'd known, yesterday would have been a pleasure.' When they reached the rice paddies again, he dreaded jumping off the dike. Twenty yards into them, he was more exhausted than he'd been all morning.

Hamilton again offered some advice. "Don't follow the trail of the guy in front of you, make your own. Step on the rice shoots. You won't sink in the mud so deep." Hamilton's advice helped, but not much.

It took another hour to reach the base of the mountains. The last half kilometer had been on high ground and relatively easy. The two columns meshed before turning left along the foothills. When the entire company had made the turn and was parallel to the road, the order to hold up was given. Chalice noticed the men checking for leeches. He pulled up his left pants leg and found three huge ones, bloated with blood, attached just above his sock. "Hey Hamilton, how do you get these things off?"

"Here, use this bug juice." As soon as the insect repellent touched them, the leeches dropped off, leaving his calf smeared with blood.

The word was passed to start sweeping. Chalice concentrated on staying even with the men to each side of him. There was constant yelling about keeping the line straight. The men moving on the better ground tended to get ahead of the men moving through the deeper paddies, so they'd have to stop every few minutes to let the others catch up. As the company approached the first tree line, Chalice thought about what he'd been taught. 'Don't go through breaks in the brush — might be booby-trapped. Better to go right through the brush than around it. Look for trip wires, but keep your head up. Have rifle ready to shoot.'

Twenty yards into the tree line the vegetation got thicker. Continually tripping over the undergrowth, Chalice decided to put his rifle on safe rather than risk an accidental discharge. He found himself more worried about keeping up than about tripping a booby trap. 'No wonder so many guys get killed. Get so tired you don't give a shit what you step on.'

The order was passed for everybody to hold up until the line straightened. Some heavy brush lay in front of Chalice. He stared at it disgustedly, chest heaving and thankful for the rest. When given the word to start moving, he pushed his way forward. The brush thickened. He struggled with all his might, hardly making any progress. Thorns covered the branches. He had to ignore them. The brush enveloped him, squeezing tighter, defining his shape and pressing into his skin like thousands of tiny spikes. It crackled loudly around him with each small movement. Choking, unable to get enough air, he had to stop struggling for a second. The silence surprised and frightened him. He couldn't hear or see the rest of his squad. They'd left him behind. He thrashed forward nervously. His feet stomped up and down, almost in place. Tongue sticking to the roof of his mouth, he couldn't breathe. Again he had to stop, dizzy and exhausted. Only the thick brush kept him from falling to the ground.

"*Chalice!*" Tony 5 shouted.

"Over here."

"You're way behind! Get up here! You're holding back the whole company."

"I can't get through this brush."

"For Christ sake, go back and come around it." He turned and flung himself forward. The way back out proved easier than he had expected. Circling around, he came even with the rest of the platoon. Tony glared at him. "Man! Don't get behind like that."

"Okay, I'm sorry."

"You will be if Charlie ever catches you straggling like that. . . . You really did a job on your arms."

Chalice looked at them, noticing for the first time that they were covered with blood. He quickly pulled out the thorns as the company began moving again. They hadn't gone more than a few yards before Tony 5 yelled, "Kovacs, I got a bunker here."

Kovacs yelled back, "Hold up, everybody. Go ahead and frag it, Tony."

Tony 5 called Chalice over. "Watch how I do this." The bunker was so well camouflaged that Chalice came within a step of falling into it. The entrance was a hole barely large enough for a man to pass through. Tony took a grenade out of his pouch and pulled the pin. "When I let go of this frag, hit the deck." He lobbed it in the bunker, yelled "Fire in the hole," and dove to the ground. The blast filled the air with dirt and small rocks. Tony told Forsythe to check out the bunker.

When he got inside, Forsythe yelled, "Nothing here," and crawled back out.

The pace began to slow as more bunkers were found. Each one had to be checked. Somebody would call out "Fire in the hole," then a grenade would go off. Everything had gone all right for a half hour when suddenly a grenade went off without any warning.

Tony 5's head shot up and he looked in the direction of the blast, thinking, 'booby trap.'

Kovacs yelled, "*What the fuck was that?*"

A meek voice replied, "Fire in the hole."

"Well *no* shit," Kovacs called back, and everybody started laughing. The incident took Chalice's mind off his fatigue, and he felt a lot stronger.

Around noon they reached the last tree line and set-in under its shade. Most of the men were in a talkative mood, and they kidded each other as they opened cans of C-rations. Kovacs called the platoon together. By the look on his face, it was evident that he had some good news. "The company's gonna pull out around four o'clock. Our platoon stays behind to set up an ambush in case any Gooks are following us. When the company leaves, I want everyone to keep hidden in the tree line. Tomorrow morning we'll hump over to Liberty Bridge and set up some bridge security. The CP is gonna be at Ladybird State Park, and we'll be by ourselves."

As the men dispersed, they seemed satisfied with the news. Forsythe sat down and started cooking a can of ham and eggs. Chalice sat down next to him and opened a can of franks and beans. "Why's everyone so happy about going to Liberty Bridge? Is it close to here?"

"No, it's a good five klicks; but since it's on the river we'll get to take baths, and the ground is white sand instead of mud — easy to dig in and cleaner. The important thing is the CP is setting-in at Ladybird State Park. That means the captain and gunny won't be around to fuck with us."

"What's Ladybird Park?"

"A sandy place on the riverbank with a lot of shade trees. It's pretty nice. That's why the CP always sets-in there. . . . I'm the one who named it."

Chalice unwrapped a heat tab and set it under his can of franks and beans. He lit the tab and leaned back against a tree. A stiff breeze rustled the brush around him. For the first time since he'd gotten off the hill, he felt relaxed. A few minutes later he took the can off of the heat tab. Surprisingly, the franks and beans tasted delicious. As he dropped the empty can, Chalice said, "Good company, good food, a big shade tree, and a nice breeze; what more could you possibly want?"

An hour after the company pulled out, Kovacs called the squad leaders together. "If any VC are around, they're probably over there," he said pointing to the mountains. "I'd set up an L-shaped ambush, but they can approach from too many directions. We'll have to set-in at the bow in the tree line. Our fields of fire won't be too hot, but it'll be safer." The squad leaders nodded agreement and he assigned them their responsibilities.

The men hid in the tree line until a few minutes before dusk, then took up their positions. Chalice started digging a foxhole, but Forsythe stopped him. "This is an ambush. You never dig in on an ambush." Glad to get the news, he flipped away his entrenching tool. As Chalice sat watching the sun dip behind the mountains, mosquitoes began to swarm around him. Forsythe saw him slapping them and handed him a bottle of insect repellent.

Kovacs had just walked over to Tony 5, and now Tony came towards their position with a disgusted look on his face. "We just got word over the radio that somebody spotted a whole company of NVA in the foot-hills. There's about two hundred, and the flyboys are probably gonna work out on 'em. We better dig in; two two-man holes. Chalice, start digging one for you and me. Hurry up."

The ground was hard. Chalice didn't finish digging until an hour after sunset. When he dropped the E-tool on the back lip of the foxhole, it landed with a clang. "What was that?" Tony asked.

They both felt around in the dark until Chalice found a large metal object about a foot-and-a-half long. "Here it is."

As Tony cleared the dirt away, he kept saying, "Oh no."

"What is it?"

"A dud 105 shell."

Chalice ran his hand across it. "What're we gonna do?"

"We can't move it. It might go off."

"But it's right in back of our hole. What if a round hits it?"

"We'll never know what happened. I'll guarantee you that. Listen Professor, if we get hit tonight, don't fire your rifle. The muzzle flash'll attract their fire. Just keep heaving frags." A series of loud blasts came from the foothills. "Let's hope they're dropping those bombs in the right place."

The bombing continued halfway through the night. During his watch, Chalice kept looking in the direction of the explosions. Tony 5 had pointed out the different types of bombs being dropped, and now that he was alone Chalice identified them to himself. There was a large billow of orange flame — 'Napalm.' This was followed by some louder blasts and some white flashes — 'Regular bombs, HE.' He then heard a small explosion followed by many more small explosions — 'Must be Corfam.' The first explosion was the casing scattering hundreds of small grenades which exploded a few seconds later when they hit the ground.

Aside from the bombing, the night passed quietly. Chalice stared at the terrain around him, trying to imagine what an attack would have been like.

His curiosity caused him to feel cheated. What he had feared the night before became his disappointment the morning after. Then he spotted the 105 round on the edge of the foxhole and figured it was just as well. The CP called on the radio and said the bombing had killed over a hundred NVA, and that Second Platoon was to go up and see if they could find anything interesting. At first the men grumbled about the three additional hours of marching, but soon thoughts of easy souvenirs buoyed their spirits and made them anxious to get started.

Kovacs kept the pace slow and there was very little complaining along the way. Hamilton thought about finding an SKS — the Russian design, Chinese Communist–made rifle that some of the NVA carried. Unlike the AK-47, it was semiautomatic and could be kept as a souvenir. Chalice thought about what the bombs must have done to the NVA. He pictured a hundred bodies lying scattered on the ground; some missing limbs or decapitated, some charred by napalm. His thoughts tinged more with curiosity than horror; he was anxious to reach the spot where the bombs had dropped. They crossed over the first set of hills and walked through an area of fresh bomb craters without seeing any bodies. Hamilton warned Chalice not to step on any of the shiny metallic objects scattered on the ground. They were dud Corfam bombs. Chalice heard Tony 5 say, "Not a fucking thing, not even a blood trail, they didn't get a fucking Gook."

Chalice thought, 'A hundred dead NVA, that's where they get those ridiculous casualty figures.'

Kovacs called the CP on the radio and told them what they had found, or hadn't found. He then ordered the point to angle back towards the road through the high ground. The men plodded on dejectedly, far more irritated about the senseless marching than at not finding any souvenirs. By five o'clock, they reached Liberty Bridge. Kovacs immediately set the perimeter. He told Alpha Squad, half of Charlie Squad, and half of Guns Squad to dig their holes in a semicircle around the far end of the bridge. Bravo Squad and the other halves of Charlie and Guns Squads did the same thing on the near side. Everybody was worn out, but the white sand proved easy to dig in and the mood of the men gradually lightened. Forsythe and Payne kidded Chalice about his being in the Arizona for the first time, "If you can call thirty yards from the bridge the Arizona." After digging in, they had just enough time to heat some C-rations.

During his watch that night, Chalice was startled by some muffled explosions in the water around the bridge. When Payne relieved him, he found out they were from sticks of C-4 thrown into the water every hour to keep the VC from swimming up and blowing the bridge. Aside from these explosions, the night was quiet and uneventful.

64

Nobody bothered to wake Chalice the next morning. At nine o'clock when he got up, most of the platoon was already milling around the area. Forsythe walked up to him holding a machete. "You wanna build a hootch together?"

"Sure, it beats sleeping out in the open." Chalice followed him to a clump of bamboo on the riverbank. A few other men were already hacking away at the stalks.

"We need three poles; one about ten feet and two about six." Forsythe pulled a large bamboo stalk from the thicket and motioned for Chalice to hold it bent while he cut it down. "Don't run your hands over the stalk. It's full of tiny splinters." Forsythe cut it down with three whacks of the machete. He then cut two smaller stalks and six pegs. They carried the bamboo back towards their foxhole, and Forsythe picked out a little knoll twenty yards behind it on which to build their hootch. First he drove the two shorter poles into the ground about nine feet apart. After hunting in his pack, he came up with some pieces of string and tied the longer pole across the tops of the two shorter ones. He and Chalice snapped their ponchos together and laid them athwart the crossbar. They tied six pieces of string to the ponchos' dangling edges, then attached the free ends to the wooden pegs. After hammering the pegs into the ground, Forsythe stood back and looked over the hootch. "Not bad. All we have to do is dig a rain trench around it. But that can wait. Let's eat."

As they finished eating, Tony 5 walked over. "I just got the word on how we're gonna operate. It'll be like the last time: Every day we send out a squad on patrol and every night we send out an all-night ambush. We've got the patrol today, tomorrow the ambush, and the next day we skate."

"How long is the patrol?"

"A klick out and a klick back."

"Sounds good to me," Forsythe commented. Then looking at Chalice, he added, "I hope you're gonna appreciate this, Prof. It's the best you'll have it during your thirteen months."

As Tony walked away, he called back, "We're gonna move-out on that patrol in about an hour, be ready."

The machine gun team on Alpha's side of the bridge was building a hootch a few yards away. Forsythe walked over and Chalice followed him. The machine gunner was a Mexican-American named Pablo. His sharp, clean features seemed always set in the same placid yet alert expression. He wasn't very talkative, but because of his patient manner he often found himself on the listening ends of long conversations. His assistant machine gunner, Sinclaire, talked constantly in a deep southern drawl as he helped Pablo build their hootch. He was a skinny, towheaded youth whose long

65

legs seemed to make up four-fifths of his body. They had a radio playing, so Forsythe and Chalice sat down next to it. When Pablo and Sinclaire finished, they also sat down near the radio. Sinclaire started the conversation, "Well Professor, how do you like the bush?"

"Haven't seen much of it yet."

Childs walked up behind Sinclaire and said, "Don't worry about it. He hasn't seen much of it either."

"I've seen enough to know I've seen as much as I wanna see."

"Don't sweat it. Chances are you won't be around here too much longer."

Pablo gave Childs a hard stare, then changed the subject. "You guys got the patrol today?"

"Yeah."

"I'm going with you. How far is it?"

"Two klicks; one out and one back."

Pablo nodded his head. "We'll have plenty of time to take a bath when we get back. It'll be the first time in three weeks for me."

They sat listening to the radio until Harmon came over and told them to form up for the patrol. As Chalice swung the machine gun ammo can over his shoulder, he asked Forsythe, "How come Pablo looked at Childs that way when he said Sinclaire wouldn't be around too long?"

"Oh, you noticed that. Sinclaire is Pablo's third A-gunner. The other two got blown away. While the machine gunner is firing, the A-gunner has to hold his head up and sight him in. That gives the Gooks a real nice target, and the first thing they go after is the machine guns. His first A-gunner got it right in the eye. The second one got it through the front of his helmet."

The purpose of the patrol was to check out the riverbank. Hamilton's fire team led off. They formed a wedge with Childs at the point. Roads walked along the bank twenty yards to his left and ten yards behind him. Bolton, a tall, awkward-looking youth, took the same position on the right. Hamilton walked ten yards behind Childs. Harmon followed directly behind Hamilton. Then came Payne with the radio and the rest of Tony 5's fire team.

Chalice realized they probably wouldn't find anything, but the idea of being on his first patrol excited him despite himself. Just as they had gone a kilometer and were about to turn around, Roads called out, "Got some spider holes."

Harmon walked over to have a look, telling Chalice to follow him. There were three holes along the riverbank about two feet in diameter and five feet deep. "They're spider holes all right, VC or NVA. . . . Looks like they been here a long time. Don't really mean much."

"How do you know VC or NVA dug them?" Chalice asked.

"They're one-man holes. We always dig holes for two or four men."

Harmon sent the patrol a hundred yards further down the bank. Not finding anything, they turned around and headed back to the bridge. Instead of following the bank this time, they walked fifty yards away from it in case some VC had seen them head out and had booby-trapped their trail.

The patrol returned to the perimeter by one o'clock. The men spent the next few hours reading and cleaning their rifles. Kovacs passed word for a swim call for those on Alpha's side of the bridge. Skip and Flip brought their machine gun over to provide cover. Everybody stripped down and headed for the river carrying their M-16's.

Though the river was over forty yards across, it was only about five feet deep. When Chalice got out far enough, he started swimming, as fast and as hard as he had ever swum before. Memories of school days spent playing hooky at hidden streams ran through his mind. Now experiencing the same relaxed excitement, a sense of freedom overwhelmed him. He remembered how refreshing — and far away — the river had looked on the march out, and how much he had wanted to throw off his pack and dive into it. The other members of the platoon — their rifles lying on the bank — seemed no longer soldiers, but boys, like the ones he had played hooky with, older, less innocent, but boys. He heard them making the same comments, saw them enacting the same childish pranks. Chalice swam back towards them, for the first time realizing he was one of them, not only a member of their platoon, but a friend; their friendship based not on likes, dislikes, or abilities, but on the vagaries of chance that had put them in the same place, at the same time, sharing a common danger, possessing a common hope, all of them dependent upon the others, the symbols of their common bond lying abandoned on the bank — their rifles.

Chalice, standing waist deep in the gently flowing river, had just finished shaving. He handed the razor to Forsythe and dove forward to wash the lather from his face. The warm water felt suddenly cool against his skin. Never before had he received so much pleasure from the act of shaving. Looking towards the bank, he noticed someone filling a canteen. "Hey, what's he doing?" Forsythe looked at Chalice questioningly. "I mean, is he going to drink *this* water? Look at it. It's dirty."

"Of course he is. This stuff is great compared to some of the piss we've had to drink. We don't even put halazone tablets in this stuff. The only time we do that is when we drink bomb crater water, and that's half mud."

Skip and Flip started yelling and pointing towards the water. At first Chalice thought they had spotted trouble, but then he saw some naked men chasing a large buck on the riverbank. One of them tried to grab it around the neck. The buck bolted forward and left the naked Marine lying in the sand. The frightened animal dashed towards the river and splashed by only a few feet away from Chalice. A number of men had been yelling, "Shoot him! Shoot him!" Appleton, a big, heavyset member of Charlie Squad, got to his rifle and drew a bead on the deer as it swam downstream. A few of the others yelled "Don't shoot it," and one of them ran up and raised the rifle barrel.

"What the fuck you do that for?" Appleton said angrily.

"Why kill it, man?"

"Whata you mean? That was a beautiful buck." As he walked away, he mumbled to himself, "Like to ride home with that thing tied to the front of my car."

During the next few days, Kovacs saw to it that the patrols and ambushes went according to plan, but otherwise let the men enjoy a sense of freedom that had been so lacking on the hill. On the third day a small convoy brought a load of supplies. Tony 5 distributed his fire team's share — food, grenades, rounds, a claymore mine, C-4, and a lot of blasting caps. When he divided up the blasting caps, Forsythe objected, "I've already got five of them."

"Here's five more."

"I'm not gonna carry ten blasting caps."

"Your old ones might be duds."

"Then I better blow them. We've got plenty."

"It's all right with me . . . but you better ask Kovacs first."

Forsythe walked across the bridge, and came back smiling. "It's okay with him. C'mon," he said to Chalice, and they walked over to get Hamilton. "Kovacs said I should blow these blasting caps."

Hamilton picked up an entrenching tool and pointed to the bank. "Let's go down there."

When they got to the bank, Hamilton dug a hole about a foot deep and buried a blasting cap, careful to leave the tip of its fuse above ground. Forsythe lit it and they took cover. A muffled explosion sent up a small puff of sand. Hamilton started digging another hole, but Forsythe said, "Wait a minute. Let's put a little C-4 on the cap," and he ran back to the perimeter. While he was gone, Sinclaire and Appleton came down to see what was going on. Appleton was shirtless, his paunch undulating as he walked up to Chalice. "What you guys doing, Prof?"

"Getting rid of some blasting caps."

"What are you waiting for?"

"Forsythe went to get some C-4. Here he comes now." By the time Forsythe reached them, he had already broken off a piece of the white plastic and molded it into a ball. Hamilton put it on the cap and buried it. The explosion was much louder than the first. Everybody seemed to be getting a kick out of it, so with each succeeding cap Forsythe made the ball of C-4 a little larger. Soon a dozen more men had gathered around. Forsythe was down to his last blasting cap when he got a sneaky look in his eyes. Hamilton knew right away what he was thinking. He started smiling and nodding as he said, "Go 'head, do it."

Forsythe quickly unwrapped the remaining half stick of C-4 and rolled it into a ball. Everyone gathered around him laughing, most of them acting like little kids playing with matches. The large ball of C-4 completely covered the blasting cap. Hamilton dug the hole a little deeper this time. Forsythe was just about to light the fuse when Appleton stopped him. "We better not take any chances." He picked up a sandbag and dropped it on top of the hole. Laughing, he clapped his hands together loudly and said, "Let her rip."

As Forsythe bent down to light the fuse, everyone else started running toward a large sand dune thirty yards away. They already lay behind it when he came rushing towards them at full speed. Forsythe dived over the dune feet first, turning over on his stomach in midair so as not to miss anything. Just as he hit the ground, a large explosion shot sand in all directions. The sandbag flew fifty feet in the air. They watched in awe as it slammed down in the middle of the bridge with a loud thud. Practically the whole platoon came running towards them to find out what had happened. They lay stunned behind the dune for a few moments, then started laughing and slapping each other while rolling around in the sand.

Kovacs had been sleeping in his hootch. He came running across the bridge and tripped over the sandbag, nearly losing his balance. Red-faced, he tapped it with his foot a few times before yelling towards the men standing around the crater. "*Forsythe,* you motherfucker, what the hell was that?" Forsythe looked up wearing an expression of childlike guilt. Kovacs continued to glare at him. Forsythe lowered his head and began moving one foot back and forth in front of the other tracing an arc in the sand. "*What — was — that?*" Kovacs repeated.

Forsythe answered meekly, "It go boom."

"So I fucking noticed. *What* go boom?"

"One of those blasting caps you said we could blow."

"*Blasting caps my ass,* you dumb sonofabitch. *I'll stick a blasting cap in your ear.* Dig a shitter. NO! Dig three shitters."

Forsythe had just finished digging the second latrine when Hamilton and Chalice walked up to him. "You do nice work."

Forsythe flung a shovelful of sand into Hamilton's chest. "Hey man, what was that for?"

Forsythe lifted himself out of the hole and sat on its edge. "It was worth it. No question about it, it was worth it."

"I know," Hamilton agreed.

"What the fuck are you talking about? You don't have to dig any shitters."

"I'll give you a hand." Hamilton started digging the third latrine. "You know your fire team's got the tower tonight."

"We do? That means we can't sleep in our hootches again." Forsythe looked up at the sky. "Doesn't look like rain. I don't mind."

Chalice said, "I don't think Kovacs believed you when you said it was just a blasting cap."

"Yeah, he *was* just a little suspicious."

Hamilton handed Chalice the entrenching tool. "Your turn, friend."

They finished digging shortly before dusk. Forsythe and Chalice picked up their gear and headed across the bridge to the tower. Tony 5 and Payne were already laying out their ponchos and poncho liners at its base. The gear the men had to carry and their stiff flak jackets made the seventy foot climb both awkward and tiring. Just before he reached the top, Payne dropped his rifle. As he started down after it, Tony said, "I woulda bet a million bucks you couldn't have gotten all the way up without dropping something. That's why I made sure I climbed up ahead of you."

The platform on top of the tower had four-foot walls and a tin roof. Tony sat on the floor while Chalice and Forsythe looked out over the valley. Only a faint glow remained where the sun had slipped behind the mountains.

"Tony, how 'bout let's partying tonight?" Forsythe asked. "We ain't gonna get hit."

"I don't like the idea of doing it at night. Besides, Payne is a big enough shitbird straight."

"Send him back to your hootch for something," Forsythe suggested.

"Okay, but only one joint, and let's not make this a habit." Tony called down to Payne, who was three-quarters of the way up the tower, "Hey Payne, go over to my hootch and get some bug juice out of my pack."

"C'mon man, you don't need it up in the tower."

"Get it anyway."

"That was a good idea. I didn't bring any," Forsythe commented.

"Chances are Payne won't either. I haven't got any in my pack." Tony 5 took out a joint and lit it. They squatted down so the ash wouldn't be

70

visible from below. The bouquet sent Chalice off before he had even taken a drag. The grass was strong, one joint being enough to get them high. Chalice stood up and looked around. The transparent blackness of the sky took on substance and dimension, surrounding the stars as if they were vacant globes of light. A cool breeze rushed against his face, leaving him with a sense of drifting motion. He took a long, refreshing drink from his canteen. Feeling the need to relieve himself, he refrained, not wanting to lessen the effect of the grass. Finally, he spoke, as if thinking the words themselves would make the act unnecessary. "Hey you guys, I gotta take a piss."

Tony 5 and Forsythe stared at each other. After a long pause, Tony said, "You asking permission?"

"No, no, I was just telling you," Chalice answered dreamily.

"Oh, you know that's one thing you never have to ask. I wouldn't want you to wet your pants, never want that to happen."

"No, I was just telling you."

"What made you think we were interested?" Tony asked, his voice indicating deep curiosity.

"Man, I'm stoned. I can't be held responsible for what I say."

Forsythe cut in. "What are you guys talking about?"

"He wants to take a piss," Tony answered with dreamy satisfaction.

". . . What, you mean all that talking was about him taking a piss? Go 'head, Professor, it's all right with us."

"Okay." Chalice climbed up on one of the walls.

"Not that side," Tony said. "That's where our gear is."

He climbed down slowly and walked over to the opposite wall. As he stood atop it, Payne's voice called out from below. "Cut that shit out. It's bad enough being your errand boy, you don't have to throw water on me."

As Payne climbed over the wall, he found them rolling on the floor trying to muffle their hysterical laughter. Without knowing why, Payne also began to laugh as he handed the insect repellent to Tony 5.

"Where'd you get this?"

"Out of your pack."

"I didn't have any bug juice in my pack."

"How come you told me to get it out of your pack?

"I just remembered. Where *did* you get it?"

"Out of the first pack I saw."

"That's what I thought."

The next day Alpha had a short patrol. They went out early and got back before twelve. The sun burned down from a cloudless sky, turning the light brown river into a slowly undulating mirror. As soon as they dropped their gear, most of the men headed over the bridge to buy soft drinks from the soda boys who hung around just outside the perimeter. The kids were from six to fourteen years old, and all of them spoke English surprisingly well. When they saw the Marines approaching, they ran towards them, cigarettes dangling from most of their mouths. "Hey Marine, you want bucoo cold soda?" "You souvenir me chop-chop?"

Chalice, Forsythe, and Hamilton sat down and drank their sodas under a large shady tree. A few of the Vietnamese kids sat down next to them and started talking. When Forsythe took out a pack of cigarettes, they immediately stuck out their hands and he passed a few around. Another kid rode up with a cooler on the back of his bike. "Marine, you want ice?"

Hamilton said, "Yeah," and walked over to him.

Chalice called to Hamilton, "What's he got?"

"Popsicles. They're good. You want one?"

"Sure." Chalice got up and walked over.

Still sitting down, Forsythe said, "Get me one too."

Hamilton bargained with the kid until he settled for five cigarettes for each Popsicle. "Sure beats fifty cents for a Coke," Chalice commented. The kid took the top off the cooler. Four bars of ice lay inside, each about a foot-and-a-half long. He sliced off three four-inch pieces, then stuck a sliver of bamboo in each and handed them to Chalice and Hamilton. "Where do they get the electricity to make these?"

"They bring them in from Da Nang every morning. We're not supposed to buy them because they can be poisoned, but I've never had any trouble with 'em."

They walked over and handed a popsicle to Forsythe who had been talking to one of the Vietnamese kids. "Hey, Van here says he can get us two syclo girls."

"Decent. How long will it take to get them here?" Hamilton asked.

"He says about an hour." Turning to the kid, Forsythe said, "Get going, hurry." The kid took off running. "Maybe I should of asked Kovacs first."

"Yeah, you should have, but he won't mind. Ask him now. No, he's a little pissed at you. I better ask him. C'mon, let's go."

Hamilton straightened everything out with Kovacs, the only stipulation being that Kovacs had firsts. The three of them then walked around looking for Sugar Bear and Valdez, the squad leaders of Bravo and Charlie Squads. They found them both playing cards with Skip and Flip. Sugar Bear was a good-natured black about five foot ten and two hundred twenty pounds. Valdez was a wiry Mexican-American who took every chance he got to ride somebody. But the men were used to him and he was generally liked.

Forsythe said, "We've got two whores coming in about an hour. Find out how many of your men want in." Both Sugar Bear and Valdez took the news with satisfaction, then got up to tell their squads. Forsythe eventually got word that eighteen men were interested. He, Chalice, and Hamilton were sitting around listening to Hamilton's radio when Roads approached them. He wasn't wearing a shirt, and his taut muscles flexed as he walked. When he reached them, he nodded to Forsythe and Hamilton, then spoke to Chalice. "Here's the book. Thanks a lot."

"Did you get anything more out of it this time?"

"You always do."

"With some books."

"With most books. . . . The person who reads it the second time is always different from the one who read it the first time."

Chalice nodded his head in agreement. "I guess you're right." Roads started to turn away, but Chalice spoke first. "Listen, would you like something else to read?"

"Yeah, I would."

"I just finished *Absalom, Absalom!* You want it?"

"Yeah, I heard it was good."

"It is." Chalice reached inside the hootch and pulled out his books, wondering whether Roads had been to college. He didn't want to come out and ask him, so he asked instead, "Where'd you go to school?"

"Syracuse."

"I had a cousin that went there, Don Gardner."

"Didn't know him."

Chalice felt awkward looking up at Roads, but he knew that if he asked him to sit down he'd refuse. "What was your major?"

"Philosophy. What was yours?"

"English. How long did you go?"

"I graduated."

Hamilton, who hadn't been paying much attention to the conversation, cut in. "Roads, you gonna get in on those syclo girls?"

"No," he answered curtly.

Hamilton asked kiddingly, "What's the matter, you don't like hairless pussy?"

"I can do without it." Roads nodded and walked away.

"Not very friendly, is he?" Hamilton commented. "I shoulda known better than trying to talk to a nigger with a book in his hand."

"How come you guys never told me he graduated college?" Chalice asked.

Forsythe, not seeing any importance in the question, answered, "I didn't know. He never told anybody, I guess."

Roads went back to his hootch and started reading the book. Eyes moving down the page mechanically, he conceived no meaning from the words before him. He started again, this time speaking each word aloud, but still they had no meaning. A rage rose within him, and when he realized he was shouting each meaningless word as if it were a curse, he flung the book aside.

'Not gonna fuck no Gook chick got nothing against these people that's why they hate our guts we're fucking their women if they were white I'd fuck them *fuck 'em fuck 'em.* Did those bastards hate my guts supposed to be their first string halfback special plays for me I had to rip my knee apart woulda given anything to hear them talk behind my back must of cursed the day I was born *Dumbrowski Dumbrowski* my buddy good old coach Dumbrowski always went out of his way always always to say a nice word to the nigger before he *before before* he I fucked up my knee he knew the dirty cocksucker knew I didn't give a shit why the hell should I bust my ass for eighty thousand screaming morons that hate my guts because they're inside my skin pissed them off keeping that scholarship figured the nigger 'ud drop out soon as he couldn't play their stupidassfuckinggame fucked them *good* laughing at their faces at that fucking athletic department picking up my money every fucking month when the most of them 'ud be around to see my black ass taking their fucking check rubbing their noses in it getting a fucking high that their fucking hundredyard freakshow could never give me in a hundred years as good as fucking their foul-smelling daughters. Let my teammates down awwww too bad great buncha guys always ready to glad hand me little remarks about how the best fuck they'd ever had was black thinking what a nice compliment they just gave the big nigger. They found out fast the looks on their faces knowing the best white cunts on campus were mine anytime anyfuckingwhere I wanted them all the cool candyassfraternitystuds pinned to bitches I'd fucked the shit out of fucking bitches wouldn't leave me alone — fifty-six in four years — not bad not fucking bad wish I could of sent their parents pictures of my black ass between their daughters' legs wish I'd been pig enough to brag my head off so they'd never forget but they knew they fucking knew I was getting mine fuck 'em. . . . Why . . . the hell . . . does it bother *me* so fucking much? . . . You can't kill them all. You *can't* kill them all. . . . *Fuck 'em Fuck 'em!*'

Somebody sent word that the syclo girls had arrived, and most of the platoon gathered on the road side of the bridge. One of the girls was exceptionally beautiful. Chalice repeatedly shifted his stare between her

74

angelic face and the eager faces of the men standing around him. Forsythe tried talking to them, but they spoke very little English. Chalice had to take over. They wanted five dollars a man, but he talked them into fifty dollars for everybody. He thought he had everything straightened out, when the better-looking one pointed to Sugar Bear and whispered, "Him no. Vietnamese, Chuck tee tee; Brothers bucoo."

Suppressing his laughter, he spoke to the men. "She says they won't fuck for the Brothers because their cocks are too big."

Chalice's explanation brought on a lot of backslapping and laughing. Sugar Bear didn't feel the situation was all that humorous. He kept on saying, "No bucoo, no bucoo," as he pulled out his cock and pointed to it. Then the laughter really started. Chalice told the girls it was everybody or nobody, and they finally relented. Kovacs and Forsythe took them inside a large clump of brush. Two lines formed on the edge of it amidst a lot of good-natured shoving and arguing about who was ahead of whom.

When it was over, Chalice walked back to his hootch in a sullen mood, thinking, 'I've changed,' telling himself the Marine Corps or Parris Island hadn't been the reason.

4. A Hundred Miles from Nowhere

"Welcome to Parris Island. . . . YOU GOT THREE SECONDS TO
GET OFF THIS BUS AND TWO OF 'EM ARE GONE!" They scram-
bled off and were herded from the dark sidewalk into the glaring lights of
a dilapidated building. Chalice was still squinting when he found himself
in a line of men backed against a wall.

"Get at attention!"

"MOVE IT!"

Before he and the men with him were aware of what had happened,
they'd been herded from one point in the room to another until everyone
was stripped of his civilian possessions, searched, fingerprinted, fitted with
a gas mask by having one shoved on his face, and finally driven up a dark
stairway to a barracks.

No one was shouting anymore, telling him what to do. Chalice stood
motionless. The men with him, also dazed, wandered around in the dark
looking for empty beds. Only after he found himself standing alone did
Chalice remember how tired he was.

He lay awake, flinching as the contracting pipes cracked like rifle shots.
This too seemed to be done on purpose. He'd prepared himself, told
himself to expect the worst; but still he was shocked, realizing he was no
longer a civilian and the difference that made, wondering, 'What the fuck
have I got myself into?' Exhausted, wanting to sleep, he listened to the
pipes crack — disbelieving his own fear.

The lights flashed on. *"Get at attention in front of your racks!"*

Chalice jumped to his feet. He had lain in bed for five hours without
sleeping, wondering what they had done to scare him. Nothing — they'd
shouted, herded him around like an animal in a slaughterhouse. Why was
he scared? Because they'd treated him like an object? What had they taken
from him? How had they done it so fast? He glanced at the men around
him, at first not seeing them. One man drew his attention. Head already

76

shaved, he must have arrived the day before. Chalice saw his own fear in this man's face. At least there were two of them. Seeing the men around him for the first time, he realized they all looked just as bewildered. He wasn't alone. It was almost humorous, no longer frightening. And he was different — not one of these juvenile delinquents trying to prove how tough they were.

"*Fall out for chow!* NO TALKING!"

The men rushed down the stairs. Chalice tried to keep himself in the middle of the mob. It was still dark. The men bunched together on top of some footprints painted on the street.

"GET ON THE YELLOW FOOTPRINTS! MOVE IT!"

They shifted around until each man stood upon a set of footprints — as if they had all fallen into separate slots. Chalice found himself in the center of a precisely spaced formation.

"*Forward,* HARCH!" As soon as the men were off the footprints, they began to jam together.

Chalice glanced around as he entered the mess hall. "EYES FORWARD! *This ain't no sightseeing tour.*" They were the only men in civilian clothes. The smells of milk, eggs, and hot cereal nauseated him. Row upon row of shaved heads sat silently eating while shouting drill instructors paced up and down between them.

Chalice sat with his tray in front of him. He wasn't hungry. The food jelled upon his plate like plastic vomit. The other men were eating. Seeing how ridiculous they looked, he became more relaxed, assuring himself, 'They can't kill all of us.' He ate, able to do so only by refusing to taste what he put in his mouth.

The men around him started to get up. He followed them as they cleaned off their trays and headed outside. By themselves, they got into formation. Uniformed recruits passed by on the way to their own formations. Nearly every one of them whispered out of the side of his mouth, "You'll be sorry."

'What do you mean, *will be?*' Chalice thought to himself.

It was two days before enough recruits had arrived to form a platoon. The men were herded downstairs and lined up at attention along some rows of tables. They waited. Finally, three drill instructors burst shouting through the door. One of them leaped upon a table and began waving his arms wildly as he yelled:

"ALL RIGHT YOU HORRIBLE HOGS, *this is what you've been waiting for.* I'M STAFF SERGEANT MORTON, *your senior drill in-*

structor. You're gonna see a lot of me for the next eight weeks. I'm gonna *eat* with you, *sleep* with you, *and watch you sweat.* You're hogs now, but when I get through with you you'll be Marines or you'll be dead, and it don't make no difference to me which. *Get your seabags and* START RUNNING! We'll tell you where, *and you* BETTER *not stop!"*

The men bunched at the door, struggling fiercely to get outside. A drill instructor stood waiting for them. He began shouting and pointing down the street. In less than a minute the entire platoon was running in a confused mass while the three drill instructors drove them along by shouting, shoving, and directing them like cattle. Men tripped and were immediately buried by piles of other men. Chalice began to tire. The heavy seabag on his shoulder seemed trying to drive him into the pavement. Some men passed him while others dropped back. The platoon began to string out, and two of the drill instructors concentrated on those lagging behind. If a man collapsed, they hovered over him screaming until he got to his feet and began running again. One of the fatter men collapsed for the third time and pleaded that he couldn't get up.

Bent double over him, Morton screamed, "YOU CIVILIAN PIECE OF SHIT, GET ON YOUR FEET."

"I can't," he moaned breathlessly.

Morton picked up the man's seabag and held it over his stomach. "GET UP YOU GUTLESS MOTHERFUCKER!"

"I can't. I can't."

"GET UP!"

"I'm a Communist. I'm a Communist."

Morton slammed the seabag down on the man's stomach. He and another drill instructor yanked the man to his feet. Morton flung the man's seabag onto his shoulder, and he again collapsed. "TAKE CARE OF THIS GUTLESS CUNT," Morton screamed to the other drill instructor before dashing after the pack.

While being yanked to his feet, the man moaned, "I'm a Communist. I'm a Communist." He staggered in the direction of the rest of the platoon — the drill instructor yelling directly into his ear — barely moaning, "I'm a Communist. I'm a Communist."

The barracks was in a dilapidated frame building. Two rows of bunks separated by a wide aisle ran the length of it. The men stood at attention with their backs towards the bunks.

"ALL RIGHT, HOGS," Morton shouted, "now that you know the position of Attention, we can teach you the position of At Ease. BUT WE

78

WON'T! As long as you're on your goddamn feet, you will remain at attention. You get six weeks' practice at it before we teach you At Ease.

"Now I'm gonna tell you something about where you are. YOU'RE A HUNDRED MILES FROM NOWHERE! There's only two fucking ways to get off Parris Island — right through the main gate as Marines, or through the swamps. Hogs, there ain't a swingin' dick here that could make it through those swamps. Unless you plan on spending your whole enlistment here, you better make up your minds you're gonna be Marines — little green machines that make up the Big Green Machine.

"MARINES ARE THE BEST FIGHTING MEN IN THE WORLD. We're the best marksmen, the best hand-to-hand fighters, the most fearless motherfuckers that ever lived. You sure ain't Marines yet, but you're in the Marine Corps. It don't rain in the Marine Corps. You don't get tired in the Marine Corps. It don't get hot, and it don't get cold. There's only two ways to do things — the wrong way and the Marine Corps way. That's what me, Sergeant Green, and Sergeant Hacker are here for — to turn you disgusting civilians into Marines. You ain't standing on no corner and you ain't sloppin' no hogs. You're professional men now, each and every one of you worthless cunts has a profession. YOU'RE PROFESSIONAL KILLERS *in the service of the United States government.*"

The men remained at attention as Sergeant Green read their names off the roster and assigned each man a laundry number. "White."

"Here, sir."

"Seventy-two. . . . White, take one step forward."

"Aye aye, sir." A large black stepped into the aisle.

"You sure ain't, cocksucker. GET BACK!"

"Aye aye, sir."

When Green finished, he, Morton, and Hacker walked down the aisle giving each man a closer look, as if debating whether to kill him now or later. Hacker stopped in front of a dark recruit. He slowly moved closer until his mouth was within an inch of the recruit's nose, then shouted. "YOU A SPLIB OR A SPIC?"

"Splib."

"SPLIB, WHAT?"

"Splib, sir."

"COCKSUCKER, if you want to live, the first word out of your mouth will be, 'sir'. . . . ARE YOU A SPLIB OR A SPIC?"

"Splib, sir."

"LISTEN, COME BUBBLE, WHAT DID I TELL YOU?"

"Sir, splib."

"SIR, SPLIB!"

"Splib, sir."

"SIR, THE PRIVATE IS A SPLIB!"

"Sir, the Private is a splib."

"LOUDER!"

"Sir, the private is a splib."

"I CAN'T HEAR YOU."

"SIR, THE PRIVATE IS A SPLIB."

"Remember that, you high-yellow come bubble."

Sergeant Green slowly walked up to the recruit standing next to Chalice, his expression changing from pure hate to loathing amusement. With gritted teeth, he shook his head before asking, "You aren't a Jew, are you?"

"Yes, sir."

"No . . . you couldn't be that dumb. Kikes ain't that dumb. . . . WHAT'S YOUR NAME, JEWBOY?"

"Sir, the Private's name is Cowen."

"Cowen? *Cowen?* COWEN? Hog, what's wrong with your old man? CAN'T HE SPELL COHEN?"

"No, sir."

"I bet he can make out his income tax."

"Yes, sir."

Green turned his head away and shouted down the aisle, "Staff Sergeant Morton, guess what we've got."

"*No!*"

"*Yes!*"

"It ain't a JEW, is it?"

"IT SURE THE FUCK IS!"

Morton and Hacker converged upon Cowen until the heads of all three drill instructors were within an inch of his. Cowen tried to keep from trembling as Hacker shouted, "God, *look at the beak on this motherfucker.*"

"What are you doing in MY Marine Corps?" Morton asked.

"Sir, the Private doesn't know."

"JEWBOY, YOU MUST NOT. . . . *Don't you know I don't want Jews in MY MARINE CORPS?"*

"Sir, the Private didn't know."

"HE KNOWS NOW, *don't he?"* Hacker asked.

"Yes, sir."

"How come you're not working in your father's jewelry store?"

"Sir, the Private's father doesn't own a jewelry store."

"PAWN SHOP?" Green shouted.

"Sir, the Private's father doesn't own a pawn shop."

"What does he own, Hymie?"

"A dress factory."

"HUH?"

"A dress factory."

"I CAN'T HEAR YOU!"

"HUH?"

"HUH?"

"SIR, THE PRIVATE'S FATHER OWNS A DRESS FACTORY."

"Jewboy's father owns a dress factory."

"You must wear the prettiest dresses on the block, kike."

"You made a mistake, Abie."

"You *are* a mistake, Abie."

"What are you trying to do to MY MARINE CORPS, *Hymie?"*

"HUH?"

"YEAH, JEWBOY?"

"HUH?"

"Sir, the Private doesn't know."

"THE PRIVATE MUST NOT KNOW."

"The Private's out of his ass."

"YOU'RE A DEAD MAN, ABIE," Green shouted in his face at the same time Morton screamed, "I AIN'T GONNA LET YOU RUIN MY MARINE CORPS, HYMIE!"

"You're gonna be sorry, Jewboy."

"YOU'RE SORRY ALREADY, AREN'T YOU, HYMIE?"

"Yes, sir."

"WHAT!"

"No, sir."

"HUH?"

"MAKE UP YOUR MIND, ABIE."

"NO, SIR."

"You will be though, won't you?"

"Yes, sir."

"WHAT!"

"HUH?"

"HUH?"

"NO, SIR."

The drill instructors backed off while Green sneered, "You will be, Abie. You'll be the sorriest motherfucker that ever lived."

Chalice stood dazed, again wondering what he'd gotten himself into. Morton shouted, "Any of you hogs that have been to college take one step forward." Five men stepped into the aisle. The drill instructors interrogated each man, reaching Chalice last. "How many years did *you* waste, hog?"

"*Four, sir,*" Chalice replied, wishing he could have said, "One."

"HUH?"

"I CAN'T HEAR YOU!"

"HOW MANY?"

"SIR, THE PRIVATE SPENT FOUR YEARS IN COLLEGE."

"SPENT?"

"HUH?"

"SIR, *the Private wasted four years in college.*"

"HUH?"

"You didn't graduate, *did you*, hog?"

"*Yes Sir, the Private graduated.*"

"HUH?"

"I CAN'T HEAR YOU!"

"YES, SIR."

"*We got a graduate!*"

"*I DON'T fucking believe it!* How could *anyone* with balls spend FOUR YEARS in college?"

"A college graduate."

"What was your major?" Green asked.

"Sir, the Private's major was English."

Morton took a step backwards. "ENGLISH!"

"*You wasted four fucking years learning how to speak English?*" Hacker asked.

"That means poetry," Green corrected him.

"POETRY?"

"POETRY! THE HOG STUDIED POETRY?"

"Recite us a poem."

"Sir, the Private doesn't know a poem."

"THE PRIVATE DOESN'T KNOW!"

"*Four years* and he doesn't know a poem?"

"How come you can't recite us a poem, Private?"

"Sir, the Private forgot."

"FORGOT?"

"HUH?"

"FORGOT!"

"*The Private* BETTER FUCKING REMEMBER!"

"Let's hear one, Private."

"I never saw a moor,/ I never saw the sea;/ Yet know I how —"

"SHUT THE FUCK UP!"

82

"STOP! FUCKING STOP!"

"YOU DON'T KNOW SHIT!"

" 'Know I how' — *you call that English?*"

"FOUR FUCKING YEARS?"

"COME BUBBLE, your education has *just* started."

"REVEILLE! REVEILLE!" Morton shouted as the lights flashed on. Chalice jumped to a sitting position in time to see a garbage can bounce past his rack. Green flung the lid and then another garbage can against the wall while shouting, "ON YOUR FEET! ON YOUR FEET!" Hacker ran around pushing over any rack with somebody still in it. Eyes blinking, Chalice stood at attention in front of his bunk. He flinched at each sound, amazed to see that all the noise was coming from only three drill instructors. Dazed and scared, he found no humor in the thought, 'So this is what the Marine Corps uses instead of alarm clocks.' The shouting and noise continued even after all the men were standing at attention. Again Chalice wondered what he had gotten himself into.

Morton shouted, "WHAT'S THE MATTER, HOGS? DON'T YOU LIKE GETTING UP IN THE MORNING? You don't act like it. Push-up position; *ready*, MOVE!" One hundred sixty hands slapped the floor. "Four-count push-ups, twenty-five of them; *ready*, BEGIN!"

The men's voices became strained and quieter as they continued, ". . . One, two, three, eighteen. One, two, three, nineteen."

"I CAN'T HEAR YOU, LADIES. . . . I STILL CAN'T HEAR YOU. . . . STOP! FUCKING STOP!" Arms straightened in front of them, the men hovered in the up position while Morton shouted, "Ladies, you turn my stomach. WHAT ARE YOU TRYING TO DO TO MY MARINE CORPS? Why didn't you fags join the Navy?" A man collapsed, his chest slapping the floor sharply.

Green stood on the man's back while addressing the rest of the platoon. "This little lady is tired. We're gonna let her rest a minute." Choking sounds came from the man beneath Green's feet. "While she's resting, you can rest too — *in the up position.*" The men who had collapsed on their chests immediately pushed themselves up again. Green asked the man beneath him, "What's your name, little lady?"

The recruit gasped, "Sir, the Private's name is Private Colson."

"You hear that, hogs? This little rest period is courtesy of Private Colson. Private Colson doesn't like to do push-ups. As soon as *Private Colson* is ready, we'll start again. Are you ready, Sweet Pea?"

"Sir, the Private's ready."

"That's just lovely, Sweet Pea, *just fucking lovely.*" Green jumped off Colson and shouted, "Four-count push-ups; *ready*, BEGIN!"

"One, two, three, twenty. One, two —"

"I CAN'T HEAR YOU."

"— three, twenty-one."

"I STILL CAN'T HEAR YOU!"

"One, two, three, twenty-two."

"STOP! FUCKING STOP! . . . Ladies, the last number I heard was ten. Start from there. *Ready*, BEGIN!"

"ONE, TWO, THREE . . ."

After fifteen minutes of exercise, Morton decided his men were fully awakened. He ordered them to get dressed. They took too much time, so he had to interrupt them twice for bends and thrusts. He then ordered them to make their beds. They took too much time, and he interrupted them for a set of side-straddle hops. He ordered them to clean the barracks. They took too much time, so he interrupted them for a set of sit-ups. Dissatisfied with the job they had done, Green overturned the garbage cans as the platoon left for breakfast.

It was still dark when they returned to the barracks. First they swept the floor — on their hands and knees using small scrub brushes. After the third time, Morton decided the floor was clean enough to be mopped. Instead of mops, the men crawled around with wet rags in their hands. They then dried the floor with dry rags, wet it again with buckets of water, scrubbed it with scrub brushes, dried it with rags, and repeated the operation one more time. None of the drill instructors seemed satisfied, but there were other things to do.

Sergeant Hacker stood in the center of the aisle explaining and demonstrating About Face. As Hacker went over everything for the fourth time, Chalice stood thinking, 'What kind of idiots does he take us for?'

"All right, hogs, we're gonna try it now; and NOBODY better make a mistake." Hacker remained in the center of the aisle while Morton and Green walked to opposite ends of the barracks, eyeing each man along the way as if they were moving in for the kill.

"*About*, HACE!" At least ten men turned to the left, and a few more ended up with their legs crossed. All three drill instructors exploded into action. Sergeant Green was glad for the opportunity to have another conference with Private Colson. Colson squinted his right eye as Green's teeth clicked within an inch of it. "Are you winking at me, Sweet Pea?"

"Sir, the Private wasn't winking at you."

"*You?* YOU?"

"Sir, the Private —"

84

"DID I GIVE YOU PERMISSION TO SPEAK?"

"NO, SIR."

"LISTEN, COME BUBBLE, *if you want to say something to me,* you say, 'Sir, the Private requests permission to speak to the Drill Instructor.'"

"Sir, the Private requests permission to speak to the Drill Instructor."

"Oh, does he?" Green cooed. "What does the Private have to say that's so important?"

Colson remained silent.

"WHAT DOES THE PRIVATE HAVE TO SAY?"

"Sir, the Private forgot."

"Oh, the Private forgot," Green replied in a soothing tone. "THE PRIVATE FUCKING FORGOT!" Green's hand shot towards Colson's neck. He squeezed as hard as he could — his face turning red while Colson's turned white. "THE PRIVATE'S GONNA FORGET HOW TO BREATHE, *isn't he?*"

"Aaaacccchhhh," Colson replied.

"ISN'T HE?"

"Aaaacccchhhh."

Green pulled his hand away just before Colson's saliva reached it. "ISN'T HE?"

"Yes, sir," Colson answered in a hoarse whisper.

"HUH?"

"YES, SIR."

Green stepped back into the aisle as Hacker shouted, "*All right, hogs,* let's try it again. . . . *About,* HACE!" Only three men turned in the wrong direction, one for each drill instructor. Morton was immediately nose to nose with a tall, skinny black. "That was lovely, Sambo, *just fucking lovely! You did that on purpose,* DIDN'T YOU?"

"No, *sir.*"

"HUH?"

"NO, SIR."

"Are you trying to tell me you don't know your left from your right?"

"NO, SIR."

"Then you did it on purpose. *You're trying to beat the system.* You're making fun of me, AREN'T YOU?"

"No, sir."

"HUH?"

"No, *sir.*"

"HUH?"

"NO, SIR."

"WHAT'S YOUR NAME, PRIVATE?"

85

"MOBLEY."

"WHAT?"

"MOBLEY, SIR."

"WHAT?"

"SIR, THE PRIVATE'S NAME IS MOBLEY."

"What's your first name? *Thaddeus? Ambrose?* WILLIE?"

"NO, SIR. *The Private's first name is Reginald.*"

Morton staggered backwards. "Reginald, *fucking Reginald?* Tell me something Reggie Baby: How do those black mammies think up all those fancy names?"

"Sir, the Private doesn't know."

"The Private doesn't know a lot of things, doesn't even know his left from his right. *You better get your shit together*, REGINALD, or you'll find that *fancy* name of yours on a TOMBSTONE!"

"YES, SIR."

The platoon continued practicing About Face for another hour. This allowed almost a third of the men the opportunity to have personal instructions shouted in their ears. Chalice managed to get by unnoticed. As frightened as he was, he still found some of the drill instructors' comments amusing. What really astounded him was the stupidity of the men around him. Only six times had the entire platoon been able to perform About Face correctly, and never twice in a row. It seemed as if the men were taking turns at making blunders. Without much confidence, Chalice told himself that his own superior intelligence would prove useful.

Upon order, the men rushed out to the street and into a formation. Morton called cadence and headed them toward the mess hall. Green and Hacker ran around tripping and stomping on the feet of anyone who was out of step. Again Chalice had managed to place himself safely in the center of the formation. A distant humming sound baffled him. The sound increased to a harsh roar before Chalice realized what it was — a large group of Marines growling as they ran. Thinking that he was hearing at least a thousand men, Chalice didn't dare turn his head.

"Hippity hop, *mob, stop!*" Morton shouted. The men bounced off each other like billiard balls.

Green sneered, "Lovely, just fucking lovely."

"Left, HACE!" Morton commanded. It was a few seconds before everyone was facing in the right direction, many of the men having taken the long way around. *"Take a look, hogs."* Chalice was surprised to see a company of three hundred men run by instead of the thousand they sounded like. They looked ridiculous, but each man was in step. They looked stupid but confident. They looked will-less but brutal. They looked like

86

"professional killers in the service of the United States government." Chalice was most astonished to see that they didn't look anything like the confused sheep standing around him.

After the company passed, Morton waited over a minute before saying in an almost civilized tone, "Believe it or not, hogs, that's what you're gonna look like."

"I don't," Chalice mumbled, knowing that he did.

The men went quickly through the serving line, all three drill instructors breathing on their necks. By having commands shouted in their ears, Chalice and the rest of his platoon quickly learned that there was a "Marine Corps way" to hold your tray, to carry your silverware, to focus your eyes, to place your tray on a table, to sit down, to sit up, to chew, to drink, and to lose your appetite.

Sergeant Green emphasized his instructions by leaping upon the table and pacing the length of it between the trays. Not daring to look anywhere but directly to the front, the men could hear Green's shouts become louder and feel the table vibrate violently before they saw his boots stomp by at the edge of their trays.

"GET YOUR HEAD UP! *You're sitting at attention*, JEWBOY!" Chalice was sitting next to Cowen. By reflex, he looked up at Green. "*Why the fuck are you eyeballing me*, YOU DUMB COLLEGE FAG?" Chalice jerked his head down, but Green wasn't satisfied. He squatted directly in front of Chalice, and purposely spit saliva all over his tray as he shouted, "YOU GOT A CRUSH ON ME, FAG? *You wanna smoke my pole?* You'll get it, BUT NOT IN YOUR MOUTH. *Fag*, if I ever catch you eyeballing me again, *I'm gonna gouge your eye out and* SKULL FUCK YOU!"

Chalice stared straight ahead at the lower half of Green's enraged face, praying to be left alone, thinking, 'He'd like to. He really would.'

The shouts from Hacker, Morton, and Green became more agitated as they warned the men they only had five minutes to finish every crumb of food on their trays. Chalice frantically stuffed his mouth, too busy to notice Green until his shiny boots were right in front of him, not even realizing he had glanced up until after he felt the metal tray slam against his chin and chest, heard it reverberating upon the concrete floor.

"What did I tell you about eyeballing me?" Green cooed. "HUH?"

Chalice remained motionless, his mouth still stuffed with food. It seemed to be hardening, trying to choke him. The rest of his food oozed slowly down his chest and settled between his legs. He felt as if he were swimming in a garbage can, slowly fighting his way to the surface for air.

"How about a poem, college creep?"

For the first time since he'd arrived at Parris Island, Chalice didn't feel the least bit more intelligent than the men around him.

That night the recruits were herded into a small lecture room. It looked exactly like a college classroom, exactly like a college classroom invaded by a horde of Mongols. Four platoons of recruits sat at attention while their drill instructors shouted and stomped insanely up and down the aisles. But the real show was on the stage. The lecturer was an officer, a captain. He wasn't speaking to the men, he was tyrannizing them. Shouting, waving his arms wildly, he tore back and forth across the stage like a gorilla trying to break out of a cage.

Dazed and awed, still able to smell the food caked across the front of his uniform, Chalice heard every word. He heard them because he couldn't believe them. For almost an hour, the captain had been explaining to the men their rights under the Military Code of Justice. Each right he enumerated, each prohibition placed upon drill instructors, was a perfect example of a military law that had been flagrantly and continuously broken during the previous nine hours. "A recruit will be addressed by his superiors in no manner except that which indicates his rank, by the term 'Private.' . . . A superior is prohibited from placing his hands upon a subordinate except by permission of that subordinate, and solely for the purpose of adjusting that subordinate's uniform."

Chalice sat stupefied. He could make no connection between what he was hearing and the things he had seen during the day. For a few minutes he almost had himself convinced that he was involved in an experiment, that for scientific purposes the United States Marine Corps had taken three hundred recruits and was seeing how quickly it could drive them all insane.

The captain suddenly stopped shouting. He walked to the edge of the stage and stared at the recruits. Chalice knew something important was about to happen, and all he could think of was, 'God, what's next?'

"PRIVATES, I've spent a fucking hour up here explaining your rights under the Military Code of Justice. You skinheaded motherfuckers better know every one of them. I've saved your most important right for last. It's the most important one because it's the only way you have to see that your other rights aren't violated. Every swinging dick in the military service of the United States government — and that includes you horrible hogs — has the right of Request Mast. Anytime you feel your rights have been violated, you can take your gripe right up the Chain of Command. That means right up to the President of the United States. If anywhere along the Chain of Command, someone agrees with you — either your sergeant, or your lieutenant, or the President himself — then you'll get your way.

"NOW YOU HOGS GET THIS STRAIGHT, *because this is the most important part:* The President of the United States hasn't got time to fuck with every dipshit civilian that lands on Parris Island. *The only way you can get up the Chain of Command is step by step,* STARTING AT THE BOTTOM. If you see anything you don't like on Parris Island, all you have to do is go up to your drill instructor and say, "Sir, the Private requests permission to Request Mast. . . . HA-ten-TION! . . . Drill instructors, get these disgusting skinheads out of my sight."

The men rushed into the barracks and were standing at attention in front of their racks when the drill instructors entered. Chalice waited. The three drill instructors moved quietly up and down the aisle. They too were waiting. Chalice couldn't remember a moment as silent, a time when he wasn't standing at attention in a baggy green uniform, when his life wasn't in the hands of three psychopaths wearing Smokey the Bear hats. 'Somebody's gonna do it. Some idiot's gonna do it.'

No one did. The drill instructors eyed each man. The silence continued. 'Maybe they're not so dumb after all.'

It was Morton who finally spoke. "*On your bellies.*" The bodies of eighty men slapped the floor. "*On your backs.*" In an instant, they flipped themselves over. "*On your bellies.*" For ten minutes Morton paced back and forth along the floor flipping his men over as if this were a trick he'd taught them, the only one they were capable of learning. Finally, he stood them up for some side-straddle hops, knocked them down for some push-ups, flattened them out for some sit-ups, and finished them off with some squat thrusts. Green and Hacker paced the aisle, generously providing personal instructions when necessary.

Morton called the men to attention. Dark blotches of sweat stained their uniforms as they tried to muffle their heavy breathing. After carefully eyeing his men, Morton turned to Green. "I guess it's time to find out."

Green slowly paced the aisle as he addressed the men in a loud but civilized tone. "So now you know what it's all about. Parris Island isn't supposed to be any picnic. The Marine Corps builds men, not interior decorators. A lot of you hogs are never gonna make it. You just won't measure up. We can't waste time on you. There's a war going on. It's not the greatest war, but it's the only one we've got. Our job is to turn out fighting men, the best fighting men in the world. We can't waste time with cunts that'll never make it. Not everyone can be a Marine. It isn't that much to be ashamed of. You've been here a whole day. You should know by now whether you can measure up. You should be able to save us some time and trouble —"

Chalice sensed what Green was leading up to. Remembering that no one had been stupid enough to call for a Request Mast, he wasn't sure what would happen; but he told himself, 'This'll be a real test of their intelligence.'

"— To be a Marine, you have to want to be a Marine. That's the only way we can make men out of you. Think it over. In a few seconds you'll have to decide." Green stopped talking. He moved his stare along both sides of the squad bay, allowing the men to feel his eyes upon them. When he began speaking again, it was even more slowly than before. "Anybody who's had enough, who wants to go home, take one step forward."

Chalice winced as three men stepped into the aisle. There was silence. Chalice waited, now unsure what would happen. Had he missed his chance to go home, his chance to escape from this maximum security insane asylum?

Finally, the drill instructors walked up to the men who had stepped forward. No hostility in their stares, they looked each man in the eye as if to thank him for his honesty. All the recruits waited uneasily, but especially the three that had stepped forward. Colson, who had been standing next to Chalice, was one of these men. Green stared at him calmly, a pleased expression on his face. He turned away and began pacing the aisle, his footsteps the only sound in the squad bay. Finally he spoke:

"Three men . . . that's not bad — three out of eighty. These three men have saved us some trouble. I hope the rest of you know what you're doing. Maybe I should give you another chance to decide —"

Confused and no longer sure of what was happening, Chalice debated what to do if Green did give him another chance.

"— I shouldn't do this, but I'm going to. Anybody else that wants to go home with these three men, take one step forward."

Three more men stepped into the aisle. Chalice, immobilized by fear and confusion, wasn't one of them. If Green had said, "Anyone who wants to stick it out, take one step forward," Chalice still would have remained stationary, unable to decide because the decision necessitated physical action. Knowing that he might have made a mistake, Chalice waited to see what would happen.

Again Green walked up to Private Colson. "Where you from, Colson?"

"Sir, the Private's from Meridian, Mississippi."

"No shit, Private. Meridian's a pretty big city, five thousand people at least. I never would have picked you for a city slicker. . . . What's your old man do?"

"Sir, the Private's father is a farmer."

"Is that right? Where's his farm, in back of the courthouse?"

"No, sir. The Private's farm is ten miles outside of Meridian."

90

"That's what I thought, grit. . . . What made you decide you couldn't hack it, the push-ups?"

"Sir, the Private isn't good enough."

"I'll have to agree with you, red-neck. You'd be a fool to stick around here. A boy should know his capabilities and act upon them. Isn't that right?"

"Yes, sir."

"Only a fool would ignore his own capabilities. Isn't that right, grit?"

"Yes, sir."

"No it isn't, is it?"

"No, sir."

"ONLY A FOOL OR A MARINE!"

"Yes, sir."

"But you're going back to Mississippi where you're needed . . . to slop the hogs, clean the cow pies out of the barn, move the outhouse around. Isn't that right, red-neck?"

"Yes, sir."

"You think you've learned anything at Parris Island, red-neck?"

"Yes, sir."

"*What?*"

"*Sir, the Private's learned he isn't good enough to be a Marine.*"

"You should have learned some other things too, like how to keep your gig line straight. Take a look at the way your shirt's sticking out." Colson started to glance down but caught himself. Green said calmly, "Go ahead, Private, you can look. I'm not gonna waste any more time trying to make a Marine out of white trash like you." Colson glanced down at the front of his shirt and quickly returned to attention. "Well, I guess I can take time to show you how to straighten your gig line again. It might come in handy around the barnyard, impress the hell out of the pigs and chickens." Green started to reach for Colson's shirt, but suddenly stopped short. A smirk on his face, he said calmly, "Excuse me, Private, I forgot all about that lecture we just heard. Private, do I have permission to adjust your uniform?"

"Yes, sir."

Still looking him in the eye, Green buried his fist in Colson's stomach. Colson bent double and staggered backwards. His rack scraped loudly on the floor before crashing into the wall.

"YOUR COLLAR TOO, RED-NECK," Green shouted while swinging Colson into the aisle by his lapels. He leaped in the air, kicking Colson between the shoulder blades and sending him through the swinging double doors to the bathroom. Green crashed through after him.

Morton and Hacker exploded into action as if awakened by a mortar round. Shouting, snapping their teeth, and adjusting uniforms, they quickly convinced three of the remaining five recruits to give the Marine Corps another try. The fourth recruit whimpered, "I'm a homosexual." When the fifth recruit saw Morton step back laughing, he too remembered that he was a homosexual. Morton quickly segregated the two homosexuals in the center of the squad bay where he interrogated them as they did calisthenics.

Green and Colson emerged from the bathroom ten minutes later. "ALL RIGHT, *hogs*, let me have your attention. Private Red-Neck has an announcement to make."

Colson couldn't have looked any more frightened than he had all day. The only change in his appearance was a slowly enlarging smudge of blood at the corner of his mouth. Trying but unable to hide his fear, he called out, "*Fellow recruits, I have decided to reenlist in the Marine Corps.*"

Green called the platoon to the center of the squad bay. As they had been taught, the men converged violently upon one another, staggering into a tight mass. Satisfied, Green gave the order to sit down. "Hogs, if you're wondering what that siren was a few minutes ago, I'll tell you. One of those outstanding recruits from next door decided he just couldn't hack it in the Marine Corps, so he decided to hack his wrists instead. . . . He botched the job of course. He'll live. Let me tell you what's going to happen to him as soon as he gets out of the hospital: He's gonna be court-martialed and get sent to the brig for a *long, long time*. When you signed that little white enlistment paper, you signed your putrid bods over to Uncle Sam. Each and every one of you is government property. Our friend is gonna get court-martialed for the destruction of government property.

"Because I'm such a nice guy, I'm gonna tell you how to keep the same thing from happening to you. The civilian turd did it the wrong way. I'm gonna show you the *Marine Corps way*." Green waved a double-edged blade slowly over his head. "Privates, courtesy of Uncle Sam, you've all got a pack of these government issue items in your footlocker. If you're in a real hurry, you can take the dirty one out of your razor. It won't be quite as sharp, but it'll get the job done. First take it by the ends and press the blades together until they snap. Be careful not to cut yourself." Green held up his hands, half the blade in each one. "You really only need one of these babies, but save the other in case of emergency. Now here's the way *not* to do it — the wrong way." Green moved the blade across his wrist. "HERE'S THE MARINE CORPS WAY!" Green moved the blade up and down his forearm. "Now if you really press it in, you're home free. You'll never have to worry about a court-martial. *Remember,* up and down, not across — that way you get all the arteries instead of just one.

"Here's some other tips. Do it in the shower room. It's the darkest part of the head (you won't be so squeamish if you can't see what you're doing, and it'll be harder for some jerk to spot you and blow the whole operation). Doing it in the shower also makes it easier for your fellow hogs to clean up the mess — no use having anybody knocking the dead. Also, don't do it right before dawn — give yourself plenty of time to bleed. One more thing, wait till the fire watch (you'll learn more about him later — he's one of you hogs that stands guard at night) wait until he gets out in the hall. You don't want him interrupting you."

Chalice stood at attention in front of his rack. In a few minutes his sixth day of training would end. The squad bay was quiet except for Melton's voice. He was doing push-ups in the center of the aisle and counting them for himself. Melton still claimed to be a homosexual. After three days of doing calisthenics in front of the rest of the men, the other recruit had admitted he'd been lying. As if Morton, Green, and Hacker weren't enough, drill instructors from the other platoons in the series had constantly dropped by to taunt them — asking for blow jobs and exposing themselves. While wondering how much longer Melton could take it or if he really was a homosexual, Chalice told himself that at least he knew one way *not* to get off Parris Island.

Since the second night of training, Sergeant Morton had been trying to teach the men to count off before going to bed. Each man had to call out a number one higher than that called out by the man to his right. The final man was to say, "Sir, the count on deck is seventy-eight privates." Although they tried four or five times a night, never had the men been able to complete the count without making a mistake. Sometimes a man would repeat the number that had just been called or shout out a number one less than the preceding number. A few times the count had suddenly stopped because a recruit had forgotten the previous number. But the most common mistake was for a recruit to blurt out his laundry number. On one occasion the count got all the way up to seventy-three before the next man yelled out in a sharp, military tone, "FOURTEEN."

Counting off was the only thing about Parris Island that Chalice began to look forward to. It meant the end of another brutal day, and he also found the men's mistakes amusing. Rarely did the drill instructors get too upset over them. They were usually satisfied with merely shouting in the offending man's face, only occasionally choking or shoving him.

Chalice was expecting the command to count off, when Sergeant Green said instead, "Hogs, I've got some good news for you. I know you've been worried about Private Shockley for the last few days. Well, you'll be glad to know he's fine. He tried to get off the island by hiding in the back seat of a car. Fortunately, the car belonged to a drill instructor. Private Shockley is now safely in the hands of the MP's. He had more balls than I thought — got a little violent when they captured him. From what I hear, he'll probably spend the rest of his two years in the brig." Green turned to Private Melton. "Stay out of this, fag. We count queers separate. . . . *Count*, OFF!"

". . . EIGHT," Chalice called out. He listened to the count increase without a mistake all the way down his end of the squad bay.

". . . FORTY-THREE."

"FORTY-FOUR."

'God, we might just make it this time.'

". . . SEVENTY-FOUR."

"SEVENTY-FIVE."

'We will. I don't believe it.'

"SEVENTY-SIX."

"SEVENTY-SEVEN."

"SEVENTY-EIGHT. *Sir, seventy-eight privates in the brig, sir.*"

At first nobody really believed what he had heard. Then Green staggered backwards, speechless for the first time in six days. Sergeant Hacker began laughing, quickly followed by Morton and Green. It wasn't the vicious, sadistic laughter the men were used to hearing. It actually had a relaxing quality about it. Not wanting to be choked or punched, the recruits struggled to keep from smiling. They couldn't. The drill instructors moved towards them, Green placing his hands around a man's neck. But it was useless. They'd need until dawn to get to everybody. Morton and Hacker merely walked out the door. Before Green followed them, he said in a soft, disbelieving tone, "Seventy-eight privates in the brig," then added defeatedly, "Good night, ladies." It wasn't until Green switched off the lights that he realized these words might have made him appear human, or even sane. In the darkness, he added, "You'll pay tomorrow, hogs. *You'll* FUCKING *pay!*"

Chalice was still laughing as he lay in his rack. For the first time since he'd arrived at Parris Island, he began to think about his excuse for going into the service, his reason for joining the Marine Corps — to write a book. 'Who needs to go to Vietnam?' he asked himself. 'It's all here, every bit of it.' Again, while laughing quietly, he thought about the seventy-eight privates in the brig. 'Who'd believe it?'

"Chalice," someone whispered.

94

He turned towards the next rack. "Cowen?"

"Yeah. Wasn't that a riot?"

"Almost a massacre," Chalice answered.

"This place is unbelievable, isn't it?"

"God, it's good to hear someone else say that. At least I know I'm not hallucinating."

"Anybody that'd try to sell that pill 'ud go broke."

"Yeah," Chalice agreed. "If he didn't get shot first. . . . I don't know how much more of this shit I can take."

"Are you serious?"

"Hell, yeah."

"Shhh," Cowen warned. "Some of it's pretty funny."

"If it was happening to somebody else it would be."

"This fucking island is loaded with guys it's happening to."

"That don't help me."

Cowen propped his head up and leaned closer to Chalice. "They just want you to be able to say, 'This ain't as bad as Parris Island,' no matter where you are or what's happening to you."

"But what are you supposed to say when you *are* on Parris Island?"

" 'At least I only got so many days left.' "

"That's just it — so many. . . . I guess you're right. They can't kill all of us."

"They'd probably take away their PX cards or something if they did."

Amused by his own thought, Chalice mumbled, "Thank God for the Military Code of Justice."

"Yeah. Only the Marine Corps would take an hour to explain all minus thirty of your rights to you. I could have given the whole speech in one sentence. 'Hogs, there ain't one of you swingin' dicks that's got the right to wipe his own ass.' "

"That reminds me —"

"Shhh," Cowen warned.

"— I haven't taken a shit in six days."

"No one has. As soon as you get your cock out, they run you out of the head. We're lucky they let us piss."

"How long can they keep this up?"

"I don't know," Cowen answered. "Maybe they think it turns to muscle."

"It's got to be going somewhere."

"The Marine Corps builds men. I guess they start with toilet training. . . . If they don't let us take a shit tomorrow, I'm gonna have the fire watch wake me in the middle of the night."

"I'll have to do the same thing, but I'm so dead in the morning anyway."

"I guess we're wasting Zee's right now."

"Fuck it. This is the first time I've talked to a human being in six days."

"What about when you were reading poetry? 'I never —' "

"Fuck you. I said human being."

"You don't appreciate what a public service the Corps is doing by keeping these psychopaths off the street."

"I'm not on the street. I'm in the same cage with them. Green's the worst. Man, he hates your guts."

"I ain't so sure," Cowen answered.

"Then you haven't been paying attention."

"He's the funniest."

"I'll admit that. He's also the meanest . . . the smartest too."

"And Hacker's the dumbest," Cowen added.

"Man, it's so great to talk to somebody. I feel sane again. The thing that drives me nuts is there's always at least one of them watching you. We aren't even allowed to seal the letters we send."

"They can't read all of them. It'd take Hacker an hour to read the label off a Budweiser can."

"If they'd just give us five minutes a day when we could be sure no one was watching us."

"What about now?"

"Yeah. I —" Chalice started to answer before Sergeant Green whispered, "What about now, Jewboy?"

Cowen remained silent, hoping that he was hearing things and knowing that he wasn't. Chalice's body stiffened. A tap with a hammer would have transformed him into sand.

Green, in his stocking feet, moved silently between their racks. "If it isn't the college fag. What would you do with the five minutes — discuss poetry?" Chalice couldn't have answered if he'd wanted to. "I should have waited till you ladies got in the same rack. Get on your feet, both of you. . . . So Miss Chalice and Miss Cowenburg aren't tired. Let's see if I can entertain you sweethearts for a while. How'd you like me to teach you a new exercise? It's called, 'In the Riggings.' "

Using the same malicious whisper, Green explained the exercise as if he were acquainting Chalice and Cowen with a rite for a secret society he'd just admitted them to. He had them get into the push-up position, then lay their bare ankles on the sharp metal railings of their bunks. With their legs pointed forty-five degrees up in the air, he ordered them to do push-ups, "many, many of them."

Chalice felt as if his body weighed a thousand pounds. It pressed down

96

on his hands, forcing his face towards the floor. The bunk railing knifed into his ankles as if it would slice his feet off any second. After only a few minutes, Chalice and Cowen could do no more than collapse with their faces on the floor at the end of every push-up. Soon they couldn't even straighten their arms. For a few minutes, Green left them collapsed on the floor, their feet still hanging from the railings. He finally ordered them back into their bunks. Though both men saw Green leave the squad bay, neither of them had anything to say.

The footlockers were arranged in two perfectly straight rows along the aisle. The recruits kneeled in back of them polishing their boots.

"Barnett," Sergeant Green called out.

"*Here, sir.*" Barnett ran up to Green who was holding a letter.

"Who's Susan Smith?" Green sneered.

"Sir, Susan Smith is the Private's girl."

"Does she smoke your pole?"

"No, sir."

"*Bullshit*. A cunt that writes on the outside of envelopes sucks any dick she can find." Green handed Barnett the letter. "*Get out of here.*"

"*Aye aye, sir.*"

"Colson."

"*Here, sir.*"

Chalice felt relieved, glad that he hadn't gotten a letter and wouldn't have to face Green. Even receiving mail was something to be dreaded in the Marine Corps.

"Who's Henrietta Colson?" Green asked.

"Sir, that's the Private's sister."

"How old is she?"

"Seventeen."

"Does she fuck good?"

"Sir, the Private doesn't know."

"Grit, are you trying to tell me there's a red-neck in Mississippi who doesn't fuck his sister? . . . HUH?"

"Yes, sir."

"How come, hog? Doesn't she like white men?"

"Sir, the Private doesn't know."

"*Beat it*, grit."

"*Aye aye, sir.*"

"*Private Abie.*"

"Here, sir."

"There's something inside this, Jewboy. Open it here." Cowen withdrew some photographs and handed them to Green. A sneer on his face, Green flipped through them before shoving a photograph in Cowen's face. *"Whose dog is that, Abie?"*

"Sir, that's the Private's dog."

"No, the other one."

"Sir, that's the Private's mother."

"Jewboy, did I ask you anything about your mother? WHOSE DOG IS IT?"

"Sir, that's the Private's father's dog."

"Get out of here."

"Aye aye, sir."

". . . White."

"Here, sir."

"Good news, White. You got a package. Open it." The box contained fruit, candy bars, and gum. After sifting through it for a few seconds, Green asked, "What is this, a coon Care Package?"

"No, sir."

"What's the difference between this and a coon Care Package?"

"Sir, the Private doesn't know."

"Does he know that he's not supposed to receive packages at Parris Island?"

"Yes, sir."

"HOW COME HIS MAMMY DOESN'T KNOW?"

"Sir, the Private wrote her."

"Maybe the Private better start drawing pictures. . . . It'd be a shame to waste all this nourishing food. Pick out a piece of fruit, a candy bar, and some gum." Green dumped the remainder of the package into the garbage. *"Eat the orange first."*

"Aye aye, sir."

"What the *fuck* are you doing, Private?"

"Sir, the Private was peeling the orange."

"HOG, *how many times do I have to tell you that you don't fart around here unless you're ordered to? . . .* Eat the orange." After watching White eat half of it, Green got impatient. *"Throw it away and start on the candy bar."*

"Aye aye, sir."

"PRIVATE, WHAT THE FUCK ARE YOU DOING?"

"Sir, the Private was . . . unwrapping the candy bar."

Green shook his head while saying softly, "Uh uh, Private. *That's* a no-no." White ate the candy bar, wrapper and all. He then chewed the gum, along with its package. Green handed him a glass of warm water to wash it all down. "We wouldn't want you to get fat, Private. Sit-up position, *hit it! Ready,* BEGIN! . . . You can stop at one hundred or when you puke." White was able to stop at thirty-two.

After cleaning the squad bay for the fifth time that day, the men counted off without a mistake. Chalice was amazed. The platoon had only been in training two weeks.

"*Prepare to hit the rack*," Green commanded.

"PREPARE TO HIT THE RACK. AYE AYE, SIR," the men replied, all except Chalice. He had done far more than prepare. Before he could get back on his feet, Sergeant Green came over and started tucking him in.

"No, no, don't get up, hog. You're tired, aren't you?" Green clucked his tongue a few times. "You college boys need all the rest you can get. Just relax. We'll talk about it tomorrow."

"Prepare to hit the rack."

"PREPARE TO HIT THE RACK. AYE AYE, SIR."

"HIT IT."

The men scrambled into their bunks, and Green turned off the light. As Chalice lay wondering if Green would remember the next morning, he heard Cowen trying to muffle some laughter. "Shut the fuck up."

"Sure man, you must really need the sleep."

The men had just returned from the armory with their newly issued M-14's. Morton paced the aisle, his hands squeezed white around one of the rifles. Eyes on fire, he looked as if he saw the whole world cringing before him.

"*Hogs,* today is your most important day of training. Today you made the most important friend of your Marine Corps careers. A Marine's rifle is his best friend. Marines are the best marksmen in the world. They're the best marksmen in the world because they're the best trained marksmen in the world. They're the best trained marksmen in the world because they're taught to shoot the Marine Corps way. I could name some Marine Corps marksmen you should know, but you don't. So I'll just name two that you do know — Lee Harvey Oswald and Charles Whitman. You *can't* beat marksmanship like that! Don't worry. When we get through with you, you'll be just as good. . . . Tell everyone who Charles Whitman is, college hog."

"Sir, the Private doesn't know," Chalice answered.

"I figured as much. Private Hymie, let's see if you know."

"*Sir, Charles Whitman was the Texas Tower Killer,*" Cowen called out.

"That's right, Hymie. Tell everyone what he did."

"Sir, Charles Whitman killed sixteen people from the University of Texas tower."

"THAT'S *what I call shooting,*" Morton replied.

Green stared at Chalice while saying, "That's what I call educating people."

Morton continued, "Now some of you worthless hogs are gonna spend the rest of your time in the Corps pounding on a typewriter, slinging hash, or polishing airplanes. But . . . remember one thing: A Marine is a rifleman first and that bullshit second. When you get to Nam with your fancy MOS's, don't be surprised if you find yourself up to your balls in rice paddies. Every Marine, no matter what his MOS, takes at least some training as a rifleman when he leaves Parris Island. Remember this, hogs: A professional killer without a weapon ain't worth *shit!*"

Morton began demonstrating the manual of arms. Chalice watched closely, sensing a slight change in the way Morton looked at the recruits — sensing a hint of respect in his glare. The first movement he demonstrated was Port Arms from Order Arms. Slowly, five times, Morton moved the rifle from a position on the floor against his right leg, to a position diagonally in front of his chest. He did so in two simple, distinct motions. The men watched, confident they could duplicate this movement.

Morton eyed them warily before finally giving the command. "*Port,* HARMS!*"

Morton had been prepared for mistakes, but what he saw stunned him — seventy-seven variations of Port Arms. Not satisfied with two distinct movements, some of the men had combined them into one awkward gesture while others added two or three additional movements. There weren't five men in a row with their rifles pointing in the same direction, and a few of the men switched directions three and four times before finally deciding upon one. At the same time glad and sorry that his own rifle wasn't loaded, Morton merely ordered the men back to the starting position.

Chalice was more concerned with his own ineptitude than that of the men around him. The movement had seemed so simple when done by Morton. He watched carefully as Green demonstrated the same maneuver. Green had the platoon try it a step at a time, and the results were somewhat better. He kept the men practicing for over an hour, adding a few more movements such as Right Shoulder Arms. Not once did the entire platoon perform any of these maneuvers correctly. The drill instructors always had a choice of men to scream at. As the practice continued, the screaming became louder.

Chalice's rifle began to feel like it weighed a hundred pounds. All three drill instructors had had a turn to spit words in his face, and he was praying that the drill would soon be over. Suddenly, Hacker came rushing towards him. *"College fag,* IS THAT RIFLE TOO HEAVY FOR YOU?"

"No, sir."

"HOLD IT OUT STRAIGHT!"

"Yes, sir."

The drilling continued. Green showed particular interest in Private Cowen while Hacker and Morton distributed their insults more evenly. Green noticed that Cowen's little finger had a tendency to slide away from the rest of his fingers. Tired of pointing this out, Green smashed Cowen's hand with a rifle stock. "How's that, Abie? In a few minutes you'll look like you're wearing a pretty red mitten."

Hacker rushed towards Chalice, "HOG, *what did I tell you about that rifle?* We've got an exercise for weaklings like you." Chalice found himself in the center of the aisle with his arms straight out in front of him and his rifle lying across his palms. His forearms hardened and began to ache. The pain moved slowly towards his shoulders. Each second seemed to be the last possible one before his arms would collapse. One by one, other men joined him in the center of the aisle. He could actually feel them straining like himself. The sound of a rifle barrel hitting a bunk railing distracted him. Green and Cowen seemed glued together at the chest.

"Jewboy, what are you trying to do?"

"Sir, the Private was trying to do Right Shoulder Arms."

Green buried his fist in Cowen's stomach. His face red and twisted, Cowen straightened his body to attention. "What's the matter, Jewboy? Did that hurt?"

"No, sir."

"Oh, I can't hit." Again Green smashed his fist into Cowen's stomach. "Did *that* hurt, Jewboy?"

"Yes, sir."

"Oh, you can't take it." Green punched Cowen again. "How about that time?"

"No, sir."

"Kike, I don't know why I'm wasting my sweat." Green paused as if to calm himself, but continued in the same angry tone. "As soon as you get out of here, they'll probably stick you behind a typewriter. You'll be like any other cunt secretary. You'll shine your shoes just good enough to stay out of trouble. The same for your uniform. You might even make some

rank. If they start giving Purple Hearts for broken fingernails, you'll probably get a few of those. Everything'll go along just fine . . . *but then it'll
happen*, hog: Some candyass colonel'll walk by your desk and you'll drop
your typewriter on his foot. . . . You know what they'll do to you, hog?
They'll *take . . . you . . . out* . . . AND SHOOT YOU! . . . You
need a shower, Abie."

One by one, more men were sent into the aisle. Soon a fourth of the
platoon stood arms outstretched, rifles balanced across their palms. Chalice's arms throbbed violently. No longer did they feel ready to collapse.
Instead, he became gradually dizzier and more worried about falling on
his face. Suddenly, his arms did drop. He quickly raised them before any
of the drill instructors noticed. Other men weren't as lucky. Faces twisted
in pain, sweat gushing from their pores, they also had to endure the drill
instructors' rebukes.

Finally it happened. A man dropped his rifle to the floor. Forgetting his
pain, Chalice waited to see what the drill instructors would do. All three
of them converged upon Stevens, a lanky, delicate-looking black.

"PICK IT UP, HOG."

"GET THAT RIFLE OFF THE DECK!"

Stevens picked up the rifle, but was unable to stretch out his arms.

"GET IT OUT THERE, CUNT."

"STRAIGHTEN THOSE ARMS."

"Sir, the Private can't."

"CAN'T?"

"CAN'T, MY ASS!"

"*Why you gutless coon*, GET THAT RIFLE UP."

"Sir, the Private's trying."

"TRYING!"

"FUCKING TRYING!"

"WHO THE FUCK CARES WHAT YOU'RE TRYING?"

"I didn't ask you to *try*, hog. Now GET . . . THAT . . . RIFLE
UP!"

"Sir, the Private can't."

"THE PRIVATE'S GUTLESS."

"THE PRIVATE'S GONNA EAT THAT RIFLE."

"I AIN'T TELLING YOU AGAIN, coon."

Stevens made a feeble effort before his arms again collapsed to his sides.
Morton yanked the rifle away and smashed it against Stevens's chest, sending him sprawling to the floor.

Morton spun around and shouted, "ALL RIGHT, *you miserable civilian*
TURDS, *you don't deserve these rifles. Stow 'em* . . . right *now!*" The

men quickly put away their rifles, then stood at attention in front of their racks. "ON YOUR BELLIES!"

At first Chalice was glad to be rid of his rifle, but after a half hour of calisthenics he couldn't remember ever being glad about anything. For the past five minutes he'd been doing push-ups. His arms felt as if they were going to tear off at the shoulders. Sweat dripped rhythmically from the tip of his nose. He could see his reflection in the puddle beneath his face. All three drill instructors paced the aisle yelling at individual men. Morton stood over Cowen for a few minutes continually asking, "How 'bout a shower, Hymie. You look like you need a shower."

Finally Morton and Hacker left, leaving Green to conduct the calisthenics. It was Green that the men feared most. Whatever had to be done, he was more adept at making it painful. Green seemed to get the most pleasure from torturing them. All he had to do was look at a man to tell him he'd slit that man's throat for a laugh. Morton and Hacker had their limits, no matter how unbearable these limits might be. But Green was capable of anything.

Chalice listened to him call out the exercises, Green's pleasure increasing his own suffering. The platoon was doing side-straddle hops, all the men facing in the same direction. Chalice noticed Green standing atop a rack. He sprang silently to the next one, only the men he passed aware of him. Stevens stood in place, moving his arms to appear as if doing the exercise. Green sprang to the next rack. He crouched, teeth clenched in a smile. Chalice stared in awe, rapt by Green's image. He wasn't even human. It was a jungle cat eyeing an unsuspecting kill, waiting for the right moment. It came. Green sprang with lethal quickness, soaring dizzily over the heads of a file of men. In an instant, Stevens lay sprawled on the floor, face up with Green straddling him. He stood motionless, as if at any second he'd dive down and tear out a chunk of Stevens's neck with his teeth. Green's hands shot downward, jerking Stevens to his feet as if he were made of straw. One hand squeezed white around Stevens's neck, he hissed some words Chalice couldn't understand. Stevens stopped gagging, and his eyes squeezed tightly shut. Green flung him against the wall, then turned on the men. Within seconds the entire platoon was mopping the floor with rags. No water was needed! The men used their own sweat.

The hand-to-hand combat instructor stood upon a wooden platform. Each of the recruit battalion's four platoons made up a side of the square that surrounded him. Bayonets fixed, the men held their rifles in the Guard position.

"Butt stroke!" he yelled.

In unison, the men stepped forward, viciously swinging the butts of their rifles at an imaginary enemy, screaming, "KILL!"

"Smash!"

"KILL!"

"Slash!"

"KILL!"

"Jab!"

"KILL!"

Again and again the drill was repeated. The rifles grew heavier and the pain increased; but so did the viciousness of the attacking movements, and also the shouts, "KILL!"

The instructor paired off the four platoons, arranging the men in order of their size. Instead of a rifle, he now held a pugil stick, a thick broom handle with canvas cushions at both ends. One of the cushions was painted red to indicate the bayonet end of a rifle.

"All right, men, now you're gonna prove to me I haven't been wasting my fucking time; and you better do just that. We're also gonna find out which platoon has the most guts. *Remember,* that motherfucker coming at you with a pugil stick's got one thing on his mind — TO KILL YOU! And there ain't nothing you can do but *kill him first.* This *ain't* no ballet. You aren't supposed to impress him with your footwork. You're gonna charge right at that dirty motherfucker screaming your fucking heads off and swinging that fucking pugil stick. If you wanna live, the first thing you gotta do is prove to that cocksucker that you're the craziest, most vicious, bloodthirsty sonofabitch that ever lived — *that you're a* MARINE!"

Chalice watched the successive pairs of combatants. The viciousness with which the men fought surprised him. They looked ridiculous. He felt ridiculous, knowing that soon it would be his turn. Chalice glanced at the faces around him. Without exception, the men were eager for their turns. He too became curious to see what it would be like.

The instructor blew his whistle. It was Chalice's turn. His opponent charged towards him — screaming, looking like a maniac. Chalice ran to meet him, also screaming, feeling like an idiot, a screaming idiot. It was an absurdly odd feeling. But it wasn't bad. They closed upon each other. The hate in his opponent's eyes was real. He wanted to kill. Chalice expected a Slash, received and parried it, followed with a Butt Stroke, then a Smash to his opponent's face and a Slash that ended with the red end of his pugil stick at the base of his opponent's neck. A whistle blew.

The instructor pointed his finger in the man's face. "You're dead, cocksucker."

Chalice ran back to his platoon. The men were smiling, some of them holding their fists in the air. It had happened so fast, so easily. He ran by Green.

"Not bad, hog." Green's tone seemed out of character. Still brutal, it almost acknowledged equality. Chalice rejoined the line, anxious for another turn.

Colson ran to meet his opponent while Morton yelled, "*You better not lose this one, RED-NECK.*" Both men were big. They swung clumsily at one another. Colson seemed determined not to lose another match. He drove his opponent backwards. A jab in the stomach staggered him. He began to tire. Backstepping, Colson lost his balance. His legs twisted underneath him and he squirmed in pain. A jagged spear of bone stuck out ridiculously from a gash in his leg. He stared numbly at it while blood seeped out from the yellow and white tissue.

Green ran towards him, yelling joyously, "Finally got rid of him." A sickened expression on his face, Colson sat quietly, trying not to move. A dozen drill instructors gathered around him, laughing and slapping each other on the back.

Chalice heard Morton say, "So long, red-neck. I couldn't have done a better job myself."

"Too bad, hog. It looks like it'll be a long time before you get off this island."

"Don't look so sad, hog. If you can get them to cut it off, they'll have to give you a discharge."

"How does a clumsy turd like you get out of your rack in the morning?"

Green said loudly, "Cancel that ambulance. I think it's just a hard-on."

Green glared at the men while they did side-straddle hops. The count was up to three hundred, not including the times they'd had to start over. Private Stevens stood at attention. Green asked him, loud enough for everybody to hear, "You like watching the rest of the platoon do PT, don't you?"

"*No, sir.*"

"*No?* Well how come you weren't doing it with them, Queen Bee? If you had, they would have been done long ago."

"Sir, the Private's got a sore foot."

"NOBODY *gets a sore foot in the Marine Corps!* Is that what you're gonna tell the Gooks in Vietnam — 'Don't shoot! I got a sore foot'?"

"No, sir."

"STOP!" Green shouted to the rest of the platoon. The men came to attention, all of them breathing heavily. Green jumped upon a table. "Hogs, you can thank Queen Bee for that little workout. She's got a sore foot, so you had to do her side-straddle hops for her. That's the way it is in Nam: if one man doesn't do his share, the rest of his platoon has to make up for him. Here it's side-straddle hops. In Nam, it's more bullets you have to dodge. Here you pay with sweat. In Nam you pay with your lives . . . your arms, your legs, your balls. Stevens, tell these hogs why they had to do two hundred extra side-straddle hops."

"*Sir, the Private's got a sore foot.*"

"Awww, Queen Bee's got a sore foot. . . . HOW COME THE DOCTOR SAYS YOU'RE A MALINGERER?"

"*Sir, the Private doesn't know.*"

"Maybe he doesn't like coons. . . . Isn't that right, Queen Bee?"

"Sir, the Private doesn't —"

"BULLSHIT! *I saw the chit.* Tell these hogs who *Dr. Tolbert is.*"

"Sir, Dr. Tolbert is the doctor that said the Private was malingering."

"THAT AIN'T WHAT I MEAN!"

"Sir, Dr. Tolbert is —"

"*Is the big black* SPADE *that struts around in a white coat over at sick* bay. . . . ISN'T HE, QUEEN BEE?"

"Yes, sir."

"*Is he the same one that said there was nothing wrong with your arm two weeks ago?*"

"*No, sir.*"

"Queen Bee, you're the most gutless cunt in this platoon. AREN'T YOU?"

"*No, sir.*"

"WHAT, HOG?"

"NO, SIR." The men winced as Stevens repeated his answer. Never before had anyone contradicted a drill instructor.

"Get over here, *cunt.*" Stevens walked up to Green who was squatting upon a table. "You're gutless, aren't you, *cunt?*"

"No, sir. The Private's got a sore foot."

"DID I ASK YOU ABOUT YOUR FOOT, CUNT?"

"*No, sir.*"

"Queen Bee, you've been to sick bay twice as much as anyone in this platoon. First it was your stomach, then your ear, then your arm, then your leg. THERE AIN'T A FUCKING THING WRONG WITH YOU EXCEPT YOUR GUTS. . . . College hog, how many push-ups has this platoon done for *Private* Queen Bee?"

"Sir, the platoon has done about two hundred push-ups for Private Quee— Stevens."

"And about a hundred bends and thrusts, *and a hundred sit-ups*, AND THREE HUNDRED SIDE-STRADDLE HOPS. . . . Hog, you're gutless. Everytime this platoon does PT, I see you scratching your ass. You're gutless, *aren't you?*"

"No, sir."

Green sprang up and down on his haunches. "WHAT?"

"No, sir."

"I said you were, cunt. *You're a worthless turd that's gonna get people killed in Nam.* AREN'T YOU, CUNT?"

"No, sir."

"I SAID YOU WERE."

"Sir, the Drill Instructor can't say that about the Private."

In an instant, Stevens lay flat on his back with Green squatting upon his chest. Stevens gagged as Green bounced upon his haunches. "Aw, the hog can't breathe. . . . You're gutless, aren't you, cunt?" Attempting to answer, Stevens could only gag. "*Choke*, hog. I hope you *die*." Green sprang to his feet, landing with his boots straddling Stevens's head. "Get up, hog." Stevens sat up slowly. "GET UP, HOG!" Coughing, Stevens stood up. "You're the most worthless turd I've seen in years. *What did I write on the blackboard the first day?*"

"Sir, the Private doesn't remember."

"THE PRIVATE BETTER REMEMBER! . . . It was about pain."

"Sir, the Drill Instructor wrote, 'Pain is good.'"

"That's right, Queen Bee. PAIN IS GOOD! . . . Side-straddle hops; *ready*, BEGIN!"

Stevens attempted the exercise but stopped, favoring his right leg.

A vicious smile on his face, Green shouted, "I GOT YOU now, hog. I GOT YOU! It was your left leg, REMEMBER? . . . Make up your mind, hog. WHAT LEG IS IT?"

"Sir, both the Private's legs are sore."

"Push-up position, HIT IT!" Stevens dropped to the ground. "*Ready*, BEGIN — many, many of them." Stevens did twenty push-ups before collapsing on his stomach. "DID I TELL YOU TO STOP, HOG?"

"Sir, the Private can't do any more."

"*Abie*, fill your bucket. . . . Hog, you ain't even a coon. You're a NIGGER, a GUTLESS nigger! . . . Aren't you?"

"Yes, sir."

Cowen returned with a bucket of water, and Green shouted, "PUSH-UP POSITION, MOVE!" Stevens made no attempt to lift himself off the floor. "Dump it on him, Abie." Stevens lay motionless in the puddle of water. "UP POSITION!"

"Sir, the Private can't."

Two drill instructors from another platoon, one of them black, entered the squad bay. "Take a look at this cunt," Green shouted.

The black drill instructor bent over Stevens and cooed, "What'sa matter, mean old Sergeant Green picking on you?" Stevens didn't answer. "GET UP, TURD!"

Another black drill instructor entered the squad bay. "You tired, hog?"

"Push-up position, *move!*" Green shouted.

Stevens lay motionless. One of the black drill instructors nudged him with his foot. "Don't you like to do push-ups, hog?"

"Sir, Drill Instructor Sergeant Green called the Private a nigger." The black drill instructor smashed his foot into Stevens's side, lifting his whole body by the waist. Stevens rolled over, writhing and stunned.

The other black drill instructor kicked him in the leg. "GET UP, HOG!"

Stevens tried to crawl away, accidentally grabbing Green's foot. "THE HOG ATTACKED ME!"

Hacker ran into the squad bay, laughing, *"Queen Bee's finally getting what he asked for."*

"The cunt tried to attack me."

"That's right."

"We all saw him."

"GET UP, CUNT!"

"On your feet!"

Sobbing, Stevens moaned, "I can't." The two black drill instructors began kicking him down the aisle. He screamed, again and again, defeatedly. The drill instructors surrounded him — kicking and shouting, drowning out his cries.

Disbelieving what he saw, Chalice remembered wanting Stevens hurt, remembered the times he'd had to pay for Stevens. Sure he deserved it. *But not this!* nothing as brutal as this — being kicked down the aisle by five drill instructors, moaning and crying like a child, begging them to stop.

The drill instructors had Stevens surrounded. He tried to crawl away, screaming in pain. They shouted, kicked, and spit on him. A black drill instructor jerked Stevens to his feet by the neck, flung him near Chalice. Blood and snot dripped from his nose. His mouth stretched open in pain.

Spasms shot through Chalice's stomach. He fought to keep from vomiting. Stevens collapsed at his feet. The drill instructors circled him, frenzied, shouting and kicking, shoving Chalice and Cowen out of the way. The black drill instructors seemed most enraged, did the most damage. By themselves, they kicked him ten yards. One of them dragged him by the leg all the way down the aisle while Green shouted to the rest of the platoon, "Get a look at this worthless cunt."

Finally, they dragged him into the bathroom. Hacker phoned the MP's while the other drill instructors remained with Stevens. Green returned to the squad bay, the vicious expression on his face asking, "Who's next?" Sneering, he scraped his boot through the blood splotches on the floor.

"GET OUT YOUR RAGS! CLEAN THIS SHIT UP!" Still queasy, Chalice ran his rag over the floor. It came away stained with the sickening brown color of blood.

The men were back at attention when the MP's arrived. They dragged Stevens, half-conscious, out the door. Green seemed calm as he paced the aisle, but Chalice had no doubts that his rage had been real. As Green's stare passed over him, Chalice wondered, 'Are you satisfied now? . . . That's what you wanted, isn't it?'

Green began speaking in his usual sadistic, arrogant tone; but beneath it Chalice sensed something more than the desire to terrorize. "Hogs, I hope you enjoyed this as much as I did. There's nothing that says you can't have some good, clean fun on Parris Island. I did you a favor, hogs. You may not appreciate it now, but when you get to Nam you will. When you get to Nam and find yourself in a foxhole with some other Marine, you won't have to sweat it being Stevens. I'd rather see that cocksucker *dead* than as a Marine. I can't kill him myself, but there's two things I can do: try to turn him into a Marine or try my best to keep him on this island. *You* won't see him again. When he gets out of the brig, you'll be long gone.

"Maybe some other drill instructor can turn *Private* Stevens into a Marine. I've seen worse turds salvaged. *But at least I'm through with him.* I've already spent one tour in Nam, and it won't be long before I go back. Too many Marines get killed because of cunts like that to let another one off this island. *If he can't take it here*, then he can't take it in Nam. . . . Sometimes a shitbird slips through. If you meet one in Nam, do your platoon a favor: BLOW HIM AWAY! Blow him away before he gets someone else blown away."

Green paused. When he began speaking again, it was in a still loud but less arrogant tone. "Hogs, the Marine Corps is my life, *my whole fucking life*. I intend to stay in it a long time. When I put my hands on one of you turds, I put my career on the line. Who the hell knows when some pencil-pushing cunt in Legal might decide that a gutless turd like Stevens is worth more than the Marine Corps, worth more than this uniform I risk my life to wear. See these stripes on my arm, they've come off before and I don't give a shit if they come off again. I don't care if they bust me to private — just as long as I can keep turds like Stevens from wearing the same uniform as I wear, just as long as I can keep turds like that from ending up in Nam where they can get me or any other decent Marine killed because they can't hack it."

Green stopped talking. He walked over to the blackboard and wrote in large, block letters, "JEROME ALLEN GREEN 1991666."

"Hogs, that's my name and serial number. I want every one of you to write it down and memorize it. If you don't like something I do, you figure out a way to get that name and serial number over to Legal. You fix up a nice little story to go along with it. You can even save it until after you get off Parris Island. It might be easier then. *But remember something, hogs:* There ain't one of you cunts that's gonna get off this island until I think he deserves to be called a Marine. There ain't one of you cunts that's gonna wear this uniform unless I'd be proud to share the same foxhole with you."

Green walked out of the squad bay, leaving the men alone and at attention. Still sickened by what had happened to Stevens, Chalice asked himself what could excuse such brutality — certainly not the gung ho speech he'd just heard. Green was less than an animal. He was a sadistic perversion of a human being. Or was it that simple?

The men stood facing each other in two files, a painfully cold wind gusting towards them from the opposite side of the rifle range. Morton stood between the files holding a can of Sure Grip. "Today's the day, hogs. Today's the day you get to fire your M-14 Destroyers. This goo is to keep your rifle stocks from slipping. When I walk by, scream out, '*Left-handed,* sir,' if you're left-handed."

When Morton reached him, Chalice shouted, "*Left-handed, sir.*"

Morton slapped a spoonful of Sure Grip on the left side of Chalice's chest. "Rub it in, hog."

Chalice pressed the glob against his shooting jacket. The grainy gluelike mass oozed between his fingers, webbing them together. He pressed harder, trying to rub off as much of the Sure Grip as possible. Even after his arm was at his side, Chalice kept working his fingers apart only to have them stick together again.

Morton started on the men across from Chalice. He slapped some Sure Grip on a recruit's shoulder. As if awakened, the recruit shouted, "*Left-handed, sir.*"

Chalice saw Morton's fist squeeze white around the spoon. He waited for him to explode. Instead, Morton said calmly, "Open your mouth, hog."

Morton heaped the spoon with Sure Grip. He waved it slowly in front of the recruit before resting it upon his lower teeth. "Bite, hog." The teeth clamped down with a metallic cling. Morton withdrew the spoon. "Chew, hog." The recruit's jaw ground slowly. His face reddened. Morton jumped back to avoid the vomit.

Chalice found himself trying to suppress a laugh. Between wheezing coughs, the recruit's face twisted with nausea. Chalice tasted the Sure Grip in his own mouth, felt his stomach convulse. Guiltily, he tried to keep from smiling.

The rest of the day went quickly. It had been strikingly different. Not until the platoon was ready to leave the rifle range did Chalice try to figure out why. The men stood in front of him in formation. He, the college hog, was waiting for all the wind hoods to be passed forward so he could count them. He felt relaxed, noticed the same feeling on the other men's faces. It had something to do with the rifles. During the day, the drill instructors had seemed to look at the men differently — almost as equals. Their words, even their shouts, hadn't been meant to taunt or harass. The drill instructors had been on their side — teaching them how to shoot, spotting their rounds, adjusting their sights. Chalice stared at Morton, intrigued, seeing him for the first time as something other than an adversary.

"ARE YOU EYEBALLING ME, *college fag?* COUNT THEM GODDAMN HOODS!" Nervously, Chalice began stuffing the wind hoods into a canvas bag. He lost count and had to start over, sure that Morton was glaring at him. The wind slashed against the side of his face. His numb fingers grabbed clumsily at the hoods. Relieved to stuff the final hood into the bag, he called out, "Sir, seventy-two hoods."

Morton spun around. "*There should be seventy-three.*" Chalice remained silent, sure that he had miscounted. "Hog, you *better* not have made a mistake. . . . *Count 'em again.*"

Chalice emptied the bag as Morton turned towards the men. "*Which one of you cocksuckers didn't turn in his wind hood?*" Morton froze, spotting something. Shoving men aside, he burst through the ranks. A recruit in the back row stood rigidly at attention, eyes directed forward, still wearing his wind hood. Morton rushed up to him. "HOG, DID YOU TURN IN YOUR HOOD?"

"*Yes, sir,*" the recruit shouted uneasily, wondering why Morton had singled him out.

"Are you sure, hog?" Morton asked softly.

"YES, SIR."

"You remember turning it in?"

"Yes, sir."

"Who'd you give it to, hog?"

"Sir, the Private handed it to Private Stanley."

"YOU'RE LYING!"

Now even more bewildered, the recruit replied, "Sir, the Private turned in his wind hood."

"Oh, is that right?" Morton slammed his hand down on top of the recruit's head. He jerked him forward by the hood and dragged him gagging through the ranks.

"OPEN THE BAG!" Chalice held it open while Morton stuffed the hood and the head it contained into the bag. The chin buttons finally snapped and the recruit staggered backwards.

"GET BACK IN RANKS!" Morton screamed.

The lights flashed on and Morton said calmly, "Rise and shine, kiddies. Rise and shine." Bewildered, the men staggered out of their racks. Any change meant trouble, but Morton's easy tone was startling. Blinking, still half asleep, they stood at attention in front of their bunks.

"Hogs, I don't like to see Marines smile, and I don't like to hear them sing. *But today* is a special occasion. *We* have a birthday. I wanna hear every swinging dick singing happy birthday to our sweet little birthday boy." Morton started singing. The men joined him hesitantly, unsure of what was happening, gradually realizing as the singing became more boisterous. "Happy birthday to you./ Happy birthday to you./ *Happy birthday dear Jesus./* Happy birthday to you." By the time the song ended, most of the men were smiling. Morton restored the platoon's military bearing by good-naturedly pounding a few of the men on the sides of their heads.

Christmas proved no different from an ordinary Sunday, and aside from church services, Sunday was never very different from any other day. Few of the men had expected any difference. Christmas at Parris Island was as inconceivable as finding Parris Island under a Christmas tree.

After breakfast, Morton marched the platoon to church to hear "that fucking pansy of a chaplain tell us about Candyass Jesus." When the men returned to the squad bay, Morton assured them that if he'd been around at the time, "the slimy Jew wouldn't haven't gotten off so easy." The recruits spent the next few hours hand washing their clothes, polishing their boots, and shining their brass. As often happened when they were doing these tasks, Morton left them alone in the squad bay. As rarely happened, he didn't come sneaking through the door or windows every ten minutes to choke any man he caught talking or loafing. An hour before lunch, he did rush into the squad bay.

"ATTENTION!" Startled, the men jumped to their feet. Morton's tone and angry expression seemed ready to prove that Christmas was the most miserable day of the year. "*Any of you hogs seen the duty roster?*" No one answered. "*Chalice, Cowen, Boyd, Richardson,* . . . see if it's in the Dempster Dumpster." The four men rushed outside.

Chalice reached the garbage bin first. He swung the door open and saw that the bin was over half full. "God, we'll never find it."

All four men glanced inside. They stood around for a few minutes urging each other to climb into the bin. Placing himself farthest from the door, Chalice warned, "We better get started."

"Yeah," Richardson agreed, making no effort to climb inside.

Boyd had his head through the door. Cowen placed his hand on Boyd's shoulder. "Yeah. The garbage ain't gonna come to us. See if it's in there, Boyd."

"What's the duty roster look like?" Boyd asked, knowing exactly what it looked like and playing the dumb Southerner that he wasn't.

"It's a white paper with typing on it," Chalice informed him.

Boyd reached inside and started shuffling the garbage. "Sure a mess a white papers in here." Boyd reached farther into the bin and began thrashing the garbage around.

"Find it?" Cowen asked, all but pushing Boyd inside.

"No, but I found a pack of Hershey bars," Boyd answered excitedly.

"Huh?"

"Where?"

"Hand 'em out." All four men squeezed their heads through the door. "Take it easy. You're smothering me."

"One at a time," Chalice suggested while climbing Richardson's back. "*Hey,* I see some pistachio nuts." Cowen dived over Boyd, and Richardson followed him inside.

"*Ow!* Get off me!" Chalice lifted Boyd's legs and dumped him into the bin. Cowen pulled Boyd's head out of the garbage while Chalice climbed in. The Dumpster was full of candy sent to the men for Christmas. The drill instructors had gotten tired of making the recruits eat it wrappers and all, then exercising them until they puked. Garbage flew furiously around the bin as all four men burrowed through it.

"Cup cakes!"

"*Clark Bars!*"

"Let me have one."

"More gum."

"*Brownies!*"

The men stuffed their mouths as they searched, and the announcements became less intelligible. Finally tiring, they piled all the loot in the center of the bin and began devouring it. Cheeks stuffed like hamsters', the men suddenly stopped grabbing for the candy. They stared at each other. Convulsed by laughter, Cowen fell over backwards. Candy spurted from his mouth as he wallowed in the garbage. They all started laughing, each one noticing how ridiculous the other three looked. As their mouths emptied and the laughter became louder, Chalice reached over and shut the large metal door. Just enough light seeped in for them to see each other and the candy.

Richardson, a small, frail black, was almost invisible beneath his green hat. Teeth flashing from nowhere, he said. "This reminds me of Candyland in the fairy stories."

"Except for the smell."

"Who cares?"

"I forgot what candy tastes like without the wrapper."

"I almost forgot to take it off."

"You know this is the best Christmas I ever had."

"Me too," Cowen agreed.

Chalice said, "Dear Mom and Dad, I had a beautiful black Christmas . . . inside a Dempster Dumpster. . . . This is the first time in two months I've felt safe."

"Yeah. No drill instructors in here."

"Can't see us either."

"It's a damn good thing."

"Parris Island wouldn't be so bad if they'd let us sit in garbage cans more often."

"Yeah," Cowen agreed. "This is almost as good as being back in the States."

Boyd said, "It's a mite cramped, but a damn sight cozier than the squad bay."

"Yankee Stadium would be cramped with me and three drill instructors inside."

"One drill instructor wouldn't be much better, Abie."

"Not iffin' it was Green. Abie, I don't think he likes you *at* all."

"He don't like anybody."

"Especially Abie."

"I ain't so sure," Cowen said softly, willing to let the matter drop.

"He sure don't like Jews."

"He don't like anybody."

"Jews especially."

Chalice asked, "Doesn't it bother you being called Jewboy or Hymie or Abie all the time?"

"Naw — well at first it did. But it got pretty funny after a while. Guys were always sneaking up to me after chow — half of them asking, 'Abie, how come they call you Hymie?' and the other half asking, 'Hymie, how come they call you Abie?' "

"Hey Hymie, what is your name?" Boyd asked.

"Abie, stupid," Richardson cut in.

"No, it ain't. It's Robert."

"How come they call — "

"Well, doesn't it bother you being called kike?" Chalice asked.

"That's the whole idea of Parris Island: to teach you how to take anything. . . . Richardson, how much does it bother you to be called coon?"

"Nothing new."

Chalice said, "They keep on telling us we're all Marines, all equal; but then they call us kikes, niggers, red-necks — "

"College hogs."

"That too. They're just teaching us how to hate each other."

"Bullshit! Do you hate me more because of what they call me? Or Richardson? Or red-necks like Boyd?"

"I kinda like red-necks," Boyd cut in. "I figgered it was a compliment."

Richardson said, "Since I been at Parris Island, I ain't figgered nothin' was a compliment."

"I still think it's wrong."

"My oldest brother was in the Corps — "

"A Marine Corps family!"

" — He went through the same bullshit. I knew what to expect."

"Then why'd you join?" Chalice asked.

"Because he said Parris Island was the last place he heard any of that bullshit. . . . My middle brother was in the Army — "

"No! a doggie."

" — They called him private in boot camp and kike for the rest of his hitch. He got in so many fights, they court-martialed him twice."

"I still say it's wrong," Chalice insisted.

"You're wrong. They figure if they put us through enough shit, we'll respect each other more."

"Yeah," Boyd agreed. "I'm glad we've got Abie around. Green messes with him so much he ain't got nearly enough time for the rest of us."

"He sure makes time for me. Chalice, what happened to the rest of those pistachio nuts?"

Chalice handed Richardson the remainder of the bag. "Maybe so, but why does he spend so much time fucking with you if it isn't because you're Jewish?"

"Maybe it is," Cowen mumbled, but then added in a louder tone, "He don't hate Jews."

"Ain't crazy about 'em either," Boyd said. "Hey, how come they're always telling you to take a shower, Abie?"

Changing the subject, Cowen said, "Remember when Stevens got the shit kicked out of him, it was the black drill instructors that did most of it." Chalice had noticed the same thing, but was unsure of Cowen's point. "Richardson, how'd you feel when that happened?"

"The turd deserved it."

Chalice said, "He didn't deserve *that*."

"How'd you like being in the same foxhole with him?" Boyd asked.

"Yeah?"

Richardson said, "I wouldn't."

At first surprised at their remarks, Chalice began to think about what Boyd had said. "I guess I wouldn't. . . . But they shouldn't have beat him up as bad as that."

"He's all right now," Richardson replied. "I saw him marching around with some prisoners a few days ago."

"I saw him with a new platoon yesterday. They just set him back two weeks."

"I saw Melton too. He's just starting training with a new platoon."

"God!"

"Who's Melton?"

"The one who said he was queer."

"Must of kept saying it for two months."

"Maybe you're right," Chalice said to Cowen, as if he hadn't heard the last few comments.

"Me?" Cowen asked.

"Yeah. I remember what Green said after Stevens got beat up. The gung ho psychopath really believed it — that he didn't want any of us getting off Parris Island unless he'd jump in a foxhole with us. . . . He sure does hate Jews though."

"No he doesn't."

"Well how come he's always on your ass?"

In exasperation, Cowen finally said what he didn't want to say. "Because he's a Jew."

"Green?"

"Him?"

"You shittin' me, Abie?"

"*No!*"

"He is?"

"Abie said 'No.'"

"*No*, I said he was."

Remembering how the black drill instructors beat Stevens, Chalice was sure Cowen was right. "God, I never would have believed it."

"No, you wouldn't have," Cowen mumbled just loud enough for Chalice to hear.

Embarrassed, Chalice was trying to think of something to say when he noticed his hands were stained red from the pistachio nuts. "God, look at this." He tried to rub the dye off on his pants.

"You better not let Morton see that."

"Tell him it's blood."

"It will be."

"What about the duty roster?"

"Yeah?"

"What duty roster?"

Chalice stood at attention in his Dress Green Uniform, thinking about the time he'd spent polishing his shoes and brass, feeling ridiculous. Morton's eyes passed over him as he glanced down the row of men.

"This is it, hogaroos: Command Inspection. If the candyass colonel likes the way you look, you'll be leaving Parris Island in two days. You know the questions he'll probably ask you; and you *better know* the answers. I don't want to hear any stammering. Shout right in his face. If he asks you what you cleaned your rifles with, don't say WD-40. They don't like us using it."

The colonel arrived on time. He had a question for each man. Chalice watched him move down the ranks, distrustful of the way the colonel tried to seem friendly without sacrificing his stiff, military bearing.

"Private, where are you from?"

"Sir, the Private's from Turtletown, Tennessee," Boyd answered.

"Where exactly is that, Private?"

"Sir, it's about ten miles outside of Ducktown."

Chalice tightened his facial muscles to keep from smiling. Boyd had probably been waiting for that question. Chalice glanced at the men around him, admitting that they were smarter than he'd first thought.

The colonel moved to the next man. "Private Brown, you did a fine job on your rifle. How'd you manage to get it so clean?"

"*Sir, the Private used WD-40.*"

Chalice winced. 'Some of them are smarter.'

As soon as the colonel left, Morton stepped back into the aisle. He

117

glanced at his men, making little attempt to hide the pride in his expression. "Hogaroos, you did all right today . . . and you'll do all right in Nam. There's not a man here I'd be afraid to fight alongside . . . at least not more than one or two. We got rid of the real shitbirds. When you get off Parris Island, you're supposed to be Marines. That's a lot of bullshit. It'll take Nam to make you Marines, and you might end up corpses first. Marines or not, you're the best trained fighting men in the world. Don't *ever* fucking forget it."

Amused while Morton had been talking, Chalice was a little disappointed when the speech ended. He'd expected more, at the same time knowing that anything Morton could have said would have seemed ridiculous. 'Green could have done better,' he told himself. But this didn't matter — not what they said. He looked at the men around him, surprised by the confidence he had in them. They'd undergone everything he had, more than seemed possible. He didn't hate Morton or Hacker, or even Green; but more surprisingly, he respected them. They lived in their own simple world — competitive, destructive, brutal. But in this imaginary world, all their actions had made sense. Absurd as this world seemed, within itself it contained no absurdities. They had succeeded. They'd turned seventy-two "civilian pieces of shit" into Marines, whatever that meant. Chalice stared at the faces around him — confident, likable, *brutal*. Marines: one thing he was sure the word meant — "professional killers in the service of the United States government."

5. The Cemetery

A truck with supplies came out to the bridge. As the men unloaded it, a Marine jumped off and asked for Sergeant Kovacs. Kovacs was sitting outside his hootch cutting his toenails. Out of the corner of his eye, he spotted a new pair of boots walking towards him. 'New man, we can use him,' he thought without looking up. The boots stopped directly in front of him.

"I've been assigned to this platoon."

"Congratulations, what's your last name?" he asked, still cutting his toenails.

"Kramer."

"Okay Kramer, you'll be in Charlie Squad. Go find Valdez."

"I'd rather not."

'Just what I need, another wise guy.' Kovacs finally looked up. "What *would* you like to do, hotshot?"

"I think I'd like to be Platoon Commander."

Suppressing a grin, Kovacs slowly rose to his feet and stuck out his hand. "Glad to meet you, Lieutenant Kramer. Wanna take a look around?"

"No hurry." Kramer took off his pack and they both sat down. "How long ago did Lieutenant— your last lieutenant get killed?"

"None of us could pronounce his name either. We called him Lieutenant S. Got killed about three months ago."

Kramer stretched out on the ground and rested his head on his pack. He lit a cigarette and took a few drags while Kovacs went back to cutting his nails. "What kind of platoon have we got here?"

"They're the best, more brains than the rest of the company combined . . . a few shitbirds too. In a place like this where there isn't much chance of getting hit, they're a little more trouble than most platoons; but when the shit does hit the fan, they're a bunch of cool heads."

"What was Lieutenant S like?"

"If you're worried about the men comparing you to him, you've got a lot to worry about."

"Not worried, just curious."

"He was a hell of a dude. The first time I reported to the platoon, they were out in the Arizona and I was choppered in with some supplies. Right after I got off the chopper this guy wearing a couple a strings of love beads and a peace symbol comes swinging up to me. Right away he sticks out the glad hand, and I'm standing there thinking, 'No shit, it's the Chamber of Commerce.' We stood there talking for about ten minutes — you know, the usual stuff: Where're you from? Who do you know? Do you eat pussy? I couldn't think of the lieutenant's name, so I asked, 'What's Lieutenant What's-His-Fuck like?' He told me he was the greatest; good guy, knew his shit, lotta guts, didn't bug anybody. I said, 'I better check in with him. Where is he?' He says, 'You're talking to him.' "

Kramer sat up, shaking his head with amusement. "You really have a knack for making good first impressions with your lieutenants."

"Yeah, I guess I do. . . . You want me to call the squad leaders up here now, sir?"

"No, I can meet them later when I check out the perimeter. You always call your lieutenants 'sir'?"

"Not if I don't have to."

"You don't have to."

Whereas Kovacs seemed indifferent, Kramer noticed that most of the other members of the platoon carefully avoided him — doing so without exhibiting any outward hostility, but at the same time refusing to recognize him as their lieutenant. He realized that they thought of him as an outsider and wasn't particularly bothered, certainly not to the point of doing anything about it. The inward hostility of the older members of the platoon would have been more evident to him if he could have heard them talk among themselves — not by any direct comments about him, but by their reminiscences about Lieutenant S. The real reason for their hostility was always carefully avoided. To them Vietnam had become a question of odds. Kramer had changed these odds. Every day that had passed, every round that had missed them, and even every friend killed had improved the chances of their own survival, or so they thought. To them it was merely a question of their tours running out before their luck. So far it had been good, but now the odds had changed and so could their luck. In the backs of their minds was the same thought: 'A few days ago somebody steps off a truck and says he's our new lieutenant, so now our lives depend on him even though Kovacs knows more shit than he'll ever know, and all he has to do is make one little mistake and a few more of us get blown away.'

Alpha's next patrol was a short one with little chance of contact. Harmon took advantage of it to give Chalice some experience at walking point. Even though he realized this, Chalice still felt a deep sense of responsibility for the other members of his squad as he carefully led them along a thick tree line. Upon reaching the end of it, he saw a small stream. His eyes followed its course until, fifty yards in the distance, they came upon an old Vietnamese peasant talking to a younger man. At first his mind attributed little importance to what he was watching, then suddenly he became conscious of the actual situation and the danger involved in anything unusual. He passed the word back and was told to sneak up on them. Before they could get close, the younger man hurried off into a huge tree line.

"*Haul ass!*" Harmon shouted. The old man saw them running towards him and froze. When they reached him, he immediately started jabbering with a forced smile on his face. Harmon told Chalice to ask him who the young man was. Chalice had trouble understanding his answers, but he finally made out that the old man claimed to have just met him. Harmon felt he was a VC sympathizer, but he realized that they didn't have any evidence and he'd just be let go if they brought him in. He decided to have Payne radio back to the bridge and find out what Kramer wanted them to do. Kramer radioed Trippitt and was told not to bother with the old man. Harmon ordered Chalice to start heading back to the bridge. As they left, the old man nervously bowed and mumbled continuous thank-yous.

Upon returning to the perimeter, they found supplies and mail waiting for them. Hamilton had gotten a big package full of candy bars, Kool-Aid, and canned food. The whole squad stood around eagerly while he passed out a few of the candy bars. As Payne got one, he said, "Hey Hamilton, this is the first time I've ever seen you get a package when we didn't have to move-out."

"Yeah, that pisses me off."

Just then Harmon walked over. "Well, I guess you know what the story is."

"Whata you talking about?" Payne asked.

"Hamilton got a package, didn't he?"

"Are you shitting me? Are we moving out?"

"There it is."

"Where the fuck to?"

"Ladybird Park."

Hamilton, who had been holding a can of ravioli in his hand, threw it violently into the box and shouted, "I don't *fucking* believe it!" As everybody started walking away, he called out different names and flipped each man something out of his package until it was empty. Turning to Tony 5, he said, "I sure as hell wasn't gonna hump all that shit."

Forsythe and Chalice had just started to tear down their hootch when Harmon called out for everybody to pick up six meals of C-rations. Chalice threw down his poncho in disgust. "Why can't they drop off the supplies at the place we're going instead of making us hump them?"

"I dunno," Forsythe answered. "I can't ever remember moving out except on a day we got supplied."

After the men finished tearing down their hootches and fixing their packs, they had to sit around for an hour until First Platoon arrived to relieve them. They gathered in small groups wherever they could find some shade. Though Ladybird Park was only three kilometers away, nobody was very happy about moving out. As soon as First Platoon arrived, they headed back in the direction of Hill 65 following the road all the way.

Chalice expected the march to be easy because it was short and he now knew what to expect. After only a few minutes of marching, he felt exhausted and the shorter distance seemed unimportant. Only the psychological advantage of knowing exactly how far he had to go made this march any easier than the previous ones.

Ladybird Park was on the river side of the road and separated from it by a marsh. A small ville fronted the road on the opposite side. Three dike-like paths led across the marsh to the park. As soon as the platoon turned off the road onto one of them, a few dozen Vietnamese kids came running from the ville. They tagged along, palms outstretched, begging for food and cigarettes.

"Hey Marine, you souvenir me chop-chop?"

"You give me sigmoke?"

Most of the men were exhausted and simply ignored the kids. Chalice noticed Appleton reach into his pocket and throw a small object to them. One of the smaller kids snatched it up. He unwrapped it and was about to put it into his mouth when an older boy grabbed it away, at the same time yelling at Appleton, "You bullshit, this no chop-chop. This heat tab."

As soon as they crossed the marsh, Chalice saw why the place was called Ladybird State Park. Wide canopied shade trees dotted an area of white beach sand a hundred yards long and almost as wide, giving it the appearance of a picnic ground. Alpha Squad was assigned the side of the perimeter that fronted the river. Their positions were fifty yards from the bank, the area in between being free of obstacles and resembling a beach. First Platoon had left up the frames of their hootches, so setting up new ones involved little effort. The foxholes were already dug, and everybody just sat around and rested during the hour before dusk.

Kramer found little to complain about, and had even enjoyed his first week in the bush. Effortlessly, he'd fallen into the role of platoon commander. The narrow bounds of this role necessitated little thinking or decisiveness. The situations and choices were familiar — all of them covered by the boring nonsense he'd learned in OCS. The lines that circumscribed him were those he'd read in leadership manuals. All he had to do was remember them, to pick and choose the most appropriate. "An officer must —" and he was that officer, that military cliché. It wasn't the role that Kramer enjoyed, but rather the freedom from freedom it afforded him. However distasteful the military, it had a skill for rigid simplification.

Casually, Kramer's mind became occupied with thoughts about gaining the confidence of his men. He perceived their dislike for the captain and the gunny, and his encounters with both of them led him to share it. They were exactly as he had expected them to be — ambitious career men whose lives centered on and had no meaning outside of the Marine Corps, "yes men" to those with more power and tyrants to those with less. Kramer knew that they'd soon find out he wasn't their idea of a platoon commander. He decided it would be best to avoid them as much as possible — to keep his role uncomplicated.

The first time they were resupplied at the park, Kramer got a letter from his parents. The handwriting on the envelope was his mother's. He scanned the neat, attractive characters. Without opening it, he walked back to his hootch and sat down. Holding the envelope at opposite corners between the thumb of one hand and the forefinger of the other, he spun it around by tapping it with his free forefinger. Whatever the letter said, it would be an accusation. Finally, he took his bayonet and sliced open the envelope.

Dear David,

We hope this letter finds you well. We received the oriental calendar you sent us from Okinawa. I hung it up in the kitchen and everybody thinks it's beautiful. I've circled your return date on it. Thirteen months is a long time, but I'm sure the wait will be forgotten on the day you come home.

Danny's grades weren't as high as he had hoped, and it looks as if he has given up any idea of finishing engineering. He switched his major to advertising. I guess it's just as well. The only important thing is that he'll be happy whatever career he decides on. He says he will try to come home for a weekend this month.

Your father and I have been very busy around the house. There are a lot of things for us to do, and maybe you'll find us a little handier when you get home. It's helping us adjust to being retired.

Please be careful and write as often as you can. Write Danny also. Tell

him to study hard. He always thinks highly of his older brother's advice.
It's hard to believe you're 10,000 miles away, and we miss you very much.
Don't forget to write. Do you want us to send you anything?

                                                            Love,
                                                    Mom and Dad

Kramer reread the letter, thinking about how much he had wanted to hear from them, and yet how depressed he now was, thinking about them, alone, in a large, empty house, memories making it even emptier, waiting for letters from a son halfway around the world and for those weekends when another son would come home from college, waiting, having nothing but time, and little of that. 'Only memories,' he thought, knowing that now that was all they would ever have of him. 'Is that why?' he asked himself, 'not out of hate, but out of compassion.' He wondered why a person's life can't be a possession, a piece of property to throw away if one chooses; knowing the end of his own life would tear away a part of theirs, their only crime being to have outlived a son to whom war was an excuse, a means rather than a force; thinking, 'Is that why? Is that why people — did I ever want to kill them?' And again he thought about the house, them coming home to it, turning on lights in empty rooms.

Each day at three o'clock, half the platoon would go down to the river to bathe. One day as he stood waist-deep in water shaving, Chalice noticed a bunch of little children leading four water buffaloes down to the river. Before they went in, the kids took off their clothes and threw them on some bushes along the bank. As the huge animals were led into the river, they dropped to their stomachs and the children ran around splashing water on them. Captivated by the simple beauty of the scene, Chalice started to walk towards it, as if to become a part of it. One of the water buffaloes bolted to its feet, its formerly placid, bovine eyes now locked in a suspicious, catlike stare. Chalice froze, then walked back towards the rest of the men.

When the swim call ended, the men returned to the perimeter carrying their freshly washed clothes. They spread them on the bushes to dry and sat around naked on their poncho liners. Gunny Martin walked by and yelled for everybody to get their shirts on. Somebody replied that they were wet, but Martin yelled back that he didn't give a shit and that it was a company rule that everyone had to wear a shirt at all times. Though the men grumbled as he walked away, all of them put on their shirts.

An hour later Captain Trippitt passed by Bolton who was walking around without a hat on. "Where's your cover, Marine?"

"Left it on the other side of the perimeter. I was just going to get it."

Trippitt grabbed him by the shirt and flung him violently against a tree trunk. "Did you forget how to say, '*sir*'?"

"No, sir," Bolton answered in a bewildered voice as he looked down at the top of the captain's head.

Rather than look up, Trippitt just stared at his chest. "Don't *ever* let that happen again."

"Yes, sir."

Childs, who was sitting next to Chalice, tapped him on the shoulder. "You never see the Skipper act like that out in the Arizona. He knows somebody'd blow his head off first chance they got."

The next afternoon Kramer told his platoon they were moving out. Ignoring the march, the men were glad to get away from the CP. Tony 5 learned they were to set-in with a company of Arvins, and reminded Chalice to buy a pack from one of them. Though the day had been overcast, by the time the platoon moved out there wasn't a cloud in the sky. Hamilton set a fairly slow pace, but after only a few minutes of marching everybody's senses were numbed.

Chalice found himself performing some newly acquired idiosyncrasies — switching his rifle from hand to hand, sliding the strap of his ammo can along the top of his shoulder when it started to dig in, and spasmodically hunching his shoulders every few steps in order to keep his pack straps from cutting off the circulation to his arms. Dully, he began enumerating the items in his pack, trying to think of something he could discard. His mind focused on his discomfort, he paid little attention to the possibility of an ambush or a booby trap. The sight of a fresh crater in the road jolted him. A charred truck, still smelling of burnt rubber, lay off to one side. He tightened his grip on his rifle and scanned the area for dangerous signs. But after only a few minutes, his head dropped down again and he plodded on as before.

The Arvin camp lay just off the road, about two kilometers from Ladybird Park. It encircled the remains of an abandoned ville. Hamilton led the platoon through the center of the camp to some high ground in back of it. The Arvins greeted them with friendly smiles and waves. Their appearance surprised Chalice. Most of them seemed over thirty years old. They had evidently arrived just before the Marines, and were wandering around in a disorganized manner setting up their hootches.

Kovacs assigned positions even before the men had their packs off. The perimeter partially enclosed a cemetery, one obviously used by the richer families because most of the graves had concrete headstones. Each grave

125

was covered by a flat mound of dirt anywhere from six to ten feet in diameter and a few feet high.

The men dropped their packs and rested for a few minutes before starting to dig in. To save a little work, most of them dug on the edges of the burial mounds. When the Arvin lieutenant saw this, he sought out Kramer and led him to one of the holes. Kramer had a good idea what he wanted, but called Chalice over to translate anyway. After talking to the Arvin lieutenant, Chalice turned to Kramer. "He doesn't want us digging into the burial mounds. He says the spirits will come up."

Before Kramer could answer, Forsythe cut in, "That's great. We can have five-man watches instead of four, more sleep for everybody."

Speaking to Kramer, Chalice added, "They worship their ancestors."

"Oh really? Tell him the holes are already half dug, and the men don't want to start over. See what he says."

When Chalice finished translating, the Arvin pointed to the hole and said with a look of disapproval, "Numba ten, numba ten." He then pointed a few feet to the side of the mound and said with a smile, "Numba one, numba one." Kramer told Chalice to tell him okay. He then ordered his men to move their foxholes away from the graves. Many of them were almost finished digging, and they received the news with loud curses and flying shovels.

As they started new holes, a few of the Arvins walked among them. The first one to come around was carrying a large metal ice chest. "Hey Marine, bucoo cold soda, beer, fifty cents. You want?" Chalice found the sight of a soldier in uniform selling cold drinks humorous. He was less than five feet tall, and the cooler he carried weighed almost as much as he did. Tony bought four cans for the fire team. The Arvin stayed around and talked to them in pidgin English for a few minutes before pointing to a poncho liner on Forsythe's pack. "You souvenir me this?"

Forsythe said no, and with Chalice's help tried to bargain with him. The Arvin offered to give eight sodas or beers for it. Forsythe told him that if he could pick up an extra one, he'd trade him. Someone in the next position yelled for the "Soda Man," so he carried his cooler over to them. After he left, Chalice remarked that he should have asked him about a pack.

"Don't sweat it," Forsythe replied. "Somebody else'll come around."

A few minutes later two more Arvins walked over with a potful of rice. They offered to share it and sat down to talk while it was being passed around. Glad for the opportunity to eat something that hadn't come out of a can, the Marines greedily stuffed themselves, repeating "Numba one, numba one" as they did so. One of the Arvins pointed to some cans of

126

C-rations: "You souvenir me?" Forsythe handed him a can of ham and limas, and the Arvins headed for the next foxhole with what was left of the rice.

Another Arvin came around with a pack. He pointed to it and said, "Numba one, you want?"

Chalice looked at it disparagingly. "Numba ten." After a few minutes of haggling, he bought it for four dollars and his Marine Corps pack, the usual price.

Dusk came on quickly. The men sat around their foxholes talking and enjoying their last cigarettes before dark. Everyone was relaxed, and most of the comments were about how good it was to get away from the CP. As the last glow of light disappeared behind the mountains, Tony ordered out the cigarettes. All conversation stopped, and only then did the men become aware of the flittering insect sounds of the night. Suddenly Tony 5 grabbed his rifle and jumped into one of the foxholes, his men following suit. Chalice didn't know what was happening. He started to ask, but Tony 5 raised his hand for him to be quiet. He then whispered over to the next foxhole, "Forsythe, you hear it?"

"Yeah, in front of us."

Chalice hadn't heard anything. His eyes strained as they searched the darkness. He could see a grenade gripped in one of Tony's hands, a finger of his other hand through the pin ring ready to pull it. Chalice pressed his forefinger gently against the trigger of his M-16, more in anticipation than fear. His mind speeded with thoughts about what was out there and what he would do if he knew — should he fire his rifle on automatic or semiautomatic? His finger pressed nervously against the selector switch. Or should he do the same thing as Tony, throw a frag? Should he take his rifle off safe now and risk the metallic click, or wait until the action started, sacrificing a possibly fatal second? Suddenly he heard it, a few yards in front of him, plodding footsteps and heavy breathing. Every muscle in his body tightened and seemed ready to snap — What's Tony waiting for? Chalice slowly raised his rifle and pointed it towards the sound. A quick glance to his side told him that Tony now had the grenade in front of his chest, ready to use it. He could almost feel the tension between Tony's two hands, set to jerk apart in an instant and separate the pin from the grenade. Without warning, a voice came from a few feet in front of the hole. "Marine, you want bucoo cold soda?" Chalice's muscles relaxed with a wilting motion and his back settled against the rear of the foxhole. Tony 5 cursed through clenched teeth, "Get the fuck out of here, Soda Man."

It was Alpha's turn to loaf around the perimeter. Chalice lay in his hootch reading a book — something he had been looking forward to doing — when he heard a few of the men complaining. Having a good idea what the answer would be, he hesitated to ask what was going on. Instead he flipped the book down with disgust and waited for someone to walk over and give him the bad news. Forsythe eventually wandered back to the hootch and told him to saddle up, they were going on a platoon-size patrol to check out an abandoned ville a few kilometers back down the road.

It took them less than an hour to reach the ville, but the time was spent trudging through rice paddies and they were wet, tired, and irritable when they got there. Kramer set the platoon on-line for a sweep of the high ground. As he expected, they found nothing. He arranged the fire teams in positions encircling the ville, telling them they'd stay set-in for a couple of hours and to keep an eye out for anything unusual.

Chalice leaned his back against a banana tree and pulled out a cigarette. Payne started complaining to Tony 5 about "the stupid patrols they send us on just to fuck with us." Tony, only half paying attention, was on the verge of telling him to shut up. Chalice noticed Forsythe vacantly daydreaming, a depressed expression on his face. It was the first time he'd ever seen him in that type of mood. "You look like you're about to blow your brains out."

Forsythe looked at, but right through him, his head slightly tilted to one side. When his eyes finally focused on Chalice, he said, "Funny, but I *was* thinking about something like that." He hesitated, as if considering whether to go on. Picking up a twig and scratching it in the dirt, Forsythe began to speak in a slow, serious tone that seemed so out of character Chalice was a little embarrassed to be caught listening to it.

"When I was in high school there was this girl I had a crush on, but I didn't ask her out because I knew she was wild about this other guy named Scott. He'd been taking her out, but he was also dating a few other girls. Had a reputation for getting what he wanted from a girl. I guess I hated him a little because I knew I liked her a lot more than he did. I didn't blame her for liking him. Scott could have had any girl he wanted. You know, he was one of those guys you see in the movies; great athlete, real smart, good looking. I mean he was *really* good looking, probably the best looking guy in school — tall, dark, the whole bit." Forsythe held up his forearm in front of his face and studied it. "I always wanted to be dark. Everytime I got a good tan I'd start peeling. It really used to piss me off.

"I started going with a different girl that I got to like and forgot about

128

the other one. This girl's best friend also dated Scott — a real good-looking bitch — and we used to double a lot. He was banging the shit out of her. Wasn't the type to shoot off his mouth, but it was pretty obvious. We used to use his car, and when his parents were out we used to take them over to his house. You wouldn't believe that place, a fucking castle." Forsythe paused, debating whether to continue, knowing that he would. Chalice remained silent, still too surprised by Forsythe's tone to do anything but listen.

"We got to be good friends, not real close, but he wasn't close with anyone. I'd always thought he was conceited, but I got to realize he was just the quiet type, like he was depressed about not being able to have something he really wanted. When we doubled, I never had anything to worry about — he always knew where to go or what to say. He really impressed me; had real class — not the kind you learn, he had that too, but the kind you're born with.

"One day after school he had to pick up something for his father and I went with him. We passed this gun shop and he stopped and looked in the window. He pointed to an ivory-handled automatic with a blued finish like a mirror, and he said he'd like to buy it. I was kind of surprised because his father had a whole case full of guns and he told me he didn't like them around the house.

"We went back to his place and fucked around in his room. There was an old picture of him and his younger brother on the desk. He started talking about him. I knew he was dead, but I didn't know the whole story. He was two years younger than Scott. It turns out that when Scott was ten years old his brother got kidnapped — said it seemed like a game, exciting, like in the movies where the cops always make the rescue at the last minute. Found him in a ditch a few days later. At the funeral everyone was crying and he cried too, even though he really didn't understand what was going on. When they walked by the casket his brother looked like he was just sleeping. Scott tried to talk to him and when his brother didn't answer he reached out to touch him, but his mother grabbed his arm. Said he couldn't get used to the idea his brother was dead. For a year after it happened anytime the doorbell would ring he'd run to open the door to see if his brother had come home.

"I don't think he'd ever told anyone else the whole story. He seemed changed afterwards — more relaxed, a lot happier. From that time on we were real close. We fucked around a lot more — always putting each other on. One day he came over to my house all wild-eyed, I forget about what; but after he told me, I said 'So what?' just as a joke. At first he thought I was serious, but when he realized I was kidding he dug it. From then on,

129

anytime either one of us said something, the other'd say 'So what?' — joking around, kinda like a ritual — sorta identifying with each other.

"About two weeks before the end of school he drove over to my house so we could polish his car; we were going to double for the prom. You know how it is just before graduation. I never could figure out what the big deal was until I went through it. Everybody was real excited; kinda happy and sad at the same time. We were going to room together at Duke. He could have gone to some Ivy League school if he wanted. I guess I was the reason he decided on Duke. When we finished polishing his car, I went to put what was left of the polish in his glove compartment. I couldn't get it in because there was a package in there about the size of a book. I took it out and asked him what it was. Just as I finished it hit me, I don't know how I knew, but I knew. He said it was nothing, just a present, and started the car — there was sort of a smile on his face, like he knew I knew, like he put it in the glove compartment knowing, for some reason (like putting the polish away instead of just flipping it on the seat) that I'd find it and know, not for any reason, just so I'd know, me and him would know, as if it was important, not making any real difference, just making it right. I asked him to come in the house, knowing he wouldn't, because it was settled, settled the first time I ever met him, like we were just going through the motions, for no reason but that we had to, to make it right, and I was nervous, he was calm, you know sometimes when you're nervous and you see everybody else is nervous, then you don't feel nervous anymore, me being nervous made things easier, made them right. I asked him again, knowing he wouldn't. He said he'd come over after supper, and I believed him, I wanted to, because he was dependable, if he said he'd do something he'd do it, but at the same time I knew he was lying, not really lying, because you can't lie with just words, because if you say something you know the other person doesn't believe, then you're not really saying it. Do you understand?"

Chalice nodded his head, knowing that he really wasn't sure what he understood, but that he understood it, and that it was important to Forsythe that he did. Forsythe continued to stare at him, and Chalice knew he should say something. All he could think of were comments like "You never can tell" or "That's a bust," so he just shook his head.

A light spray of rain began to fall. Forsythe flipped away the twig in his hand and took cover under a nearby tree. The rain became heavier. He was facing the mountains, watching the slow quiet drizzle envelop them. He hunched his shoulders so the droplets flowing down the back of his helmet couldn't drip inside of his shirt. A penetrating chill seeped through his limbs. He folded his arms tightly in front of his chest. A somber stare

130

on his face, he scanned the rice paddies, not seeing anything but the thoughts in his mind, oblivious to the rain.

Scott had graduated first in the class and was supposed to have given the valedictory. The English teacher who had been helping Scott suggested that Forsythe, who had graduated third, give Scott's speech. Forsythe refused, but the teacher persisted until he finally agreed. As he looked over Scott's speech his stomach tightened with anger and disgust. Eyes darting back and locking on phrases such as "make the world a better place," he pictured Scott saying and being sickened by them; the phoniness, the sad phoniness of the whole idea gripped his throat as if it were going to choke him.

During the commencement, all Forsythe could think about was the time Scott had told him about his brother, and the way his parents had looked at the funeral. His dulled senses barely caught the sound of his own name when he was introduced. By the time he got to the podium he was in a daze. Staring at the audience, he noticed tears in the eyes of some of the mothers and the somber expressions on the faces of those fathers that weren't half asleep — all of them watching this different kind of funeral. He just stood there looking out at them, unable to remember what or why — not embarrassed, just not caring; feeling sorry for all those parents. He tried to concentrate, knowing he better say something fast or get the hell out of there.

"I'm supposed to give a speech. I had one memorized, but I can't remember it now." He paused, and there were a few chuckles; but the tone he proceeded with cut them short. "It was one of those about helping mankind and making this world a better place. You've heard it all before. I don't believe a word of it. Since I'm up here already, I might as well give some sort of speech, and I might as well say something I *do* believe."

"This world was a *fucked-up* place on the day I was born, and if I live to be a hundred years old, it'll be *just as fucked up* on the day I die." Even the fathers — some just awakened — sat up and stared at him in disbelief. The room filled with murmurs; but as he began again, his words quickly silenced them. "I was going to tell you you now had an opportunity to change the world, and all that other bullshit. That's the same thing they probably told your parents. The same thing they've been saying ever since the first idiot put on these ridiculous hats and ten pound nightgowns. They keep saying it and nothing changes. Sure you can change the kind of car you drive, the food you eat, the houses you live in; but how important is that shit? *You can't change life.* Everybody gets a ticket, and all the trips are different, but every one of them ends up in the same place and all the important stops are the same."

"Two weeks ago my best friend blew his own brains out — the whole

131

Richard Cory bit. All any of you could say was 'Why?' That's a good question — the best question. Anytime anything happens you can always ask 'Why?' I'll bet *he* asked the same question just before he pulled the trigger: 'Why, why the hell doesn't everybody else do the same fucking thing I'm doing?' I doubt he had an answer, and I don't either. But I'll tell you one thing, I'm gonna stick around for a while to try and find one.

"The first thing I'm gonna do is forget about all those phony answers we've been getting ever since we were kids. Most of us are stuffed so full of bullshit we're gagging on it. When we were little kids there was one phrase we used to hear all the fucking time, '*They lived happily ever after.*' Every fucked-up story they ever told us ended with the words, 'They lived happily ever after.' I'm seventeen years old and I still haven't met one fucking person who's lived happily ever after. They give us all kinds of rules to live by. Take a look around you. Those rules didn't work for them and they won't work for you. I've got a rule for you. It may not be a good one, but it's no worse than any of the others you've been given: 'If you feel like doing something, do it.' I'm not telling you to go around killing people. You can't go around doing everything you want, but there's a lot of things you can do. If your old man wants you to take over the insurance business, but you want to live in the woods like a bum, live in the woods. If you're a fag and you gotta suck somebody's cock, go 'head and suck it. I could really give a shit, as long as it's not mine. If you're a girl that likes some guy, go ahead and sleep with him. I'm not telling you to go out and be the high school punchboard, but that wouldn't bother me either. In fact I'd probably be the first in line. If your old man catches you smoking grass and he tries to hit you over the head with his whiskey bottle, you don't have to take that shit. Sure there's a lot of people you don't want to hurt — I'm not telling you to forget that — but don't forget something else either — it's *your* goddamn life."

Forsythe's mind went blank. He sensed the immaturity, not in what he had said, but in how he had said it. He wanted to say something intelligent, to explain himself, what he was doing, to the shocked and hostile faces staring at him. Grasping for ideas, he found only memories. Fragmented, swirling through his thoughts, they further confused him. Wondering if he were crying, he perceived an idea without any means of expressing it, heard himself say, "I just . . . I just don't want to spend my life thinking about things I never got to do, thinking about how I *should have* done it."

Kovacs walked around to the positions and told the men to get ready to move out. The rain had stopped, but water still dripped from the leaves and a fresh, clean scent pervaded the air. The platoon moved out in two columns, trudging back in the direction of the camp. As soon as they reached it, the men took off their wet clothes and hung them on the tops of their hootches. Most of them were naked and either walking around the area or lying on their ponchos when word was passed that the lieutenant wanted a formation. Forsythe started to walk towards it in the nude, but Harmon told him to get some trousers on. As they straggled over, they found Kramer waiting for them.

"This won't take long. We're going on a company-size operation up Charlie Ridge. We'll pull out at three o'clock and get as high as we can by dawn, then sweep across and come down by tomorrow evening. You can leave your hootches up. We won't be taking packs. Bring enough C-rats and water. That's it."

6. Charlie Ridge

No ambushes were sent out that night. The watches ran from nine o'clock until three and were cut to an hour and a half each. Tony 5 took the last watch in his fire team and woke everybody up at a quarter to three. As they moved out in the direction of Ladybird Park, the night air was damp and chilly; but after only a few minutes of marching their shivering bodies warmed and started to perspire. The men had carefully adjusted their equipment so as to keep it from rattling, and there was no talking along the columns. The only sounds were the soft, steady scrapings of boots along the dirt road.

A third-quarter moon made it possible for Chalice to see the silhouettes of the first three men in front of him. When the ammo can strap started digging into his shoulder, he switched it to his other arm. He tried to do so quietly, but as he swung the can in front of him it struck his rifle with a sharp crack. Childs, who was in the column to Chalice's left, turned his head sharply but didn't say anything.

They had marched for what seemed like a short time when both columns came to a halt. Tony 5 walked around to each of his men to tell them they were at the park, that two of the other platoons had already started moving out, and that Second Platoon would go last. A few minutes later they peeled off the right side of the road and meshed into one column.

The ville bordering the road extended back almost a hundred yards. More from curiosity than fear, Chalice scanned the hootches for signs of life. His head turned to one side, he was startled by the snort of a water buffalo penned a few feet away on his other side. He wasn't the only one startled, and a low hum of muffled laughter came from the men around him.

The pace quickened as they reached a path on the other side of the ville. It took them across a few hundred yards of rice paddies and ended at a small stream. They crossed it on a plank less than six inches wide and a few feet below the surface of the water. Chalice thought the stream was shallow and that the men in front of him were walking through it. When he placed his foot in the water he barely got it on the board and nearly lost his balance. He felt a little stupid until he reached the other side and heard the splash of someone behind him falling in.

There was no path on the opposite bank, so the column moved along the top of a rice paddy dike. The crepe soles of their boots soon became clogged with mud, and the men were continuously falling off the dike. It finally led them to some high ground. They skirted its perimeter, then followed another dike on its opposite side. This one was somewhat wider than the first and much easier to walk on. It led them to another stream. There was no bridge this time so they had to wade through the cold, chest-high water.

By the time Chalice had mastered walking along the slippery dikes, the column abandoned them and moved straight through the rice paddies. About every thirty yards they would have to climb over the dikes running across their path. Some of the paddies were practically dry, while others were two to three feet deep. The pace increased. Chalice's leg muscles became taut from the continuous struggle to lift his feet from the mud, which seemed to be trying to suck him under. He'd had this same sensation in the daytime, and was glad he knew what to expect. When he finally reached the high ground at the base of the foothills, he estimated to himself that the company had moved about four kilometers, looking at this distance as something accomplished and gotten out of the way.

The column moved along the base of the mountains until it came upon a crude path through the foothills. The pace quickened substantially. Chalice found himself running in spurts to keep up. He was constantly telling himself that every step was one more he'd gotten out of the way. Not realizing what lay ahead, he was surprised that the mountains weren't as steep as he had expected. He soon found himself going downhill, and was relieved at first by the relative ease with which he moved. He then realized that any movement downhill would have to be made up for on the next slope. The grade leveled off for a short distance before starting up at a much steeper angle than before. As he climbed, sweat from his forehead poured down his face and began to sting his eyes. Instead of a path, they were now traveling on a stream bed that sometimes narrowed to a few inches. The loose rocks that lined the bed kept slipping out from beneath his feet, and his mind was completely occupied with keeping his balance. The path was often bordered by huge boulders that made it necessary for him to turn sideways in order to pass between them. He found himself running as fast as he could in long spurts, occasionally catching up with the man in front of him only to fall behind again almost immediately. Sometimes his rifle or ammo can would hit the rocks with a

135

sharp crack, and a whisper would come out of the darkness saying, "Cool it."

The column kept passing through small valleys followed by progressively steeper slopes. Chalice stumbled constantly over the loose rocks, often falling to the ground. At first the pain of the sharper rocks cutting into his knees was almost unbearable; but as his falls became more frequent, a numbness enveloped him and he hardly thought of anything except getting to his feet and catching up. After one such fall he sprang up only to bump into the man in front of him — 'Thank God, must be taking a break.' To his chagrin, the column started moving again almost immediately. After traveling less than fifty yards, he found out what the holdup had been. The stream bed had led them to a huge boulder surrounded by brush thick enough to make passage through it impossible. Each successive man had to be lifted across the face of the rock by two other men on top of it. The noise of banging ammo cans and rifles was ignored in the struggle to get each soldier over the rock. By the time Chalice had scaled it and helped two others do the same, he was so far behind that he couldn't even hear the men in front of him.

For the first time that night a cloud moved in front of the moon cutting off all but a hint of its former light. He ran as fast as he could, judging direction only by the sharp, shifting rocks beneath his feet, which in a lost instant disappeared, leaving him running over an area of low brush. On the verge of panic, he stopped to listen for the sounds of the other men. He couldn't even hear the sounds of those behind him, only his own forced, heavy breathing which seemed so loud that at first he couldn't believe he was the source of it. Again he ran, not because of any rational thought, but from fear. His feet slipped out from under him, and his chest and legs crashed forcefully against some sharp rocks. Oblivious to the pain, a feeling of relief swept over him — 'The stream bed!' Before he could have made any conscious effort to get up, he was already on his feet running, the fall having only changed the position of his body and in no way having stopped him even for an instant. The bed followed what seemed to be level ground — 'Maybe I'm going in the wrong direction. *Maybe it's the wrong stream bed!*' His own panic scared him. By a conscious act of will, he forced his mind clear of thoughts, at the same time deciding to run as fast as he could until he dropped. Not until his panic had waned to fear, did he realize how exhausted he was. The movement of his legs gradually slowed. His mind seemed to separate from his body, as if watching it slowly wind down from a distance. Panic again took hold. He burst forward, his own stamina surprising him. The thought, 'I can't keep this up,' flashed through his mind, but he again realized how alone he was

136

and with this realization came another thought, 'Fuck if I can't! I'll catch them.' An instant later, the mass of his body crashed into a similar mass, only larger. Both tumbled to the ground. He lay on his back, someone straddling his stomach and a rifle pressed hard against his neck.

"Professor?"

He muttered a choked "yes," as the rifle was removed.

"God! You scared the shit out of me. Are you crazy? What the fuck are you doing?"

"Got lost," he coughed, as loose phlegm clogged his throat. "Bolton?"

"Yeah, I'm the last man in the column. If I would of heard you sooner, I'd a shot."

Chalice leapt to his feet. "We better catch up."

Bolton grabbed his pants leg. "Hold on before you go crashing into someone else. The column's stopped."

"For what?"

"We're there, I think." Bolton pointed his rifle to a soft glow above the opposite chain of mountains. "Look, it's dawn already."

The company hadn't gone quite as high as planned. The point of the column had reached an area containing a few caves and the beginning of a path across the ridge. Trippitt ordered the first two platoons to follow the stream bed up to the next ridge and then travel laterally along it, Third Platoon to move slowly along the path, and Second Platoon to check out the caves and then catch up with Third Platoon.

Kramer placed a machine gun above and below the caves for security before ordering his men to check them out. Only a few men were needed, so Chalice was able to sit down and rest. Exhausted and thirsty, he took a long drink from one of his canteens. The water loosened some phlegm in his throat. He spit it out and took a second drink. The warm water had a soothing effect, but he still hadn't got used to the metallic taste it derived from the canteen.

Forsythe, who had been poking around in one of the caves, walked over to Kramer and showed him some things he'd found — empty cans of fish, propaganda leaflets, and a pouch full of AK-47 rounds. He took Kramer's flashlight and headed back towards the cave, passing out a few of the rounds as souvenirs.

"Over here," Chalice called.

Forsythe flipped him a round and said, "C'mon, let's see what we can find." Chalice put the AK round in his pocket and followed him.

The entrance was small and they had to crawl in. Once inside, they could stand in a stooped position. Chalice had never liked cramped places, but the excitement of being somewhere the Viet Cong had recently been took his mind off this. He stood breathing in the damp, musty air while his eyes adjusted to the lack of light. Forsythe started scratching around on the dirt floor with a stick.

Chalice walked over to a crevice in the rocks. He couldn't see in, and was about to put his hand inside when he thought better of the idea. Forsythe came over and pointed the flashlight into the crevice. They could see two aluminum cylinders about four feet high and ten inches in diameter. "What the hell are those?" Chalice asked.

"Illumination tubes. They're from the big flares they drop by plane. Here, hold the light while I get them out." Forsythe removed the first tube. It was full of rice. The second tube contained clothing, some documents, and three Chinese-type grenades. Forsythe handed one to Chalice while referring to it as a "chicom." It was a C-ration can stuffed with explosives. A hollow wooden handle protruded from its bottom, and a piece of string with a bamboo ring on the end hung from within the handle. The other end of the string was attached to a friction-type detonating fuse within the grenade. Forsythe placed the ring over his forefinger and showed Chalice how the pin pulled out automatically as the grenade was thrown. He then said, "Don't ever underestimate Charlie. He can kill you with your own garbage."

They looked around for a few more minutes before dragging the tubes out of the cave. Kramer had Forsythe scatter the rice on the ground, and two of the men began pissing on it. They found some important looking documents and a diary in the second tube. Kramer looked them over and said, "Well, Forsythe, you found them so you get to carry them. Put them in a sandbag."

A quick series of rifle shots echoed from the ridge above. Everyone dived to the ground, Forsythe and Chalice behind the same rock. Forsythe nonchalantly tossed the AK-47 round in his hand while mumbling, "These things look like they can go right through you." He then glanced above the rock to see if he could spot anything. "Bet he got away."

"How do you know *he* wasn't the one doing the shooting?"

"Those were M-16's. You can tell by the sound. A 16 goes bang. An SKS or an AK goes crack, like a whip. You'll be able to tell after a while."

Milton, the platoon radio man, had taken cover a few yards away from Kramer. He called over to him, "They got a confirmed, no rifle or chicoms. They want us to move-out."

"Looks like he didn't," Forsythe mumbled to Chalice.

Kramer ordered his men to catch up with Third Platoon. For twenty minutes he kept them at a rapid pace, but still they failed to make contact. Overgrown as the trail was, they might have easily missed a fork.

Kramer scanned the brush apprehensively, knowing that if they approached Third Platoon from any place but its rear, there might be some shooting.

Milton, who was walking behind him with the radio, tapped Kramer on the shoulder. "Alpha found something they want to check out."

The column stopped and Kramer looked back at Milton. "Let's see what they've got."

As Kramer approached, Tony 5 walked back towards him. He pointed to some boulders fifteen yards off the trail. "There's a wire hanging down from one of those rocks."

Kramer had to squint his eyes for a few seconds before finally being able to see it. "We've got to catch up with Third Platoon. They probably checked it out anyway. . . . Well, okay, but hurry up." He turned to Milton. "Call the captain and tell him what we're doing. Pass the word back to Valdez that I want Charlie Squad to stay where they are as rear security, and tell Sugar Bear to set Bravo up as security in front of us."

Tony 5 and Hamilton made their way up to the caves. Tony carefully followed the wire into a crevice and called back down to Kramer, "I think we've got something here. This wire's attached to some flashlight batteries, probably a booby trap."

Milton received a reply from Trippitt. "The Skipper says okay, but to hurry up."

Kramer called to Tony, "Check it out good, but don't waste any time."

As Kramer approached, he heard Tony say, "Get a load of this baby." Tony passed a large, green object out to Hamilton.

Hamilton handed it to Kramer. "It's a B-40 rocket. They can really do a job on you. They're Red Chinese, see the writing."

Kramer gently ran his hands over it. Tony handed out three more rockets, two mortars, and a box of mortar fuses. Kramer looked over the find, thinking, 'Good thing we found 'em. Wouldn't want to dodge this shit.' He didn't want his men carrying it either, so he told Harmon to blow it up. Harmon piled the mortars and rockets on a stick of C-4. As soon as he lit the fuse, the platoon moved out at a dead run. The pace had gradually slowed to a fast walk by the time they heard the explosion.

An hour passed and they still hadn't caught up with Third Platoon. The trail led them off the top of a ridge and into a small valley running parallel to it. Trippitt kept on calling up over the radio to see if they'd made contact, so Kramer constantly ordered the point to increase the pace. This had little effect in that they were already moving as fast as possible.

The brush closed in over their heads providing some shade, but also cutting off what little breeze there was. Chalice found it hard to believe he could be any hotter without the shade. His own rifle thwarted him, tried to prevent his movement, by continually tangling itself in the brush. He felt as if he were swallowing the heavy, humid air instead of breathing it, and his saliva seemed to have turned to paste. From the position of the sun as it burned through the brush, he estimated it was about nine o'clock. *But that was impossible!* Could there be that many hours left in this day?

Every mile or so the trail led into some steep-faced rocks, making it necessary for the column to halt while the men helped each other scale them. These pauses were short and didn't give Chalice enough time to sit down, but he was still grateful to be able to take an unhurried drink. At ten o'clock he finished his fourth canteen and decided to go easy on the last one, hoping they would cross a stream soon so he could refill the others. Forty minutes later he drank the last of his water without knowing the point man had halted the column to fill his own canteens.

It was shortly after twelve o'clock when Kramer passed the word for the platoon to take a half hour to eat. A few of the men ate cans of fruit, but most of them were too hot and tired. Even if they had been hungry, the bother of opening the cans would have dissuaded them. Some sat up hoping for a breeze they knew had no chance of reaching them. The others lay back on the warm, slimy ground.

As they started to move out again, Kramer got word over the radio that Third Platoon had taken the high branch of a fork in the trail. He was told to take the lower branch. It led them through the bottom of a gulley. At first, movement along it was easier because there were less large rocks blocking the way. After a few kilometers, they came upon sections where the trail was completely overgrown and they had to push their way through the often thorny brush. Emerging from these thickets, their arms would be covered with scratches and large blotches of blood.

Chalice struggled to keep pace. The thick underbrush constantly entangled his feet, keeping him off balance and often tripping him. He frequently landed on the sharp edges of his ammo can or on his rifle. If not for the dulling effect of his fatigue, the pain would have been intense. After an hour of unsuccessfully trying to place his feet to avoid falling down, he ignored the underbrush completely and dragged on as if he had spent his whole life falling on his face and getting up again every thirty yards.

The platoon crossed another small stream, and Kramer had the pace slowed so everybody could fill their canteens. As they did so, the men splashed the cool water on their faces and backs. There was no trail on the opposite bank and the underbrush was thicker than any they had previously encountered. Chalice felt as if it was willfully trying to stop

140

him and only him. His mouth became clammy, and he removed one of his canteens from its pouch as he marched. The sensation of the cool water running down his throat brought some relief; but even before he put the canteen away, his mouth was clammy again.

As the trail started a steep downward grade, the brush closed in from above leaving less than three feet of vertical clearance. The men experimented with many different positions — plowing through the brush upright with their hands in front of their faces; bending double at the waist; walking sideways. Soon the trail became slippery causing them to fall to sitting positions on the hard, slimy mud. They would slide downhill a few yards before getting up and falling again a few feet farther down the trail. Only the comfort of repetition made this process bearable. They completely forgot about the pain they were enduring except when glances at their scratched, blood-covered arms reminded them.

When the trail finally leveled off, they found themselves in a field of elephant grass reaching a few feet over their heads. The farther back each man was, the better the trail he had to follow. The point man had the hardest time, but it was still preferable to the heavy brush they had just come through. Chalice was in the center of the column and found the elephant grass a welcome relief. Occasionally a sharp, quick pain in his hands would cause his whole body to flinch. In his fatigue he ignored this until, more from curiosity than pain, he looked down at his hands. They were crisscrossed with barely bleeding cuts similar to those made by a razor blade. His forearms, which had been covered with blood a few minutes earlier, were now cleansed by his own sweat. A blade of elephant grass slid against the web of two fingers, and he again felt the sharp pain. Drawing his hand towards his face, he noticed a new, clean cut. His mouth broke into a tired smile of recognition.

The point eventually located a well-defined trail. They followed it for over an hour before stopping at a small stream to fill their canteens. Just as they started moving again, the hot, stagnant air around them exploded with numerous bursts of rifle fire. Chalice heard a few of the men say "16's" or "ours," but he hadn't been scared or even excited by the shots anyway. He was too exhausted for either emotion. The firing continued. It seemed to be coming from above and ahead of them in the direction where Third Platoon was likely to be.

The pace of the column accelerated to a dead run. After only a few minutes, the front elements reached a high clearing and joined up with Third Platoon. As the rifle fire continued, the call "Ammo up" echoed down the column. Chalice just stood there trying to catch his breath until Forsythe shoved him and he realized what he was supposed to do. He ran clumsily down the trail, passing and bumping into members of his platoon. Spotting the machine gun, he dashed towards it only to fall on his face ten yards short. As he struggled to get back to his feet, Pablo said in a calm voice, "Take it easy, Professor."

The shooting had stopped. Chalice looked up and saw a few of the men laughing. He felt like an idiot until he noticed that the smiles were friendly. Realizing the humor of the situation, he also began to laugh. Sinclaire walked over and took the ammo can. Appleton helped him to his feet while saying, "You don't have to kill yourself for anybody, Prof."

They were in a rocky clearing above a thirty foot cliff. As Chalice stood on the edge of it, a welcome breeze rushed against his face, the first one he could remember that day. He scanned the clearing, seeing nothing. Kramer called the rest of the platoon up and set them in positions along the edge of the cliff. Pablo and Sinclaire had their machine gun set up in Chalice's position, and he asked them what had happened.

"We're on top of a big cave." Pablo took a reed from his mouth and pointed down to the clearing with it. "About ten Gooks took off running just as Third Platoon got here."

"Did they get any?"

"They think they wounded a few, but no confirms. They're sweeping down there now to look for blood trails."

Milton called Kramer to the radio. The captain was with First and Fourth Platoons. They had already started back down the mountains when they heard the shots, and they wanted to know what had happened. Trippitt told Kramer to head back as soon as possible. Third Platoon hadn't found anything on its sweep, and had already started moving down towards the lowlands. Kramer passed the word for Second Platoon to do the same with Alpha at the point.

When Childs had finally broken a path to the plateau below, he found himself standing directly in front of a huge cave. He and Forsythe talked Tony 5 into asking Kramer if they could check it out. Hesitant at first, Kramer finally agreed. Childs, Forsythe, and Hamilton went in while the rest of the platoon sat scattered in front of the entrance.

Chalice leaned back against a rock. He had become dizzy on the march down from the ledge, and now welcomed the rest. Hearing excited voices coming from inside the cave, he was too tired to go and see what was happening. The mouth of the cave was about twelve feet high by six feet wide. The ceiling heightened to almost twenty feet at its rear. There were twelve hammocks, some of them hanging in tiers of two and three. Tony 5 entered to hurry his men, and came back out with an armload of loot — documents, clothing (including two brassieres), cans of food, AK-47 rounds,

142

a straight razor, and over twenty pounds of rice. Kramer had a fire built in front of the cave, and anything lacking intelligence value was burned. More men entered the cave while others carried out armloads of loot.

Valdez shouted to the men inside, "For God's sake, let's get out of here before dark." Other men voiced agreement, and Kramer checked his watch. He called to the men in the cave, but finally had to go in himself to get Forsythe and Childs.

Bravo led off with Bolton at the point. When Chalice saw this, he mumbled, "Look at the legs on that freak. He's six feet at the waist."

The pace was slow at first, but the more experienced members of the platoon were worried about getting caught in the mountains after dark and they frequently shouted for it to be increased. Bolton heeded them. While he was able to lope along with ease, most of the other members of the platoon were moving at full speed. They followed a dry stream bed. The brush around it was light and only knee deep. This would have made movement easy but for the pace. The stream bed narrowed to a sharp V at its bottom, making the footing precarious. The sometimes steep downward grade added to the difficulty.

Chalice began to get dizzy. The weight of the ammo can hanging to one side made matters worse. He struggled to keep pace with the man in front of him and also to retain his balance. All along the column, men were continually falling, Chalice more often than anybody else. He became progressively dizzier after each fall. Skip warned him to keep up a number of times before finally passing him. As a matter of pride, Chalice tried to regain his position. After a few minutes he gave up and concentrated merely on keeping pace. When he fell again, Flip passed him saying, "I gotta stay with my gunner." As Chalice made it to his feet, Forsythe rushed by and picked up his ammo can without saying anything. This further hurt his pride, but the relief he felt from not having eighteen pounds of metal banging into his side kept him from asking for it back. He staggered forward, just as dizzy as before but better able to keep up.

The frenzied pace continued until they reached the valley floor. An hour of sunlight remained, hardly enough time to get back to camp before dark. Kramer passed the word to break into two columns. He also told the point to slow the pace. Chalice dreaded walking through the paddies, but he noticed that he wasn't as dizzy as he had been in the mountains. He was further relieved when he saw that the other members of the platoon looked as tired as he felt.

Instead of cutting across the paddies at an angle and moving straight towards camp, Kramer took advantage of some scattered high ground and headed his men directly for the road. When they hit it, Chalice found himself loping along with little effort while those around him were dragging their feet. A feeling of confidence ran through him. Then he noticed Forsythe carrying his ammo can. Catching up with him, he said, "Sorry, man. Let me take the ammo back."

Forsythe handed it to him. "Don't sweat it. You'll get used to this shit."

They reached their perimeter a half hour after dark. As they passed by the smiling Arvins, numerous sneering comments were made: "Have a nice day, Gook?" "Their fucking country, and we do all the dirty work." "Bet you motherfuckers were worried we weren't coming back."

Chalice slipped off his magazine pouch and flak jacket. With a forgotten sense of freedom, he stretched out on the ground and took a long drink from one of his canteens, then mumbled, "Let's see; started with five, filled five the first time, four the second, got one left. *Holy shit!* Thirteen." Chalice got up to urinate but found he didn't need to. He called to Forsythe, "Thirteen canteens of water today, and I can't even take a piss. . . . That's a lot of sweat."

As Kramer lay in his hootch, he wondered if he would have quit if he hadn't been the lieutenant. He then wondered what kept his men from quitting, and finally said to Kovacs, "They're a humping bunch of motherfuckers."

"Yeah, they don't know how to quit."

Milton walked over to them with a piece of paper in his hand. "Here's the ambush position. I just got it over the radio."

"The ambush!" Kramer sat up and took out his map. He figured the coordinates, then looked at Kovacs. "It's only a klick and a half out."

"Yeah, the Skipper's really got a heart."

"Who has the ambush tonight?"

"Bravo."

"Send someone to get Sugar Bear. . . . No, fuck it! There won't be any ambush tonight. Trippitt can go on his own ambush if he wants to." Kramer flipped the map away and lay back down.

The next morning Chalice awoke to find his left arm a little better. The weight of the ammo can had caused its strap to dig into his shoulder during the march. Standing watch that night, he couldn't lift his arm more than a few inches away from his body. He now sat in front of his hootch massaging it as Forsythe crawled out. "What was all that yelling about?"

"They caught Payne cheating at cards again. Why the hell do they keep playing with him if he cheats all the time?"

"They all cheat. That's why I never play. It's just that Payne doesn't cheat as well as the rest of them."

144

"That's ridiculous. What's the point of playing cards if they all cheat?"

"I don't know. I guess it evens out. Besides, winning is one thing and collecting another."

There was some commotion in another direction and Hamilton's voice could be heard yelling, "Those dirty, slant-eyed motherfuckers, I oughta kill 'em all."

Chalice and Forsythe walked over to his hootch. Hamilton was inside rummaging around and cursing, while Childs sat out front with his glasses off and his forearm held close to his face as he studied his lump. "What's going on?" Chalice asked.

"Oh nothing, the Gooks stole that radio Hamilton bought off them a few days ago."

Chalice peered in and saw Hamilton dumping out his pack in disgust. "Hey Childs," he called out, "you better get in here and check your pack."

"I don't have anything to steal. . . . Wait a minute!" Childs hurriedly crawled in as Hamilton came out.

"I hid it in the bottom of my pack so those fucking Gooks wouldn't steal it, but they found it anyway. I'll bet they stole it from some Marine in the first place. *That's it!* The same guy who sold it to me probably stole it back."

"*Sonofabitch!*" Childs cursed from within the hootch.

"What'd they get?" Hamilton asked.

"*Sonofabitch!*"

"What'd they steal?"

"Wait a minute. Here it is." Childs emerged from the hootch holding his billiard ball. "Had me worried."

"Didn't they steal anything?" Hamilton asked.

"Just my food."

"How much?"

"All of it."

At first Chalice felt the whole affair was humorous, but then the idea of being robbed by their "allies" while they were "killing" themselves up in the mountains got to him. Ignoring this, he said, "We seem so rich to them, they really can't look on it as stealing." His defense of the Arvins satisfied neither the others nor himself.

"C'mon," Hamilton said in an angry voice, "let's see if we can get it back." They followed him to the Arvin side of the perimeter. As they walked around looking for the man that had sold Hamilton the radio, they were met by grins and pleas for handouts. They brusquely snubbed these Arvins and eventually found the one they were looking for. Hamilton immediately started yelling at him. The Arvin seemed to have no idea what Hamilton was shouting about, and he just stood there with a bewildered grin on his face. Hamilton, red with frustration, angrily turned to Chalice. "You know how to talk to these thieving Gooks. Tell him I want my radio back."

The Arvin told Chalice he didn't know anything about it. Hamilton reached across and grabbed the radio that the Arvin happened to be holding. "When you bring me mine, you'll get this back." He then added sarcastically, "Numba one, numba one," before walking away. The Arvin protested loudly as Chalice tried to tell him what Hamilton had said. By the time he finished, Hamilton, Childs, and Forsythe were already on the Marine side of the perimeter. He rejoined them as they were telling Tony 5 what had happened. Payne walked over and also got the story. They were sitting around laughing when they heard the Arvin yelling to some of his friends, exhorting them to follow him in Hamilton's direction. The Arvin walked over and stood in front of Hamilton. "You give radio!"

Hamilton stared up at him and said, "No, numba ten, you give me my radio first."

The Arvin raised his rifle and pointed it in Hamilton's face. Hamilton stood up slowly without saying anything. "You give radio," the Arvin repeated while shaking the rifle in his face. Hamilton just stood there glaring back at him. Childs walked behind the Arvin and pointed his rifle at his head. Another Arvin pointed his rifle at Childs's head.

Payne ran to get Kramer. He and Kovacs arrived in time to find fifteen Arvins and Marines standing alternately in line with their rifles pointed at the heads of the men in front of them. Startled into silence, Kramer glanced at Kovacs who began yelling for everyone to put their rifles down. No one heeded him. Rifles in hand, the large crowd of Arvins and Marines circling the line moved in closer. The Arvin lieutenant came running up. Kramer tried to talk to him, but he couldn't make himself understood. His eyes darted around the area looking for Chalice only to locate him standing in the line with his rifle pointed at an Arvin's head. Without lowering his rifle, Chalice explained what was happening to both lieutenants.

Kramer heard some shouting behind him. He spun around in time to see Appleton shove an Arvin to the ground. The Arvin started to raise his rifle towards Appleton, but Harmon kicked it from his hands and stood on it. The yelling became louder and another Arvin shoved Harmon off the rifle. Harmon turned to see Appleton shove an Arvin towards him. Valdez stepped between them and flattened the Arvin. Two more Arvins ran for Valdez. Harmon grabbed one around the chest, and Appleton kicked the other in the groin. The shouting increased as Kovacs ran over and started shoving people out of the way. By this time the group was a mass of swinging fists and rifle butts. The only motionless bodies were those of the men still standing in the line. An Arvin slammed his rifle butt

146

into Appleton's neck, at the same time accidentally pulling the trigger and sending off a deafening burst of automatic rifle fire. In that split second all movement froze except for the jerking of heads towards the line of men still standing with raised rifles.

There was complete silence, no one moving or speaking for fear that the men in line would start shooting. Kramer slowly let out a deep breath as he watched their intense stares. It was a few seconds before he finally stepped towards them. Everyone else remained completely frozen and silent. His eyes searched out the Arvin lieutenant who now also stepped forward. Kramer pointed to the last Arvin in the line. The lieutenant nodded, then gently tapped him on the shoulder. The Arvin slowly lowered his rifle and stepped back a few paces. Ski was the next man in line, and Kramer got him to do the same. Everyone else remained silent as Kramer and the Arvin lieutenant cautiously worked their way down the line until the last rifle was lowered. There were some murmurs from the men, but after a few seconds they again became silent. The soldiers slowly split into two opposing groups with their lieutenants between them.

After some discussion, Kramer said to Hamilton, "All right, give him back the radio."

"What about *my* radio?"

"He," referring to the Vietnamese lieutenant, "is going to search his men and see if he can find it."

"Yeah. I'll bet that'll do me a lot of good."

"Give it back," Kovacs shouted.

Hamilton threw the radio in the Arvin's direction. It bounced in front of him and landed at his feet in two pieces. This was followed by a lot of commotion and a few raised rifles, but eventually the two groups of soldiers were herded back to their respective sides of the perimeter.

As they walked to their hootch, Kovacs said, "Not bad, Lieutenant."

"Not bad, just lucky."

Three o'clock that afternoon supplies and mail came in on a convoy. Chalice picked up a letter for Forsythe. When he handed it to him, Forsythe muttered, "The cheap bastard," and threw it aside.

Chalice, knowing how much he'd have liked to have gotten a letter, asked, "Aren't you gonna read it?"

"I'll wait till after I eat. It's from my old man and I don't wanna lose my appetite." He picked up the letter and handed it to Chalice. "Look at the stamp. As soon as I saw it wasn't sent airmail, I knew it was from him, the Last of the Big Time Savers."

"He can't be *that* cheap."

"Bull fucking shit he can't! Why do you think I'm in the Marine Corps? The bastard wouldn't give me the coins to go to college."

"Couldn't you get any financial aid?"

"Not a chance. He's too loaded. I was accepted at Duke. I didn't apply for any financial aid because he said he'd pay for it. Besides, when they'd find out how loaded he was, they'd think I was nuts asking for it."

"How come he decided not to pay?"

"I handed him a good enough excuse. I gave one of the speeches at graduation. All the phonies got pissed off at what I said, and they wouldn't give me my diploma. I had to get a lawyer from the Civil Liberties Union to get it for me. My old man sure wasn't gonna spend his 'hard earned money' for one."

"He still wouldn't pay for college?"

"Hell, no! He said I disgraced the family name, and I should work my way through like he did. Family name my ass, the only thing our family name stands for is penny-pinching."

"Is your mother the same way?"

"No, but she hasn't got the guts to stand up to him. He bought this wreck of a boat and everytime the fishing was good, that's all we'd eat. We once had fish for supper twenty-three nights in a row. . . . Maybe that's why I still can't eat pussy."

"You must of went nuts."

"Not a chance, seventeen years of anything and you'll get used to it. I'll tell you one thing, as soon as I got the diploma I got the fuck out of there."

"Is that when you headed for California?"

"Yeah, the day the lawyer got it for me I went home, folded it up like an airplane, put it on my old man's desk, and went out to get drunk. I couldn't find anyone to go with me, so I went alone. I wanted to get drunk as fast as I could.

"It wasn't even four o'clock, and the only open bar I could find was just about the raunchiest place I'd ever seen. The whores were so ugly they'd of had to pay me. I started guzzling as soon as I sat down. There was this big clock in front of me and I was timing myself on every glass. I was getting pretty fucked-up, but not as fucked-up as I wanted to be. If you're drinking alone, always drink enough so you don't know you're alone. I looked at the clock and saw it was seven-thirty: 'No sweat,' I thought, 'still plenty of time to get really shit-faced.'

"Then this fat-assed, big-titted whore walks up and leans her elbow on the bar right next to me. You should of seen her. She was wearing this shiny blue dress, almost as blue as the eye shadow she had smeared all

148

the way up to her eyebrows. That may not seem like any big thing, but her real eyebrows were plucked and she had a set penciled in halfway up her forehead. She had this big mop of frazzly bleach-blond hair. Ordinarily I don't go for bleached blonds, but she also had this cool, black mustache to go with it, would of taken me a week to grow one like it. I'm sitting there trying to see my reflection in her lipstick, must of had five coats of the reddest stuff I'd ever seen, when she says, 'Hey good looking, how about buying a lady a drink?'

" 'Sure,' I said. She was still leaning on the bar with her elbow and playing with these giant pearls around her neck. They were all about the size of golf balls except the one in the middle. That one was just a little smaller than a cue ball. The bartender brought the beer over, and I said, real suavelike, 'Put it on my tab,' then I gave her a big grin. I could tell she really dug me.

"Man, could that broad guzzle beer. She wrapped her claw around the glass and just poured it down. Both her arms had about ten pounds of bracelets on them. When she put the glass down, she gave me a big smile with her yellow teeth and said, 'Thanks Mack, you're a real gentleman.'

"As soon as she said that I got the greatest idea: I'd take her home to meet Mom and Dad. I knew their faces would really be something to see. I was so excited I didn't know what to say. I wanted to come out with a really cool line, and I finally thought of one I thought was just right. I said, 'Tell me something, gorgeous, what's a nice girl like you doing in a place like this?'

"I remember seeing a big, meaty arm covered with bracelets come swinging at me, then the next thing I remember I was lying on the floor sprawled out on my back with the whore and two Neanderthal Men standing over me. She's yelling, 'The queer insulted me! The dirty little fag insulted me!'

"One of the Neanderthal Men bent over and started waving his thumb in my face. He said, 'If you don't know how to talk to a lady, you better beat it, pal.'

"I got up and staggered to the door when the bartender started yelling, 'He's trying to get out without paying his tab.' One of the Neanderthal Men dragged me back to the bar. As soon as I paid, they threw me out the door.

"Here I was flopped over this big Triumph motorcycle, so I threw my leg over it and sat down. That thing was huge. It was blue like the whore's dress and I thought maybe it was hers. I could even picture her tearing around town on it."

Chalice sat captivated by Forsythe's story. He noticed for the first time that Forsythe's teeth were slightly bucked. This and the expressions that flashed across his face as he talked added to the effects of his words. "You stole the bike and headed for California!"

"Yeah! No, wait a minute. The key was in the thing. I fucked around with it for a while and somehow started it up. The next thing I knew, it lurched onto the road carrying me with it. I tried to slow it down, but it accelerated instead. The wind was smashing against my face and I felt great, so I opened the throttle all the way and flew down the road not giving a shit where I was headed. I kept going for about an hour when I started to get sick. I pulled off the road to puke and the next thing I knew I was shading the sun from my eyes. I must of spent the night sleeping in the bushes.

"I couldn't figure out where I was, so I hopped back on the cycle and headed for home, or where I thought was home. I passed this sign that said I was heading west, so I slowed down to turn around. But just as I turned I got the idea to fuck everything and head for California. I made a full circle and was on my way."

Valdez walked by in front of them. Changing his mind, he turned around and sat down next to Chalice, slapping him on the back as he did so. "Well Prof, you almost saw your first fire fight today."

"If there would have been a fire fight, I wouldn't have seen much at all, not the way that Arvin had his rifle pointed between my ears."

Forsythe cut in, "The way they shoot, you still would of had a fifty-fifty chance."

Chalice leaned back and stretched out on the ground saying, "I like my odds a little fatter than that."

Valdez reached over and helped himself to a cigarette out of Forsythe's pocket. He lit it and leaned back on his elbows. "Around here, you have to take any odds you can get." He quickly sat up again. "Hey, what day is today?"

"Saturday," Forsythe answered.

Valdez fumbled with the button on one of his shirt pockets. "Shit, I almost forgot." He pulled out five cards and displayed them to Chalice and Forsythe: the ace, king, queen, jack and ten of spades. "I gotta write my letter," he said while getting to his feet. "See you later."

"What was that all about?" Chalice asked.

"A month after he got in-country, his girl sent him a package with a deck of cards in it. He sends one back to her every week. The ace of spades goes with him on the plane. It's a good way to keep track of time."

"That *is* kinda cool. Maybe I'll do something like that."

"A lot of the other guys have ways of keeping track of time. One guy

150

started out with a bottle of fifty-six malaria tabs. Every week he'd take one, but he got sent home before the bottle was half empty."

"What did he get sent home for?"

"Malaria."

"How the hell could he get malaria three times if he was taking the tabs."

"I already told you. Those things aren't good for anything except givin' you the shits."

Kramer and Kovacs were sitting in front of their hootch cooking some C-rations when Kramer said, "Everybody seemed kind of surprised when we ran into those Gooks up on Charlie Ridge."

"I was as surprised as anybody. It ain't often you catch Charlie with his pants down, and I'm sorry we did."

"Why's that?"

"Now you can bet your ass we'll be going back up there."

Kovacs was right. Trippitt started sending the platoons up one at a time. Third and Fourth Platoons went up first. Neither one of them made contact, but Fourth Platoon found a small ammo cache and some documents. It was Second Platoon's turn, and they were to follow the same procedure as before — leaving at three in the morning so as not to be spotted.

Kramer had taken the last watch that night to make sure they left on time. He crawled into the hootch to wake Kovacs. "It's time. Let's go."

"Okay," Kovacs replied in an alert voice. He'd been awake and merely waiting for Kramer to call him. Kovacs woke Preston and Milton. Walking back towards Kramer, he could make out the dark forms of the rest of the platoon as they put their gear on and gathered in groups.

They were to take a different trail this time. Alpha's patrol the day before had led them by it, so Kramer gave them the point. The squads lined up in one column. Hamilton assigned Bolton the point; but when Childs complained that he walked too fast, Hamilton switched Childs to the point. By the time the platoon had reached the foothills, he was glad he had made the switch. Childs's pace had been slower and steadier than that of the last operation, and they seemed to have reached the foothills in half the time with much less effort.

The trail followed the ridge lines as it twisted through the mountains. This eliminated a lot of needless movement up and down the valleys. The marching didn't become strenuous until the last hour when the steepness

151

of the grade increased enough to necessitate more climbing than walking.

The platoon was strung out vertically along a rocky slope when they took their first break. Chalice tapped Forsythe on the shoulder and whispered, "How much farther?"

"I'm not sure, but I think this is it."

"Are you sure?"

"I said I wasn't."

"Okay. . . . It sure was a hell of a lot easier this time." Moving off the trail, he fumbled in his pockets for some toilet paper. He had forgotten to place it inside his helmet, and it was soaking wet. He dropped his pants and squatted down while rushing to separate the sheets of soggy paper. 'Here it comes. Learned a lot of things lately, wish pissing through my asshole wasn't one of them.'

The men in the column started moving around, and Forsythe whispered, "Chalice, let's go."

Sticking what was left of the toilet paper in his helmet, he jumped up and fastened his pants. 'Only Nam could make taking an undisturbed shit a rare privilege.' He joined the column in the middle of Bravo Squad. By the time he caught up with Alpha, the platoon had turned off the trail and stopped moving. "Where's Hamilton's fire team?" he asked Forsythe in a whisper.

"The lieutenant sent them up ahead as security. This is as far as we're going. We'll stay here till dawn, then sweep across."

"You got any shit paper?"

"A little." He took some out of his helmet and handed it to Chalice. "Didn't you just take a shit?"

"I've been shitting twenty-four hours a day for a week. If this keeps up my ass'll get sunburnt." He stepped off the trail and laid his rifle and magazines down. After squatting in some high grass, Chalice immediately realized his mistake and stood up. Holding his pants with one hand and his rifle with the other, he moved over to some clearer ground. The sound of his shit splattering on the dirt was interrupted by a burst of rifle fire. 'What the fuck is that?' he thought while making quick use of the toilet paper. As he ran back to the column, the night exploded with bursts of rifle fire and concussions from grenades.

Harmon yelled, "Over here!" A bright flash of light and a loud explosion ended in a rapidly expanding globe of thousands of orange white particles that disappeared at the same instant, seemingly leaving the sky darker than before.

A voice tinged with disbelief came from the rear of the column. "Did you see that chicom?"

152

Sugar Bear was kneeling on the trail where Forsythe had been. "Where's my fire team?" Chalice asked.

"They moved up to help. You better wait here a while."

Kramer reached the head of the column just as the shooting stopped. "*Harmon,* what's going on?"

Harmon's voice shot back from twenty yards in front of them. "A Gook. He was sitting on a rock. I got within five feet before I saw him."

"Did you hit him?"

"I don't know. He ain't dead. We've either got him trapped in this cave, or he headed up the next ridge. It's too dark to tell."

Kramer turned around and shouted back down the column, "Valdez, take your squad up the next ridge and circle around." Kramer and Milton moved forward until they reached Harmon. "Anybody hit?" Without waiting for an answer he turned to Milton. "Call in. Get some illumes up here."

"Tony, Hamilton, everybody okay?"

"Yeah."

"Yeah."

"Keep an eye on the cave."

"What cave?" Kramer asked.

Harmon pointed to a group of barely visible boulders. "You don't want us to move up, do you?"

"Hell no, not till it gets light. Have them throw some frags."

"Hamilton."

"Over here."

"Can you get any frags in there?"

"Maybe."

"Give it a try. Everybody stay down."

Just as Hamilton started to pull the pin on a grenade, there was a short burst of rifle fire from above. It was followed by some longer bursts.

"Valdez, was that you?" Kramer shouted.

"Yeah, he walked right into us. I could hear him breathing."

"Did you get him?"

"I don't know. He took off."

"Stay where you are. We should be getting some illumes soon."

Within minutes the entire area was lit up with the flickering glow of illumination flares. Charlie and Alpha squads searched for blood trails without finding any. In the meantime, Bravo Squad was checking out one of the caves. They found a lot of clothing, rice, and Chinese Communist grenades. By the time Alpha and Charlie joined them, the hazy light of dawn had replaced that of the illumes. Most of the platoon stood around

153

watching Bravo empty the cave. Valdez took a lot of ribbing about his marksmanship, which he excused by saying that the way the "Gook" walked right up to him he thought it might have been someone from Alpha.

Ski came running out of the cave waving a .38 Smith and Wesson revolver. "Hey motherfuckers, look at this." As they passed the gun around, they congratulated him on his find. Holding the pistol in his hand, Chalice became envious. Though he'd never owned a gun in his life, he made up his mind that he wanted something like it to take home as a souvenir.

There were two more clusters of boulders that had to be checked out. Kramer assigned them to Alpha and Charlie squads. Thinking about the possibility of getting some souvenirs, the men hurried towards them. Alpha immediately found a large cave with three small entrances. Knowing that his men might get careless thinking about Ski's souvenir, Harmon decided to check out the cave himself. He handed Payne his M-16 and took Payne's .45, then crawled into one of the openings. After a few minutes he called for Tony 5 and Hamilton to come in. Chalice started to follow them, but Tony 5 turned around and told him to climb to the top of the cave and stand security.

Chalice slowly scaled the smooth gray boulders. The next ridge towered above him like a huge, forbidding parapet. He scanned it, feeling alone and vulnerable. Upon reaching the top, Chalice turned and began to kneel. The sight of the soft green lowlands stopped him. He stood high above them, and above the sun — alone.

Only a diaphanous hint of the once thick morning mist remained, and this too was quickly being burned away by the sun's slanting rays. Bound within the parameters of his sight, lay a minute replica of the only world he had known the past few weeks. All links between the man standing free above the valley and the soldier who trudged through its mud and dust dissolved. He pictured himself as one might picture an intriguing stranger. His eyes followed this stranger's path from Hill 65 on his left, that orange scab upon the valley floor, to the toylike silhouette of Liberty Bridge on his right. Between these two points flowed the calm, wide river — its breadth belying its shallowness. It bowed gracefully around that white arc of sand he knew to be the park. The dusty, crater-scarred road was now no more than a thin yellow line, twisting parallel to the river. It touched upon a group of tiny gray rectangles that marked the camp they had set out from just a few hours earlier. Between the mountains and road lay a checkerboardlike configuration of multicolored rice paddies. There was something strange and methodical about them, as if constructed by ants. And across the river, stretching to the dark mountains that formed the southern boundary of the valley, lay a tract of land so feared as to give it an aura of mystery — the Arizona. A feeling of serenity engulfed Chalice, not as in one who has found an answer, but as in one who no longer cares to ask. Again he traced the paths he had taken, seeing himself not as a person, but as an insignificant, slowly moving speck against the many-hued mosaic below.

The sound of a rifle banging against one of the boulders brought Chalice out of his reverie. Forsythe was making his way towards him. "Quite a view."

"I can't remember seeing anything like it." Chalice pointed to a group of boulders about fifty yards away on the opposite side of the trail. "Do you think there might be a cave over there?"

"Probably, you wanna check it out?"

"Yeah, I wouldn't mind getting some souvenirs."

"We have to turn in most of the stuff we find."

"What about the pistol Ski found?"

"He's supposed to be able to keep it, but somebody in the rear who sits on his ass all day while we're in the bush will probably steal it. You never heard about Armstead, did you?" Chalice shook his head. "They shipped him home with one arm blown away, blind in both eyes, and burns all over his face. When his parents came to visit him in the hospital, he asked them if they got his SKS. He was the only guy in the platoon with one. It was practically new, a lifer's dream. They said they didn't know anything about it, and when they checked they found out it had been stolen the same day his lieutenant left country. From what I hear, nobody ever tried to get it back for him. . . . I'll ask Tony if we can check out those rocks anyway."

A few minutes later Chalice, Forsythe, and Tony 5 headed towards the boulders. They found a narrow trail that led right to them. Tony immediately spotted a cave. He had the .45, so he entered it while Chalice and Forsythe waited outside. Chalice felt cheated because Tony would get to keep anything he found even though Chalice had spotted the boulders. Tony came right out dragging two rusty cans. As they sorted through them, Forsythe pulled out a roll of material. He started to unravel it, at the same time saying, "What the fuck is this?" It turned out to be a banner about ten feet long and two feet wide with two rows of large printed writing on it.

Tony pulled out another one just like it, only with different words. "Hey Prof, what the fuck do they say?"

Chalice only recognized a few words. "I can't make it out. What do you suppose they use them for?"

155

Forsythe started laughing. "Maybe they're gonna have a convention. *That's it!* We've captured the Viet Cong convention center."

Tony had been unwrapping a small package, and he now held a Viet Cong flag in his hands. "Hey you guys, get a load of this. Looks like I got my brother a hell of a souvenir."

Chalice became jealous and started to say something about being the one who spotted the cave, but he changed his mind and walked to the mouth of it. "Is there anything else inside?"

"No, not a thing," Tony answered.

"Can I check it out anyway?"

"Sure, here's the .45."

Chalice took the pistol and crawled in. It was shaped more like a small tunnel than a cave. There wasn't enough room to stand up, and the walls were slanted making movement inside even more awkward. Chalice crawled to the rear without finding anything. He moved back towards the entrance. Just as he was about to crawl out, he spotted a small crevice right inside the mouth of the cave. "Tony, did you check this hole?"

"I checked the whole cave."

"This hole by the entrance?"

"Everything."

Chalice looked down the crevice again, but turned around and started to crawl out. As he was doing so he thought, 'What the hell,' and turned back towards the crevice. It was about two feet across at the top, but widened out towards the bottom. He checked carefully for signs of a booby trap, then lowered himself down. There was a small opening at the base of one wall. Peering into it, Chalice could see two big aluminum tubes with a rifle butt sticking out of one of them — 'An SKS, maybe.' He pulled the rifle from the tube without checking for a booby trap.

Forsythe had crawled into the cave and was peering down at him. "What have you got there?"

"Just an SKS," Chalice answered excitedly.

"Are you shittin' me? *Tony!* He's got an SKS."

"No shit! Bring the motherfucker out."

Chalice handed the SKS up to Forsythe, then lifted himself from the crevice. When he got outside, Tony 5 and Forsythe seemed as excited as he was.

Tony said, "God, how could I have missed it. I've wanted one of these things ever since I got over here." He opened the magazine and took out a handful of rounds. After putting one in his pocket, he gave another to Forsythe and handed the rest of them and the rifle to Chalice. "One of those bullets could of had our names on it."

156

Tony 5 and Forsythe each picked up a tin can, and the three of them headed back to the rest of the platoon. As they approached, Forsythe saw Sugar Bear standing on a boulder and yelled out, "The Prof found an SKS."

Sugar Bear jumped off the boulder and met them. "Nice going, Professor. That's a beauty." By the time they reached Kramer, practically the whole platoon was there to meet them.

Everyone was slapping Chalice on the back and congratulating him when Kovacs said, "Sorry Prof, that's not an SKS. That's an AK-47." Chalice stood mute, knowing that an AK-47 is an automatic rifle and can't be taken home as a souvenir. There was a few seconds' silence, then everybody started laughing. "I'm fucking with you, Professor. You've got yourself a lifer's dream."

Appleton slapped him hard on the back. "You shoulda seen your face. You looked like somebody cut your balls off."

Kovacs took the rifle and opened the bayonet. Instead of the knife type, it was aluminum colored and round with four large blood grooves. Kovacs pressed it against Chalice's stomach. "Prof, the advantage of this ice pick bayonet is that when you pull it out of somebody's stomach, his guts come out with it."

The SKS wasn't the only topic. Appleton told everybody about what had happened to Hicks. "Yeah, Good Old Hicks found something interesting too. There was this little old wire strung across one of the caves, and our boy Hicks decided to kick it out of the way." Hicks remained silent with an embarrassed look on his face. As everybody turned towards him, he lowered his head to avoid their stares. "Now I know he says he didn't see it, but I can't believe that. I'm standing behind him and I hear this nice, loud pop. When I got off the ground — Hicks bowled me over on his way out of the cave — I found this pretty little 60-millimeter mortar round all rigged to go off. The primer blew, but the mortar didn't. It's a good thing too. It would of taken us a week to find enough of Hicks to fill a C-rat can."

They stood around for a few minutes kidding Hicks and passing the SKS to each other, then Kramer told Harmon to form up the men. As the platoon started along the trail, Chalice was thinking about the SKS. He remembered the way those few Marines had carried them around at the Da Nang airfield on the day he arrived in-country — the superior looks on their faces. He could picture himself strolling around in the same manner — 'The most wanted souvenir there is, and I've got it.' Realizing he was the only man in the platoon with one, Chalice felt a little guilty about it. He'd only been in-country a few weeks while some of the other men had been there twelve months. If there was any animosity towards him, it was far outweighed by the pride the others took in the fact that a member of their platoon had gotten an SKS, and that there was now one less rifle to shoot at them.

Roads walked the point with Hamilton right behind him. Although being point man usually made him uneasy, there hadn't been another sign of the Viet Cong and he was in a relaxed but cautious mood. This caused him to set a fairly slow pace, and no one bothered to rush him. The trail petered out and he had to blaze his own for more than an hour, but he preferred doing so because this eliminated the chance of hitting a booby trap. Pushing through a thicket of heavy brush only to be confronted by some steep rocks, he instinctively kept moving along the lower edge, not wasting time to figure out whether to go above or below. As soon as he got to their base, he found himself in a sea of elephant grass well above his head. He held his hands against his chest to protect them from being cut, and moved forward taking short, high steps. Just when he started wondering whether the grass would ever end, it opened onto a group of large, flat boulders separated by wide crevices that necessitated long jumps over them. He slowed down his pace a little in order to make it easier for those behind him. The boulders ended in a small cliff above a clearing.

While deciding how to climb down, his eyes caught the color black — Viet Cong uniforms. Eleven of them were sitting on the edge of the clearing not more than twenty yards away from him. Roads crouched, his heartbeat quickening as a heavy warmth spread within his body. Hurriedly, he aimed his rifle, at the same time feeling a sense of absurdity about what he was doing. With his sights held steady on the back of the nearest Viet Cong, he pulled the trigger. It wouldn't move! He pulled harder. Finally realizing his rifle was on safe, he clicked it on semiautomatic. Now afraid that the Viet Cong had heard the click, he opened fire without aiming. Instead of the loud, percussive burst of an exploding cartridge, his ears caught the sharp, hollow sound of metal hitting metal — the rifle had misfired.

The Viet Cong scrambled to their feet and headed towards the elephant grass in a panic. Hamilton moved up alongside of Roads and got off a few quick shots aimed below the moving tops of the grass. Roads kneeled next to him thinking, 'Good, got nothing against these people.'

The rest of the platoon came tearing across the boulders only to see an empty clearing before them. Kramer ordered a search of the elephant grass. They swept through it without finding a trace of the Viet Cong. When they reached a path, Kramer told Valdez to put Charlie Squad at the point and head the platoon back to camp.

Valdez figured that this was Hicks's lucky day, so he made him point man. He soon regretted his choice. Hicks knew the slim chances of one man tripping two booby traps in the same day, and he set a rapid pace. All the men, especially those at the tail end of the column, were out of breath within a few minutes. Only the psychological advantage of knowing that they were headed back to their perimeter enabled them to keep up. The fast pace became more of a joke than a sore point, and the frequency of the men's bantering complaints and curses caused Kramer to order them to keep the noise down. After an hour of steady marching, he thought about calling a five minute break. Spirits seemed high and stopping might give the Viet Cong time to set up an ambush ahead of them. Kramer decided to wait.

Just as the front of the column started up a steep ridge and the tail end of it was descending the preceding slope with most of the platoon strung out in the barren valley between, a burst of rifle fire came from above and behind them. Kramer's first thought was to have the men take cover. But the valley floor offered none.

"MOVE IT!" he ordered.

The sniper fire continued in short bursts as they ran. When the last man had reached the heavier brush of the slope, Kramer halted the column and told the men to take cover. He turned to Kovacs. "Doesn't seem like much of a shot."

"He's just harassing us."

Kramer called out asking if anybody thought they knew where the fire was coming from. Receiving no reply, he turned back to Kovacs. "You think there's only one of them?"

"That's what it sounds like."

"No use calling in any fire then."

Kovacs was stretched out on the ground nonchalantly lighting a cigarette. He offered the pack to Kramer. "Just be a waste of time."

Kramer shook his head at the cigarettes. "That's what I think. Let's get out of here." He turned to Ski who was sitting in front of them. "Tell 'em to move-out fast."

In a few seconds the entire platoon was traveling at a dead run, and the sniper fire started again. The trail curved around a small knoll at the top of the ridge. Just as Kramer reached the front edge of the knoll, a loud blast came from the opposite side and some light debris rained down on him.

"What was that?" Kovacs yelled across the knoll.

Valdez's voice rang out, "Corpsman up. Booby trap."

Kramer nervously looked around. Seeing he was the only one standing, he began to kneel. The corpsman rushed by him, and he and Kovacs followed. By the time the three of them reached the head of the column, the other corpsman had already split Hicks's trousers exposing his blood-covered legs. Stung by the sight, Kramer blamed himself. His distress was apparent, and as soon as the corpsman injected Hicks with morphine, he turned to Kramer and said, "It's not as bad as it looks." Both corpsmen started wrapping the legs in bandages.

Kramer turned around to call to Milton only to find himself standing face to face with him. "Call in a medivac chopper and a casualty report." He then turned to Valdez. "Anyone else hit?"

"Chief got a scratch on his elbow."

Kramer looked towards Chief who was wrapping a bandage on his own forearm. "Any shrapnel inside?"

"Don't think so. Just a scratch."

"What type of booby trap was it?"

"Sounded like a frag."

As Chief said this, the sniper fire began again. Kramer turned to Milton. "Call in an air strike on that motherfucker. Make sure you get our co-ordinates right." He then said to Kovacs, "I really fell for it, didn't I?"

"Yeah, he sucked us in. You can't outguess Charlie all the time."

Kovacs told Harmon to have the men clear an LZ. A few minutes later, Sugar Bear came running up to the corpsmen. "Can one of you guys come over to the LZ? Graham cut his leg pretty bad."

Kovacs asked disgustedly, "How'd the asshole do that?"

"I can't figure it out. He must of thought his leg was a tree stump and gave it a whack with his machete."

One of the corpsmen went to the LZ with Sugar Bear. Kramer told Milton to call in another casualty report before following them. Just as he got there, two broncos — propeller-driven planes with mounted machine guns — roared overhead.

Graham sat with sweat dripping from his face as the corpsman wrapped his leg. Sugar Bear, Forsythe, and Chalice stood around shaking their heads at him. "How bad did Hicks get it?" Forsythe asked the corpsman.

"Not too bad. There's a lot of shrapnel in him, but nothing's ripped away."

"I'd rather have shrapnel in me than rifle lead," Chalice commented.

"Why's that?" Forsythe asked.

"I'd rather have a lot of little scars than one big one."

The corpsman looked up. "Those holes might be little now, but by the time the doctors get that shrapnel out they'll be plenty big."

"Well, at least he gets a vacation," Chalice remarked.

"Better than that, he's got a sure ticket home."

A loud burst of machine gun fire from one of the broncos sent Chalice

160

to his knees. While Forsythe looked down at him with amusement, he got back on his feet, saying meekly, "I'm glad they're not shooting at us."

"You should be. Those guys are pretty good. They usually put on quite a show."

The broncos proved Forsythe right. They took turns diving in at treetop level and strafing the area — seeming to wait until the last second before banking to avoid crashing into the ridges. As Chalice and Forsythe stood watching, Tony 5 walked up behind them and asked, "You dudes don't mind helping us clear this LZ, do you?" They joined the rest of the platoon in time to find the area already cleared and the medivac chopper circling.

Graham and Hicks were loaded aboard seconds after the helicopter landed. As soon as it took off, Alpha Squad led the way back towards camp with Childs at the point. The last slope before the lowlands was quite steep. He had to drag his feet to slow himself. After losing what there was of a trail, he led the men through some thick, waist-high brush. A few yards into it, his ankle caught on a sharp object and he fell flat on his stomach. Childs sat up to rub his ankle and saw what he had tripped over — a two hundred pound bomb. "Hold up. I've got a dud two hundred pounder here."

Kramer made his way to the front of the column. "Where is it?"

"Next to your boot."

Kramer backed away from the bomb while saying, "Nice work, Childs. I don't see how you spotted it."

"I make it a point to keep my eyes open," Childs answered, still rubbing his ankle.

Kramer turned to Harmon. "Have somebody set a charge under it."

Harmon called out for a stick of C-4 and a blasting cap. When none was forthcoming, he asked again only to find out that nobody in his squad had brought any. "That's just fucking outstanding. Instead of leaving it in camp, why don't you guys mail it home. That way your mothers can send it to you when you need it." Somebody in Bravo had brought some along, and it was passed up the column. Tony 5 stayed behind to light the fuse, while the rest of the platoon moved out at a dead run. This proved unnecessary because the charge never went off.

Second Platoon got back to their perimeter an hour before dusk. Alpha had the ambush, and Harmon walked over to Kramer's hootch to find out the site. Kovacs was sitting in front cleaning his rifle while Kramer looked over his map. "It's a short one tonight," Kramer said as he pointed to the map. "Just go straight across the road and set up on the last tree line before the river."

As Harmon studied the map, Kovacs said, "Don't forget the Little

People." Lately they had been taking four Arvins on each ambush, but Charlie Squad had forgotten them the night before. Harmon nodded and left. On the way back to his squad, he looked up at the sky and saw a solid canopy of rain clouds.

A few minutes before dusk, Harmon ordered Alpha to saddle up. The men moved around sluggishly as they put on their gear. Tony 5 called to Guns Squad, and Pablo and Sinclaire walked over with their machine gun. The men were tired. Aside from some grumbling, they remained silent as they lined up.

Tony assigned Forsythe the point. Four Arvins were waiting for them at the far edge of the perimeter. Forsythe motioned them into the column. He found the tree line where they were supposed to set in, but it offered little cover and poor fields of fire. Harmon told him to head up the river a little farther. They moved another fifty yards without finding a better location. The front of the column peeled back around and stopped at the original spot. Forsythe and Harmon walked down the river a few yards by themselves. The men waited restlessly, tired and anxious to set in.

A light drizzle started. Chalice moved to the side to see what was going on. Most of the men in the column were kneeling. Barely enough moonlight glowed through the clouds to outline Pablo's upright silhouette. He stood in profile — motionless with his machine gun on his shoulder. The rest of the men began getting to their feet. Finding nothing better, Harmon had decided to set in where they were. He divided the squad into two positions, giving a third position to the Arvins.

Chalice sat down and took out his mosquito repellent. Payne smelled it and stuck out his palm indicating that he wanted some. The sound of the rain as it pattered on the brush became louder, but over it Chalice could hear the Arvins talking in loud whispers. The thought of them giving away the ambush site made him nervous. Someone walking in a hunched position came towards him. "Chalice," Harmon's voice whispered.

"Over here."

"The Gooks are making too much noise. You better set-in with them and keep them quiet."

Chalice moved as quietly as possible to the Arvin position. He explained to four sets of smiling teeth that he was going to stand watch with them. Just as he got them quieted, one lit up a cigarette while making a crude effort to cup the match. Chalice pointed towards him. "Numba ten." The Arvin sitting next to Chalice touched the other's arm and got him to put out the cigarette.

They gave Chalice the last watch and he lay back to get some sleep. The rain had just stopped, but at that moment it started again, harder

162

than before. Placing his soft cover over his face, he tried to fall asleep. Though he was completely exhausted from the day's march, he lay shivering for more than an hour, returning many times from the verge of sleep as rain beat down upon him. His neck sank into the mud and he finally sat up in disgust. Wringing out his hat, he decided to move from the puddle he was lying in. He felt around with his hands and found a small clump of grass to lay his head on. The rest of his body remained in a puddle a few inches deep. The grass tickled the back of his neck while chills ran through his limbs. Changing position every few minutes, he was able to get a little sleep; but the next morning he was more tired than he had been the night before. It was still raining when he got back to his hootch. After taking his clothes off and laying them on top, he crawled in and wrapped himself in his poncho liner. Within minutes he dropped off into a deep sleep.

"Let go!" Chalice said half asleep.

"Get up."

"Cut it out."

"C'mon, we've got a patrol."

Chalice sat up and saw Tony 5 pulling on his ankle. "Okay. . . . *Wait a minute!* We had the ambush last night. Bravo's got the patrol today."

"We've got one too," Tony said.

"What time is it?"

"Eleven."

"How come we got a patrol?"

"We've got to go up and blow that two hundred pounder."

"We've got to go back up *there?*"

"You wouldn't want Charlie to find it, would you? He could make bucoo booby traps out of that baby."

Chalice stood up. Finding himself completely naked, he took his shirt from the top of the hootch. 'At least it's dry. . . . Where the fuck are my pants?' They were lying in the mud beside his hootch. He picked them up with two fingers. 'Nothing like putting on a slimy pair of pants.' Buttoning them, he noticed a spot of pus on his forearm.

Forsythe came strolling over with a big grin on his face. "*Good* morning."

"Shut the fuck up."

Forsythe took a step backwards. "Sorry, sir. What's your problem?"

"If there's one thing I can't stand to see when I get up in the morning, it's a smiling face."

163

"Oh, excuse me. Next time you get up I'll kick you in the balls first thing."

"Thanks. Anything'll be an improvement." Chalice held out his forearm. "What do you think this is?"

"Looks like the forearm of a hairy fourteen-year-old girl to me."

"The pus, stupid."

Forsythe grabbed Chalice's forearm and studied it intently. "Very interesting." Letting go, he said, "It's nothing, just a Gook sore."

"It'll go way in a few days?"

"No, usually takes a month or two."

"Are you serious, a little thing like that?"

"It won't be so little in a few weeks. You'll get enough pus out of that to fill your helmet."

"Why would I want a helmet full of pus?"

"Why are you in Nam? Why'd you join the Marine Corps?"

"Only my psychiatrist knows for sure. You *do* guarantee it'll disappear in a few short months? I'd sure hate to have my arm fall off."

"It will, everything but the scar."

"The scar!"

"Yeah, look at these." Forsythe showed Chalice a small purple scar on his wrist. He then rolled up his pants legs, exposing two large purple blotches on his knees. "This country's got everything — eight out of ten of the original Plagues."

"Isn't there any way I can keep it from scarring?"

"Sure; bathe three times a day, eat a balanced diet, and get plenty of sleep."

"Oh, is that all."

"Don't sweat it. Everybody gets them. You'll get plenty more before you leave here."

"That's great."

Harmon walked by, turning his head to say, "Hurry up and get your gear on so we can get this over with."

Once outside the perimeter, the men forgot their irritation at having to go on the patrol. The sky was overcast and the pace slow. They followed the tree line that ran parallel to the road. It was a little less than two kilometers long and ended in a circle of high ground containing a small ville. By following the trails leading away from the ville, they could reach the foothills without crossing more than a kilometer of rice paddies. As they approached the village, Childs talked Harmon into holding up the column so he could get some grapefruit off a tree. The Vietnamese usually picked the fruit as soon as it was ripe, and finding any ready to eat was a

164

rare occurrence. This time they were lucky. Childs threw down eight. Only three were ripe, and these were passed around and quickly devoured. The men moved out with buoyed spirits and a sense of accomplishment. The incident, though seemingly insignificant, endowed the rest of the patrol with a mood of cheerfulness. This mood prevailed even after the mad rush back down the slope after setting a new charge that also failed to explode. Harmon surmised that a batch of defective blasting caps was the problem, so he headed the squad back to the perimeter instead of returning to the bomb. The men knew they would have to come back the next day, but it would be their turn for a patrol anyway. On the way back to the perimeter, even the tedious, often-performed ritual of picking the leeches off their legs was given lighthearted significance by a pool of one dollar per man to be divided between the two men with the most and largest leeches. Ski won half of it with eight, and Payne won the other with a five-inch specimen.

The next day a small convoy brought supplies and mail. On one of the envelopes, Kramer recognized the nearly illegible handwriting of his brother. The original address was wrong, and the correct one was written over the mark of a large, red stamp. He hurriedly ripped it open and started reading.

Hi Dave,

You really got yourself into it this time, didn't you? I hope everything is okay so far. Write and tell me what it's like.

My grades kind of hurt last semester. In every course that I was on the borderline, I got the lower grade. Maybe I could have done better, but engineering would have been a mistake anyway. It's definitely out now. My classes are crip this time. I've been studying hard since the beginning of the semester (two whole weeks), and if I keep it up I'll come out all right.

Write Mom and Dad. The last time I was home Mom kept running out to the mail box all morning. It's a major catastrophe anytime the mailman comes without a letter from you.

I hope you'll have some good ideas about how to make a lot of money when you get out. I'm not looking forward to working for a living.

I'm rooming with four other guys. We've moved into this real cool house. This should be a good semester for girls. The football team is supposed to be lousy this year, but I have a feeling they're going to be all right. Send me some cool souvenirs right away; some rings, beads, or anything cool.

Don't do anything stupid. If you're at some place you can get shot, try and get out of there. Be careful. You know what it would do to Mom and Dad if anything happened to you.

Danny

P.S. — Make sure you write Mom and Dad right away. Don't forget about the souvenirs.

Although the letter was from his brother, Kramer's thoughts turned to his parents. He withdrew the stationery from the bottom of his pack and set the pad on his lap. Not knowing the date, he looked around for somebody to ask. Nobody was in less than shouting distance, so he guessed at it. After writing "Dear Mom and Dad," his pen moved down the page, but he couldn't think of anything to write. He finally decided to look at their letter for ideas. His eyes caught the section about souvenirs he had sent from Okinawa — a woven silk calendar and a tiny bean with an ivory elephant on top and a hundred minute ones inside. Surprised that his mother hadn't made a fuss over the elephants, he decided to ask about them. He thought of the trees he had planted just before he'd left home, deciding to ask how they were growing. He remembered to tell his parents not to worry about his brother. After thinking for a few minutes, he began to write about Vietnam. He tried to describe the simple beauty of the country, not mentioning the marks now upon it. As he put his thoughts down, his mind reflected upon a troubling question. After a moment's hesitation, he ended the letter with the words, "Be home soon. Love, David."

Kramer looked up to see Alpha coming in off its patrol. The men dropped their equipment and immediately headed for the right guide's hootch where they had seen the new supplies stacked. Preston was waiting for them with their mail in his hand. He tried to get them to divide the supplies first, but Harmon took the mail from him and started calling out the names while flipping each letter in the air without looking up. He then divided up the supplies where they were, and left it to the men to carry them back on their own.

As usually happened when they received mail, each man wandered off alone to read his letter. In a few minutes they would gather into groups, with one member reading parts of his letter to the others. Chalice sat in front of his hootch listening to a small transistor radio when Hamilton called him over. "Here's some pictures of my girl. I took them just before I left home. Man, I'm so glad they came out. She looks so cool, doesn't she?"

166

As Chalice thumbed through them, he noticed Hamilton's grinning face looking up at him waiting for an answer. He unconsciously hesitated for a few seconds, then glanced at the pictures again. To him, Hamilton's girl appeared far less than "cool." Suddenly realizing an honest opinion was not what the situation required, he nodded his head and said, "Yeah, yeah, real nice." Surprised at how unconvincing his answer had sounded, he handed back the pictures searching Hamilton's face for any sign of displeasure. Hamilton, still grinning like a little kid, took the photographs and thumbed through them again.

Chalice got up and started walking away when Hamilton called to him as if he'd done something incomprehensible. "*Hey*, where are you going?"

"Back to my hootch."

Hamilton saw the questioning look on Chalice's face and said, "Oh. . . . Hey, I gotta show these to Forsythe." He stood up and brushed past Chalice. Hamilton handed Forsythe the pictures as he and Chalice sat down. "This is my girl. I told you about her. Pretty nice, isn't she?"

"Definitely all right," Forsythe answered. He then noticed Chalice watching his face and almost broke into a grin.

'Handled it better than I did,' thought Chalice.

Childs approached unnoticed from the rear of the hootch, both arms wrapped around a large, battered pot. He tripped over one of the guy wires and stumbled to his knees in front of them. Chalice turned to inspect the damage. "Nice hootch we used to have here."

"Fuck the hootch. Look what I got." He withdrew some foil packages from the pot.

Forsythe reached for them with a pleased expression on his face. "Gook long-rats. Outa sight."

"What are long-rats?" Chalice asked.

"Food, man. You just add water and heat them up. They're better than the crap they feed us. How many did you get?"

"Four meals."

"Great, that's enough for all of us."

"What'd you trade for them?" Hamilton asked.

"Two cans of meat."

"You got *four* long-rats for two cans of meat?"

"Hell no! That was my share. You guys all owe me two meats each. I told the Gook I'd bring them over later."

Childs was opening the packages into the pot when Hamilton shoved the pictures in front of him. "Hey man, take a look at these." Childs gave them a quick glance and dumped them in the pot. He opened another package on top of them as Hamilton fished them out. "Quit fucking around. That's my girl."

"What good is a girl if you can't eat her, I always say. . . . Chalice, give me one of your canteens."

As Childs poured in the water, Payne said, "Hey, that's too much."

Still pouring, Childs stared at him a few seconds before saying, "Payne, if you saw me taking a shit, you'd come over and start telling me how to wipe my ass, wouldn't you?"

By the time Childs finished cooking the long-rations, half the platoon had gathered around with spoons in their hands. There was much more than four people could eat, so the pot eventually got passed around to anybody who wanted it.

As soon as Chalice finished eating, he was overcome by a now familiar need. "Goddamn it. I got the shits again. Food's been running through me like I was a sewer."

"You should eat a lot of peanut butter," Hamilton suggested.

"That doesn't do me any good. Just changes the color."

"A little variety never hurt," Forsythe kidded. "Ask the corpsman to give you some pills."

"I've taken every kind of pills they've got: pink ones, white ones, blue ones."

"Maybe that's what's givin' you the shits."

"Gee Forsythe, I never thought of that. You're a real help sometimes." Chalice picked up an entrenching tool and headed for the edge of the perimeter.

It started to get dark, and on the way back he failed to see a detonating cord running from an automatic tear gas launcher to one of the foxholes. Chalice didn't realize what had happened until he turned around and saw the sky filling with twenty trails of white smoke from the falling canisters. He stood motionless for a few seconds before dropping the E-tool and tearing across to the opposite side of the perimeter. The ensuing scene resembled something out of an old-time movie — the whole platoon scurrying around looking for their gas masks. Within a minute or two everybody had gathered on the Arvin side of the camp and stood huddled in a large group. Half of the men had on gas masks, and practically anybody that didn't was arguing with somebody that did about whose mask he had on. But the humor of the situation was evident to them, and they welcomed the incident as a break in the monotony. This was true at least until it became obvious that the wind was carrying the gas straight towards them. Soon those without masks started gagging. Equally irritating was the sound of laughter from inside the masks of the other men. A free-for-all broke out. Those without masks stumbled around trying to rip off the masks of those wearing them. By the time the gas dissipated, everybody was sitting around coughing and laughing at the same time.

168

The rain started a few minutes before dusk. 'I should of known it,' Chalice thought. 'We've got the ambush.' He crawled inside his hootch to wait for the word to form up. As soon as he lay down, Forsythe came over. "Tony says to bring your rain suit."

"I thought we couldn't use them on ambushes because they shine when they're wet."

"This isn't gonna be much of an ambush; we're sandbagging it. They want us to go on a long one to some low ground and Harmon doesn't feel like sleeping in two feet of water. C'mon, I see them forming up."

After the entire squad had gathered, Harmon carefully shifted his men around until they were in the order he wanted them. He placed Stoker, the new corpsman, in front of Chalice. Stoker was about five eleven and extremely broad shouldered. Chalice moved to the side to see the other men in front of him. 'Shit, if it wasn't for his albino neck, I'd swear I was standing behind a water buffalo.' Since his arrival, Stoker had been a common topic among the men. His brutelike appearance was incongruously matched with a mousy disposition and a squeaky, high-pitched voice that caused astonishment every time he spoke. Standing next to Stoker made Chalice feel like a battle-hardened veteran.

Alpha Squad left the perimeter at a different point than usual to avoid picking up the Arvins who were supposed to accompany it. Clouds completely covered the moon, giving the sky a faint, eerie glow. The column crossed the road in front of the perimeter and walked through the remains of a burned-out native hootch. Fifty yards past it, Harmon halted his men and walked up to Tony 5. "What do you think?"

"I dunno. It's complete shit right here, and it's bound to get worse the farther we go. You thinkin' about that old hootch back there?"

"Yeah, it doesn't have a roof, but at least the ground's high."

"I'd hate being so close. We'd have to be bucoo careful."

The rain became heavier. Harmon looked back toward the hootch. "Fuck it, let's peel back around."

As soon as they reached the hootch, Harmon got everybody down and warned them to keep low and quiet. Chalice stretched out on the hard ground placing his bush cover over his face as a shield against the rain. His rain suit offered little protection and in minutes the chilling water had seeped through it and completely soaked him. He crossed his arms tightly over his chest knowing this would make him feel warmer. Exhaustion overcame him, and he dozed off.

Chalice awoke while it was still dark, surprised that he had been able to sleep at all and with a feeling that something was wrong. Slowly sitting up, he scanned the prone bodies of the rest of the squad and realized that the person on watch had fallen asleep. Whoever's turn it was would be by the radio. He crawled around until he located it, Payne holding the receiver. Chalice poked him in the chest. Payne bolted to a sitting position and called out in a sharp, startled voice, "I'm awake!"

Wincing, Chalice watched a few of the other men squirm around in their sleep. "A lousy one-hour watch, and you crash."

"I was awake," Payne whispered nervously.

"Sure you were. That's why you were nice enough to stand my watch."

"No!"

"Forget it. You better wake up Hamilton. It's his watch now." Chalice crawled back in the corner and tried to get some more sleep, but he kept waking up every few minutes. Stoker had the last watch, and Chalice saw Hamilton wake him. After Hamilton went back to sleep, Stoker stood up and walked outside the hootch. Chalice couldn't figure out what he was doing. Stoker dropped his pants and squatted down, seemingly in answer to Chalice's thoughts. Stoker being red haired and very light complected, Chalice mused, 'Looked like an eclipse of the moon.' Suddenly, excited shouts in Vietnamese rang out from inside the perimeter. Chalice immediately realized what had happened: the Arvins had been told where the ambush should have been, so they naturally assumed any movement outside the perimeter was VC. 'The sonofabitch would have to have a neon sign for an ass.' He lay motionless, not sure what to do and hoping the Arvins would stop yelling. Stoker was the only other person up, and his advice wouldn't be worth much. Chalice decided to count to *ten*. If the Arvins hadn't stopped shouting by then, he'd call out to them to try to prevent any shooting. Just as he got to *four*, a burst of automatic rifle fire whizzed by a few feet over his head. The other members of the squad scrambled around on their stomachs grabbing for their rifles.

"Marines! Marines!" Chalice yelled. The Arvins continued to shout, but held their fire. Dumbfounded whispers came from the men around him. "What the fuck's going on?" "Who yelled, 'Marines'?" "What were those shots?" Ignoring them, Chalice again called out, *"Marines! Marines!"*

Vietnamese voices answered, "Okay, Marine. Okay."

Knowing that the Arvins didn't need much of an excuse to start shooting, the rest of the platoon didn't bother to ask any questions when Alpha returned to the perimeter. The men went back to their hootches to catch a few more hours' sleep. As they awoke one by one, they were greeted with some unwelcome news: at three that night the whole company was to leave on a six-day operation up in the mountains, carrying full packs. The third day they would reach the heavy canopy of trees, much farther up than they had previously gone. Because the canopy would prevent their resupply until the fifth day, every man was to be issued eight meals of

C-rations, two for each of the first four days. The impossibility of getting this much food into their packs, no less carrying it, would force them to leave much of it behind. Ordinarily, for an operation of this length in the mountains, the lighter and more compact long-rations would be issued. But Captain Trippitt had neglected to order them in time. Most of the men were resentful about the operation, not only because of the marching that lay ahead, but also because they felt it was Trippitt's idea to help him get his major's oak leaf.

7. The Canopy

The company moved out that night with no sense of excitement, only dread of the physical torture to come. Kramer's platoon was second in the column and the CP traveled behind its first two squads. Having the captain move with them bothered Kramer as much as it did the men, even though they knew that if any dirty work were to be done, they wouldn't have to do it.

The point chose a trail that proved somewhat easier than the ones the men had previously traveled. By daybreak they were high above the valley floor. Their unusually heavy packs had made the climbing far more strenuous. But the men had completed this same march before, and repetition dulled their minds and the pain they were enduring.

As the sun glided towards its apex the pace of the column gradually slowed. Trippitt compensated by not taking any breaks until one o'clock. A few of the men were already suffering from the first effects of heat prostration, and the corpsmen had little time to eat after attending to them. When Trippitt passed the word to "saddle-up," the commander of Fourth Platoon got on his radio and called in that some of his men were in bad shape and needed to rest a while longer. Trippitt rebuked him furiously before giving the company another half hour.

When the word was again passed to get ready to move out, a number of men had to be wakened from fatigue-induced sleep. A few minutes after resuming the march, they were just as exhausted as before the break, trudging forward in inattentive stupor. For another two hours they climbed steadily upward, watching for and seeing nothing but the heels of the men in front of them. Suddenly — the one thing that could have had any effect on them — a thunderous burst of rifle fire rang out from the front of the column. Not even this completely brought them back to their senses. Without bothering to take cover, they merely dropped to the ground, thankful for the unexpected respite and heedless of any danger.

Kramer got word over his radio that First Platoon had surprised five VC at the mouth of a cave. They had gotten two confirmed kills and had probably wounded some of the others. "Big fucking deal, that makes my day," he mumbled under his breath, purposely loud enough for Milton to hear. Handing the receiver back, he looked over his exhausted men. 'At least they're just as fagged out as I am. We'll be in great shape if we get ambushed.'

He heard Trippitt's excited voice. "Kramer!"

Standing, he saw the captain's grinning face searching him out. "Yes, sir."

"Get this platoon moving. I wanna see what we've got."

Kramer issued the command in an unconcerned tone. "Move-out."

As they approached the cave, Chalice was the third man from the front of the platoon. Some members of First Platoon came into view as he made his way up the rocky slope. Nearing them, he could see that they were standing over the contorted, black-clad bodies of two Viet Cong — 'The first dead I've seen so far,' he thought. Chalice found himself drawn closer by a morbid curiosity, at the same time conscious of an aura of guilt enveloping him, not about the killing, but about the callousness of his curiosity.

The bodies lay side-by-side on their backs, in opposite directions. The nearer one was of a young boy, probably not even eighteen. One of his hands stretched out towards Chalice, palm up. The other hand lay across his blood-soaked chest, fingers apart with the blood drying between them. 'Shot in the chest, two holes, at least two . . . God! Look at his mouth. Look at it!' The boy's head was tilted as far back as it could go. His hair nearly reached his tightly shut eyes, and his mouth was wide open. A row of perfectly formed upper teeth was almost entirely visible. Chalice couldn't take his eyes off the boy's mouth. 'As if his life, his whole life, escaped from inside him through his throat in one long scream.' A series of hideous cries echoed through Chalice's mind, none of them even closely matching the horror on the boy's contorted face.

The rest of the platoon made their way up the trail and gathered around the corpses. Nudged by men in back of him trying to get a better look, Chalice decided to walk away. Instead, he moved closer to the other body. Its face, almost covered by unbelievably long blood-matted hair, appeared older than the first. The black Viet Cong shirt, spread open down to the waist, revealed a flabby chest. One of its pants legs was rolled up above the knee. Chalice stared at the skinny leg thus exposed. "It's a woman," someone said. 'My God! It is a woman,' Chalice thought. 'The hair, of course, the hair, and it's a woman's breast.'

Appleton placed the barrel of his rifle just above her crotch. "Get some, Ramirez. It's still warm."

There was some laughter. Chalice glanced up at the men around him. Shocked to see smiles on most of their faces, he suddenly became conscious of the smile on his own face. 'Why the fuck am I standing here?' he thought, making no effort to move away.

Kovacs took a quick look at the corpses. "C'mon, break it up. You guys have seen dead bodies before." Chalice withdrew before Kovacs had finished. Once more he glanced back. A few of the men still stood around the bodies, seemingly transfixed by the mystery the dead hold over the living.

First Platoon was scattered to one side of the caves trying to follow two blood trails and at the same time searching the brush. Trippitt stood next to the company radioman, his lips wet with excitement. Kramer, conscious of the captain's presence, arranged his men in a half circle to provide security for the CP. Not wanting to waste any time, Trippitt ordered Third and Fourth Platoons to continue marching up the mountains. Just before the last man of Fourth Platoon passed by, he told Kramer to have his men follow them. The CP placed itself in the middle of Second Platoon as Trippitt ordered the commander of First Platoon to call his men in and take up the tail end.

The point platoon used the danger of an ambush as an excuse to slacken the pace. Trippitt, gratified by the day's work, didn't bother to speed them up. By late afternoon the slower pace had made little difference; the men were completely exhausted. The good fortune of finding themselves on an exceptionally large plateau, rather than anyone's concern over the condition of the men, enabled the company to set-in somewhat earlier than had been planned. Gunny Martin delineated the perimeter and assigned each platoon's responsibility. He also told the platoon commanders to report to the CP in forty minutes.

Kovacs had seen to the placement of the foxholes. Kramer, relieved of his pack and lying with his back against a rock, watched his men dig in. Fatigued by the march, thinking no farther ahead than to the approaching night and its promise of sleep, he was in a placid, almost fulfilled, state of mind, grudgingly admitting to himself that Trippitt's performance had been impressive. Throughout the day he had always seemed in command of the situations that arose — never wasting words and always impelling the desired results. Although he had driven the men hard, they weren't asked to do anything he hadn't done. Yet still Kramer wondered, considering the jaded condition of the company, what the results of an ambush along the trail would have been.

He got up and made his way to the center of the perimeter. Not finding the CP there, he continued across until he located them just inside the far positions. They had set up in an area pockmarked with small bomb craters, eliminating the need for digging foxholes. Trippitt and Martin were heating their chow in canteen cups, the other platoon commanders sitting around them. Lieutenant Forest said in a loud drawl, "That was a smart idea, Skipper, bringing long-rations. These C-rats sure get heavy."

"I tried to get them for the whole company, but they said there wasn't enough. No reason why some of us shouldn't have them."

"No, no sir, not at all," Forest agreed.

'No reason my ass,' thought Kramer. 'Only the best for the CP.'

Trippitt noticed Kramer. "Let's get started." He pulled a map out of his flak jacket pocket and spread it on the ground. The platoon commanders gathered around. "We're here right now," he said, pointing with his stocky index finger. Kramer was surprised to see that the nail was bitten to the quick.

"We're going to split up tomorrow," Trippitt continued. "Forest, I want your platoon to move out at dawn. Follow the stream bed for half a klick, then bear left up this hill, here. Go right to the top of it and back down. Do the same thing with these other two hills that overlook the stream bed. You'll be security for the column. Set-in on the last one. Kramer, I want you to do the same thing on the right. Set up on this fourth hill, here. Write down the coordinates. That way you and Forest will be overlooking the trail from opposite sides. I'll be traveling up the stream bed with the rest of the company. When I pass between you two, you'll peel off and follow us. We'll make camp about two klicks higher up."

Kramer noticed that the last hill Trippitt pointed to had another, lower one, between it and the trail. Not seeing any reason why they should have to climb the higher hill, he pointed to the map and asked, "Sir, you want us to climb *this* hill?"

Trippitt, feeling he had made himself perfectly clear, answered gruffly, "That's what I said, Lieutenant."

The captain gave each platoon commander the coordinates for their night's ambush before sending them back to their sectors. On the way, Kramer thought about the CP carrying long-rations while the rest of the company had to carry C-rations. It bothered him more and more as he thought about it, even though he realized that his anger stemmed as much from his dislike for Trippitt as from the fact itself.

Upon reaching their foxhole, Kramer took out his map and began explaining the next day's plan to Kovacs. When he finished, Kovacs picked up the map and tried to match it with the terrain in front of them. "Why the hell do we have to set up on that last hill? We won't even be able to see the stream bed from there."

"That's the way I see it," Kramer answered disgustedly.

"The hill right next to it is only half as high and gives the column better security."

"I know, but that's the way Trippitt wants it, so that's the way we'll do it."

For most of the men dawn came too quickly. Even before they were able to get to their feet, the soreness in their bodies reminded them of the previous day's march and forewarned them of what was to follow. Within a half hour after dawn, Second Platoon had filled in its foxholes and started moving out. The first few minutes of marching drove the early morning chill from their bodies. They reached the stream bed as Forest's platoon started up it. Kramer's men fell in behind.

The two platoons split off the trail at the same place. Charlie Squad had Second Platoon's point with Ramirez as the lead man and Valdez right behind him. Ramirez became vexed when he saw the thick brush that covered the hill. Without looking back towards Valdez, he angled off along the base, searching for some semblance of a trail. They moved a third of the way around the hill before Valdez, who was just as perplexed by the thought of breaking a trail, finally stopped him. "C'mon, let's start up."

"I'm looking for a trail."

"No shit, but you ain't gonna find one. Let's get it over with."

Mumbling under his breath, Ramirez started up. He plowed ahead by kicking up his knees as far as they would go, then leaning forward on them to push the brush down until his foot hit the ground. He bulled his way upward for twenty minutes before looking back to see the last few men in the column still at the base of the hill. "Madre Dios," he mumbled to himself. "Not even a fourth the way up yet." Realizing that stopping was the worst thing to do, he quickly started pushing his way forward again. The brush was just over waist high, and his short legs made each step more strenuous. 'All the same, same shit all the way up.' He received some comfort from the sound of Valdez's heavy breathing behind him. 'He is taller, but just as tired. I hump as good as any of them.'

The undergrowth sprung back as each man passed over it, giving little advantage to those towards the rear of the column. The newer men continued to make the mistake of looking up or back in order to determine their progress. The more experienced men kept staring at the ground a few feet in front of them, occasionally glancing warily to the sides or up at the sun. To them it was more of a fight against the sun than against the terrain. They knew that the higher the sun, the more intense the heat. Their

176

thoughts centered around getting as far as possible before noon because every step afterwards would be many times harder.

Kramer radioed ahead to hold up at the summit. When Ramirez finally reached it an hour and a half later, he looked around for the tallest bush and sprawled out in what little shade it offered. The others joined him, forming a circle around the top of the hill. Kramer, Kovacs, Milton, and Preston sat down in its center. Milton took a long drink from one of his canteens. "Humping this radio sure is a motherfucker."

Kramer turned his head towards him. "Call the CP. Tell 'em we're at check point one. . . . What time is it?" he asked rather than taking the trouble to look at his watch.

"Nine forty-five."

"Tell the men to take fifteen."

After a few minutes, Kovacs stood up and looked toward the next hill. "The next sonofabitch is even higher."

At first Preston didn't know what he meant. "Next sonofabitch? Oh, the next hill. *Sonofabitch*, it sure is."

Kramer looked at his watch. 'Five after ten. . . . Fuck it. A few more minutes. Nobody'll complain about that.'

When they moved out, Valdez switched Redstone, a full-blooded Kiowa, to the point. His reddish brown skin stretched tautly over his muscular frame as he moved through the brush with the same light grace that never failed to impress the other members of the platoon. Reserved but not unfriendly, he was liked by most of the men though not particularly close with any of them. Like most Indians in the Marine Corps, his nickname was Chief and he seemed to take a lot of pride in it.

As Redstone led the way down the opposite side of the hill, he continually looked back to make sure the pace he set wasn't too fast or slow. Although moving downhill is a welcome relief in itself, he knew that it could be made even easier by allowing the men to keep just the right momentum — letting the slope of the hill set the pace so they wouldn't have to worry about keeping up or slowing themselves down. The quick trip to the bottom left many of them with the same thought — 'Same distance, same brush, quite a difference.'

The lower part of the next hill was covered with a similar type of undergrowth. As the column made its way to the top, the terrain became rockier and the brush sparser. The frequent need to overcome obstacles changed the slow, steady pace to one of spurts and short waits. Once, after climbing atop a huge boulder, Redstone was faced with a chasm twenty feet deep between himself and the rocks in front of him. He quickly checked both sides for an alternate route. Not finding one, he decided to make his way across using the numerous tree limbs overhead. Hanging from the strongest limb, he moved hand over hand for a few feet until he reached a maze of other limbs that he could stand on while still grasping the one above. Valdez hesitantly followed his example complaining, "Chief, from now on let's keep this shit down to a minimum. I ain't no monkey."

It was twelve o'clock before the platoon reached the summit. Milton called in and gave Kramer the message that the CP was moving out soon. Hearing this, Kovacs commented, "That's just fucking lovely. I hope they had a nice time sitting on their asses while we were playing Tarzan up here."

"Yeah," Milton agreed, "and I guess they'll have just as nice a time walking up that stream bed while we climb every mountain in Nam."

As they started back down the hill, the last few clouds in the sky disappeared over the horizon and the sun besieged them with an intense white heat. A large stream ran along the base of the hill. Kramer passed word to stop and fill canteens. The men did so sitting down immersed to their necks in the cool, clear water — letting the swift current rush over their sweat-soaked bodies. The unexpected relief was enough to momentarily buoy their spirits and make them forget the exertion they had undergone or that which was to follow.

Once started again, the effects of their respite soon wore off. Halfway up the next hill Kramer noticed a blotch of fresh blood on the trail. Ten yards further he noticed some more on the leaves of a bush. Kovacs, who was walking in front of him, pointed his rifle at another bush with blood on it. "Somebody up there must be having a period."

"Pass the word up to find out who's bleeding." Word came back that Chief had gashed his leg. "Tell him to step off the trail and wait for us." When they reached him, Redstone was standing expressionless, the bottom of his trouser leg soaked with blood. Kramer bent down and lifted it up exposing a three-inch gash. "Hold up the column. . . . Corpsman, up!"

Kovacs kneeled down to have a look. "Not real deep, but deep enough. How'd you manage that?"

"Sharp rock," Chief answered, as if bored by the whole incident.

Stoker, sweat pouring from his face, pushed his way past the men in front of him. Kovacs had rolled up Redstone's pants leg and Stoker saw the gash immediately. "God," he gasped, "how did you do that?"

Redstone made no effort to reply. "Cut it on a rock," Kovacs answered disdainfully, thinking, 'Oh, this turd's gonna be great. Wait'll he sees somebody really get messed-up.'

Stoker fumbled with the bandage as he wrapped it around Redstone's shin. Kramer was watching the bored expression on Chief's face with

178

amusement when Milton approached him. "It's the Skipper. He wants to know where we are."

"Tell him," Kramer said nonchalantly.

Milton relayed Trippitt's message. "He says to hurry up or we'll hold back the column."

"Tell him to kiss my ass. We're moving as fast as we can." Milton relayed Kramer's reply, omitting the first part.

"He says we've got to move faster."

Stoker finished bandaging Chief's leg and Kramer angrily ordered the men to move out.

Upon reaching the top of the hill, they started back down without stopping. Kramer couldn't keep from staring at the next summit. "That gung ho motherfucker," he mumbled audibly. "You don't see that dirty cocksucker busting his ass." Kramer sent word to quicken the pace; but realizing that he was taking his resentment out on his men, refrained from doing so again. When they finally reached the top, he threw his pack down in disgust and almost shouted at Milton, "Tell the CP we're at check point four."

Milton relayed Trippitt's reply. "The Skipper says he can't see us."

"Of course he can't. There's another hill in the way."

Again Milton gave Trippitt's reply. "He says that's because we're on the wrong hill."

"I'll be *goddamned* if we are." Kramer grabbed the receiver and spoke into it with obvious anger. "We're on the right hill. I've got the coordinates right here on my map."

There was a pause as Trippitt checked his own map. "You're supposed to be on the one bordering the trail."

"That is *not* the hill you assigned us."

Now Trippitt's voice was also angry. "You may be on the right hill, but you're not doing me any fucking good, so *get* there." There was a pause as Trippitt waited for a reply. "Is that clear?"

"Roger, over." Kramer answered in an emotionless tone. He handed Milton the receiver and yelled, "Get ready to move-out."

"Where to?" Kovacs asked.

"On top of that hill, there," Kramer answered pointing in the direction of the stream bed.

"A lot of fucking sweat for nothing," Preston remarked. "That hill would have been half as hard to climb in the first place."

The rocky, sparsely vegetated slope allowed the men to reach its bottom quickly. Once there, however, the brush towered above their heads. Denser than anything they'd encountered so far, it forced them to use the machetes. After each stroke the blades would spring back at them with almost the same force with which they had been swung. It was as if they weren't cutting through the brush, but pushing it ahead of them, each step increasing in difficulty. As the grade steepened upward, the brush became only slightly less dense.

All Kramer could think about was Trippitt. 'Anything's possible as long as he has somebody else to do it. That dumb motherfucker, can't even read a map. A captain in the glorious service of the United States of America and he can't even read a map.' The pace slowed almost to a standstill before they were halfway up. Realizing they'd been "busting their asses" because of somebody else's mistake, the men were enraged and cursed continuously. 'Never gonna reach the top at this pace,' thought Kramer. About to order them to move faster, he changed his mind. "Pass the word to go around to the other side and start heading down. We're up far enough."

The main column started passing by just after Second Platoon reached the stream bed. Kramer's eyes darted back and forth between their relaxed faces and those of his exhausted men. A hatred swelled within him; a hatred for Trippitt, for the senselessness of what they were doing, and for the men in the column — for the simple reason that today they'd been a little luckier than he or his men.

The company moved a few kilometers up the trail and set-in. Milton walked over to tell Kramer that the captain wanted to see the platoon commanders. He stood up thinking, 'Man, I wish they'd leave me out of their stupid games.' He reached the CP and sat down, carefully avoiding Trippitt's eyes.

"Tomorrow we'll move in a single column. We should reach the canopy by afternoon. Any questions?" There weren't any. "We're only sending out two ambushes tonight. The other two platoons will send out two listening posts each. First and Second Platoon have the ambushes." Trippitt noticed Kramer wince. "Something wrong, Lieutenant Kramer?"

Kramer hesitated for a few seconds, then, without looking up, spoke slowly in a calm voice. "First and Second Platoons had the worst of it today. I would think they'd get the listening posts instead of the ambushes."

Trippitt grinned and spoke in an overly sympathetic manner to make it obvious that he was toying with Kramer. "Nobody has it any easier than anybody else in this company, Mr. Kramer. It all evens out. But if you like, Third and Fourth Platoons can have the ambushes."

As Kramer nodded, Forest's fawning drawl cut in. "My platoon doesn't mind getting the ambush."

'I bet they're real proud of you,' thought Kramer.

"Okay," said Trippitt, "First and Third Platoons will take the ambushes. Gunny Martin has the coordinates. That's all."

Trippitt remained seated as the platoon commanders got up to leave. "Mr. Kramer, I'd like to talk to you a minute." Kramer turned and stared down at him. The captain slowly rose to his feet while returning the stare. "I've been getting the impression you don't like the way I run this company."

"What makes you say that, sir?"

"Your tone over the radio this afternoon for one."

"I'm not sure I understand what you mean, sir."

"I think you do. I can't be held responsible when you make mistakes like climbing the wrong hill."

Kramer started to protest, but — realizing Trippitt knew he had been wrong and was just toying with him — caught himself and said instead, "I was just thinking of my men, sir."

"Very good, Lieutenant. You should always think of your men. But you should also remember something else — mission over men. That'll be all."

"Yes, sir." Kramer walked away with a wry smile on his face. 'They've all got their little phrases, a phrase for every occasion. Mission over men, mission over men — gotta remember that.'

Again the company moved out shortly after dawn, Second Platoon on the tail end of the column. The trail running along the stream bed gradually widened and appeared more often used. While this gave the point more to worry about, it made things easier for the rest of the company. The sky had been continuously overcast and a light drizzle started around ten o'clock. The men greeted it with welcome relief, hoping it would continue all day. Around eleven o'clock Trippitt called a twenty minute break. The men sat in small groups eating cold C-rations, the rain dripping from their helmets. The mood was lighter than at any time since the operation had begun. When they finished eating, many of the men lay on their backs to let the rain drizzle upon their faces.

The sky cleared shortly after the company started moving again. But within an hour they reached the canopy, and huge trees completely blotted out the sun. The light that filtered through the leaves took on a relaxing green hue. As they proceeded farther into the canopy the air became heavy and damp, negating the advantage of shade. The thicker brush sometimes made the use of machetes necessary, but at other times the column was able to follow the remains of seldom-used paths.

Around four o'clock the company suddenly halted. They had just taken a break an hour before, and Kramer was puzzled by the delay. "Milton, keep your ear to the radio."

Milton overheard a conversation between Trippitt and one of the platoon commanders. "The point's got a wounded prisoner."

Kramer was surprised. "I didn't hear a shot."

"There wasn't any," Kovacs remarked.

In a few minutes the column started moving again. As they were marching, Milton handed Kramer the radio handset. "The Skipper wants to talk to you."

"C-2 here."

"Is your interpreter any good?"

"Pretty good."

"I've gotta use him."

"Should I send him up?"

"No, I'll wait till your platoon gets here."

When Kramer reached him, Trippitt halted the company. A wounded Viet Cong lay on his stomach at Trippitt's feet. His skin was a purple yellow color from loss of blood, and his pants were pulled halfway down his thighs, exposing a large wound on his buttocks where a hunk of flesh the size of a fist was missing. Already something less than human, he seemed to be waiting — like a flattened, run-over dog. Kramer took a step backwards, more from the stench of the wound than the sight of it. "Chalice, up," he called to the rear. A fading series of voices repeated, "Professor, up."

When Chalice reached the prisoner, he was still lying on his stomach, motionless except for the slow blinking of his visible eye. Trippitt told Chalice to find out how many others there were, and he kneeled down at the prisoner's head. Instead of answering him, the prisoner said in a weak voice, "*Chieu hoi, chieu hoi.*"

Trippitt interrupted irritably. "I know. You're a *chieu hoi*. Okay, okay."

Chalice asked the question again and got a barely audible answer. "He says he's alone."

"No fucking shit? How many *were* there?" Trippitt turned to Kramer. "Do you think he's one of those we wounded two days ago?"

"Probably," Kramer answered indifferently.

"Is that enough time for him to get those maggots?"

Kramer noticed for the first time that the wound was seething with maggots. "I don't know."

Chalice looked up at Trippitt. "I can't get anything out of him. He's in bad shape."

"I thought you were an interpreter. If I'd wanted a corpsman, I would have gotten one." He turned to Kramer. "No way we can get a medivac chopper through this canopy."

182

Kramer made no reply. 'Who's he kidding? He wouldn't call in a medivac anyway.'

"We can't take him with us. He'd never make it, lost too much blood." Trippitt paused, but Kramer remained silent. "They probably left him to slow us down." Kramer knew what Trippitt was thinking, but he refused to abet him. Trippitt told his radioman to pass the word to move out. When the men in front of Kramer started moving, Trippitt motioned for him and the company radioman to follow. As Kramer started walking, he stared over his shoulder at the prisoner, still motionless except for his slowly blinking eye.

Trippitt stood calmly as the last few men in the column passed by him. Kramer continued to march without looking back, placing one foot carefully in front of the other, ready to flinch. He waited anxiously for the sound, each step making it less likely, though he knew it would come, thinking, 'What difference — Maybe I could, if I turned' — and it did come, the sound of a .45, but louder, much louder, and he thought, 'Out of my hands.' A few seconds later Trippitt caught up with his radioman. Kramer didn't look back as he heard the order to halt the column being radioed ahead.

The company made camp a half hour before dusk. The canopy hid the sunset, gradually blending day into night. Darkness caught the men unawares, even before they had finished digging their foxholes.

Kramer sat by himself, knowing he should be trying to get some sleep. The picture of the wounded Viet Cong — the slowly blinking eye — refused to leave him. He'd made no attempt to stop Trippitt, hadn't even said a word. 'Why?' And why did it bother him *now*, now that it was too late, 'I could have — *What difference does it make?*' 'None,' Kramer told himself, 'not to me, anyway.' Why *should* it make any difference? Why should he place any more value upon someone else's life than he placed upon his own? 'The Gook probably would have died anyway. Just put him out of his misery.'

Kramer lay back on his poncho liner. Leaves ruffled above him, yet he felt no breeze. The canopy seemed to bring the heavens closer, diffusing the resplendence of a clear but hidden sky into a soft, eerie glow. Cathedral-like, it calmed him, its indifference offering a strange sense of safety. He saw it in his mind even after his eyes closed. Kramer slept well.

The next morning Trippitt was in an unusually good humor as he explained the day's plan. "We're gonna try and catch Charlie with his pants down." He pointed to their present position on the map. "Charlie usually follows us around to pick up shit-canned or lost food and ammo. Lieutenant Kramer," he looked up from the map at Kramer, "the rest of the company is going to travel along this ridge until we reach here to set-in for the night." He indicated a path parallel to the mountains that would take them no higher or lower than they now were. "Your platoon will stay set-in here all day. Be sure and keep out of sight. If Charlie comes scrounging around, you'll be ready for him. An hour after dawn you'll head down at a forty-five degree angle. We'll do the same." Trippitt pointed to a large plateau about five kilometers above the edge of the canopy. "We should be able to meet here by three o'clock. Write down the coordinates." Trippitt looked up at him as if they were sharing a private joke. Kramer gave no indication that he caught it. "It's important that we rendezvous by three o'clock. If we don't, we won't have enough time to get out from under this canopy by dusk. That'll mean no resupply." Trippitt's tone became more severe. "I understand some of the shitbirds in this company are out of chow already. We issued four days' rations per man. It was the job of you platoon commanders to see that your men brought it along. Obviously some of you were lax —"

Kramer cringed at Trippitt's remark. He himself had left much of his food behind. There was no way the men could have carried it all. 'Of course the sonofabitch had had the foresight to get long-rations for himself and the rest of the CP.'

" — Are there any questions?"

Kramer couldn't resist finding fault with the plan. As he spoke, he looked at the map rather than at Trippitt. "If Charlie knows we're here now — and I'm sure he does — isn't it going to be a little difficult to keep a whole platoon hidden? He might even notice that the main column is shorter than it should be."

Trippitt hesitated as he seriously considered Kramer's comment. Then, slapping his hand on his leg, he stood up and said, "Well, we'll give it a try anyway. Let's get ready to move-out."

Kramer walked back to his men and told them the plan. They seemed happy about getting to sit around for the day. Kramer was looking over the area for a good place to keep hidden when a member of the CP walked up to him. "The captain changed his mind. He says to keep a squad and send the rest of your platoon with the company."

Kramer's stomach tightened as the messenger walked away. He sought out Kovacs thinking, 'I really fucked myself this time.'

Kovacs took the news with surprise. "Charlie might show up now whether he thinks we're here or not. You better hope he doesn't."

"What squad should I take?"

"Alpha."

"How many men will that give me?"

"Tony's fire team with Forsythe, Chalice, and Payne; Hamilton's with Roads, Bolton, and Childs; plus Harmon, Milton, two men from Guns, a corpsman (better take Fields) — that's thirteen. I guess Preston'll go with you and I'll stay with the other two squads. Including yourself, that makes fifteen." Kovacs paused. "If you want, you can send Preston with Charlie and Bravo and keep me instead."

"Yeah, that'll be better. Tell the men."

When the company pulled out, some of the men in Alpha went back to sleep while others stood watch. Harmon saw Bolton furiously rummaging through his pack, and asked him what he was doing. Bolton answered disgustedly, "Before we left, I traded a spiced beef for some pound cake. I've got a can of peaches to make shortcake out of it, but I must of forgot it. . . . Pisses me off. I've been saving it for when I had some time to enjoy it."

A few minutes later Chalice was rummaging through his pack looking for something to eat, when he suddenly exclaimed, "I don't believe it. I can't be out of food. I know I brought more than I've eaten."

Hamilton offered to give Chalice some food, but when he looked in his own pack he found only a can of spaghetti. Bolton had overheard Chalice, and had thought nothing of it until Hamilton also complained of being short of food. He called over to him, "Did you eat that spiced beef I traded you?"

A look of realization came across Hamilton's face. He quickly emptied his pack while exclaiming loudly, "Sonofabitch! Sonofabitch! Those thievin', slant-eyed motherfuckers stole —"

"Quiet," Harmon cautioned, then checked his own pack and found some food missing. The other members of the squad began rummaging through their packs. Forsythe and Payne said they thought they might be short some food, but none of the other men seemed to be missing anything.

Sickened by the incident, Chalice mumbled to Hamilton, "I gave them half my food, didn't trade it, *gave* it to them. But that wasn't enough. They had to steal some more out of my pack."

"We're doin' their dirty work, and they steal us blind," Bolton commented disgustedly.

Again Hamilton began to complain loudly, and he finally said, "I'd give anything to go back and find their throats slit by the VC."

Both Harmon and Tony 5 cautioned Hamilton to keep the noise down. He lowered his voice, but continued to curse the Arvins. Each slur brought words of agreement from the men around him. Chalice again realized how hungry he was; but he couldn't make himself ask anyone for food. It didn't seem right that he should eat the food somebody else had carried. Without being asked, Pablo gave him half a can of spaghetti.

Though the men remained irritated about having some of their food stolen, this did not completely prevent them from enjoying the first bearable day of the operation. They spent the rest of it sleeping and cleaning their rifles. At dusk Kramer divided them into only two watches so they would have more time to sleep. He took the last watch in his group for himself. When the preceding man came to wake him, he was already up. Kramer had been mulling over his situation and continued to do so during his watch. The night was chilly. Instead of getting used to it, he became colder and colder. His teeth chattered uncontrollably. In order to stop them, he began vocalizing his thoughts, actually mumbling to himself.

"Twenty-five years old and still playing soldiers. Worse than that, not playing. What the fuck am I doing here? Four years of college — an accounting degree — *that* fits: Nam, accounting; both ridiculous — figuring out how much money some jerk makes — no more absurd than anything else, more *obviously* absurd — accounting: the defining profession — symbol of Twentieth Century Man.

"Like to be able to think of one thing I'd change. . . . *What difference would it make?* . . . Least I don't fool myself — *bullshit*: what am I *doing* here? Playing for time my ass. No guts: can't blow my own brains out. Let the VC do it for me — walk around like a hero, die like a man; easy as getting up in the morning — the perfect solution: bullet in the head: the great simplifier: no second thoughts, no regrets . . . no time."

The thought of his own death relaxed him — brought no sense of fear, of anguish. To him it *was* a solution, and its existence — as would the existence of any solution — calmed him, slowed his mind. It was always a truth he could fall back on — a limit in a world of infinities, a door that could always be opened, irrevocably opened, enabling not escape to escape, but escape from escape.

He moved his head in a half circle to scan the area. A slight glow appeared in the east. Looking down at his watch he thought, 'Yeah, 'bout time for sunrise.'

Just before Kramer was going to wake the men, Kovacs sat up. They nodded to each other. "Do you want me to wake them?"

"Yeah, it's about time. The radio was acting up last night. Do you think it's because of the trees, or maybe the batteries?"

"Both, probably."

"I'll tell Milton to put a new battery in. Tell Payne to do the same."

Kovacs stood up and started waking the men. When he came to Payne, he kneeled down and shook him. "Okay, I'm up."

186

"Put a new battery in your radio."

"Yeah, okay. . . . Wait a minute! I don't have a radio."

"You what?"

"Bravo has it." The platoon had three radios. Milton kept his and the other two were rotated among the three squads.

"You dumb cocksucker! Didn't you get it back from them?"

"Nobody told me to."

"Oh, I forgot you wouldn't have enough brains to think of that yourself."

Kovacs stood up, Payne still looking at him. "It wasn't my fault."

Kovacs's foot flew into Payne's thigh with enough force to lift him up and knock him on his side. "*Sorry*, I guess it was *my* fault."

Kramer shook his head when he got the news. "I should have told him."

"Any other radioman would have known. He just didn't want to hump it."

"I should have made sure anyway. . . . Finding the company isn't gonna be easy." He turned to Milton. "Try a new battery."

"I just changed it last night."

"Was it working all right before you changed it?"

"I think so. It just seemed weak."

"Do you have another one?"

"No, I only brought one extra. Do you think we might be in some sort of a valley?"

Kramer pulled out his map and studied it. "We're practically on a plateau. We should be getting something."

"You can bet Payne doesn't have one." Kovacs turned to Harmon. "Tell Payne to get his ass over here." Payne walked towards them hesitantly. "No chance you've got a spare battery, is there?"

Payne's face lit up. "Yeah, I got one."

"Congratulations. Get it over here."

Milton put in the new battery as soon as it was brought over. "Well, at least now we know it's not the battery."

"Maybe it's the handset. Did you bring a spare?"

"Yes sir, already tried it."

"Keep fucking around with it. We're gonna stay here another hour anyway."

The hour went by slowly. When it had passed, Kovacs got the men on their feet; and he and Harmon put them in the order they wanted them. Before they moved out, Kramer checked with Milton again. "Anything yet?"

"Nothing."

"No use giving our position away with the whip antenna. Put on the tape." Milton broke down the long antenna and replaced it with the short one. "Pass the word to move-out."

They headed back down the mountains bearing forty-five degrees to their left. Bolton walked the point, his feet sinking deeply into the soft mulch of decaying leaves. Harmon walked behind him with the compass, calling out different objects for Bolton to guide on. Harmon had to concentrate. He couldn't see very far and it wasn't easy. 'Vectors,' he thought. 'Practice, it'll take practice.' Lost in concentration, Harmon was looking down at his compass when the damp heavy air exploded with bursts of rifle fire and the sucking sound of three loud TWAPS.

Harmon dove to the ground. Bolton flew backwards and crashed down upon him. A trace of black disappeared into the brush. Shoving Bolton's gangling leg out of his way, Harmon emptied a magazine at the fleeing Viet Cong. A second's silence brought a hollow gurgling sound. He squirmed around towards Bolton and turned him on his back. Wide, vacant eyes stared up at him. The gurgling sound became louder, interspersed with coughs. Blood, it had never seemed so red before, covered Bolton's chest, and a steady stream of it drooled from the corner of his mouth. Harmon ripped open his shirt as Bolton gave out an anguished moan. His body convulsed with hacking coughs, spitting blood into Harmon's face, wheezing, more blood bubbling from the wounds that ran across his chest in an almost straight line. The firing resumed as Harmon fumbled to take the plastic wrapping off his bandage. He pressed the dressing on one of the wounds. It was hopeless. "CORPSMAN UP! CORPSMAN UP!" he screamed above the rifle fire. But he had to keep trying. The plastic wrapper from the bandage lay at his knee. He grabbed it, then the cellophane off his cigarettes. "CORPSMAN UP! CORPSMAN UP!" The wounds had to be kept airtight. His blood-smeared hands refused to move fast enough. He tried futilely to hold all three makeshift bandages in place while Bolton convulsed with coughs and bullets flew inches over their bodies. "CORPSMAN UP! CORPSMAN UP!"

Somehow, Fields got the word to come forward. He scrambled frantically along the ground on his hands and knees. Just as he got past Chalice, he actually heard Harmon's yells for help. Instinctively, Fields shot to his feet. At the same instant a chicom grenade exploded a few inches from his ear, knocking him — limbs flying aimlessly — against a large tree. Chalice, firing blindly in the direction of the incoming rounds, felt a dull thud as Fields's helmet landed on top of his flak jacket. Another chicom exploded towards the head of the column, followed by one exploding harmlessly in the brush behind them.

188

There was silence.

The men on both sides of Chalice lay motionless. He slowly turned his head and saw Fields's lifeless body propped feet in the air against a tree. Chalice hesitated, hoping someone else would go over to it. No one did. He began to crawl over. A helmet lay in his path, one side crushed and peppered with holes. Chalice reached out and picked it up. His hand felt wet. He looked down at the helmet and saw his fingers pressing a large piece of scalp against its side. Fragments of skull and brain lay in the bottom of it. Chalice's nostrils filled with the stench of death, a stench that existed only in his mind. His stomach tightened in spasms as the helmet fell from his hand. Hamilton crawled over to what remained of Fields.

Kramer sat up, feeling helpless and inadequate. "Keep trying on that radio," he told Milton in an excited voice, at the same time thinking, 'Is anybody dead?' Seeing Kovacs already headed towards the front of the column, he called after him, "Find out if anybody's wounded."

Hamilton, kneeling next to Fields's body, shook his head as Kovacs rushed by. Ten yards further up, he came upon Harmon leaning over Bolton — a pair of stunned eyes staring down at a pair of vacant ones. Kovacs kneeled at Bolton's head. "Dead?" Harmon nodded. He noticed Harmon's blood-soaked clothes. "You hit?" Harmon shook his head. Kovacs placed his hand on Harmon's shoulder as he stood up. "We'll be getting out of here in a few seconds. Be ready." He headed back down the column checking for other casualties. As he approached Kramer, Milton was still trying to raise the company on the radio. "Fields and Bolton are finished, Roads and Childs got nicked by some shrapnel."

"Bolton too? I already saw Fields. Listen, I think we better get out of here right now."

"You *know* it."

Kramer suddenly remembered the bodies. "What about Fields and Bolton?"

"Better take 'em the way they are. No time now." Turning around, Kovacs told Payne, "Pass the word to get ready to move-out."

Hamilton and Chalice stripped Fields of his medical gear and passed it down the column. Roads rushed forward to help Harmon with Bolton, but when Harmon stood up he fell back down in pain. He hadn't realized a chicom had ripped off the heel of one of his boots, taking a hunk of flesh with it.

"*Move-out*, fast!" Kramer shouted.

Roads threw Bolton over his shoulder. Forsythe rushed past them to take the point. By the time Kovacs reached him, Harmon had made it to his feet and was limping slowly forward. Without stopping, Kovacs grabbed Harmon's arm and pulled it over his shoulder, half carrying him down the trail.

The squad had been moving at a frantic pace for ten minutes when Chalice, who was carrying Fields's legs, tripped. Jerked backwards, Hamilton fell down. Kramer tripped over Chalice, barely managing to keep his balance. As Chalice tried to get up, he again fell down. "Hold it up," Kramer called forward. "This should be far enough," he gasped to Kovacs, and they both dropped to their knees.

The entire squad sat exhausted, trying to catch their breaths. Kramer ordered security positions at both the front and rear of the column. Kovacs told Payne to cut down four saplings to use as stretcher poles. Roads sat emptying a canteen on his shoulder trying to wash away the excrement that had discharged on him from Bolton's corpse. Harmon limped over to the body with a poncho to wrap it in. Kramer and Kovacs looked over the map. "We're about here, and the rendezvous point is here." Kramer ran his finger between the two points. "This canopy is gonna make things harder, but we should be able to find our way. We'll keep angling off at forty-five degrees until we hit this stream here, then we'll try and figure out our position and a new heading from there. No point in sending up a flare now, is there?"

"Not much," Kovacs agreed. "Probably never make it through the canopy. . . . Charlie'd be the only one to see it."

"You think we're doing the right thing heading for the rendezvous point instead of straight down?"

"That's what I'd do. Most of the men ran out of chow last night. The bodies and Harmon will slow us down plenty if we try it by ourselves. . . . Getting a chopper in won't be any problem once we hit the company and get hold of a radio."

"*If* we hit the company," Kramer mumbled.

"They should be there."

"I hate to depend on Trippitt; besides, they might have heard the ambush."

"Sounds are tricky up here. Even if they heard it, they wouldn't be sure where it was coming from."

"We can get fucked no matter what we do. Better move-out as soon as we get the stretchers made."

Kramer stood watching as his men spread two ponchos on the ground and placed the poles on top of them. They worked with an almost detached quickness while folding the ponchos over the bodies and poles. Only now did Kramer grasp the reality of the deaths, the first of his men to die. He asked himself what he had done wrong, knowing there was nothing — feeling guilt and at the same time knowing he was free of it. He felt as if, in his own struggle for life or death or whatever he was struggling for or against, he had needlessly involved others, others who had died in his place, not by accident, but by his own hand.

The squad moved out at a fast pace. Roads took it upon himself to help Harmon. Forsythe walked the point, Childs using the compass to direct him. Although there was no trail, the compass needle led them along a surprisingly easy path. Forsythe was able to follow descending ridgelines most of the morning, only rarely leading the men uphill. At twelve o'clock Kramer halted the squad for a half hour break. He was looking at his map when Kovacs asked, "Any idea where we are?"

Kramer shook his head. "I'm hoping we'll hit that stream by three. It's only about four klicks from there."

Kovacs pointed to a place on the map. "I'd guess we're about here."

"I hope you're right. If you are, we should meet the company by five."

"There goes resupply."

"I know. Tell the men to save any food they've got."

"Doubt they have much. If they did, they'd be eating it now. I'll tell them anyway."

Soon after they started moving again, Forsythe had to use his machete to cut a path almost a kilometer in length. This slowed their pace considerably. An hour later he again had to use the machete. The blisters on his hands quickly burst, leaving them painfully raw. After a few minutes of practically no progress, Childs came forward to take the machete and the point. An hour of hacking through the brush exhausted him, so Forsythe called up Payne. Payne tired in a few minutes, and Childs noticed he was merely pushing his way forward without following any set course. After reminding him a few times, Childs gave up and again took the point himself. Forsythe called back for someone to spell them and Tony 5 came forward.

Tony's arms swung back and forth rhythmically as he slashed the brush. The pace increased considerably, never slackening. The undergrowth gradually thinned, making the use of the machete unnecessary. It continued that way for a couple of kilometers before again thickening. Tony never once looked back for relief, and Childs was amazed at his stamina. The only sign of fatigue was his switching of hands more often.

He was finally about to pass the machete to someone else when a faint sound caught his ear. A few moments later the other members of the squad also heard it. There had been very little talking, but now a steady murmur ran back and forth along the line — was it water or just the wind rushing through the trees? As the sound grew louder, Tony's strength returned. He used the machete ever more furiously than before. The sound continued to increase and the air took on a cool freshness not felt since the operation had begun. Finally, the machete sliced a large opening in the wall of brush revealing a crystal-clear stream slashing its way down to the valley.

Tony opened his hand to drop the machete. It peeled slowly away from his skin and fell to the ground. He kneeled and lowered his hands into the stream, moving his fingers as the soothing water rushed through them. Forsythe, Childs, and Payne did the same.

Childs asked Payne, "What the fuck are *you* doing?"

"My hands are sore."

"From what?"

As soon as Kramer reached the stream, he took out his map and studied it while the rest of the men dropped their packs and waded in. Kovacs saw him and walked back over, his body dripping with water. "Figure out where we are?"

"I think so. That fall back there makes it pretty easy." He pointed to a spot on the map.

"Not as far down as I thought we were."

"No, but we did a pretty good job considering. We're a little over four klicks above the company and about thirty degrees to the side. Let's see, we can follow the edge of this stream till we hit this ridge, follow it, cross this valley, and the next ridge will take us right there."

"How long do you think it will take?" Kovacs asked.

"Two, three hours."

"How much daylight we got left?"

Kramer checked his watch and shook his head. "Less than two hours. I dunno."

"We can't take a chance on approaching them in the dark, . . . not without a radio."

Roads walked up and said in his usual emotionless tone, "Harmon's burning up. Got somethin' for him?"

"Do you think it's from the wound? It didn't seem that bad."

"It's pretty swollen up now."

"Keep a damp cloth on his forehead. I'll check Fields's gear." He turned to Kovacs. "Guess that settles it. We'll camp here tonight."

For more than one reason, but mainly hunger, the men spent a restless night. When morning's first light filtered through the trees, most of them were already on their feet. They had stood shivering in those long moments before dawn waiting to light up their first smoke of the day. The only cigarettes left were Pablo's half pack of Luckies and a few Marlboros belonging to Kovacs. They lit one of each and passed them from hand to hand. Kovacs squeezed the last drag out of the Marlboro — half tobacco, half filter — and flicked it on the ground. He walked up to Kramer who was kneeling over Harmon. "How is he?"

"He'll be all right." Kramer stood up and walked away, Kovacs following him.

"Lieutenant, maybe I better take the point to make sure we get there." Kramer nodded. "Harmon's burning up."

"He is, eh. Wonder if it's just the wound."

"I don't know," Kramer answered in a depressed tone.

"I wouldn't sweat it, Lieutenant. I've been around Harmon a long time. He ain't gonna die from that wound — a round between the eyes, a mortar, sure; but not from that dinky wound."

"I can't see it either. I think we better have the men make a stretcher for him."

In a few minutes the stretcher was finished. No order to move out was given. When the men saw Kovacs put on his pack, they did the same; and when he started moving they followed him. Kramer watched his men divide up the extra gear without any haggling — a very unusual occurrence. He then realized that they couldn't very well argue about who was going to carry the stretchers. 'No matter how cheap life becomes, they don't lose their respect for the dead.'

Even though he didn't have to use the machete, Kovacs kept the pace fairly slow. The added danger of running into the rest of the company unexpectedly and of being shot by their own men made him especially wary. He'd survived this long. Either Charlie was going to "do the job" on him, or no one was.

Still, Kovacs was nervous, more nervous and for less reason than at any time during the last twelve and a half months. It wasn't his guts, reflexes, or cunning that worried him. They'd kept him alive so far, and he'd seen enough men die for lack of them. If that was all there was to it, he'd survive, he'd be the last man on earth. But that wasn't all. Chance stalked him and Kovacs knew it. Arbitrary, moody, capricious — she eyed him like a bitch. He could have been with the rest of the company, but he'd flaunted her, chosen to stay. That's what scared Kovacs about Vietnam. For the first time in his life, he was responsible for more than just himself. He risked his life for others, knowing that their pathetic luck might rub off on him. Wondering why he had volunteered to stay, he never even doubted he would make the same choice again. Chance was his worst enemy, and Kovacs knew it.

The men marched on tirelessly. Their hunger, contrary to exhausting them, kept their minds off the marching. A few hours later when Kovacs stopped for the first time, everyone thought they were just taking a break. He walked back down the line to Kramer. "Well?"

"Well what?"

"This is it."

"It is?" Kramer checked his watch. "Yeah, I guess that's about right. I hadn't realized we'd been humping that long." He pulled out his map to check the topography. "Yeah, this is definitely it. Nice work. I'd guess this plateau is about a hundred and sixty yards."

"We'll have to sweep it."

"Looks that way. There's the back edge." Kramer indicated it by jerking his head. "Let's start over there."

As they moved towards it, a heavy rain began to fall. The water collected on the leaves above them and fell in sheets and rivulets whenever the wind picked up. The short distance through the brush they were previously able to see was now cut in half. As soon as they reached the base of the plateau, Kovacs spotted a cave. The men backed up in a dangerously close group. Pointing to it with his rifle, he looked towards Kramer. "Better check it out." Before Kramer could answer, Childs — seeing a chance to get out of the rain — volunteered. "Watch out for friendlies," Kovacs warned.

Childs entered the cave while Kovacs covered him from its mouth. The rest of the men stood where they were. After a few minutes of waiting, they started to grumble. "What the hell's he doing in there?"

"Probably fell asleep."

"If I know Childs, he's looking for chow."

"Let him look. I've only eaten three crackers in the last two days."

Childs walked back to the men shaking his head. "Nothing?" Kramer asked.

"Uh, uh."

Kramer noticed Tony 5 trying to shield Harmon's stretcher from the rain. He asked Childs, "Is there another entrance?"

"A small one."

Kramer motioned towards the cave with his head. "Let's go in for a while."

The opening to the cave was rectangular — about three feet wide and four feet high. The cave itself was almost circular and about twenty feet in diameter. A small hole in the ceiling enabled a steady stream of rain to enter. The water dropped along some large rocks and ran out another opening at the base of the wall without draining onto the floor.

The men placed Harmon's stretcher in the rear, and those of the two corpses in front of the opening. After some shuffling around, they arranged themselves against the walls. "Running water, all the comforts of home," Forsythe joked.

"Charlie's home, not mine," Childs added.

"Is everybody out of chow?" Kramer asked.

Most of the men nodded their heads or answered "Yeah." Pablo looked through his pack. "I've got two crackers and some jelly."

Roads held up a small tin. "Peanut butter."

Kramer flipped a can into the center of the cave. "Fruitcake."

"Where's Fields's and Bolton's packs?" Kovacs asked. The men looked at each other with discomfort. Payne stood up and tossed a pack at Kovacs's feet.

"That's Fields's."

"Who's got Bolton's?" Kramer asked.

There was a pause, then Tony 5 said, "Left behind, I guess."

"That's great," Kovacs commented while searching through Fields's pack. Tossing two cans to the center, he said, "Fruit salad and date pudding." Pablo and Roads then tossed their food onto the center of the floor.

Kramer said, "We'll need a chef. Childs, I guess you're drafted."

Childs walked to the center of the cave. "It only hurts the first time."

"Not much food for thirteen men. See what you can do."

"Could be worse," Childs mumbled.

"How?" somebody asked.

"Could be fifteen." A few of the men looked around, but nobody was really shocked — nothing Childs could say would shock any of them. Besides, he was right.

Childs played around for a few minutes dividing up the food, but even *he* couldn't make it come out to more than a mouthful per man. By the time they were done the rain had let up a little and Kramer asked for a green pop-up — the proper signal to designate a position as containing friendlies. The men fumbled in their packs and came up with three red pop-ups — the signal to designate enemy in your area. As Tony 5 mentioned that Bolton had two in his pack, Chalice came up with a green star cluster. Kramer took it and Kovacs followed him out of the cave. They walked far enough away from the cave so as not to tell the Viet Cong exactly where they were. "Never get through the canopy," Kovacs commented. "If they aren't on this plateau, they'll never see it."

"Probably won't even see it if they are."

Kovacs took the top off of the aluminum tube and placed it on the bottom. He banged the bottom down hard on the palm of his hand. There was a loud swoosh followed by five green flares bouncing among the tree branches and falling back to the ground.

"Maybe. No harm done anyhow." Kovacs then noticed a large welt on Kramer's neck. "What's that?" he asked pointing to it.

Kramer touched the welt gently with his fingers. "Nothing. Got nicked in the ambush."

"Did Harmon eat that food?"

Kramer shook his head. "He was sleeping. Wasn't gonna wake him up for that."

"How is he?"

"His temperature might be down a little. I gave him some dope. We'll get him out okay. If the rest of the company doesn't show up today, we'll head back tomorrow. We should be able to make it in two days."

"Without any food?" Kovacs asked.

"What do you think?"

"Yeah, shouldn't be much of a sweat. With a little luck, we might even find some sort of fruit tree."

"That's pretty optimistic for you."

"I'm getting short. Just a couple more weeks. Living through over twelve months of this bullshit'll make an optimist out of anybody."

"Quite a confession."

"It ain't really true. I just can't see myself dying because of an empty stomach. Let Childs walk the point. That sonofabitch can smell food a mile away."

Kovacs took most of the squad on a sweep of the plateau. Kramer and Milton remained behind, each alternately staying with Harmon and guarding the mouth of the cave from a short distance away. The rest of the squad finally returned, soaking wet, without having seen any sign of the company. Staying inside the cave was risky enough, so Kramer decided not to add to the danger by building a fire. He placed two men on watch outside the cave. The rest of the squad took off their wet clothes and sat around naked, wrapped in their poncho liners. Childs — his sense of humor working overtime — started describing the most delicious meals he had ever eaten and was only stopped after numerous threats on his life. Milton sat fiddling with the radio. When Kramer asked him if he thought he could fix it, he replied, "Not a chance. Just fucking around." There were five cigarettes left, and it was decided that they'd be saved for special occasions. While Childs was cleaning his rifle, the bolt went home and smashed his thumb. Everyone, him excepted, agreed that this was a special occasion.

As the hours wore on, the men became moodier. Sinclaire commented that he was going to beat up every hippie in sight when he got back to the States. One or two of the men mumbled agreement. Not wanting to miss the opportunity, Childs mocked him in an exaggerated southern drawl. "Don't forget you won't have your M-16." Sinclaire answered with a diatribe against those "peace creeps back home." "Were you drafted?" Childs asked.

"No, I enlisted."

"Well, what the fuck are you complaining about? You got what you asked for."

Chalice kept waiting for the argument to end. Knowing that most of the squad probably sided with Sinclaire, he debated whether to get involved. Finally, more in hopes of ending some of the inane comments than anything else, he asked Sinclaire, "Do you think we should be in Vietnam?"

"Sure," answered Sinclaire, astonished at the stupidity of Chalice's question.

"Why?"

"To stop the Communists."

"To stop them from what?"

"From taking over this country."

"What the hell do you care?"

Chalice heard some mumblings of agreement, and Forsythe repeated the question. "Yeah, what the hell do *you* care?"

"We've gotta stop 'em somewhere, and I'd rather do it here than back home."

Childs stood up and slunk toward Sinclaire while making furtive glances around the cave, then asked in a loud whisper, "Do you mean to say that if they win here they're gonna get in their little boats and come take over the United States?"

"Hell yeah," Sinclaire answered with conviction.

Payne yelled out, "He's right, they'll push us as far as we let them."

Childs turned toward Payne and said in mock horror, "You mean they'll take over our whole country? Brooklyn? South Philly? Disneyland?"

Hamilton spoke up in an excited voice. "That's it! They're going through all this bullshit because they want Disneyland. If we don't stop them here, in ten years Mao will be riding the monorail."

The laughter encouraged Childs. "Mickey Mouse'll speak Chinese."

"You're making a joke out of this whole thing," Sinclaire protested.

"You're making a crusade out of it."

Kovacs spoke up in a poor imitation of Sinclaire's southern accent. "They don't want Disneyland. What they really want is our white women." Kovacs's remark brought quite a few laughs. Although it went unnoticed, one of them belonged to Roads.

Sinclaire started to say something, but thought better of it and remained

197

silent. Payne felt obligated to continue the argument. "What about the Geneva Convention?"

Chalice saw an opening. "What about it?"

"They double-crossed us. You can't trust 'em." Sinclaire and a few of the others voiced agreement.

"How?" Chalice asked.

"By starting the war."

"The Geneva Accords divided Vietnam into two parts, but they also provided for a national election in 1964. We knew we'd lose, so *we* double-crossed *them* and didn't hold it."

"We'd a won."

Tony 5 cut in, "C'mon Sinclaire, how many times have I heard you say all these fucking Gooks are Communists?

"We wouldn't a lost."

"*Bullshit!*" Chalice said. "We couldn't even win an election in South Vietnam."

"You sound like one a them protestors."

"I was," answered Chalice.

The men stared at him with surprise. "You shitting me, Professor?"

"You were a hippie?"

"Were you ever on the news?"

Chalice felt his admission had been a mistake. "I've been against this fucked-up war from the start. I had just as much right to make my opinion known as the people who favored it."

"What are you doing here instead of Canada?" Tony chided, more to make the irony of his position apparent than to personally embarrass him.

"I don't go for that flag-burning bullshit," Kovacs cut in contemptuously.

Seeing the futility of the discussion, Chalice became defensive and lost all desire to continue. "I never burned any flag. Besides, a flag's a piece of cloth. Nobody dies when you burn a flag."

This remark brought moans of disapproval from most of the men. But they also seemed tired of the subject and willing to let the discussion die when, breaking a short pause, Childs spoke out in general disgust. "Most of the protestors are assholes, but so are most of the guys in Nam. We're just dumber assholes." He received a few laughs and continued. "The Prof's right though, a flag's made out of the same stuff your underwear is."

"I can't see it that way," Kovacs commented in a tone more factual than argumentative.

Childs decided to take one more stab at getting in the last word. "C'mon Sarge, if one of those times you had the runs and were out of

198

shit-paper and looking around for something to use, if you just happened to see Old Glory lying around doing nothing, tell me you wouldn't use it."

Interested more in the argument as a contest than as a discussion, the men felt Childs had made a good point and most of them started laughing. Milton, who had been standing watch outside, walked back to find out what was happening. He arrived in time to see a few cans and rocks flying in Childs's direction. Kramer quickly quieted the men. As he did so, Harmon sat up. "What's going on?" he asked in a dazed voice.

"Nothing, everything's okay," Kramer answered. "How you feeling?"

"I'm all right, but it's awful hot in here." Kramer placed the back of his hand against Harmon's forehead. "I'm okay," he protested drawing his head away. He still had a fever, but it didn't seem any higher.

"Here, I've got some food for you." Kramer handed him his own and Harmon's portion. At first he refused, but then slowly ate it while Kramer searched through Fields's gear for some medicine to give him.

The men spent the rest of the day quietly withdrawn into themselves, waiting for the rest of the company to arrive. As dusk approached with no sign of them, they became more aware of their isolation and speculated about what might happen the next day. Darkness came more suddenly than it would have if they had been outside the cave. The only things that could be seen were the luminous dials on some of the wristwatches. Hunger made the men restless, and they could hear each other moving about. Every sound became more audible and what little talking occurred was done in eerie whispers.

Kramer had felt a headache coming on for a few minutes. It was a familiar, helpless feeling, and for some reason he hadn't undergone it since joining the Marine Corps. Now one side of his forehead throbbed unbearably while he lay with his forearm pressed tightly against it. His mind beset by numerous, unrelated thoughts, he tried to clear it in order to fall asleep. 'Would have to get one of these now. If I could only sleep, for just a minute, it'd go away.' The pain increased. He pressed harder against the side of his forehead. 'One bullet, one fucking bullet would cure this thing. Right above my eye. It'd feel so good, burn right through.'

Chalice sat watching the jerky movements of Childs's watch dial. Suddenly it disappeared. His eyes were wide open, searching for it in the darkness, while Tony 5's question repeatedly came to mind. 'What am I doing here?' He began to doubt whether he had ever really believed in his own or anybody else's activism, telling himself that at first he had, thus admitting to stupidity rather than hypocrisy, but no, he couldn't accept this either. It wasn't stupidity, at least not the idea. 'You have to look at it rationally,' he told himself. 'Special case — can't generalize.' He tried to

199

slow his thoughts in order to gain control over them. 'They just wouldn't listen,' he argued to himself, knowing that "they" couldn't have helped but listen. 'What more could we have done?'

Suddenly remembering something he had read, a seemingly irrelevant magazine article, Chalice tried to discover a connection between it and his thoughts. The article had been about a wolf, raised from a cub by a family in their home. Everytime the wolf was brought into the house and something had been rearranged, it would immediately freeze to a point, staring at the object that was out of place — a candlestick, a small ashtray. Now seeing the relevance, Chalice refused to accept it, very logically telling himself, 'You can't generalize. . . . We just tried to do too much.'

But again he found himself left with Tony's question. 'What am I doing here?' He wondered if he, alone and separated from those who believed as he did, would do more than "them," would someday write the book, reach the fools who seemed unreachable. Now he began to question this also, whether it had ever been more than an excuse, if fear of jail and gang rapes, or exile hadn't been more important, or maybe it was the desire to create something indestructible, something that wouldn't die with him. 'Sure, write a book . . . but *kill* in the meantime.'

Kramer had the second-to-last watch that night. Milton gently shook his shoulder. He sat up. No words passed between them. Unable to remember exactly how high the cave was, Kramer got to his feet slowly. Surrounded by darkness, he also wasn't sure where the entrance was. Remembering he had gone to sleep with his feet towards it, he moved in that direction taking short, wary steps to keep from tripping over anyone. Now he could barely make out the opening a few feet away. On his second step towards it, he fell hard across two of the men. They didn't move. For a few seconds he couldn't figure out why. He lay motionless on top of the corpses listening to his men squirm around, awakened by the sound of his fall. Drawing his legs up under him and over the corpses, he slowly rose to his feet and ducked out the entrance.

It was a little lighter outside, but not much. Kramer moved through the wet brush until he was about ten yards from the cave. There was no breeze, but the damp, chilly air still pierced through his clothing. 'Should of brought my poncho liner.' He then remembered the time Gunny Martin had caught Appleton standing watch wrapped in a poncho liner, and had bashed a rifle butt over his head. Kramer began to shiver, but decided it was too much trouble to go back for it now. He longed for a cigarette to warm his insides, knowing that if he ever caught any of his men smoking on watch he'd want to kill them. 'Can't believe the company didn't show,' he thought before deciding that they'd probably heard the ambush and had headed towards it. 'You'd think they would have sent at least one platoon here.' His thoughts turned to Trippitt — 'Sonofabitch can't read a map for shit,' but he knew that somebody in the company should have been able to lead them there. Kramer became conscious of the tightness in his stomach. The idea of a two day march to the lowlands without food worried him. Only the fear that another day of waiting would make it three days caused him to decide to start back in the morning. 'Maybe they'll spot us on the way down. Possible.'

Suddenly, the cold, quiet air was shattered by the roar of bombs and the screech of jets. Kramer spun around in the direction of the explosions. He watched with surprise as the soft glow of napalm filtered through the trees. More blasts and the sounds of more jets followed. 'Two, maybe three klicks away . . . Wonder what they're after.' The bombing continued for ten minutes. He checked the time. 'Kovacs has last watch. Should have woke him five minutes ago.' Kramer made his way back towards the cave. As he bent down to enter, he could barely make out the outline of a face staring up at him.

"Really going at it," Kovacs whispered. Muffled voices agreed from inside the cave.

Kramer stepped back as Kovacs made his way out. "The jets woke everybody up. Weren't getting much sleep anyway, not on those empty stomachs."

"What do you make of it?" Kramer asked.

"The bombing? Could mean anything. They don't have to see much to unload."

"I hope they *didn't* see much."

"I wouldn't sweat it. I was drinking with a few of them on my R and R and they were bragging about killing elephants, tigers, water buffaloes — they just like to drop bombs."

Kramer nodded from habit, Kovacs being unable to see him. "That's real nice to know. Listen, we'll get out of here as soon as we can tomorrow. Unless there was a foul-up, they wouldn't be dropping bombs if they knew we were anywhere near here. Make sure everybody's up at dawn. No use letting them sit around thinking about their stomachs."

As Kramer stooped to enter the cave, his nostrils caught the smell of decaying flesh. Nauseous tremors ran through his body. He quickly stepped over the corpses and made his way to the back of the cave. Instead of lying down, he propped his back against the wall and thought over his plans for the next day.

When Kovacs returned to the cave, most of the men were sitting up. "Lieutenant?"

"Over here."

"Daybreak."

"Okay," Kramer called out. "Let's get everybody and everything out of the cave." The men filed out dragging their equipment.

"Pablo, how many cigarettes we got left?" Kovacs asked.

"Two."

"Sunrise, special occasion. Let's run one," Forsythe suggested. Pablo lit a cigarette and the rest of the men stood around him shivering as they waited their turn.

When the last puff was squeezed out of it, Kramer, who had been giving some medicine to Harmon, turned towards the rest of the men. "We should be able to make it back in two days. I know you're hungry now and you'll be hungrier tomorrow, but we'll be moving fast enough to take your minds off your stomachs. Let's get rid of any extra weight. Empty your packs of everything except ponchos and poncho liners. Get your bayonets out and shred anything you leave behind. Dump your flak jackets too." Kramer looked toward Kovacs and received a nod of agreement. "That's fifteen pounds you won't have to worry about. We should be able to make it without hitting any booby traps. Childs, you'll be walking the point at first. You can keep yours if you want it."

"No thanks." Childs pulled off his flak jacket and started to cut it up.

"Sir, what about the mortar rounds?" Hamilton asked.

"Mortar rounds, you should have pawned those off on somebody that went with the company. They're worthless to us without tubes. How many of you have rounds?" Five hands went up. "Okay, we'll get rid of them and some C-4 to boot. Tony, when we get all this shit inside the cave, put those rounds in and set a charge under them. Use two blasting caps to make sure."

A few minutes later, Kramer told Childs to move out and Tony 5 to light the fuses. At first Childs's pace was as fast as the ones Bolton used to set. By the time they heard the charge go off he had slowed down a little, but not much. There were no complaints from the rest of the squad — hunger and the desire to get back to camp drove them on as fear never could. Childs's skill, or luck, enabled the squad to move over fairly easy terrain and kept them constantly traveling downhill. In an hour they reached the spot where the napalm had been dropped the night before. Nothing remained of the canopy except a huge oblong blotch of charred and smoldering tree trunks. Childs cut through it, keeping as close to the edge as possible. They were practically to the other side when Kramer held up the column. "Pass the word to take ten." Turning to Kovacs, he said, "We can shoot a pop-up over the canopy from here. It's a long chance, but maybe somebody'll see it."

"Good idea," Kovacs agreed.

"Think Charlie's around?"

"Doubt it. Haven't seen any bodies."

"Send up a red one. We'll head for the trees, wait five minutes, pop a smoke, wait another five, and beat it." By this time Kovacs had the pop-up ready. He banged the bottom, and a large red flare burst over the burned-out canopy.

As the men moved towards the edge of the brush, a gray object caught Hamilton's eye. "Hey, look at this."

Kovacs walked towards him with Kramer and Milton following. At Hamilton's feet lay an oddly shaped object that took each of them a few seconds to recognize. "Looks like they did get something," Kramer said slowly as he stared down at the charred remains of an upper torso. One arm was missing and the head was barely connected. "Where's the rest of him?" Kramer wondered out loud.

Kovacs pointed his rifle where the waist should have been. "Must have been wearing a belt of chicoms. Exploded when the napalm hit them. Probably around here somewhere — in more than one place." The tip of his rifle nudged the remains of the body and the ashes crumbled around it.

By this time the rest of the squad had all taken a look. Some of them were still standing around it and others were checking the brush when Childs's voice called out, "Here's the rest of him." The entire squad walked over and found Childs standing beside two barely connected legs. "This part's only medium rare."

"Smells like hamburger meat, don't it?" Sinclaire asked.

Childs raised his head slightly, his tongue protruding from his mouth for a second and his eyes shifting from side to side. Chalice, who was standing directly across from him, immediately realized what Childs was thinking. The others saw Chalice's blank expression and followed it to its object — Childs. No one said a word, but most of the others also realized what was going on in Childs's mind. They began thinking about it to themselves, some of them biting their lips and slowly rubbing their stomachs. "Why not?" Childs asked sneeringly.

Kovacs nodded agreement. Then Tony 5, who had just realized what was going on, stepped back. "Are you crazy? *No!*"

Pablo shook his head. "Uh, uh."

"I'm starved," Forsythe said demurely.

There was a pause, then Hamilton spoke. "I'm so hungry I'd eat anything."

Tony took a step backwards. "Not *that* hungry! . . . Just *two* lousy days — we can make it."

"Count me out," Payne said, his voice tinged with guilt for even thinking about it.

All faces slowly turned towards Kramer. He remained silent for a few seconds, then, as if to wash his hands of the matter, said, "It's up to you. Help yourselves if you want."

Childs dropped to his knees, pulling his knife out as he did so. Pablo, and then Tony 5 turned away. The rest of the men stood watching in silent awe as the blade of Childs's knife scraped the burnt crust away just above the front of one of the knees. He made two slashes a few inches long and an inch apart, then joined them and removed the piece.

Payne watched him carefully, while saying, "You shouldn't have cut it there. It'll be too tough."

Childs looked up with disgust. "You can have one of the wings." He then looked back down at the piece of meat while turning it over in his hand. Quickly lowering his head, he grabbed the end between his teeth. The blade cut off a small piece just below his lips. He pushed it into his mouth and slowly began to chew. The men watched, some smiling, all astonished. Childs started to nod as he chewed. "Damn tough, but not bad. Not bad at all."

"Let me try some," Kovacs commanded, while grabbing the meat away. Childs proffered the knife, and Kovacs quickly cut off a piece and started to chew. He also began to nod, then spoke with his mouth still full, "He's right. This ain't bad. Tough, but I've tasted tougher."

The others were now anxious to try some. They urged Childs to cut them pieces in excited, childlike voices. Some of them even giggled and Chalice began laughing madly, staggering about holding his sides. Unnoticed, he made his way to the other remains of the corpse. With a wild grin on his face and still laughing, he stuck his rifle barrel into the eye socket of the charred skull and ripped it away from the rest of the body. He staggered back to the group holding the rifle and skull over his head. A few of the men turned towards him with wild smiles on their faces. Chalice tried to speak, but he was laughing so hard he couldn't get the first word out.

Soon all of the men were gathered around Childs in a circle. Kramer had already fed some to Harmon without telling him what it was. Everyone was eating except Tony 5, Pablo, and Payne. The others continuously bugged them until Payne finally gave in. While he chewed, he found it

204

necessary to try to convince Tony 5 and Pablo to try some. After Payne had been at it for a while, Tony blurted out, "It's a sin."

This drew some disparaging sounds until Hamilton's voice rang out over them. With one arm and finger raised in the air, he quoted, "The Lord hath provideth." This brought some unsuccessfully muffled peals of laughter. Before it had ended, Chalice commented, "It's a sin to kill."

Saving Tony the necessity of thinking up a reply, Sinclaire cut in, "Not if you eat it. That's what my old man used to say. If you kill it, eat it. The bastard once made me eat a mole."

Hamilton recoiled at the thought, his face screwed up as if he had been sucking on a lemon. "*God*, how could anyone eat a mole?"

"How did it taste?" Pablo asked.

Sinclaire hesitated for a few seconds, then, looking at the piece of meat in his hand, he said, "Not as good as this."

Childs stopped carving and stared up at Tony. "Look at it this way, we didn't rape his wife."

Payne asked, "Would you eat a woman, Tony?"

In a nonchalant tone, Milton spoke for the first time. "I once had a pet duck, and I eat duck all the time."

Kovacs demanded another piece. Childs started to use the knife, then hesitated. "Light meat or dark?"

"Yellow, please."

Forsythe decided to raise the level of the conversation. "Who says man is basically bad? He's delicious. Just think how good he'd be with a little seasoning."

"Yeah," Chalice agreed, "if only the Hunger Artist had known about this." He hadn't expected anyone to catch his remark, but to his surprise Roads half smiled while nodding to him.

Kovacs said to Tony 5, "The Prof's really flipped his lid, now."

Childs wrapped a piece of meat in a leaf and started eating it. Sinclaire was baffled. "What the fuck you doing?"

"Tastes like lettuce. Besides, a balanced diet's gotta have green vegetables in it. Got chlorophyll — good for your breath."

"No shit. You haven't got anything for my armpits, do you?"

The men finished what Childs had cut and sat around quietly. Childs picked up the knife again. "Any of you guys want some more? Could be your last meal for two days." He had no takers.

"Maybe we oughta pack a lunch," Kovacs suggested. The only reason the men didn't react wildly, was because they were tired of laughing. Kramer pulled a red smoke grenade off of Milton's pack. He was just about to get up and throw it when five cracks from an AK-47 split the air.

Before the second shot, most of the men were already flat on the ground.

They lay motionless until Kramer shouted, "Get your gear and let's get out of here." He tossed the smoke grenade. A red cloud billowed down the slope, and Childs ran the squad along its edge. For over an hour they crashed through the brush at a frenzied pace — no thoughts of stopping or slowing down, only running — both away from and towards something. Hamilton and Chalice were carrying Fields's stretcher directly in front of Kramer. He watched them struggle with it as they ran, barely keeping their balance. Kramer knew the men couldn't keep up this pace for long. Just as he was about to order Childs to slacken it, the column slowed by itself. The reason for this was made clear by the sharp, hacking sound of Childs's machete.

The men bunched up and became frustrated by the slower pace, their feet moving up and down nervously. As the thicker brush enveloped them, the air became stiflingly heavy and sweat poured from their faces. A few of them struggled to get their canteens out and took long, greedy drinks. Vines and branches scraped against their faces, especially those of the men carrying stretchers. The further they went, the thicker the brush became. They took deep, forced breaths, seeming never able to get enough air in their lungs.

Childs used the machete viciously to attack the brush, which seemed to take on a sinister air — fighting back at him, blocking his path, sucking the air from his lungs. His arms weakened and he started to use his body more than the machete, pushing forward and letting his momentum clear a path with his chest. The brush finally stopped him — the machete at his side and his body leaning on and supported by the branches and vines in front of him. The men bunched up in back of Childs. Hamilton offered to take the machete, but Childs refused to give it to him. He stepped back and started using it again.

For during that instant when he had stood motionless, a familiar sound came to his ears unmuffled by the brush, the brush which stood between him and the sound — a sound that meant respite, comfort, and even pleasure; a sound that would break a path for and lead them to the lowlands — the sound of surging water. It quickly grew louder and every step seemed to promise the sight of it before his eyes, but no, it just increased with thunderous power — louder than it could possibly be, louder than the ocean itself. The noise of the machete and even his own breathing was muted by it. Then, with one powerful slash, the orange white light of the sun burst upon his face and left him blinded. His head jerked downward and away from it as his staggered steps left the brush behind — to his right a solid wall of rock, beneath his feet a ledge. His steps unconsciously lengthened. Then, as his stare moved from the ledge itself to its edge, he saw it — a hundred feet down and directly below him — a broad river of raging foam. He continued to walk, but with a dreamlike slowness, awed by the sight below. Finally, he stopped. The entire squad bunched along the ledge behind him — all of them staring numbly at the majestic violence of what lay beneath them. They put down the stretchers, and even Harmon sat up and leaned toward the edge. Each of them felt as if he were looking at something never before seen by man, and that no one besides himself could possibly be viewing it.

They were on a ledge thirty yards long and a few feet wide. To their left, a stream of cool, flowing crystal burst from within the canopy. To their right and above them, a slashing river of foam cascaded over the rocks and fell a hundred feet straight down, leaving a crystal-covered passage along the ledge. Directly beneath them, the two currents met in a violent whirlpool. Thus joined, they cut a winding, eddy-filled path between rock and foliage until finally reaching the now visible valley below.

The men stood transfixed, for how long none of them knew. Kramer felt a tap on his shoulder and turned to see Kovacs holding a star cluster. He gave an unconcerned nod. Kovacs sent it up, its swoosh muted by the thundering water. Five red flares soared above them. Kramer watched as they arched gracefully against the clear blue sky. He turned to Tony 5 and motioned with his head to pass the word to start again. Each man in turn picked up his ammo can, stretcher, or anything else he had laid down. They waited for Childs to start moving, their eyes still fastened on the river below. As Childs stepped between the sparkling curtain of water and the cliff, the strap on Chalice's ammo can broke. Jumping back to avoid having it land on his foot, Chalice lost his balance. He dived away from the edge, unconsciously pushing his end of Fields's stretcher over it. Hamilton, who was in front of him, still held fast; but as he let go with one hand so as to face the stretcher, Fields's mutilated corpse slid from beneath the poncho.

The men watched, motionless, faces reft of all save placid wonder, as the body moved, without falling, not even downward, merely hurtling away from them, farther and farther away, suddenly disappearing, tracelessly beneath the foam. They continued to stare — waiting, knowing that this was all they could or had to do. Finally, it surfaced and spun from the whirlpool. The river took it in its power; carrying it, like an insignificant piece of wood, between rocks and through eddies, spinning it furiously all the while like some compass needle gone wild — bearing it down towards the valley below.

BOOK TWO

And yet is not mankind itself, pushing on its blind way, driven by a dream of its greatness and its power upon the dark paths of excessive cruelty and excessive devotion? And what is the pursuit of truth, after all?

JOSEPH CONRAD, *Lord Jim*

1. Da Nang

Colonel Nash entered the officers' hootch on Hill 65 and saw a lone, motionless figure lying on one of the cots. He walked towards it, recognizing Kramer even though he lay with his forearm across his eyes. "A little late to be sleeping, isn't it?"

Kramer slowly sat up. "Not sleeping, sir. Just trying to get rid of a headache." Colonel Nash sat down facing Kramer on the adjacent cot. Even within the darkness of the hootch, Kramer had to squint as he nodded to the colonel. He lowered his eyes to the floor and shielded them with the palm of his hand. "What time *is* it, sir?"

"A little past eleven." Nash pointed to a bandage on the side of Kramer's neck. "What's that all about?"

Kramer pressed his hand gently against the bandage. "Caught a little shrapnel in the ambush."

"Still in there?"

"The Doc thinks he got it all out, but the swelling hasn't gone down yet. I may have to go to Da Nang to get it X-rayed."

"That's where I'm headed in a few minutes. . . . You didn't waste much time getting your first Heart, a cheap one at that. If you were an enlisted man, one more would get you a job in the rear. . . . But, two more and you've got a ticket home."

"I'd settle for that."

Nash's voice showed interest. "You would, eh?" Kramer made no reply. "I read your report. You're lucky. It could have been worse."

Kramer looked up with a wry smile on his face, then lowered his head again. "I was just thinking about that — two men dead and I'm lucky."

"They won't be your last."

"I don't imagine they will."

"You can count on it, especially where you're going."

"The Arizona?"

"You heard already?"

"Five minutes after I got off the chopper."

"Two days ago, the same day I told the company commanders. Word travels fast. I guess Charlie knew it before I did."

"When are we going in?"

"Thursday."

"Five more days."

"Four."

"That's right."

"I don't want to go in there minus any of my officers. Maybe you better go to Da Nang with me."

"One of my men's at First Med. I wouldn't mind checking on him."

"Harmon?" Kramer nodded. "I've got a Purple Heart for him. You can come with me. . . . What exactly happened with that chopper that spotted you?"

"He saw us when we were trying to get Fields's body from the river. It —"

"No, he saw you on the ledge. I heard him on the radio. He saw the body fall, only he didn't know the man was already dead."

"He was there then? I guess we couldn't hear him because of the falls. We didn't see him for another hour, not until we first saw the body again."

"That's right. He radioed-in that he lost sight of you when you climbed down from the ledge. He said he came in real low, but he couldn't get your attention."

"The trail at the base of the ledge was covered for about a klick. We knew the body had gone farther than that, so we didn't follow the edge of the river until the trail led us there. The body was a few hundred yards further down, caught between some rocks. Two of my men waded out to get it, but they slipped on the way back and it got loose. One of them almost drowned. We were getting him out when we spotted the chopper."

"That's when you sent up the red star cluster?"

"Yes sir, we were out of green. We'd already sent up one from the ledge."

"He saw both of them. He wasn't sure whether you were out of green or you were warning him to stay away."

"Is that why he took off and came back with the gun ships? We weren't even sure he saw us."

"No, that was another chopper. The first one had been looking for you for a long time. He was low on gas. You must have been pretty disgusted when you saw him leave."

"No, we were too busy trying to get the body. . . . We'd have made it down by ourselves."

"It took you another hour."

"Yes sir, we caught up with it two more times only to have it get away just before we reached it."

"I don't have to tell you there was no excuse for only taking one radio."

"No, sir."

"You still should have made contact with Trippitt at the rendezvous point."

"We couldn't get there until the day after."

"Trippitt says he waited."

"I *know* we were there. We couldn't have missed the whole company."

"By the time you got there, he'd sent one platoon down to the edge of the canopy to get the resupplies, and another one back up to look for you."

"If there was anybody —"

A corporal entered the hootch. "Sir, your chopper's ready." Nash stood up.

"If *anybody* was there, we would have seen them."

"Well, either you or Trippitt can't read a map."

"That's what *I* think."

"As it turned out, the extra day didn't make any difference anyway." A wry smile appeared on Kramer's face as Nash continued, "C'mon, let's get to the LZ."

Neither Kramer nor Nash spoke as they walked to the landing zone. A four-man helicopter was waiting on the pad, its engine running. The corporal jumped into the back seat and Kramer followed him. Nash sat in front. As the helicopter left the pad, Kramer took a quick glance out the window, then stared straight ahead.

He walked along the edge of the road, not to or from anywhere, just walking, making no progress, merely moving the distance between two points he neither knew nor was concerned about. Pablo walked towards him on the opposite side of the road — the person he wanted most to avoid. Pablo looked up, right through him. "Where you skatin' to, Professor?"

Chalice merely shook his head and kept walking, avoiding Pablo's eyes, thinking, 'Where *am* I going? Not skating,' and he wasn't. The one time he had actually anticipated going on a working party, hoping that the meaningless drudgery would dull his mind to blankness, this one time it had been canceled. Now he would have to remember, to think things out, to write them down.

He actually didn't know where he was going, at least not consciously. He knew he wanted to find a place where he could sit down, stop walking, where Pablo, where no one would be looking at him — to be alone. There was no conscious thought involved when he turned off the road, moved slowly between the ammo bunkers, found himself standing in front of the Buddhist shrine. "Yeah, I'll go inside it," he mumbled, as if chance had led him there.

Chalice sat down against one of the inner walls, hidden, alone — the physical state helping to make the mental state more bearable. His eyes scanned the geometric designs painted upon the walls. He liked the shrine. It was something apart and insulated from the rest of the hill. He felt calmer, glad he had come upon it.

Again his thoughts redrew the scene under the canopy. Comments that had been made repeated themselves randomly in his mind. They were funny, some of them; and for an instant a faint smile appeared on his lips. He saw himself sitting with the others around the burnt corpse. It all seemed less grotesque than before. But suddenly, a figure appeared, madly laughing, waving a rifle with a charred skull atop it: himself. Yes, this seemed, was grotesque.

The scene became less vivid, and Chalice's mind began to function rationally, as if the matter that concerned it was being absorbed by and carried along the very grooves of his brain. At first he made no attempt to penetrate the actions of the others, only his own actions. 'Why — What caused me to become a part, a willing part?' He tried to remember if he had been hungry. He recalled the dull pangs in his stomach as they stood outside the cave, his desire for a drag from the cigarette to stave them off. He was hungry then, undeniably; but that was the last time. There had been no thoughts about hunger as they rushed down the slope, no resentment about having to carry the stretcher, no sense that he was becoming weaker.

Childs's face appeared before him, looking up, the unseen knife in his hand. 'Why did he look at *me?* Why was I the first one to know his thoughts?' Chalice was sure that it never would have happened if Childs hadn't been there. But it had happened. He saw Kramer's impotent stare, waited for him to stop Childs, to say, "Are you crazy?" Instead he heard, "It's up to you. Help yourselves if you want." Yes, Chalice was sure Kramer could have stopped it. But he hadn't. It was up to somebody else. Kovacs demanded the flesh. They all respected him. Tony 5, he could have stopped it. He tried, protested — "Just two days." Chalice knew Tony was right. They all knew it — 'two days, could have made it even without a copter' — but Tony had stepped back, horrified, as he had said this. It was already too late. Pablo knew it — his eyes. He could see into their minds. It was too late. Still, Chalice remembered waiting for someone to stop it, to take

214

the knife away from Childs. Instead there were only hands, reaching out greedily, begging for flesh.

These same thoughts repeated themselves in Chalice's mind, but their force gradually lessened. He still asked himself, 'Why?' And while his own guilt continued to scare and bewilder him, a single question fought against this guilt. 'Could I have stopped them?' He derived both absolution and degradation from his answer — 'No!' It was true, undeniably; but what about himself? No one had made him reach for the flesh. Pablo — of course — refused. Tony 5 also. Even Payne hesitated. Chalice searched for an answer, never believing he would find one. Had he done it from fear — scared his refusal would isolate him? No, he was sure this wasn't the reason. He tried to recapture his thoughts, to see behind the wildly laughing jester he had been. 'Laughter? Why was I laughing?' Maybe the answer to this question would explain everything. He tried to picture himself madly waving the skull. It seemed even more pathetic now. Suddenly, the mad figure fused with the one now huddled against the wall of the temple. By trying to understand that figure, Chalice realized he had become him. Without consciously searching for a description, the word despair seemed to fix upon both of them. Chalice felt himself to be close to the truth. 'But despair over what?'

Searching for the cause, he felt a revulsion for the state itself. For the first time he realized that only he had waved the skull, only he now sat alone and brooding in the shrine. His own 'weakness' disgusted him. He refused to think about it anymore. Even now, when he had finally derived at least a scantling of sense from it, perhaps been on the verge of understanding, he willfully cast these thoughts from his mind, forced himself to stop.

He took the small, red notebook from his pocket. In an unsure hand he began to write, refusing to delve for meaning, telling himself he was still too close to it and now wasn't the time. He nervously thumbed through some earlier pages, remembering forgotten incidents, glad he had written them down, saying to himself, 'It's all here.' There had to be a pattern. Only by putting everything together into a book would he understand this pattern. He came to the pages he had just written, again seeing Childs with the knife. Chalice shook his head as he got to his feet and put the notebook back into his pocket. 'Who'd believe it? God, who the hell would believe it?'

Hamilton was walking towards the LZ when he spotted Childs leaning against an ammo bunker. Childs had his head down as he massaged the lump on his arm. He heard Hamilton's footsteps and looked up. "What have you got your fighting gear on for?"

"I'm going in to An Hoa."

"How'd you manage that?" Childs asked with disgust.

"I got a letter from my parents saying they haven't gotten my allotment for two months. Kramer's sending me to the paymaster to straighten things out."

"I don't wanna bring you down, but guess what I heard?"

"We're going into the Arizona," Hamilton said calmly.

A surprised look crossed Childs's face. "How'd you know?"

It was now Hamilton's turn to be surprised. "We are? Sonofabitch! I just said the worst thing I could think of. Are you sure?"

"One of the Gook chicks that works in the officers' mess told me."

"Maybe it's just a rumor," Hamilton said with relief.

"No chance. Remember how I found out a week ahead the last time?" Hamilton nodded. "Well she was the one that told me."

"It still might be a rumor."

"What difference does it make? The bad rumors always turn out right, and the good rumors always get forgotten."

"Well, at least I get to go to An Hoa for a day."

"Wish I was going with you. These fucked-up working parties are gonna drive me nuts. . . . Wait a minute! What do you say we go to Da Nang for some R and R?"

"How the fuck can we manage that?"

"Let's see." Childs paused as he began thinking to himself. "I got it! Don't check in at An Hoa. Go straight to the paymaster and get it taken care of right away. When we get back, you can say you had to stay over an extra day, and by the time you got through you couldn't get a chopper out. That'll give us tonight and tomorrow in Da Nang."

"Sounds good, but what if I do have to stay over in An Hoa?"

"We'll worry about that if it happens."

"Okay, but how are *you* gonna swing it?"

Childs paused for a few seconds, then said, "I just saw Kramer get on a chopper. That means Kovacs is in charge. I'll tell him the doc's sending me to Da Nang to get my leg X-rayed to see if there's any shrapnel in it."

"Kovacs knows it was just a scratch. Besides, he'll want to see your orders."

"Naw, even if he thinks I'm trying to skate, he'll let me go. He's only got a few more days in-country and he don't give a shit." Hamilton's expression indicated that he was having second thoughts. "What's the matter?"

"I don't know. . . . We're taking a big chance."

"Chance about what? Da Nang, baby, Da Nang — it'll be worth it."

"Okay, let's hurry up."

When Childs told him his story, Kovacs immediately became suspicious; and after staring at him for a few seconds, he was sure it was a lie. About to ask to see the orders, Kovacs realized that there wasn't much point in keeping Childs around just for the working parties. "You better be back as soon as you can. Now get the fuck out of here."

Hamilton and Childs reached An Hoa in less than an hour. They went directly to the paymaster without checking in at the company office. Within another hour they were on a helicopter headed for Da Nang. As soon as it landed, Hamilton became nervous. "What if the MP's ask for our orders?"

"Listen man, you keep walking around with that look on your face, and they sure as hell will."

"What look?"

"Man, you gotta walk around like you own this place. As long as you do, nobody'll bug you, I don't care if you're in VC pajamas with an AK slung across your shoulder."

Childs and Hamilton stashed their packs and other equipment in one of the barracks at the Ninth Motor Division, then hitched a ride into Da Nang on a supply truck. As they got closer to the center of town, the streets became clogged with old cars, motorcycles, and bicycles. The truck was hardly making any progress when Hamilton noticed young girls standing in practically every doorway. He flung open the door and started to jump out just as the truck lurched forward. Childs was barely able to grab him before he could fall to the street. "What the fuck you doing?"

Hamilton answered in an excited voice, "This place is loaded with syclo girls."

"Well, *no* shit. What did you expect?"

"C'mon, let's get out."

Childs turned to the driver. "You better let us out before my partner comes in his pants."

The truck stopped, and Hamilton was halfway out when he found himself staring at two sets of MP armbands. He casually spat on the street and slammed the door shut. The driver also saw the MP's and quickly accelerated the truck. "Man, that was close," Hamilton commented.

Childs said irritably, "If you can't keep that paranoid look off your face, we'll get picked up in two minutes."

The driver went another few blocks before letting them off right in front of a whorehouse. A young girl was standing in the doorway, and

Hamilton almost knocked her over on the way inside. "Will you please take it easy?" Childs begged him.

"I am, I am," Hamilton answered as he stared at the prostitute, his tongue running over his upper lip.

"You want boom-boom?" she asked with a smile.

"Yeah, yeah, boom-boom."

The prostitute coyly stuck out her hand. "Five dollar."

Hamilton fumbled in his pocket for the money as another prostitute came from the rear of the room and stood smiling in front of Childs. The shack was a crude combination of bamboo, cardboard, and thatch. A few carelessly placed candles provided the only light.

The girls led them to the rear of the shack where two cribs were separated from the rest of the room by cardboard partitions. As soon as she and Childs were alone, the girl began undressing, giggling as she did so. The musty smell of the crib nauseated Childs. He nervously began to undress as the girl slipped off the last of her clothing and sat down upon a thin mattress lying on the floor. She coyly motioned for him to finish undressing, and he became more nervous as she watched.

Childs hesitated as he stood naked staring down at her. Then, in one self-conscious motion, he practically dived on top of her. She gasped and tried to support him with her hands until she could catch her breath. For the first time, he became aware of the laughter and strenuous breathing coming from the other side of the partition. He lay motionless on top of the girl until he noticed her peering questioningly through his glasses.

Childs cleared his throat and started shifting his body around trying to enter her. She waited patiently for a few seconds before reaching down and helping him. He nodded his head to thank her, and she began to giggle. Now even more self-conscious, he again became aware of the laughter and heavy breathing coming from Hamilton's side of the partition.

Childs lay motionless until the girl started moving beneath him. Remembering what was expected of him, he also started to move. Sweat dripped down his forehead onto the lenses of his glasses. When he tried to wipe them, they fell on top of her. Her laughter stopped him from putting them back on.

They began again. After she had to replace him inside herself two more times, Childs decided to let her do most of the work. He soon became a dead weight on top of her. Still struggling beneath him, she finally realized he'd reached a climax and collapsed with a laugh. "You baby," she giggled as Childs scrambled off her.

Childs dressed hurriedly and walked out of the crib. He was waiting for

Hamilton to finish when the prostitute joined him. She tried to suppress a giggle as Childs shifted his glance away from her. Seeing this, he called out in an exasperated tone, "Hamilton, hurry up!"

The sounds from the other side of the partition stopped, and Hamilton asked with disbelief, "You're done *already?*"

"Yeah," Childs answered irritably, "why? — I mean I was horny."

"You *sure* must have been."

"I was. Now hurry up!"

A few minutes later, Hamilton came walking out with a big grin on his face. "That sure was good, wasn't it?"

"Yeah, let's get out of here."

"Sure man, but what's your hurry?"

"We ain't gonna be here very long, so we might as well make the most of it."

"That's exactly what I was doing, *exactly.*"

They emerged into the street to find it even more crowded than before. The air was tainted with the smells of automobile exhausts, raw sewage, and cooking food. The street seemed to be lined by two endless rows of bordellos, each with a young girl at the entrance beckoning them to enter. On numerous occasions, Childs had to grab Hamilton by the arm and drag him away. Young children continually approached them begging for handouts. A line of slowly moving cars clogged the street, many of them honking their horns. Motorcycles squeezed between and beside the cars, seemingly mocking their impotency. Bicycles were forced to move along the crude paths that served as sidewalks, doing so by weaving between the street vendors' wares that lined them. These wares ranged from goods stolen from American supplies to exotic-looking vegetables. More than once Hamilton was approached by teenagers offering to sell him *thuoc phim*, the Vietnamese words for marijuana. He'd shake his head and walk by, knowing that Childs had brought plenty. After ten minutes of trying to keep pace with Childs, he grabbed his arm and asked, "Hey, *where* are we going?"

"Let's see what's here. Maybe we'll find a bar."

"Who needs a bar? You brought some herb, didn't you? Let's run one now."

"Where?"

"Let's go in one of these whorehouses."

"We just got laid," Childs protested.

"So what? . . . Well, if you don't wanna get laid, we can just give them a buck to let us smoke there."

Hamilton stepped into the next whorehouse, and Childs followed. It was almost a replica of the previous one. The prostitute at the door immediately asked, "You want boom-boom?"

Hamilton pointed to Childs who was pulling a joint from his pocket. After a few seconds of pantomime, the girls accepted a dollar each and led them to one of the cribs. Childs was about to light the joint when he heard someone enter the shack and call out, "Mamasan, it's the tax collector." He stashed it just as an MP stuck his head inside the crib. "What the *fuck* you doing here?"

"Just getting laid," Hamilton answered nervously.

"You know damn well these whorehouses are off limits. Get the fuck out of here, and hurry up before I change my mind."

Hamilton scrambled to his feet and headed for the door, while Childs casually followed behind him.

"I'm doing you a favor. You might have got the black siff in here."

When they were outside, Hamilton said, "That was close. Those guys are usually real bastards."

"What the fuck are you talking about? He didn't impress me as anything *but* a bastard."

"He could of taken us in."

"Didn't you hear that taxman bullshit. He was just in a hurry to get laid."

Hamilton stopped walking. "Why that sonofabitch! Here he's got a skating job in Da Nang while we're busting our asses in the bush, and he can't even let us get laid."

"You mean smoke a joint."

"That's got nothing to do with it. . . . Let's go back."

"Are you crazy? What for?"

"To kick his ass."

"You sure as hell got fearless all of a sudden."

Hamilton's tone became even angrier. "I sure as hell wasn't scared of that pussy. It was the armband he was wearing."

"He's still wearing it."

"I don't give a shit. Let's go back. What can they do — send us to Nam?"

"Guess the brig's no worse than the Arizona."

Hamilton headed back towards the whorehouse at a fast walk. Bursting through the entrance, he went directly to the crib with the drawn curtains and flung them open. The startled MP lay naked between the girl's legs. He started to curse, but seeing the expression on Hamilton's face, cut himself short.

"You sonofabitch," Hamilton spit through his teeth.

220

"I —"

Hamilton took a step towards him. "You cocksuckin' sonofabitch."

Childs restrained him. "Wait, I got a better idea."

"Nothing could be better than beating him to a pulp."

The prostitute moved out of the way, and the MP faced Childs and Hamilton in a kneeling position. "Take it easy you guys. I'm just doing my job."

"Nice job you got there," Childs sneered. Hamilton began to walk forward. "Wait, I told you I got a better idea. Get his gun."

The MP reached for the pistol that lay on top of his clothes. Hamilton leaped forward, smashing his heel down on the MP's hand and picking up the pistol in the same motion. Holding it a few inches from the MP's face, he asked, "Okay, what's your idea?"

The MP inched backwards on his knees as Childs spoke. "Let's take his clothes."

Hamilton broke into a grin. "Yeah, get 'em."

As Childs gathered the clothes together, the MP pleaded, "C'mon, you guys. You can't do that to me. . . . I'm a Marine too."

Childs replied. "We're doing you a favor, *Marine*. You could of got the black siff in here."

"You're a skatin', chicken-shit sonofabitch," Hamilton cursed through his teeth before turning to Childs and saying, "Let's get out of here."

When Hamilton turned back towards the MP, he saw him getting to his feet and moving closer. Hamilton viciously kicked him backwards, then stomped on his balls. Incited by the MP's moans, Hamilton smashed his other foot down on his face, and was about to stomp him again when Childs jerked him away.

They ran down the street, Childs holding the bundle of clothes and Hamilton waving the pistol. Noticing people staring at him, Hamilton shoved the pistol into his belt. Childs began to tire. He spotted a garbage can and stuffed the clothes into it.

As they walked away, Hamilton said, "You know, that should of been funny; but I'm so pissed off at that sonofabitch, it isn't."

"I know what you mean. All they've got to do is stick an MP armband on those turds, and they've got an instant lifer. . . . It'll get funnier as we think about it."

It did get funnier. They wandered casually through the streets until the sky began to darken, then decided to look for a bar. They had completely forgotten about the MP when two more MP's rode by in a jeep. A third American sitting in the back seat wrapped in a kimono began to point wildly at them. The jeep driver attempted a U-turn only to end up stuck between a truck and a car. Hamilton and Childs ran into an alley. As they darted across the street at its opposite end, another jeep made a U-turn and followed them. They dashed down the sidewalk only to be cut off by this same jeep. Hamilton put his hands up, but Childs recognized the driver, a lanky, black Marine. *"Delaney!"*

They dove into the jeep and told him to get moving while explaining that the MP's were after them. The jeep shot backwards, then tore down the street. After Delaney had taken numerous corners on two wheels, Childs's nervous pleas finally got him to slow down. Delaney smiled as he said, "I thought it was you guys, especially when I saw you running."

"How the hell did you recognize us?" Hamilton asked.

"I recognized Childs. He's the only Marine in Nam that wears portholes for eye glasses."

"Bullshit," Childs replied. "What are you doing in Da Nang?"

"This is my job since I got my second Heart. I drive between here and An Hoa every few days — delivering mail, supplies, lifers."

Hamilton said with surprise, "I thought you got a real skating job."

"This is!"

"Hell, it may be skating compared to the bush, but traveling between here and An Hoa by jeep ain't such a sure thing."

"It is if you do it right. I always put myself one-third the way back from the front of the convoy."

"Childs picked up his second Heart a few days ago. He'll be skatin' the rest of his tour too."

"Serious?"

"Just a scratch," Childs answered.

"I almost forgot, what did the pigs want you for?"

By the time Childs finished telling him, Delaney had driven them to a cluster of shantytown bars. He also told them about a nearby Air Force barracks where they'd be able to sleep.

The sun had just gone down and most of the bars were still empty. Childs and Hamilton decided to enter the next bar they came upon, crowded or not. It was dark and empty except for five bar girls. Rhythm and Blues album covers nailed all over the walls did little to lighten the depressing atmosphere. The counter behind the bar had a number of candles on it. Hamilton excitedly read the names on the bottles of American liquor while repeating "Just like back in the world."

The bar girls seemed to be ignoring them. Childs finally called to one, "Hey Mamasan, you give me rum and Coke."

"Are you shittin' me?" Hamilton asked. "All this good American liquor and you order rum and Coke?"

"I can't tell the difference. I just wanna get drunk."

"Hey man, the reason you can't tell the difference is because you never *had* good liquor. . . . Mamasan, two Jack Daniels." The bar girl had ignored Childs, and now she ignored Hamilton. He jokingly banged his fist upon the bar and said, "Hey Mamasan, how 'bout a little service." She slowly walked over to them. Hamilton pointed to the Jack Daniels. She poured some of it into two large glasses, and was about to add Coke when Hamilton stopped her. "Mamasan! You know you'd get arrested in the States for polluting good liquor like that?" She gave no indication she understood all he had said, but she did bring over the straight liquor and asked for two dollars. Hamilton was practically drooling as she set the glasses down. "Man, this is the finest stuff you've ever tasted. Stick with me and you'll learn something about drinking."

Childs ran the liquor around the glass while saying, "I'm not used to drinking this stuff straight."

"Trust me, man, trust me. This stuff is just like honey. Let it glide down your throat *real* slow."

"I don't know about this," Childs said as he lifted the glass.

"Trust me. Just let it go down real slow."

Childs took the glass to his lips and tilted it hesitantly, finally letting a little of the liquor drip into his mouth. He immediately put the glass down, and his face screwed up in distaste as he shook his head from side to side, finally gasping, "That stuff's a little rough."

"What the *fuck* are you talking about? Poor Jack Daniels is probably turning over in his grave. You did it wrong. You gotta let it flow down your throat *real* slow." Hamilton lifted the glass and gave Childs a self-satisfied grin before slowly pouring the liquor down his throat. When the glass was almost empty, his mouth puffed up in disbelief. He made one final effort to swallow before spewing a mouthful of liquor over the bar. Gagging and gasping, Hamilton squirmed on his barstool trying to evade Childs's hand as it pounded him on the back. Still not sure he could keep from vomiting or that enough of his throat was left to speak, he finally rasped after a few choked attempts, "Man, I'd like to know how much they pay for those Jack Daniels labels. That's the raunchiest horse piss I've *ever* drunk."

Trying to keep a straight face, Childs waved off this explanation. "No, no man, you did it wrong. Let it go down *reeeeal* slow, like honey, like honey."

Hamilton noticed the bar girl looking angrily at them, and he quickly ordered two rum and Cokes. While they were drinking them, three black Marines entered the bar. They stood in the doorway staring at Hamilton and Childs before Hamilton noticed them and gave a friendly nod. It was returned by three unfriendly glares. They sat down at a table as far away from Childs and Hamilton as the room would allow. "What was that all about?" Hamilton asked.

"Hell if I care," Childs shrugged.

A bar girl immediately went over to the table. Before giving their orders, one of the men asked her a question and she shook her head. Hamilton picked up his drink and walked over to an old-fashioned jukebox in the corner of the room. When he came back, Childs asked, "What did you play?"

"Nothing. All that thing's got on it is soul music. I can't stand that shit."

More people started coming into the bar, usually in groups, all of them black, and always with hard stares for Childs and Hamilton. Aside from a few remarks such as, "What a friendly bunch of motherfuckers these guys are," Hamilton and Childs ignored the other men in the bar and simply stared straight ahead over the counter. Someone played the jukebox, and it stayed on continuously. Every few minutes someone else would make it louder until the music became deafening. All the tables filled, and every barstool except those on each side of Childs and Hamilton. Suddenly the plug to the jukebox was pulled. By the time the record wound to a stop, the bar was completely silent. Childs and Hamilton turned to see all the faces in the room focused upon them in hard, threatening stares. Both of them knew that whatever was going to happen would happen soon. They turned back to the bar.

"Let's beat it," Childs whispered out of the corner of his mouth.

Hamilton whispered back, "Fuck it, no! We've got as much right to be here as them."

A shrill whistle came from the back of the room. Others joined it, then more, until the entire bar seemed to be vibrating. Childs tapped Hamilton and said, "Let's go."

His words were muted, but Hamilton had seen his lips move and knew exactly what Childs must have said. He shook his head "no" while pressing his hand against the pistol he had stolen from the MP. But when Childs got up, Hamilton followed him out the door. The instant they passed through it, a burst of wild laughter cut short and replaced the whistling.

Childs walked down the street with an unconcerned look on his face, while Hamilton nervously smashed his fist into the palm of his hand. "Goddamn it! Didn't that piss you off?"

"Who the fuck cares? I saw the same thing happen to a splib in Okinawa."

"But . . . but it's the damn niggers that want it this way!"

224

Childs shrugged his shoulders. "So let them have it this way."

"I mean doesn't it piss you off? Don't you hate them?"

"There aren't many people I can stand. The splibs were just giving you the same bullshit they've been taking for years."

"*Yeah!*" Hamilton practically shouted, "but why should they do it to *me!*"

As they were walking, four black Marines approached from the opposite direction. Hamilton edged toward the street to give them room, but the nearest black went out of his way to brush against Childs. Hamilton became enraged. "See what I mean! Don't you hate those bastards?"

"Believe me, I've got no love for splibs; but I'd act the same way if I were them. I'm just glad I ain't. . . . If they bug you so much, stay away from them."

"I wish I could. I just fucking wish I could. . . . You know during all that segregation bullshit back home, my old man was on the school board. He had to take all kinds of shit from both sides. Everytime the phone rang, it'd be some red-neck calling him a nigger lover. We had to get an unlisted phone number. Even some of my friends started givin' me dirty looks. I was always taking up for the niggers, saying the same bullshit my father did. Look what it got me."

"What'd you think it would get you?"

"I mean I was nice to them. When one came out for the football team, I was the first guy to be friendly with him. I even got to be *good* friends with —"

"Double-date much?"

"Fuck you!"

"First you say you hate them, then you say you're good friends with —"

"*Now* I do. Honest, I didn't hate 'em then, but I sure do now."

"What about Delaney? If it wasn't for him, we'd probably be in the brig now."

"When they're alone, they're all right. It's when a few of 'em get together. . . . It's the ones that don't know you."

"Why get so uptight? Look, when they see some chuck they don't know, they just assume he's a bigot; and nine out of ten times they're right. . . . I'm a bigot myself. Just don't let it bug you."

They'd passed a number of bars, all of them deserted or crowded with blacks. As they approached another one, they could hear a hard rock record being played inside. A number of white Marines stood in front of the door. These Marines gave them friendly nods as they entered. The bar was crowded with men, none of them black; and the air inside was hot, humid, and smoky. It was a few minutes before they were finally able to

225

get seats at the bar. While they waited, a number of men introduced themselves and asked what unit they were from.

The relaxed atmosphere soon enabled Hamilton to forget what had happened. He and Childs were enjoying themselves when a chorus of "oohs" and "ahhs" came from the men in the bar. Childs and Hamilton were amused to see the cause — two MP's standing in the doorway. Then remembering their earlier encounter with the MP, they both became tense. The MP's scanned the room before heading straight for a bespectacled Marine of similar build to Childs. This made them more nervous; and as the MP's checked his pass, Hamilton debated to himself whether to ditch the pistol he'd stolen. He finally decided not to take the chance. After the MP's had talked to the man, they left without bothering anyone else. Hamilton turned to Childs and saw that he had removed his glasses, leaving two large, blanched circles around his eyes. While laughing at Childs's appearance, he said, "Wow, that was close."

"You ain't shittin' it was. Let's get out of here."

"Who's paranoid now? . . . They won't be back for a while. Besides, I wanna get drunk."

Before they could finish their drinks, two more MP's came in. They approached the same Marine with the same results. When they left, Hamilton walked over to him and then returned to Childs. "They're after us, all right," he whispered.

"That's what I thought. Let's get out of here."

"I guess we better."

They were walking towards the Air Force barracks when a Vietnamese teenager approached and tried to sell them what he called "moon juice." Childs said no, and started to walk away; but Hamilton called him back. "Wait, I heard about this stuff. It's supposed to be wild."

"What is it?"

"Cough syrup with speed in it."

"Where'd you get that bullshit. I don't know shit about drugs, but I know cough syrup is the opposite of speed."

"Not this stuff," Hamilton insisted. "I know a lot of guys that have tried it. Even Forsythe says it's speed, and he knows more about drugs than any pharmacist's mate in Nam."

Hamilton bought two bottles for a dollar apiece, and they continued on their way to the Air Force barracks. "What's this stuff supposed to do to you?" Childs asked.

"It makes you speed."

"Well *no* shit. . . . What the fuck is that supposed to mean?"

"Hell if I know. Grass is my limit."

226

"That's just fucking dandy. What are we supposed to do with it, stick it up our asses?"

"No, you drink it."

"Well, what are we waiting for?" Childs said as he uncapped the bottle.

In what seemed like a short time, they found themselves in front of the Air Force barracks. They told the sentry they were looking for a friend, and he allowed them to enter. Neither one of them was tired, so they just wandered around the area continually asking each other if they felt anything yet. Childs insisted that they'd been gypped, but Hamilton refused to admit it. Two men walked by, one of them saying that he was going to "hit the rack." Childs and Hamilton trailed him to a large, rectangular building. When he walked inside, they both stood awestruck at the doorway. "I don't believe it!" Hamilton gasped. "Did you ever see anything like this?

"Yeah, but it was a long, long time ago."

"I know what you mean — *beds*, just like back in the world, and mattresses too." Hamilton pressed down on a mattress with his hand. The person in the bed turned over, and Hamilton drew his hand away. "Soft, just like real mattresses."

"They *are* real, you idiot."

"I know, but I mean just like mattresses back in the world."

"It's almost like a hotel."

"I know," Hamilton agreed. "I didn't think they had barracks like this in Nam. . . . Hey, wait a minute! Maybe this is a generals' barracks."

"Don't be ridiculous. Look at all the beds. There aren't that many generals in Nam."

"Well then it must be an officers' barracks."

"It has to be," Childs agreed.

Hamilton walked down the darkened aisle as if he were in a trance. He kept mumbling to Childs until a sleepy voice told him to shut up. The aisle ended at a door, and Hamilton stopped in front of it. "What's that?" Childs asked.

"A door."

"A door to what, stupid?"

"How am I supposed to know?"

"Well open it, you jerk."

"All right, take it easy." Hamilton pushed the door open and they were both blinded by a bright light. When they turned their heads back towards the door, they could see that it opened into a large bathroom. "Look, real sinks!" Hamilton gasped.

"And mirrors!"

Someone yelled for them to close the door, so they entered the bathroom. Hamilton stuck his head into an open passageway before saying, "Look, showers, indoor showers."

They walked around the bathroom in wonder, as if they were inside an elegant palace. Soon an Airman entered with a shaving kit. He nodded to them before walking over to a sink to wash his face. They drew closer and stood on both sides of him as he began to shave. Finally, Hamilton said, "Nice place you got here."

The Airman stared at him questioningly. "Huh?"

Childs cut in, "What rank are you?"

"Airman second class."

"You mean this is an enlisted man's barracks?" Childs asked.

"Sure," the Airman said with surprise. "You don't see any air-conditioners, do you?"

"Air-conditioners!" they both repeated.

"Hey, are you guys speeding?"

Both Childs and Hamilton straightened up and shook their heads. "No," Hamilton answered. "Why'd you ask?"

"Your eyes for one."

Hamilton leaned towards the mirror. "Holy shit," he mumbled before straightening up and adding, "They always look like that."

"Oh yeah, I can imagine."

Hamilton and Childs stayed in the bathroom for over two hours anxiously questioning each Airman that wandered in. Finally, after they had been alone for a long time, Childs remarked, "Man, this is ridiculous. Here we've got a chance to sleep in real beds, and instead we're hanging around a bathroom like a bunch of perverts."

"Hey, that's right," Hamilton agreed.

They left the bathroom and wandered down the aisle of the barracks until they found two empty, adjacent beds. As they undressed and got into them, they each said, "Just like back in the world," at least three times. They lay silent for what seemed like an hour before Hamilton sat up and asked, "Hey Childs, are you asleep?"

"Yeah," Childs answered in a wide-awake voice.

"Bullshit."

"What'd you ask for if you weren't gonna believe me?"

"How the hell did I know you were gonna lie?"

At this, Childs also sat up. "It's no use. I'm not even tired."

"Me neither."

"Do you think it's the beds?" Childs asked.

"Hell no. It's the moon juice."

"How long is it supposed to last?"

"I don't know," Hamilton shrugged.

"Why the hell did you talk me into it? We might as well be back in the bush."

"How the hell was I supposed to know we were gonna find real beds? Besides, if it wasn't for the beds, we'd be havin' a real good time you gotta admit."

"Yeah," Childs agreed, "this stuff isn't bad; but it makes you talk a lot."

"I guess that's what it's supposed to do. . . . Tell me something, Childs, did you ever dream we could have such a good time in Nam?"

"No, but I never dreamed I'd end up in Nam. Besides, what's so great about this? It's only because the rest of Nam is so shitty."

"C'mon, you knew you'd end up in Nam when you joined the Crotch. . . . Hey, why *did* you join the Crotch?"

"Seemed like the worst thing I could do, I guess." Childs hesitated for a few seconds, then added, "When things are going bad, you just wanna do anything to change them, even if it's for the worse."

"What kinda bullshit is that — 'Things going bad'? I heard you had it made."

"Oh yeah, how?"

"Your old man's loaded, isn't he?"

"What gave you that fucked-up idea?"

"You used to live in Hong Kong, the Philippines, all them places . . . and you went to that school in Switzerland, the one with all the queers."

"That was because of my old man's job."

"Some job."

" 'Some job,' bullshit. He's just a flunky in the State Department."

"What's that?"

"What's what?" Childs asked irritably.

"I mean what does he do?"

"He's a consul. They ship him around a lot."

"Oh . . . what does a consul do?"

"Drink a lot, cheat on their wives — they're just ambassadors without political pull."

"Really?" Hamilton's voice showed surprise. "Your old man is a diplomat?"

"It's no big thing."

"Tell me something, what do those guys do all day?"

"Sign papers."

"You mean that's all they have to do is sign papers?"

"No, but that's all they do do. They're supposed to prevent wars and unimportant garbage like that."

"No shit! He didn't do a very good job, did he?"

"Sure don't look like it."

"Sure don't. He should get fired."

"They don't have to go to the trouble. They just bury them alive."

"Huh?"

"Send 'em to some trading post in Africa."

"No shit, is that what they did to your old man?"

"Something like that."

"You must of been pissed."

"What do I give a shit?"

"He's your old man, isn't he?"

"That don't mean I have to like him."

"Well . . . it ain't fair to your mother."

"Who says it ain't? She didn't have to marry him."

"Oh, I get it; you're pissed-off 'cause they sent you to Switzerland."

"*Bullshit!* That's the best thing that ever happened to me — getting away from them. I got tired of hearing them fight all the time, drunken brawls every weekend."

"About what?" Hamilton asked with interest.

"None of your fucking business!"

"Don't get pissed."

"Who's pissed?" Childs practically shouted.

"Stop yelling."

"Who the fuck's yelling?"

"You are."

"So what? I don't care if I wake up every flyboy in this fucking barracks."

"Take it easy, man."

"What are you asking me all these questions for? Why the hell are *you* in Nam?"

"I dunno," Hamilton shrugged. Then, after a pause, he added, "Just wanted to get away for a while."

"From what?"

"You know — when I quit the football team — well I didn't feel much like staying in school, wasn't learning anything except how to cheat. I wanted to get married. You've seen the pictures of my girl — she's so cool — but she said she wanted to graduate first. She's real smart — gets straight A's. I got pissed off at her, so I enlisted. Ever since I was a little kid, I wanted to be a Marine. I was sorry later, but it was too late. . . . She was mad for a while, but we're still gonna get married, as soon as I get out of the Crotch."

While Childs and Hamilton were talking, an Airman staggered into the barracks. He stood in front of Childs's bed, then counted the racks from there to the wall. He repeated the process one more time, then stood in front of Childs's bed again. "Hey, you're in my rack," he slurred.

"Don't be ridiculous," Childs replied. "I oughta know my own rack."

Again the Airman counted the beds before returning. "Hey, you're in my rack."

"So what?" Childs answered. "There's plenty of empty ones."

"Hey, you're in my rack."

"You said that before."

Hamilton cut in, "C'mon Childs, let him have his rack."

Childs got up and moved to an empty one on the other side of Hamilton. They continued talking until the man in the bed next to Childs's asked in a disgusted, sleepy voice, "Are you guys speeding?"

"Where'd you get that idea?" Childs replied.

"Because it's four o'clock in the goddamn morning, and I've been listening to you bullshit for two hours."

Two more Airmen had entered the barracks, and they now stood in front of the beds that Childs and Hamilton were lying in. One of them finally asked, "What are you doing in our racks?"

"We didn't know they were yours," Childs answered.

"What do you mean?"

"It was dark."

"Well they *are* ours!"

There had been pleas for quiet before, but they now turned into demands, and half the barracks was awake. Somebody asked, "Who are those guys?" and somebody else answered, "They're jarheads. I heard them talking."

The Airman standing in front of Hamilton's bed asked gruffly, "What unit are you with?"

"Hotel Company, Second Battalion, Fifth Marines," Hamilton answered with pride.

"Well get the hell out of my rack."

Hamilton's refusal was followed by some loud arguing. Before long a dozen Airmen stood around the beds demanding that they leave. One of them pulled out a pistol, and Childs said, "Take it easy, Jack. We can tell when we're not wanted. . . . C'mon Hamilton, let's flee this dump."

Childs and Hamilton were walking towards the gate trying to figure out what to say to the sentry, when they saw someone peering underneath the hood of a jeep. "Need any help?" Hamilton asked.

"Yeah, start her up for me, will ya?" Hamilton got inside, and the jeep started immediately. As Hamilton was getting out, the driver asked, "You need a ride?"

"No, just a place to sleep."

"You're Marines, aren't you?"

"Yeah."

"I can drop you off at a Marine armoured company."

Childs jumped into the jeep and the driver took off. They reached the armoured company in a few minutes, and the driver took them through the gate so they wouldn't have any trouble with the sentry. They were walking down a dirt road looking for someone to give them directions, when they saw a huge figure standing motionless in front of them. Hamilton walked up to it and asked, "You know where we can find some empty racks around here?" The figure stared straight down at him without making a sound. Hamilton repeated the question with the same results.

Childs dragged Hamilton away, whispering nervously, "Man, don't give anybody that big a hard time."

"*Hard time!* I was just trying to find out where we could find some racks."

"Well he sure wasn't anxious to tell you."

"Maybe there's something wrong with him."

"Dumb probably," Childs suggested.

"Or maybe he's an officer."

"Both, probably. . . . C'mon, let's find some racks."

"What's the use? I'm still speeding."

After a few seconds' silence, Childs said, "I got it. We'll smoke a joint. That'll slow us down."

They walked to the edge of the road and stood in a ditch. Childs lit a joint and was holding in the smoke when he tried to hand it to Hamilton. Instead, Hamilton just tapped Childs on the arm and pointed directly behind him. Childs turned to see the same huge figure peering down at them. He quickly snuffed out the joint and threw it away. The huge figure said in a soft, dreamy voice, "You were blowing grass, weren't you?"

"Hell, no," Hamilton answered nervously.

"Yes you were," the figure said in a childish tone.

"No we weren't," Childs answered. "It was a cigarette. Here, you want one?" Childs lit a cigarette and tried to hand it to the figure, but he chose to stare at the still-burning match instead. Noticing this, Childs waved the match while the figure moved his head to follow it. When he held the match closer to the figure's face, Childs could see two dilated pupils staring at the flame in awe. "Hey, this dude's on something."

"How do you know?" Hamilton asked.

"You should see his eyes. . . . Hey man, what are you on?"

"Acid."

"No shit. What's it like?" Hamilton asked.

The figure's calm words indicated no desire to explain. "You either know, or you don't know. . . . Did you see Thompson?"

"Who's Thompson?" Hamilton asked.

"Thompson," the figure repeated.

"Who *is* he?"

"Me and Thompson, we were trippin' together, watching the illumes. He disappeared, just vanished."

"No, we haven't seen him." Childs had pulled out another joint, and asked, "You want a few tokes?"

The figure stepped back shaking his head. "No! Don't do that."

"Why?"

"You shouldn't do that."

"Why?"

"MP's everywhere."

"Where can we smoke?" Hamilton asked.

The figure stood mute for a few seconds, seemingly ignoring the question; but he then blurted out, "By the tanks, behind the tanks." He slowly led them forty or fifty yards until they were between two rows of tanks. Just as Childs started to light the joint, a sentry walked by. "Wow!" the figure gasped. "That was close."

"This is worse than the road," Childs complained.

"Do you know a better place?" Hamilton asked.

Childs said irritably, "What the fuck you asking him for? He's out of his mind."

"My tank," the figure said. He paused in front of numerous tanks before stopping in front of one with "Son of a Gun" painted on it. "This — it belongs to me."

Hamilton had always wanted to see the inside of a tank. Childs held back, but Hamilton finally convinced him, the idea being that it was a safe place to get stoned and rebreathing the smoke would get them higher. Once inside, Hamilton began acting like a little kid. He ran his hands over the dials and clutched the different devices, all the while asking childish questions that the figure seemed unable to answer. Childs found it hard to understand Hamilton's excitement. The inside of the tank was surprisingly smaller than what he'd imagined. The stiffling air was thick with the smells of fuel, lubricants, and metal. He began to sweat, and tried to talk Hamilton into going back outside. Hamilton refused these requests by ignoring them, instead urging Childs to "run one." When Hamilton tried to get the figure to close the hatch, Childs objected and was able to prevent it by finally lighting the joint.

Soon the only odor was that of marijuana. Childs became more relaxed and even a little curious about the array of dials in front of him. All this time, the figure had remained silent. Hamilton had been curiously watching him peer through the viewer, and after continuous inquiries about what he was looking for, he finally answered, "Thompson." It was still dark, and all Hamilton could see through the viewer was a black field occasionally lighted by the faint flickerings of illumination flares. Hamilton soon lost interest in the viewer. He and Childs began asking each other if the marijuana had slowed their speeding. They were interrupted by an excited command from the figure. "Look!" They saw him staring into the viewer, but only Hamilton was in a position to look through it. He saw nothing. The figure noticed his questioning stare. "Don't you see her?"

Hamilton strained his eyes as he studied the viewer. "See who?"

"The fat lady!"

Hamilton and Childs glanced at each other with amusement. Hamilton turned towards him and asked, "The fat lady?"

The figure looked at Hamilton as if he were crazy. "*Can't* you see her?"

Hamilton peered intently at the viewer. "I can't see a thing. . . . Maybe it's Thompson."

"Are you crazy? Thompson isn't *that* big!"

Again Hamilton peered at the viewer. "How big is she?"

"At least twenty feet tall," he answered in an excited voice.

"Twenty feet!" Childs said with surprise. He leaned across Hamilton trying to get a look.

"She's coming towards us," the figure warned.

"Let's get out of here," Childs whispered to Hamilton.

"Okay," the figure agreed as he tried to start the tank.

"*Not you!*" Childs screamed. The tank stalled and Hamilton was able to draw the figure's attention back to the viewer.

Instead of whispering, this time Childs mouthed, "Let's get out of here."

Hamilton was enjoying himself, and he whispered back, "How can we get by *him?*"

The figure became more agitated. "She's coming closer! She's coming closer."

Hamilton tried to calm him by telling him to close the hatch. He did so, but became even more agitated as he said, "She's still coming!"

Hamilton asked nervously, "Is she Gook or American?"

Excited as he was, the figure realized the stupidity of Hamilton's question and glared at him derisively as if to emphasize it. Glancing back at the viewer, he became even more agitated. "She's still coming! What are we gonna do? What are we gonna do?" Then, in answer to the question he had thought so ridiculous before, he said, "She's a Gook, but she's got red hair, right down to the ground."

"Is she still that big?" Hamilton asked.

The figure's voice indicated horror. "Maybe even twenty-five feet." He started pulling knobs and levers while metallic screeches reverberated against the inside walls of the tank.

"Is it moving?" Childs asked in fear.

Hamilton knew it wasn't, but he ignored Childs's question and instead asked the figure, "What are you doing?"

The figure continued to maneuver instruments, seemingly ignoring Hamilton's question, but finally answering, "I'm gonna have to blow her away."

"*What!* You —"

Childs cut Hamilton off. "You can't do that! She's a civilian! They'll court-martial us!"

Hamilton pointed at the viewer as if he could see the fat lady. "He's right! She hasn't got a gun."

"But she's so big!" The figure's eyes darted between the faces of Childs and Hamilton and the viewer. His features took on a perplexed cast and his voice became almost hysterical as he asked, "What are we gonna do?"

"She can't get us," Childs answered.

"Yeah," Hamilton agreed, "the hatch is closed."

For an instant the figure became calm, but then returned to his former state. "*She can! She can!* She's so big." Nervous as they themselves were, neither Childs nor Hamilton could think of anything to say to calm him. After a few seconds' silence, he blurted out in horror, "She's on top of us! We'll have to run for it — only chance." Before he had finished speaking, his hands were moving wildly from one lever to another eliciting strident screeches from the meshing and grinding gears. The tank lurched forward, and these sounds were soon drowned out by the harsh strains of its accelerating engine.

Still disbelieving what was happening, both Hamilton and Childs were more awed than frightened. For brief instances, they even accepted the idea that there really was a fat lady chasing them; and as Childs squirmed around unsuccessfully trying to get a look at the viewer, Hamilton asked, "Is she still after us?"

Over the deafening rumble of the tank, he could barely make out the figure's excited reply. "She's gaining on us!" The speed of the tank accelerated until it finally leveled off, and the driver shouted in exasperation, "It's wide open and she's gaining!" Sweat glistening on his face, he added, "Have to ram her. It's our only chance."

The tank spun around while Hamilton and Childs bounced helplessly off its walls and each other. They regained their balance in time to see the driver staring determinedly into the viewer as he again accelerated the tank. Suddenly, all the determination on his face transformed into fear. "She ain't running!" he screamed. "Coming right at us! Hold on!" The tank swerved recklessly, again throwing Childs and Hamilton off balance.

"Did you get her?" Hamilton asked with nervous excitement.

The driver sat dazed, making no effort to control the runaway tank. He began to shake his head while saying in a defeated tone, "Chickened out, I chickened out."

Childs and Hamilton waited helplessly for something to bring an end to this absurd and unreal experience. In the few moments they had to wait, they became calm and merely stared at the interior of the tank, bracing themselves for the end, any end no matter what the consequences, hoping it would come soon. The tank still seemed to be moving fast, but they could tell it was decelerating. In one ponderous effort, the front end lunged upward, leveled off, and crashed to the ground; all the while accompanied by the sound of crunching metal. Markedly slowed, the tank still groaned forward, not even phased by the new sound of splintering wood. Without warning, it stopped dead, violently propelling Childs and Hamilton against its interior.

Now aware of his own safety, Hamilton remained motionless — calm and thankful. A nervous shove from Childs reminded him of the need to get away. The tank had them trapped in its belly, and panic took hold as they struggled to free themselves. The driver sat dazed while Hamilton climbed on top of him in order to open the hatch. His confused hands, in their random movements, somehow managed to fling it open, exposing a dawn blue sky. First dazed, then calmed, Hamilton scrambled out into the light he hadn't expected. No one was in sight. He nervously urged Childs to hurry. More dazed than either of them, the driver, with help from both, barely managed to crawl out of the hatch. A renewed sense of fear took hold of Childs and Hamilton. They jumped to the ground, pulling the driver with them, all falling to their knees. Nervous glances failed to detect anyone watching them. They staggered away under the weight of the driver who they were practically dragging, listening to his dazed voice repeat, "Chickened out, I chickened out." As they rounded the corner of a bunker, Hamilton looked back to see the tank standing a few feet in front of the two remaining walls of a supply shed, and behind this a jeep crushed within a foot of the ground. He didn't notice the red

236

and gold pennant with a general's star on it lying in the dirt in front of the jeep.

Colonel Nash and Kramer located Harmon a few hours before he was medivacked back to the States. His fever gone, only the large bandage on his foot gave any indication that he was in less than perfect condition. Neither he nor Kramer made any reference to the ambush or the men killed. Rather than being eased by their meeting, Kramer left it somewhat unnerved. He felt as if he had been playing a role, that of the concerned lieutenant, even though Harmon was no longer his 'problem' and he was glad of it.

Nash walked with Kramer to the reception room, arranged for an examination, and left immediately. The doctor took a quick look at Kramer's neck and told him that they'd take X-rays and he'd probably be out of the hospital by the next day. Kramer was assigned a ward and left to himself to find it. While looking, he passed by the operating room, a large bunker with curtains at the entrance. The curtains were only half drawn, and he could see a number of doctors crowded around one of the tables. A set of blood-soaked jungle fatigues lay beneath it in a pile. One of the doctors held a saw.

Kramer reached the officers' ward and found it to be a Quonset hut with two rows of beds. A noisy air-conditioner protruded awkwardly from one of the walls. He hesitated in front of it. A corpsman walked up to Kramer and assigned him a bed in the center of the hut. Across the aisle, a young officer stared blankly at the ceiling. He lay beneath a blanket stretched flat against the mattress where his legs should have been. An older man sat on the bed next to Kramer's. A large cast enclosed his entire upper torso, except for one arm he was using to deal a game of solitaire. The bed on the other side of Kramer's was empty. Even after Kramer had put on a pair of pajamas and lay down, the man in the cast hadn't looked up from his cards. Kramer had lain there a few minutes when a patient walking with a cane made his way to the next bed. Before sitting down on it, he nodded to Kramer and asked in a friendly, rasping voice, "What they got you stuck here for?"

Pointing to the bandage on his neck, Kramer answered, "Just a nick." Then catching a glimpse of the amputee across the aisle, he quickly added, "Probably be out of here tomorrow."

"Wish I could say the same. My name's Donaldson."

"Kramer."

Donaldson took a quick glance around the hut before removing a flask of liquor from under his mattress. "Want a taste?" Kramer shook his head. Shielding the bottle with his body, Donaldson took a long swig. He noticed Kramer staring at him as he placed the bottle back under his mattress, and said almost apologetically, "This place'll drive you nuts." Kramer nodded. "Hey, why don't we get some liberty tonight — see if we can find some good liquor and bad women?"

Kramer immediately had visions of noisy, rundown bars filled with sweaty Marines and prostitutes. "I'd just as soon take advantage of this mattress and get some sleep."

A few minutes later a corpsman came over and told Kramer he was due in the X-ray room. On his way there, he passed some soldiers wearing jungle fatigues. It had been less than an hour since he had taken his off; but when he looked at these soldiers and then at the pajamas he was wearing, he felt weak and almost impotent compared to them. This feeling stayed with him even after the X-rays were taken. Instead of going back to his ward, Kramer walked to the rear of the hospital complex in hopes of being alone for a few minutes. The back of the hospital was protected by a wall of sandbags. While leaning on it, he could see the helicopter landing pad a few yards away, and beyond it endless miles of rice paddies.

Kramer wanted a cigarette. Knowing he'd left his pack in the ward, he searched the pocket of his robe anyway. He felt a tightness in his stomach and realized that he hadn't eaten anything all day. A wry smile came to his lips as thoughts about what had happened under the canopy again resurfaced. He remembered saying "It's up to you," never dreaming Childs would go through with it. He saw the scene as he had seen it then, hearing the different remarks, watching each additional man hold out his hand for a piece of flesh, himself looking on at them as if they were voting. 'Nine to two,' he thought now as he had thought then. Kramer relived the scene with the same grotesque excitement, not realizing that he had again left himself out of the count, or also that even while it was happening, he had never thought of himself as a part of it, as anything more than a detached observer — except for one small act. He had fed Harmon some of the flesh without telling him what it was. Since then, there were times when this had slightly bothered him; but thoughts such as, 'What he doesn't know won't hurt him,' had always served to diminish any sense of guilt. Now Harmon would never know. 'Why shouldn't I have done it once before I die?' he thought, again outside himself and a separate entity from that "I" who had eaten the flesh, who had been in a position to prevent any of it from happening.

An almost gloating look on his face, Kramer heard the faint drone of a helicopter. The sound grew louder, and his eyes finally spotted an insignificant dot cast upon the iron gray sky. The glare was intense, but he squinted his eyes rather than turn his stare from this now expanding dot. As the sound grew louder, he was able to make out the silhouette of the helicopter. Kramer ignored the wind from its blades as the chopper descended upon the pad — forcing himself to watch. Only now did he see the group of men in white coats waiting anxiously for it to land. They ran aboard, emerging a few seconds later with a stretcher. Their white coats flapped furiously as they rushed towards the operating room. One of them held a bottle of plasma high over the stretcher, while another banged viciously on the soldier's chest. Although they passed within twenty yards of Kramer, he watched with a detached curiosity, and to him they seemed miles in the distance.

Long after they were gone, he continued to stare out at the LZ. His mind replaying the scene, he moved his gaze across the now empty landing pad in the same manner as when the stretcher was being carried to the operating room. Kramer heard the faint sound of another helicopter, but made no effort to seek it out. Instead, he headed back to his ward, telling himself that he wanted a cigarette. When he got there, he walked over to Donaldson. "Some liberty might be a pretty good idea after all."

It was the fifth bar they'd been to, but neither Kramer nor Donaldson would have been sure, each bar being a replica of the others. From the start Kramer had had the feeling that he would end the night with a prostitute, so he'd been forcing himself to drink in hopes of getting drunk as soon as possible. The only effect of the liquor had been a warm glow in his stomach. But still, he began to anticipate picking up a prostitute. The ones he had seen didn't have the fucked-out eyes of American prostitutes, and so many other American women. They'd had a playful yet shy quality about them that became more and more attractive each time he saw it.

Donaldson, while making no effort to get drunk, had been outdrinking Kramer at every bar. His voice had become increasingly louder, and he was now talking about the ineptitude of the Arvins within his area, all the while waving his cane for emphasis. Kramer continually tried to quiet him while taking quick glances around the room. He always expected to find people staring at them, but no one seemed to be paying much attention. Just as he was about to give up, Donaldson's mood changed to one of quiet sullenness.

People started leaving, and the bar girls began collecting glasses and cleaning up. One he hadn't noticed before came from somewhere in the back of the room and stood behind the end of the bar. She made no effort to help the other girls, and said nothing to them. Instead, she merely stood motionless except for occasional turns of her head as she stared across the room. Most of the other bar girls Kramer had seen that night had walked around with overly seductive smiles on their faces, going out of their way to be friendly. Their delicate, almost shy, mannerisms had given their behavior a childlike innocence, behavior that would have seemed cheap and forward in American women.

Kramer realized he was staring at the one standing motionless behind the bar. Without turning his head away he tried to figure out why she had attracted his attention. Her shiny black hair was no different from that of any other girl he had seen that night. Her features seemed attractive, but the room was too dark and she too far away for him to really tell. There was something intriguing about her. The longer he looked, the more beautiful she seemed. But he realized it wasn't a question of beauty. If anything, it was her bearing, especially the way she held her head. Her face had a seriousness about it that somehow resulted in a calm beauty rather than sullenness. He told himself it was merely the absence of that childlike quality he had become so accustomed to in oriental women, at the same time knowing there was something more.

For no obvious reason, she walked in Kramer's direction and stood directly across the bar from him and a few feet away. He now saw that she was far more beautiful than he'd imagined. What had been interest became something close to awe. She seemed cold, yet at the same time so indifferent as to be incapable of coldness. As Kramer stared at her, he felt the need, ridiculous as it seemed to him, to change the expression on her face, to elicit some form of recognition from her — to make her feel. Confused thoughts ran through his mind and he became uneasy as he tried to combine them into a single clear idea or impression that would explain his reaction. One inadequate thought kept returning to him, a thought so seemingly deficient that he consciously tried to reject it — 'To be able to see her face when she comes.'

Kramer felt a tap on his arm. Donaldson had been unusually quiet, and he hesitated to look towards him. When he finally did turn his head, he was met by a sly, knowing grin. Donaldson pointed towards the woman behind the bar. Liquor reeking from his mouth, he leaned towards Kramer and said, "You'd like to fuck her, eh?"

Disgusted, Kramer glanced across the bar to see if she'd heard. Her face gave no indication that she had, and Kramer's eyes returned to Donaldson. He was met by the same knowing grin and the slow nodding of Donaldson's head. Kramer tried to think of something to say that would keep him from making another remark. He couldn't, and merely stared back at him in an irritated manner, admitting to himself that however crude the remark, it had also been accurate. Instead of pacifying him, this made Kramer more resentful. Sensing Kramer's attitude, Donaldson was offended by the self-righteousness of it. Kramer noticed a sudden belligerency on his face. To avoid a scene he quickly offered to buy him another drink. Donaldson grudgingly accepted.

Kramer glanced at the woman again. Instead of trying to get her attention, he looked around for one of the other bar girls. They were all busy, so his eyes returned to her. She seemed to be looking directly over his head, her eyes still focused in the distance. He pointed to his empty glass anyway. She immediately caught his gesture. Barely moving her head, she shifted her eyes to a girl who had just stepped behind the bar, then back in Kramer's direction. The girl walked towards him.

Donaldson hadn't caught this. "I'll get her," he said to Kramer. "Hey Mamasan, how —"

Kramer grabbed his arm and pointed to the bar girl walking towards them. Donaldson gave him an irritated look as Kramer said, "Scotch and soda," then pointing to Donaldson, "bourbon and water."

Sensing Kramer's uneasiness about the woman behind the bar, Donaldson decided to make him more uneasy by getting her attention. "Hey, Mamasan," he called out, then added, "lai dai," the Vietnamese words for, "come here."

The woman behind the bar ignored and seemed not even to notice him. Kramer put his hand on Donaldson's shoulder and it was quickly shrugged off. Now more determined to get her attention, Donaldson became even louder. Embarrassed as he was, Kramer felt more ridiculous for caring. The woman, oblivious to Donaldson, retained a cool poise as she continued to stare directly over their heads, refusing to leave or turn away.

Suddenly, Donaldson stretched his cane over the bar and in an awkward gesture grabbed the woman's arm within its crook. Kramer started to reach for the cane, but caught himself when he saw Donaldson stop pulling on it. The woman stood motionless, her eyes focused upon Donaldson. The crook of his cane still around her arm, he was leaning awkwardly over the bar, seemingly frozen by the silent superiority of her stare. Kramer watched with amazement as Donaldson tried to save face by giving a slight tug on the cane before withdrawing it and turning his head away.

He quickly downed his drink, then said to Kramer, "Let's get out of here. I'm tired of these slant-eyed bitches." Kramer ignored him and continued to stare at the woman. Seeing this, Donaldson said, "High class whore," then asked gruffly, "Are you coming?"

Still smiling, Kramer finally turned and said, "I'll stick around a while."

"What for?" Donaldson demanded. When he saw no answer coming, he pulled a few bills out of his pocket. *"Here,* this is for the drinks. See you, *pal."*

Kramer's eyes shifted back and forth between the woman and his drink as he thought about what had happened. She stood with the same distant, superior stare on her face, seeming not to notice him. 'Big, tough Marine,' he thought, remembering how Donaldson had been humiliated by a stare. *'Quite* a bitch.'

Kramer remained at the bar for another half hour hoping something would happen to enable him to speak to her. He felt ridiculous at not being able to merely start a conversation, telling himself, 'What have I got to lose?' and berating himself for acting 'like some high school kid.' He tried to figure out why he was afraid, as he had never been before, knowing that one of the reasons was the sense that she was somehow superior to himself as well as Donaldson, and also knowing that this couldn't be the only reason.

The bar girls started asking people to finish their drinks. He'd have to do something fast or forget about it. Kramer made up his mind to say something, and for the next few minutes he mulled over different lines. None of them seemed right. While he hesitated, she walked away. Furious with himself, and at the same time furious about 'giving a damn,' Kramer knew that it was too late. He decided he should have merely apologized for Donaldson's behavior — it seemed so obvious now. He sat regretting his failure to do so, wondering what she would have been like, until only one other Marine besides himself remained in the bar.

A bar girl eyed Kramer impatiently. He finished his drink and walked towards the door. Disgusted with himself, he almost bumped into one of the girls on his way out. As he stepped back to let her pass, he was stunned to see that it was her. She stopped, seemingly staring right through him. A jaunty expression came across his face as he started to apologize about Donaldson. Before he could speak, she turned away and he blurted out, "I —" To his surprise, she turned back towards him. "Listen, I'm —"

She looked right through him.

"— I'm sorry about what happened."

Kramer stood amazed at the feebleness of his own words until she answered, "I do not speak English."

Her words were cold, yet there was a sad quality about them that caught him off guard. Knowing he'd have to say something immediately or she'd walk away, he blurted out, "Sounds all right to me."

"I do not speak English."

Wanting one more chance, ready to say anything he could think of:

"Parlez-vous français?" She gave an almost imperceptible nod. Trying to remember his high school French, Kramer clumsily apologized for Donaldson's behavior.

She seemed anxious to get away from him and said in French, "He's an American." Realizing her slight had cut Kramer, she assumed the wrong reason. Her cold stare softened a little, and she said in French, "It's all right."

Encouraged by the change in her look, Kramer was again at a loss for words. He finally asked, "Where did you learn to speak French?"

"In school," she answered. Kramer told her that that was also where he had learned. With no coldness in her tone, she replied in perfect French that he hadn't learned very well. Amused and a little embarrassed, Kramer agreed with her. She said she had to clean up and started to walk away. He began to apologize again.

She politely cut him short, repeating, "It's all right," then turned and walked towards the rear of the bar — now looking no different than any of a hundred Vietnamese women Kramer had seen that night. But she had been different. By the time he reached the hospital, he wasn't even sure exactly what she had looked like. Her features blurred and changed within his memory. This shouldn't have mattered. He'd never see her again anyway. But it did matter.

The next morning Kramer awoke with the same thoughts that had kept him awake the night before. After breakfast, his thinking became more practical and he tried to figure out a way to stay in Da Nang one more night. He was almost resigned to the impossibility of this when the doctor told him there was still a piece of shrapnel in his neck. They'd remove it that afternoon, and he'd *have* to stay one more night.

As much as he had hoped for it, Kramer found this "bad" news hard to believe. He spent the rest of the day thinking about how to make the most of his luck — how to get her attention again, and what to say afterwards. He felt childish, yet he enjoyed the feeling, as if he were trying to recapture a time or experience that had somehow evaded him. He even spent an hour in what was referred to as the hospital library, fruitlessly searching for a French dictionary. He did so just as much as a means to kill time as in hopes of finding one.

After what seemed like his longest day in Vietnam, Kramer left the hospital. It wasn't until he neared the bar where she worked that he began debating to himself whether to go through with his plans. He felt as if he'd been acting like a fool, and berated himself for the fantasizing and scheming he'd been doing all day. As he approached the door of the bar, he became increasingly hesitant. Only the rationalization that ·nothing would come of it and that by trying and failing he would at least get her off his mind enabled him to finally enter and take a seat at the bar.

She was nowhere to be seen. Instead of being disappointed he became relaxed, knowing that he'd at least made an effort and there would be no chance to second-guess himself. The fact that she wasn't there seemed only logical, his good luck in being held over in Da Nang now counterbalanced by his inability to take advantage of it.

Kramer felt no desire to leave, as if his presence affirmed something he'd always believed and found necessary to continually prove to himself. A faceless girl brought him a drink, and then another. He drank slowly, savoring the flavor of the Scotch as he was rarely able to do. Within the glass he could see the reflections of his thoughts — the walk down the dusty road to the landing pad at Ninth Motors, the wait beneath a glaring sun for a helicopter, the sight of Hill 65 beneath him, and the walk across the hill to rejoin his platoon.

Kramer quickly finished his drink. He started to place the glass down on the bar, but his hand froze a few inches from the surface. She was there, a few feet in front of him, as if she had always been there and he'd refused to see her. Her face carved with that same coldly superior expression, she stared across the room, seemingly unconscious of him. Thoughts raced through his mind. Had she seen him, and if so, why did she refuse to look at him? He decided to leave, but instead sat staring at her face, trying to take it apart feature by feature, wondering what he saw in her that he'd never seen before. Unable to explain her effect on him, he tried to dismiss it by telling himself that she was 'just another bitch.' But then an old realization returned — bitches had always attracted him, often instilling a hatred, yet always keeping their attraction. For the first time he began to feel superior to her, looking at her as some frustrated object to satisfy a man's, a certain type of man's, sexual desire.

But as he continued to stare at her face, he attributed to it a mysterious type of intelligence, a knowledge of something of which he felt ignorant. He'd *rip* it away from her. Rip *what* away? 'Nothing! She's just another bitch.' But not like any bitch he had ever known. Her face — *what was there about it?* Baffled by the intensity of his own reaction, he knew that no other face had ever affected him as hers had, and unlike any other he had ever seen — 'For *some goddamn reason*' — it would refuse to fade within his memory. Unless — he'd *change* it, within his mind, see it helpless, pathetically helpless. And there was only one way this could happen. 'If I could — *I will!* I'll fuck the living shit out of her and walk away.'

She continued to gaze across the room. It seemed to him that this was a cold refusal to see him, to admit that he was there. He mulled over the different ways he had planned to get her attention, the things he had decided to say to her. But the immature excitement that had been connected with these thoughts during the day was now absent. Instead, he schemed with a destructive determination that ruled out any kind of results except sadistic relief, its object being to leave her in his wake, forgotten, reft of all mystery.

He pushed his glass towards the edge of the bar indicating he wanted another drink. The only other girl behind the bar was standing a few feet away talking to a customer. His eyes returned to the woman standing in front of him. This was his chance. She still seemed unaware of him, but to his surprise she slowly turned towards the bar girl, spoke her name, and then indicated without saying a word that Kramer wanted another drink. As the bar girl walked away with his empty glass, Kramer nodded to the woman to thank her. She returned his nod with an almost imperceptible nod of her own. Sitting with the drink in his hand, Kramer found it impossible to merely call her over. Instead he kept staring at her. At first she gave no indication that she realized he wanted to speak to her, but she soon stepped forward and stood against the bar.

He finally asked her in French what she was looking at. Instead of answering the question, she asked where his friend was. He looked up and said that Donaldson had been bad, so he had put him to bed early. She remained silent, giving no indication that she saw any humor in his reply. He asked her if she owned the bar. Still refusing to look at him, she answered with a nod. In poor French, he tried to ask her if owning a bar was what they had taught her to do in school. As he finished speaking, Kramer realized that she might take this question as an insult. Her tone gave no indication she had, but her reply did. She told him they had taught her to speak French.

Kramer found the remark more amusing than cutting. "I need more practice."

"Then you should be in France, not Vietnam," she replied in French.

He chose to ignore her implication. "I've always wanted to go to France." His purpose in saying this was to get her to look at him. It would be a sort of victory over her.

"Then you should go," she answered, implying that he should not only leave Vietnam, but also her bar.

Her bitchiness began to irritate him, but he sluffed it off by asking, "How can I?"

"Fight with the French."

He realized her words had been intended as an insult, but there was so obviously a sad quality in the way she had said them that he felt as if he had been the one insulting her. His guilt caused him to try and picture the expression on her face when she had spoken. He continued to want her to look at him, but no longer as a symbol of his will conquering hers. His desire to see her face was now founded upon a compelling curiosity about her. He spoke again, not to make conversation, but merely to receive an answer. Had he been aware of the feeble sincerity of his words, he would have regretted speaking them. "Did you ever want to go to France?"

Aware of his change in tone, she was surprised enough by it to finally look down at him. It was Kramer's eyes that were now turned away, staring blankly at the glass between his hands. "A long time ago," she answered slowly.

At first her words were meaningless to him, but he then recalled them and his mind translated what she had said into English. He raised his eyes to meet hers. There was no coldness in her look. But gradually, as if by reflex, her stare hardened. He suddenly felt weak in comparison to her, and only by a conscious effort was he able to harden his gaze. "Why a long time ago?"

"I will never go back."

Kramer noticed that she had seemed weaker when she had spoken, her stare less piercing, and for this reason he desired her to speak again. "You were in France? . . . How long were you there?"

She was looking directly at him, but while she spoke her mind seemed far away. "Almost a year. . . . I went to the Sorbonne." Before he could ask her another question, she turned and walked slowly to the end of the bar.

Only two other Marines were left in the bar. Kramer sat nursing his drink. 'Wouldn't you know it? . . . Guess every fucking whore and barmaid in Vietnam spends a year at Sorbonne.' Kramer laughed to himself, knowing that as much as he'd like to, he wouldn't be able to laugh her off so easily. Believing and surprised by her words, Kramer refused to admit to himself that he wanted her somehow to be different; wanted to hear things such as he'd just heard. There was no question of his leaving without trying to speak to her again, but she refused to walk near him. The bar would be closing soon. He ordered another drink, first gulping down the liquor still in his glass. Scotch was now the last thing he wanted, and he had trouble swallowing it.

Soon he was the only Marine left in the bar. One of the girls came over and told him they were closing. He nodded as if agreeing to leave, but continued to sit nursing his drink. When only one bar girl remained a naval officer walked in to pick her up. The woman nodded to her, leaving herself and Kramer alone in the bar.

She was standing a few feet away from him when she said softly in French, "We are closed."

Kramer wanted to say, "I'd like to talk to you," but was unable to. "I have to go home."

He began speaking with a jaunty air, but by the time he finished the sentence his voice trailed off into a self-conscious request. "I thought maybe you could tell me about Paris."

She came very close to laughing in his face, but for some reason caught herself. "I cannot tell you. You have to see. . . . It is a beautiful city."

"You could tell me about it."

There was a calculating expression on her face as she looked down at him and asked, "Is this what you want, to hear about Paris?"

"Yes," he answered, while thinking, 'No, but I want to hear you talk about it.'

Not believing his answer, but now curious about him, she began describing the Seine and the broad avenues. Her words were lost to him as he watched the faraway expression on her face, staring at her dark eyes which had lost their hardness as soon as she began speaking. This hardness soon returned, and by the time she had finished, her eyes were again focused on him in a cold stare.

It was now Kramer's face that possessed the faraway look, and he said, "They say it's the most beautiful city in the world." She shook her head slowly in disagreement. Surprised at this, Kramer asked, "What is, Saigon?"

She met his question with calm arrogance. "Saigon is ugly."

His face indicating weak apology, Kramer said, "I thought maybe you were born there." She shook her head. "Where were you born?"

"Hanoi."

"How did you come to Da Nang?"

"My father worked for the government, the French. When they divided the country, we fled the Communists."

"You came to Da Nang?"

She shook her head. "No, Hue. My mother did not want to leave Hanoi. Hue is closer."

"You must have been very young."

She looked questioningly at Kramer, then answered, "Sixteen."

"How *old* are you?"

"You think I am very young. I am thirty." Kramer stared at her in disbelief, and she asked, "How old did you think I was?"

247

Still surprised, he lied, "Twenty-four, twenty-five, like me."

"Now you think I am an old woman."

Kramer studied her face. She seemed even more striking than before. "No, a beautiful woman is most beautiful when she's thirty."

While Kramer judged his own comment as childish, she replied, "I think you are right."

There was a pause before Kramer asked, "So it's Hanoi you think is more beautiful than Paris?"

"They are very much alike. Perhaps I liked Paris because it reminded me of Hanoi. . . . The French liked Hanoi more than any other city in Vietnam."

"You sound like you want to go back." She slowly shook her head. "If it's so beautiful, why don't you want to see it again?"

"I like Hanoi, but it is very French." A proud and distant expression appeared on her face. "Hue is the most beautiful city in the world. When we left Hanoi, I was very sad. My father told me Hue was more beautiful. I did not think this was possible. When I first saw Hue, it appeared more beautiful than even my father had said. Much of Hanoi was built by the French. Hue is Vietnamese, very old and beautiful. It was the ancient capital of Vietnam, and it made me very proud."

She paused, and Kramer said, "But Saigon is the capital now."

"It is ugly, like pictures I have seen of the United States. The buildings are American, not Vietnamese, like New York."

Amused by the inappropriateness of the comparison, Kramer refrained from commenting on it.

Before, she had been content to speak French and let him struggle to understand her, but now as she talked about Hue, she felt a sudden need to make herself understood. She abandoned French, and instead spoke in perfectly understandable English. Though there was an urgency beneath her words, it remained hidden and she retained the same proud, calm tone. "Hue, it is the ancient capital of Vietnam. The buildings are very old and beautiful. At first, when I walk among them, it seems I am in the past, before the French have come — hundreds of years. All the stories I have heard of the ancient empire seem to be living. I see them in my mind and believe them. Then I know all the French have bring is nothing." She noticed a slight smile on Kramer's face and immediately paused, thinking that he was laughing at her. Irritated and sorry she had begun talking to him, she said with a calm assertiveness, "Is true. I never hear one person say is not. . . . Everyone who see Hue say is the most beautiful city in the world. When I go to Paris, I think I will see things more beautiful. But I never see them. Paris, is beautiful, yes; but like Hanoi,

248

only very dirty. I go to the Versailles Palace, and I like it very much; but for me the Imperial Palace in Hue is even more beautiful."

She told him of her house less than a mile away from the Imperial Palace, how it stood upon a corner of the Square of the Four Dragons. Each side of the square was guarded by a bronze dragon upon a marble base, and they all looked inwards towards a huge, stone Buddha. The Buddha faced towards the south, and around it were concentric squares of brightly colored flowers. She told him how she would sometimes wait before dawn, looking out her window as the sun's light increased in intensity allowing each flower to gain its natural brilliance.

At first Kramer had merely wanted to hear her voice; but as she continued speaking, he began to picture the things she described. He could see the vaunted grandeur of Emperor Khai Dinh's Tomb. Each of its details appeared before him, her very words illuminating them like rays of light cast within a shadow-darkened room. Her voice came to him as if he were actually standing within the timeless marble halls she described. The light of a thousand candles reflected upon columns of smooth, patterned stone. Gentle smells of hidden incense hinted of forbidden temples. Shards of brightly colored porcelain swirled in intricate frescos upon the walls that surrounded him — telling the story of her people, their suffering and their triumph. And above it all, a gilt bronze likeness of Emperor Khai Dinh himself passively surveyed his vain, self-justified compromise with death.

She told him of the Imperial Palace. Its roof of orange tile curved gracefully against the sky, each corner protected by a huge stone dragon. He stood amidst the sacred urns of brass and porcelain. Ancient teak columns cast their shadows upon floors of brightly painted tile. The surrounding gardens and ponds added to the still grandeur of the palace itself. And the solemn beauty of all she described stood eternalized by an encircling wall seven feet in thickness, this wall in turn protected by an emerald-hued moat.

As Kramer listened, he realized that however beautiful these things she described, much of this beauty would have been lost to his own eyes. He knew that it stemmed as much from the way she was able to see things as from the objects themselves. Her eyes were directed towards him, yet he knew she was not seeing him. He was fascinated by the way she held her chin, giving herself a quiet pride, now with no sense of haughtiness. Her lips moved slowly and with an assurance that somehow lent her words an aloof intimacy. But it was her eyes that astonished him, possessing a soft, black depth he could not make himself believe existed. He tried to tell himself their appearance was due to the lighting in the bar. Never darting, they moved with a slow scanning motion, seeming not to focus, yet capable of piercing all that surrounded them. He imagined them to be seeing so much more than his own eyes, and he felt blind in her presence.

When she stopped speaking, Kramer remained silent, hoping to again hear her voice, remembering its proud yet sad quality. But she remained silent, looking directly at yet through him. A long moment passed without words before Kramer spoke the one coherent thought in his mind. "You never told me your name."

"Tuyen," she answered, then hesitated before asking in the manner of an afterthought, "Your name is?"

"David."

For the first time that night, something close to a smile appeared on her face. "I know him." Kramer looked at her questioningly. "He is in the Bible. We read it in school. . . . Is a lesson. I have to."

"Oh," he answered, wanting to hear her voice, not his own.

"I really like him," she said, trilling the *l*'s in "really."

"Why do you say that?"

"He sings and plays music and writes poems. He is good, and yet he kills a man to get his wife. He seem real, not like the others."

Again Kramer became intrigued by her way of looking at things; to be told something about his own name that he'd never realized before, something so obviously true as to amaze him with his ignorance of it. 'Maybe she's a Catholic,' he thought. 'They fled the Communists.' "Are you Buddhist?"

She shook her head. "I am —" she paused while trying to think of the right word "— atheist."

Again he waited for her to speak, wanting to hear her voice and yet unable to think of any questions. Finally she said, "I think I should go home."

This was the last thing he wanted to hear, yet there was never any question in his mind of trying to get her to stay. He followed her to the door and watched as she padlocked it. Kramer had no intention of walking with her, but she started in the direction of the hospital and he followed. He now realized for the first time, that since her description of Hue, she had been speaking English. "I thought you couldn't speak English."

"I say I do not speak English."

"Why not?"

"Is ugly."

"Why do you say that?"

She looked at him as if to ask, "What is there to explain?" then said, "Is an ugly language, like German."

They were no longer walking between the disheveled shacks of the bar district, but instead along a street of drab concrete buildings, "American buildings," she told him. Tuyen stopped in front of a door to one of them. "This is where I live." He made no effort to leave. "I think you should go."

"Go where?"

"Wherever you should go. . . . I am tired."

"I thought maybe we could talk awhile," Kramer suggested, and this was exactly what he had in mind, nothing more.

"Is late," she said coldly.

"I'm going back to An Hoa tomorrow." She shrugged her shoulders indicating this meant nothing to her. "Maybe I could come in for a few minutes," he suggested with no hope of her agreeing.

Without answering him, Tuyen unlocked the door and stepped inside. As he followed her in, she said, "For a minute."

Tuyen walked towards the center of the room and pulled the cord to a rice paper-shaded lamp hanging from the ceiling. Kramer's eyes scanned the sparsely furnished room. The concrete floor was highly polished and immaculate. A red silk bedspread covered a thin mattress and the pallet it lay upon. The room's only window was curtained with this same material. A narrow, silk-screen painting hung on each of the walls. In the corner stood a carved, black enamel dresser. On the opposite side of the room was a small table with two pictures on top of it. In front of the pictures lay a pack of Salem cigarettes and a candle. Kramer noticed Tuyen take a quick glance at the table before saying, "Is late. Maybe you should go." He remained silent, so she walked to the door and held it open for him. As he walked through it, he made no effort to hide his disappointment.

Turning in the doorway, he said, "I'd like to talk to you some time." She made no reply, nor did her face give any indication that this would be agreeable to her. He stepped out into the quiet deserted street and headed towards the hospital. Her face remained in his thoughts as clearly as if it were before him; and he wondered why. It never occurred to him to wonder why she had spoken to him at all, or about the things she had chosen to tell him. Knowing that he would never see her again and that now she was even more of a mystery, he regretted the entire evening. When he reached the hospital, Kramer was irritated to find himself repeating her name.

Childs and Hamilton were walking along the orange dirt road back to Ninth Motors. They had spent their second day in Da Nang at Freedom Hill, the huge PX complex wandering through and around it while eating hamburgers, french fries, and carrying Cokes in their hands. That night they had slept at the Marine Air Wing facility, and they were now heading towards the helicopter landing pad to get a ride back to Hill 65. Childs was in an unusually good mood, and he asked Hamilton, "Aren't you glad I talked you into this?" Hamilton, walking with his head down, made no reply. "What the hell's wrong with you? This was almost as good as an R and R, wasn't it?"

"I guess so," Hamilton answered sullenly. It wasn't Da Nang that he was thinking about. Now that they were heading back to Hill 65, Hamilton's thoughts returned to what had happened under the canopy. All during the time they had been in Da Nang, these memories had been forgotten. Only now did he relive that scene, and he did so with no sense of horror. What had happened did trouble him; but only because he had so easily accepted it, and this seemed vitally wrong. Something told him that he should be horrified by the memories of what had happened; and yet it was merely the absence of this guilt that bothered him. Hamilton kept reminding himself that only Pablo and Tony 5 had refused, but this seemed more a reason for guilt than an excuse against it. He remembered how the men had been purposely avoiding each other's eyes on Hill 65, and sensed that it was each other's knowledge of the act that was painful, not the act itself. Only Chalice had been greatly affected, had acted the way it seemed all of them should be acting; but this merely suggested that he was somehow weaker than the rest of them.

Hamilton now refused to let himself again forget the act. It seemed his responsibility to keep thinking about it until these thoughts brought on a feeling of guilt. Without really being conscious of it, he sensed a deep incongruity in his reaction — either he should feel guilty or he should search out the hidden flaw in his consciousness that misled him into thinking that he should. He was only able to state this idea to himself in the simplest of terms — 'Something is wrong, fucked up, really fucked up.' He walked along in silence, pondering the problem without results or even the hope for any, sure that he hadn't really understood what had happened, that the eating of human flesh must be something more than merely that, something horrible. For the first time he felt a need to talk about it; to have his guilt explained to him. As of yet he had not heard anyone else mention what had happened, and this made him hesitant to do so. He realized that the fact that no one even dared to joke about it was of even greater import. When he finally spoke, Hamilton found no significance in his own choice of words or the guiltless tone that he used. "Childs, do you remember when we ate part of that Gook up on Charlie Rid—"

"What the *fuck* do you want to bring that up for?" Childs cut him off

252

angrily. "I'm glad we did! So what?" And Childs believed what he said, or most of it. He *was* glad. It seemed to prove something, his whole attitude maybe. He wasn't completely sure what, but it did prove something. Hamilton remained silent, and Childs now became conscious of the angry tone he had used. He wondered how Hamilton could refer to the eating of human flesh, this act which had to be so important in order to prove anything, how he could refer to it as if he were asking, "Do you remember that hamburger we ate at the PX yesterday?" Hamilton's tone had illustrated with such unequivocal clarity the single aspect of the incident that bothered Childs — the fact that it never would have happened if not for him. It had been *his* act. He *was* glad it had happened; but only about the part involving himself. The fact that he had eaten human flesh proved something, but the fact that he had induced others to commit this same act caused him nothing but guilt.

Childs remembered how he had stood with the knife, determined to go through with it even before the others had realized what he was thinking. It had seemed impossible that anyone else there would also be capable of this same act. He had relished the idea of having the others stand horrified while he ate the flesh, chewed and savored it while smiling at their aghast stares, telling them how good it was. He had been so excited by the thought of it, that his amazement at the reactions of those around him had remained hidden. Childs remembered seeing Kovacs nod for him to go ahead, and how he couldn't believe that Kovacs — 'the guardian of the flag' — actually understood what he was thinking, how he wanted to explain it to him and see the horror on a face seemingly incapable of horror. He remembered Forsythe — 'of all people' — saying, "I'm starved," and Hamilton saying he could eat anything. Then, right then, he wanted to shout, "*Idiots!* Don't you realize what this means?" Childs remembered Kramer saying the only thing he was capable of — "It's up to you" — saying nothing at all. Only Tony 5 had reacted the way Childs had expected — "Are you crazy?" Childs wanted to answer, "No, motherfucker, you are; and I'm gonna prove it!" Pablo had refused, but quietly, knowing. Only Tony 5 — 'Who would have thought? . . .' — had acted the way Childs had anticipated. Still, he was sure that he had proved something, maybe even more than he had imagined possible. Only one thing bothered him. Some of them — 'Hamilton: "Remember when we ate that Gook?" ' — did not have the slightest perception of what they were doing. Some of them did know — 'all the better' — but some of them had 'no fucking idea, as if they were at a picnic,' not realizing that they were eating the 'filthiest, sickest, most putrid sewage imaginable — human flesh.'

They continued walking in silence, Hamilton's presence reminding

Childs that through this person's 'ignorance or stupidity or innocence' he had acquired guilt. Hamilton hesitated to speak again, sensing that Childs had mistakenly taken his last question as an accusation. Finally Hamilton did speak, in the same tone as before, to ask about something that he felt bothered him much more than it should. "Remember when we were trying to get Fields's body?"

"What the fuck do you want to bring that up for?"

Hamilton continued as if he hadn't heard Childs. "Remember all the trouble we went through? Didn't you feel stupid?"

"I've felt stupid ever since I arrived at Parris Island."

"Cut it out, will ya! I mean shouldn't we have left him in the river?"

"We didn't," Childs answered. "Why the hell are you worrying about it now?"

"We — I mean, I mean if it was me in the river, I wouldn't of cared."

"You're damn right you wouldn't. When you're dead, you don't care about nothing."

"I mean I would of said, 'Forget it you guys. I'm dead. Get the hell out of here.'"

Childs was anxious to drop the subject. "Ain't no way, motherfucker. If you were dead, you wouldn't a said shit."

Hamilton stopped walking and glared angrily at Childs. "You're *pissin'* me off."

Childs regretted having made a joke out of it. "Relax, will you."

"All I want to know is why we went to all that trouble."

"Oh, is that all you want to know?" Childs said sarcastically. "I'll tell you: It's a Marine Corps tradition never to leave dead or wounded behind."

"*I* know that, but it seems like it would have been so much simpler to just leave him."

"It."

"Huh?" Hamilton asked.

"*He* was dead. *It* was a corpse."

"*Childs*, will you cut that shit out."

"All right, just relax. It's a Marine Corps tradition. That means it's naturally stupid." Childs realized this explanation was far from adequate, so he added, "I suppose it's because sometimes you don't really know if a guy's dead. This way you go back and find out. Once you're there, you might as well take the body with you."

"But we knew he was dead."

"*Sonofabitch*. . . . I'll tell you what. Let's smoke some herb." As he said this, Childs pulled the last joint out of his pocket. They were walking

254

down the side of a busy road, but when he saw Hamilton's troubled expression he lit it anyway. Hamilton waved the joint away. Childs kept holding it out until Hamilton finally took it. Before the marijuana could possibly have affected them, their mood lightened and they both began walking with carefree gaits. Childs remarked about how good the hamburgers had tasted, and from then on they traded excited reminiscences about the previous two days.

As Childs and Hamilton approached Ninth Motors, they noticed a young girl walking in front of them. Her red silk dress ruffled gracefully in the breeze. All they could see was her back, and each knew the other was trying to imagine how beautiful she was. Anxious to see her face, they began to walk faster. Suddenly, she turned — faced them with a single transpiercing eye that erupted from a mass of napalmed flesh. Neither of them could move. Seeing their horror, the girl refused to turn away. First Childs, then Hamilton, burst madly by her. They continued to run at full speed long after they were exhausted, neither one daring to look back.

Kramer was the last man to board the helicopter to Hill 65. It failed to take off immediately, and he saw a member of the ground crew waving someone else aboard. Hamilton and Childs came running up the loading ramp and collapsed in some seats directly across from him. Kramer knew that he should at least act angry. His mind on other things, it took some effort to face them with an irritated stare. Unaware of Kramer, Childs and Hamilton continually gasped to each other, "What a freak-out!" The helicopter was halfway to Hill 65 before they noticed him. Kramer continued to stare at them coldly. Hamilton gave a nervous nod of recognition and Childs hunched his shoulders as if to ask, "So what?" When the helicopter landed, Childs and Hamilton scurried off without looking back. Kramer was glad to be rid of them, but he realized he'd have to say something and figured now was the time to do so. "Wait a minute!" he called out. As they approached, Hamilton was visibly nervous, while the expression on Childs's face alternated between insolence and nonchalance. Kramer said calmly, "If anything like this happens again, I'll screw you to the wall."

2. Hill 65

Kramer found Kovacs in the platoon hootch cleaning his rifle. He knew that Kovacs had only five days left in-country, and was glad he would still be with the platoon for their first three days in the Arizona. Kovacs's first question was about Harmon. His second was a request to remain behind when the platoon left for the Arizona. Surprised, Kramer asked for the reason.

There was no hint of pleading in Kovacs's answer, only a statement of what he considered facts. "I been here thirteen months. And I've stuck my neck out a lotta times when I didn't have to. There ain't a reason in the world I shouldn't be dead now. I've got three days to spend in the Arizona. I ain't gonna tell you what it's like. You'll have to see for yourself. If I played it safe, I'd make it; but if I get a chance to stick my neck out, I'd probably be stupid enough to do it. I just don't wanna give my luck a chance to catch up with me."

From what he had seen of Kovacs, this argument made sense to Kramer; but he also knew that he'd feel more confident having Kovacs with him, even if it was only for three days. "I don't blame you, but it'll be a lot safer for the men with you around. I'll see you don't stick your neck out. Besides, Preston got to the rear somehow, and you two are my most experienced men."

Kovacs made no effort to hide his irritation as he replied, "Preston never was worth a shit. You're lucky he's gone. Now Tony 5 can move right up to platoon sergeant."

"What about Valdez?"

"He's got the short-timer's jitters — wants to stay with his squad."

"But you've had more experience than Tony."

"Come off it, Lieutenant. I've been here three months longer than Tony. I'm him three months later. You know what the story is: If a man's worth a shit, he gets better according to how many more lives depend on him." Kramer remained silent, so Kovacs added harshly, "I don't beg."

Both of them were thinking about the time Kovacs volunteered to stay behind under the canopy; Kovacs with irritation and Kramer with guilt. "All right, I'll talk to Trippitt." Although he kept from showing it, this reply incensed Kovacs. He knew that Trippitt would make him stay until the last possible minute. Kovacs had previously reserved judgment on Kramer, but he now looked upon him as gutless and was sorry he had even asked the favor. As Kovacs started to walk out of the hootch, Kramer asked, "What do you think he'll say?"

Kovacs realized that Kramer knew exactly what Trippitt would say. He stood staring at Kramer, making no effort to answer. "All right, stick around the hill for three days, then go in to An Hoa on your own." Kovacs was still irritated at Kramer for not agreeing immediately. He turned his back on him and left without a word. Kramer remained sitting in the hootch, realizing he had made a mistake with someone whose opinion he valued, but thinking, 'At least he won't be around to remind me.'

Kramer sent for Tony 5 and Sugar Bear. While he waited, he tried to think of some words to add when he would tell them they were now the platoon's sergeant and right guide. After a few sterile minutes, he realized that no pompous words were necessary. When they did arrive, he merely gave them the news and headed for the officers' hootch.

Tony 5 and Sugar Bear took their promotions matter-of-factly, as if they had been assigned to a different working party. Tony's only concern was having to give up his blooker. It was a grenade launcher that looked like a single-barreled, sawed-off shotgun. Each of the three rifle squads in the platoon had a man that carried one, and Tony had been in charge of Alpha's for the last six months. Now that he was Platoon Sergeant, he would have to leave the blooker with his squad. He found it hard to imagine himself without it. The blooker had become a part of him, not something ignored, but rather something unthinkingly depended upon. He gave it credit for saving his own life twice, and those of his friends many other times. Tony thought about who should receive it in the same manner a person would think about conferring a family heirloom upon someone sure to outlive him. Hamilton would now be Alpha's squad leader, and was therefore eliminated. Childs had two Purple Hearts and would be sent to the rear in a few days. He didn't trust Payne; and besides, as long as Payne carried the radio, Hamilton had an excuse to keep him from becoming a fire team leader. Tony felt Roads had been hostile towards him, and he would not consider giving it to anybody but a friend. This left Forsythe who had only a little over four months left in-country, and Chalice who was too inexperienced. He kept thinking he was leaving somebody out until he finally counted these men on his fingers, then added Bolton who was dead, Harmon medivacked, and himself promoted.

257

Though he would have liked to assign the blooker to someone with more time left in-country, he finally decided on Forsythe.

Knowing that Forsythe had probably skated out of his working party, Tony didn't even bother to go to the S-2 office. Instead he decided to check out the few time-killing haunts available on the hill. The second one he tried was the shack that served as a Vietnamese souvenir store, referred to by the men as the Gook shop; and it was there that he found Forsythe sipping a Coke and talking to the Vietnamese girl who ran it.

Forsythe objected to the idea of trading his rifle for the blooker. The reason he gave was that he'd been lucky with his M-16 for almost nine months, and he didn't want to do anything to change his luck. Tony realized how dependent a man could become upon his particular weapon, and was hesitant about forcing him to switch. Instead, he tried to convince Forsythe by telling him he was the only man in the squad he was sure of. Still reluctant, Forsythe suggested Roads instead. Tony 5 rejected this suggestion without giving the actual reason. Forsythe then suggested Chalice. Tony replied that he wasn't sure enough of him, but finally agreed to give him a chance.

Chalice was also hesitant about switching his M-16 for the blooker, but he felt he was in no position to argue. In order for Chalice to get some practice, Tony 5 took him and a sack of ammunition to the area on the hill that served as a dump. He gave Chalice an old oil drum as a target. The first thing Chalice did was raise the blooker to his eye and sight it in. This wasn't the way Tony wanted Chalice to fire it, but he kept quiet and watched as the round landed within five yards of the oil drum. This impressed Tony. He then explained to Chalice that because the rounds exploded upon impact it was only necessary to come within five yards of a target; and therefore the ability to fire quickly was more advantageous than extreme accuracy. He also explained that he wanted Chalice to shoot from the hip without aiming, and to practice reloading as quickly as possible. Chalice tried this, and the first round landed twenty yards in front of the oil drum. He quickly loaded another round and placed it fifteen yards in back of the target. Tony was impressed by the fact that both shots were directly in line with the oil drum, and he was more impressed when the next three rounds landed within five yards of it.

Chalice's aptitude with the blooker surprised even himself. He continued firing it with excitement as Tony explained the characteristics of the different types of rounds. The blooker was capable of firing a standard grenade round, a shotgun round, white phosphorus, and signal flares. When Chalice had emptied the sack of ammunition, he asked Tony if they could get some additional rounds. Tony told him that he didn't need any more practice. Chalice would have been flattered by any favorable reaction from Tony, but this compliment stripped him of any qualms about exchanging his M-16 for the blooker.

Tony mentioned Chalice's prowess with the blooker to Forsythe, and it wasn't long before the whole platoon was making complimentary remarks to him. A few of the men mentioned something about the Phantom Blooker, as if it were Chalice's sole responsibility to kill him. Chalice had heard references to him before, and he'd always assumed this Phantom Blooker was merely a mythical Viet Cong representing a number of Viet Cong soldiers who prowled the Arizona with captured American grenade launchers. It wasn't until they were standing bunker watch that night, that Forsythe realized Chalice had no real knowledge of exactly who the Phantom Blooker was. Chalice listened incredulously to Forsythe's explanation, unable to decide how much of it was reality, and with the claustrophobic feeling that he had somehow been trapped.

At first Forsythe's story seemed to focus upon Kovacs. He had joined Second Platoon as they were finishing the third month of what had been planned as a ninety day, battalion-size operation in the Arizona. The conversations and thoughts of the men were centered upon that approaching but uncertain time when they would be able to cross the river and leave the Arizona behind. Each day brought with it the prospect that it might be the last; but then something happened, and no longer did the operation's end depend upon days.

Each of the battalion's four rifle companies was camped in a different section of the Arizona. The helicopter that had brought Kovacs to Hotel Company had also brought in a load of supplies. The men were busy dividing them when this same helicopter radioed back that it had spotted five Viet Cong escorting an American prisoner. The CP and one platoon were left behind to guard the supplies, while Hotel Company's other three platoons immediately headed in the direction of the hovering chopper. Moving at an exhausting pace through the rice paddies, the men took quick glances at the circling copter to see how much farther they had to go. Only a dense tree line and three hundred yards remained between the column's point and the helicopter when the men were startled by a burst of rifle fire from the other side of the high ground. They watched as the helicopter hung motionless for a few seconds, then plummeted behind the tree line.

The column had seemed to be moving as fast as possible, but the pace quickened to a frantic run. The men could hardly keep their balance by the time they burst from the opposite side of the tree line and saw the scattered and half-burned wreckage of the helicopter. It took more than an

259

hour to recover all the bodies. Besides the crew, there had also been five members of Hotel Company on board. Two were headed for R and R's, and the other three had just finished their thirteen month tours. It was now too late to get another helicopter in to pick up the dead, so the men carried them to the tree line and set-in for what was to be the most terrifying and longest night many of them had ever spent. At roughly fifteen-minute intervals, they would hear the faint pop of a grenade launcher discharging its round, and a few seconds later the explosion of this round within their perimeter. The next morning two more bodies and six wounded had to be loaded on the incoming chopper, and it was then that the men of Hotel Company started making references to the Phantom Blooker.

During the next few days there was very little speculation about when the battalion would leave the Arizona. Instead, all talk centered upon the rescue of their fellow Marine which everyone knew would have to come first. Surprisingly, the morale of the men improved to a point far better than at any other time during the operation. They no longer saw themselves as searching out a ubiquitous yet impalpable enemy. Every march through rice paddies and every sweep through tree lines had a single cogent purpose — the rescue of one of their own. Each man was able to sympathize with this lone captive who waited helplessly for them to free him. They imagined themselves in his place, and required nothing more to drive them on. Each man's actions were defined by what he himself would expect from those around him if he were the captive.

A week passed with no sign of the prisoner. Then one night their perimeter was again besieged by a blooker attack. At dawn they received word that less than a kilometer away a helicopter had spotted five Viet Cong with a prisoner disappear into a nearby tree line. It was obvious to the men that an air strike would endanger his life, and that this man's only chance was to be rescued by a rifle company. All four of Second Battalion's rifle companies became involved in the search. The captured Marine was sighted numerous times, usually at intervals of five or six days, and always by the helicopters. Almost every one of these sightings was preceded or followed by a blooker attack upon the nearest company. In the first three weeks of the search, twelve Marines were killed and almost forty wounded. It became obvious that the prisoner and the Phantom Blooker always traveled together. The men's obsession to rescue their fellow Marine now took on another and often more dominant aspect — the destruction of the Phantom Blooker. No rifleman had ever seen the elusive captive, but there were very few who had not endured at least one blooker attack and seen its results. In their imaginations, it was the Phantom Blooker who prevented the intended rescue, and by doing so pre-

260

vented their leaving the Arizona. His ability to continually outwit them caused the men to begin equating him with death itself; and the American prisoner who had never been seen by any of them began to fade farther into the background. It was obvious that the Phantom Blooker was using him not only as bait, but also as insurance against indiscriminate fire. Seldom was the prisoner spoken of except in connection with derisive comments about his intelligence or bravery. Perhaps this wouldn't have happened if they had been able to see him themselves, to be sure of his existence. Unquestioningly, they continued the search, now without distinguishing the Phantom Blooker from the prisoner. They crossed and recrossed the same ground, occasionally coming upon the footprints of a single pair of boots, and once finding two live blooker rounds. Still, they weren't sure that these tracks or rounds were not their own. The night barrages continued, but less frequently and of shorter duration. For almost a month, not even the helicopters had been able to spot the American, but numerous terrifying nights attested to the continued presence of the Phantom Blooker.

The men no longer thought of the operation as something that would come to an end. Instead, they looked with anticipation towards the terminations of their tours or their upcoming R and R's. For this reason, many of them were actually dumbfounded when the entire battalion was suddenly reunited and choppered back to Hill 65. They searched for reasons to explain why the operation had been so unexpectedly terminated. At first the general conclusion was that because the prisoner hadn't been spotted for over a month, the colonel had decided he'd probably been either executed or evacuated. But soon another explanation spread among them. Usually it was received with doubts, but even the skeptics served to relay it to others. Few men admitted to accepting it as fact, but fewer challenged the possibility that it was true. Each new man that joined the battalion soon heard about that one additional time the American and five Viet Cong had been spotted, supposedly two days before the battalion pulled out of the Arizona, and about the helicopter pilot who swore it was the American who carried the blooker.

For two months the rumor hovered over the battalion — seldom argued about but often mentioned. It wasn't until the men received word that in a few days they would again enter the Arizona that the arguments started, often loud and sometimes ending in fights. In the last few minutes before the operation began, all speculation was stopped, and what had been rumor was finally accepted as fact. When the men formed up to board the helicopters, the platoon commanders said their standard few words, but in addition they added the instructions that if any American prisoners were sighted in the company of the Viet Cong, shoot first and ask questions later.

Second Battalion returned to the Arizona expecting the same conditions they had experienced the last time. With each day they anticipated contact; either booby traps, sniper fire, or ambushes. Previously there had never been five days in a row without some sort of action, but the first two weeks of the operation passed without any sign of the enemy. Instead of causing the men to become lax, this tended to make them nervous, and it was repeated many times that, "When the shit hits the fan, it'll really hit." These predictions proved correct, and for the following three weeks they were constantly harassed by booby traps and sniper fire. It was only then that the men began to comfort themselves by saying, "Things can't get worse." This time they were wrong, and each of the four rifle companies walked into at least one daylight ambush. However, at no time did they come under fire from a grenade launcher, and therefore all talk of the Phantom Blooker ended.

Their luck finally began to change, and soon they were springing the ambushes on the Viet Cong. A week before the operation was to end, battalion headquarters estimated that that they had inflicted ten Viet Cong casualties for every one inflicted upon them. The men had no knowledge of this, and their estimates approximated five to one. A more realistic ratio would have been two Viet Cong casualties for every American casualty.

The Viet Cong saw no reason to worry about relative casualties yet. They had intelligence information saying that Second Battalion would pull out within a few days. To them, this meant that the Americans might get careless, and therefore the opportunity for revenge. They took advantage of this opportunity with a late-afternoon ambush and an all-night attack. Golf Company was the victim, and it was necessary for Hotel Company to help recover some of the bodies. At first it seemed as if the Viet Cong hadn't had time to loot these bodies, and this was partially true. It was Tony 5 who first noticed that something was wrong. The dead Marines still had their watches and rings. Their new M-16's lay beside them, some jammed and half taken apart. Two of the bodies were those of blooker men, and although both of their grenade launchers lay in plain view, no rounds were to be seen. Even if they had used all of them, they would still be wearing the empty pouches in which these rounds were carried. Tony was quick to mention this to Lieutenant S, and it was received with interest. A day later the entire battalion pulled out of the Arizona, still without coming across any sign of the Phantom Blooker.

Two months later, when Second Battalion returned to the Arizona, there was little talk of the Phantom Blooker. On the third night of the operation, Echo Company came under a four-hour barrage from a grenade launcher. It was then that old memories were repeated and exaggerated until again few words were spoken without reference to the Phantom Blooker. During the next month, only Fox Company escaped contact with him. The other three rifle companies in the battalion and also Headquarters and Supply Company all took casualties from these encounters. At no time during this period had there been any sightings of a lone American prisoner.

Late one afternoon when Hotel Company was returning from a patrol, Kovacs suddenly stopped walking and began pointing his rifle towards a tree line three hundred yards away, yelling, "Look! There they are, over there!" He raised the rifle to his eye and began shooting. All along the column, men squinted while trying to make out what he was aiming at. After a dozen quick shots, he lowered the rifle and said, "Four VC disappeared into that tree line," and then after a pause, he added, "one of them had on a Marine bush jacket." There wasn't a man in the company that didn't know what this could mean, yet Kovacs's later claim that this one man had been the Phantom Blooker was met with skepticism. It seemed much more likely that he was merely a Viet Cong soldier wearing an American bush jacket. Kovacs refused to push his contention, but when asked why he was so sure, he replied, "The sonofabitch didn't walk like a Gook." Even though Kovacs was only a fire team leader at the time, no one in the platoon, including Lieutenant S, would dare laugh in his face. Yet this is exactly what many of the men felt like doing. It seemed impossible that anyone could somehow distinguish the walk of an American from that of a Vietnamese at three hundred yards, and it also seemed strange that Kovacs had been the only one to spot anything.

Regardless of his own beliefs and those of his men, the company commander decided not to take any chances. He immediately directed the column towards the tree line. The brush was much denser than they had expected, and dusk came on before they were able to sweep through half of it, thus making it necessary for them to set-in for the night. As the men dug their foxholes, there was a lot of kidding about digging them deep enough for protection against the Phantom Blooker; but this is exactly what most of them did. Shortly before midnight, they were awakened by a quick series of exploding blooker rounds, seemingly proving Kovacs's claims. The men scurried and dived into their foxholes, some of which were the deepest they had ever dug. Although these holes seemed all too inadequate at the time, they were the sole reason every man in Hotel Company survived the night. Three men were wounded badly enough to be medivacked. One of these men was Alpha's squad leader, and before Second Platoon moved out that day, Lieutenant S told Kovacs to take over his squad.

Second Battalion remained in the Arizona for three more weeks, but only once more did it come into contact with the Phantom Blooker. It was during Kovacs's third day as a squad leader. He was on a platoon-size patrol with his squad, Alpha, at the point. They were following the edge of an overgrown path through some very heavy brush. Kovacs was the fifth man in the column, with Tony 5 directly in front of him. The squad radioman was right back of Kovacs. He in turn was followed by Forsythe, Childs, and Hamilton. The dense brush prevented anyone from seeing past the back of the man in front of him.

Within a span of five frightening seconds, it happened; and no one there was sure about all of it. First there was the staccato burst from the point man's rifle, then the silencing of this rifle by the explosion of a blooker round which ripped away half of the point man's face. A few pieces of shrapnel from the same round entered the skull of the second man, killing him instantly. Next there was a burst of two rounds from an SKS. The first of these rounds grazed the third man's shoulder, while the second pierced his neck, at the same time knocking him backwards into Tony 5, and both of them to the ground. In that instant the reeling body flew towards him, Tony 5 saw the profile of a man wearing Viet Cong slacks and a Marine bush jacket, a man he would later swear was an American.

Kovacs had seen nothing. He scrambled up the trail a mere fifteen yards before it widened into a small clearing. Within this clearing, the corpse of a Viet Cong soldier lay sprawled face down on the ground, one leg drawn up under him — caught in the same frantic position it had been in when the bullet found him. Across from this corpse was the body of another Viet Cong, sitting in the same position in which he had been surprised, and with the tin of food he had been eating still clutched in his hand. On the ground lay an SKS and four live blooker rounds. Kovacs returned to his squad to find two of his men dead and another critically wounded.

Chalice had the third watch that night. At nine o'clock, he laid his poncho liner on the ground in back of the bunker, realizing then that he would not be able to sleep. No longer was he thinking about what had happened under the canopy. This was part of the past, and Forsythe's story had purged these thoughts of their immediacy. However disturbing they were, Chalice now imagined himself faced with something far more threatening. In less than forty-eight hours the battalion would enter the

264

Arizona. He now understood the meaning behind the remarks made to him that day, the belief among many of the men that the Phantom Blooker would have to be destroyed by his own weapon, a weapon that Chalice was to carry. Their comments had almost made it seem as if they would be mere observers, and that Chalice would be representing them in a macabre duel upon which their fates depended. He felt it absurd that this superstition should bother him, and yet it did more than that. When Forsythe came to wake him for his watch, Chalice was lying motionless with his eyes open, no closer to sleep than he had been at any time during the previous four hours. Only after he was inside the bunker, silently looking over the valley and seeing nothing but darkness, only then did he become tired. The two hours and fifteen minutes of his watch seemed to stretch on insufferably. When it was over, he almost staggered back to his poncho liner before lying down and falling into a deep sleep.

Chalice awoke with the sense that something was different, yet everything seemed the same. There was no unusual activity on the hill, and the men straggled to the mess hall in the same manner as always. The food was as bland and tasteless as usual. It did seem to stick in his throat slightly more often as he forced himself to eat it. By taste alone, he would have had a difficult time distinguishing exactly what he was eating. Only after he finished and sat scanning the room was Chalice able to detect small differences in the men. Some were more animated than usual, others less; and the mess hall was a little quieter than normal. It was then he realized that no one was talking about the Arizona. The word that had been so often spoken during the past few days seemed now to be forgotten.

The next hour was spent in the same manner as during previous days on the hill. It was only as he stood in the working party formation in front of the S-2 hootch that Chalice began to really question this. It seemed incomprehensible that tomorrow he would be in the Arizona Territory, yet today should be a monotonous, grinding replica of past days on the hill. As the men were divided into different details, they moved with even more lethargy than usual, seemingly having built up some unfeeling inertia within themselves. Though Chalice didn't notice it, none of the men complained about the different working parties they were assigned, accepting them and their meaninglessness with indurate resignation.

Lunch was a repeat of breakfast. When the men returned to the platoon hootch, many of them shoved the equipment off the cots and lay down. Payne tried unsuccessfully to get up a card game. No one seemed to want to move, their faces exhibiting a quiet belligerency. Sugar Bear overheard a few of the men remark that they weren't going back to their working parties. He was now the right guide, and seeing that they did was his responsibility. To avoid having to make them, he left the hootch with plans to stay away from it for the rest of the day.

Childs was lying on the floor when he suddenly got up and walked over to Forsythe. They were talking with disturbed expressions on their faces when Hamilton joined them. Chalice became curious, and he walked over to find out what was going on. They led him outside before explaining. Childs had suddenly realized that no one in the platoon had any marijuana. They wouldn't be able to get it in the Arizona, and today was their last chance to do so. "I thought you didn't blow grass in the Arizona," Chalice remarked.

Childs gave him a deprecating glance as he answered, "When it's safe, we do."

Forsythe explained, "Sometimes we set-in for a few days with H and S Company, or even the whole battalion."

"We don't smoke too often, and never at night," Hamilton added.

"But it's nice to have around," Forsythe said, and this was the main reason they wanted it — to know it was there and to be able to look forward to using it if the chance came.

They stood for ten minutes while each man made suggestions only to have them rejected by the others. Finally, Hamilton remarked that it was too bad they didn't have a patrol through the ville scheduled. "*That's it!*" Forsythe shouted. He then explained that they would run their own patrol. At first the others merely laughed at him, but soon they were all making suggestions as to how it should be done.

"We'll need a radio," Childs pointed out.

"Payne'll go," Forsythe said.

Chalice asked Forsythe why he was so sure, and Hamilton cut in, "Because I'll kick his ass if he doesn't."

It was then a matter of deciding who else would go. They needed a machine gun. Neither Pablo nor Sinclaire smoked marijuana; so it was decided that they would ask Skip and Flip, knowing that if one could be convinced, then the other would also go. Ski was an obvious addition to the patrol. Ramirez didn't smoke much, but they knew he'd never let them think he was afraid. Roads was eliminated when no one agreed to ask him to go, or even to ask him if he smoked. In a few minutes the entire group stood outside the hootch suggesting other additions to the patrol. Ski went back inside hoping to get two more members. Both Hemrick and Valdez refused, but Appleton overheard Ski asking them and volunteered.

Within five minutes, they were lined up in back of the platoon hootch with all their equipment on. The road bisected the ville just a third of a mile from the base of the hill. After asking him four times if he thought he could find it, Hamilton assigned Chalice the point. Chalice then received some lyrical instructions from Forsythe: "Follow the yellow dirt road. Follow the yellow dirt road." The other members of the patrol picked this up, and they were all singing it as Chalice headed down the slope. To avoid being spotted, he led them behind the bunkers that lined the hill. The men were all laughing and passing humorous orders back and forth when Chalice motioned for them to halt and get down. At first they thought he was kidding, but when they saw what he had spotted, the men all hit the ground as if under a mortar attack. They lay silent and motionless as Gunny Martin and Captain Trippitt walked by less than ten yards in front of them. After a few minutes, Chalice got up and started leading them towards the road. They remained silent for a while and seemed to be taking the exploit more seriously until Hamilton passed congratulations up to Chalice for the "fearless" job he was doing. Chalice in turn passed the word back that he would have had two confirms if his rifle hadn't jammed. This returned the men to their previous joking mood, and they passed continuous warnings back and forth about booby traps and ambushes. As they approached the guard bunker at the base of the hill, the men became more serious. They exchanged nods with the sentry, at the same time placing rounds in the chambers of their rifles. Once off the hill, the men retained their serious mood. Knowing the relative safety of the road to the ville, they were mainly concerned about being spotted by a battalion officer. They moved slowly and with the care and precautions customary on a regular patrol.

The ville was alive with waves of people who streamed along both sides of the patrol giving the Marines barely enough room to move. Hamilton halted the column in front of a stand displaying black-marketed C-rations and other American goods. He arranged his men in a half circle around it for security and told Chalice to see if he could "score." Chalice approached the counter, but waited until the other customers had left before asking the twelve-year-old boy behind it in a whisper if he knew where they could get some marijuana. The boy casually reached beneath the counter and produced a small package wrapped in newspapers. Chalice repeated the question to make sure he was being understood. The boy unwrapped the package exposing ten cellophane packets of ten joints each. Chalice quickly rewrapped them while asking the price. The boy answered fifteen dollars. Chalice gave him a disapproving look and said, "Numba ten, numba ten."

The boy remained silent, so Chalice finally told him they'd pay ten dollars. It was now the boy's turn to reply, "Numba ten."

After a few minutes of haggling, Chalice got the price down to twelve dollars. Forsythe called over instructions to get three hundred. Chalice did this, at the same time asking Forsythe for some money. Forsythe made a quick collection and approached the counter. As he laid thirty dollars on top of it, Chalice said, "He wants thirty-six."

Forsythe shook his head admonishingly at the boy who was busy counting the thirty dollars. The boy made no complaint, and Forsythe picked up the package and walked away. They were about to leave when Appleton decided he wanted to buy some liquor. While they waited for him, Forsythe walked over to a boy selling the straw, cone-shaped hats the peasants wore. He bought one, put it on, and walked back to the men. They kidded him as he modeled it for them. Forsythe remarked that he wished he had brought his camera, whereupon Ski produced one out of his pocket. Ski was just about to take a picture when Forsythe stopped him. Forsythe then took out a pack of cigarettes and called a few kids over. Soon he was surrounded by a host of small, outstretched hands. The kids, some of them five and six years old, lit their cigarettes as Forsythe arranged them in front of him. They stood with cigarettes dangling from their smiling faces as Ski focused the camera. Forsythe again stopped him and moved all the kids in front of a stand displaying some brightly colored yard goods. For a few more cigarettes, he got the old woman running it to join the picture. Her husband approached, and he too was bribed into taking part. As Ski snapped the picture, Forsythe stood smiling with his arms around the old couple. They were also smiling, as evidenced by their black-stained teeth. The little kids stood in front of them puffing on cigarettes and making faces into the camera.

Appleton was tasting his liquor when he noticed a peasant trying to drag a spooked water buffalo past the men. "Hey Ramirez, bet you can't ride that baby."

"*Maaan*, I'm from *Tex*as. I can ride anything."

Before the rest of the men had a chance to coax Ramirez on, he was already headed towards the water buffalo. The animal became even more spooked, shifting its feet nervously upon the dusty road. The peasant pleadingly motioned Ramirez away while being dragged around in a circle. Appleton held up a dollar bill; but the peasant was too busy to figure out what the Marines wanted. When Chalice explained to him, the peasant refused. Soon they were holding up five dollars. This seemingly extraordinary amount of money and his fear of angering the Marines caused him to relent.

Ramirez circled behind the water buffalo. He stared determinedly at its huge gray rump, glanced at the Marines around him, and took off running. Just as he left the ground, the animal shifted its hindquarters into him and knocked Ramirez flat on his back. Hamilton lunged for the rope and was barely able to jerk the water buffalo away before it could gore him.

Ramirez jumped to his feet and insisted on trying again. Chalice held him by the arm, but Ramirez broke away and leaped on top of the water buffalo. The bewildered animal nervously shifted its feet without trying to throw Ramirez. He sat atop it with his helmet fallen down over his eyes and a big smile on his face. Ski quickly snapped a picture. Ramirez yelled for Forsythe to give him the peasant hat. Just as he held it out and Ramirez reached for it, the water buffalo jerked violently in a half circle and threw Ramirez to the ground.

The crowd of villagers converged upon him, some of them helping the peasant drag away the water buffalo. Ramirez lay unconscious in the middle of the road while Chalice nervously slapped his cheeks. In the meantime, Appleton managed to pour some liquor down Ramirez's throat. He convulsed with coughs, and they turned him over on his stomach. Spittle and liquor drooled from his lips, and then he puked. Still coughing, Ramirez kept trying to speak and finally managed to say, "I rode him." He repeated this a few more times between coughs as they helped him to his feet. His legs were wobbly, so Appleton had to hold him up. Their repeated inquiries as to whether he was all right were always met by the same dazed reply, "I rode that motherfucker."

Hamilton headed the patrol back to the hill. Ramirez was still dazed, and Appleton had to support him. He continued to babble all the way to the hill. "I'm from Laredo. I can ride anything."

"Sure, Mex," Appleton assured him.

" 'Mex,' bullshit! I'm a Chicano!"

"Sure, Ramirez, toughest Chicano in the Marine Corps."

"I can ride anything."

Before they even reached the platoon hootch, they found Tony 5 waiting for them. He had learned exactly what they were up to soon after they had gotten off the hill. Chalice cringed when he saw the furious look on Tony's face, and even Forsythe became ill-at-ease. Tony rushed by Chalice and headed directly for Hamilton, who was now back-stepping with his hands held out in front of him to fend off Tony. Hamilton continued stepping backwards as Tony berated him through gritted teeth. After both of them had made a complete circle around the squad, Tony was finally able to control himself enough to stand in one place. His forearms held tensed in front of him, he almost hissed his words while spittle flew from his mouth. Hamilton assured him that they'd never pull anything like the patrol again, and also that they'd get Tony's permission before smoking the marijuana.

When they reached the platoon hootch, they found both mail and replacements waiting for them. Of the five new men, Alpha received two. Each rifle squad was supposed to have a squad leader and three fire teams of four men each. Rarely did more than one of Second Platoon's three rifle squads have enough men to make a third fire team. Instead of the standard thirteen men, Alpha now had eight. The two replacements didn't even make up for the loss of Bolton, Harmon, and Tony 5. One of the replacements was a pudgy, blond-haired kid from Ohio named Fuller. The other was a slender black nicknamed Rabbit. It was now necessary for Hamilton to rearrange his fire teams. Until they received another replacement, he would have to act as both squad leader and a fire team leader. Payne and the radio would have to remain in his own fire team. Childs had more time in-country than any of the other men in the squad, and he should have been the other fire team leader; but Hamilton figured that Childs would be sent to the rear pretty soon because of his two Purple Hearts. This and the fact that Childs didn't care anyway, caused Hamilton to make Forsythe the other fire team leader and keep Childs in his own fire team. Forsythe was left with Chalice, Roads, and one of the replacements. Hamilton could see that Rabbit would be quite a bit better than Fuller; but Payne objected to having a "nigger" in his fire team, so Hamilton took Fuller and gave Rabbit to Forsythe.

As soon as he assigned the two new men, Hamilton began opening a large package at his feet. The other members of his squad gathered around him. The first few layers were canned goods, and he gave most of them away. He then picked up a box of candy bars and a dreamy smile appeared on his face as he said, "Almond Joys, wow!" Forsythe reached into the package and pulled out a small box. This drew the same reaction from Hamilton. "Turtles, wow! . . . Let me have one."

Forsythe drew the box away. "No, save them." Their eyes met, and Hamilton knew exactly what Forsythe was thinking. There were numerous other types of candy in the box. Hamilton kept less than half of it for himself. He sat thinking about how it would taste that night, when he suddenly remembered his promise to Tony 5.

Hamilton sought him out and asked permission, but Tony again became furious. "Not a fucking chance!"

"But Tony, it may be our last time to smoke for two months."

"Tough shit! You're lucky I didn't stuff that dope up your ass."

"C'mon Tony, you'll use just as much of it as I will."

"Fuck if I will. I'm not smoking anymore."

"Bullshit."

"I'm tellin' you, I'm laying off the stuff."

270

"What's the big deal, just because you're platoon sergeant?"

"You're *damn* right! I don't want anybody gettin' an extra hole in his ass 'cause of me."

"But you're just as good when you're stoned."

"*I know that*, but I don't want to give some punk that can't handle it an excuse to get wrecked."

"Why the hell can't *I* smoke?"

Tony hesitated before saying, "Because Payne is a shitbird and I don't want him smoking, and because you got two new men."

"So what? I'll stick Payne and the new men with Roads tonight."

"Quit buggin' me!"

"C'mon, Tony?"

"Oh get the fuck out of here."

"It's all right then?" Hamilton asked before leaving. Tony made no reply.

Chalice, Hamilton, Childs, and Forsythe sat quietly on top of the bunker's shooting counter, their legs dangling over the front edge. The only movement was the occasional passing of candy from hand to hand as they stared across the valley, waiting silently for the popping of the variously colored illumination flares. It was a common understanding among the men of Second Platoon that if all the men in a bunker had been smoking marijuana, no one would be left alone on watch until the effects had worn off. For this reason, they had smoked the first joint a few minutes after sunset, knowing that by nine o'clock it would be all right to leave one person on watch. Forsythe held the still unlit second joint in his hand as he scanned the area around the bunker. Something told him not to light it yet, and a few seconds later he heard approaching footsteps. Chalice was the first to speak the challenge. "Halt! Who is there?"

"Three fucking guesses," replied the now familiar voice of Valdez.

Ski was with Valdez, and the first thing he asked for was one of the joints. Forsythe turned around, and with his body lying across the shooting counter and his head hanging inside the bunker, he lit the second joint. After taking a drag, he passed it to Ski.

Hamilton's voice asked dreamily, "How come you guys aren't on watch?"

Ski was trying to pass the joint, but Valdez refused it saying, "No man, not tonight."

"C'mon," Ski insisted, "this is just what you need."

Again Hamilton asked, "How come you guys aren't on watch?"

"What's wrong with him?" asked Forsythe, referring to Valdez.

"He's got short-timer's jitters," Ski replied.

In a serious tone, Valdez said, "Wait till you get 'em. It won't be so funny."

"That right, man?" Forsythe asked.

"Hey, how come you guys aren't on watch?"

"That's right," Valdez answered. "Sunday I mail the king of spades home." His tone became more reflective as he added, "The ace goes home with me on the plane."

"That's the death card," Childs interrupted. "Ask any Gook."

Valdez's anger was real as he replied, "Your death card if you don't shut the fuck up."

Forsythe tried to calm him. "Take it easy, man. . . . Maybe a few tokes 'ud do you some good."

"Hey, how come you guys aren't on watch?"

"No man, leave me alone."

"Whata ya eatin'?" Ski asked Childs.

"Almond Joys."

"Pass me one."

"No." Ski reached over and took what was left of the candy bar from Childs's hand.

"Wait a minute! Listen!" Hamilton commanded. Everybody froze in silence as they listened intently for the sound Hamilton had heard.

"I don't hear anything," Forsythe whispered.

"Of course, I didn't say anything yet."

"Huh?"

"What?"

"I'm *gonna . . . ask . . . a question.*"

"Shit."

"I don't fucking believe it."

"Okay Hamilton, ask your goddamn question."

"How come you guys aren't on watch?"

"Because we're squad leaders," Valdez answered.

"Oh, that's right! You're Bravo's squad leader now, aren't you, Ski? . . . Wait a minute! I'm a squad leader too."

"Yeah, but you're dumb," Childs cut in.

Valdez said irritably, "We've got nine men in our squads. You got eight."

"Oh . . . wait a minute! You shoulda had five-man watches."

"But we didn't," Ski replied. "Nine months in the bush and this is the first time I didn't have to stand lines, and probably the last too."

While Ski had been talking, Chalice said, "Puff the Magic Dragon,

I think he's gonna work out." They all looked in the direction Chalice had pointed. Two huge illumination flares designating corners of Puff's grid square had already been dropped. They watched intently as the other two burst over the Arizona. Waiting for the machine gun tracer rounds, they were now able to enjoy the calming effect of the marijuana. Then it appeared, a bright red dotted line, seemingly created out of nothing but the blackness of the sky — manmade lightning. This same sight that he'd seen so many times before, hypnotized Chalice as always; and he said to himself, 'So beautiful, like a thousand falling stars.' Then the muffled staccato of the machine guns that created it reached his ears, seemingly as an afterthought of whoever it was that had been capable of such an act of beauty. They all continued to watch for those brief seconds when the red line of fire would cut the darkness in half.

Forsythe heard someone's footsteps approaching the rear of the bunker, and all he could think of was 'Go away. Go away.' Now the others heard them also, but each man refused to give the challenge. They stared in the direction of Puff, not wanting to break the spell. Only when the footsteps had reached the door did Forsythe speak — not the mandatory "Halt! Who is there?" but instead a resentful "Who's that?"

"Commander of the Guard," came a voice from outside the bunker.

'So what?' thought Childs.

The commander of the guard waited outside for the command, "Advance and be recognized!" When he realized it wasn't coming, he entered anyway.

Chalice sat thinking, 'Uh oh, now we've had it.'

As the commander of the guard entered the bunker, a green flare burst in the air above it. He could now make out the distinct outlines of four men sitting upon the shooting counter. They heard him walking around behind them, yet no one took his eyes off the green flare.

"Who's on watch here?" asked the fatherly voice.

Hamilton realized that it was his responsibility to reply, and while thinking, 'What a bummer,' he answered, "We all are."

The commander of the guard continued to walk behind them. Without saying anything, he placed his hand on the shoulders of each of the four men. Still with their backs to him, they wondered what he was doing. As if in reply to their thoughts, he asked casually, "Where are your flak jackets, men?"

Again there was a pause before Hamilton answered, "We don't put them on until we go on watch."

"I thought you said you were all on watch."

"I mean when we divide up the watch at nine o'clock."

The voice said calmly, "You know it's battalion policy for everyone on watch to wear a flak jacket and helmet." He received no reply, nor did anyone attempt to put on his flak jacket. After a long pause, he again spoke in a fatherly tone as he walked up and down behind them. "I know you men have seen quite a bit of action, but that's no excuse for getting careless. Charlie can't keep this up much longer. It looks like we've got this war just about won. . . . How would one of you like to be known as the last man to be killed in Vietnam?" Again no one answered him. "You men make some pretty fine targets up there." None of them made any effort to climb down off the shooting counter. He paced back and forth behind them a few more times before leaving the bunker without saying another word.

The men sighed in unison, and Forsythe spoke the thought they'd all been thinking. "I thought he'd *never* leave."

Chalice said, "God, what if it had been Trippitt?"

Hamilton answered immediately. "We would have gotten our asses kicked, court-martialed, or both."

"He wasn't a bad guy," Chalice commented.

Childs gave a sarcastic grunt, then said, "A lifer's a lifer. The fatherly type can get you killed just as dead as any other type."

"Yeah," Ski agreed, "but if I had to take my choice, I'd take the fatherly type."

"Do you think he knew we were stoned?" Chalice asked.

"Who cares?" Childs replied.

Forsythe said, "I doubt it. If he knew what it was like, he'd a been stoned himself."

"They all know we blow grass," Childs cut in. "What do they expect. We never get any time off. We'd go nuts if we didn't."

"What about the Second World War?" Valdez asked.

"What are you talking about?"

"They didn't get any days off and they didn't smoke marijuana."

"Sure they didn't," Hamilton replied, "but they sure as hell got drunk a lot."

"Not when they were standing bunker watch," Valdez insisted.

"That's different," Forsythe said. "You're a hell of a lot better off on grass, sometimes even more alert than when you're straight. Besides, they were always getting shipped to the rear. Our rear is Okinawa."

"There it is," Ski agreed.

The men soon lost what little desire they had to talk, and their attention shifted back to the flares exploding in front of them. At nine o'clock, the effects of the marijuana had practically worn off, and Chalice was left

274

alone to begin his watch. Hamilton, Forsythe, and Childs spread out their poncho liners on a little knoll in back of the bunker. Ski and Valdez had followed them, and they were all lying down gazing at the sky when Valdez broke the silence by saying, "If anything happens to me, I want one of you to write to my family." They all tried to laugh off this remark, but Valdez spoke again as if he hadn't heard them. "I want you to tell my brother to stay home and take care of my parents, not to join the Crotch."

"How come you're talking like that?" Hamilton asked.

Valdez hesitated before answering slowly and with conviction, "I'm not coming back from the Arizona. Ain't no way I can make it."

They no longer tried to laugh off what Valdez was saying. They knew that they had to convince him otherwise, and their reason for attempting to do so was spoken by Forsythe. "C'mon man, you know what the story is: If you think you're gonna get it, you will."

"There it is."

"I know, I know, but I just can't help it. . . . I know."

No one said anything for a few seconds, then Childs spoke. "For Christ's sake, Valdez, you've made it for twelve and a half months. Next Sunday you'll send home the king of spades. Five days later you'll take the ace home with you. You said so yourself."

"That's the death card. *You* said so."

"Oh come off it. I was just riding you."

"The Gooks think so too, and they oughta know about death."

"Jesus Christ! Will you cut it out! What the hell makes you think you won't make it."

Valdez hesitated before answering, "I've come too close too many times."

Now Hamilton spoke. "We all have. You know that."

"That's not all I know."

"All right," Childs moaned, "where'd you get your information?"

"In the hospital. . . . When I woke up in the hospital I didn't know if I was dead or alive, and I didn't give a shit. . . . I knew if they sent me back to the Arizona, I'd had it."

"You hardly got hit," Hamilton protested, "a few pieces of shrapnel, that's all."

"It don't matter. I knew if they ever sent me back there I'd be finished. . . . You don't know what it was like coming back to An Hoa. I thought you guys were still in the Arizona. All the time since then, I've been sending home the cards, knowing that my only chance to go home was if the cards ran out before we got sent back there. . . . So close," he added softly, then gave a slight laugh before saying, "I came so close."

Forsythe repeated what he had said before, knowing the truth in it. "Listen Valdez, you can't think that way. If you do, you've had it."

"I can't help it. I just can't help it."

Childs said, "Well, don't go back."

At first Valdez ignored Childs's suggestion. In all the time he had been worrying about the Arizona, Valdez had never considered doing something to keep himself from returning. Still not taking the suggestion completely seriously, he asked, "How do you suppose I could manage that?"

"Ask Kramer," Hamilton suggested.

Valdez shook his head. "I can't ask him. Maybe if Lieutenant S was still —"

"It wouldn't make any difference," Childs cut in. "Trippitt's the one that has to decide, and he wouldn't let you leave *ten seconds* early. . . . Why don't you tell them you're sick?"

"I don't wanna do that. Besides, it 'ud look kinda funny going over to sick bay tomorrow morning."

"Who the fuck cares what it looks like?" Childs asked.

"*I* do!"

"It's better than looking dead."

Forsythe became irritated. "Lay off him, Childs. . . . Listen Valdez, what if you had something real obvious like a broken leg?"

"A broken leg? What —"

"It doesn't have to be your leg, maybe just your finger." Valdez didn't reply. "Well, how 'bout it?"

"Quit asking me dumb questions. How am I gonna get a broken finger?"

Up to this point, Valdez actually had no idea what Forsythe was getting at; but he suddenly realized, and even in the darkness Childs and Forsythe could see the whites of Valdez's eyes as they shifted nervously between them. Valdez could not make himself answer the question, so Childs said harshly, "If you're so scared, let me do a job on you."

The word "scared" was a mistake. "I can't, man. It wouldn't be right."

"Sure it would," Childs insisted. "You owe it to yourself."

"There it is," Ski agreed.

Valdez remained silent, so Forsythe finally said, "They're right. You owe it to yourself. Anyway you can get out of it, do it."

"You mean I wouldn't be letting you guys down?"

"Fuck no!"

"Hell no!"

"Are you fucking serious?"

"But I'm a squad leader."

Childs was getting impatient. "Who the hell needs *you*?"

276

"What do you mean by that?" Valdez asked angrily.

Forsythe tried to calm him. "Take it easy, man. You'd be going home in less than two weeks anyway."

Valdez hesitated before saying with nervous excitement, "Okay, okay, hurry up."

Childs immediately began to scramble around on the ground. "What are you doing?" Forsythe asked.

"Looking for something to use."

"Use my rifle butt."

"No, I need something harder."

"Harder!" Valdez exclaimed. "What's he trying to —"

"Just take it easy," Forsythe insisted.

"Harder?" Valdez repeated.

Forsythe motioned to the engineers' hootch in back of them. "Go up there."

Childs scrambled to his feet and started running. They could hear him as he fell and got up again. They then heard the clanging of tools, followed by the noise of Childs running back towards them. Before he was even in sight, Valdez called out nervously, "What'd you find?"

"A saw."

"A saw!"

Childs fell to his knees in front of Valdez. "Take it easy, man. It's just a hammer."

"Just a hammer!"

"Will you relax. I ain't gonna hit you in the head."

"You're fucking right you ain't."

Childs held up the hammer ready to use it. "Just on the finger."

In an instant, Valdez drew his hands up to his chest and leaned away from Childs. "Wait a minute. Just wait a minute."

"For what?" Childs asked impatiently.

"He ain't gonna hit you with all his might," Hamilton cut in.

"Besides, he's the weakest guy in the platoon," Forsythe pointed out.

Childs raised the hammer threateningly. "Who says so? I could knock your fucking hand off."

It was now Valdez who said, "Take it easy, man."

Childs became angry. "Let's get this abortion over with." There was a few seconds' silence before he added in a calmer tone, "C'mon, put your hand down."

Valdez slowly lowered his hand to the ground, then instantly drew it away. "You ain't gonna hit me hard, are you?"

"Hell no, not half as hard as I'd hit Forsythe."

Forsythe couldn't resist saying, "That'll be the fucking day you ever get near me with a hammer."

"What do you mean?" Valdez asked nervously.

"I'm only kidding."

"Well don't kid around."

Childs said impatiently, "If you'd put your hand down, I'd be able to get this abortion over with and start on Forsythe's head."

Valdez put his hand down and Childs aimed the hammer. "Not too hard now."

"Hell no, just a tap."

"Just a tap now," cautioned Valdez.

The instant Childs raised the hammer, Valdez drew his hand away. "Wait a minute!"

"For what?" Childs asked disgustedly.

"I changed my mind."

"How come?" Hamilton moaned.

"It's a chicken-shit thing to do."

Childs banged the hammer on the ground. "Jesus Christ! I thought we settled that."

"Well I changed my mind. I've stuck it out this long. I'm not gonna turn yellow at last."

"Who's turning yellow?" Forsythe asked. "You owe it to yourself."

"There it is," Ski agreed. "It's either a little job by Childs, or a big one by Charlie."

Hamilton cut in, "What's worse, going home with a sore finger, or going home in a box?"

Childs held out the hammer. "Don't be an idiot. If you don't let me use this, you're a dead man."

Valdez began to look at the situation logically. "Maybe not. I only gotta last eight days."

Childs really began to lose his patience. "Goddamn it! You said yourself you were a dead man if you didn't."

"Maybe not. I'll be careful." Valdez's voice indicated he was having as hard a time trying to convince himself as he was those around him.

Childs dropped the hammer disgustedly and lay down, at the same time saying, "Cries for an hour, then changes his mind."

"*Who* was crying?"

"Ski, it must have been Ski."

"You're gonna get your wise-ass face pushed in."

Forsythe was now irritated with both Valdez and Childs. "Cut the shit, will ya?"

278

"I can't see what the big deal is, one lousy finger," Ski commented.

"What about your parents? How are they gonna feel if you come home dead?" Hamilton asked.

"After waiting twelve and a half months for you," Forsythe added.

This last comment had an effect on Valdez, and he asked somberly, "Do you guys really think I should do it?"

"Hell yeah!"

"Yes!"

"What do you think I got this hammer for, to commit suicide?"

"Okay, I'll do it," Valdez said with conviction.

His hand was already on the ground. Childs drew the hammer back slowly. A flare exploded above the hill. When Forsythe saw Valdez grimacing with his eyes closed and the look of concentration on Childs's face, he couldn't keep from laughing. Childs also began to laugh. Valdez quickly drew his hand away, and he too began to laugh. Hamilton and Ski joined them, and soon they were all rolling around on the ground in hysterics. It was a while before they sat up, ready to start again. Each man tried to be serious, but every few minutes one of them would lose control, precipitating muffled laughter from the others. Childs finally said impatiently, "C'mon, let's get it over with."

Valdez was still laughing as he said, "Okay, okay, I'll do it." He placed his hand down. Just as Childs was about to strike, he again drew it away and brought on another round of laughter.

Finally, Forsythe said the only thing he could think of that might stop the laughing. "What about your family? Who's gonna take care of them if you get killed?"

The laughter stopped immediately. Valdez placed his hand on the ground. As Childs aimed the hammer, they could again hear each other's muffled laughs. It wasn't until the hammer was already on its way down that Valdez drew his hand away, at the same time exclaiming, "There's the insurance money!"

Forsythe asked seriously, "How long do you think that'll last?"

"Yeah, most of it'll go for taxes," Childs lied.

"Really?"

"Sure, it'll put them in a higher income tax bracket."

Even though he realized Childs was lying, Valdez placed his hand down. "Okay, I'll do it." Before Childs could raise the hammer, Valdez drew it back again. "Wait a minute. There's no hurry."

They finally got him to put his hand down again, but this try ended in the same laughter as the others. After some harsh words, it was decided that Forsythe would hold Valdez's hand in place. By the time Childs raised the hammer, they were all laughing again and Valdez jerked his hand free. Impatient and irritated, some of their anger was real as they berated Forsythe. It was finally decided that both he and Hamilton would hold Valdez's arm. As they did so, everyone became completely serious, and Valdez cautioned, "Just a tap."

"Okay, just a tap," Childs agreed.

They were now weary of the entire effort and anxious to get it over with. Each man remained completely serious. Hamilton and Forsythe leaned forward, placing as much weight as possible on Valdez's arm. Childs aimed the hammer with the care worthy of a surgeon. Ski held his breath as he watched. Childs put the hammer down and started fumbling with his shirt.

"C'mon," urged Valdez nervously.

"What are you doing?" Hamilton asked.

"My glasses fogged."

Childs heard someone trying to control a laugh. He knew that he'd better act fast. Quickly replacing his glasses, he grabbed the hammer. The laughter became louder. Childs nervously swung the hammer down. As soon as he heard it hit the ground, he knew he had missed.

This last failure was too much for the others. They collapsed in hysterics. During those brief intervals when they were able to control themselves, they directed angry curses at Childs. As stupid as he felt, even Childs had to laugh. One by one the men sat up. Too exhausted to be really abusive towards Childs, they did their best. None of them had the strength or patience to try again, and their only consolation was that at least it was over. Childs accepted their rebukes silently. Valdez leaned forward on his hands to get up and leave. The sound of the hammer's dull thud was followed by an anguished but muffled scream. While Valdez writhed on his back in pain, he was somehow able to kick Childs in the crotch. Now there were two moaning figures on the ground, and three hysterical ones above them. Chalice came running out of the bunker, nervously asking what was going on. No one had the ability nor desire to tell him, and the only words spoken were those of Valdez. "Childs, you motherfucker, you crippled me. . . . I'll kill you. My hand is *destroyed*. . . . Oh, *God* it hurts. . . . Thanks, Childs. Thanks. . . . I should kill you. *God* it hurts. . . . Thanks, man. Thanks."

3. The Arizona Territory

During the night, Echo, Fox, and Golf had joined Hotel Company on the hill. It was barely light, but already a line of men completely encircled the mess hall and stretched fifty yards away from it. Their faces displayed no fear or anxiety. In less than two hours they would start boarding the helicopters, and there was no longer time to worry. The men were constantly spotting friends from other companies, shouting greetings and kidding remarks to them as they all waited in line.

  Right after breakfast, Kovacs sought out Kramer to wish him luck. They walked together to the platoon hootch. Kramer mentioned that Valdez had somehow had an ammo crate dropped on his hand, and that he'd have to be left behind. Kovacs had heard a different account of this, but he didn't mention it to Kramer. When they reached the hootch, the men were already busy filling their packs. Kramer knew that most of them had a better idea of what to expect than he did, so he stayed out of their way as they bustled around the platoon area. It was Tony 5 who gave the few orders that were necessary, and he did so with a demanding self-assurance reminiscent of Kovacs.

Hamilton's main concern was making sure that Fuller packed his gear correctly. He'd check on him every few minutes, then walk away as quickly as possible to avoid hearing again how glad Fuller was to be headed for the "Arizona Territory, right off." Fuller directed all his questions to the extremely receptive Payne. This made Hamilton more uneasy, and he strained to hear the advice Payne offered. Rabbit, Alpha's other new man, asked very few questions; but instead watched the men in his fire team, especially Forsythe. Having expected Roads to be the most friendly towards him, Rabbit found him appreciably colder than either Chalice or Forsythe.

Ramirez was the fourth man that morning to remind Childs to bring his hammer. As the men began to stage their packs outside the hootch, Valdez approached sheepishly with a large bandage on his hand. At first Tony 5 gave him a sideways glance, but then walked over to wish him

281

well. Soon a large group of men had gathered around Valdez commenting about his "accident" and slapping him on the back.

Childs avoided the group. The men began to call out jokingly for him to come over and say good-bye to Valdez, and he finally had to do so to silence them. Most of the men were sincerely glad that Valdez wasn't going with them. Thinking that someday they would also be in the same position, they drew from Valdez's example a vicarious sense of relief. There was also the feeling that with each man they saw leave Vietnam, their own return dates drew closer.

After all packs were staged outside the hootch, word was passed that Captain Hindman wanted to speak to the men before they left. Nearly a third of the battalion stood in front of the chapel when Hindman began.

"First of all, let me say that I know you men have things to do, so I'll make this short. Nobody told you that Vietnam was going to be any picnic; and for those of you who've never been to the Arizona, this operation will prove it isn't. Nothing worthwhile was ever gained without sacrifices, and for the next few months it will be your turn to make these sacrifices. The weaker of you might see things that will cause you to question your faith, but remember that the Lord works in strange ways. It is not our job to question these ways. Instead, we must always keep in mind what we're fighting for — freedom, yes, but freedom under God. Through our faith in God we will overcome our enemies, for this is the one powerful weapon they can never capture from us.

"I don't have to tell you how much I wish I could fight alongside of you, but that's not my job. When God chooses our life's work for us, he does so with far greater understanding than we could ever have. While you brave men are fighting for your country, you can rest assured that I will be fighting for your souls; and I'm not bragging when I say my victory will be greater than yours. But remember, we're all Americans, and a victory by each of us is shared as a common victory."

Colonel Nash had stood restlessly listening to Hindman, but finally had to step up and whisper something to him. Hindman continued: "I guess I'm going to have to wrap things up, but let me say one last thing. There's a lot of people back home that don't understand why it's necessary for us to be fighting here. When you write home, tell your folks what we're doing, and have them tell others. In fact, if you have the time, write a letter to your hometown newspaper. We're Americans, and this is one of our rights.

"There's no reason a good soldier can't be a good Christian. Don't lose your faith in God, and as you make sacrifices, remember the sacrifices made for us by Our Savior, Jesus Christ. God bless you, and good luck."

282

As soon as Hindman finished speaking, the harsh shouts of platoon sergeants rang out over the hum of the men's voices, ordering them back to their staging areas. They returned in time to hear the order given to "saddle-up." There were the usual moans and complaints as they helped each other put on their packs and equipment. As soon as the men were ready, Captain Trippitt and Gunny Martin appeared. Trippitt retained his somber, disapproving appearance as Martin yelled out the order to form up.

Soon the entire battalion was strung out in two columns along the edges of the road. Echo Company paralleled Hotel, and they would be the first to board the helicopters. It was only a few minutes before the first one was sighted. Hotel Company watched each succeeding copter boarded until all of Echo Company was off the hill. It was now Hotel Company's turn. The men were already divided up into different loads, and there was no confusion as the helicopters were filled.

Kramer didn't look out his window until he felt the chopper descending. They were headed for a small patch of high ground surrounded by a kilometer of rice paddies. He could barely make out the irregular circle formed by the men of Echo Company who were serving as security for the landing. The chopper touched down in the middle of this circle, and Kramer now saw that the patch of high ground was the remains of a small, burned-out ville. A man from Echo Company waved them by as they rushed off the copter. They didn't stop to form up until they were standing in two feet of water. Kramer waited impatiently while the choppers brought in the rest of Hotel Company. As each succeeding helicopter took off, he and his men were overcome by the sense that they were now stranded.

In less than an hour, the entire battalion had been choppered-in. Hotel Company was given the battalion point, and Second Platoon the company point. Soon the battalion was heading towards some high ground a kilometer away. Hotel Company moved in a single column. Headquarters and Supply Company, with Colonel Nash and the rest of the battalion officers followed behind them in two columns. Echo Company, in a single column, took up the rear. Fox Company, also in a single column, marched as flank security fifty yards to the left of the battalion's main body. Golf had the same position on the right.

By the time they were halfway to the tree line, the men were exhausted and already staggering under their heavy packs. Alpha was the lead squad in the column, and Childs the battalion point man. Chalice was now remembering the agony of marching through rice paddies, doing so the only way possible, by experiencing it. Each step he took seemed to be the final

283

one before collapse. His pack straps dug into his shoulders as if they were a gradually tightening tourniquet. The sharp edges of his ammo can kept banging into his sides, and he was continually trying to adjust the sling to prevent this. The familiar thought came to him that no one in the platoon could possibly be experiencing the agonizing pain that he was now enduring. For the first time since he had been in Vietnam, the absurdity of this thought became apparent. The cause of this realization was the sight of Rabbit staggering in front of him. For the first time, he felt physically superior to another member of the platoon. The reason for this was not the belief that he was less tired than Rabbit, but merely the knowledge that he'd had some idea of what to expect. A smile crossed his lips as he imagined Rabbit's thoughts. Chalice was able, at the same time, to sympathize with Rabbit and yet to receive some pleasure from the example of his suffering. In a voice, the strength and assuredness of which surprised him, Chalice called forward the same helpful lie he had heard so often from others. "Take it easy, Rabbit. You'll get used to it."

Kramer was also exhausted. As he watched those in front of him staggering through the rice paddies, he found reason to again ask himself what caused his men to endure such suffering, not admitting that he was actually trying to figure out why he himself was enduring it. Sweat dripped from his face, and he began performing that now familiar idiosyncrasy of using his forearm to cock back his helmet, knowing the advantage gained from this would be negligible. Before drawing his arm away, he roughly brushed the sweat from his face. It was then that he heard the faint, almost moaning sound of someone in front of him singing. His disbelief quickly turned to amazement that someone would have the energy to even attempt to sing. Kramer strove to hear it, and was barely able to make out the words sung by the straining, off-key voice. "*If I had a hammer, I'd hammer in the mor-or-ning./ I'd hammer in the evening, all over this land./ I'd hammer out da-an-ger. I'd hammer out war-or-ning./ I'd —*"

"Who is that?" Kramer asked the man in front of him. The singing had already stopped by the time word was casually relayed back to him that it had been Childs. Kramer felt like laughing, but was too exhausted to do anything more than smile. Now that no one was singing, he passed the word forward to tell Childs to "knock it off." As Kramer heard his message relayed up the column, he tried to think about the incident disparagingly. Despite himself, a feeling of pride took hold — 'A singing point man, a singing point man — what an unbelievable platoon.'

Two hundred yards from the tree line, Colonel Nash gave the order to halt. The companies on flank security were told to draw even with Hotel Company. When this was done, the first elements of each of these companies turned at right angles and marched parallel to the tree line until all three companies were on-line and facing the high ground. Headquarters and Supply Company remained behind Hotel, and Echo in turn behind H and S Company. The order to move out was given, and the three forward companies moved on-line towards the high ground.

It was now that the men's thoughts shifted from their own pain to their fear of contact. Not one head hung down. All eyes remained focused upon the tree line in anticipation and dread of what it might be hiding. Each step closer increased their fear, even after they had passed the point where they would have been most vulnerable.

They did not stop upon reaching the tree line, but immediately began to sweep through it as fast and as carefully as possible. The men constantly raised and lowered their heads, alternately looking for an ambush or booby traps. A few hundred yards into the tree line, Hotel Company came upon a large, burned-out ville. Every deserted hootch had a bunker beneath it, and now began the troublesome job of fragging and entering each one. The entire battalion halted as Hotel Company methodically checked out each bunker.

Hardly a minute went by without the warning "Fire in the hole," and then the sound of an exploding grenade. They found no sign of the enemy, and many of the men remembered having gone through these same procedures, in this same ville, with the same results during the last operation in the Arizona.

As soon as all the bunkers had been checked, Hotel, Golf, and Fox Companies resumed their sweep through the high ground. H and S Company made camp in the ville, while Echo acted as rear security. When the three sweeping companies reached the far edge of the high ground, they backtracked until Fox and Golf had made contact with Echo Company. These four rifle companies then formed a perimeter around the ville and H and S Company. Word was soon passed to take a half hour for lunch.

During this break, the company commanders were told to report to H and S Company where they found Colonel Nash waiting for them. He went over the plans for the next three days. The battalion would retain its camp in the ville. Each day three rifle companies would go out on separate patrols while one would stay behind as security for Headquarters Company. After explaining this, Colonel Nash nodded to an unassuming-looking man wearing thick glasses. Major Lucas rose to his feet and held up a map of the area. He then explained the routes of the different patrols to the company commanders. Although he had the appearance of a bookkeeper wearing a set of oversized jungle fatigues, his voice was sharp and possessed a concise, military tone. Nash had only given him a rough idea

285

of what he had wanted. It was the major who had planned the patrols, as he would plan all future movements of the battalion. Lucas finished his explanation by asking if there were any questions. The satisfied look on his face unequivocally indicated that he felt none were necessary.

Trippitt hurried back to his company and explained the day's patrol to his platoon commanders. Its object was to search for signs of the enemy by sweeping a small patch of high ground two kilometers away. Hotel Company moved out almost immediately. Rabbit and Fuller were glad to be able to leave their packs behind; but after a few minutes of walking through rice paddies, they were just as exhausted as before. Fuller marched directly in front of Hamilton, and his every action made Hamilton sorry he had chosen Fuller over Rabbit. He staggered through the water as if he were crushing grapes; and even though there was nothing but rice paddies for a kilometer in any direction, Fuller shifted his head warily from side to side as if he expected a company of Viet Cong to pop up in front of him. Hamilton realized that Fuller was trying to impress him, and this made his actions even more ludicrous.

As Hotel Company approached the high ground, the men became increasingly wary and uneasy. Eyes straining, they searched the brush for any sign of danger. The company was in two parallel columns. When it came within a hundred yards of the high ground, the forward elements peeled off at right angles until the entire company paralleled the front edge of the tree line. The men then moved towards it on-line. Chalice glanced nervously at his blooker, wondering whether he and the other blooker men would be ordered to fire into the brush in preparation for the sweep. No such order was given.

The patch of high ground was crisscrossed by worn and recently used paths. The men warily avoided these paths for fear that they might be booby-trapped. As sure as they were that the Viet Cong had been there, they were just as sure they weren't there now. A careful search affirmed this. Trippitt headed them back towards the camp, and they reached it in time to heat some C-rations.

As the sky darkened, most of the men took occasional glances at the all-but-hidden sun, experiencing at once the anomalous feelings of camaraderie and isolation. No one needed to be told to dig his foxhole deeper. Soon they were surrounded by blackness, but the more experienced men knew that at any instant it could explode upon them. Nash had decided that hootches would make too easy a target, so the men were prepared to sleep on top of their ponchos. The damp air retained the smell of insect repellent as bottles of it were passed around.

Forsythe noticed a man already in his foxhole, and immediately realized it was Fuller. Out of curiosity and amusement, Forsythe walked towards the foxhole. Fuller stood leaning forward with only the top of his head protruding above the lip of the hole. He constantly shifted it from side to side while holding his finger on the trigger of his rifle. "How's it going?" Forsythe asked in a purposely loud voice.

"Okay," Fuller whispered.

"See anything," Forsythe asked with mock concern and in an even louder voice.

"Not yet, but I'm ready," Fuller answered in a whisper.

"Well keep up the good work."

"You can count on me."

While most of the men went to sleep expecting to be awakened by the sounds of rifle fire or incoming mortars, the night passed quietly, disappointing no one. Two more days went by without contact. Instead of becoming lax, the men became increasingly edgy. They felt that each day without contact merely increased the likelihood of it coming the next day. Their uneasiness was also heightened by the fact that they were now experiencing something they hadn't expected.

The battalion moved out at dawn on the fourth day. They marched without stopping until noon. After a short break for lunch, Golf Company was left as security for H and S Company, while the other three rifle companies headed for the different places where they would make camp that night. Hotel set-in an hour before dusk.

Trippitt called together his platoon commanders in order to go over the daily plan that would be used for the next few weeks. They would move out each day at dawn and march until noon. One platoon would remain behind with the CP, while the other three went on separate patrols. They would return before dark; whereupon two of the platoons would send out ambushes, while the other two placed listening posts fifty to a hundred yards outside the perimeter. Before Trippitt dismissed his platoon commanders, he relayed the news he had just heard over the radio. The commander of Echo Company, his radioman, and one other soldier had been killed by a booby trap.

When Kramer mentioned this to Tony 5, his reply was, "We had him for a couple of weeks before we got Trippitt. He was almost as shitty. . . . Too bad the other dudes got killed."

"Seems kind of funny that they only got three men and one of them was the company commander," Kramer mused.

"Not funny, just smart. It was probably a command detonated booby trap. The Gook waits till half the company passes, then pulls the cord to detonate the booby trap as soon as he sees a radio. Has a pretty good chance of bagging himself a lieutenant, maybe even a skipper. He just hit the jackpot this time. . . . I wonder if they got him."

Hotel Company continued to make camp in a different place each night. Ten days after leaving the battalion, they had still failed to make contact, or even to come upon any civilians. During that time, Echo Company had hit four more booby traps and Fox had hit two. Kramer was glad that so far they had been lucky, but he knew their luck couldn't possibly continue. Each dawn threatened them with contact, and there was such a feeling of inevitability about it that he almost wished to get it over with. In addition to being edgy, his men were frustrated by the constant movement. They would set-in each night with the disgusted feeling that the next day at dawn they would again have to break camp, march all day, and set-in somewhere else. With nothing to look forward to, they became fatalistic and sometimes a little careless. All their actions seemed so meaningless, that they longed for that first bit of contact — picturing it as a fire fight, not a booby trap or a mortar attack — to prove to themselves that the physical torture of the marches and the discomfort of sleeping on wet ground were actually necessary. This was true even though they knew that their constant movement was as much for the purpose of avoiding the Viet Cong at night, as it was for seeking them out in the daytime.

The depression of the men was most obvious in Childs, and this surprised those who had known him longest. It wasn't that he was more irritable, this being impossible; but rather, as Forsythe put it, he wasn't "his old, sarcastic self."

Dusk had just come on when Hamilton noticed Childs's brooding figure sitting a few feet away from him. Hamilton slid over and said, "Well, we've been lucky so far."

"Guess so," Childs answered somberly.

"Every day without Charlie's a lucky one."

"Guess so."

"What's wrong with you, man?"

"What's wrong with *you?*"

"Cut the shit. You're the one looking like you lost your best friend."

"Lost enough of them, haven't I?" Childs answered gruffly.

"Bullshit, you never had one."

Childs grinned as he lay back on the ground. "Guess you're right."

288

"I don't know what you're so down about. We've been through this before."

"Who's down?"

"*Oh*, I know." Hamilton lowered his voice as he said, "It's what happened on Charlie Ridge."

"Hell no!" Childs answered truthfully.

"Then there *is* something wrong."

"Maybe." Childs paused for a long time before asking in a falsely casual manner, "Remember that Gook chick we saw with the napalmed face?"

"How could I forget? What a freak-out."

Childs continued in a dreamy tone, making no attempt to belittle his own words. "I thought she was going to be so beautiful."

"Me too. That's why it was so bad."

"You know, I bet she *was* beautiful . . . before that."

Hamilton would have found it hard to understand why anyone would be lastingly affected by this incident, but such a reaction from Childs seemed even more puzzling. Incapable of handling the situation in any other way, he tried to sluff it off. "All them Gook chicks look alike."

"Fuck you."

Hamilton attempted to change the subject. "Look, I don't know what you're so down about. You'll be going home before I will."

"Not if you get blown away."

This remark in no way irritated Hamilton. Childs was beginning to sound like his old self. "Besides, you can always think of a way to skate back to the rear."

Childs again became serious as he said, "I'm tired of that shit. . . . It's too much trouble."

"Too much trouble? It's better than the bush. . . . Hey, maybe your lump'll get bigger."

Childs rubbed the lump on his forearm and shook his head while saying, "It's the same."

"You'll think of a way."

"I shouldn't have to. I've got two Hearts already. . . . That got Delaney and a lot of other guys a job in the rear."

"But both of yours were skatin'."

"I can't help it if I didn't get my arm blown off. Anybody else and they would have sent him to the rear."

"But you wouldn't of went."

"I would now."

"Why don't you say something to the lieutenant?" Childs thought about Kramer catching him and Hamilton in Da Nang, and he shook his head.

289

"You got nothing to lose." Childs remained silent. "I mean he ain't Lieutenant S, but he may be all right."

"No!"

"Go ahead. You got nothing to lose."

"All right."

Childs found Kramer and Tony 5 talking near their foxhole. Tempted to turn around, he stared down at Kramer and said, "How come I didn't get a job in the rear after my second Heart?" He'd asked this question in the only way possible for him to do so, by using a cocky, sarcastic tone.

Kramer's first reaction was surprise. "Why didn't you say something about this on the hill?"

"*They're* supposed to ask me."

"I don't know what you expect me to do now. I can't just send you in." Childs realized that this was true, but he continued to stare at Kramer. "I'll tell you what, I'll have the next man that goes to the rear say something about it to the company master sergeant." Still unsatisfied, Childs realized that this was about all Kramer could do. He nodded and walked away.

After Childs had left, Kramer asked Tony 5, "How come they didn't send for him?"

"It's kind of fucked up the way it works. After two Hearts, they're supposed to let you have a job in the rear — except officers — or if you want to, you can sign a waiver and stay in the bush."

"He didn't sign any waiver."

"Well you don't always have to. We're about twelve men short, and they might figure we need every man we can get in the Arizona. . . . It could be because both his Hearts were skating."

"That shouldn't make any difference. Who's to decide how bad you have to be wounded?"

"I'll tell you what the reason probably is. Childs has got a reputation for being a fuck-off, and they probably don't want him."

"I don't see how they can do that. Besides, he seems to know what he's doing."

"He does. Next to Chief, he's the best point man we've got. But that's in the bush where you have to know what you're doing. When things get slow, he can be a pain in the ass."

Kramer remembered the incident in Da Nang, and realized Tony was right. "You seem to think they should keep him out here."

"No. If he wants to go, they should let him. . . . But I hate to see us lose anybody now, especially a good point man."

"Is he the only man in the platoon with two Hearts?"

"No."

"How many others are there?"

"Just one, I think."

"Who?"

"Me."

"How come you're out here?"

"I signed the waiver."

"What'd you do that for?"

Tony hesitated before speaking; and when he finally did answer, he failed to mention the most important reason. "You have to take a lot of crap in the rear, real Mickey Mouse bullshit. . . . One time we had about six guys that signed waivers. I think only one got killed. . . . Kovacs had two Hearts."

The next day the company broke camp at dawn as usual. It would again be a long march before they would set-in. Trippitt was more short-tempered than usual, and he constantly ordered the point to quicken the pace. It was after two o'clock when they finally set-in. Trippitt radioed their position to battalion, and then passed the word to "take thirty" for lunch.

Kramer and Tony 5 sat eating their C-rations with Charlie Squad when Ramirez asked Redstone, "What are you gonna do when you get out of the Crotch, Chief?"

Redstone shrugged his shoulders and Appleton said, "Go on the war path?"

"They'd have to pay me more money than the Crotch does."

"Gonna stick around the reservation, eh?" Appleton joked while slapping Redstone on the back.

Chief realized that no slight had been intended; and he was so used to this type of remark, especially from Appleton, that it had little effect on him. Although Redstone seldom did much talking, he now had the urge to speak about the main thing he'd been giving thought to since joining the Marine Corps. "That land ain't good for anything except fillin' holes with. My oldest brother's been workin' on a cattle ranch in Texas for ten years. He knows a place we can get nearby for twenty-five thousand dollars. My two cousins and my younger brother and me all joined the Crotch on the same day. When we get out, we'll take the money and go partners on the land."

Kramer sat wondering how the money they saved could possibly add up to twenty-five thousand dollars. He didn't doubt that Redstone was telling the truth, but he couldn't see how and what chance there would be of them getting the rest of the money. Ramirez was thinking the same thing, and after waiting a few seconds, he asked, "Chief, how's that gonna come to twenty-five thousand dollars?"

Redstone did not hesitate to answer. He and his relatives had been too serious and careful in their plans to have left them incomplete. He shrugged his shoulders before saying, "There's four of us — all grunts, all in Nam. Chances are we all won't make it back."

For a few seconds, Kramer failed to make the connection between what Redstone had said and the fact that all servicemen were covered by ten thousand dollars military insurance. Even afterwards, he couldn't believe what he had heard. During the time he'd been in Vietnam, little he had seen or heard had shocked him as much as these calmly spoken words. From the moment he'd stepped off the plane in Da Nang, Kramer realized he was in a new and referenceless matrix. Purposely and ruthlessly, he had stripped his mind of all inflexible preconceptions, preparing himself for anything. Yet Redstone's words did not stem from this new matrix, but rather from the world they had all left behind; and for the first time, Kramer sensed a valid, logical connection between the two.

Second Platoon was given one of the day's patrols. Kramer told Charlie Squad to lead off. Ramirez was now the squad leader, and he assigned Chief the point. The men no longer assumed each patrol would finally make contact. They had gone too long without seeing any sign of the Viet Cong. This did not cause them to get careless, for they knew that eventually they would make contact. However, it was no longer a question of catching Charlie, but rather of waiting for Charlie to strike.

The objective of the patrol was a large area of high ground, too large not to have at one time contained a ville. Chief realized this, and he approached it cautiously. A number of banana trees stood at its near edge. Redstone veered the column towards them. He spotted one with the remainder of a large bunch of bananas hanging from it. None of those left were ripe, and he scanned the ground looking for remains of the rest. Their absence told him that someone had been there recently, but he still wasn't sure they would find anybody. Twice since the operation had begun, he'd noticed the same thing; and both times they had failed to come upon a single person. After passing a warning back down the column, he avoided an existing path and instead broke a new one.

Chalice was fifty yards into the brush when Pablo tapped him on the shoulder and said in a low voice, "I smell Gooks." At first Chalice thought he was kidding, but then he remembered that Pablo rarely said anything on patrols and never without a purpose. As Chalice turned and looked at him questioningly, Pablo motioned forward with his head and said, "Pass it up." Rabbit was the man in front of Chalice. He passed the word forward only after Chalice insisted he do so, and still thinking it was a joke. By the time Chief got the message, he stood at the edge of a clearing that contained a large, inhabited ville.

Redstone carefully scanned the village. Few faces turned towards him, and those that did quickly turned away. The villagers weren't surprised. It was as if they had known exactly when the Marines were coming, what they would do, and how soon they would leave. Redstone had expected this. If the peasants had acted in any other way, it would have been far more disturbing to him, for it would have been something out of the ordinary. Only after he had carefully scanned everything before him, did Redstone move far enough into the clearing to allow the rest of the platoon to enter it. Tony 5 quickly divided the men into their squads and spread them out. Kramer assigned each squad leader responsibility for a particular section of the ville.

Chalice strained his eyes to get a look at the villagers, immediately aware of how different the Arizona side of the river was. The ville looked exactly the same as those on the other side of the river, but was strikingly quieter. No children played around the hootches. Instead they stood inside them, behind their mothers or grandparents; and their large, innocent eyes stared back at him with fear and distrust. Most of the elders refused to look at the Marines. They stared down at the cooking, sewing, or whatever else they were doing. Except for a few young mothers, all the people were either extremely elderly or children. Even if he had not been told numerous times, Chalice would have sensed that the absent villagers were either dead or Viet Cong.

In the first hootch Chalice's fire team was to check out, a young woman sat sewing in the middle of the floor. A small boy peered from behind her back. Only once did she glance up at him, somberly and for a second. "Chao, Ba," he said to her, using the Vietnamese greeting meaning, "Hello, Mrs." She ignored him, and he wondered how many times she'd been abused or molested by Marines, sat listening to words she did not understand, yet knowing she was being insulted and derided. He walked towards the child and it shrank away from him. Chalice clumsily took a chocolate from his shirt pocket. So many times before, children had begged him for candy; but now he had to coax the boy to take it. The boy nibbled at the chocolate slowly, his eyes suspiciously fixed upon Chalice. The woman spoke no words, but clearly she was screaming at him to go away. Now he further understood why so many of the men had told him that every living thing on the Arizona side of the river was Viet Cong.

Forsythe had been checking the inside of the bunker behind the hootch.

He emerged from it and led his men to the next hootch. An old couple sat on the packed dirt floor. Their reactions were the same as those of the young mother. Forsythe handed Chalice the flashlight and the .45. Chalice took them to the three-by-two entrance of the bunker. Kneeling on his hands and knees, he cautiously crawled inside. Even after his eyes had adjusted to the darkness, he could see nothing; so he turned on the flashlight. The musty smell almost choked him as he crept along the damp floor. It was covered with rough boards. He squeezed his hands through the cracks between them and felt nothing but dirt beneath. Next, he felt along the bamboo walls. Chalice was being extremely careful, yet his mind was only slightly concerned about the possibility of a booby trap. Instead, he tried to imagine what it was like for the old couple to spend all their nights huddled inside the bunker, listening to the bombs being dropped, knowing that the mud and bamboo would be of no value if one even came close.

For two hours Second Platoon searched the hootches. While the faces that met them were different, the reactions were the same. As Tony 5 formed up the platoon, Chalice couldn't help but look back at the ville. He tried to understand why these people had chosen to stay in a free-fire zone, enduring the random bombings, unable to stray from their village and its surrounding rice paddies, knowing that they lived at the mercy of every Marine with a gun who in fear might choose certain death for them to prevent his own possible death.

Childs was assigned the point for the march back to camp. Knowing the dangers of returning by the same route they had used to approach the ville, Childs broke a new path through the sparse brush. As he neared the edge of the high ground and was able to see the rice paddies beyond it, he felt the natural tendency to become careless. But his experience caused him to overcome this. While Hotel Company had yet to hit a booby trap, Childs knew that every other company in the battalion had. Chalice was walking directly behind Childs, and his eyes were fixed upon the rice paddies a few yards away when Childs suddenly stopped and mumbled, "I knew it."

Chalice waited impatiently for Childs to start moving again. Instead he heard Childs repeat, "I knew it."

"Knew what?" Chalice asked. Childs pointed to the ground at his feet. Chalice didn't see anything. "What is it?" Childs again pointed to the ground, but all Chalice could see was a reed bending across an opening in the brush. "What are you pointing at?"

"Just a goddamn trip wire."

Chalice continued to strain his eyes without being able to see anything. "Where?"

"Practically leaning against my ankle, stupid."

"The reed?"

"Yeah!"

Childs bent down to examine the reed. Still bewildered, Chalice was about to ask "Where?" when he moved his head and saw a glint of light flash above the tip of the reed. Whoever had set the booby trap had threaded the trip wire through the reed. Although Childs had been extremely careful, his spotting the wire was more the result of luck than anything else. The men behind them became restless, so Childs sent back word of what he had found. By the time Kramer reached the head of the column, Childs had traced the wire to a C-ration can with a grenade in it. The delay had been taken out so the grenade would explode instantly when pulled from the can. Kramer was trying to think of a way to detonate the booby trap when Childs placed his hand over the top of the can and casually yanked it away from the bush it was tied to. He handed it to Chalice, then got down on his hands and knees to search the brush for additional booby traps. In this manner, Childs crawled the twenty yards to the edge of the tree line. He took back the can with the grenade in it and placed it on top of a rice paddy dike. When the column was thirty yards away from it, Appleton, the last man, turned and shot the can off the dike, thus detonating the grenade.

An hour after they had returned to the perimeter, Trippitt called together his platoon commanders. He explained to them that the next day they would make camp in a tree line adjoining the village where Second Platoon had found the booby trap. Around noon, three of the platoons, with Second Platoon at the point, would circle behind the ville and approach from its opposite side. The remaining platoon would stay set-in as a blocking force in case any Viet Cong were flushed from the village.

The men were told the plan at dawn the next morning. Nobody was surprised, and they were all less than anxious to return. Chief was given the point. As soon as he was within three hundred yards of the ville, he began leading the column across the rice paddies instead of on top of the dikes. When he reached the high ground, he avoided anything resembling a path and pushed his way through the brush. The closer he approached to the village, the more often he had to jump over trails that angled across his path.

Chief soon found himself at the edge of the clearing with the ville in front of him. Three trails adjoined the clearing within a few feet of where he stood. Realizing this was a bad place to enter the ville, he hesitated going forward and tried to decide what to do. Trippitt radioed ahead to ask what the hold up was. Chief eyed the ground in front of him. It seemed hard packed and undisturbed. He moved slowly forward while

295

shifting his eyes cautiously between the ville and the ground. Suddenly, as he was looking towards the ville, the ground beneath his feet gave a fraction more than it should have. He stood motionless for a protracted instant, as if awaiting retribution for a fatal error. Nothing happened. "Stay back!" Redstone cautioned sharply.

Appleton was right behind him. "Booby trap?"

"I think so."

"A dud?"

"Maybe it's pressure-release," Redstone answered, referring to the type of booby trap that is detonated after pressure is removed instead of when it is applied.

"Don't move. I'll get the lieutenant."

'That's the last thing I'm gonna do,' thought Redstone. 'The very last thing.'

Kramer approached and found Redstone in the exact same position as when he had first felt the earth give beneath his foot. "You sure it's a booby trap?"

'No. I'm just fucking around.' — "I think so."

"Okay, don't move."

'Sure am gettin' some great advice.'

Kramer turned to Ramirez. "Get some E-tools, fast." Two shovels were quickly passed up the column. Ramirez and Appleton held them as they looked questioningly at Kramer. "Dig a trench just off the trail. Be careful." Ramirez moved forward on his hands and knees. "That's far enough. Start digging, *carefully*. Make it just deep enough for Chief to dive into."

Redstone also wanted to remind them to be careful, but he realized this was unnecessary. "Won't do much good," he commented somberly, doubting that the trench would do *any* good.

"Won't do any harm," Kramer replied. "Did you hear a click?"

"No, but that doesn't mean anything. . . . It *might not* be a booby trap."

"We can't take that chance."

'I can't,' thought Redstone.

In order to keep calm, Kramer began thinking out loud. "If it's a dud, we're safe."

'You're safe,' thought Redstone.

"If it's pressure-release, we've still got a chance. You'll dive into the trench, right?"

Redstone nodded while thinking he'd be "lucky" only to lose his legs. This thought seemed bad enough, but then a worse one came to him, and he asked Kramer, "What if it's a Bouncing Betsy?"

296

This frightened Kramer. He pictured a metal canister popping a few feet above the ground, hanging for a second, and then exploding in all directions. "Then we're wasting our time," he thought out loud. "Maybe we could do it some other way. . . . Do you want to try and put a board under your foot?"

"Never be able to do it."

A few seconds later, Kramer got another idea. "Should we spread some flak jackets around your leg?"

"Too risky. I might of missed the fuse. You might hit it."

Until now, Redstone's muscles had remained in the same tensed condition as when he had first felt the earth give. Feeling the strain and afraid of getting a cramp, he carefully relaxed his muscles without moving his foot. Redstone immediately felt surer of himself. He was further relieved to see sweat dripping from Kramer's face, knowing that his own face was dry. Still frightened, he felt Kramer was doing enough worrying for both of them, thus leaving his own mind free to react.

In a few minutes Ramirez and Appleton finished digging and returned to their places in the column. Redstone eyed the trench nervously, planning exactly how he would dive into it. Kramer motioned back the men behind him. He asked Redstone if he was ready. Chief nodded while thinking, 'If you'd get out of here, I'd get this over with.' Kramer started to walk away, but Redstone called him back and explained that he wanted a small hole dug next to the sole of his back foot. As Kramer was doing this, Redstone said, "Make it gradual so I can put my foot in it without putting any more weight on my other foot."

Kramer finished digging and stood waiting for Redstone to put his foot into the hole. Instead of doing so, Redstone motioned Kramer back. Only after Kramer was fifteen yards behind him, did Chief ease his foot into the hole. Very gradually, he shifted more weight onto his back foot while trying to retain pressure on his front foot. He leaned slowly forward, and at the right instant, shot his body towards the trench. Even before he landed in the bottom of it, Redstone knew there hadn't been a booby trap or else it was a dud. For a few seconds he lay motionless in the trench, relieved by the sound of his own heavy breathing. He got to his feet and spit some dirt from his mouth.

Kramer walked forward and found Redstone standing near the spot where his foot had been. "No booby trap?"

Redstone pointed to the spot. "It's there all right." As Kramer kneeled, he could see a pinlike detonating device. If the rest hadn't been covered by dirt, he would have seen a circle of them less than an inch in diameter. They had been placed in the ground upright, and all that should have been necessary to set off the mine was for one of them to be bent more than thirty degrees from the vertical. Clearly this had happened. Chief pointed to the needle that lay almost flat. "A dud."

Kramer returned to his position in the column as Redstone again began to crawl forward. Appleton stood well back while he watched him. First Chief would run his hand over the ground while gently pressing to see if it would give. He had gone about ten yards when the weight of one of his knees depressed the ground. There was a pop. A canister burst up from the ground. The thought, 'Maybe a dud' — his only chance — shot through his mind the same moment the canister exploded beneath him.

The instant before Appleton was knocked backwards by the concussion, he saw a mass of arms and legs fly up in front of him. Ramirez, who was in back of Appleton, caught some shrapnel in the leg. They scrambled to their feet and reached Redstone at the same time as Kramer and Stoker. All of them had to turn their heads away as soon as they saw what lay in front of them. Redstone's calm face, his eyes wide open, stared up at the sky. Shreds of dripping flesh hung from his rib cage, then nothing. His legs, cut off at the waist, were lying at a right angle to his upper torso and facing down. Only a thin strip of flesh joined the two sections of his body; and below his rib cage lay a green and brown iridescent mass that had once been his stomach. Stoker stepped backwards and began to vomit. Kramer was only able to keep from doing so by turning his back to the corpse. He noticed Ramirez's blood-soaked pants leg, and began to tell Stoker to take care of him before changing his mind and calling for another corpsman.

There was nothing to do but to try and cover the body. They had left their packs at camp, and therefore their ponchos and poncho liners. The first hootch was only twenty yards away. Appleton started to walk towards it, but Kramer shouted, "Wait! There may be some more booby traps."

"I ain't goin' nowhere," Appleton called back harshly. An old man was sitting on the floor of the hootch. Appleton screamed, "Lai dai!" the Vietnamese words for "come here." The old man didn't move. "Lai dai!" Appleton screamed again. Still the old man sat motionless. Appleton aimed his rifle and emptied a magazine above the old man's head. "LAI DAI!"

The old man rose to his feet with great effort, and tottered towards Appleton. The frightened look in his eyes clearly indicated that he thought he would be killed. When the trembling old man reached him, Appleton spun him around and shoved him towards the hootch. Appleton followed a few yards behind until they reached it. He grabbed a straw mat off the floor and began shoving the old man back towards Redstone's corpse. By this time Trippitt had reached the front of the column. Appleton threw the old man to the ground at Trippitt's feet.

Now that he was standing above the corpse, Appleton hesitated. He couldn't figure out what to do. His eyes avoiding as much of the sight as possible, he finally turned over Redstone's legs and pushed them against his upper torso. He still could not look at the grotesquely shortened form, so he laid the straw mat on top of it. With great effort, and some help from Kramer and Ramirez, he rolled the mat around it.

Trippitt yanked the old man violently to his feet, at the same time ordering his men to round up all the villagers and burn their hootches. They did so with vengeance. Old people and mothers were pulled from their hootches, children still clinging to them. The soldiers shoved and kicked them from hootch to hootch, at all times making sure the villagers walked in front of them as a shield against booby traps. Constant screams from the children and moaning cries from the elderly added to the madness. Grenades continued to explode as each bunker was fragged, every hootch burned, and the peasants were herded into the center of the ville. Those too elderly to walk were dragged by their arms or legs. As more and more peasants were shoved, kicked, and dragged to the center of the ville, the moaning and screaming increased. This seemed to further incense the soldiers. Those few villagers who had tried to bring some of their valuables — a battered pot, a bag of rice, a wooden bowl — had them grabbed away and flung to the ground.

Soon the entire ville was in flames, and all of the inhabitants pressed into a frightened mass at its center. A few of the Marines spat on them as they walked by. The elderly sat cowering, glancing up at their tormentors, wondering if they would soon see their own deaths and those of their grandchildren who now pressed against their mothers, bewildered and crying, too frightened to ask "Why?" maybe sensing that even their elders wouldn't be able to answer them. Only the younger mothers sat stoically, never having known anything but war and never having possessed illusions that life could be something more than what they were now enduring.

Trippitt called in a medivac chopper for Redstone's corpse and Ramirez. He also called for a helicopter to evacuate the villagers. Chalice was one of the men assigned to guard them until it came. The pathetic scene before him was enough to temporarily obscure the memory of Redstone's death and their complicity in it. He knew they would be sent to Duc Duc, a resettlement camp — not a village but straight rows of tin-roofed hootches no more than four feet apart. His mind ignored the stench of it, and he kept telling himself that it was for the best, anything would be better than living in a free-fire zone. Chalice knew they feared much worse. When no one was standing near him, he told them not to worry, that they wouldn't be harmed. His words had no effect on them. It was not only fear that they were suffering. They looked at those standing before them with guns, these men with the watery eyes; and they knew there was a difference between themselves and these men. Yet they were not sure what this difference was. They were cruel, yes; but still different. They could not know that it was impossible for these men to think of a thatch-covered shack as a home, to see any difference between one piece of high ground and another, to find meaning and importance in the simple graves of unknown ancestors and remembered parents, to look upon battered pots and straw mats as valuables, or to know they were unwanted and terrifying strangers.

The medivac chopper arrived in a half hour, but the Marines had to wait another two hours before a helicopter came for the detainees. When the company headed back to camp, it wasn't necessary for Trippitt to push his men. The fear of being caught in the open at night kept them at a fast pace. They reached camp just before dusk. Not enough time remained to heat C-rations, and it was another hour before they had finished digging their foxholes and were able to eat their food cold from the cans in the dark.

Tired as they were, no one in Second Platoon found it easy to sleep that night. It was just as well. Shortly after one o'clock in the morning, they were awakened by a series of explosions inside their perimeter — too small to be mortars or rockets, they had to be blooker rounds. The men scrambled into their foxholes, now wishing they had dug them deeper. They had no idea where the rounds were coming from. All that was left for them to do was sit cringing beneath the lips of their foxholes.

Forsythe and Chalice were in the same hole, both of them thinking that sooner or later one of the rounds would land in somebody's foxhole, hoping it wouldn't be theirs. They knew that their hole was deeper than most of those on the perimeter, and they were thankful. Chalice pressed his back against the wall of the foxhole. The smell of damp earth, once nothing more than a repugnant odor, a reminder of the filth he'd learned to accept and live in, was now something reassuring. Unconsciously, he rubbed his fingers into the dirt. The feel of it somewhat calmed him, promised protection. He could ask for no more, except maybe a deeper hole to burrow himself into.

The intervals between explosions increased to twenty and thirty minutes. During the long waits for a new explosion, the newer men would continually tell themselves, 'That might have been the last,' but an additional explosion seemed always to prove them wrong. Those who had been through this before, though just as frightened, were outwardly calmer. They knew the "odds" were with them. There was also the strange, added comfort that the Phantom Blooker was no longer a stalking shadow, but rather a tangible force that had finally seen fit to declare itself. They knew that even when the barrage ended, it would only be for the night; and if they were "lucky," they would witness this same scene many more times.

Though he continued to react with the same flinching tenseness in his muscles, Chalice almost grew accustomed to the recurrent explosions. The barrage had lasted too long without any apparent damage. He began trying to locate the rounds in his mind, following their sound from one point in the perimeter to another. Awed by the skill with which each round was aimed, he identified with whoever was firing the blooker, as if he himself were doing the firing. With each additional round, Chalice began to experience the barrage more as an event of mysterious interest than one of great danger.

Trippitt had called in Puff the Magic Dragon. It slowly circled the perimeter, spraying thousands of machine gun bullets around it. The roar of Puff's guns seemed always an afterthought to the dotted red line of fire that sprang from its invisible underside. As if to taunt both the Marines on the ground and those above, the Phantom Blooker continued his barrage unaffected. Puff circled the perimeter for over an hour without being able to silence the incoming blooker rounds. They continued landing with undiminished accuracy. A round exploded to the side of Chalice's hole. Globs of mud fell into it. Just as Chalice started to whisper "That was close," an anguished moan sickened him.

"I'm hit. Help me," a voice called out in pain and disbelief.

This same cry was repeated. It came from the position ten yards to the left of Forsythe's. Chalice started to climb out of the foxhole, but Forsythe pulled him back. "What are you doing?"

"Help! I'm hit."

"I'm gonna help him."

"Shhh," Forsythe warned. "We've got to stay —"

"*Corpsman! Corpsman!*"

"— in our positions."

"But he's hurt bad."

"You don't know who's out there. If a Gook gets inside the perimeter, there'll be a lot more people yelling for —"

"Help me. I'm hit."

"— help. . . . What could you do anyway?"

"We've gotta do something," Chalice said nervously.

"Just take it easy." Forsythe turned to the foxhole on his left. "Payne, get a corpsman over there."

Hamilton's angry voice replied, "Shut up! One's on the way."

Chalice realized that merely for his sake, Forsythe had wrongly called to Payne.

"Corpsman, get me a corpsman."

"Do you recognize his voice?"

"No," Forsythe answered irritably. "He's from Third Platoon."

Chalice heard someone running towards the wounded man's foxhole. The moaning continued, but more quietly and without words. He heard the same voice say in a calmer but still distressed tone, "See if Cox is all right."

"Quiet. Don't worry about him," came the reply.

"He's all right?"

"He's all right."

A round hit the opposite side of the perimeter. Chalice heard a faint, distant voice cry for help. No longer was he looking upon the blooker barrage as something to be experienced. Scared for his own life, horrified by the cries around him, and anguished by his inability to do anything but cringe within his foxhole, Chalice became increasingly nervous and agitated. He watched Puff shoot its line of fire directly in front of his hole, gritting his teeth and hoping that this would silence the Phantom Blooker.

It wasn't until an hour before dawn that the blooker barrage ceased. A few minutes later the sergeant of Third Platoon found two of his men dead in their hole. At first light, a helicopter was already circling above the perimeter. Someone set off a smoke grenade to guide it in. The wounded man in the foxhole next to Chalice's was carried aboard unconscious. The other man from this hole went with him, wrapped in a poncho. Three more bodies were carried aboard. Five wounded men, who now regretted that they hadn't dug their holes deeper, were also helped to the copter. Numerous other men walked around inside the perimeter wearing bandages for less serious wounds. It was not until he saw all this, that Chalice was able to comprehend fully the damage done during the night.

Trippitt told his platoon commanders that they would march all day, covering as many tree lines as possible. The men put their gear on lethargically, their minds on the previous night instead of the day that was to follow. These survivors knew they had merely had a warning, a glimpse of a scene that would be repeated again and again.

After a few minutes of marching, the men's thoughts shifted to their own discomfort. Fuller no longer spoke of how glad he was to be in the "Arizona Territory, right off." Each march left him more tired than the previous one. At first Rabbit had believed the men who kept telling him he'd get used to the marching, but he now had lost all hope of this and was continually amazed by what he misconceived as the superior stamina of those around him. It was too soon for him to realize that this was merely a stoic acceptance of the torture they were all enduring combined with the will to take one more step.

Shortly after twelve o'clock, Trippitt halted the column on a sparsely vegetated patch of high ground and passed word for the men to "take thirty." They received this order with gasps of relief as they dropped their gear on the ground. Only a few men remained standing as they all began arching their now unweighted backs and rubbing their shoulders. Knowing that they would continue marching until dusk, the men comforted themselves with the thought that at least they would be able to leave their packs behind. While they were enduring it, all degrees of pain seemed equally torturous; but now as they thought ahead, they were thankful that for the rest of the afternoon they would be enduring a lesser degree of torture. These thoughts merely increased their distress when they learned a few minutes later that the rest of the march would be "with packs."

No one really wanted to eat, but they knew their strength would have to come from somewhere. Only a few of the men bothered to heat their food because of the added trouble and the realization that as tired as they were, nothing could possibly taste good. Kramer ate his spaghetti cold from the can. After a few mouthfuls, he was no longer conscious of the greasy, doughy taste. It was the flies that were bothering him — something about Vietnam he knew he would never get used to. They swarmed like mosquitoes around him and his men. As they ate, everyone would continually shake their heads and arms to scare them off. The flies buzzed suspended a few inches away until the men stopped moving, then landed again.

Kramer watched three flies perched upon the lip of his C-ration can. Knowing the futility of it, he still blew them away with a short burst of air. One buzzed in front of his eye and another landed on the spoon as he drew it towards his mouth. Kramer flicked the spoonful of spaghetti to the ground, thinking of this act as an inadequate bribe, an offering. He began to jiggle the spoon each time he drew it towards his mouth. The flies seemed to hang around the can waiting for the short ride on the spoon. Soon he even stopped bothering to look and see if he was eating them along with the spaghetti, figuring that he could always spit them out if he felt one in his mouth. Kramer half smiled when he heard Forsythe say, "Hey Hamilton, how 'bout moving over. I think you're attracting these flies."

"Sorry, I forgot to take a shower this morning."

Childs said in his normally sarcastic tone, "Don't worry about the flies. They're gonna get theirs no matter what you do."

The afternoon proved to be a repeat of the morning — long marches through rice paddies punctuated by on-line sweeps through patches of high ground. The only villes they came upon were burned-out and abandoned. Occasional signs of life failed to lead them to any Viet Cong or even any peasants. The men walked in stupors. Staggered, splashing steps would end with falls into the brown water of the rice paddies. With each tree line the men approached, their hopes rose with the thought that maybe this would be where they would set-in for the night. But again and again they found themselves trudging through the rice paddies on its opposite side.

Barely an hour of sunlight remained when a small, meagerly vegetated patch of high ground stood a half kilometer in front of Hotel Company. Each man knew that this would have to be where they would make camp. All eyes stayed fixed upon it. To many of the men, it seemed as if they were marching and marching without making any progress towards it. Finally, the high ground seemed gradually to rise up in front of them. When the head of the column was a hundred yards away from it, Trippitt ordered the company on-line. The men reacted with despair, knowing that this meant more time before they would be able to take off their packs. They moved grudgingly while arranging themselves parallel to the front edge of the high ground.

The order was given to move out. Continued reminders to stay even were ignored as the men's thoughts fled to that moment when they would be able to drop their packs, or when they would be able to lie down and sleep for the first time in two days. The pace quickened by itself as the formation came within twenty yards of the high ground. Many of the men were driven by the desire to place their feet upon something solid instead of having them covered with two feet of water and four inches of mud. As each man stepped from the rice paddies onto the dry ground, he would hesitate, straightening his back and savoring the hard feel of dry earth beneath his feet. They could see the rice paddies on its opposite side, a mere fifty yards away; and they knew it wouldn't be long before they could drop their packs.

Before the men began their sweep, word was passed to watch out for booby traps. Most of them were too exhausted to value this warning, and they merely concentrated on staying even with those to their sides. In a disbelieved instant, a deafening explosion tremored the ground beneath them and pushed a gust of hot, dead air along the formation. The concussion and shrapnel knocked an entire squad from Third Platoon to the ground. Amidst the moans of the wounded, men all along the line dropped to their knees, some even collapsing on their faces. Frantic orders were shouted. Corpsmen staggered to the spot where a dud 105-millimeter shell had been turned into a lethal booby trap by those it had tried to destroy.

All sounds seemed distant and hollow, as if echoing off the inside of a huge, vacant sphere. Nothing short of necessity could have prodded the

304

men into movement. Orders were quickly followed, for lives depended upon them; but all activity was tainted by dull confusion. The faint hum of the approaching medivac chopper soon turned into a relentless drone. The men were barely able to finish sweeping the remainder of the high ground before it landed. Five wounded Marines and the remains of two others were rushed aboard.

Darkness came just as the men took up their positions within the perimeter. All the promises about digging deeper foxholes that they had made during the blooker barrage of the previous night were now forgotten. The ground was hard, and only a small fraction of the holes were deeper than a few feet. Exhausted himself, Kramer had to be aware of the condition of his men. Instead of keeping them up until nine o'clock, he gave orders for the watches to begin immediately. Each man was assigned two short watches instead of a single long one. Their fatigue drove all thoughts of danger and all awareness of pain from their minds. No one had trouble getting to sleep.

Trippitt explained the day's plan to his platoon commanders with an assuredness that had been absent for the past two weeks. The operation had been under way for almost a month, and each rifle company had taken heavy casualties. During this period, not one Viet Cong had been confirmed killed. There had been fire fights, but nothing more than a blood trail had ever been found. While Hotel Company had had its share of casualties, they were all the result of booby traps or the Phantom Blooker. Not only had they failed to get off a single shot, but they had not even seen anything to shoot at. The expression on Trippitt's face clearly indicated that he was expecting all this to change.

He explained that for the next few days they would be operating in the Thousand Islands. Kramer noticed that this name seemed to mean something to all of the platoon commanders except himself. It referred to four square kilometers of small patches of high ground. Very few of them were isolated by more than two hundred yards of rice paddies. At one time they had been cultivated with banana trees, papaya trees, sugarcane, corn, and various other vegetables. The remains of these fields now lay abandoned.

As soon as Kramer returned to his platoon, he told Tony 5 where they were headed. Tony's expression indicated that he had been there before and had no desire to return. "Bad place?" Kramer asked.

"The worst."

"Trippitt seems to think we'll find some VC there."

"We will. . . . Wait'll you see it — wall-to-wall bomb craters."

"And there's still VC around?"

"They don't stay. Not even Charlie can take all that bombing. . . . They just go there for food. Anything above ground looks like a vegetable patch. There's probably more shit growing there now than there ever was. You won't believe it — bomb craters lined with everything from sugarcane to eggplant. Five minutes after we get there, Childs'll look like a walking fruit salad."

"How can it be any worse than the shit we've been traveling through for the last month?"

"It's got all the disadvantages and then some. I've never been in a place that we've taken more sniper fire. You never know where it's coming from. If you call in gun ships, they don't even know where to start." Tony had been speaking in a callous, unconcerned tone, but a grim sneer appeared on his face as he added through gritted teeth, "The Phantom Blooker'll be there."

When Trippitt gave his men a break for lunch, they were already set-in on a crater-scarred patch of high ground just inside the Thousand Islands. Second Platoon had one of the afternoon patrols, and Roads was assigned the point. Even though the terrain was conducive to ambushes and sniper fire, Roads was far more concerned about tripping a booby trap. He couldn't imagine himself being cut down by the crossfire of an ambush or by the carefully aimed round of a sniper; but the vision of himself stepping on a booby trap, a Bouncing Betsy, was always with him — an innocuous pop, a gray canister hanging in the air in front of his groin, the telescoped second in which his body strove futilely to escape, but as in a nightmare, became caught in a mysterious, exhausting inertia that limited all his movements to slow motion until an explosion so deafening as to be silent left him lying helpless, knowing the extent of his own mutilation and lacking the will to kill himself.

Childs was well back in the formation, no less edgy than he would have been if he were at the point. But he saw something that took his mind off the possibility of an ambush. The front of the column was moving across a lush green patch of high ground. Childs strained his eyes as he studied it, then called over his shoulder to Hamilton, "Get ready."

"For what?" Hamilton asked nervously.

"Supper, baby, supper."

"What do you see?"

"Don't know yet, but I think we're on to something."

As soon as he stepped from the rice paddies to the high ground, Childs began scampering around picking vegetables. He called ahead, "Tell Roads to slow down."

"We're gettin' behind," Hamilton warned.

"Fuck it, man. Just start picking."

"That shit's green."

"It's okra, stupid. It's supposed to be green."

"Okra? Is that the stuff you made last time we were here?"

"Yeah. That's it."

"That shit was horrible. It tasted like come."

"How do you know what come tastes like?"

"Fuck you."

"Quit arguing and start picking."

"I told you I can't stand that shit."

"It don't come out of a can, does it? . . . Look, there's squash here too. You can pick that."

Squash wasn't one of Hamilton's favorite vegetables either; but after a sarcastic "Oh boy," he also began to pick as they walked. While Childs stuffed his pockets, he noticed that Forsythe wasn't picking anything and urged him to help. Forsythe also remembered what the okra had tasted like, but picked some anyway just to quiet Childs. He found some cucumbers, and all three men began frantically picking as they walked. When their pockets were full, Forsythe took out his bayonet and began eating one of the cucumbers. A distant burst of rifle fire interrupted him. Everyone in the column turned their heads towards the sound, many of them recognizing the unmistakable cracks of AK-47's.

Kramer immediately headed his men towards the firing. The pace quickened by itself, but when Kramer received word over the radio that First Platoon had run into a dozen Viet Cong, he gave orders to further increase it. By the time they approached within five hundred yards, the firing had become more sporadic and was mostly from M-16's. Thoughts of the losses they had taken without being able to fire a shot caused many of the men to be more concerned about revenge than their own safety. The pace through the rice paddies was exhausting them, but they drove themselves on in hopes of reaching the Viet Cong before they'd all escaped or been killed by First Platoon.

Soon the firing stopped completely. The last shots had come from within a tree line less than a hundred yards away. To prevent First Platoon from firing on them, Kramer had Milton call Forest. Word came back that First Platoon was sweeping through the high ground and heading straight towards them. As Roads moved within twenty yards of the tree line, First

Platoon emerged from it. The two platoons met, and Kramer sought out Forest.

First Platoon had gotten three confirmed kills. They were the first by any rifle company in the battalion, and Forest was beaming. He and Kramer decided to combine their platoons for a quick sweep back through the high ground before returning to camp. Realizing that some Viet Cong might still be in the tree line, the men moved through it cautiously. This was the closest Fuller had come to being in a fire fight, and he was especially nervous. Chalice and Forsythe watched with amusement as he moved forward in a crouch, his head shifting quickly from side to side. Suddenly he started firing and yelling. The men around him crouched nervously, trying to see what he was shooting at. "I got 'em," Fuller yelled, "three of 'em." By now they could see what had happened. The bodies of two Viet Cong, their legs folded in front of them and their backs propped up against two trees, sat facing each other with unlit cigarettes in their mouths. Between them lay a third body, its hands folded across its chest. It was obvious to everyone but Fuller that these were the three Viet Cong killed by First Platoon.

Appleton noticed something on the chest of the prone body. He pushed aside the dead Viet Cong's hands with his rifle barrel, exposing an ace of spades with "Hotel 2/5" scrawled across it. Appleton bent down and replaced the corpse's hands over the card, at the same time saying, "When his friends see that, they'll know not to fuck with Hotel Company anymore."

The platoons returned to camp in plenty of time to dig foxholes and heat C-rations. It took Childs over an hour to cook the okra and squash in a canteen cup. After the first few men who tasted it had spit it out, no one else in the squad would try it. Payne told Childs he overcooked it, and suggested some more salt. Forsythe asked him if he still had the billiard ball, saying he preferred to eat it instead. Childs got up and walked away from the other men. He sat down by himself to finish what was left. After a few mouthfuls, he emptied the canteen cup on the ground, still hearing the other members of his squad joke about how good he had made the cucumbers.

Every night since the operation had begun, Hotel Company had sent out two ambushes and two listening posts. The listening posts always consisted of a four-man fire team placed fifty to a hundred yards outside the perimeter, and their instructions were to fire only if fired upon. The ambushes consisted of an entire squad and a machine gun team placed at least half a kilometer from the perimeter. It was Second Platoon's turn to send out an ambush, and Alpha's turn within Second Platoon.

Shortly after dusk, Hamilton gathered his men on the edge of the perimeter and warned them to keep the noise down as he always did before an ambush. He realized the Viet Cong knew that every Marine company in Vietnam sent out from two to four ambushes a night. They had been known to set their own ambushes outside a perimeter to catch the Marines as they left it. Because of the difficulty in finding their way around at night, it was usually necessary for the squads to return by the same routes they had used to reach the ambush site, and this was an added danger. Most of the companies in the battalion had taken close to twice the number of casualties on ambushes than they had inflicted. In addition to being the most risky and fruitless of all operations the Marines were asked to perform, they were also disliked because of the added marching and loss of sleep involved.

Alpha's ambush was a short one. This didn't cause the men to be any less wary than usual. Until they set-in, the noise of their movement would put them at a disadvantage. It made no difference whether they traveled over dry ground or through rice paddies. Tree lines supplied more cover from which they themselves could be ambushed, and the noise made by moving through rice paddies could enable the Viet Cong to pinpoint their position. Most of Alpha's ambush route necessitated movement through water.

Hamilton could tell that Fuller and Rabbit were making more noise than anyone else in the squad, but he realized there was no way to teach them to be quieter. This was a skill he and the rest of his men had picked up without any conscious effort, and it could only be learned with experience. The sharp sound of a rifle banging against an ammo can caused Hamilton to flinch as if he'd received an electric shock. Knowing that passing a rebuke down the column would only create more noise, he kept silent. This type of carelessness always left him frustrated, and he mulled over the incident as he walked.

The moonlight revealed the nebulous outline of some high ground that would have to be skirted in order to reach the ambush site. This by itself would have increased the men's nervousness, but the noise that had just been made caused them to be even more uneasy. Forsythe, the point man, had the choice of leading the squad on top of a rice paddy dike or through the water. Traveling along the dike would be faster and quieter, but it would place them between the tree line and the moon, thus making them better targets. Forsythe was about to choose the path through the water when a cloud passed in front of the moon and he changed his mind.

They hadn't traveled more than thirty yards along the dike before a loud splash caused the men to freeze in place. Fuller had fallen off it into a waist-deep rice paddy. Surprised by the water's depth, he went completely under. Hamilton stood cringing on the dike as Fuller tried to muffle his coughing. "Do you have the ammo can?" Hamilton asked in a whisper.

"Yeah."

"Well get back on the dike."

"I can't find my rifle."

"I don't fucking believe it," Hamilton mumbled under his breath.

"Here it is!"

"Shhh. . . . Get on the dike."

They were already more than halfway to the ambush site. Forsythe led them the rest of the way without incident. If the squad had been at full strength, Hamilton would have divided them into three concurrent watches; but there were only ten men in the ambush party, so he divided them into two five-man groups.

Chalice had the second watch in his group. The chilling effect of his wet clothing helped to awaken him fully as soon as his watch began. He felt uneasy, and was bothered further by his inability to figure out why. Suddenly, he realized the cause — a complete absence of sounds except for those he himself was making. No insects droned around him, no breeze stirred the brush, and no rain fell. His own breathing soon lulled and relaxed him. He remained alert for those dangers that were his responsibility, but the placid radiance of the night seemed to make this wariness unnecessary. Hearing a faint, innocuous pop, he listened intently for a repeat of this sound. Instead, he heard a distant explosion, then another.

Hamilton had also been on watch. He crawled over to Chalice and asked, "Did you hear it?"

"Yeah. The Phantom Blooker's working out on the rest of the company."

"Sounds like he's in that tree line we passed."

"I think so."

"I'll call in what we know. You start working out on the tree line."

Chalice could barely see the patch of high ground where he thought the blooker barrage was coming from. After hearing another pop, he aimed his blooker and shot in that direction. The sound of the exploding shell returned to him unmuffled by water, and he knew his round had landed on dry ground. Chalice had no hopes of getting the Phantom Blooker. His only purpose was to silence him. He quickly reloaded and shot numerous times, all the while listening for the faint pop which he failed to hear again. It seemed impossible that he had ended the barrage so easily.

A series of flashes came from the distant tree line. The sounds of exploding mortar rounds followed them. Hamilton had radioed the suspected position of the Phantom Blooker, and now the company mortars had zeroed in on him. Trippitt had also called in Puff the Magic Dragon, and within minutes some blinding flares burst above the suspected tree line. Their light illuminated not only it, but also the ambush site and the company perimeter. The brightness of the haloed flares awed Chalice. They seemed to illuminate the ground with a light far more intense and whiter than that of the sun. Soon he saw the tracer rounds from Puff pointing directly at the tree line. The rumble of its machine guns added to the eerie effect of the illumination flares. Chalice remembered being told that Puff's guns could cover every square foot of a football field in less than a minute, and he felt sure that this meant death for the Phantom Blooker.

During the four hours that the mortar and machine gun barrage continued, nothing was heard from the Phantom Blooker. At dawn the company moved on-line towards the battered patch of high ground. Alpha had been told to approach slowly from the opposite side, thus serving as a blocking force while the company moved through it. Chalice was positive that the Phantom Blooker would be found dead, and also that it had been his round that had killed him — as if the mortar and machine gun barrage had been ineffectual, and only by Chalice's hand could the Phantom Blooker have been destroyed. He took no pride in this act. Something in his mind tried to disassociate it from himself, making it an act of fate rather than will, performed by a helpless and unthinking entity, everything having been decided when Tony 5 had handed him the blooker.

As Chalice watched Hotel Company emerge from the tree line, he waited silently for someone to tell him that it was over, the body had been found. Yet he knew that more than just a life had ended. Through the haze of his thoughts, he heard Forsythe say, "Bet he got away."

"Why? What makes you say that?"

Struck by Chalice's tone, Forsythe searched his face while answering, "I just think so."

Soon Chalice was to know that Forsythe had been right. He wasn't the only one that found this hard to believe. Trippitt ordered his men to sweep back through the high ground. Chalice's disbelief increased as he noticed that no foot of earth remained unmarked. Areas of adjoining mortar craters sometimes stretched over twenty yards. Flattened globs of lead from Puff's machine guns lay scattered on the ground. Not a single tree had been left untouched. Again the company reached the spot where the empty shells had been ejected from the Phantom Blooker's weapon. Some of the men pointed to a stain on the ground that looked like blood, and Chalice thought, 'I did that. It was my round.'

After returning to camp for their packs, Hotel Company began searching

311

the surrounding tree lines. An hour of daylight remained when Trippitt decided to head for a new patch of high ground to make camp. As they marched between two parallel tree lines, a burst of sniper fire came from the high ground on their left. Trippitt advanced the column on-line towards the sniper fire and ordered the blooker men to prep-fire the brush. There were continuous pops all along the formation as the blookers were fired. Then the machine guns opened up on the tree line. As they approached within a hundred yards of it, the firing of M-16's became constant. The sniping continued, but it was drowned out by the noise of their own weapons. Also drowned out were the cries of their wounded. All eyes focused upon the tree line as the formation continued to advance. Only the corpsmen stayed behind to help the wounded. Long before they had reached the tree line, the sniper fire ceased; but their own firing continued until they were well inside it. A careful sweep revealed nothing but some abandoned Viet Cong spider holes.

Five men had been wounded, two seriously. By the time they had been medivacked, only a few minutes of daylight remained. Trippitt radioed their position to the battalion CP, and ordered his men to set-in for the night.

Tony 5 assigned Second Platoon's positions, and checked them a few minutes later. When he came to Chalice and Forsythe's hole, Chalice started to ask him a question, but decided against it. As Tony walked away, Chalice changed his mind and followed him. "Tony, wait a minute." Tony looked at Chalice as if he wanted him to hurry up and speak. This made him even more hesitant, but he fianlly said, "They say you're the only one that's seen the Phantom Blooker." Tony remained silent, his expression clearly indicating that he wasn't in any mood to get involved in a conversation, especially about the Phantom Blooker. "It it true?"

"Is what true?" Tony asked irritably.

"That you've seen the Phantom Blooker."

"That's what you heard, ain't it?"

"You think he's a Marine?"

"He's an American," Tony replied with obvious hatred.

"Are you sure?"

"I *seen* him."

Tony turned to leave, but Chalice stopped him. "What did he look like?"

"Like an American."

"I mean did he . . . have blond hair . . . or something?"

"You ain't gonna give me that al —, al —"

"Albino."

312

"Yeah, that albino bullshit. Well he wasn't."

"What color hair did he have?"

"Light brown, a little lighter than yours. Maybe about the same, but it was longer, and *no pink eyes.*"

"What —"

"I'll talk to you some other time. I've gotta check with Kramer."

No one was surprised that night when blooker rounds started falling within the perimeter. The men had dug their foxholes deep enough, and morning found them all unharmed. For the next ten days, Hotel Company moved from tree line to tree line within the Thousand Islands. Sniper fire became a habitual occurrence, and each incident was usually a repeat of those that preceded it. Unless the firing was extremely heavy, Trippitt didn't bother to call in helicopter gun ships to strafe the presumed hiding place. He'd merely march his men towards it on-line. Though they repeated this same procedure over a dozen times, only twice was it successful. One time a sniper was found dead as a result of the air support. Another time, one was killed because he waited for the formation to get within ten yards before opening fire. After killing two Marines, he in turn was shot — more than two hundred times.

Not once since the company had been operating within the Thousand Islands had they run into any booby traps. The more experienced of the men realized that this was because the Viet Cong constantly combed the area for food and didn't want to lose men to their own booby traps. These men also felt that eventually they would come across some command detonated booby traps. As much as they feared this, the one occurrence they feared more had so far failed to happen. Never had their camp been subjected to a night ground attack and its accompanying barrage of mortars. To carry out such an attack, the Viet Cong would have to gather in strength. So far there had been no indication they were doing so. While somewhat assuaging the men's anxiety about a ground attack, this also frustrated their attempts to make contact. There was no question that they feared a fire fight, but in their thoughts at least, they found the idea of one preferable to the constant loss of men to sniper fire in the daytime and blooker barrages at night.

The men of Chalice's platoon had given him credit for silencing the Phantom Blooker on the night of the ambush. Formerly all of the platoon's blooker men had been urged to get the Phantom Blooker, but now the men directed most of these remarks at Chalice. Though they did so jokingly, their fear was real and it was obvious they believed there was some truth in the superstition that he would have to be killed by his own weapon. Each time the Phantom Blooker attacked, Chalice felt a forced responsibility to silence him.

One day nineteen replacements were choppered in with supplies. Second Platoon received three of these men. This still left the platoon well below full strength, even counting Forsythe who had received orders for his R and R. Kramer sent him in grudgingly, and with instructions to ask about a job in the rear for Childs. Roads was made a temporary fire team leader, and Alpha was given a huge, pudgy replacement named Wilcox. Though they retained the same number of men and were able to divide the watches as usual, Alpha's morale declined with the departure of Forsythe. He'd always had the ability to point out something humorous in the worst of circumstances, and now this ability was lost to them.

Trippitt and Martin became more and more irritated about Hotel Company's failure to make substantial contact. They took their frustration out on the men by seeing that they kept their hair short and their faces clean shaven. In order to shave every few days, the men had to carry additional water. After numerous long marches, many of them decided that the extra weight was too exhausting a hindrance. Instead they began giving themselves "bush shaves." Without lathering their faces, they would methodically shave themselves by placing their index fingers through the slots of double-edged razor blades, literally scraping the whiskers from their faces. Whenever Gunny Martin noticed a man with what he felt was overly long hair, that man would be ordered to the CP where Martin quickly lopped it off in the "skin job" style he himself preferred.

Trippitt and Martin's frustration resulted in more than harassment of their men. Though ambushes were ostensibly offensive actions, their main purpose was actually defensive in that they prevented the Viet Cong from approaching a perimeter at night with impunity. For this reason, they were seldom sent out more than a kilometer. Trippitt saw no indications of a ground attack, and he decided there was little risk in temporarily ignoring the possibility of one. He also believed that the only tangible measure of a company's effectiveness, and therefore that of its commander, was the number of confirmed kills it registered. By this criterion, Hotel Company had been extremely lacking. He decided to extend the lengths of the ambushes. The change came about gradually as dictated by the fruitlessness of each succeeding ambush. It was not until the men found themselves continually traveling over two kilometers to their ambush sites that they realized such ambushes had become Trippitt's policy. In conversations among themselves, they constantly complained about the disadvantage Trippitt was placing them under.

314

One night at dusk, Chalice and Hamilton were arranging their equipment in back of their foxholes. It was a full moon, and Chalice remarked that he was glad Alpha didn't have that night's ambush.

"Don't get too happy about it," Hamilton replied. "It'll be just as bright tomorrow, and then it'll be our turn."

Chalice asked in a depressed tone, "Why don't we sandbag it?"

"No chance."

"Why not?"

"I don't wanna be in the wrong place if Puff or mortars start working out. At least if we don't sandbag, they know where we are."

"But if we keep marching all over the place at night, we're gonna get ambushed ourselves."

"Maybe, but so far it hasn't happened. If it does, then Trippitt'll have to start making the ambushes shorter. I just hope it doesn't happen to us."

Chalice put on some insect repellent, then handed the bottle to Hamilton. Too tired to do any more talking, he lay back and watched the clouds drift in front of the moon. A cool breeze softly ruffled the brush. There was something very reassuring about the quiet beauty of the night. Unlike the distant and oppressive daytime sky that glared down upon them as they marched, its darkness descended and enveloped them in a cool radiance. It seemed incongruous to Chalice that now, under these conditions, he had developed for the first time a real appreciation for something so unchanging and indifferent as nature. He continued to watch the moon, sensing a harmony in all that surrounded him. Even the sounds of mosquitoes failed to be a bother, and he accepted them as part of something beautiful.

Chalice and Hamilton had been lying silently for a half hour when a distant burst of rifle fire startled them to sitting positions. Neither one of them spoke, both realizing that nearly all of the shots had come from AK-47's. Whispers from the men around them confirmed this, and everyone knew what must have happened. "I hope not," Hamilton murmured as he headed for Payne and the radio. Chalice followed behind him, angrily mumbling to himself about the "power of negative thinking."

All over the perimeter, men gathered around radios to listen while Fourth Platoon's lieutenant futilely tried to make contact with his ambush party. Trippitt called in some illumination flares. Soon the sky glowed with their light. First Platoon was quickly gathered together, and within minutes they were on their way to the ambush site. Trippitt put the company on full alert, but this was unnecessary because no one was even thinking about sleeping.

The men waited restlessly around radios and in their foxholes for what

315

they knew would be bad news. Soon they heard Puff's propeller-driven engines above them. Flares continued to drop over the ambush site. A medivac helicopter began circling invisibly overhead. One of the men gathered around Milton's radio asked Kramer if it was all right to smoke. It was Tony 5 who took the trouble to rebuke him. The men heard someone directing the medivac chopper in. They knew this meant at least one member of the ambush party was still alive, otherwise no one would risk a night landing. As the medivac chopper descended, it was met by bursts from AK-47's. The men could see the Viet Cong tracer rounds streaking through the darkness. The chopper struggled to regain altitude as its accompanying gun ships strafed the area. Again it tried to descend, but sniper fire quickly drove it away. Three more times it tried to land only to be chased away by sniper fire. The gun ships were unable to knock out the Viet Cong positions, so Puff began to spray the area with machine gun rounds. On its sixth try, the medivac chopper was finally able to land. The men who sat watching and listening from within the perimeter felt relieved as they heard the engines of the helicopter fading in the distance. They soon found out that only two of the thirteen men in the ambush party had survived long enough to be medivacked, and later that these two had died aboard the chopper.

Hotel Company set-in early the next afternoon. To the men in Alpha, this meant little. All day their thoughts had concerned the coming night's ambush. Hamilton walked over to Kramer's foxhole to receive its coordinates. His men waited restlessly for him to return, telling themselves that the ambush might be called off while knowing it wouldn't, or comforting themselves with the thought that at least it would be a short one. Hamilton's expression was enough to tell them that even this wasn't the case. They watched in disbelief as he traced on his map a two kilometer path to the ambush site.

Ordinarily the machine gun team chosen to accompany an ambush would join it just before dusk, but Skip and Flip reported to Hamilton a half hour early. Hamilton, Childs, and Skip carefully decided upon a route to the ambush site and a slightly different one for their return. They also exchanged comments about those points on their route that offered the most danger.

At dusk Hamilton gathered the ambush party together and carefully arranged them in the order he wanted. He walked down the line jostling each man to make sure his equipment didn't rattle. As he did this to Wilcox, the new replacement, Hamilton's ears caught a jingling sound. "How come you don't have your dog tags taped together?" he asked angrily.

"Nobody ever told —"

"Well I'm telling you now. Take one of them off and put it in your pocket." Wilcox slowly removed his dog tags and chain, then placed them in his pocket. "Listen asshole, what's the difference if they're jangling around your neck or in your pocket? Now take one of the fucking tags off and put it in your pocket. Then put the other tag around your neck."

At first Hamilton watched as Wilcox slowly did this, but he soon lost patience and walked away. Before giving Childs the order to move out, Hamilton again warned those with ammo cans to keep them quiet. As if in answer to this warning, Fuller banged his rifle against his ammo can before he was ten yards outside of the company lines. Hamilton immediately ordered the column back to the perimeter. He walked up to Fuller, and without a word shoved him to the ground and took away the ammo can. Returning to his place in the column with the ammo can on his shoulder, Hamilton again ordered Childs to move out. From that moment until the time they reached the ambush site, not one word was spoken.

The ambush site was a small patch of barren high ground twenty yards distant from a large tree line. With a minimum of talking and movement, Hamilton set-in his men for an L-shaped ambush facing the tree line. At the base of the L, he placed the machine gun team.

They hadn't been set-in for more than ten minutes when they were startled by a burst from Fuller's rifle. As their eyes searched in the direction Fuller had aimed, Hamilton crawled over to him and whispered, "What did you see?"

Fuller pointed to the tree line. "Movement, over there."

Payne was sitting next to Fuller, and he whispered, "I didn't see anything."

Hamilton doubted that Fuller had either, but he realized that this was no time to start an argument. Instead, he turned to Payne and told him to radio in that they were moving the ambush. He then told Childs to head to the last tree line they had passed on the way out. Within seconds, the men were on their feet and moving in the direction of the perimeter.

A half hour after they had reset the ambush, Fuller again opened fire across the rice paddies. No one else had seen anything, and Hamilton was barely able to control his anger as he gave orders to again move the ambush. The others also felt like cursing Fuller, but they knew the satisfaction their words would give them would be insignificant compared to the added dangers they would involve. They had been edgy before leaving the perimeter. Now that every Viet Cong within miles knew just about where they were, the men were even more nervous.

At the new ambush site, Hamilton placed himself next to Fuller, and instructed him not to fire unless ordered to. Despite this, Fuller again opened fire twenty minutes later. Neither Hamilton nor anyone else bothered to ask him what he was supposedly shooting at. Payne contacted the perimeter, and Hamilton took the receiver from his hand. Recognizing Kramer's voice on the other end, he immediately asked for permission to bring in the ambush. Kramer gave it without hesitation.

Hotel Company's lack of success during the operation was not singular. The other three rifle companies had suffered similar losses with the same absence of results to show for them. Colonel Nash and Major Lucas realized that a change in strategy was mandatory, and information from a *chieu hoi* helped to decide exactly what that change would be. According to this information, the continued American bombings had made it necessary for the Viet Cong to mass and regroup under the protection of the mountain range that formed the southern boundary of the Arizona. Only a few snipers and harassing squads remained in the lowlands. This explained the battalion's failure to make substantial contact. The Viet Cong had decided to stay in the mountains until they received an expected resupply of weapons and ammunition. By doing so, they remained cut off from the lowlands which was their source of food. Much of the rice at the base of the mountains was now ready for harvest. It was Major Lucas's guess that the Viet Cong would soon be sending patrols down to tax or buy the villagers' rice. He decided to converge upon these paddies from three sides. Fox and Golf Companies were to sweep towards each other along the base of the mountains. Hotel and Echo would accompany Headquarters and Supply Company in a sweep straight towards the mountains. In this manner, the battalion would at least be able to prevent much of the harvested rice from being carried away by the Viet Cong.

On the march to the mountains, H and S Company traveled between Hotel and Echo, these two rifle companies alternating the point. Two members of the Vietnamese National Police were sent in to assist the operation. It was their job to interrogate the peasants and weed out Viet Cong sympathizers. Since any Vietnamese who risked his life by staying in the Arizona was considered a probable Viet Cong sympathizer, the National Police had never been known to use much restraint with these peasants. Among the Marines who had seen them operate, their efficiency was sometimes questioned, but never their ruthlessness.

Hotel Company had the point on the second day of the march towards the mountains, and it was then they came upon the first inhabited ville.

318

A thorough search uncovered four large caches of rice buried in huge earthen jugs. This alone was enough to feed the villagers for a year. Because he knew that rice was harvested four times a year, Trippitt immediately assumed the surplus was destined for the Viet Cong. While the search continued, he called for the National Police to interrogate the villagers. Only two hours of daylight remained, so when Colonel Nash heard about the rice, he decided to set-in for the night around the ville rather than rush the search.

Headquarters and Supply Company dug in at the center of the village. Echo and Hotel arranged their foxholes in a circle around it. After the men had finished digging their holes and eating, many of them returned to the center of the ville. They found the National Police interrogating a young woman while the rest of the villagers sat huddled together a few yards away. So used to seeing nothing but old people and mothers, the Marines were surprised by the attractiveness of the young woman. Chalice stared at her intently, finding it impossible to associate her with the enemy that had been constantly harassing them.

Suddenly the policeman doing most of the interrogating began to shout. The young woman stared at the ground, refusing to look at him. When he again began to shout, she did look up, and with obvious hatred. The interrogator's hand sliced across her face, knocking the woman to her knees. At first stunned, she finally raised her head and exhibited the same hate-filled stare. The interrogator grabbed her arm and began dragging her along the ground. Her long, black hair flailed wildly as she tried to get to her feet. The second interrogator grabbed her other arm, and they both dragged her towards a mud hole.

Chalice stood dumbfounded — wanting to help her and wondering why no one else attempted to do so. He was unable to take his eyes off her until he heard someone chuckle. Glancing at the face of the Marine standing next to him, he wondered what sort of person could see anything humorous in what was happening. Not until he noticed that most of the men around him were smiling did Chalice begin to question his own reaction. A quick glance back at the girl cut this questioning short. The interrogators were holding her head beneath the muddy water as she struggled to free herself. Each time they allowed her to raise her head and breathe, their questions would be met by the same obdurate stare.

"Professor, don't take any pictures. They don't like it." Chalice didn't recognize the face of the man who had said this. He quickly looked back towards the girl, his dazed mind surprised that someone from another platoon had known his nickname. The interrogator began holding the girl's head under water for longer and longer intervals. Suddenly Chalice real-

319

ized what the Marine had said to him. Ski had asked him to try and fix his camera, and Chalice hadn't even been aware that he was holding it. An idea flashed through his mind, and the feeling of helplessness left him.

Chalice pushed his way to the front of the crowd and aimed the empty camera at the girl. No one seemed to notice him, so he took a few steps forward. One of the interrogators then waved him back. He ignored this gesture, and immediately a few of the men behind him urged Chalice to put away the camera. He continued to aim it anyway. When the girl was finally allowed to raise her head from the water, she was coughing violently and the obdurate stare had left her face. The interrogators again waved Chalice away. He refused to put the camera down, so they jerked the girl to her feet.

As they shoved her towards the rest of the villagers, she noticed Chalice holding the camera. Her hostile expression numbed him. For a second he actually considered trying to explain his actions to her. A couple of the men made critical remarks to him, but the rest cared little and the crowd dispersed. The shock of the woman's stare soon wore off, and a faint smile appeared on Chalice's face as a feeling of potency took hold of him. He hadn't moved and was still staring at the mud hole when he heard Pablo's voice behind him. "Maybe you shouldn't have done that, Professor. They might have found out something to save one of our lives." These words were spoken softly and without recrimination. There had been no assuredness in Pablo's tone, and even the sense that he wasn't sorry Chalice had done it; but there was obviously the desire to make Chalice aware of exactly what he had done. For a second Chalice wondered how Pablo had known, but memories of dead and wounded Marines drove this question from his mind. No longer was Chalice sure he had done the right thing.

A half hour before dusk, Colonel Nash called together Trippitt, the commander of Echo Company, and all of their platoon commanders. Major Lucas then proceeded to reexplain the plan by the use of his maps. When he finished, Colonel Nash began to speak. "I don't have to tell you that nearly all the villagers we'll come in contact with will be hostile to us. Many of them have good reason to be, but that makes little difference now. As you know, the Arizona is a free-fire zone, and they've all been warned to leave. For reasons you and I may find hard to understand, they've chosen to stay. This may make them subject to random bombings and artillery fire, *but remember*, we're a rifle battalion. We don't have the same *privileges*. It's our responsibility to distinguish between combatants and noncombatants. I don't care how you feel about these people.

They will be considered noncombatants unless caught in a hostile act. When as today, we find a village giving support to the Viet Cong, we'll call in a helicopter and evacuate them to the resettlement camp at Duc Duc.

"There's no point in making these people hate us any more than they already do. That just makes things worse. I never expect you to risk the lives of your men unnecessarily, but I want to make it very clear that you are responsible for your own acts and also the acts of your men. I'm not appealing to your consciences. I've seen it here and I've seen it in Korea — when a man becomes worn down, the first thing to wear away is usually his conscience. You can take this as advice or a threat, but make sure you take it.

"One more thing. I hear a lot of talk about confirmed kills. High body counts may be what they want at headquarters, but I'm the only one that has to deal with headquarters. The rest of you have to deal with me. As far as I'm concerned, a talkative prisoner is worth a hell of a lot more than a corpse. This little operation may prove that. I'm not going to start issuing Boy Scout badges for prisoners. The two-day R and R we give is incentive enough. Unfortunately, not many men have gotten them. I want you to remind your men about them. Then maybe they won't be so anxious to pull the trigger. That's all."

Nash looked over his officers, doubting that his warning had been anything more than a waste of time. Seventeen years in the Marine Corps had taught him to place a low value upon words. His main purpose was to state his own views, thus preventing the ignorance of these views from being used by the men under him as justification for acts he was helpless to prevent. As the group dispersed, he doubted that anyone there had related the warning to himself.

Kramer was walking back to his sector when he noticed the villagers quietly huddled together in a hootch under the watch of four armed Marines. He felt uneasy looking down at them, yet something prevented him from turning his head away. The old men and women sat with their heads bowed, enduring this act of degradation with the same stoicism with which they endured their advanced years. The young mothers stared blankly at the horizon. It was the faces of the children that left Kramer most uneasy. Their large eyes stared up at him with the same questioning look he had seen so many times before, but behind this there was a mixture of fear and suspicion that made it clear to Kramer that he was something far worse than a stranger. He would now have been able to turn his head away, but a different face caught his attention. It was that of a young woman. Despite her disheveled and mud-caked hair, she retained a hard pride as she stared coldly up at him. The girl's face reminded him

321

of an older and more beautiful face — one that he had tried to keep from his thoughts, knowing that he would never see it again.

A helicopter arrived to pick up the detainees shortly after dawn. Colonel Nash immediately ordered his men to move out towards the mountains. After a break for lunch, he switched Hotel Company back to the point. It was still early afternoon when they began sweeping towards a large patch of high ground. Before they got within a hundred yards of it, they came under a burst of sniper fire. All along the formation, men began firing their rifles and blookers as they moved swiftly forward. There was no return fire, but the Marines continued shooting until they reached the high ground. A quick sweep through it revealed a small ville and a dozen peasants. One of them, a little boy, had suffered a serious head wound from a blooker round. He was left behind as they continued the sweep.

When the Marines swept back through the ville, they found the National Police interrogating the villagers. Off to the side, the boy's weeping mother hovered over him. She kept pleading with the National Police to help her son, but they ignored her. Chalice walked over as soon as he saw this. The sight of the still unbandaged wound and the knowledge that it might have resulted from one of his own rounds sickened him. Adrift in a feeling of guilt and helplessness, Chalice spotted Stoker lying on his back thirty yards away. He ran over and told him about the boy.

Sweat dripping from his face, Stoker gasped, "Wait . . . let me rest a minute."

"But he's hurt bad," Chalice said frantically.

"Wait a minute. . . . I'm beat."

Chalice scanned the area looking for another corpsman. Instead he saw Kramer standing a few yards away. Chalice ran up to him and said breathlessly, "There's a kid hurt bad over there."

"Where?"

Chalice pointed and began running back to the boy. Kramer and Milton followed. A few Marines were now gathered around. One of them had inexpertly placed a bandage on the boy's head. Even without removing it, Kramer could see the seriousness of the wound. The mother's anguished face was pleadingly staring up at him as he said, "Get a corpsman! Why didn't you get a corpsman?"

"Stoker says he's too tired."

"Where *is* that cocksucker?" Chalice pointed to Stoker, and Kramer ran over to him. Stoker was still lying down. Kramer kicked off his helmet before saying, "Get up, slob."

Stoker scrambled to his feet and ran over to the boy. After checking the wound, he said, "He's hurt bad."

"No shit," someone mumbled.

As Kramer watched Stoker fumble with the wound, he couldn't help but be glad it wasn't he Stoker was trying to help. Kramer turned to Milton. "Call Trippitt. Tell him we've got a badly wounded noncombatant."

In a few seconds Milton relayed Trippitt's message, "He says what do you want *him* to do?"

"Tell him it's a kid and he has to be medivacked."

A few seconds later, Milton gave Trippitt's reply. "He says he's busy now. He'll be over in a few minutes."

Kramer mumbled audibly, "What did I expect?" He turned to Tony 5. "Get another corpsman over here in the meantime."

Ten minutes later Trippitt walked calmly up to Kramer and said, "These brats are always getting in the way." Kramer remained silent, and Trippitt added, "He's probably the one that was shooting at us."

"Who the *fuck* are you kidding?"

Trippitt stood dumbfounded, his lips quivering in an attempt to reply. Before he could, Nash walked up and asked, "What's going on here?"

It was left to Stoker to answer. "This kid's hurt bad, sir."

Nash gave Trippitt an incensed look as he asked harshly, "Why wasn't I told about this?" Trippitt again found himself embarrassed and speechless. Nash turned to Milton. "Get a medivac in here right away. I don't want that kid on *my* conscience." Before leaving, he said to Stoker, "Do what you can till it gets here."

As soon as the boy had been medivacked, Nash ordered his men to move out. They marched the rest of the afternoon without stopping, and set-in an hour before dusk. Hamilton's fire team had one of the listening posts, and he was trying to figure out what to do with Fuller when Wilcox walked up to him. "I need a new pair of boots. These are too small."

Still thinking about the listening post, Hamilton answered, "Tell the right guide."

"Who's the right guide?" Wilcox asked.

"Sugar Bear."

"Who's Sugar Bear?"

"Oh fuck . . . never mind. *I'll* order them. What size do you wear?"

"Eleven."

Hamilton also needed a pair of boots. Wilcox's were new, and he figured he might be able to wear them. "What size are those you've got on?"

"Eleven."

"I thought you said you wear elevens."

"I do."

"Oh, never mind. I'll order you twelves. Just beat it."

Hamilton found Sugar Bear rubbing insect repellent on his arms. "How's our skating right guide?"

"Nobody skates in the Arizona."

"Guess you're right. . . . Wilcox needs a pair of twelve boots."

"Ain't he the new man?"

"Sure is — new and dumb."

"He must be if *you* think so," Sugar Bear said with a smile.

"Fuck you."

"What's wrong with the ones he's got on?"

"Too small."

"I ain't runnin' no shoe store. He should of taken care of that when he was in the rear."

"He should of stayed in the rear."

"Was he the John Wayne that blew your ambush three times?"

"No. That was Fuller, another jerk."

"You oughta put 'em both on point. That'll get rid of 'em."

"I should. I've only got two point men now — Roads and Childs. I've been walking it myself sometimes."

"What about the Professor? He's been around long enough."

"Yeah. I guess I'll start using him, but I hate to have my blooker man walking point. . . . Listen, get me a new pair of boots too — ten, wide."

"I'll try, but you know what the story is: you gotta be an office poag to get anything out of supply. Ski's been waitin' a month for a pair of nines. He's wearing twelves right now."

Hamilton stood up and started to leave. "Well, give it a try."

By the time he returned to his squad, Hamilton had decided to replace Fuller with Chalice for the listening post. A few minutes before they were to leave the perimeter, Childs told Hamilton he was feeling sick. Wilcox was sitting near them, so Hamilton told him to take Childs's place.

Hamilton took the point himself. He led his men to a small patch of brush seventy yards from the perimeter. Less than ten yards wide, the only vegetation on it was some waist-high bushes. He placed Chalice and Wilcox back to back, then he and Payne sat down in the same manner a few feet away. This allowed the men in the listening post to face in four different directions.

They all remained sitting up until nine o'clock when Chalice took first watch. As he started the second hour of it, he became drowsy and had to continually jerk his head up after it fell to his chest. To prevent this and

324

keep alert, he began shaking his head violently every few seconds. This didn't help much, so he tried to think of a better way. After rejecting a number of other ideas, he decided to picture a fully dressed girl and then remove her clothing piece by piece. At first this worked, but he soon found himself rushing things, thus making it necessary to keep picturing new girls. After a while he had to start repeating some he'd already undressed. Chalice lost interest in the game and reluctantly decided to think of another method to stay awake. After pondering the problem for a few minutes, he suddenly realized that he'd been wide awake for quite a while and all his thinking had been unnecessary.

As he thought with amusement about what had happened, Chalice heard a faint sound. He strained to hear it again. Ready to conclude it had been his imagination, he did hear it again. It seemed like the movement of somebody through the rice paddies. He jostled Hamilton awake. Hamilton in turn woke Payne while Chalice shook Wilcox. Wilcox brushed Chalice's hand away. Not until Hamilton twisted his leg did Wilcox sit up.

The sound grew louder and louder as Hamilton and Payne, and finally Wilcox and Chalice, arranged themselves back to back. Hamilton called in to the perimeter and reported that they were hearing movement. Tony 5 was on the other end, and he cautioned them not to open fire. The noise grew continually louder. It sounded like at least fifty men walking through the rice paddies towards the listening post.

Chalice couldn't believe what he was hearing. He glanced backwards to see if Wilcox was also hearing it. Wilcox's head lay collapsed upon his chest. He was asleep. Frightened and nervous, Chalice jabbed Wilcox with his elbow. Wilcox grunted sleepily and said, "I'm awake." Still cringing at these words, Chalice became aware of Wilcox's heavy breathing. But what could he do? He poked him again. This served only to irritate Wilcox, and after what seemed like an unbelievably loud grunt, he whined in a drowsy voice, "Cut it out."

The sound was now coming from the edge of the high ground not five yards away. The sloshing through the water continued, but in addition, Chalice could hear footsteps. His awareness of whoever was there made it seem that they must also be aware of him. He sat motionless, his heightened senses amplifying all sounds, scents, and sights — experiencing at once the fear of the hunted and the thrill of the hunter.

The scent of Vietnamese body odor came to him. Just as Chalice leaned to the side so his head would be below the tops of the bushes, a Viet Cong soldier appeared not two yards away. Chalice could barely perceive his outline and that of his rifle. He fingered his blooker nervously, knowing that at this range it would do almost as much damage to himself as to his tar-

325

get. The sloshing through the water continued as a second soldier carrying a large sack joined the first. Chalice sat petrified, eyes as wide open as they had ever been in his life. Conscious of his own breathing, he tried to quiet it. *There wasn't any pressure on his back*. He carefully turned to see why.

Wilcox, sitting with his head and chest leaning forward, was obviously asleep. Chalice could even hear him breathing. He quickly turned his head back towards the Viet Cong soldiers. There were now three of them whispering and pointing in front of him. Chalice tried to figure out what they were saying, but soon realized he'd forgotten every Vietnamese word he had ever learned. Hearing Wilcox move his foot, Chalice waited breathlessly to see if he would make any more noise. The sloshing sound continued. Another Viet Cong soldier joined the first three. Instead of waiting behind them, he stepped in front of Chalice who was sitting with his knees drawn up to his chest. Even by raising his eyes as high as they would go, he could see no higher than the closest Viet Cong's shoulder blades. Suddenly this soldier dropped his bag. It grazed Chalice's knees before coming to rest on his foot — 'Feels like rice.' Chalice became so conscious of his own breathing, he couldn't understand why the Viet Cong soldiers were unable to hear it. A word from one of these soldiers cut the conversation short. The bag of rice was jerked off Chalice's foot, and the soldiers began walking back into the rice paddies.

The sloshing sound became louder as more Viet Cong soldiers paraded in front of Chalice. He continued to sit petrified, but gradually the eerie sense that he was invisible overcame him. Some of the soldiers passed by so close he could have grabbed their arms, and the parade of them began to seem endless. Occasionally one would turn his head back and say something to the man behind him, or a soldier carrying a bag of rice would grunt or sigh. As they continued to pass in front of him, the scene became increasingly unreal. Finally there was a break in the column. Chalice waited impatiently for it to resume. He soon realized that all the noise was now coming from the side of the high ground closest to the mountains. Finding it hard to believe that this unreal experience had ever occurred, no less ended, Chalice remained motionless for a few more seconds. As much from exhaustion as from the knowledge that no more soldiers were coming, he finally let out a sigh and felt his body melt towards the ground.

The sound of Hamilton's voice whispering into the radio revived him. Trippitt was on the other end, and his first question was, "How many are there?"

"About thirty," Hamilton whispered.

"Where are they headed?"

326

"Straight towards the mountains."

"Sit tight and keep your ears open."

Chalice turned to Wilcox who was still sleeping. He had the urge but not the strength to jab his elbow violently into his back.

One of Hotel Company's ambushes was right in the path of the Viet Cong. Trippitt quickly alerted them. Everyone aware of what was happening waited nervously for the sound of the ambush being sprung. An hour passed in silence before Trippitt concluded that the Viet Cong had somehow slipped by it. He then did what he would have done if the ambush hadn't been in position, he called in Puff. Soon the sky was aglow with illumination flares as Puff sprayed the rice paddies with machine gun bullets.

Dawn came with no hint as to how successful Puff had been. The main body of the battalion was less than a day's march from the mountains. Fox and Golf were converging at their base and only six kilometers apart. The Viet Cong platoon had to be somewhere in between. Nash realized that Lucas's trap had been sprung; and although he had seen Viet Cong platoons vanish before, there seemed no chance of that this time. He called in helicopter gun ships. They ceaselessly patrolled the area between the three elements of the battalion. By ten o'clock, Echo Company had reached a deserted ville. A quick sweep through it uncovered some freshly turned earth. Nash ordered a few men to start digging. One of the shovels caught on something just below the surface and dragged it straight up. When Nash saw the lone, human hand reaching out of the ground, he ordered the hole covered and the men to move out. Puff had done its work.

They marched at a reckless pace until two o'clock, when a long and heavy burst of M-16 fire came from their left front. There were also some scattered replies from SKS's. Fox Company had made contact. Next it was their turn. A burst of sniper fire came from a tree line in front of them. They answered with a deafening barrage of rifle, blooker, and rocket fire. The bodies of two Viet Cong snipers were discovered at the edge of the tree line. They had been dug in, and their actions were obviously suicidal delaying ones to enable the rest of their platoon to escape. Nash realized that there would be no escape.

He didn't have to order the pace increased. It quickened by itself, the men pushing anxiously forward like wolves upon an ever-freshening trail of blood. Within an hour, two more Viet Cong sacrificed themselves in payment for the six added minutes it had taken to kill them. Nash received word that Fox and Golf companies had made contact and were heading back towards the rest of the battalion.

As Echo company emerged from a tree line, they could see and hear a helicopter gun ship firing at the center of a vast stretch of rice paddies. It was joined by three other gun ships. They swung back and forth over the area spraying it with machine gun bullets. A gun ship exploded in the air leaving no doubt as to the fate of its crew, one of whom was sent hurtling away from the rest of the debris, arms and legs flailing wildly. This seemed to incense the other gun ships. They became more daring as they swung on lower and lower trajectories, all the while maintaining a deafening barrage of fire. When the main element of the battalion came within range, the gun ships ceased firing and gained altitude. Small moving specks appeared across the rice paddies as Fox and Golf companies emerged from the opposite tree line. Echo was the first to reach the remains of the Viet Cong platoon. They were met by the sight of fourteen contorted bodies lying in the rice paddies and across the dikes. Hardly any of them had less than a half-dozen gaping wounds from the huge machine gun rounds.

Nash made his way forward. He could already see a few of the bodies, the water around them taking on a slightly darker tint. Echo Company's commander stood a few yards away, but Nash stopped short of him. The arm of a Viet Cong soldier lay across a dike. It reached up from beneath the surface of the water, fingers still digging into the gray mud. As Nash stared down, Lucas came over to him and said, "That takes care of that."

The success of Lucas's plan buoyed the morale of many of the men. The Viet Cong had lost their invincibility. No longer were they a force capable of striking at will, yet impalpable enough to dissolve like mist. As Lucas's plan had proved, they too could die.

Nash realized that the loss of an entire platoon would cause the Viet Cong to be more cautious. The need for food would again drive them into the lowlands, but in smaller, less conspicuous numbers. For this reason, Nash redivided the battalion into four groups. Three rifle companies worked separately, while the fourth stayed with H and S Company.

Hotel Company returned to its previous plan of operations. Each night, the platoons set-in together. At dawn they moved out and established a new camp. During the afternoon, three platoons went on separate patrols while the fourth stayed behind with the CP. The first few days were uneventful. Forest's platoon was the first to make contact. The two confirmed kills they recorded didn't surprise anybody, but the fact that they were NVA regulars did. Curious why his men had more respect for the North Vietnamese regulars than the Viet Cong, Kramer asked Tony 5 the reason.

"We lose more men to the VC, but how can you respect someone who

328

runs when the shooting starts? . . . If the VC get you, chances are it's with a booby trap or a sniper. The only time they attack is at night. They do pull some hairy shit then, but it's usually done by sappers. The NVA are hard core, like us. They do the same things we do — with less equipment and no air support. When they come at you, they don't stop; and when you go after them, they don't run. They're just a bunch of slant-eyed Marines."

Kramer still couldn't understand why the men would have more respect for soldiers that ignored disadvantages such as the lack of air cover and inferior weapons, and seemingly sacrificed themselves to an enemy. "If the VC are more effective, why do the men have more respect for the NVA?"

Tony had no clear answer, but he attempted to explain. "It isn't that they're not as effective. See, the Gooks are smart. There's certain things disciplined soldiers like NVA can do better, like attacking in force and laying a lot of fire power on you. Other things the VC can do better, like knowing the terrain well enough to harass the hell out of you with booby traps and sniper fire. If the VC are working alone, they have to do both. Same with the NVA. But when they operate together, like here in the Arizona, each does what he can do best."

"So why are the NVA any better?"

"Well, because — It's hard to explain. You know how they tried to make us in boot camp? Well that's how the NVA are — hard-core mother-fuckers." Tony realized he wasn't getting through to Kramer, and he added almost in exasperation, "They know how to stand up and die."

Kramer now understood what Tony was trying to say, but this conflicted with things he had heard about the Viet Cong sapper squads. They had the reputation for being able to penetrate any Marine perimeter, regardless of its defenses, and of doing so with nothing on them but chicom grenades and satchel charges to be used for blowing up certain planned targets. "But what about the sappers?"

"They're different. There ain't anybody as hard core as the sappers, but how the hell can you respect a crazy man trying to kill himself and you along with him? They're not regular VC, anyway. They got more training, like us and the NVA. Instead of staying in the same area, they move around a lot and do their specialty."

While Tony 5 was speaking, Ramirez, who had returned from the hospital on the supply chopper, approached Kramer to get the coordinates for the ambush Charlie Squad was to go on that night. The site was two kilometers from the perimeter, and Kramer couldn't help but feel guilty as he pointed it out on the map. He watched Ramirez walk away, wondering if it was his turn to lose an ambush party. As soon as Milton relayed the

329

message that Charlie Squad was leaving the perimeter, Kramer sat down by the radio. He waited in the darkness until Ramirez called in and said that they had made it to the site. Only then did Kramer try to get some sleep.

The next day Second Platoon drew a short patrol. Alpha was to be the lead squad, so Kramer sent for Hamilton and his point man. Kramer and Tony 5 were already looking over the map when Childs and Hamilton arrived. Kramer traced the route on his map for Childs. It was almost a straight line and involved sweeps of only two areas of high ground.

Childs set a rapid pace through the rice paddies, and the platoon reached the first patch of high ground before two o'clock. A quick sweep through it revealed nothing, so Kramer ordered a twenty minute break. From where they rested, the men could see the next patch of high ground to be swept. It looked exactly the same as the first, and they were anxious to be done with it and return to camp.

Again the platoon moved out at a fast pace. The sky was a bright blue. Small, billowy clouds drifted across it, affording some occasional shade. For a change, a strong breeze was blowing, and most of the men were relaxed enough to enjoy it. When the platoon approached within three hundred yards of the high ground, Kramer arranged his men on-line and ordered them to sweep towards it. He watched with satisfaction as they obeyed this order.

Kramer hadn't written home in two weeks. He was thinking that this evening he would have time to do so when a great swarm of birds floated up from the tree line. Drifting higher, the swarm expanded against the bright blue sky. His own feet anchored in mud, Kramer followed their flight, shared their freedom.

"THE BIRDS! THE BIRDS!" Tony screamed. "*Prep-fire the tree line.*" Startled, Kramer glanced at the tree line, then at Tony 5. It seemed impossible that Tony could get so excited. Bewildered, eyes darting nervously, Kramer tried to figure out what was happening. "PREP-FIRE! I said. PREP-FIRE!"

Suddenly Kramer realized that it was he Tony was shouting at, that neither Trippitt, Nash, nor anyone else was around to give the orders — that *he*, Kramer, was in charge. Now even more nervous, knowing he had to do something, Kramer shouted, "*Rockets*, work out!" His own voice and the swoosh of the rockets gave him confidence. He ordered the laws fired. Even before this was done, the crackling sound of AK-47's came from within the tree line. *Tony had been right.* The orders he himself had given had also been right. Bullets from the tree line splashed all around the formation. The prep-firing had caused the ambush to be sprung prematurely. A tracer round burned a glowing red path a few feet above Kramer's head,

330

increasing his excitement instead of scaring him. A line of men, *under his command,* was rushing forward in the face of fire. It was *he* who had given the order. The crackling of AK-47's continued, but was all but drowned out by bursts from M-16's. The deafening confusion of sounds both numbed and exhilarated him. A quick glance to his side revealed Chalice loading and firing his blooker with mechanical precision. The rounds from it arched beautifully before dropping and exploding just within the tree line.

Even over the roar of their own fire, Kramer and the rest of his men were hearing rounds whizzing above and by them. For an instant he did become scared, but his fear was overshadowed by thoughts of his own responsibility — 'Am I doing everything right, everything I can? . . . Too late for air support.' Should he send a flank squad ahead — 'Impossible. No time.' He swung his head from side to side, watching his platoon hurl itself forward like a huge wave, he at the same time leading and being carried by it, swelled by its impetus into something of ascendant power, experiencing within himself a sense of destructive potency both bestial and godlike.

The broad wave of men climbed from the rice paddies to the high ground and began crashing through the brush. All the firing was now their own. Kramer almost shouted, "I see! Now I see!" Suddenly, twenty yards before him appeared a bomb crater with an abandoned rifle lying upon the lip. For the first time, Kramer fired his own rifle, spraying sand along the rim of the crater and emptying his magazine in a few seconds. Tony 5 lofted a grenade into the crater. A gray-clad human form exploded into the air, a chicom in one hand and its arm still cocked in an attempt to throw it. The Marines rushed past the crater, firing at the lifeless forms lining its sides.

The tree line was only forty yards across. The men quickly burst through to the rice paddies on its opposite side. Kramer ordered a return sweep, his exhilaration now replaced by numbness. But still he repeated to himself, "I see. I see." When he reached the bomb crater and the bodies of the three NVA soldiers it contained, he looked down at them with some pity, as much for himself as for them, but with no sense of regret.

He had been just as reckless with his men's safety as with his own, and now for the first time he became concerned about them. "Is everybody okay?" he shouted. News of three slightly wounded men came back to him. Kramer was amazed that in all the firing not one of his men had been seriously hurt. Remembering the dead bodies, he called out, "Any of 'em still alive?"

"No," was the reply from both sides of him.

331

"How many bodies?" he shouted.

"Two."

"Two."

'Seven . . . seven men dead.' He remembered the NVA soldier who had, until the last second of his life, tried to throw a grenade — to kill. Struck by the courage in that act, and also by the fact that he could have been the target, Kramer again glanced at the bodies. A cigarette now in his shaking hand, he awkwardly lit it while thinking, 'I see.' For the first time it was apparent to him what the lifers lived for, those few seconds of reckless exhilaration that he had so often heard both glorified and denied. They existed. He knew that now; and he thought to himself, 'So that's what it's all about. . . . At least I see.'

"Ski," someone called out.

A moment's silence.

"Where's Ski?"

"He was right next to me."

"*When?*"

"SKI!"

Sugar Bear splashed back through the rice paddies. All the men watched, some of them following him. Sugar Bear jerked his head from side to side as he scanned the first dike. He kept running. When he reached the fifth dike, Sugar Bear didn't have to scan the paddies behind it. Ski lay at his feet, face down in the water with blood swirling around him in delicate marbleized patterns. Knowing there was no chance but refusing to believe it, Sugar Bear jerked Ski from the water as if he were a weightless rag doll. Now the others also saw him, head collapsed on one shoulder and a gaping wound on his neck.

Chalice sat alone in the darkness. He heard footsteps and saw Childs walking towards him. His stomach tightened. He glanced around, looking for a place to go, to hide. Childs saw him. Their eyes met for a second before Childs half turned and sat down. He didn't want to talk either — 'Thank God.'

But then Hamilton walked over. He saw Childs, not Chalice, and sat down near him. "We were lucky, man." Childs remained silent. "Man, were we lucky."

"Yeah," Childs said grudgingly.

Tony 5 came over, checking positions. Hamilton repeated, "Man, were we lucky."

Tony hesitated. "Yeah . . . except for Ski."

"Yeah, except for Ski. . . . God that was close, worse than the last time."

'The last time!' Chalice thought, only now realizing that what had happened could happen again.

Tony 5 started to leave; he didn't want to talk either. But Hamilton called to him, "Wait. Wait just a minute. . . . Man, didn't that scare the shit out of you."

Childs cut in irritably, "Jesus Christ, we were all scared shitless. Who wouldn't be?"

"Who wouldn't be?" Tony repeated.

"Man, I didn't know what the fuck I was doing."

"But you did the right thing."

"Yeah . . . it —"

"Jesus Christ, let's drop it," Childs said.

Tony was ready to, but not Hamilton. "It all happened so fast, but everyone did the right thing. It was like fast and slow motion at the same time. . . . How can it be like that?" Tony remained silent. "I don't —"

"It *is* like that!" Childs still didn't want to talk, had never before talked about it; but he had to shut up Hamilton. "It's always like that —"

'Always?' thought Chalice.

"— It happens faster, but you see it faster. You see it all, like in slow motion. . . . Let's drop it."

"But you can't do anything about it."

"But you did," Tony said.

"But it seems like you're not doing things fast enough."

"But you are — you're alive."

"Something makes you," Childs cut in. "It always does."

"Fast and slow motion at the same time," Hamilton mumbled.

"Yeah."

"Yeah . . . yeah, that's it."

'Yeah,' Chalice thought, knowing that at least for him, "that" hadn't been *all* of it. He recalled the sensations that had swept through him during the advance, a fear so intense as to be exhilarating, the sense of freedom as the yoke of individuality dissolved and he merged with the men alongside him to share the primeval instincts of the pack, the satisfaction he felt while watching the rounds from his blooker land exactly where he had wanted, as if he had not aimed, but willed them to their targets.

On the sweep through the tree line he had passed by the lip of the crater, but refused to look into it. Only on the return sweep did he actually glance inside, seeing the bodies of three NVA soldiers, one of them obviously killed by a blooker round. His head turned away quickly, at the same time remembering his first reaction to the shot. It was then that he forced himself to admit it, to mumble audibly and in disbelief, "I enjoyed it. *God*, I enjoyed it."

4. The Arizona

The men waited anxiously as the supply chopper descended. It had been almost two weeks since they'd received any mail, and the hope for it was all that was on their minds. This was not because of any concern or curiosity about what was happening at home, but because the very act of reading about a place other than the Arizona was a needed form of escape to that place. As the chopper hovered above the ground, the men struggled under the turbulence of its blades to unhook the cargo net. Their eyes vainly searched the load of supplies for the bright orange mailbags. Instead of ascending when the net was detached, the helicopter flew forward and landed. A Marine carrying a huge mailbag staggered down the loading ramp. A large peace medallion and a dozen strings of love beads hung from his neck. As other Marines approached to help him, he waved them into the chopper to get the rest of the mail. Chalice and Hamilton immediately recognized the Marine struggling under the weight of the bag as Forsythe, and they rushed forward to welcome him back. Soon he was surrounded by members of his platoon questioning him about his R and R or kidding him about running out on them.

While some of the men divided the supplies and sorted the mail, Childs, Hamilton, Chalice, and Forsythe sat talking in Alpha's sector of the perimeter. It was Forsythe who began asking the questions, avoiding the one that bothered him most. He had learned of Ski's death in the rear, but he now hesitated asking about it. Each man began telling some part of what had happened while Forsythe was away, starting first with generalities and only after a while giving details. It wasn't until almost all conversation was exhausted that Hamilton told him exactly what had happened to Ski.

Forsythe also had something to tell them, and only now did he begin. "Do you guys know why you haven't been getting mail?" They shook their heads. "Charlie got the last batch. We'll never see it."

"How'd that happen?" Hamilton asked.

"Remember the Brother from Third Platoon that got the job riding the

335

jeep?" Forsythe knew the name of this Brother, but he felt uneasy about using it.

"Sure, Delaney. What about him?" Childs asked.

"He got blown away."

Childs's stomach tightened and he remained silent while Hamilton asked with surprise, "How'd it happen?"

"Who's Delaney?" Chalice asked.

"You don't know him," Forsythe answered before continuing. "You guys know Fowler and Combs, don't you?"

Childs nodded and Hamilton said, "Yeah. One's the big red-headed guy, and the other's the dude from Wyoming."

"Delaney drove them into Da Nang for some reason. He went there to pick up the mail. They were supposed to meet him before the convoy pulled out, but they got there a few minutes late. Fowler didn't have a pass, and he wanted to get back to An Hoa before anyone missed him. So Delaney took off after the convoy. . . . Never made it. The Gooks ambushed 'em a few miles outside Da Nang. . . . Delaney and Combs got killed. The Gooks stole the mail and cleaned their pockets — leaving Fowler for dead. But he's all right now."

Hamilton remembered what he had said to Delaney in Da Nang. "I knew that was no skating job. . . . He was a good dude."

Neither Childs nor Hamilton cared to continue talking. They hadn't seen Delaney killed, so they both found it hard to believe he was dead. All they could picture in their minds was the way he had looked in Da Nang. They remembered envying the fact that he got to ride in a jeep all day. Many times before they'd had friends killed, and their reaction was now the same as always — sorrow over the loss of a friend, relief that it hadn't been themselves, and guilt that they felt this relief. As Forsythe watched their faces, he knew that they would have wanted him to tell them, yet he was sorry he had. Suddenly he remembered something. A big smile on his face, he rummaged through his pack, finally pulling out a large, orange disk.

It was a Frisbee, and they were soon tossing it around the perimeter. Forsythe and Chalice were the only ones who already knew how to throw it, but Hamilton learned quickly. Childs was hopeless. Everytime he tried, the Frisbee wobbled a few feet in front of him and fell to the ground. As they were able to throw it longer distances, they began to spread out. Other members of the platoon saw them, and soon twenty men were chasing and fighting over it. They forgot how tiring the day's march had been. Even some men from the other platoons came over and joined them. Each time the Frisbee approached the ground, a group of men

336

would be waiting for it, shoving each other out of the way and cursing among themselves. As soon as someone caught it, a few of the others would try to tackle him and grab it away. They quickly tired and became content to let the man it came to throw it. All eyes would fasten on the bright orange disk as it floated effortlessly through the air, seemingly ignoring some law they were all subject to.

Suddenly Gunny Martin's whiskey tenor rang out among them. "Put that fucking thing away. This ain't no playground." A hatred rose up within them, as if Martin's words had taunted them into remembering something that for an instant they had been able to forget. Many of them smiled when these words were ignored and the Frisbee again floated above them. Martin repeated his order in an even gruffer tone. This time someone handed the Frisbee to Forsythe, and the men dispersed while cursing Martin under their breaths.

Their anger was soon forgotten as the mail was passed out. Forsythe received a large, brown envelope, and he sat down near Pablo, Chalice, Hamilton, Childs, and Ramirez. As soon as Forsythe opened it, he jumped to his feet and shouted, "It's here! I *finally* got it!" He held out a white piece of paper. "It's my ordination. I'm an ordained minister now." These words were met by skeptical remarks until Forsythe passed around the paper. "I'm now an ordained minister of the Universal Life Church."

"What kind of bullshit is this?" Childs asked as he handed the paper to Hamilton.

"It's true," Hamilton said with surprise. "It says so right here."

"You're damn right it's true."

"What the hell's the Universal Life Church?" Chalice asked.

"It's a registered religious organization, just like the Catholic Church."

"Oh some more of that bullshit," Childs commented.

Ramirez immediately jumped to his feet. "Whata you mean by that?"

Pablo reached up and grabbed Ramirez by the tail of his shirt. "Don't get excited. He didn't mean anything."

"Yeah. You oughta be used to Childs by now," Hamilton added.

Ramirez reluctantly sat down as Forsythe began speaking. "No bullshit. It's a real religious organization, incorporated and everything. I can turn my house into a church and not pay taxes on it. I can get all kinds of discounts on plane tickets and garbage like that. I can —"

Childs cut him off by asking in a sarcastic tone, "Can you get out of the bush? Can you get rid of that asshole chaplain we've got now?"

These questions somewhat deflated Forsythe, but he refused to let them stop him. "I can perform marriages just like any other sky pilot. I can perform funerals."

As soon as he said this, Forsythe realized that he had made a mistake; Childs immediately pointed it out to him. "Funerals, I ain't interested in. Marriage neither, as a matter of fact."

While carefully studying Forsythe's paper, Ramirez asked, "Hey man, what'd you do to get this?"

"Sent in my name and some postage stamps."

"Is that all." Ramirez again looked at the paper. "Hey man, this sounds phony to me."

"Read it yourself."

Ramirez did so before finally asking, "You mean all I have to do is send them my name and I'm a priest."

"Hell no, a minister."

"Well what good's it gonna do me to be a minister? I'm Catholic."

"It'll get you all kinds of discounts."

"Can I still be Catholic?"

"It's all right with me."

While sitting with a big grin on his face and thinking about the difference it made to have Forsythe around, Chalice asked, "What's this Universal Life Church supposed to believe in?"

"That's simple: What you believe, is right."

Chalice nodded his head as he replied, "That is simple."

"Tolerant bunch of motherfuckers," Childs added.

"Sure are," Forsythe agreed. "For the price of an envelope and a stamp, they'd even tolerate you."

"This still sounds phony to me," Ramirez commented.

As usual, Pablo was doing more listening than talking. Amused by Ramirez's puzzled look, Pablo placed his hand on Ramirez's shoulder and said, "Don't sweat it. I think you and me just better stay Catholics."

Ramirez looked up at him questioningly, knowing that he could trust Pablo not to kid him. "They fucking with me, man?"

"No. I think somebody's fucking with Forsythe."

As Pablo said this, Appleton walked over and picked up the Frisbee. He tossed it from hand to hand for a few seconds before saying, "Let's try this thingamajig out again."

"Naw," Forsythe answered. "The Gunny's got a hair up his ass."

"What the hell's he gonna do, send us to the Arizona?"

This was all Appleton needed to say. Within seconds they were again on their feet throwing the Frisbee. Other members of the platoon came over and joined them, but this time there was much less of the rough horseplay and they were content to let the disk float slowly between them. Soon each man was calling out the name of someone across from him and trying to throw it to that person.

338

Gunny Martin noticed them and stared on in rage, taking their actions as a personal insult. The temptation to shout for them to stop was strong, but he got a better idea. Martin picked up a nearby rifle. As the men watched the Frisbee float above them, they were startled by a burst of rifle fire. The Frisbee tumbled awkwardly higher before another burst from the M-16 knocked it to the ground. All of the men were staring at Martin by the time he lowered the rifle from his shoulder, the smile on his face indicating satisfaction with his marksmanship. When Martin saw the glares of the men, he was at first pleased that he had so effectively made his point; but as they continued to stare insolently at him, he grew uneasy and finally shouted, "Get back to your positions and act like Marines. . . . Do you want Charlie to walk right up here and blow us all to hell?" Forsythe alone remained staring at him. Martin refused to be the one to turn his back. "Hey you, when was the last time you had a haircut?" Forsythe remained silent. "Get over here, Marine." Hoping that Martin would try to manhandle him, Forsythe approached slowly and with the insolent stare still on his face. "Follow me. You need a haircut," Martin said in a calmer but still harsh tone.

"I'll cut it myself."

"Oh you will!" Forsythe remained silent. "Are you refusing an order?"

"I don't have to let you cut my hair."

Martin knew that Forsythe was right, but this was the first time anyone had stood up to him. His only choice was to use physical force or to try and bluff his way out. "Oh you don't, do you? I'm writing you up, Marine. You can expect to hear from Legal. . . . And don't let me see you wearing that fucking jewelry again. You look like a fag." Martin then turned his back and walked away. Even though Forsythe realized that this was a bluff and he had come off the better of the two, his rage was not spent, nor would it be for a long time.

It had rained for five straight days, never stopping for more than a few hours. However discomforting this made the marching, it was mainly at night — when the wet chill of their clothes kept their bodies shivering and awake — that the men of Hotel Company cursed the rain, doing so with the knowledge that for the next few months all that could be hoped for was an occasional day without it. Weeks had passed since the last time they'd camped in an area safe enough to build hootches. The loss of sleep due to the rain caused the men to become even more irritable than usual, and the absence of night attacks encouraged a willingness to undergo the added risk of hootches. Rather than having his men and himself endure a sixth straight night of rain, Trippitt was forced to allow them to erect hootches. Knowing that they would have to take them down the next morning, the men built these shelters carelessly. When finished, they could see the moonlight reflecting off their wet hootches and they knew another danger had been added to those they were already enduring.

Hotel Company went a week without any contact except for occasional sniper fire. Helicopter pilots had spotted Viet Cong in their area, but so far none had been seen from the ground. It was shortly after twelve o'clock as the company approached the large tree line that was to be its camp for the night. Kramer watched his men stumble through the rice paddies, realizing that for the last two days he had not heard one of them complain about the constant marching. All curses and gripes had been directed at the weather. They had endured the marching long enough to finally accept it, and he knew that soon they would also accept the rain.

The company got on-line and swept the high ground. It contained a large village and no one was surprised to find it abandoned. However, they were surprised at its size and the presence of a few concrete structures. All that remained of most of these buildings was a battered wall or two protruding up from a pile of rubble, but a couple of them still had roofs.

Trippitt called together his platoon commanders. They met him in the shelter of what had once been a small pagoda. Three of its walls were still standing, and the roof remained largely intact. Trippitt was sitting on a hunk of concrete and removing his boots and socks as he assigned the patrols. Kramer noticed Lieutenant Howell, the commander of Fourth Platoon, staring at Trippitt's feet. When Trippitt finished and asked if there were any questions, Howell spoke up. "Sir, what are we going to do about the men's feet?"

Howell had spoken in a relaxed tone, and Trippitt replied in the same manner. "What do you mean, Lieutenant?"

"Some of the men are having trouble walking."

There was a hint of irritation in Trippitt's tone as he answered, "They seem to be doing all right."

"Yes sir, but it's been two weeks since we've had anything but rain. They're starting to get immersion foot."

Kramer had noticed the same thing with some of his own men, and he listened with curiosity for Trippitt's reply. "Lieutenant, it's your job to see that your men take care of themselves."

"But sir —"

"Make sure they dry their feet at least once a day."

"*But sir,*" Howell almost shouted, "the only time they get a chance to

340

take their boots off is every fourth day when they don't have an afternoon patrol. You don't expect them to sleep without their boots?"

"You're *damn* right I don't! We'll be in bad enough shape if we get hit at night." Trippitt now began speaking to all of his platoon commanders instead of just Howell, and he did so in an angry tone. "Listen, you and I know there's a lot of shitbirds in this company that'd like nothing better than an excuse to get out of here. It's your job to see they don't. I know damn well their feet'll be all right if they just dry them off once a day. Make sure they do."

Trippitt's platoon commanders remained silent, each of them wondering when this was supposed to be done.

Second Platoon had one of the afternoon patrols. It rained continuously as they marched to a patch of high ground two kilometers away. When they came upon some deserted hootches, Kramer debated with himself whether to let his men take advantage of them to dry their feet. The only way this would be possible was if they were allowed to build fires. There was no dry wood around and it was getting late, so he decided to head back immediately. As his platoon reached camp, he noticed a few of the men limping and he knew that they wouldn't get a chance to take their boots off and dry their feet until the next afternoon when it was Second Platoon's turn to remain behind with the CP. Kramer was wondering how many more of his men would be limping by then when he received word of something else to worry about. Forest's platoon had surprised a squad of NVA, killing four before the rest had gotten away.

At dawn the next morning, Trippitt moved the company to the area where this had happened. The other platoons went out on their patrols while the men of Second Platoon set up hootches, built fires, and removed their boots for the first time in four days. As Kramer checked their position, he noticed that his men's feet were sickeningly blanched and shriveled, and that some of them were raw and bleeding.

The next day Second Platoon drew a short patrol. Roads walked the point. A decent hootch and a rain trench around it had enabled him to get his first good night's sleep in weeks. But by the time he halted in front of the patch of high ground that was the object of the patrol, Roads was exhausted. In their rundown condition, the luxury of one night's sleep had proved of little value to him or the other men.

The rain became heavier as Second Platoon started sweeping through the high ground. Though he could hardly see the length of one stride, Roads forced himself to search the brush — looking for that booby trap that had a better chance of finding him first. He'd find it though, somehow he'd find it. There was no way he'd let it find him — *no matter how many fucking tree lines they made him walk through.* Their game. Their rules. But this was one nigger that was gonna beat them at it.

The brush cleared in front of Roads. He looked up to see the rice paddies that meant he had made it through another tree line. Instead he saw something else — 'A fucking ville.' Each abandoned hootch meant one more bunker that had to be searched. 'Fuck it!'

Roads stood shivering, anxious to be finished with the job and head back to camp. At least then the marching would warm him. He waited impatiently for Rabbit and Forsythe to finish searching their bunker so he could get the flashlight and .45, and start on the one that had been assigned to him and Chalice. At least then he'd be out of the rain — 'Maybe some Gook had the same idea.' He heard Rabbit complain that the flashlight wasn't working and decided not to wait for the .45. Without throwing a frag in first, Roads crawled into the bunker. The supply chopper was two days late because of the rain, and Kramer had told his men to conserve their grenades.

Roads hesitated a few seconds just inside the entrance. He still couldn't see anything. The bunker was too dark. They always were. Always empty, too — the ones he had checked. Still, always frightening. But it was a calm type of fear, a fear that repetition makes bearable. At least he was out of the rain. Roads crawled forward on his hands and knees, carefully checking the floor for booby traps. Suddenly he stopped — aware of something different about this bunker — the smell. The damp musty odor, that was always there. But not the other one — 'Different' — warm, heavy — 'Living? . . . *What the fuck is it?*'

Roads drew his rifle forward, regretting he had not waited for the .45. He fingered the safety — 'On.' If there was another person in the bunker, that person had to be aware of him. But still, he hesitated taking his rifle off safe — 'Might panic them. . . . Panic. Panic. . . . Don't panic.' Roads adjusted his grip so that with one hand he would be able to click his rifle on semiautomatic and begin firing almost instantly — 'Good.' Feeling along the floor with his other hand, he crawled slowly forward. A board creaked beneath his knee. He froze, waiting, waiting for another sound — that of a shot. None came. Still trembling, he remembered the sound of the creaking board — deafening within the silence of the bunker — 'Deafening. Deafening?' — firing his M-16 would burst his own eardrums. He pointed it straight ahead anyway. This was merely a fact, nothing to be considered.

Sweat burned his eyes — only a few seconds ago he had been shivering — 'Keep cool.' If someone was there wanting to kill him, that person had

342

lost the perfect opportunity. Roads became slightly more relaxed. He sensed that the bunker's opposite wall was within his reach — 'Little more to go.' Feeling almost relieved, he swept his hand over what remained of the floor.

Suddenly, against the wall — '*Cloth!*' He jerked his hand back, freezing with his rifle at the ready. The cloth had contained something soft and warm — 'Flesh. I'm not alone!' Again he waited. The silence demanded he do something, demanded he 'GET IT OVER WITH!' Not sure what to do, he clicked his rifle off safe, at the same time shouting, "*Dung lai!*" — Vietnamese for "Don't move."

No response. No sound.

Fingering the trigger, Roads fought the urge to fire blindly into the darkness. '*Do* SOMETHING!' — he thrust the rifle forward to pin whoever was in the bunker against the wall. The barrel hit bamboo. Baffled, he drew it back quickly. 'What to do? *Can't just sit here!*' He stretched his hand forward to the spot where he had felt the warm flesh. Again he found it — 'Soft, but no sound' — this time trying to define its shape with his hand. It moved. He flinched, wiltingly, now knowing that whatever was there was too small to be a threat. It squirmed beneath his grasp. He could lift it with one hand. Roads scrambled back across the floor in search of light. Before reaching the entrance, he knew what he held. He would have realized sooner, but it was hard for him to believe that what had once seemed so threatening was merely a half-starved puppy.

Chalice watched with surprise as Roads crawled out of the bunker. This surprise stemmed in part from what Roads held, but more from the expression on his face. Roads, who he had never even seen smile before, was now actually grinning and on the verge of laughter.

The sky cleared before them as the men of Second Platoon approached the company perimeter. This change in weather only lasted an hour, but that was long enough for the supply choppers to finally reach them. They also found H and S Company camped within their perimeter. As much as they had hoped for mail and supplies, the presence of H and S Company was far more gratifying. For they knew that it probably meant they would remain stationary for anywhere from a few days to a week.

Colonel Nash noticed that many of the men were limping around the perimeter. He immediately ordered the corpsmen to examine each man's feet. Nearly every member of Hotel Company showed signs of immersion foot, and a few of them found it difficult if not impossible to walk. A corpsman came over to Nash and told him that a number of the men in First Platoon would have to be medivacked. His battalion was at less than three-quarters strength already, and Nash was enraged — not at the men themselves, but at the officers who were responsible for them. He quickly sought out Trippitt, and together they headed for First Platoon's sector of the perimeter.

Lieutenant Forest sat heating some C-rations when Nash gruffly ordered him to follow them. They approached a corpsman who was helping a man remove his blood-soaked sock. Each time the sock was touched, the man would cry out. Finally, the corpsman had to cut it with a razor blade. But part of the sock still remained stuck to his instep. The corpsman slowly pulled it away as the man squirmed in pain. Before discarding it, he held the piece of sock up to Nash. There was a patch of flesh over an inch in diameter still sticking to it. The corpsman then washed the man's instep, exposing a mass of bloody tissue.

Nash was barely able to control his anger until he could get Trippitt and Forest far enough away from their men to berate them. He knew that conditions like this were inevitable; but he was also aware that Trippitt hadn't done anything to try and prevent them, and that they could have been put off a while longer. Now it was probably too late to keep the rest of the company from ending up in the same condition as the man he had just seen. Making no effort to hide his anger, Nash ordered Trippitt to see that his men dried their feet and kept them dry for at least an hour before moving out each morning.

When the men of Hotel Company awoke the next day, no one was surprised to see that it was raining. Kramer immediately passed word for his men to take off their boots. All their gear was either soaked or very damp, so they still had no way of drying their feet. Kramer decided the only thing to do was to have them build fires. But there was no dry wood around. It was Sugar Bear who got the idea to use the wooden floors of the abandoned bunkers. Though this wood was damp, they were finally able to start a fire with it. From this main fire, the men took burning pieces of wood and started smaller fires within the dryer hootches. Six to eight men would gather in these hootches and take turns drying their feet.

Trippitt had three patrols planned for the day. Nash told him to eliminate one and shorten the other two. The entire company remained within the perimeter until eleven o'clock when the medivac chopper came for the six men with the worst cases of immersion foot. As soon as it took off, the patrols left camp. Anyone with a bad case of immersion foot was left behind. Since most of these men were members of First Platoon, the remaining men in it were divided up and sent out with Fourth and Second Platoons.

An hour after leaving the perimeter, Fourth Platoon got pinned down

344

by some heavy sniper fire. Judging by the fire power they were receiving, Lieutenant Howell estimated that it was at least a squad firing at them. He immediately called in some helicopter gun ships. It took three of them over an hour to silence the snipers.

Howell swept his platoon towards the heavy brush from which the fire had originated. He did so expecting the usual results — none at all. It made little difference whether the Americans who searched for them believed the Viet Cong had escaped unharmed or had somehow managed to carry off their dead and wounded. All that was usually left for the Marines to see was their own casualties. To Howell's surprise, this incident ended differently. They discovered the bodies of two NVA soldiers, but some of the more experienced men were sorry they had. Fourth Platoon carried the reasons for this discomfort back to the perimeter with them.

When Nash saw what they had found, he immediately called for a meeting with Trippitt and his platoon commanders. They arrived to find Nash in front of his hootch with two NVA pith helmets in his hand. He stared hostilely at the men before him for a few seconds, then began speaking in a disgruntled and angry tone. "Fourth Platoon found something you should all be interested in." Nash held out the helmets. One of them had some writing on it that numerous bullet holes would have made illegible if similar writing had not been clearly printed on the other helmet. "Hotel 2/5" was written in large, black letters on the front of it. "I'm not sure about the reason for this, but I've got a pretty good idea. I'm warning all of you: You're responsible for the actions of your men. It's beyond me to figure out why someone would think of a dead body as a toy. Once you've killed a man, that's damn well enough. I want you to make it clear to your men that anyone caught fucking with a dead body will be court-martialed. You'd think what happened to Charlie 1/9 would be warning enough, but I guess it isn't. A few years in the brig might not teach anything either, but you can bet your ass I'll do my best to send someone there if I get the chance. That's it!"

It was obvious to Kramer what Nash had warned them about, but he was puzzled by the reference to Charlie 1/9. As soon as he reached their position, Kramer asked Tony 5, "Does Charlie 1/9 mean anything to you?"

Tony laughed derisively before answering, "Those jerks could get ambushed in South Philly."

"What do you mean by that?"

"You never heard about the ghost platoon?" Kramer shook his head. "I ain't sure how it started, but it was probably Charlie 1/9's fault. Some guys — I've seen a few of them — get a kick out of fucking with dead Gooks — carving the name of their company across their chests, shaving

345

their heads, cutting their ears off — real fun stuff like that. Well the Gooks don't like you fucking with their dead, so they decided to teach Charlie 1/9 a lesson. Wherever Charlie 1/9 went, a platoon of Gooks used to follow them. Every chance they got, they'd hit 'em somehow — ambushes, mortars, rockets. It got so bad, the guys in Charlie 1/9 used to think they were haunted. Sometimes they'd knock off a few Gooks in the ghost platoon, but they still got the worst of it. They knew it wasn't any accident because some of the dead Gooks had Charlie 1/9 carved on their rifle stocks. I don't know whether they wised up and quit fucking with the dead bodies, but the ghost platoon sure as hell didn't. More than one guy from Charlie 1/9 got found by his buddies with his balls cut off and his cock in his mouth. You find your best friend like that, and you do some heavy thinking. The Gooks kept 'em thinking. Last I heard, they sent 1/9 back to Da Nang to guard some PX or something."

As Kramer listened to Tony 5, he purposely kept his face expressionless. This wasn't because he was surprised or worried, but rather because the story amused him. In a macabre way, it seemed to exemplify so many other things he had witnessed, to testify to the cheapness of human life and make a sham of actions and ideas that 'hypocritically' placed value upon it. His mind flashed back to those intense moments when he and his men had recklessly advanced in the face of fire, and his senses partially relived the shrill intoxication of that advance, that zenith of sensation when the value of life became submerged and lost in the feverish excitement of the moment. Since then he had often tried to dissect those few minutes — not because he found them disturbing, but because they puzzled him, and hidden within them he sensed there was a reality on the verge of exploding before him as testament to and justification of the 'truths' he refused to ignore. A hatred rose within him, not for what he viewed as his own pathetic existence, but for the 'hypocritical' faces in his past who had tried to place a value upon their own meaningless lives by torturing him into the belief that life itself was something sacred and to be prized, that his blindness to the beauty it contained would someday fade and leave him also possessed with this vision that somehow, for some perverted reason, had eluded him. He suddenly 'realized' that those faces that clogged his past, in their own tortured striving, had deceived themselves with the very poison they had offered him, and with this realization his outrage waned to amusement. He looked on them as creatures more pathetic than himself, fools not even satisfied with the 'lie' that life was something to be endured. Kramer took sadistic pleasure in the wish that they could somehow be with him, here in this pitiable country where war had obliterated all facades of false meaning, where it was not enough to rob a man of something as

346

meaningless as his own life, where even the violence of this act was incapable of drawing from the man that killed all the lie-produced venom which made the act possible, here, where there was even a need to disfigure and mutilate the hollow, already decaying corpse that had once enclosed that life.

Childs sat by himself, violently cutting shavings from a stick with his bayonet. It had been almost an hour since Kramer — 'the worthless prick' — told him to go to the battalion CP and talk to the sergeant major. Two Purple Hearts weren't enough. They wanted him to grovel and beg his way to the rear. Childs promised himself that if he ever got the chance, he'd make the company master sergeant pay. He pictured him sitting in his office in An Hoa, evading Forsythe's question as to why he was still in the bush, not even bothering to lie that he would try to get him a job in the rear. No, Childs knew they wanted him to beg, and even then they would do everything they could to keep him in the bush. He flung away the remainder of the stick and sheathed his bayonet, but still hesitated before getting to his feet. As he walked towards the battalion CP, he thought of the things he would like to say to the sergeant major, to all of them.

The first few men Childs asked said the sergeant major hadn't even been there, but finally someone told him that he'd been choppered back to An Hoa. At first Childs was relieved, knowing that now he wouldn't have to beg. But then it began to seem like a plot, of everyone and everything, against him. He stopped walking, as if doing so itself was an act of defiance, knowing that if he stood there a week no one would even bother to ask him why. His outrage increased. If the master sergeant had been standing in front of him, Childs would have been able, driven to kill him.

Childs remained standing in the same place, paralyzed by the impotency of his rage. He heard a voice say, "I see them now." Major Lucas had said this to the battalion artillery spotter. They were sitting together, a few yards away, while Lucas squinted through a pair of binoculars. "They might be children," he added before handing the binoculars to the spotter.

After a long look, the spotter said, "I think they *are* children."

"Can't be sure," Lucas replied reflectively.

"You want to go ahead?"

"Might as well."

The spotter yelled a set of coordinates to a mortar position thirty yards away, then called for some rounds of white phosphorous. Childs stood motionless, glaring at the backs of the two men as if he were looking at germs through a microscope. After the mortar rounds were fired, the artillery spotter casually called out an adjustment and yelled for two more. Childs raised his rifle, knowing he wouldn't use it, and sighted in on the back of Major Lucas's neck. He pressed hard enough to remove the play from the trigger, but no harder. While Lucas and the spotter speculated about how successful the rounds had been, Childs lowered the rifle and walked back towards his foxhole.

Dusk fell upon a cloudless sky. For the first time in weeks, the men were allowed to fall asleep without the discomfort of wet clothing, and most of them were tired enough to take quick advantage of this. Their comfort was short lived. Two hours before dawn, the rain started again. It fell harder than at any previous time during the operation, flooding the ground beneath their hootches and turning it to mud. Sleep became impossible. One by one, the men sat up and wrapped their soaked poncho liners around themselves. In this manner, they sat shivering in the mud until the sun rose slowly above the mountains, its light and heat all but dissipated by a barrier of rain.

Colonel Nash would have slept little regardless of the rain. The incident of the NVA helmets emphasized something he was already aware of — the lack of control he held over the men in his battalion. He knew the gulf between himself and them was caused by the absence of responsible leadership beneath him. Again the paradox had proved itself: war demands superior leadership; war dilutes leadership. The battalion was already five officers short, and it would be absurd to remove any of the remaining officers. This would merely place the lives of his men in the hands of less experienced and probably even less competent officers. It was not the fear of losing lives that bothered him. The possibility of such losses had to be accepted along with the responsibility for them. It was needless loss of life that worried him. He wondered how many men would die because they were in no condition to fight, or because a 'fatalistic' enemy had been goaded by atrocities upon their dead to sacrifice even more of their lives to take those of his own men.

All logic and all of his training told Nash that it was just a matter of time before the enemy would succumb. Yet his experiences and intuition overruled this conclusion. The Americans had been constantly able to raise the price of a Viet Cong victory without being able to put it out of reach. He knew the possible reasons — the presence of a foreign race upon their land, a normal standard of living little removed from that demanded by war, the belief in their cause, the patience inherent in their culture — and yet none of these reasons nor all of them together seemed to explain the amount of suffering they chose to endure. It wasn't the question of defeating the Viet Cong that bothered Nash. It was the realization that all

348

the destruction he had witnessed was endured by a population so indifferent to the struggle before them that if not for the suffering they would refuse to recognize it.

What little of the idealist that had ever been in him had gradually succumbed to his experiences in the military, but never before Vietnam had Nash considered himself a fatalist. His first few months in-country left him convinced that he was witnessing the destruction of a people and a cause so stubborn as to deserve, by their very obstinance, to survive. Now this destruction seemed no longer imminent, and was replaced by the destruction, not of his country, but of the myth that gave it life and in which he had once believed.

The heavy rain prevented the men from building fires to dry their feet. They sat huddled in their hootches until an hour after dawn when word was passed for them to form up for a company-size patrol. Because they were to return before dusk, they left their packs behind. Those men with the worst cases of immersion foot remained in camp to guard the CP.

The exertion of marching warmed the men's bodies and made them oblivious to the chilling rain. Dark clouds limited visibility to less than a kilometer. While this made those at the point of the columns edgy about the possibility of an ambush, it had little effect on the men of Second Platoon. They were at the tail end of the formation and it was only necessary for them to be able to see the man marching directly to their front.

The object of the patrol was, as nearly always, a careful search of a large patch of high ground. The men knew the march would be a long one, and they were grateful to be free of their packs. They quickly grew tired anyway. Before they had gone a kilometer, the rain again began to chill their bodies. As usual, their fatigue gave rise to a resentment of the constant marching and its seeming purposelessness; but as this fatigue increased, their resentment waned and was replaced by acceptance. The sight of their friends enduring the same torture as themselves forced them to endure it also. Regardless of their curses and complaints, each man was determined to continue. The root of this determination was as always, their individual pride.

At ten o'clock Trippitt ordered the first break. The columns halted in the center of a field of rice paddies. The men sat down on dikes, making no effort to draw their feet out of the water. The heavy rain would have made this purposeless. Only a few of them bothered to open cans of fruitcake or date bread. The commander of the point platoon tried to match the obscured outline of some high ground with the topography printed on

349

his map. As soon as he was sure they were headed in the right direction, he radioed Trippitt and was told to move out. The men viewed the short duration of the break indifferently. Lack of movement had caused them to become colder. It was merely a question of being tired and relatively warm or rested and cold. They also deceived themselves into thinking of the patrol as something that could be gotten over with instead of an all-day maneuver as most turned out to be.

Shortly before twelve o'clock, they reached the high ground that was the object of the patrol. A tedious sweep through it revealed a small but heavily populated ville. Though this was no surprise, the sight of it dejected them because they knew they would have to search it before starting back to camp.

Pablo and Sinclaire were standing security inside one of the hootches when Appleton took cover from the rain and joined them. He walked over to a small fire in the corner, asking Sinclaire gruffly, "No chance you had enough brains to bring that whiskey your bitch sent you?"

"She ain't a bitch, she's my girl; and there's a chance I brought it, but none of you getting any."

Appleton's tone immediately became more friendly. "No shit, did you really bring it?"

"Won't do *you* no good one way or the other."

"Hey man, you sure were ready to drink with me when it was my bottle."

Sinclaire remembered how free Appleton had been with his own liquor, but was still hesitant to share the little he had left. Sinclaire also realized that Pablo would resent his drinking on a patrol, and he was now sorry he'd admitted to bringing it. "I'll let you have some when I drink some."

"What's wrong with right now?"

Sinclaire glanced at Pablo, receiving nothing more than an indifferent look. Pablo didn't want Sinclaire drinking and he knew Sinclaire realized this, but he refused to play the part of Sinclaire's nursemaid. "We'll be heading back soon," Sinclaire said to Appleton.

"Not for a while yet. C'mon, I'm freezing."

Childs and Hamilton had just walked into the hootch, and Childs asked, "What do you want him to do, put his arms around you?"

"No, but I'd like to get my arms around *him*. The bastard's got some whiskey and he's holding out on us."

"No shit?" Hamilton asked with surprise. "How 'bout it, Sinclaire? I could use some warmin'-up myself."

If he took out his liquor now, there would be even less for himself. But Sinclaire didn't feel right about refusing to share it. He withdrew the plastic squeeze-bottle from his pocket. As he lifted it to his mouth, Pablo said coldly, "Not here — with all these lifers around. Take it in the bunker."

Sinclaire led Appleton, Hamilton, and Childs into the bunker. They sat down quickly and started passing the liquor around. When it was Hamilton's turn, he held the plastic bottle in front of his mouth and squeezed a long stream of liquor down his throat. The warmth of it hit him immediately, and he fell back against the wall of the bunker in satisfaction. It was too dark to see what he was doing, so those around him became startled when he scrambled away from the wall and yelled, "*Dung lai!*" All of them backed towards the entrance as they asked him what had happened. "The wall gave when I leaned against it."

Childs was far from unfrightened, but he couldn't resist saying, "Hey man, people like you shouldn't drink."

Hamilton ignored him and again yelled, "*Dung lai! . . .* I tell you it gave and then pushed out again."

The others were now convinced that Hamilton was neither mistaken nor kidding. Appleton could make out two silhouettes in the dim light of the entrance. "Some of you guys get out of here." Childs and Sinclaire crawled out of the bunker while Appleton and Hamilton moved cautiously towards the wall. Appleton reached it first, and he shouted, "*Dung lai!*" while pressing against it. "You're right, it's phony. Stay back and cover me." Appleton began to shake the wall while cautioning, "*Dung lai.*" It continued to give without falling, and he became more and more nervous as he tried to bring it down. Knowing the darkness would hide whoever was there even after the wall was removed, he was anxious to get whatever was going to happen over with.

Hamilton was also nervous, and he said, "Let's get out and throw a frag in first." Part of the wall collapsed upon Appleton before Hamilton had finished speaking.

"*Dung lai,*" he cautioned while crawling behind it. He heard the nervous breathing of someone too frightened to muffle it. A quick grab forward filled his hand with flesh, and he dragged the unresisting body from behind the wall. "I got him," he yelled, pulling his prisoner towards the entrance. "See if there's any more of them."

When Appleton emerged from the bunker, he was shocked to find he was holding a frightened and beautiful young girl. Immediately, men gathered around to find out what had happened. Hemrick walked over, and Pablo said to him, "I thought you checked out that bunker?"

"I did. You saw me. I was down there ten minutes."

"You must have been beating-off," Childs commented.

Their attention was drawn away from Hemrick by Hamilton's excited voice from within the bunker. "Sonofabitch, look what I got!" He crawled out with a grin on his face and an SKS in his hand. The girl was forgotten as the men gathered around the rifle. "Been wantin' one of these babies since I got here."

Without malice, Appleton said, "Hey man, I was the one that did the dirty work."

Realizing that this was true, Hamilton said, "I'll flip you for it — two out of three and I'll give you the first." Appleton agreed, whereupon Hamilton produced a coin and won two straight flips and the rifle.

Appleton was still cursing and kicking his helmet at anybody in sight when Trippitt came over to look at the prisoner. He ordered the men standing around her to get on with the search. A few minutes later, someone in Third Platoon discovered a cache of rice. It had been buried in a huge urn. The men probed the ground around it with sticks, uncovering two more urns. Another half hour yielded nothing, but Trippitt ordered his men to continue searching. They did so grudgingly, knowing there would be barely enough time to get back to camp before dusk. Trippitt was too excited by the find to be worried about this now. Regretting that the hootches were too wet to be burned, he decided to send all the villagers to the detention camp at Duc Duc. The weather made it impossible to call in a helicopter. They would have to be marched back to camp with the company. He ordered his men to round them up. When this was done, Kramer reported to Trippitt, thinking that the company would now start back to camp. Instead, Trippitt told Kramer to make sure that his men were conducting a thorough search. "Don't you think we ought to head back?"

Kramer had hesitated asking this, but to his surprise Trippitt merely glanced at his watch and said without irritation, "In a few minutes."

Forest then walked up to him with a Chinese Communist grenade. "We found about a dozen of them in the roof of a hootch." Trippitt immediately ordered a search of every roof. The men did so grudgingly, while worrying about getting caught out in the open at night. Most of them were soon gathered under the protection of the hootches, halfheartedly poking their rifle barrels into the roofs.

A half hour passed without the men uncovering any more weapons or rice. Feeling he had waited until the last possible moment, Trippitt reluctantly ordered the company to form up. The presence of over thirty villagers prevented him from arranging his men in two columns as on the march from camp. Instead, he formed them into a single column with the villagers placed in the middle of it and Second Platoon on the tail end. Aside from a few young mothers with babies in their arms, all the peasants

352

were small children or old people. Many of them had been able to gather a few possessions together, and they clutched them nervously as they were herded around. While their stares had been passive and sometimes hostile within the ville, their eyes now darted around apprehensively.

After only a few minutes of marching, it became clear that the villagers were incapable of keeping pace with the Marines. Trippitt reluctantly ordered the point to slow down. The rain increased, and some of the children started to cry. The men became even more worried about making it back to camp before dark. Many of them thought to themselves that they wouldn't have been stupid enough to wait as long as Trippitt had.

The sky grew darker as much from the angle of the sun as from the clouds that hid it. The point man could see no farther than twenty or thirty yards to his front. After they had marched for over an hour, the cries of the children became less frequent. Then suddenly, there was a burst of rifle fire at the head of the column. The rain muffled the sounds of the shots, making it impossible for those men in the rear to tell whether they were AK-47's or M-16's. Each man searched the grayness around him in fear, knowing that if it had been an ambush, it couldn't have come at a more dangerous time. A medivac chopper would find it almost impossible to make it to them; and if one did, it was doubtful it could pick up the wounded without being shot down.

No medivac was needed. The point man and two of the men behind him were beyond help. The haze before them had suddenly exploded with the muzzle flashes of numerous AK-47's. The shots had been fired not at the soldiers themselves, but at the sound of their movement through the rice paddies. The point platoon had returned the fire in the direction of the previous muzzle flashes, then swept towards them. Thirty yards away, they found a wounded NVA soldier. He had been shot in the buttocks as he fled.

It was only a few minutes before the column started moving again. The platoon formerly at the point took up the tail end. There had been no time or material to make stretchers, so four of the stronger men carried the three bodies and the prisoner. Third Platoon moved ahead of the villagers while Second Platoon placed itself behind them. Unable to see the peasants through the haze, most of the men in the column could hear their frightened words and the cries of their children. Many of them had at first felt pity for the villagers. Now all they felt was resentment. The sky had grown menacingly darker, leaving no chance of a return to camp before nightfall. The noise that the peasants were making increased the probability of a second ambush. It also added to the confusion. Every man knew that this confusion would multiply if the company were attacked again.

Each minute made them more vulnerable, and the knowledge of this increased their edginess and shortened their tempers. Trippitt, the primary reason for the danger they were undergoing, was all but forgotten as they listened to the noise that the villagers were making. It was these peasants who now endangered their lives. Every few minutes a frustrated Marine would make matters worse by shouting at them to shut up, doing so in a language the villagers didn't understand. Even if they had understood, they would have been too confused and nervous to obey.

Kramer marched on disgustedly. Each labored breath left him unsatisfied. He felt as if he were choking on the darkness that surrounded him. Despite the rain, he was sweating profusely and could feel the thick salt slime that coated his entire body. Everytime he stepped over a dike he wanted to say, *"Fuck this shit!"* and sit down upon it until he could no longer hear the villagers, the men around him, and his own heavy breathing. Tony 5 was only a few yards away, but the darkness made it necessary for Kramer to follow solely by the sound of Tony's footsteps. He felt the rotting skin being rubbed away from his insteps, and knew that his socks were already soaked with blood. Kramer began to dread each step and the painful necessity of pulling his feet from the mud. Yet he realized that many of his men had far worse cases of immersion foot. The eerie luminescence of his watch dial caught his eye. It was almost eight o'clock. At least it wouldn't be long before they were back at the perimeter.

Chalice scanned the blackness around him, expecting it to explode at any moment with bursts of rifle fire. He cringed each time the peasants made a sound and silently cursed them. Stumbling forward, he felt as if he were dragging all of them behind him on a rope while they cried out and pulled in different directions. It was as if he would never be free of them, and would soon collapse and in turn be dragged by them. He heard Hamilton shout at one of the villagers, and was actually surprised by the fact that they were in front of him. It wasn't until Chalice bumped into him that he realized Hamilton was bent over, trying to lift an old woman off the ground. He did so roughly, and Chalice saw the old woman's hand reach back to grab a battered pot at his feet. The absurdity of that pathetic act made Chalice want to cry out in laughter. There was a smile on his face as he mumbled, "A pot, a lousy fucking pot." Barely able to see Hamilton reach for it, Chalice heard the pot splash into the water a few yards away. Hamilton continued to urge the old woman on, now almost compassionately.

The column halted. Chalice felt relieved, thinking they had reached the perimeter. The men in front of him started moving again, but much more slowly. He then realized they had come upon some sort of obstacle. The

354

children began to cry louder than at any time before. He couldn't figure out what the obstacle was until he reached it — a wide stream. They hadn't crossed one on the way out to the ville — 'We're lost. Shit, we're lost.' Their return to camp — which even in his fear and misery had seemed just a matter of time — was now an uncertainty. Disheartened, he held his rifle over his head as the cold water rose within a few inches of his armpits. Peasants bunched in front of him, waiting to be helped across by the Marines. The cries of the children became louder. Chalice knew he'd do almost anything to silence them. Hamilton grabbed the arm of an old woman and placed it around his neck. Chalice saw a figure struggling before him and heard the choked coughs of a child. Its mother had slipped, allowing the panicked child to splash away. She cried out for somebody to help her child just as Chalice reached it. At first the mother tried to grab her child away from Chalice, but was soon content to let him hold it. He pressed the child against his chest with his free hand. It continued to cough and cry as the mother held on to Chalice's shoulder. The water deepened. He had to sling his rifle and hold the child with both hands. The stream remained at the same depth for twenty yards. Just as Chalice started to think he would never get across, the water gradually began to get shallower. Again there were people bunched in front of him on the opposite side.

Chalice wondered what new obstacle lay ahead. It proved to be the riverbank itself. Extremely steep and covered with hard, slimy mud, no one seemed able to scale it on the first attempt. Finally his turn came. The distance to the top was only ten yards. Chalice decided to try it standing up. Placing his feet carefully, he got halfway up before losing his balance and sliding back down on his stomach. On his next try, he leaned forward, at all times grasping the small tufts of grass that lined the trail. Twice his feet slipped, leaving him stretched out on the slick mud; but the grass tufts saved him another trip to the bottom.

The column halted thirty yards ahead in order to give everyone time to catch up. The men had been exhausted before; now they were close to collapse. All along the column the same two words were repeated again and again — "We're lost." The men would have been satisfied to lie down and sleep where they were regardless of the danger. A green flare burst above them. Each man dropped to his knees, knowing that any Viet Cong within a mile already knew where they were, but still refusing to let himself become a target. The purpose of the flare had been to get a bearing towards the perimeter. As soon as it burned out, the men stood up and searched the black horizon for a return flare. Few of them saw it, and those that didn't became even more disheartened.

The column began moving again — away from the river. The men were relieved, thankful that they wouldn't have to recross it. Though all the peasants had had time to regain their place in the column, they soon began to straggle back and intersperse with Second Platoon. This made the men more nervous, and they realized there was nothing they could do about it. Many of them ended up with children clutched in their arms as they stumbled forward. Chalice was among these. He held one of the older children against his chest, and felt himself fortunate that at least the child wasn't bellowing in his ear.

Each man was fearful of losing the column and becoming lost. When someone carrying a child would fall back, a few of the others would pass him to keep contact until the column halted long enough for each man to regain his position. In this manner, Chalice found himself among the members of the last platoon. He knew that he had fallen too far behind, but the hope that the column would soon halt and his jaded condition prevented him from trying to regain his place. The man in back of him was continually cursing. Chalice turned and saw that he was carrying the wounded and moaning NVA soldier. The warnings to shut up were far louder than the moans of the soldier. Suddenly, there was a loud splash. Chalice was pushed forward and almost lost his balance. He turned to see the Marine behind him jerk the prisoner from the rice paddy, at the same time saying venomously, "You better shut up, motherfucker, or I'll throw you down again."

Chalice blurted out, "Take it easy. You want to kill him?"

The Marine's tone became even more vicious as he answered, "You're damn right I do, cocksucker. You wanna fucking carry him?" Chalice made no reply. When the column finally halted, he stumbled back to his platoon. This wasn't really necessary. The point man had merely halted outside the perimeter to make sure they weren't fired upon.

Colonel Nash was waiting for them as they entered. He arranged for the peasants to be sheltered under the remains of a hootch and ordered a guard placed around them. A few yards away, Nash spotted the red glow of a corpsman's flashlight. He approached and saw a few men bent over and attending to the prisoner. There was a small wound in his buttocks, and Nash asked, "Is that the only place he's hit?" A corpsman answered affirmatively. "Well, do all you can for him. We won't be able to get him on a medivac until morning." Nash walked back to his hootch without taking the trouble to criticize Trippitt, knowing the uselessness of doing so.

As exhausted as the men were, there was a lot of movement within the perimeter while they searched out their packs and the C-rations inside them. Most of the men hadn't eaten since the previous evening. Now

356

that they had time, they remembered how hungry they were. Chalice sat contentedly with an open can of franks and beans in his hand. It hadn't been raining for almost an hour, but now was the first time Chalice became aware of this. Surprised to find himself smiling, he tried to figure out why. Everyone around him also seemed happy. Glad to be within the relative safety of the perimeter, they looked back on a night of fear that had seemed interminable while they were enduring it. Chalice watched with surprise as the glowing ashes of cigarettes made patterns in the darkness. Never before had he seen anyone dare to smoke at night in the Arizona. The men weren't even bothering to cup their ashes. Even if they had, they could still be court-martialed. Of course if any Viet Cong were around, the noise from within, especially that being made by the crying children, would be a far better guide to their perimeter. But it was still a rule they were breaking. As they looked back on the fear and exhaustion of the night march, they did so with relief, and there arose in them a need to celebrate its end, to say to themselves and those around them, "I'm still alive. They'll never get me now," even though by doing so they were increasing the danger of just this. As Kramer watched them, the same feeling prevented him from ordering the cigarettes out. Besides, it was all four platoons, not just his; and he knew the men would soon put out the cigarettes anyway.

A glance at his watch told Kramer it was almost eleven o'clock. He turned to Tony 5 and asked, "Did you arrange for some men to guard the girl?"

"Not yet."

As Tony rose to his feet, Kramer remembered how pretty she was and he realized that many of his men must have had the same thought as himself. "Make sure you warn them not to mess with her."

It rained for most of the night, but by dawn the sun was shining and the air was dry. No one woke the men. Morning found them still exhausted and lying on the ground. Through the haze, Kramer watched their listless movements as they slowly sat up — gaunt faces and tattered, mud-covered uniforms testifying to what they had undergone. He found nothing in his past to relate to this sight. There was a sneering sullenness about them, as if they'd been buried alive and had clawed and kicked their way above ground out of sheer stubbornness merely to face again those who had buried them.

Chalice rose to his feet and began walking around the perimeter. The eyes of the villagers followed him as he passed by their hootch. A few yards away someone was standing guard over the blindfolded girl. She had sat in the rain all night, and he wondered if anyone had covered her with

357

a poncho. Some men were standing around the wounded NVA soldier. He lay motionless in front of Trippitt and Martin's hootch, his knees partially drawn up and pointed stiffly towards the sky. The thought flashed through Chalice's mind that he might be dead, but Chalice then remembered he'd only been hit in the buttocks and this seemed impossible, at least until he found himself standing over the body. The soldier's eyes were closed and his features stiffened in pain. He lay in a blood-tinted pool of water. It was obvious to Chalice that he'd been left out in the rain all night, and had died of exposure or loss of blood. As Chalice looked down at the corpse, a voice said casually, "How do you like that, he's dead?"

"He died happy. I gave him plenty of morphine."

Another voice said, "I had first watch on him. He was alive when I went to sleep, moaning so loud Martin told me to kick him."

Someone said gruffly and with conviction, "The sonofabitch did it for spite, stayed alive just long enough so I'd have to carry him all the way back."

Chalice hadn't looked up at the faces of those men who had spoken, and he didn't have to for the next voice, immediately recognizing it as Martin's. "The sonofabitch must of wore himself out moaning. . . . Some of you men get him out of here before he starts to stink."

Chalice and most of those around him backed away. Two men picked up the corpse and carried it to the rice paddies at the edge of the perimeter. Chalice watched them as they swung the body and counted, "One . . . two . . . three," before flinging it into the water. Again Chalice glanced at the blood-tinted puddle where the body had lain.

Nash had sent for Trippitt, and as he watched him approach, he regretted having to speak to him. Trippitt also had no desire to see Nash, but to his surprise he was greeted indifferently and no mention was made of the previous day's mistake. "I've already sent for a medivac chopper and one to evacuate the detainees."

"Won't need the medivac, sir. The Gook's dead."

Nash looked up in surprise. "But I thought he was shot in the ass?"

"He was stiff as a board when I got up this morning."

Nash slowly shook his head as he replied, "Can't understand that."

"Well, they got three of my men."

'Wonder if he knew their names.' After a long pause, he said, "No patrols today. Tomorrow Echo Company relieves you. You'll set up a few klicks away. . . . Major Lucas has the details." As Trippitt started to leave the hootch, Nash added, "Check your men's feet. Make sure the bad cases get sent in with the detainees. Have the others keep as dry as they can today."

358

Kramer stood a few yards away from the detainees. He didn't want it to seem as if he were staring at them, but he found himself taking quick glances in their direction. They sat huddled together beneath the hootch, their faces now more weary than frightened. Someone spoke to him, and he recognized Nash's voice even before he turned around. "Nothing to be proud of, is it?" Kramer shook his head. "I guess they can't be any worse off at Duc Duc. At least there they won't have to worry about the bombs." Nash walked towards the villagers and Kramer followed. A very old man with a white beard on the tip of his chin sat at the edge of the hootch. Kramer watched as Nash nodded to him and the old man nervously returned the nod. "I guess this old timer's seen just about everything . . . most of it bad." Nash pointed to a primitive hoe the old man held beside him, then opened his hand for the old man to place the hoe into it. Nash turned to Kramer and asked, "If they came for you and said, 'I know you've never been more than a few miles away from your hootch in your whole life, but we're taking you away from here. You can bring one thing.' If they came and told you that, what would you bring?"

"I don't know."

"It wouldn't be a hoe, would it?"

Kramer stared at the hoe. It had a bamboo shaft with a hand-carved wooden blade tied to it by a vine. Even its battered condition helped to give it the appearance of a time-forgotten relic. "They say these people are lazy."

"You listen long enough, and you'll hear them say just about anything." Nash returned the hoe to the peasant, then added, "All they need is to be left alone . . . by the Communists too."

Echo Company relieved Hotel Company the next afternoon. The men knew it would be a long march to their new camp. Fear of again being caught in the open at night made them anxious to get started. The day's rest had done little to heal their feet, and by the time they set-in, many of them could hardly walk. It was Third and Fourth Platoons' turns to go on ambushes, while First and Second drew listening posts. Trippitt had been making the ambushes shorter, but this night he chose to send the squad from Fourth Platoon almost two kilometers outside the perimeter. Unfortunately for the men in the company, the ambush was successful. A squad of NVA soldiers walked right in front of it only to leave five of their dead behind. Because of this, Trippitt decided to use the perimeter for another night, and to send out two additional ambushes instead of the listening posts. While a few of the squad leaders were tempted to sandbag them, none did. It would have been better if they had. The squad

359

from First Platoon was itself ambushed on the way to its site. One man was killed, and three others wounded. Because it was too risky to call in a medivac so far away from the perimeter, they had to carry their dead and wounded back to the camp.

Every few nights the perimeter had been coming under heavy sniper fire, and the men were extremely nervous about the chopper giving away their position. Shortly after the medivac took off, these fears proved justified; but in a manner few of them expected. The perimeter came under attack from a rapid barrage of blooker rounds. It had been weeks since this had happened, and their fear of the Phantom Blooker had gradually waned until he was rarely mentioned. During the barrage, they had plenty of time to recall past encounters with him, and these memories involved deaths and injuries. First light broke over the mountains three hours after the barrage had ended, and it found the men of Hotel Company tired and shaken, feeling as if a mysteriously granted reprieve had suddenly been revoked without warning or explanation.

Even if Trippitt had wanted to spare his men the marching, he now had no choice but to move the perimeter. The men realized this, and as tired and pain ridden as they were, few complained as they broke camp and started marching. Soon they were too exhausted to complain. It was four o'clock when they reached the foothills. Before setting out, Trippitt had given his platoon commanders the coordinates of the hill that was to be their new camp. Kramer became bewildered as he watched the column veer away from the intended hill. He finally concluded that Trippitt merely wanted to approach it from a different angle, but a few minutes later it became obvious that this wasn't the case. Thinking he should call Trippitt on the radio, Kramer turned to Milton but changed his mind before he spoke. He was exhausted; and besides, it seemed to make little difference what hill they used. He even began to have doubts as to which hill Trippitt had pointed, and tried without success to picture the map in his mind. Something told Kramer to take out his own map, but he was too weary to bother.

The column soon reached the base of the hill. Though not very high and sparsely vegetated, it was far steeper than it had looked from a distance. The column bunched at its base as the haggard men fought their way up. Again something told Kramer to look at his map. Not seeing any point in doing so, he took out his canteen instead. The warm water somewhat refreshed him. As he watched the point platoon struggle towards the top, he dreaded the climb that he too would have to make. Again he was bothered by the impulse to look at his map. It was as if his own mind was refusing him a few moments' peace. As much for the satisfaction of

360

knowing that again Trippitt had been wrong, he finally took it out. A quick glance told him that this was the case. Seeing no point in saying anything, he nodded to himself and started to put the map away. Suddenly his dulled senses were shocked into a panic and he yelled forward, "*Stop them! Stop them! It's a minefield!*"

As the first few men disappeared over the edge of the summit, the order to halt was frantically passed forward by radio and the shouts of those men behind them. Everyone with a map took it out. Trippitt called Kramer on the radio and began to argue with him when Lieutenant Howell cut him short by agreeing with Kramer. The maps clearly showed an old French minefield atop the hill. Kramer had noticed it that morning without realizing it. Trippitt ordered those on the summit to carefully backtrack and come down. As the tenseness of the men abated, most of them began shaking their heads in relief and disgust.

It took another half hour before the entire company made it to the top of the right hill. After digging their foxholes, the men still had time to heat some C-rations. Most of Alpha Sqaud was sitting together talking about their close call when Forsythe said, "I guess Trippitt'll get another medal for guiding us out of that minefield."

A number of men agreed, and Chalice asked, "What do you mean *another* medal?"

Forsythe looked up in surprise. "You guys didn't hear?" The men around him shook their heads. "Trippitt and Martin wrote each other up for medals. Trippitt got a Silver Star, and Martin got a Bronze."

"*For what?*" Hamilton shouted.

"For nothing, of course. It supposedly had something to do with one of the times the Phantom Blooker hit us."

"What the hell did *they* do?" Hamilton asked.

"It ain't what they did," Forsythe replied. "You don't get medals for that. It's for what they *said* each other did."

"*Well*, what did they say?"

"Something about leaving their foxholes."

"What about the corpsmen?" Chalice cut in. "They were the only ones I ever saw out of the foxholes."

Childs spoke before Forsythe could answer. "What's the big fucking deal? How do you think these lifers get all their phony medals? By writing each other up. That's why they don't have time to write up anybody that does anything. . . . Who the hell wants medals anyway?"

Hamilton was still enraged, and he said, "It ain't a case of wanting medals. It's a case of having Martin and Trippitt get them."

Childs found it hard to understand both Hamilton's anger and surprise.

"Listen man, you know damn well this happens all the time, at least two other times since we've been here. Besides, the only real heroes are the ones with notches on their rifles for the lifers they've killed."

The men nodded their heads, and Hamilton added, "I just wish somebody'd get some notches on his rifle for Trippitt and Martin before those assholes get *me* killed."

Trippitt again sent out four ambushes that night, all of them long. The men allowed to remain within the perimeter were thankful that it wasn't their turn, but this could bring them little comfort, for they knew their turns would come. Few of them would have preferred the ambushes even if they had known the Phantom Blooker would again strike their perimeter, even if they had known beforehand that two of them would be dead by morning. No one was surprised that he had found them, nor were they surprised when they learned that one of their ambushes had been ambushed. Luck, nothing more, had prevented anyone in the ambush party from being wounded. The nervousness of a single Viet Cong soldier had saved their lives. He had fired too soon and with too little care. Solely for this reason, the ambush party had enough time to take cover.

The next morning Hotel Company moved out as soon as the medivac chopper evacuated the dead. A helicopter had spotted some NVA soldiers disappear into a large tree line, and this was where they were now headed. When they were within a kilometer of it, the point man spotted three NVA soldiers in the open. The columns moved out after them at full speed, but the NVA soldiers ran into some thick brush and vanished. Only the more experienced of the men found it easy to believe they had gotten away.

Trippitt immediately made camp on a small, barren patch of high ground. He then assigned patrols to three of his platoons. As soon as Second Platoon got a kilometer away from the perimeter, they came under sniper fire. No one was sure where it was coming from. Kramer picked out the likeliest thicket and advanced his platoon towards it on-line. He knew some of his men were lame, but was surprised to see so many of them struggling through the rice paddies trying to keep up. Kramer ordered the pace slowed, but this did little good.

The formation was barely into the tree line when Kramer realized the impossibility of sweeping through it. A solid wall of brush lay before them. His men were already exhausted from six hours of marching on their swollen and bleeding feet. He ordered them to back out of the tree line, then assigned Alpha the point. The rest of the platoon followed them through the brush.

362

Childs led the column. All he could think about was the possibility that the brush might become sparser. In a few minutes it did, but he was too sore and exhausted to take any real comfort from this. He merely pushed his way forward, not looking for booby traps and too tired to care, thinking that he should be in An Hoa and cursing the fact that he wasn't. Childs didn't have the strength to be angry, but he thought about his two Purple Hearts with disgust and resentment. He hated Kramer for not seeing that he was sent to the rear, and the company master sergeant — 'sitting in his office' — for keeping him in the bush. Childs was sure of one thing: something had to happen. He'd waited and waited, but nothing had changed — each day as insanely meaningless as the ones before it. Something *had* to happen, or Childs knew he would be forced to make it happen. Behind these thoughts, there were also vague, repetitive warnings to watch out for booby traps or an ambush; but he forced them aside with a fatalistic finality as he repeated under his breath, "Fuck it!"

Suddenly he found himself standing in front of a Viet Cong antiaircraft position, a circular trench with a mound of earth in the middle on which a large-caliber machine gun could be placed. Now forced to become more alert, Childs pushed his resentment aside. He turned and told Hamilton to stay back. Moving slowly forward with his eyes on the ground, Childs cleared a path for the rest of the column. Little tufts of brush lay all around him. He studied the spaces between them for trip wires. In an instant, as he was about to place his foot down, Childs awkwardly jerked his body back and gazed at a tuft of brush before him. Within it lay a dull green piece of metal he knew to be part of a C-ration can. The rest of it and the grenade it contained remained buried. The rain had washed away some of the mud. For this and no other reason he'd been able to see it. Only after studying the ground around the grenade did he spot the trip wire. A tremor chilled him as he realized that he was still alive merely because of the rain and his luck in approaching the foxhole from the direction he had.

Sure there were other booby traps around, Childs decided against searching them out. All that was necessary was for him to clear a path for the rest of the column. He pointed out the grenade to Hamilton before again moving forward, now with the same care and alertness that was usually his custom. His resentment about being in the bush gradually did return, but in no way took his mind off the dangers that lay before him.

Childs felt relieved when he finally broke through to the opposite side of the tree line. He was safe, but only for a while. There would be other booby traps, ones that could do to him what they had done to Chief, a better point man than he ever was. 'No more,' Childs told himself, 'not much longer. Something has to happen.'

The rest of the men joined him on the edge of the tree line, most of them dropping to the ground immediately. Childs watched, waited until he was the last man standing. He walked a few yards away and sat down by himself. Still he watched the men around him. They sat quietly in the rain, none of them having made any conscious attempt to avoid it by sitting under trees, or even by turning their faces from it like cattle. 'Not *even* cattle,' Childs thought. He knew that for himself as well as the rest of the men, rain had become a fact, something accepted without question. To help avert the chill and discomfort of it, he and those around him unconsciously dulled all their senses.

Suddenly these barriers were shattered by a paralyzing explosion of light and a blast of thunder loud enough to send many of the men diving to the ground. Childs remained sitting, having only flinched. He didn't even look up in the direction of the rending sound that followed, or see the huge tree branch until it had fallen around him with a dull thud. Childs sat motionless, completely enveloped in a fork of this branch which hadn't even grazed him.

Some of the still-startled men rushed forward to see if he was all right. They were met by a steady and outraged stare. Only the nearest of them heard Childs mumble, "Missed." As he got to his feet, Childs stared up at the sky in rage, finally spitting out a victorious shout. "*Missed*, you dirty *cocksucker!*" Just as he finished yelling, there was a faint rumble of thunder. A grin came to his lips and he noticed a few of the men drawing back. He began to laugh violently, and some of the men joined him. Again he looked up at the heavens and shouted with exultation, "Missed, you sonofabitch!" A few of the men continued to back away, but most of them joined him in laughter. It was just dying down when a bolt of lightning scorched the ground in back of Childs. Again the men were shocked — some backing away, others standing transfixed — while Childs, who had barely flinched, began to laugh even louder. His eyes, expression, and the sound of his laughter seemed more than insane and no less than satanic. Once more he raised his glare to the heavens and shouted in anger and triumph, "Missed again, you dirty cocksucker! . . . Give it another try!" When Childs lowered his stare to the men around him, he saw that no one was within twenty yards and all eyes were focused upon him in disbelief. This further incited him. During the few seconds he was able to control his mad laughter, Childs once more shouted to the heavens, "Try again, motherfucker! I dare you!" The startled men continued to stare at him in silence, some of them actually waiting for the lightning to strike. When Childs saw this, he taunted them with a wild, ridiculing grin and the words, "What the hell are you jerks scared of? He's after *me!*" Then looking up at the sky, he added, "C'mon, asshole, I'll give you another chance." What had started as outrage on the verge of insanity had now transformed into a performance. Childs gloried in the disbelieving stares of those around him. He sensed and enjoyed their doubts about what they were seeing and his own sanity. He would have liked to continue, but his body felt ready to wilt and melt into the ground. Even his wild expression of triumph faded to a calm, blank stare. Still there was silence, unbroken until a few seconds later by a laugh from one of the men, then a few more. But most of those around Childs remained startled and silent.

Kramer continued to stare at Childs, a disbelieving grin on his face, thinking, 'More! More! I want to see more,' once again trying to read Childs's thoughts, wondering what possessed him. All the men were on their feet, and there was no point in doing anything but forming them up and moving out. Kramer reluctantly ordered them to do so. It was now too late to finish the patrol as planned. Instead, Kramer decided to move back through the tree line and return to camp. He switched Charlie Squad to the point and placed Alpha on the tail end.

Childs was the last man in the column. Now that he didn't have to worry as much about ambushes and booby traps, his thoughts turned from his experience with the lightning to how close he'd come to being killed on that day and on many other days. For the very first time, he began to resent having to walk point more than anybody else in his squad. The fact that he was the best point man didn't satisfy him, and he kept asking himself, 'Why me? Why me, when I should be in the rear?' It was true that much of his success at dealing with booby traps had been due to luck rather than skill; but Childs convinced himself that all of it had been due to luck, and that this luck would soon run out. Memories of the way Chief had been killed seemed to confirm this belief. Childs had long refused trying to think of some imaginative way to get to the rear and stay there. Such exploits had given him the reputation that now kept him in the bush, a reputation he felt was undeserved. Never had he left the platoon when it was in danger. Only the meaningless working parties and guard duty had forced him, at the risk of his sanity, to escape from the bush. No longer could he wait for something to happen. He was now forced to make it happen.

An idea that had been recurring for weeks finally took hold — a way of leaving Vietnam that left little opportunity for subsequent guilt or regret. He could have figured out easier ways; but no, he refused to make it too easy. He knew that only by refusing to kneel, by adding a last curse of bravado that would flaunt not only the universe but also its henchman, Chance, could he look back haughtily on what he had done. Childs became excited by the absurd danger of this plan too simple even to be a scheme. There wouldn't be any phony illness to explain to doctors, or self-inflicted wounds during an artillery barrage. He'd do something crazy, yet far saner than any of the actions of those men around him. 'No hammer for me,' he thought as he withdrew a grenade from his pouch, at the same time slapping his flak jacket for reassurance of the protection it afforded.

Childs jerked the pin from the grenade. It was now too late to change his mind, and the excitement of the moment took hold of him. He tilted his helmet back until it rested on his flak jacket and protected his neck. He stopped walking, so that Chalice would be out of the grenade's range. His determination began to wane. Childs knew he had to throw the grenade immediately. He was just about to do so when a horrible thought occurred to him. He quickly reached in his pants and drew up his balls. With his hand still in his trousers, Childs flung the grenade ten yards behind him and cringed in expectation. By reflex, he almost yelled, "Fire in the hole." Seconds seemed somehow to expand and he thought the grenade would never go off. Only the part of his body below the waist lay unprotected — 'My poor ass. My poor ass.' He began to squat just as the grenade exploded. Its concussion pushed him forward without knocking him to the ground.

Chalice was startled by the explosion. He rushed back to help Childs, finding him feeling up and down the backs of his legs in disbelief, mumbling feebly, "I'm not hit."

"What happened?" Chalice asked excitedly.

"I'm not even hit," Childs said in a quietly depressed tone.

"What was it?"

"I can't believe it, not even a pin prick."

"What was it, a booby trap?"

By this time there were a number of men standing around Childs. "Yeah . . . yeah . . . a booby trap. Make sure I'm not hit."

As he said this, Childs turned around, thus exposing his shredded flak jacket. Hamilton looked at it with astonishment. "God, what a mess. . . . But not a drop of blood on you."

"Are you sure?" Childs asked hopefully.

"Not a drop," Hamilton insisted.

Only now had the shock of the incident worn off Chalice. "God Childs, you're the luckiest motherfucker I ever met."

"Yeah . . . I guess I am," Childs answered in a stunned, disbelieving tone.

Kramer had just stepped from the tree line into the rice paddies when he was startled by the explosion. His first thought was, 'booby trap.' It seemed impossible that so many men had been able to pass it without injury. Kramer was doubly surprised to find out the victim had been Childs. He couldn't conceive how Childs, his best point man, could be so effective while walking point, yet inept enough to trip a booby trap when he was the last man in the column. Kramer ordered his men to move out again, thinking, 'At least no one was hurt.'

When Second Platoon reached the perimeter, most of the men gathered around Childs to find out exactly what had happened. The failure of his attempt had left him bewildered. Even if he'd understood the questions asked him, he would have been in no condition to think up answers. To his relief, attention was soon drawn away from him by the return of Third Platoon with three NVA prisoners, all of them wounded. The body of another NVA soldier had been left behind. It was Marine Corps policy not to risk night medivac missions for enemy soldiers. Enough daylight remained to get a chopper for the wounded prisoners, but Trippitt didn't bother to send for one. This meant they would have to wait until morning.

The men didn't waste any time before starting to dig their foxholes. They not only feared a blooker attack, they expected one. For this reason there was no complaining when Trippitt passed the word not to build hootches. They wouldn't have had time anyway, and doing so would have made them easier targets. When the foxholes were finished, barely enough daylight remained to heat C-rations. All around the perimeter, men sat in small groups, their ponchos wrapped around them as protection from the light drizzle as they ate.

Kramer tossed aside his empty C-ration can. Bland and pastelike, at least the food had been warm. And tonight this was enough. His rotting uniform stuck to him like a coat of slime. How long had it been since he'd felt dry cloth against his skin? A month, at least. When was the last time he or anyone else in his platoon had gotten six whole hours' sleep? *Too many* months ago. At least the food had been warm.

Kramer watched as the last hint of light faded into the mountains. Two of his men, now no more than sepia patterns, rose up and moved across the horizon. He had no idea who they were, but he respected them. He thought about Childs — not about his curses towards the heavens, but about the way he had spotted the booby trap. Even though Kramer had been warned about the booby trap, he'd come within inches of stepping on it. How could he not respect Childs, knowing that more than one man would now be dead or wounded if he himself had been walking the point? He thought with confidence about all of his men, realizing how he had always fought against having any feeling for them. But they had somehow won much more than his respect. No longer did he look down on them, as he had done at first and would have continued to do under circumstances where the life of one man didn't depend upon those around him. He respected the newer replacements as much as the men who had been with the platoon longer than he had, knowing that in time they too could be depended upon.

Chalice and Forsythe sat silently in the darkness, legs dangling into their foxhole. During the previous few days, Chalice had often been kidded about not being able to protect his squad from the Phantom Blooker. He'd taken these remarks more seriously than they had been intended. Ever since the Phantom Blooker had renewed his attacks, Chalice thought little about anything else. These thoughts had bothered him to the extent that he refrained as much as possible from asking questions about or even mentioning the Phantom Blooker. But now, as the sky darkened, he could no longer keep his silence. "Forsythe, why do you think the Phantom Blooker laid off us so long?"

"He was on his R and R."

"No, seriously."

"Maybe he was after one of the other companies."

"No. I heard Kramer talking to Milton about it."

"You're the professor. You should have all the answers."

"Maybe I do. . . . At first I thought he might have been out of ammunition, but he sure as hell used a lot of it the last couple of nights. It got me thinking. Everytime —"

"That's dangerous."

"Everytime a supply chopper gets shot down, the Gooks come out at night and strip it, right?"

"Right," Forsythe answered in a bored tone.

"Well a lot of times they're carrying blooker rounds, so the Gooks probably give him as much as he can use. The only thing is, he can't carry them all around. He has to stash them somewhere. The choppers never see him anymore, so he must do all his traveling at night. The only way he can keep following us is if he's got hiding places all over the Arizona where he sleeps and keeps his ammo."

"So what?"

"I don't know. . . . I mean it makes him seem more like a human being, doesn't it?"

"What else would spend all its time trying to kill people. . . . I'll tell you one thing though: I'd rather stay in the perimeter tonight than go on any ambush — the odds are better, and every patrol we sent out today made contact. There's Gooks all over the place, and you can bet your ass they know we send out ambushes every night. They'll be waiting for someone."

368

Trippitt realized this also, but he was willing to take the risk. Again he assigned four ambushes, three of them long. Within Second Platoon, it was Charlie Squad's turn. Ramirez had previously decided to sandbag if assigned a long one. To his relief he drew the short ambush. Of the three squads that were assigned long ones, two decided to sandbag. This made it necessary for their squad leaders to pick patches of high ground that were close to the perimeter and large enough to afford cover. The ambush party from First Platoon chose a spot twenty-five yards outside Second Platoon's sector of the perimeter. To prevent themselves from being fired upon by their own company, their squad leader arranged for Tony 5 to caution his men. Chalice and Forsythe's foxhole faced this patch of high ground, so First Platoon's ambush party left the perimeter from their position.

As was now the custom, the men remaining within the perimeter sat quietly around the radios waiting for the ambushes to notify them that they had set-in. They heard three of the ambush parties do this, but a burst of AK-47 fire told them that the fourth never would. What they eventually heard was an excited voice telling them that three men had been wounded, two seriously. A medivac chopper was immediately called in, but sniper fire drove it away. Puff was then called in, and the men within the perimeter started worrying about their friends who had sandbagged and weren't in their proper positions. The ambushed squad finally made it back to the perimeter, and in minutes the medivac chopper landed within it and picked up the wounded. Before many of the men who had guided it in had time to return to their foxholes, the Phantom Blooker began firing. Even over the roar of the ascending helicopter, anguished screams testified to his accuracy.

Puff began spraying rounds closer to the perimeter as the men sat crouched within their foxholes, worried just as much about their friends sandbagging as they were about a blooker round finding them. Soon another medivac chopper was circling the perimeter for those men wounded on the last evacuation. The whir of its blades became deafening as it quickly descended. Just when it was a few feet above the ground and the wounded were being rushed towards it, a perfectly aimed blooker round sent sheets of flaming gasoline all over the perimeter. The chopper hung motionless for an instant before another explosion brought it crashing to the ground. Its blade tore lose and sliced through the radioman that had tried to bring it in. All over the perimeter men were shouting for help for themselves and for their friends. The burning chopper lit the entire perimeter with a hot orange light, and the only crewman able to escape rushed out of it, himself a squirming, twisting torch.

The panic diminished to a wary silence, broken only by the feeble, excruciating moans of the wounded. It took Puff's machine guns to cut the tension of those protracted moments by drowning out the moans. It was soon joined by helicopter gun ships that swung low over the perimeter as they strafed the area around it. This continued for almost an hour before the perimeter was again silent.

The Phantom Blooker had long ceased his assault when the third medivac chopper picked up the wounded. Chalice and Forsythe sat stunned in their foxhole as the engines faded in the distance and the perimeter alternated back to silence. Chalice stared out at the patch of high ground where the party from First Platoon had chosen to sandbag. If they had been any farther from the perimeter they'd probably all be dead. Suddenly he heard a moaning sound behind him. He and Forsythe turned and were barely able to discern a human figure crawling towards them. Forsythe reached out and dragged the burned and bleeding NVA prisoner up to their hole. Even in the darkness, they could tell that a pathetic few minutes would be enough to trace out the death of something already less than human. He had managed to outlive his two comrades, but these last moments were filled merely with delirium and agony.

The perimeter was again silent as Gunny Martin moved around it to check each position. He was as much shaken by what had happened as anyone else in the company. "You all right, men?" he asked in an almost fatherly tone.

"Yeah."

"We're okay."

Just as Martin turned to walk away, a metallic sound came from the opposite tree line. Forsythe and Chalice flinched in dread, hoping Martin hadn't heard it. "What was that?" he asked in an excited whisper.

"What was what?" Forsythe replied.

"I didn't hear anything," Chalice added.

Martin had pulled out his pistol, but he now reholstered it. "Guess it's my nerves." Just before he'd finished speaking, a similar sound came from the tree line. Martin jumped into their hole and whispered, "There's something out there."

Forsythe heard the faint voice of someone in the ambush party warning someone else to keep quiet, and he tried to drown it out with his own words. "We've been —"

"Shut up!"

" — watching all night."

"Shut up!" Martin repeated. He noticed Chalice's blooker and whispered, "Lob a round into that tree line. Hurry up!"

Chalice had enough self-possession to start fumbling with the blooker as he said, "It's jammed."

Martin grabbed it out of his hands and fired before Chalice could stop him. There was a moan from the tree line, and somebody called out, "I'm hit."

"They're Marines," Martin murmured in a dazed tone.

For the fourth time that night a medivac chopper had to be called in. Three men in the ambush party had been wounded, none critically. The chopper arrived just as dawn broke over the mountains. Only after it had taken off did Trippitt have time to expel his anger. Most of the men were gathered in the center of the perimeter when Trippitt called for the squad leader from First Platoon. The sight of him approaching enraged Trippitt.

"*What the fuck were you doing in that tree line?*"

Those men closest backed away, and others approached until Trippitt and the squad leader were completely encircled. The squad leader was discernibly shaken, but he stared directly at Trippitt as he answered, "We were coming in from our ambush."

Trippitt and everyone else knew this was a lie. Being lied to would have easily been enough to anger Trippitt, but having this happen in front of the whole company enraged him. "*Bullshit!* What do you take me for?" he screamed, his face within inches of the squad leader's. "Since when do you start back from an ambush without radioing in?" The squad leader remained silent, but he continued glaring back at Trippitt. "You were sandbagging, weren't you?" Again the squad leader remained silent. "You chickenshit motherfucker, you were sandbagging, *weren't you?*"

The squad leader moved his head in short, nervous jerks as he glanced warily around him. Tears of rage came to his eyes. He started backing away from Trippitt, at the same time screaming in anger and fear, "You're damn right we sandbagged, and it was *my* fucking idea!" He continued to back up as Trippitt advanced on him. "How many of us do you want to kill with your fucking ambushes? When the colonel's around you don't send us all over the Arizona."

"Shut up!" Trippitt hissed through gritted teeth.

The circle around them enlarged as Trippitt continued advancing on the squad leader, who wouldn't shut up, but screamed back instead, "How many more of my friends wouldn't be dead if they'd sandbagged? You *killed* them! You killed them just as sure as if you'd used a gun. You and the rest of the CP lying around while we kill ourselves. Go on your own fucking ambushes. They're my men. I'm protecting 'em from you, you *cocksucking* lifer!"

The squad leader stopped back-stepping and gained control of himself.

Trippitt continued to advance on him until they were chest to chest and Trippitt screamed, saliva spurting from his mouth, "You chickenshit motherfucker, you call yourself a *Marine?*" The squad leader shoved Trippitt back. Within seconds they were both on the ground with Trippitt's hands around the squad leader's neck. Sugar Bear reached them first, and with Tony 5's help he pulled Trippitt off and flung him back. The squad leader scrambled to his feet, but now Sugar Bear, Tony 5, and a few other men stood between them, glaring at Trippitt. This stunned him for a second, but he quickly turned to the company radioman and shouted, "Get me a chopper! Tell them we've got a prisoner." Trippitt turned back towards the squad leader who was still blocked from his view. "If it's the last thing I do, I'm gonna see you in the brig. You're under arrest for cowardice under fire and assaulting an officer. . . . Somebody bring me his rifle."

No one moved. Trippitt quickly turned and walked away, knowing by the silence that all eyes were glaring at his back. The squad leader, his head hanging down, started to walk away. The men moved with him, some of them placing their hands on his shoulders, their voices saying, "Don't sweat it, man. They can't do shit to you."

"That took guts."

"I'm a squad leader and I sandbag. They'll have to court-martial all of us."

"Hey man, take it easy. You're the closest thing to a hero we've got in this company."

It was over an hour before the helicopter arrived. Almost every man in the company gathered around it and stood watching as the squad leader from First Platoon went aboard. Trippitt immediately gave the order to form up. Within minutes they were marching to their new camp. The pace was unusually slow, and the condition of the men's feet wasn't the only reason. Each slow step frustrated Trippitt. Only by clenching his teeth was he able to keep from yelling the order to speed up. His memory assaulted him with all the absurd orders he'd ever had to follow, all the bastards that had owned him because they'd had one more stripe on their arms. But that was the idea — the reason the Marine Corps was something different — larger than anyone in it and all of them put together — being able to take it — keeping your mouth shut and doing what you were told. Ten years he had taken all the shit without ever regretting it; but these brats had to be different, thinking they're gonna change the system, turn the Marine Corps into the Cub Scouts. In his frustrated rage, Trippitt bumped into the man in front of him and immediately yelled, "*Speed it up!*" Teeth clenched, he waited for his order to be followed, finally yelling again, and one more time. But the pace remained the same. It was happening. He was losing control of his men. Rage and disbelief confused his thoughts as he pondered what to do, realizing his career, possibly his life was now at stake.

The company finally reached the irregularly shaped patch of high ground that was to be its camp. As Martin walked around to survey the area, he was startled by the sight of a small puppy's head sticking out of the pouch on a soldier's pack. "Hey, you!" he called out in anger and disbelief. A number of soldiers turned towards him, but Roads wasn't one of them. Martin's voice became louder and angrier. "*Hey* you with the dog-" Again Roads failed to turn around. Martin circled in front of Roads and stood face to face with him only to be met by an impassive yet belligerent stare. "Are you deaf?"

Roads answered with calm insolence, " 'Hey you' isn't my name. It's Roads, Lance Corporal Roads."

Martin couldn't believe what he was hearing. "Oh, is that right? Well let me tell you something, *Lance Corporal Roads:* This is a rifle company, not a *pet show*. See that you get rid of that dog or I'll do it for you." Before Martin could walk away, Roads turned his back on him and Martin again found himself exchanging stares with the puppy.

As soon as Martin had arranged the positions, he began looking for Trippitt, all the while mumbling incoherently. He couldn't believe what was happening — this was nothing like Korea. He'd noticed the difference immediately after arriving in Vietnam, and had become increasingly perplexed by it. These weren't Marines. They were a bunch of wise-ass punks. They had no pride in the Marine Corps, acted as if they'd been tricked into joining — no respect for the finest, proudest organization there was, *his* Marine Corps, the only meaningful thing in a world full of bullshit; and they were trying to destroy it. Someday they'd be sorry — when they got back to the States and found themselves walking around in civilian clothes — feeling like nobodies. Then they'd remember what it was like to be a Marine. He didn't demand that they love the Marine Corps. That was too much to ask of the punks. But they didn't even respect it, take pride in it. They tried to make a joke of it — right in front of him. They wanted to destroy the only meaningful thing in his life.

Martin was even more unnerved by the time he reached Trippitt, 'sitting on his ass, doing nothing.' It took all his self-control not to shout with outraged and indiscriminate anger the agitated warning that he finally issued from between clenched teeth. "We've got to do something fast."

Trippitt knew exactly what Martin meant. "Yeah, but what?"

373

"Something, we gotta do something before this gets out of hand."

Trippitt was more puzzled by what was happening than by what he should do about it. "I don't understand it. You try and go by the book — I was an enlisted man just like them, *nine years*. I'm not one of those college jerks just out of OCS. It doesn't make sense."

"Sure it does. That's just it. We can't run this company by ourselves. How we gonna control the men when all we've got for platoon commanders is a bunch of college clowns? The only decent one is Forest, and he's as dumb as any of 'em. . . . There's no discipline!"

Martin hadn't told him anything he didn't already know. "Yeah, but what am I supposed to do about it? I tried to treat them like men."

"That's just it. You can't do that anymore. They don't even *act* like Marines!"

"It ain't their guts. I've seen them in action."

"Sure it isn't. But they don't know how to take orders. There's no *discipline!* Just look at them. Some of them haven't shaved in a week. Look at their hair."

"It isn't what they look like."

"I *know* that," Martin insisted. "They think they're too smart. Their heads are so full of ideas, they can't even *hear* orders."

"Maybe it's this war. They don't realize how many people'd give their left nut to be in a war."

"That's not it! There's no more discipline. . . . Maybe if they looked like Marines, they'd act like them too."

Trippitt realized it was more than this, but he wasn't sure what. "I don't know. It's for their own good. How we gonna get through to them?"

"Not through their platoon commanders. That's for sure."

"Maybe if I talked to them," Trippitt said without conviction. He'd always felt at a disadvantage when he had to rely on words, and speaking directly to his men seemed something he shouldn't have to do. 'What's the chain of command for?' he asked himself.

Martin found the idea of Trippitt talking to the men ridiculous, but refrained from telling him so. "Yeah, maybe; but we've got to do more. You can't instill discipline with words. Let's get them to look like Marines first — *have an inspection!*"

"An inspection, *here?*"

"Well . . . we've gotta do something."

Trippitt realized this was true, but he was still at a loss about what that something should be. After a long pause, he finally said, "I'll talk to them."

Word was quickly passed for the men to form up at the center of the perimeter. They milled around like a disorganized mob while Trippitt

374

watched from a distance. This irritated him, and he remembered what Martin had said about the platoon commanders. Tempted to order them into a formation, he decided not to. There was silence as he took his place before them, studying their faces and the tattered conditions of their uniforms, thinking, 'It ain't their guts.'

He began speaking in an uncomfortable, but calm and fatherly tone:

"We've been through a lot these last few months. Many of us didn't make it, your friends and my men. There's a difference, but not that much of one. Mistakes have been made, some of them mine." The men eyed Trippitt suspiciously, but few of them were not disarmed by his tone and the surprising sincerity of his words. For many of them, it was the first time they'd ever looked on him as anything even resembling a human being. "When mistakes are made in a place like this, people die. That's the way it is." Trippitt hadn't even thought about what he was going to say. The words began to come more slowly, and with greater effort. The fear that he was showing weakness caused his tone to gradually harden. "We're in this together, whether we like it or not. They can't keep us out here much longer. It's just a matter of time. I know some of you hate my guts, but that's the way it is. I've tried to go by the book." With this phrase he lost them. Sensing what had happened without knowing why, Trippitt became even more uneasy. "Charlie isn't gonna come to us. We have to go to him. I've done everything I could to see that we'd lose as few men as possible." Trippitt actually believed this as he said it, but no one else did. The stares of the men became colder, and he could feel their distrust. Words teased and evaded him. The faces of his men seemed even more hostile than they were. He felt trapped and wanted to get away from them, but didn't know how to end his speech. For one of the very few times in his life he knew fear, intensified by his ignorance of its source, suddenly transformed into anger by the stare of one of his men, fervent with hatred, drawing Trippitt's own outraged stare. He wanted to strike out at it. "Discipline, we have to have discipline," he said without conviction. Still unable to look away from that one leering scowl, he didn't even realize it was coming from a single man. All the faces before him became duplicates of it. *"Discipline!"* he shouted harshly, and this time with conviction. "The Marine Corps is built on discipline. That's why we're the greatest fighting force in the world. Look at you! You don't even look like Marines. Some of you haven't shaved in a week. Look at your *hair!* I'm telling all of you right now; if we have nothing else around here, we'll have discipline, and we'll start right now. You have one hour to shave, cut you hair, and report back here, *in formation*, for an inspection. *Dis* . . . missed!"

Even before he turned his back on his men, Trippitt realized he had made a mistake; and he spent the time before the inspection brooding over it. His men spent this time differently. The idea of an inspection seemed so absurd to them, it was more ludicrous than irritating. Because there weren't enough razors to go around, many of them had to shave by placing their index fingers through the slots of double-edged blades. Gunny Martin had the only pair of scissors, so no one attempted to get his hair cut. The men spent the rest of the hour jokingly calling out to each other for Brasso, shoe polish, and other items they hadn't seen in months.

Most of the men were smiling when the company formed up at the center of the perimeter. Trippitt stared on somberly, for the first time realizing the danger of keeping the men in formation. But it was too late now. He ordered the platoon commanders to inspect their men.

Kramer was struck by the absurdity of what was happening, and he couldn't keep from grinning. The rain became harder as the men stood motionless in their worn boots and tattered, mud-covered uniforms. The seams of many of their trousers had rotted away, and these men's testicles hung down conspicuously in front of them. Nearly every face was mottled by patches of unshaved whiskers. When the platoon commanders had finished, Gunny Martin walked behind the formation and picked out over a dozen men for haircuts. After ten minutes of standing in the rain, the formation was dismissed and most of the men walked away smiling.

Trippitt realized the inspection had proved an even greater mistake than he had feared. Hatred from his men was something he felt he could deal with, but their laughter had left him unnerved and frustrated. He'd have to ease up on them. But doing so now would merely eliminate the small amount of control he still retained. Wanting to reduce the number of that night's ambushes from four to two, he finally decided to put this off for one more day, instead making all the ambushes somewhat shorter than those he had been assigning. Trippitt called his platoon commanders together to give them the coordinates, hoping that tonight there would be no trouble and he would have time to think.

As the men of Alpha Squad talked about the inspection, it became even more of a joke, especially when Hamilton returned from the CP with his lifer's haircut. Some of the men from the other squads had followed him, and now most of Second Platoon was sitting together in the rain joking about the inspection and Hamilton's haircut. Their morale was better than at any time since the rainy season had started, and it remained that way until an hour before dusk. It was then that they found out there would again be four ambushes that night. Tomorrow night it would be Alpha's turn, and Childs said with disgust, "That sonofabitch doesn't care how many of us he kills."

376

"I can't understand it," Chalice commented. "We lose twice as many men on ambushes than we get."

Hamilton flipped a grenade from hand to hand while saying, "It wouldn't be so bad if he'd make them shorter and cut them to two a night like he did for a while."

"What does he care?" Childs said gruffly. "He only counts the Gooks he kills, not the Marines."

"That's what they put on his record," Tony 5 commented as he sat down next to Hamilton.

"I wish somebody'd put KIA on his record," Childs replied, and then added, "I'd pay fifty dollars to see that."

"So would I," Appleton agreed.

"That makes a hundred. Are there any more donations from the house?" Hemrick asked jokingly.

Hamilton's tone was more serious as he said, "Yeah . . . I'll put twenty-five on Trippitt and fifty on Martin."

It was no longer a joke or idle talk. Somebody would call out a name and all faces would turn towards that person as they waited to hear whether the bounty would be increased. Other members of the platoon were called over and told what was going on. Within minutes there was seven hundred dollars on Trippitt's head, and six hundred and twenty-five on Martin's.

Tony 5 had watched silently, but he now said, "I've seen too many men die because of Trippitt and Martin. Add twenty-five dollars on both their heads."

"That's seven hundred and twenty-five on Trippitt and six hundred and fifty on Martin," Childs said with satisfaction.

"No it ain't," Tony spoke out, and all faces turned towards him. "I was talking to Moretti, the sergeant of first platoon. They've got five on Forest, four on Martin, and three on Trippitt."

Sugar Bear, who hadn't spoken except to add twenty-five dollars on both the bounties, now said, "I heard Grear and somebody else from Fourth Platoon talking. They've got a price out on Trippitt. I don't know about Martin."

"Can you find out?" Childs asked.

Sugar Bear rose to his feet as Hamilton asked, "Anybody got a good friend in Third Platoon?"

"I'll take care of it," Hemrick answered.

Within twenty minutes the perimeter was alive with nervous excitement. Not all, but most of the men knew that every platoon except Third had pledged money toward the bounties. There was $1,900 on Trippitt's head and $1,575 on Martin's.

The sun had just set, and Chalice and Forsythe were in their foxhole when Chalice said, "I don't know about this."

"Don't sweat it," Forsythe assured him.

"I just don't like it."

"Nobody's gonna get caught."

Surprised and disturbed by Forsythe's callous attitude, Chalice said, "I don't mean that!"

"What *do* you mean?"

"Do we have to kill them?"

"No, just pay the dude that does," Forsythe replied casually, then added in a more reflective tone, "Look, I don't like this too much either. But they've gotten too many of my friends killed. It's either us or them. . . . You're in for fifty apiece, aren't you?"

"Yeah, but do you think somebody'll do it?"

"It's a lot of money. I think so."

"Did it ever happen before?"

"Hell yeah, twice since I've been here . . . but not so out in the open. Somebody did a job on a platoon commander for three hundred dollars. There was two hundred out on a chickenshit corpsman, but he just got wounded and nobody had to pay."

"Do you think they'll pay this time?"

"Most of them. If a dude's got enough guts to blow away a lifer, he's got enough guts to do a job on a welcher. . . . Whoever does it has to have one witness with him. The witness'll help him collect."

"What if he gets caught?"

"How they gonna catch him; and if they do, who'll testify?"

"They can check the bullet with everyone's rifle."

"They could, but they won't. Most of the time an M-16 slug is too much of a mess when they get it dug out. You've seen what those things can do to a Gook, hit him in the finger and it ends up in his lung. Even if they do match it, they have to prove it was intentional. Besides, if the dude's smart, he'll use a frag. They don't leave no fingerprints."

Chalice had first watch that night. At nine o'clock Forsythe left him alone in their foxhole. The ambushes had all made it safely to their sites, and the perimeter was quiet. As he searched the darkness in front of him, Chalice was more fearful of a blooker barrage than of a ground attack. A few minutes before his watch was to end, the night's stillness was shattered by an explosion within the perimeter. Forsythe came diving into the hole with him, and they heard Roads and Rabbitt scrambling into their foxhole a few yards away. "Here we go again," Chalice whispered to Forsythe.

378

"I don't think so. It was too loud, sounded more like a frag."

It was then that they first heard Martin's voice. In a loud, delirious tone he shouted, "Did they get him?"

"Somebody might have hit the jackpot," Forsythe whispered without emotion.

"Already?"

"Go on over and find out what happened."

The perimeter was a luminescent black, but all Chalice had to do was to follow the sound of Martin's voice. Suddenly he heard Trippitt ask nervously, "Is the medivac coming?"

"I called for it, sir. But it hasn't made contact yet."

Chalice drew closer to the red glow of a corpsman's flashlight. Martin lay on his stomach, the back of his shirt drenched with blood.

"He's paralyzed," one of the corpsmen said.

Chalice stepped closer and saw that only Martin's head moved as he cried, "Did they get him? Did they get the sonofabitch?" Someone told Chalice to return to his position, but he merely backed up a few feet. Martin continued to shout as the sound of a descending helicopter began to drown out his words. In the darkness, Chalice could barely make out what was happening. The limp body was placed on a poncho. Just before it was carried to the medivac chopper, the red light flashed on Martin's face. It was grotesquely distorted as his mouth vainly tried to yell over the noise of the helicopter, "Did they get the sonofabitch?"

Soon every man in the company was aware of what had happened. All over the perimeter, voices could be heard in the darkness, often repeating, "One down and one to go."

Trippitt leaned against a tree a few yards away from his hootch. The light drizzle continued, and he had his poncho wrapped around him. Beneath it, he squeezed tightly on his .45, the safety off and ready to be used. His confused mind nervously tried to figure out what he had done wrong and exactly when he had lost control. He remembered the grotesque movements of Martin's head as it seemingly tried to free itself from the inert and useless remainder of his body. Though Trippitt had feared something like this, he never really believed his men were capable of it. Again the thought came to him, 'It ain't their guts.' He tried to make himself believe that his platoon commanders had turned the men against him. Kramer stood out in his thoughts, but he also suspected Howell, and even Forest. The cold rain seeped under his poncho, and as he stood shivering in the darkness, Trippitt realized there wasn't one man in the company he could trust. Death didn't scare him, only in rare moments had he ever been afraid of dying. It was the ignoble idea of being killed by his own men that unnerved him. Not even worried about his career anymore, he repeatedly asked himself, 'Didn't they know that some of them would die? Didn't they know that's what war is? It's nothing without death. Don't they know that?' Never once did he question the fact that he had used fear to drive his men on. Even now this accusation would have seemed absurd to him. He would have denied it, insisting that it was merely discipline that he had used; and he would not have been lying. For if he had been asked the difference between fear and discipline, he would have been incapable of answering.

Dawn broke upon a cloudless sky. The men knew this wouldn't last more than a few hours. They took off their clothing and hung it on bushes, doing so not really to dry their clothing, but more to dry themselves for the first time in four days. They also removed their boots, though they knew an hour's sun would do little to heal their feet. Trippitt was in no hurry to move the camp. He had other things to think about, but finally chose a new site only a few kilometers away. This enabled the men to stay dry for an extra hour before moving out. They reached their new site by eleven o'clock. The afternoon patrols were short, and everyone returned to the perimeter by four o'clock.

Despite the condition of their feet, it had been a relatively easy day. The men's mood did not reflect this. There was no regret about what had happened to Martin, but little gloating over it either. Today they'd had time to think, and the things they thought about couldn't help but depress them. In a week, or two, or three, they would be pulled out of the Arizona. Many of their friends had left before them — in plastic sacks or on blood-soaked stretchers. All the dead had not been Marines, far less than half of them and they knew it. Yet they would leave this place the same as they had found it — hostile, dangerous, and still a mystery.

Again they began to think about odds, knowing that now these odds were with them. Yet they also knew a booby trap, a distant shot from an invisible sniper, or a blindly fired blooker round would make these odds meaningless. They had found themselves fighting for a people they loathed, some of whom hated Americans far more than the Viet Cong. Many of the Marines hated the Viet Cong, but did so with a grudging respect. Yet the thing they feared most was something they could neither respect nor understand. It made them question everything they'd ever been told and everyone they'd ever trusted. It seemed impossible that one of them, a Marine, would turn his back on those he had fought with, the country they dreamed of returning to, and everything they valued. To many of the men he was something, perhaps a part of their experience

380

and therefore a part of them, that had to be not only destroyed, but so irrevocably erased that afterwards his existence might be denied.

Except for Roads who was off to the side feeding his puppy, the men of Alpha Squad sat in a circle either eating or heating their food. Tony 5 decided to join his former squad, and as he approached, Forsythe called out, "How's it going short-timer?"

"Slow," Tony replied as he sat down with them.

"Do you know how many days you have left?" Chalice asked.

Before Tony 5 could answer, Childs said, "You're damn *right* he does."

"Three days counting tomorrow."

"And just think, you'll get to spend them in the Arizona."

Hamilton slapped Tony 5 on the back as he said, "You're gonna miss this place, ain'tcha Tony? Admit it."

"And the Crotch too," Childs added.

Tony 5 shook his head while answering, "No. I ain't gonna miss the Crotch."

"Sure you are, Tony," Hamilton insisted.

"I ain't gonna have no reason to. I'm re-upping." As soon as these words were out of Tony's mouth, the men around him burst out laughing. Hamilton kept slapping him on the back while a few of the other men threw their empty C-ration cans. Tony 5 shoved Hamilton to the ground and the laughter died away.

"Are you shitting us, Tony?" Chalice asked.

"*Hell no,* I ain't!" Tony replied angrily, precipitating a new round of laughter.

After repeatedly hearing comments such as, "No shit, Tony's gonna be a fucking lifer," and, "I had you pegged for a decent motherfucker. *Shit* was I wrong!" Tony 5 lost his temper, and his angry words silenced all the joking.

"*Fuck* you guys! Let me tell you something, motherfuckers: The Crotch has done all right by me. I'm not sorry I joined. There ain't one motherfucker here, that if he knew he was gonna have to fight, would do it as anything else but a Marine." Tony paused, but none of those around him cared to break the silence. "*Is there?*" They still remained silent, because as much as they griped about the Marine Corps, there wasn't one of them who could conceive of himself in combat as anything other than a Marine. "Sure there's a lot of fucked-up things about the Crotch, but I ain't ashamed of being in it. I used to think I was the toughest dude that ever stood on a street corner; but when I got in the Crotch, I found out there were a lot of dudes just as tough, and they were guys you could depend on. When it was me, Sugar Bear, Pablo, Kovacs, and Lieutenant S, I just knew that whatever came up, we could handle it. And there were other guys too, that none of you ever saw." The men remained silent, remembering the times they'd had the feeling Tony described.

Finally, Hamilton said, "I know what you mean; and it's true. I never met so many guys I liked besides in the Crotch."

Even Chalice, who had often found himself puzzled by or looking down upon those around him, had to admit this. "You're right, both of you; but the Crotch can be pretty fucked-up sometimes."

Most of the men nodded agreement, and Hamilton said, "Yeah, but it ain't the guys. It's the lifers that fuck it up." After a quick glance at Tony 5, Hamilton added, "No offense, Tony."

Even before Hamilton had a chance to finish, Tony 5 replied, "Not *all* the lifers. Sure, most of them are fucked up, but there's a lot a decent ones. Most of you guys weren't here then, but the gunny we used to have before Martin was *one* decent motherfucker. He never got on anybody's ass unless he had to, and the company was a hell of a lot more squared-away than it is now. . . . How many of you guys didn't have at least one cool drill instructor at Parris Island?"

One person said "Me," but the others nodded their heads or voiced agreement.

"Ever since PI, I think I had my mind made up to be a drill instructor, and I will someday. I don't get no special kick out of killing people; but if it comes to that, you might as well know what you're doing, and there ain't a better place to learn than in the Crotch. When the skin-headed punks get out of my platoon, they'll have their shit together. They'll be somebody you can depend on — a Marine." Tony moved his stare from man to man, waiting for someone to contradict him, sure that no one would.

"Yeah," Forsythe finally agreed. "You'll make a hell of a drill instructor, Tony. Someday I'll send you my kid to beat up."

Forsythe's remark broke the seriousness of the mood, but then Childs, who had been the quietest of the group, spoke out. His tone more factual than sarcastic, what he said turned all faces towards him. "How 'bout the Phantom Blooker?"

"What do you mean?" Rabbit asked.

But the question had been directed at Tony 5. "I said he was an American, not a Marine."

"I think he's a Marine," Childs replied without emotion.

Tony 5 hesitated, staring at the faces of those around him before saying slowly and in an uncommonly demure tone, "I think he's a Marine too."

Childs was unwilling to let the matter drop with this admission. "He went to PI."

"I guess he did," Tony replied softly, but his face suddenly hardened; and when he spoke again, he spit out each word with an anger that made Chalice wince. "I'd take another thirteen months of this shit if I could go home with that motherfucker's scalp in my hand." Tony 5 paused and began to shake his head. "I can't figure that motherfucker out."

"None of us can," Rabbit added.

Chalice wanted to speak out, but his lips moved silently. Even after he had suppressed this desire, the word "us" continued to reverberate in his mind. He searched the faces of the men in his squad, picking out the ones he had the most affection for, knowing he was irrevocably isolated from even them.

It was Hamilton who finally spoke. "Just 'cause he's a Marine doesn't mean anything. There's plenty of guys in this company I hate."

"It's not the same," Tony 5 insisted somberly.

"Maybe he just went crazy," Rabbit suggested.

Wilcox asked in his usually dull tone, "How can anybody fight for the Gooks?"

The previous remarks had frustrated more than angered Chalice, but this comment enraged him. He turned towards Wilcox with the urge to shout. But the only indication of this was the nervous, almost imperceptible movement of his lips as he said to himself what he wanted to scream. "You dumb, pathetic motherfucker. That's what they tell us *we are* doing — fighting for the Gooks, except for the wrong fucking Gooks. One of us has the guts to fight for the only people in this country worth a shit, and you hate him."

Forsythe spoke out in an uncommonly slow and serious tone. "*I'd* kill him. . . . You know as long as I've been here, I don't think I've killed a man. I never told anyone this, but one time when I was walking point I surprised a Gook in a clearing. He got up and ran. I saw he was wearing a belt of chicoms. The next thing I knew, I had my rifle pointed at him and my finger on the trigger. But I couldn't shoot. I could have emptied a magazine in his back, but I *couldn't* pull the trigger. For days after that I was scared he was gonna come back and kill one of my friends. I knew it would be my fault, but I was still glad I let him get away. I don't think I could ever kill a man unless he was coming at me with a rifle . . . except for *him*. I could kill *him* and never be sorry. . . . He's blown away too many of my friends."

Was that the question, Chalice wondered. 'Friends . . . my friends — is that what it comes down to?' Never before had this word seemed so important.

Chalice heard his nickname mentioned and noticed that everyone was looking at him. It had been Tony 5's voice. "Professor . . . when I handed you my blooker and watched you fire it for the first time, I said to myself, 'He'll get him. He'll do the job on the Phantom Blooker.' I'd always thought I'd be the one to blow him away, because it had to be done with his own weapon and Alpha owed it to him more than any squad in the battalion. It was the only way he could be stopped from killing any more of my friends. When I gave you that blooker, it was like I failed, now it was somebody else's turn; but just by the way you held it made me sure you'd get him. I don't know why, but it did. . . . Maybe you will. I won't be around, but maybe you will."

That night it was Alpha's turn to go on an ambush. The site was less than a kilometer outside the perimeter, and they reached it without incident. Chalice had second watch, but he was awakened just before it was to begin by the sound of blooker rounds exploding in the vicinity of the perimeter. As he listened, he wondered if they were finding their mark, if at dawn he would return to the perimeter and see a body, or maybe a row of them, wrapped in ponchos, and then be told that one of them was a friend. When Chalice did return to camp, he saw no bodies. They were on the opposite side of the perimeter. None were friends.

The rain gradually increased while the men waited for the medivac chopper to arrive for the bodies. At eight o'clock, they heard a helicopter circling above the perimeter, but the intense rain prevented it from landing. Just before noon, a slight break in the clouds enabled the bodies to be evacuated. Trippitt had planned to move the campsite, but the ease with which the Phantom Blooker seemed always able to find them made such movements appear ludicrous. If they moved to a new site now, they would not have time to send out patrols. If they chose to stay, Trippitt felt the Phantom Blooker might also stay. An attack would be more of a certainty, but they'd have a chance to send out patrols and possibly surprise him. Trippitt chose to retain the same camp.

Second Platoon's patrol was somewhat shorter than the other two, but it necessitated a sweep through a larger area of high ground. The rain resumed even before they left the perimeter. Unusually strong winds prevented the exertion of the march from warming the men's bodies. By the time they reached the object of the patrol, they were not only tired but also shivering. It was an oblong patch of high ground, its length facing their perimeter. Kramer had his men circle around and approach from the narrowest side, thus making it possible to finish the search with one continuous sweep. He arranged the platoon on-line, the distance between the men averaging seven yards.

Eyes squinting into a wind that lashed the rain against their faces, the men could think of little besides their own discomfort. The sweep was no more than a task divorced from all purpose, something to be done, something to be gotten over with. Booby traps were a possibility, but they had no hopes of finding the Phantom Blooker. To question or to justify seemed equally pointless. All they could do was walk forward, step by step, until an hour later when the far edge of the high ground came into view.

They found nothing, not even the remains of a ville. Their thoughts were on the march back to camp when Tony 5 spotted it through the rain, an almost obscured human form walking towards them from the rice paddies. He alerted the men on either side, and they immediately froze except to alert other men. What had first appeared as a blur became sharper. Whoever he was, he was less than twenty yards away.

The men kneeled or lay prone, their rifles aimed at the approaching form. Through the rain, it appeared to be a peasant wearing a white, conical hat and a light-colored shirt. Every few steps the brim of the hat would rise up for a few seconds as he looked forward. Each time the men saw this, their fingers pressed gently against the triggers of their rifles. But the rain kept him from seeing them until they wanted him to.

He approached within six yards before Tony was certain he wasn't carrying a rifle. Both arms drawn up alongside his chin, he held a bag over his shoulder. Tony rose to his feet. The men to his sides did the same. The peasant took two more steps before the brim of his hat tilted up.

She froze, five rifles pointing directly at her. Tony remained silent, thinking that maybe someone else would approach. The trembling woman before him looked no different from any other peasant. After standing motionless for over a minute, Tony glanced to his left and told Kramer to cover him. He circled behind the woman and took the bag from her shoulder. By its weight and the metallic sound as he placed it on the ground, Tony knew what the bag contained even before he opened it. He slowly reached inside, withdrew a small object, and tossed it to Kramer.

Kramer turned to his left and said softly, "Professor, up. Corpsman, up." Chalice reached him first. Kramer pointed to Tony. "We've got some ammunition for you." Chalice knelt down and looked into the bag with disbelief. He then emptied the blooker rounds into his pouch.

When the corpsman arrived, Tony 5 took a bandage from him and gagged the woman. He then said to Kramer, "If he's here, we'll find him."

Word of what had happened was whispered down the line. The men turned in preparation for another sweep through the high ground. They knew that he might not be within it; but they also knew that if he was, he wouldn't be expecting them to return. The sweep progressed more slowly than the first time. No one thought about how cold he was, or about returning to the perimeter. Something remained to be done, done with the rifles they squeezed tightly in their hands.

The rain began to slacken. By the time they were halfway through their sweep, it stopped completely. Chalice tried to convince himself that again the Phantom Blooker would elude them. He knew that possibly he had never been there, or that the peasant was merely leaving the rounds in one of his hiding places. But the chance of coming upon him became unnerving. All logic told him that he had nothing to fear — that it was only myth and superstition which now threatened him. There were almost thirty men in the platoon — the odds were with him. Yet never had the odds seemed so meaningless. There were two other blooker men in the platoon. Yet Tony 5's words made this seem irrelevant. He told himself that he would never see the Phantom Blooker. Yet thoughts that made him question his own sanity convinced Chalice that their meeting was inevitable. Something had happened, something irrevocable, happened even before the day on the hill when Tony had taught him how to shoot the blooker; and he was now too confused even to wonder what it had been. All odds, all logic seemed meaningless. Chalice feared and believed that soon he would have to make a decision, and he had no idea what that decision would be.

The men to his sides moved forward quietly, carefully. Chalice recognized a small knoll less than twenty yards to his front. He remembered it from the previous sweep and looked upon it with relief, knowing that not more than fifty yards lay between it and the far edge of the high ground. Again their search would prove fruitless. The odds had saved him. He was sure of this.

Forsythe was to Chalice's left, and it was he who began to climb the knoll. In his hurry to get by it, Chalice had gotten a few yards in front of the formation. He stopped and began to turn his head towards Forsythe so he would know when to begin moving again. He never saw Forsythe. His eyes became transfixed upon something he couldn't make himself believe he was seeing — the form of a man, naked to the waist, sitting on the far side of the knoll. Chalice froze.

It was too unreal, a dream, reality in its cruelest and most threatening form. The figure suddenly rose and spun around towards the top of the knoll, the barrel of a blooker extending beyond its arm — a hollow click, a loud explosion. The figure spun towards Chalice — hunted, protruding eyes and gaunt Caucasian features cast into a hollow mask — then fell beneath Chalice's stare, dropping to his knees and disappearing as Forsythe yelled, *"Over here!"*

386

Men brushed quickly past Chalice, their rifles pointed ahead of them. They formed a half circle around the base of the knoll. Chalice remained where he stood. As if from a great distance, he heard Forsythe say excitedly, "He's in here! My rifle jammed. . . . The Professor ripped open his shoulder."

The men stood with their rifles pointed at a small, square opening at the base of the knoll. Beside it lay a plant in a crude, bamboo box that had formerly covered this hole. There was blood on the ground, a lot of it.

"*Spread out!*" Kramer yelled. "There may be another entrance." Most of the men backed away as Tony 5 rushed forward and threw a grenade into the hole. Soon almost everyone had a frag in his hand, and they took turns rushing forward and throwing them into the tunnel. Again and again the grenades exploded until Kramer finally yelled, "*That's enough!*" He turned to Tony 5. "There can't be much left of him now."

"Yes there can. *Get me an E-tool!*" Tony yelled.

Someone handed him one, and he rushed towards the top of the knoll. Once before he had seen a bunker like this. Using the shovel as if it were a pick, Tony swung it down frantically at the crest of the knoll. The men glanced questioningly at each other, wondering what Tony was trying to do. Suddenly he flung the shovel aside and grabbed a grenade from his pouch. He threw it at his feet and stepped off the knoll. A muffled explosion came from within as debris erupted from its peak.

Now everyone realized what Tony 5 had been doing. The entrance merely curved a few feet below the surface, leading upward to a chamber at the top of the knoll. Again they began throwing grenades, this time into the opening at the crest of the knoll. They continued doing so in a frenzy for over five minutes, nearly half the men in the platoon taking a turn. Chalice slowly approached the knoll, searching the faces of the men around him. The brutal satisfaction most of them seemed to take in this act bewildered him. Even after Kramer yelled, "That's enough!" another man ran wildly up the knoll and flung a grenade inside.

At first the men stood silently watching the knoll. One by one, their stares turned towards Kramer. His stomach tightened as he wondered what was left of whoever was in the bunker. He turned towards Tony 5. "Let's get him out."

Tony grabbed the flashlight and .45, then headed for the entrance. But he stopped short of it. Turning to the men behind him, he called out, "Professor." Some men standing between Tony 5 and Chalice moved aside and left them facing each other. "He's all yours, Professor. You earned the honor."

'Honor. . . . honor?' All Chalice could do was shake his head.

Tony kneeled by the entrance. The grenades had caved it in, so he called for the rope. Some men tied it around his waist, then lowered him into the opening at the top of the knoll. His feet touched upon a bamboo floor. Only now did he turn on the flashlight. Slowly directing it in a circle, it shone upon a stack of C-rations, then some blooker rounds — nothing else. 'He *couldn't* have gotten away.' The chamber was about four feet by eight feet. Again, more hurriedly, he directed the flashlight over its floor. This time he saw something else — not on the floor, but against the wall a few inches above it — a hand, fingers extended towards the ground. He slowly raised the beam of the flashlight up the hanging arm until it shone upon the entrance to the chamber, from which hung another arm and a limply hanging head. Tony removed the rope from his waist. He slipped the noose over the head and roughly jerked it taut.

"Pull him up!"

There was the sibilant swooshing sound of the corpse sliding from the tunnel, followed by the delicate, metallic tingling of something hitting the bamboo floor, then the dull scraping of bare feet against the box of C-rations as the body swung pendulum-like from the opening in the roof before being awkwardly jerked through it like a recalcitrant puppet.

When Tony 5 was pulled from the chamber, most of the men were standing around the corpse. There was a blooker wound just below his shoulder blade, and his arms and head were blood caked and mutilated. The face was nothing more than a featureless mass of raw flesh. Blood matted what remained of his brown, wavy hair. As Tony 5 stared down at the corpse, Sinclaire asked him, "How come there ain't a mark on him below the chest?"

"He was stuck in the tunnel, never made it into the chamber. Must of been dead before the first frag went off. . . . The Professor did it by himself."

Chalice was staring down at the corpse. Some of the men slapped him on the back while offering congratulations. He turned and walked away, but a few of them followed him. Chalice remembered everything — Forsythe's rifle misfiring, the explosion, the gaunt stare — everything except pulling the trigger. He actually waited for someone to say, "It wasn't the Professor. It was me," at the same time knowing that if it hadn't been him, then it hadn't happened. 'They double-crossed me,' Chalice thought to himself — meaning the odds.

Kramer had called Trippitt to find out what to do about the body. Trippitt wasn't sure, and he said he'd call battalion. In a few minutes, Milton handed the receiver back to Kramer, telling him that Nash was on the other end.

"Are you sure it's him?" Nash asked.

"Positive."

"Do you have his blooker?"

"No. It must be in the caved-in part of the bunker. . . . Two men saw him with it."

"How long would it take to dig it out?"

"Two, three hours," Kramer exaggerated.

"Was he wearing dog tags . . . any identification?"

"No."

"Could we get fingerprints off him?"

"Probably a few."

"You're sure he's a Marine?"

"How can I be? He's Caucasian."

"But you can't identify him?"

At first Kramer couldn't believe the stupidity of this question, but he suddenly realized what Nash was getting at. "No."

"Just as well. Leave him there. The VC'll take care of him."

Kramer told his men they were leaving the body, and to get ready to move out. Two men picked up the corpse and carried it towards the top of the knoll. Chalice stood watching them, all the while hearing his name called. Just as the two men viciously kicked the body into the bunker, Chalice felt a hand on his shoulder and heard Forsythe's voice say, "C'mon Professor, let's get out of here."

Darkness fell before they were halfway back to the perimeter. The only sounds were those of their legs moving rhythmically through the knee-deep water. The rain had stopped, and a cool, clean breeze blew across their faces. They were tired, but not exhausted. It seemed to many of them as if a trial had ended — their own. Tony 5 said to himself, 'Only two more days.' It had seemed like such a short time that morning, too little time; but now it wasn't a question of days. They no longer made any difference. Soon — it would be soon. He'd get on a plane and it would all be over. Now, in the darkness, he opened his tightly clenched fist for the first time in more than an hour; and a small, metal plate fell silently into the water.

BOOK THREE

Even as a fox is man; as a fox which
seeing a fine vineyard lusted after its
grapes. But the palings were placed at
narrow distances, and the fox was too
bulky to creep between them. For three
days he fasted, and when he had grown
thin he entered into the vineyard. He
feasted upon the grapes, forgetful of the
morrow, of all things but his enjoyment;
and lo, he had again grown stout and was
unable to leave the scene of his feast. So
for three days more he fasted, and when
he had again grown thin, he passed
through the palings and stood outside the
vineyard, meagre as when he entered.

So with man; poor and naked he enters
the world, poor and naked does he leave.

Man is born with his hands clenched; he
dies with his hands wide open. Entering
life he desires to grasp everything; leaving
the world all that he possessed has slipped
away.

The Talmud

1. Da Nang

The glare seared his eyes, and he quickly closed them again. He was lying down. There was a light. This time he opened his eyes more slowly, but again he had to close them. It was a naked light bulb, he knew that now. He continued to open his eyes until he was able to keep them open. He saw that the bulb hung from a curved roof of corrugated steel, the roof of a Quonset hut. His hands lay between smooth, clean sheets. An air-conditioner droned in the background. It was the hospital at Da Nang, he knew that now. He was there, but this seemed impossible. There was no reason. Maybe his mind was remembering the last time. Or maybe this was the last time, and all in between merely a dream. No, it had been real. He was certain. Again, he was again in the hospital at Da Nang.

A corpsman walked by, then a patient in blue pajamas. Kramer's head remained motionless as his eyes followed them down the aisle. Nobody was aware of him. Why was he here? His left leg felt stiff. Only after he moved it did he realize that it was tightly wrapped below the knee. He moved his other limbs. They weren't bandaged. He ran his hand over the upper part of his body. Everything else seemed all right. With little effort, he sat up and pushed the covers from his legs. His left shin was bandaged, but that was all. He ran his hand gently over the bandage. His leg seemed a little sore, nothing more.

A corpsman noticed him and walked over to his bed. "You all right, sir?"

"Yeah, sure, I think so. . . . How long have I been here?"

"Twenty-four hours, maybe a little longer."

"What's wrong with my leg?"

"It's got a nice gash and about thirty stitches in it."

"How'd that happen?" Kramer asked, his mind still somewhat dazed.

"Booby trap, I think."

"Booby trap? . . . Yesterday it happened?"

"That's right. You'll be okay in a few days."

"That's the only thing wrong with me?"

393

"You might have a slight concussion, nothing too serious. . . . You feel dizzy?"

"A little. . . . My ears are ringing."

"It'll go way. . . . Just lie back and relax."

The corpsman walked away. Kramer fell back on the pillow and flinched in pain. Reaching behind his head, he located a large lump. 'Booby trap. Must have got knocked to the ground. But *when?*' Kramer searched his memory to answer this question. He remembered his men pulling the body of the Phantom Blooker from the bunker, and then Martin's screams, "Did they get him?" — 'No, that was the night before.' Everything after the Phantom Blooker had been killed seemed hazy. Gradually, he remembered the march back to camp. He was sure they had reached it, but everything after that was blank. The next morning — he now remembered that also. They were marching to a new camp, but again everything after that was a blank, and he wasn't sure anything existed to fill it. Something had happened between the time they had returned to the perimeter after killing the Phantom Blooker, and the time they set out from it the next morning, something important. This was all his memory would tell him no matter how hard he searched it.

Her image came to him, cold, knowing, seeming to say, "So you're still alive." Again he was at a loss, unsure how to react to even her memory, wanting to see her again, looking at this as a weakness. Her voice, some of the words she had spoken, repeated themselves in his mind. Again he felt ridiculous, saying to himself that even if he got the chance, he wouldn't try to see her, knowing that he would. 'What the fuck did — what does she have on me?' Now admitting that he had to see her again, he tried to justify this 'weakness' by saying to himself, 'I'll fuck her. I'll fuck the shit out of her!'

Kramer was startled by a voice that asked, "What are you so mad about?" A doctor with a clipboard at his side stood at the foot of Kramer's bed.

"What makes you think I'm mad?" he asked irritably.

"You look mad. You sound mad."

"Must of been something I stepped on."

"If I were you, I'd feel more lucky than mad. You're still alive, aren't you?" With a sarcastic sneer on his face, Kramer expelled a short burst of air from his nostrils. "I knew I'd be able to cheer you up." Kramer's face broke into a faint smile as the doctor continued. "How do you feel?"

"A little doped up. It must be the medicine you gave me."

The doctor glanced at his clipboard before saying, "You didn't get any medicine from us."

394

"I feel all right."

"Dizzy?"

"A little."

"Your ears ringing?"

"A lot."

"It's amazing you can hear them over that air-conditioner. Sounds like we're about to take off. . . . You want to stand up with your back to the bed." When Kramer had done this, the doctor stepped in front of him and told him to close his eyes. "All right, you can go back to sleep."

"What was that all about?"

"You might have a slight concussion."

"How long will that keep me here?"

"Probably not more than two or three days."

Kramer hesitated before asking, "Will I be able to get some liberty?"

"Not tonight. Maybe the last night before we ship you back to your unit."

He walked the streets, through the heavy stench of liquor, garbage, and human waste. Drunken, staggering soldiers kept jostling him on the way back to their barracks. Kramer had deliberately spent the first hours of darkness waiting at the hospital, and he now headed straight for the bar that she owned. He'd been brooding all day, and there had been no fantasizing or planning. Without hesitation he entered her bar, telling himself that he would merely see what would happen.

Kramer had no expectation of seeing her right away. It was still too early. A quick glance around the bar confirmed this. He ordered a drink, then another, still sure she would appear. Behind him he heard two men arguing over a bar girl. Suddenly he was shoved forward as one of the men crashed into him, splashing most of the liquor in his glass onto the bar. He turned to see the man regain his balance and knock the other into the jukebox. There was a loud grating sound as the needle scraped across the record. Spirited shouts of encouragement came from the Marines watching the fight.

"MP's!" someone near the door yelled. The two men were pulled apart before the MP's walked across the threshold. They glanced suspiciously around the now quiet bar before turning and leaving. One of the men who had been fighting ran towards the other. Some Marines grabbed him, and while he was being held, the other Marine stepped towards the restrained man and smashed his fist into his face. The blow knocked him unconscious, and he collapsed into the arms of those holding him. Someone

395

shoved the other Marine violently into the jukebox. Again the needle scraped across the record. Both men did no more than try to stare each other down. The unconscious Marine was placed in a chair, and the crowd around the jukebox slowly dispersed.

Kramer looked at his watch. It was late. 'Maybe she won't come.' He didn't try to tell himself it made no difference. Tomorrow he'd go back to the Arizona, and tonight he wanted to see her. During the past few days he had tried to convince himself that he merely wanted to fuck her, but now he admitted that he wanted more, and that if nothing else were possible, he at least wanted to talk to her. Again he looked at his watch. The bar would be closing in less than an hour. It seemed like his last chance to ever see her again, and he began to believe that he wouldn't get that chance. He ordered a drink and downed it quickly, as much for its effect as to have something to do. His thoughts no longer made him feel ridiculous. It was important that he see her, he admitted this now. His glass was empty, and the Scotch began to dull his mind. He ordered another drink. When it came he let it rest on the bar while he moved his fingers up and down the outside of the wet glass. He now felt there was no chance of her being there tonight, if for no other reason than because it meant too much to him.

Again his thoughts drifted back to the only other thing he had been concerned about during the last few days. He tried to remember what had happened the morning before he stepped on the booby trap. He didn't expect to remember the actual explosion, but he knew something had happened a good while before that. He tried to concentrate, to carefully recall all the events that led up to that blank spot in his memory. Forest had come over to tell him that the day before, while Second Platoon had been killing the Phantom Blooker, First Platoon had killed six NVA soldiers. He remembered Forest staring at him, waiting to be complimented. He also remembered Trippitt asking him who the Professor was. It was then. It was then that something happened. Someone shouted, he couldn't remember what, and then it happened — not the booby trap. That was later. He was sure of it.

Kramer stared at his drink. The ice cubes were almost melted. He looked up across the bar. She wasn't there. Again he glanced at his watch. It was late. The bar girls were almost finished cleaning up. There were four other Marines still in the bar. Three of them got up to leave, and Kramer watched them head towards the door. He didn't want to be the only one left. A single Marine lay slouched over one of the tables in a drunken stupor. One of the bar girls began shaking him. Kramer looked towards the door in the back of the room. He had once seen Tuyen emerge from it, and he waited for it to open, thinking that it wouldn't.

396

The bar girl was now helping the drunken Marine out the front door. Kramer noticed a dim wedge of light spread upon the floor and then disappear. It had come from the back room. He saw Tuyen walking towards the far end of the bar. She had seen him. He knew it. She stopped at the other end of the bar and glanced towards him, but gave no sign of recognition.

Kramer turned away and stared at the mottled and clouded mirror behind the bar. His reflection was little more than a shadow. He waited for her to walk over to him. A quick glance towards the end of the bar revealed her still standing there. He tightened his grip on the glass, hoping that it would shatter. 'The bitch, the lousy fucking bitch. She won't even look at me.' He wanted to throw the glass at her, at the same time thinking, 'Fuck the bitch! I'll fuck the living shit out of her.'

He stared coldly at her. But his stare began to soften almost immediately. He had to admit to himself that she was as beautiful as he had remembered. There was no recognition in her face, only the same proud yet sad expression. He wanted to reach out and touch her. Even when he realized there was a slight smile on his face, he made no effort to hide it. Instead he silently moved his lips, saying, "Come here." She waited a few seconds before walking towards him, her stare hardening as she did so, a stare that looked above and past him. Again he felt weak in her presence, but also warm. Looking down at his drink and with a childish grin on his face, he asked in a serious tone, "I'm David, remember?"

"I remember," she said without expression.

Her tone in no way irritated him. He was glad merely to hear her voice. "I stepped on a booby trap so I could come and talk to you again."

"You are a fool then."

"Maybe . . . not stupid, but maybe a fool." As he said this, Kramer noticed the last remaining bar girl walk to the door.

"You know we are closed?"

"I know. It's much quieter now. I like it better when it's quiet."

"You must leave," she said, no coldness in her tone.

"I thought maybe we could talk for a while."

"We are strangers. There is nothing to talk about. I am Vietnamese. You are American."

"Maybe if you were nice to me, I'd go away and never bother you again."

Something close to a smile appeared on her face as she asked, "You promise me this?"

"Maybe."

"Maybe you buy me a drink also?" Kramer nodded and Tuyen indicated with a glance that he should move to a table in the back of the room. Kramer sat down at it while she turned out most of the lights and locked the door. She placed a bottle of Scotch and a glass in front of Kramer before sitting down across from him. "Where's your glass?" he asked.

"I do not drink?"

"Oh, you're a head?"

"Ahead?"

"A pot head." She looked at him questioningly. "You smoke marijuana."

"No. You smoke marijuana?"

"Sometimes. . . . It makes you think too much. . . . Should I have brought some?"

"I do not care."

"Would you have smoked with me?"

"No," she answered curtly.

"You don't like people who smoke marijuana?"

"This is not true. . . . I think you are smarter if you smoke marijuana."

"Smarter?"

"I think it make you smarter."

"Why don't you smoke it then?"

"I do not need to be smarter."

"Oh, but I need to be smarter."

"You are an American. . . . Is they who smoke marijuana."

"I get the feeling sometimes you don't like Americans."

"No, I do not like Americans."

"Who do you like, the French?"

"No, I do not like the French. . . . They are better than the Americans, but I do not like them."

"Who do you like?"

"I am Vietnamese. . . . I like Vietnamese people."

"You said your family fled the Communists. They're Vietnamese."

"They are better than the Americans."

Kramer knew no reason why she should think otherwise, but it irritated him a little to be told this by a South Vietnamese. "You don't care if they win the war?"

Her expression became more sad than proud. "Is too long. Many people have die."

"Many Americans too."

"More Vietnamese have die. . . . My brother he is missing three years. His plane crash. . . . They say he is dead."

Kramer hesitated before saying, "Maybe he wanted the Americans here."

"So now he is dead. . . . Too many people have die. Many years they are fighting. . . . Someday they tell my son to fight too."

398

These words were a shock to Kramer, but he suppressed it as he asked, "Your son?"

"Yes, he is in Hue. . . . I never want him to fight."

Again the sad beauty of her face left him numb. "His father?" Kramer asked, wanting to be told that he was dead.

"He also is dead, long ago."

"The war?" he asked, now sorry he had heard what he had then wanted. She nodded. "You think he died for nothing?"

"They all die for nothing, too many people."

"I know," he said softly, but then added without conviction, "Maybe if it was my country I wouldn't think so."

"Is the same. They all die for nothing."

"Maybe they didn't think so." She looked at him with a sad, questioning expression on her face. "Your husband and your brother."

"My husband I think he knew he would die. He would not say is for nothing."

"Even if he knew the Communists would win?"

Her eyes focused on Kramer for the first time. "My husband he was Viet Cong."

A feeling of guilt sickened Kramer, and he wondered how she could even look at him, an American, without spitting in his face. He felt choked as he asked her, "Did the Americans kill him?"

She stared down at the table. "No, the South Vietnamese."

Kramer felt as if he was torturing her, not even guessing that she actually wanted, needed to talk. He kept telling himself that he should leave, but he couldn't. He wanted to be able to look at her, to hear her voice. "You must hate them very much."

She shook her head. "I hate no one. . . . My brother, I love him also. He fight with the South Vietnamese." The proud, superior expression had long since left her face; but her beauty stemmed from more than this, and she retained it. It seemed to Kramer that he was somehow the cause of all her suffering, and he wondered why she allowed him to make her relive it. He made up his mind to leave, the last thing he wanted to do. Just as he was about to stand, she began speaking again, and he knew that he must wait a little longer. "You see why my son must not fight?" He nodded, and she continued, "His father, he never saw him. He always ask me where is his father, and I tell him he will someday come home. One day someone come with a message for me, the first time in a year. My husband says he is coming home for the birthday of his son. He will be four. I think I will surprise my son, but then I have to tell him. He ask me if he can have his birthday now instead. I tell him no, he have to wait. We both wait. Two days before the birthday of my son, I go out to buy things. They are waiting when I come home. They ask me where is my husband. I tell them I do not know. They do not believe me, but they leave. I know they still watch. Someone tell them. I could do nothing. I wait. I know they wait also. I can do nothing. When is his birthday, my son ask me where is his father, and I am crying and he ask me why also. I cannot tell him. It get dark, and I take my son to his bed. He is crying because his father did not come. I wait, and I hope he will not come. Then I hear them shout, and the guns. . . . I know is too late."

As she had told Kramer this, she seemed always in control of herself, yet on the verge of tears. He wanted to reach out and touch her face, to make her stop. But he couldn't. She was now looking down somberly at the table. Kramer had little desire to talk, but he was afraid she would leave him if he didn't. "Is your son all you have left?"

She nodded, but then said, "No, my aunt, she take care of him."

"They live in the house you told me about . . . on the Square of the Four Dragons?" She nodded. "You must want to go back there very badly." Again she nodded. "Why do you stay here?"

"For money."

"Is money so important?"

"With money I can send my son away when he is older."

"You were wealthy once, weren't you?" Again Tuyen nodded. "Didn't your father leave you any money?"

"They take it away. They say he stole it from the country. . . . Then they kill him."

"Did he steal it?"

"I do not know. . . . It makes no difference. I love him very much. . . . When he die, I have enough to buy this, no more."

"You could have gone to France, couldn't you?"

"Maybe . . . maybe I could have go, but I tell myself I cannot. Ahn, my husband, he is dead. I meet him at the Sorbonne. Our families they know each other, but I never have meet him before. Before I meet him, I want to go back to Vietnam. Soon I did not care. He take me everywhere in Paris, and we were very happy, more happy than I have ever been in my life. When we come to Vietnam, our families they let us be married. But soon there are many bad things. He says he must fight because the government is bad. I want to go back to Paris, but he say no. Two more times I see him, then no more."

There was a few seconds silence before Kramer said, "The war can't last forever."

"Always I tell myself this, but I do not know. Sometimes I try to remember when there was no war, but is hard."

400

"You can remember Paris, can't you?"

A faint smile appeared on her face as she answered, "Yes, we were happy. At first I always wait for it to end, but soon I forget it will. Everything was so beautiful — the cafés, the flowers, the sky. Ahn, he knew it would end, but he too was happy."

"Someday you'll go back, and it'll be beautiful again."

Tuyen slowly shook her head. "No. It cannot be . . . only when I think of it. Maybe this is why I do not want to go back. What I remember is mine. Is beautiful, and can not be taken from me. Maybe if I go back, I will see is no longer the same. . . . Hue will be the same. Is more beautiful. There I was often sad, but always it was beautiful. . . . It will be the same."

"Someday the war will be over and you can go back."

"No, I will not wait. Very soon I have enough money. Never will I need to take the money of Americans."

As she said Americans, it was clear to Kramer that the word also included him. His tone somewhat hardened as he asked, "Is our money so bad?"

Tuyen again lowered her eyes to the table. "You do not understand. . . . I am prostitute. There is no difference."

"Why, because you own a bar?"

"Yes, there is no difference. I hate them and I take their money."

"So that means you're a prostitute?"

"Is the same. They try to touch me. They offer me money. To them I am prostitute. My brother, he also would think so, maybe my son also."

"That's bullshit."

Tuyen looked at him questioningly while saying, "Bullsheet?"

"It's not true. Do you think every bar girl is a prostitute?"

"Yes, I see them."

"All of them?"

"Many of them."

Thinking, 'What fucking difference does it make,' Kramer asked, "What about those that aren't? Do you look at them as prostitutes?"

"Yes."

She had now lost some of her mystery for him, and he began to take her for granted. "Let's just drop it."

"Drop it?"

"Forget it."

"How can I forget?"

"I mean let's talk about something else," he said irritably.

Kramer's tone offended her. "Is late," she said as she started to get up.

Without thinking, he reached for her hand. A shocked look came across her face, but it quickly changed to a cold stare as she got to her feet.

"Wait. I'm sorry. . . . Please sit down."

"Really, I am very tired. I think I should go home."

Realizing that he wouldn't be able to keep her there, Kramer asked, "Is it all right if I walk with you?"

"I do not care."

They walked towards her apartment in silence, her words, "I do not care," repeating themselves in Kramer's mind. The knowledge that tomorrow he would return to An Hoa and all that had happened would come to nothing caused him to resent her even more. 'Won't even get a piece of ass,' he kept telling himself.

"You are quiet now. What are you thinking?"

"Nothing much," he answered coldly. She remained silent and he began to regret the tone he had used. "I was thinking about tomorrow. I have to go back to my unit." She chose to remain silent, and he again felt like a fool. Kramer now wanted to be rid of her. He pointed to a cardboard and thatch hovel that adjoined the sidewalk. "Your father worked for the government; what did he think of things like that?"

"You would like my father."

Her tone, and the sad sincerity of these words cut him as no insult could have. He tried to figure out why he had wanted to hurt her, hating whatever was inside himself that caused him to do so. Her profile passed before a candlelit window. He wanted to stop and put his arms around her, apologizing for what he'd said. Instead, he merely replied softly, "I would. I'm sure I would have liked him," and as he said this he realized that nothing else she could have told him would have shown more affection. He knew that soon he would leave her at her door and never see her again; but the realization that she did like him caused a warmth to rise within him, and with it the need to say something nice to her. "Someday I'll go to Hue. Do you think it will seem as beautiful as you described?"

"More beautiful. I cannot describe it."

"Tell me about it again."

Tuyen hesitated before saying, "Is said that the city of Hue is a lotus flower that grew, as something beautiful, from the ground where there was nothing. All symbols and things from the past are kept there. Is not like Saigon, where money is important; or like Hanoi, where the government is everything. You walk in the streets and there are flowers everywhere, and the buildings they are Vietnamese and beautiful. The roofs they slant to the ground and are made of bright tile. There is a river that is near the Imperial Palace. Is far across and lovely to see, and is called the River of Perfumes. Many times I have walked along it."

Tuyen stopped talking and faced Kramer. They were at her door. It began to drizzle, and as she looked up at him there were drops of water on her face. All the sad mystery had returned to her. He wanted merely to stand there looking at her face, fearing the inevitable words that would ask him to leave. "Is late. I am very tired, really." There was a tightness in his stomach as Tuyen said this, but the way she trilled the *l*'s in "really" caused him to smile. "Really," she repeated, without knowing why he was smiling. Kramer wanted to put his arms around her, to hold her close to himself. She too began to smile, but self-consciously, "Maybe you come back some time."

The smile left Kramer's face. "No . . . tomorrow I go back to my unit."

"Maybe you step on another booby trap."

"Then they'll send me home, not to Da Nang. . . . It'll be my third Heart." She made no reply, and he asked without any hope of her agreeing, "Maybe I could come in for a while?"

Kramer wondered if he was imagining the added sadness in her look as she said, "No, I am very tired, really."

"Just until the rain stops?"

She stared up at him, offering neither words nor a look that would answer his question. Again he wanted to put his arms around her, and only the fear of insulting her prevented him. She turned and moved towards the door, away from him. A tenseness rose within him as he watched her open it. He wanted to step forward and hold it open; but he couldn't make himself do this. He stood helpless, waiting for the door to close, almost admitting to himself that what had happened had been something different — not a game or a contest.

The door didn't close, not until he finally stepped through its darkness and shut it himself.

He stood just inside the threshold, listening to her footsteps move across the concrete floor to the center of the room. There was a click as she pulled the cord of a lamp that hung from the ceiling, and a soft light glowed from within a rice paper shade. Kramer glanced at the table with the candle, the pack of Salem cigarettes, and the two pictures on it. From where he stood, he could see that one was of an older man, her father, and the other a young man, her husband. His thoughts again flashed back to those hurtling moments when he and his platoon were advancing towards the tree line under fire. This time he made no attempt to fathom them, but instead tried to drive them from his mind. Only when he turned towards Tuyen and saw that same proud stare was he able to do this, no longer wanting to ask why risking his life to kill was the only thing he'd ever done that had made him feel alive. He stood facing her, trying to think of something to say but unable to. Finally, he turned from her and walked towards the only window in the room. He lifted the red silk curtain. It revealed nothing but darkness and a few flickering lights. He turned around only to again meet her silent stare. "It's still raining."

Tuyen had been wondering why she had asked him in, but she found the feebleness of his attempt to start a conversation humorous and almost broke into a smile.

Kramer reached in his pocket for a cigarette, then asked her for a light. She walked over to the carved dresser and removed a box of matches. As she handed them to him, she asked, "You do not have a lighter?"

"No, it was stolen." Kramer gave a short laugh before continuing. "They must have gone through my pockets on the medivac chopper. They took my watch too. They were nice enough to leave my wallet though. Took twenty dollars out of it, but put it back in my pocket."

"You have *on* a watch."

"It's a new one. I bought it at the hospital today."

"You did not buy a lighter?"

"No. I'll stick to matches for a while . . . in case I get medivacked again."

"Many times I hear them say the Vietnamese are thieves."

"Stealing's an international custom. . . . Do you have an ashtray?"

She took a finely painted china dish from her dresser and held it out to him. Kramer hesitated before taking it. "Is all right. I will wash it."

He handed her the matches and she walked back towards the dresser with them. Kramer felt awkward standing, so he sat down on the straw mat in the center of the room, hoping Tuyen would sit down next to him. Instead, she sat on the mattress a few feet away and facing him. Tuyen noticed his muddy boots upon the mat. At first a little irritated, she then realized she couldn't have expected him to take them off. As they exchanged glances, she became uneasy, thinking that it was Kramer who wanted to talk and yet he had nothing to say. Again she wondered why she had asked him in, or even chosen to speak to him — perhaps to make one of "*them*" know? It was she who finally broke the silence. "Is you who want to talk, and you say nothing."

Kramer had been thinking the same thing, restraining himself from using the glib little lines that kept suggesting themselves. Still her accusation irritated him. He felt like asking her, "What was I supposed to say, that I wanted to fuck you?" but instead he said sarcastically, "I thought you let me in because of the rain."

"The rain, it can last for days."

Again she noticed the muddy boots. She stared at his face, almost daring him to say something. At first this incensed Kramer, but he was able to

404

control his anger and asked her jokingly, "What was your name again?"

Thinking he was making fun of her, she said coldly, "You know this."

The stupidity of his attempt at a joke sickened Kramer, and he was also frustrated by the realization that his refusal to fall into a predatory, seductive role left him speaking nothing but childish inanities. He wanted to explain or apologize, but her uncompromising stare made this impossible. "Tuyen, I know," he said in a bored tone.

No anger in her voice, and even some regret, she said, "I think maybe you should go."

Kramer caught nothing but the words themselves. A jaunty expression appeared on his face as he said, "I thought we were going to talk."

Seeing this expression, she found it hard to believe she had ever seen anything else in his face. What *had* she seen? She just wanted to be left alone, and forced herself to assume the same tone as Kramer's. "We have nothing to talk about. You should go."

Kramer saw the entire, unreal scene exploding in his face. A few minutes ago he had anticipated against belief something beautiful, but the moment seemed to have shattered before him and he knew it was his fault. He knew this, and yet he couldn't even control the tone of his own voice. "We've got *lots* to talk about."

The thought, 'Why won't he go?' kept repeating itself in Tuyen's mind, and she said in an almost defeated tone, "What? What is there to talk about?"

'Nothing,' Kramer thought to himself, but he refused to admit this to her. For a fraction of a second he again remembered the advance on the tree line, and his thoughts reduced to a single word. It kept him from saying anything else, and it was all he could do to keep it from passing through his lips.

"What is there to talk about?" she repeated in a cold, defeated tone.

He could no longer control his own lips, and he spit the word at her in hatred. "*Suicide!* Let's talk about suicide. . . . Tell me about it like you told me about Hue."

Tuyen merely stared at him, first questioningly but then with more warmth than she had ever shown him before. 'Maybe this is why. Maybe this is what I saw in his face.'

Now Kramer possessed the questioning stare, wondering why there was no hatred in her eyes. Only now did he think about what he had said, wondering why he had said it and what it explained to her about him, realizing that he had finally admitted that he was the weaker of them, but also that she must have already known this.

When Tuyen finally spoke, it was in the calm, beautiful tone she had

405

sometimes used before, but there was even more understanding in her words. "You think about this many times." The docile look on Kramer's face before he lowered his stare to the floor told her that she was right. "I also used to think about this, even when I was a little girl. My life it seemed very long and too hard for me."

"You don't think about it anymore?" he asked weakly.

"No, it has been many years. My life, it no longer seems long. Sometimes I am even afraid I will die. Someday it will be the same for you."

Her words and the tone she used made Kramer even surer that she possessed an understanding that he somehow lacked. He believed that through her he could gain it. Glancing up from the floor for only a second, he said softly, "I'm not sure I understand you."

"No, and there was no one for me to understand. Someday you will see."

He couldn't make himself believe she was incapable of explaining. "See what? . . . Tell me."

"I cannot. . . . I — Maybe now you think of your life as a clock, each day the same and separate. Someday you will see is not true. . . . A life it cannot be divided into hours or days. There is no time, only life. There is nothing beautiful if you divide time. When you are happy, these days they leave you quickly. Sadness sometimes stays and seems never to end. . . . It cannot be explained."

Kramer continued to stare at her, but she remained silent. "Please, I want to listen to you."

"There is no more I can tell you."

"Anything, it doesn't matter," he answered, while thinking, 'I just want to hear your voice.'

"I am tired."

"But . . . but when I leave, I'll never see you again."

"And this will make no difference." Realizing the truth in her words, she still felt guilty about saying them. After a short pause, she continued speaking. "I will tell you what I think sometimes. It seems that time is longest when we want it most to end. If I am happy, my life it will be too short. If I am not happy, it will be too long. But if I am sometimes happy and sometimes sad, it cannot be too short or too long."

Having expected something profound, Kramer began to laugh despite himself. He looked up and saw that Tuyen was also laughing. She tried to cover her face with her hand. Without thinking, he reached out for it and held it away from her face. When they had stopped laughing, Kramer found himself sitting next to her on the mattress. Tuyen gently withdrew her hand as she stared down at the floor in front of her. Kramer watched as she tried to keep a smile from her lips. She seemed so different — 'Almost human.' Again he was struck by how beautiful she was. He re-

406

membered the tone in which he had spoken to her a few minutes before, realizing he hadn't merely lost his temper and feeling more than guilty. Afraid she would see the troubled expression on his face, Kramer leaned back on one elbow. He couldn't even picture himself talking to her in that angry a tone. There had to be a reason for it. He had an idea what that reason was — something inside himself, something perverted that tried to force him to look at her as nothing more than a bitch, not even that, a cunt, something that hated her for possessing a power over him, for being able to hurt him, for being someone he could love. He glanced up and saw that she had turned and was looking down at him. Tuyen also leaned back on the mattress. She lay on her side, her arm outstretched beneath her head and a tired look on her face. "You are sad," she said softly.

Kramer shook his head slightly before saying, "No. Time seems too short." He removed his hand from beneath his head and lay back in the same manner as she was lying. With his other arm, he reached across for a strand of her hair and touched it to his lips. "You're so beautiful I can't even believe what I see . . . or what I hear." He touched the side of her face, then slowly drew his hand away. "Do you like me?"

"I do not know you. . . . Sometimes, sometimes I like you very much."

"And other times?"

"Sometimes you are a little boy. . . . You are scared."

"When?"

"When you are angry at me?"

"Sometimes you want me to be scared, don't you?"

"Maybe."

"Am I scared of you now?" Tuyen answered with an almost imperceptible shake of her head. "Do you want me to be scared of you now?"

"No."

He laid his hand upon her cheek and drew himself closer until their faces were touching. She lay back and he moved his lips over her soft, warm skin. The clean smell of her hair made him want to lose himself in it, and his hand combed gently through it. She remained passive, yet the relaxed sound of her breathing told him to continue. Kramer reached his arm beneath the small of her back, slowly raising it until he was able to place her on top of himself. Strands of her silky black hair lay across his face, and he inhaled their fragrance. Pressing her closer, he experienced the soft warmth of her body. His clothing seemed as if it were trying to suffocate him. He wanted to feel her face against his chest. His hands kept passing over the zipper of her dress, and finally his almost inept fingers undid it.

Her breathing became more controlled. She seemed suddenly cold to him and the soft light of the lamp all too blinding. She no longer reacted to his touch. Kramer became more nervous. He slid from beneath her and walked towards the light. In an instant the room was dark and he felt alone. He started to move back towards the mattress, but instead turned, and in the darkness made his way to the dresser on which she had placed the matches. His fingers quickly found them, and he walked back towards her. The room was too dark; she too beautiful. He had remembered there was a candle at the head of the mattress.

Kramer removed his shirt before striking the match. Its flame seared the air and caused him to turn his head away. He lay down upon the mattress without touching her, watching the shadows of the flame glow upon her face. Even this could give it no warmth as she stared blankly at the ceiling — as if her face were carved in cool marble. She was more beautiful than she had ever been, but the moment seemed lost to Kramer. He drew her upon his chest, and there was a sad awkwardness in this act. But soon she again began to react to him, and he became more relaxed. His hands moved softly along her body, and her clothing seemed to fall naturally away from her.

She lay motionless upon him, and with each breath he was lulled by the scent of her hair and skin. He felt her weight upon his chest as it slowly rose and fell. This seemed enough, to lie there with her and in the morning find strands of her hair upon his face. He thought about how he had tried to convince himself that all he wanted was to fuck her, an act which now seemed so unimportant — not something that he wanted to happen, but something that must happen, and at the risk of losing what he now possessed.

With a delicacy that surprised him, he was able to place her beneath himself. There was little conscious thought in what followed. It seemed so natural, natural until he saw her face. The soft, flickering candlelight upon it revealed the passive blankness of her eyes. She refused to react to him, lying motionless, as if waiting for him to finish and leave her alone. He too wanted to finish, to be rid of her. A violent anger rose within him. 'Is this what I wanted so bad? Is this what I fucking wanted — to be made to feel like some filthy animal?' He had a sudden furious urge to slap her, and in a violent instant he imagined the shock and pain that would be written upon her face, and also the recognition that he was there — *fucking her*. But the blankness of her stare made this seem impossible. No, he knew he was helpless to change the expression on her face. Confused, hating himself for his own thoughts, he suddenly realized that again he was scared and like a child. The cruel look, that he hadn't even realized was there, disappeared as he asked himself, 'Did she sense this? Did she

408

know?' He looked down at her, now with a sad, questioning expression on his face, wondering what perverted thing inside him had again caused him to think of her in that way. He saw her nostrils begin to dilate with each breath. She began to move ever so slightly beneath him. Her eyes half closed, then opened again; but they were different eyes, those of a little girl on the verge of tears. They focused upon him, as if seeing him for the first time. Her breathing quickened, and he could hear it over his own. She bit her lower lip, and the delicate tendons of her neck pressed tightly against her skin. He doubted what he was seeing, never having realized that a moment like this could be experienced, feeling himself merge with her in the fulfillment of it.

Soon he found himself lying quietly upon her soft and motionless body, her arms drawn gently around his neck, remembering the look on her face; and in it he saw all the pain and suffering, and more beauty than he had ever believed existed.

He opened his eyes slowly, proving to himself that she was there. Strands of silky black hair lay upon his face. Her arm was still across his chest, and her head slowly rose and fell with his breathing. The upper part of her back, uncovered by the silk bedspread, took on an amber glow from the warm morning light. He studied each delicate curve. But it was her face that he really wanted to see, to watch her eyes as they opened. If he tried to move he would wake her. But somehow he knew that her eyes were already open.

Her hand began to move gently over his chest, and he said, "Good morning." She made no reply nor any attempt to look at him as her hand continued to move softly over his chest. He played his fingers along the hollow of her back and she squeezed herself against him to avoid them. To get him to stop, she raised her head and pressed her chin into his chest. He stared at her profile, realizing again how flawless it was. He hesitated to touch her face, first combing away the loose strands of hair that lay before it. A sincere sense of disbelief in his tone, he said what he was thinking. "You're so beautiful . . . everything about you." She retained the same impenetrable expression before finally lowering her head to his chest. Again her hand moved gently on top of it, but she soon placed her other hand beneath his shoulder and tried to turn him on his side. He made no effort to help her, instead asking, "What are you doing?"

"Turn around." He didn't answer and continued to lie on his back. "Turn around," she repeated, this time looking at his face. He shook his head and watched with amusement as she continued trying to turn him

409

onto his side. She soon stopped, and asked him again, only more softly and followed by the gentle pressure of her cheek against his shoulder. Turning away, he listened as she slid from beneath the bedspread; then rolled back over and watched her walk slowly to the closet and remove a white silk robe. She was wearing it when she turned back towards him. He was still looking at her. Again her blank stare gave no hint of what she was thinking, and his lips moved silently as he said, "You're beautiful." She turned and walked to another door. As she opened it he could see that it led to a bathroom. He had little time to wonder whether she would close the door behind her. His next thoughts were answered by the click of the lock. As he listened to the flowing bath water, her stare appeared before him. Again he wondered what she had been thinking.

She emerged from the bathroom with the same opaque stare, but her tone was gentle as she said, "If you would like, you can take a bath."

Kramer lay motionless as he watched her disappear through another door, obviously leading to the kitchen. He tried to remember how long it had been since he'd taken a bath, finally deciding it had been six months. He got up and walked into the bathroom. Leaving the door open, he turned on the water and stepped into the tub. When it was full, he lay back in the warm, soothing water, remembering the night before and still trying to figure out what Tuyen was thinking this morning. What would have happened if she hadn't known this was the last time he would see her? This didn't seem that important. He called to her. When she finally answered him, she was a few feet outside the bathroom door. "Come here."

"I am doing things."

"Come here and wash my back," he asked in a childish tone.

"No," she answered without any coldness or equivocation, then added, "When you come out, I will make you something to eat."

Tuyen was in the kitchen when Kramer walked out of the bathroom. His jungle fatigues lay neatly folded upon the now made bed. They were clean, but he stared down at them with repugnance. Instead of putting them on, he walked to the closet and looked for a robe. He found a black one. It was too small. There was also a pink one, and he decided to wear it if it fit. It barely did.

Kramer started to walk towards the kitchen, but his eyes were caught by the two pictures on the table. He stood looking down at them. Her father's stare was similar to her own, but weaker. Something forced Kramer to lift her husband's picture from the table. The hair was straight, the lips creased somberly, and the eyes slanted. It was the same face he had seen so many times before — when blindfolds were lifted from prisoners, when corpses were rolled over on their backs. He forced himself to place the picture back down on the table, thinking, 'Maybe I looked at her like that.'

As soon as Kramer entered the kitchen, Tuyen began to laugh while saying, "You look like my mother."

Kramer was still thinking about the pictures. He had no idea what she meant until he saw that she was looking at the pink robe. "You didn't like her, did you?"

Still laughing, she answered, "She diddin like me."

"She diddin," Kramer repeated. "I can't understand that."

"You are not my mother."

"But I look like her, remember?"

The kitchen was small and immaculate. Kramer sat down at the table. Tuyen noticed him looking at some wilted flowers in its center, and she said, "They die. I will buy some today. . . . When I live in Hue, we have many flowers in our house." After a long pause, she asked, "What do you want to eat?"

"I'm not very hungry."

"You want eggs?"

"All right."

"How many?"

"Six."

She realized immediately that Kramer wasn't serious. "You say you are not hungry?"

"I know. I usually have six eggs and a steak."

"If I make you six eggs, you will eat them?"

"How much do two cost?"

"One dollar."

"I want the waitress."

"She is busy."

"Doing what?"

"Making eggs."

"Okay, I'm not hungry."

"She is still busy. . . . Now you want eggs?"

"What are *you* going to eat?"

"I eat already."

"Really, I'm not too hungry. What do you have in the refrigerator?" As he asked this, Kramer leaned back and opened the door. He reached for the first thing that caught his eye, and held it up in disbelief. "A mango!"

"You have eat this before? Is good."

"I know. I have a tree in my backyard."

"Where you live they have these? . . . Where is that?"

"Miami. . . . The ones on my tree are this big." Kramer held his hands apart to show a size three times larger than the mango he was holding.

"I know this. In America everything is *beeger*."

He looked at Tuyen with mock resentment. "You want me to be angry with you now?" She smiled as she shook her head and sat down across from him. "You'd like Miami. We have mangoes, it's warm, and there's an ocean."

"We have these things in Vietnam."

"I know. That's why you'd like it there."

"But I am already here. . . . Do they grow rice there?"

"Only during the tourist season." Tuyen looked at him questioningly. "No, but they grow it in Louisiana."

"This is near where you live?"

"Right next door. . . . When you were at Sorbonne, did you study Greek Mythology?"

"You mean about the gods? Many years before I go there I study this in Vietnamese school."

Kramer held up the mango as if he was lecturing a class. "Do you know what this is?"

"Yes, I buy it."

"It's ambrosia!"

"This word I do not know."

"Ambrosia is the food of the gods." Tuyen nodded her head. "Whenever I hear the word mango, I think of ambrosia. . . . Let's eat it." Tuyen got up and brought him a knife. Kramer was about to cut the mango when he stopped and said, "This is a ceremony, we should say an invocation to the gods." Tuyen looked at him questioningly. "A prayer."

"Is the food of the gods. They do not say prayer."

"You're right." He cut the mango in half, exposing its rich golden core. He then cut a small piece, and held it near Tuyen's lips on the point of the knife. She moved her head back and took the piece of mango between her fingers. "You don't trust me."

"I think maybe I trust you."

When they were done eating the mango, they walked back into the living room and Kramer said, "The ocean is near here, isn't it?"

"Is not far."

"Will you go there with me?"

"You say you have to go back."

"I'm never going back."

"They will come for you."

Kramer's expression became more serious. "I was supposed to go back last night. A few more hours won't make any difference."

"All right, we go." The sad, proud expression had returned to her face, and only now did Kramer realize how happy she had seemed a few moments earlier. He placed his hands gently on her neck. Tuyen started to back away, but stopped herself and instead said softly, her eyes cast down in front of her, "You say we go to the ocean."

"In a while," he whispered as his hands moved along the front of her shoulders and beneath her robe before it fell to the floor.

The sky was overcast and ominous. Strong gusts of wind carried the smell of salt towards him, telling Kramer they were near the ocean. Tuyen was wearing a long white dress of embroidered silk. It was slit to the waist on both sides, revealing slacks of thin, white silk beneath it. He watched as Tuyen's hair streamed behind her in the wind. The expression on her face made her seem very far away. In the distance, he heard the breakers. The white sand was deep and soft, and each succeeding dune seemed to promise a glimpse of the ocean behind it. Then it appeared — light green purging itself to blue towards the horizon. The expanse of it made him feel insignificant, and as if he were standing on a small, barren island. Tuyen watched him as his eyes followed the furious breakers, seeing them spend their force upon the passive sand only to once again recede into the ocean, softly. "Is beautiful, no?"

Kramer answered without moving his stare from the ocean. "I love to see her when she's mad."

The wind ripped at his words.

He felt her hand pressing down on his shoulder, and turned to see her leaning up towards his face. "I diddin hear you."

He put his arm around her, and his lips searched within her hair for her ear. "I love to see her when she's mad."

Neither of them spoke as they walked towards the water. The beach gradually hardened under their feet. For a long time they stood at the edge of the wet sand, looking out at the horizon. Tuyen was at Kramer's side, and he almost lifted her off the ground as he pulled her towards himself and against his chest. The wind blew strands of her hair across his face, and he pressed her tighter against himself while saying, "I feel so strong. I feel like the strongest person in the world." He took Tuyen's hand and almost dragged her as they walked silently along the edge of the water, the sounds of gusting wind and crashing breakers numbing their senses.

Kramer saw the receding waves leave a strange object exposed. Many times before he had seen something like this happen, and now as always he wondered what he would find when he reached it. It wasn't until he pressed his foot against it that he knew — the lip of an all-but-buried combat helmet. Again he looked out at the ocean, remembering the reefs

413

off south Florida, their calm, quiet beauty, realizing that the violence before him was merely on the surface, but there. He gently pulled Tuyen back towards the dunes. The wind no longer blew against their faces, and when he looked back, her hair was flying freely in front of her. Again the sand became soft. Their feet sank deeply into it as they climbed the dunes. Suddenly the sounds of the wind and the breakers became muffled and seemed very distant. They were in a valley between two large sand dunes.

Kramer dropped to his knees, gently pulling Tuyen down in front of him. Again her stare was sad and impenetrable. He leaned back on his elbow and looked up at her. With outstretched fingers, he combed the hair away from her face. Only then did he place his hand beneath her chin. Ever so gently, he moved her face to slightly different angles, as if examining the facets of a precious stone, trying to delve into its center and find the source of its radiance. "What is it you are thinking?" she asked. Kramer made no reply, and his expression told her that he didn't know. "Your house is by the ocean?" He answered her with a slight shake of his head. "Is beautiful, no?"

Kramer realized that she was referring to the ocean, and also that his answer would apply equally well to her face. "When I see it, life seems very short."

"You are young. You will live many years." Kramer gave a quick, sarcastic laugh, and Tuyen asked, "Your father is how old?"

"Fifty-five, fifty-six."

"You will live to be a hundred."

Kramer burst out laughing as he fell back in the sand. "No! Please, no." Tuyen also began to laugh and she said, "Maybe ninety."

"Okay, that's a little better," Kramer answered, a smile still on his face. He reached out for her hands and placed them upon his chest. She leaned over him, strands of her hair hanging alongside his face. "Tell me about time again."

"I say I cannot tell you."

"Like you did last night."

"I will tell you what I think sometimes. . . . When I am sad, time seems not to move. I see my life before me, and it seem very long. But then I think, if I kill myself, there will be time before I die, less than a second maybe, but this second may seem longer than many years, longer than all the time I would have live."

Kramer sensed a fallacy in what Tuyen had said, but the words themselves and the manner in which she had spoken them made her idea soothing. "Do you really believe that?"

"Maybe is true. I do not know."

414

He wanted to hear her voice, and mainly for this reason, he finally asked, "When you are happy, doesn't it make you sad to know that time is moving so fast?"

"No, I do not think about this. If I am happy or if I am sad, is already happen, is —" she hesitated while trying to think of the right words.

"It's in the past."

"Yes, is already in the past. Many things have happen to me, many bad things. But I remember the times when I was happy. They cannot be made separate — are a part of my life which cannot be divided. The bad things, they too are a part, but is all one — cannot be divided. When I remember, the bad things they are there, not alone by themselves. Too they seem far away, not me —" Tuyen again paused while trying to think of the right words.

"They're not as real. It's as if they happened to somebody else."

"Yes, sometimes. . . . I cannot believe they happen to me . . . sometimes. Sometimes I remember, but more than only the bad things."

"And when you remember when you were happy?"

"Is like I am happy again. Everything I remember."

"Like when you remember Paris and —" Kramer suddenly realized what he had said. His voice diminished to a whisper as he added, "Hue." Tuyen knew immediately what he was thinking. She watched his troubled expression as he tried, but failed, to keep himself from asking her, "Will you remember last night?"

The slight hesitation before she said, "Yes, I will remember," and the tone of her words made it clear to him that she could have added, "but not like Paris."

Now sorry that he knew, Kramer wished only that there could have been at least some doubt in his mind. There seemed nothing for him to say, and Tuyen also remained silent. She had sensed what would happen even before she had spoken, knowing that he would somehow see beneath her words. The troubled look on his face made him seem even sadder than when she had first seen him, when he and Donaldson sat drinking in her bar, during those moments when the childish arrogance would slowly fade from his face leaving nothing but fear and doubt. Now, for the first time, it was she who reached out and touched *his* face. He couldn't help but smile as he looked up at her, realizing that she again saw him as a child — not a scared, angry child, but still a child. It made little difference now, he knew this.

"You will walk back with me?"

He was still feeling some sense of loss; but it hadn't been unexpected. He nodded and said, "Yes."

He got to his feet and watched Tuyen as she climbed to the top of the sand dune. She glanced back towards him to make sure he was coming, then started walking again. Kramer stood watching her graceful silhouette. The sun glinted off her dress as she turned away; and suddenly, in one horrible instant, her image appeared to explode before him, a deafening barrage of rifle fire reverberated within his head, and a mutilated, bullet-riddled form, flesh flying from it, collapsed in front of him.

Kramer slowly dropped to his knees. He remembered. He had finally remembered. "I knew it," he said in a dazed whisper. "I knew it. *Now, I have to remember it now! . . . All of it!*" Confused segments flashed through his mind. He tried to control himself, deciding to go over it minute by minute. Unable to rise from his knees, he called Tuyen. "Now," he said with determination. The only way it was possible for him to start was by saying everything aloud. "Forest was talking to me. Forest was talking to me. Trippitt came over and asked who the Professor was. Forest was talking to me, then Trippitt asked — Professor, then somebody shouted, 'Look! Out there. A Gook.' " Kramer remembered turning to see a figure walking across the rice paddies towards them. The figure staggered and fell. He got up again. Somebody yelled, "He's NVA!" Kramer remembered being able to make out a tattered and mud-covered NVA uniform, and saying to himself, 'He's an NVA soldier. He's trying to *chieu hoi*.'

Somebody yelled out, "He's a *chieu hoi*."

"*Fuck it!* Blow him away!"

"*I'll* blow him away."

"No!"

"No, don't!"

"Wait!"

At first the men watched in silence as he staggered towards them. They lined the edge of the high ground waiting for him. Then there was some laughter as he continually staggered and fell. It seemed to take a long time before he reached the last dike between himself and the high ground.

Kramer remembered the way he paused after climbing over this dike. Less than twenty yards of rice paddies lay between him and a hundred Marines. He stood staring at them, hands on hips, his chest heaving while he tried to catch his breath. Somebody yelled, "C'mon!" He remained standing with his hands on his hips for a few more seconds, then began taking slow, sure steps towards them. Kramer remembered staring at his tattered uniform, and then seeing the wild, fantastic look in his eyes. His steps quickened. Suddenly he drew a knife from his belt. With all the strength he had left, he began to run towards them. No one could believe what was happening. Their rifles lay forgotten in their hands. As soon as he saw the knife, Kramer's stare shot back towards his eyes. Wild and unreal, they came straight towards him, screaming, "Kill me! Kill me! You're death! KILL ME!" Kramer couldn't, made no effort to move, his rifle hanging down at his side, the figure staggering straight towards him, eyes screaming, "You're death! You're death!" There was a single shot from an M-16. The sound of it seemed muffled. With his insane eyes still glaring at Kramer and his knife held high, the figure started to take one more step. Kramer heard an awesome burst of rifle fire at the same instant all the flesh was being ripped away from his face. The burst continued as he spun completely around, turning crimson, falling in Kramer's direction.

Even after he lay motionless, just below the surface of the water, there was another shot, two more, and a final one. Again there was silence, no one really sure it had happened, the water turning red in front of them. Then someone laughed, and another laugh. A Marine jumped into the rice paddy and pulled from it, by the hair, a piece of raw, butchered flesh. A hand grabbed for its belt as a souvenir, and only came up with a bullet-riddled half of it. There was some laughter. "Did you see the crazy motherfucker?"

"Tried to take a whole company with a knife!"

Laughter.

"He must have two hundred holes in him!"

And more laughter.

"Did you *see* the look in his eyes?"

Tuyen was kneeling before him, startled by Kramer's expression. "What happen?"

"I just remembered something. . . . I couldn't remember before."

"The booby trap?"

"No, before that . . . I just remembered it."

"You remember what?"

"I can't tell you."

"You are all right?"

"Yes, yes, just wait . . . I'll go with you in a minute."

Still dazed, Kramer rose to his feet and began walking with her. He searched his memory, making sure he had remembered all of it, sometimes questioning whether it had actually happened, knowing that it had. He walked over a mile without having any idea what was going on around him, his mind completely in the past. Until he saw Tuyen glance at him with a worried look on her face, Kramer wasn't even conscious that she was there. "I'm all right," he said, making an effort to smile.

Kramer's eyes returned to the ground. He saw a single leg between two crutches, then heard a click. A Vietnamese amputee stood before him. As they passed by, he called out, "Marine, you want picture?" Kramer continued walking, but he glanced back and saw the amputee struggling with a camera while balancing himself on the crutches. "*Marine,* you buy picture?" Kramer began to walk faster, but the man on crutches caught up with him. Kramer stared at his face and wanted to escape. "One dollar." Unsuccessfully trying to avoid the amputee's stare, Kramer pulled some bills out of his pocket as he walked. The man grabbed them and shoved a picture into his hand. Kramer stuffed the photograph into his pocket without looking at it, still trying to escape the amputee.

Once inside Tuyen's apartment, he felt more relaxed. He followed her into the kitchen where she poured two glasses of water and they sat down at the table. She still had a worried look on her face, and Kramer was more thankful for it than bothered by it. "I'm all right now. . . . You understand what happened, don't you?"

"You remember something very bad you have never remember before."

"You can understand why I acted like that, can't you?"

"Yes, is a very bad thing you remember."

"You don't think I was acting like a little kid, do you?"

"No, I understand."

"It wasn't because of anything you said."

"I believe you."

"I have to go soon."

"Because you are late they will do something?"

"No, they can't do a damn thing to me. They can't *touch* me." He noticed that Tuyen was looking at the wilted flowers on the table. "You forgot to buy some."

"Tomorrow."

Kramer stood up and reached for her hand. He led her into the living room. Tuyen was hesitant to lie down on the mattress with him, but he coaxed her without words. Her head lay upon his chest, and he stroked her hair as he asked, "You like me, don't you?"

"I like you very much."

"When will I see you again?" He waited for an answer, both knowing and fearing what she would say.

"Is better if I never see you again."

"You said you liked me."

"Is why is better."

"Will you think about me?"

"Yes, many times."

"It's not because of what happened today?" he asked, knowing that this had nothing to do with it.

418

Her tone indicated that she was hurt by him even thinking this, "No, is not."

"What if I can come back?"

This idea scared her. "Is no good."

"But what if I do?"

"Soon I go back to Hue — four, maybe five days."

"What if I go to Hue?" Kramer asked, knowing the impossibility of this, and neither surprised by nor ashamed of the supplicating tone of his words.

"Please, is no good. . . . Maybe is better if you go now."

It was a long few seconds for him before she sat up. He remained lying down, playing with her hair. But when she stood, so did he, admitting to himself that it had ended. It was Kramer who first walked to the door.

"Is very bad time now. Is bad to hope for things. Something can happen, and we are more sad than before."

Kramer knew he was being lied to, and there was some coldness in his stare as he said, "That's not why."

"I like you more than I think I ever like anyone again."

"Again," he repeated, almost as a demand, thinking that now she should tell him in her own words what they both already knew.

"Many times I tell you once I was very happy. This can never be taken from me. To lose happiness like this is very bad thing. Once, no more. Never can it be the same. . . . Someday you will understand."

This Kramer understood now, and had sensed all along. It was with a feeling of some guilt that he asked, "Are you sorry?"

"No. I think I know it would happen. The reason I diddin know, but still I know. This is why I sometimes say things to make you angry."

Kramer saw no hope in being able to change her mind, but he decided to make one last effort. "Is it better the way things are? Maybe it's already too late."

"Many things can happen. For me is better this way. Now you think is too late. Is not. Someday you will see."

Kramer couldn't make himself believe this. For once he had found something he'd wanted, and he couldn't believe it would ever happen again. There were so many reasons why he should leave things as they were, to try and forget; but he couldn't accept any of them. 'Have I changed?' he asked himself sarcastically, finally admitting that he had. 'But not that much. . . . Besides, *she* changed me.' He was sure that without her he would be as he was before. Again he decided to make one last effort. "I'll leave you my address."

"No," she almost pleaded.

"You told me how much you liked me. Maybe you'll change your mind."

"This is why you must not leave it."

"Please, for me." She made no reply, but her expression begged him not to. There seemed no hope, and Kramer felt that he had to get away from her. He quickly took out a pen and wrote down his address. While he frantically did so, he actually believed that this act would somehow save him. But the look on her face when he handed her the paper told him there was no chance. In a defeated tone, he said, "The top one is my military address. The other one is my home. *Please* keep it." Her soft stare gave no answer, but it did tell him he would never see her again. He raised his hand to her cheek, touching her face, as if doing so was the only way he could prove to himself that she existed; but he was so confused that he couldn't. It was impossible to believe that all this had happened, and to him. He knew he had to get away. He wanted to say something, maybe to ask if she would remember him, but no words would come. He slowly lowered his hand from her face, knowing it was for the last time.

2. An Hoa

Kramer stood waiting for the helicopters as footsteps approached from his rear and a familiar voice said, "I bet they'll be glad to get back here." Not sure the remark was intended for him, he hoped it wasn't and made no attempt to acknowledge it. Chaplain Hindman then put his hand on Kramer's shoulder. "Heard you had a little trouble with a booby trap." Kramer gave a slight nod, but otherwise ignored Hindman who was now standing next to him. "They're a brave bunch of men. . . . Too bad the folks back home don't appreciate what they're going through." This time Kramer didn't even bother to nod. "Well, I'm glad they're taking them out of there." After a few seconds' silence, Hindman finally took Kramer's hint and walked away while saying, "See you Sunday, Lieutenant."

In a few minutes the first helicopter arrived. Kramer watched intently as the men debarked. The faces were unfamiliar, none of them from Hotel Company. Practically every man was either supporting or being supported by someone else. Their steps were slow and deliberate as they moved away from the helicopter. It was a mere thirty yards to the edge of the landing pad, but the first man took almost two minutes to reach it. Some of the men that followed were in worse shape. Kramer watched the pain on their faces each time they would lower a foot to the ground. One or two of them had their boots slung across their shoulders and nothing except bandages on their feet. The last man off the pad was ten yards behind the others. He barely lifted his feet, each slow step covering no more than six inches. Hindman walked out on to the pad to help him.

The helicopters continued to land, and the same scene was repeated again and again. It was over a mile to the battalion area, so trucks had to be called in to carry the men there. They sat waiting in large groups at the edge of the landing pad, their faces turned away from the wind and sand stirred up by the copter blades.

Kramer watched for almost an hour before he finally saw Sugar Bear leading a group of men from one of the helicopters. Hemrick hung awkwardly from his shoulder. A man dropped to his knees, and someone helped him up. As Kramer walked quickly towards his men, he saw Roads and Appleton carrying someone between them, and two other men leaning on their outside shoulders. Hamilton and Forsythe helped Childs, while Chalice followed behind. Most of the men nodded or called out to Kramer as he passed them, precipitating a sense of pride he would have found embarrassing at almost any other time. Ramirez was the last man off the chopper. Pablo stood patiently waiting for him. Ramirez took short, painful steps toward the edge of the LZ, his feet seeming barely to move. Kramer tried to help him, but Ramirez shook his head while shouting over the squall of the copter blades, "I can make it." He repeated these words again as if to convince himself. Kramer lifted off Ramirez's pack and followed behind.

When the men of Second Platoon reached their company area, a large tent upon a wooden platform stood waiting for them. They immediately threw off their packs, flak jackets, and helmets; and lay down on the cots inside it. Someone turned on a radio. For the first time since they had gotten off the helicopter, there was some laughing and joking. Word was passed that the doctor was making the rounds of the battalion, and for the men to take off their boots and wait for him.

Childs stared down at his boots. He wanted to be free of them, but dreaded the act of taking them off. Merely leaning forward and reaching for the laces increased the pain. Slowly and carefully, he removed both laces without moving his feet. Childs drew one leg up and placed it across his other knee. He hesitated for a minute, knowing the pain he'd soon be feeling. Finally, he pressed against the heel of the boot. It seemed glued to his foot. He pressed harder, increasing the burning pain on his instep, increasing it until he had to stop, the boot still snugly on his foot.

He looked around the tent. A few of the men already had their boots off, but he knew that other men were in even worse condition than himself. Seeing Chalice remove his socks, Childs called him over. He lifted one of his boots into Chalice's hands, but pulled it away as soon as Chalice tried to get it off. Instead, he had Chalice hold the boots stationary on the floor as he slowly withdrew his feet. Feeling relief as well as burning pain, Childs quickly sat down. He noticed that a few of the men still hadn't been able to get their boots off, and again reminded himself that they were in worse condition than he. This thought helped little when he tried to get his socks off. He felt as if he were skinning his own feet, and this was exactly what he was doing. It was no use. As much as he wanted his socks off, he'd have to wait for the scissors.

Childs stared down at his socks. Blood had seeped through the material and dried in large, stiff blotches. Even where there was no blood, the socks felt like burlap against his feet. Finally, the scissors were passed to him. He cut one of his socks from ankle to toe, yet it still stuck to his foot, hanging suspended from his instep. He cut away the free material. As he carefully pulled on the remaining patch, tissue ripped away with it and he felt as if he were pouring hot grease into an open wound. He had to stop for a minute, debating whether to just rip away the material that remained, deciding not to. Now able to see the open flesh, he turned his head away and continued. Finally, the material came free, a square inch of flesh still attached to it. Relieved that he was half finished, Childs stared down at his instep. Blood trickled from a large, rough wound that looked like the work of a fish scaler. 'At least it's off,' he told himself. 'At least I'm in better shape than a lot of these motherfuckers.'

Some fairly cold beer and soda were brought to the tent. Each man took two cans of whichever he chose. It was three hours before the doctor and four corpsmen reached their hootch. They tried to help the more serious cases first. The doctor had already treated over a hundred men, but his expression still indicated disbelief at what he was seeing. He finally had to send three men back to the LZ to be medivacked to Da Nang, their feet so swollen and infected that it was impossible for them to get their boots back on. He bandaged these men and gave them sandals to wear. Before the doctor left, he told the company master sergeant to get some basins so the men would be able to soak their feet. Those that could walk to the showers were issued clean clothes. Some mail and packages had been waiting for them, and they spent the few hours before dusk reading letters and eating candy.

Kramer sat on the steps of the officers' hootch drinking a warm beer. He hadn't seen Milton or Tony 5, and was afraid to ask about them. Not until the previous evening when he arrived at An Hoa did it occur to him that he might have been the one who tripped the booby trap. He could have easily found out at the company office if anyone else had been wounded, but his guilt made him afraid to ask. He decided to wait until his platoon arrived. The faces of his men gave no hint of animosity; but the more he thought about it, the surer he was that it had been his fault. Kramer remembered how dazed he was after the NVA soldier came at him with a knife, and he knew he could have been thinking of nothing else until the booby trap went off. Everytime Kramer had looked at Sugar Bear, he had searched his face for a clue to what had happened. Knowing that he wouldn't be able to sleep until he found out, Kramer got up and walked towards the platoon hootch. A large figure walked by him in the darkness. Kramer turned around and asked, "Sugar Bear?"

"Lieutenant?"

"Yeah. Where you headed?"

"I've got a friend in supply. I wanna see if he can get us some boots."

"I hope he's a good friend."

"He ain't; but now that most of the men can't wear them, we should be able to get two pairs for everybody."

"How about coming over to my hootch a minute? I wanna talk to you."

Hearing Kramer tapping a beer can, Sugar Bear said, "Sure. You got another one of those?"

"Yeah, warm as piss."

"Wet, ain't it?"

They walked inside the officers' hootch, and Kramer handed Sugar Bear a beer. After a few seconds hesitation, he finally asked, "Tony 5 get out okay?"

"Yeah. I was the last one to shake his hand before he got on the chopper."

"He must have hated to leave."

"No shit, I think he did. The dude's a lifer."

"How much longer have you got?"

"Nineteen days."

"It doesn't even pay to call you sergeant then."

"What else you gonna call me?"

"Did you pick a right guide?"

"No. I didn't wanna switch squad leaders until we got out of there."

"Who's got seniority, Pablo?"

"Yes sir."

"Tell him he's right guide then."

"You don't have to tell him anything. He can read your mind."

"Yeah, I noticed."

"If he wasn't such a good dude, it'd be spooky."

There was a long pause before Kramer finally asked, "What happened?"

"It went off right in back of you."

Kramer realized what this meant, but he hesitated to affirm his thoughts. "What was it?"

"105 round, I think."

"Milton?"

"You don't know yet?"

"I figured I'd wait."

"All we found were parts of the radio . . . some hamburger. That was it."

"That's what I figured. . . . Anyone else get it?"

"No, it was weird. Tony 5 wasn't more than seven, eight yards behind Milton. A few pieces dinged his helmet, but that was it. Both of you

424

should have been dead. All the shrapnel must have went straight up. . . . It was weird."

There was another long pause before Kramer said, "I don't remember hitting any trip wire."

"You didn't. It was command detonated. . . . Hamilton blew away the Gook with one shot."

The fact that he hadn't been to blame didn't seem so important to Kramer now. "He must of figured I'd be near the radio."

"That's the way they work it."

"Nothing else happened during the last five days?"

"Just a lotta rain and a lotta marching."

"I guess you better see about those boots." Hearing Sugar Bear place the empty beer can on the floor, Kramer reached under his cot and handed him two more. "If anybody wants a few cans, just come in and get them. . . . Wait a minute. Where the hell is Trippitt?"

"You ain't heard yet?" Kramer shook his head. "Well here's some good news: he's been relieved. Remember that Gook Trippitt shot on Charlie Ridge, the one with the maggots in his ass? . . . MacGloughlin, the dude that found him, asked Trippitt when he was gonna get his two day R and R for capturing a prisoner. Mac and Trippitt never did cut it too good, so Trippitt tried to fuck him out of it because we didn't bring the Gook back. Mac got pissed, said we would have if Trippitt hadn't a shot him. Trippitt told Mac to get lost and Mac said something. Then Trippitt said he was gonna write him up for disrespect. But Mac made it legal first. They're getting up a court-martial against Trippitt for killing the Gook."

"Couldn't of happened to a nicer guy."

"There it is."

Chalice heard someone call out, "Professor." He remained sitting on his cot, hearing his nickname repeated until Pablo finally walked up to him. "Professor, the master sergeant wants you."

Chalice rose to his feet, noticing that Pablo was still looking at him. He left the tent and walked up to the door of the company office without entering it. "Somebody want me?"

The four men in the office continued typing and examining forms for a few seconds, then someone asked in an unconcerned tone, "Who are you?"

"Chalice."

"Come in a minute," the same voice said in a more interested tone. Chalice walked towards the man who had spoken. The company master sergeant stood up. Chalice remained silent, both puzzled and uneasy, while

425

the master sergeant looked him over as if he were examining a new type of weapon. "So you're the Sandman."

Finally understanding, Chalice wanted only to get away. He'd heard the word dozens of times, mostly whispered by strangers or the newer members of the platoon, never realizing it was himself being referred to. A faint, nervous smile appeared on his face as he repeated under his breath, "The Sandman."

"So you're the one who put the Phantom Blooker to sleep." Again Chalice remained silent, now too confused to even care about getting away. "I just wanted to get a look at you. . . . Nice work."

Chalice walked slowly out of the office, repeating to himself, "So I'm the Sandman." He continued walking, in no particular direction, on the verge of laughter, hysterical laughter. But the only indication of this was a faint smile and a distant look on his face.

"*Bang!*" someone shouted.

Too dazed to be startled, Chalice turned and saw three small Vietnamese boys playing soldiers with sticks that didn't even resemble rifles. He watched their excitement as they dodged behind crates, aiming these sticks and shouting, "Bang!" It was the incongruous yet familiar look on their faces and in their eyes that stunned him most.

One of the boys ran up to Chalice. "Marine, you souvenir me chopchop?"

Soon the other boys ran over, asking for food and cigarettes. Again they were merely children. Chalice felt relieved as he opened his shirt pocket and handed out some candy and cigarettes. From nowhere, they kept running towards him, alive and innocent. Soon over a dozen kids surrounded him, smiling and grabbing at his clothing, hanging on him by their small hands — laughing as only children can. When his cigarettes were gone, Chalice began walking away, some of the children still tugging at his clothing. He reached the platoon tent and stood alone but smiling — feeling alive. A rare breeze gusted around him.

He went inside with the intention of getting a cigarette and coming back out immediately. Forsythe handed him one. Chalice reached into his pants pocket for his lighter. The pocket was empty and his fingers passed through a hole in the bottom of it. Caring little, he told himself, 'Must have lost it. Have to buy a new one.' Chalice then looked down and saw that both his pants pockets had been slit by razor blades.

It was a week before two-thirds of the men could walk without pain. The fact that they had to stand lines as soon as they were able didn't encourage any quick recoveries. Childs and Hamilton stood outside the pla-

426

toon tent raking the dirt walkways when Childs said, "A little bit of herb sure would make this job a lot more pleasant."

"No shit it would."

"Let's run a joint."

Hamilton nodded his head eagerly. "Okay."

"What are we waiting for?"

"Beats the hell out of me."

"Well, take one out," Childs said irritably.

"*Me?* I don't have any."

"Well I sure as hell don't."

"So whata you getting me all excited for nothing for?" Hamilton asked.

"I thought you had some. . . . What about all the grass we bought before we went into the Arizona?"

"The shit got soaked after the first few days of rain."

"God, what a waste."

"We wouldn't of got a chance to smoke it anyway," Hamilton pointed out.

"I know, but it's still a waste."

"Not a complete waste. I threw it in a water buffalo pen."

"Oh, that's a real consolation." Childs spotted Forsythe walking into the platoon tent. "Oh, Reverend Forsythe, sir, could we please have an audience with you?"

Forsythe walked over and put his hand on Childs's shoulder. "Yes, my son, this is why I am here."

Childs bowed his head before saying, "Sir, I think getting wrecked would improve our morale."

"Bless you, my son. What finer method is there to gain an appreciation of God's universe?"

"You sure your church allows it?" Hamilton asked.

"*My son!* Verily I say unto you: it is the holiest of sacraments."

"You wouldn't have a wafer of it on you?" Childs asked.

"No, my son. God's infinite mercy has fallen short of providing me with said holy herb."

"Maybe you ought to try another God," Childs suggested.

Forsythe again placed his hand on Childs's shoulder. "It is not our place to question the ways of the All Mighty Lifer in the Sky."

"No offense, Your Reverency."

Forsythe saw Pablo walking into the tent and called out to him, "Illustrious Right Guide, what kinda shit you up to?"

Pablo turned and walked towards them, the bottle of malaria tabs in his hand answering Forsythe's question. Childs waved him away while saying, "We don't want any."

427

Pablo ignored him and took out three tablets. "I'm supposed to hand them out. After that, it's none of my business." He did this and they were quickly tossed to the ground. Pablo started to leave, but then changed his mind. "The Professor's been acting funny lately. One of you ought to find out what's bugging him."

"Sure, Maw," Childs answered, then qualified his tone by adding, "He was acting the same way when we came down from the canopy."

"Not as bad," Pablo replied.

"He writing in that little notebook again," Hamilton added.

Childs said jokingly, "Maybe he's a plant, CID."

"It has something to do with the Phantom Blooker," Forsythe said in a more serious tone.

"I guess it's because it's the first man he killed," Hamilton suggested.

Forsythe shook his head. "I think it's more than that."

Childs said, "Maybe he's sorry he didn't let the Phantom Blooker kill *you*."

"Could be," Forsythe agreed.

Pablo wasn't sure they were taking the matter seriously enough. "One of you ought to find out what's bugging him. . . . By the way, anybody that doesn't go to church today is gonna get roped into a working party."

Forsythe thanked Pablo for the warning, then said, "We'll take the Professor with us. The sleep'll do him good."

The chapel was crowded, more men sitting on the floor than on the benches. Chaplain Hindman had already started his sermon as Forsythe walked in the door and made his way to a rear corner. Childs, Hamilton, and Chalice followed him. They sat on the floor with their backs against the wall. Hindman was out of their view, so Childs closed his eyes and tried to get some sleep. Chalice sat in a daze, fumbling with a 50-caliber machine gun round. Hamilton took out a pornographic magazine and started leafing through it. When Forsythe saw this, he leaned over Chalice to get a better look. Childs opened his eyes long enough to see the magazine, and he also began to stare at it.

"— atheists back home. She's the one that tried to get Christ taken out of our schools. I know you men find it as hard to understand as I do. She says by us praying in the schools, we're taking away her rights. All I want to know is don't we have any rights to worship the Lord Our God, Jesus Christ? Is His name filth that our schools must be cleansed of? I'll bet she believes that Americans are just lucky, that the fact we live in the wealthiest and most beautiful country in the world has nothing to do with God's

428

will. Well she's wrong. It's by God's grace that we have such fine schools. What type of evil person would begrudge God five minutes of prayers in the schools that we built with His help? I'll tell you what type of person, her, this Madelyn Murray. I cringe when I think about what God must have in store for her. She even wants to have "In God We Trust" taken off our money. Can you believe that? It bothers her that someone might look at a penny and be reminded of God's love for us and ours for Him. What would George Washington say if he knew that they wanted to take "In God We Trust" off his dollar bill, or Thomas Jefferson, or Abraham Lincoln, or William Jennings Bryan, or Andrew —"

"William Jennings Bryan, how'd he get in there?" Childs asked with surprise.

"Cross of gold," Hamilton pointed out in a self-satisfied tone.

"Ooooh, now I understand."

"Hey, you skipped a page!"

"Don't get excited, Forsythe. It was just an advertisement."

"No. I saw her tits. Turn —"

"— letters from your mothers. I can't remember how many times they've asked me if you're taking care of yourselves and not smoking too much. I'm sure you've all noticed what they're printing on the outside of your cigarettes these days: 'Caution: Cigarette smoking may be hazardous to your health.' The people in Washington put this there for your own good. Life is too great a gift to risk for what little pleasure you can get from a cigarette. Just because they give you a little pack with each box of C-rations, you don't have to smoke them. Don't even give them to your friends, even if they ask. Just throw them away. I've written to the President telling him that they shouldn't even give them to you, and I'm going to speak to Colonel Nash about the same thing. God's gift of life is too precious a thing to risk on the mere gratification of your senses. I think —"

Childs rarely smoked, but he suddenly had an urge for a cigarette. He reached across and got a pack out of Forsythe's pocket, then handed a cigarette to Forsythe. Soon their corner of the chapel was enveloped in a light haze.

Someone turned towards them and said gruffly, "Hey, you ain't allowed to smoke in the chapel."

Forsythe shifted his eyes nervously around the room before saying, "I don't see no sign."

Chalice had seemed oblivious to the entire scene, but he now started to shake his head while repeating, "Smoking is hazardous to your health." Suddenly, he began to laugh, and all the men near him turned to see what was happening.

Making no attempt to muffle his voice, Forsythe said, "Quit tickling the Professor, Childs."

"I ain't tickling him."

"Well quit goosing him then."

A tough-looking Marine sitting in front of them turned around and said gruffly, "Shut the fuck up!" Chalice stopped laughing, but he continued to grin at the Marine.

Somebody whispered, "That's the Sandman."

The Marine glanced angrily at this man and said, "I don't care who the hell he is." He then turned back to Chalice. "You better wipe that fucking smile off your face."

Chalice didn't. The Marine seemed ready to jump him when Hamilton said with a grin, "Uh uh. I'll *fuck* you up."

Now two of the Marine's friends also turned around and began staring at Hamilton. Forsythe couldn't resist getting involved. "You shouldn't talk to the Professor like that. This man's got a college degree."

Childs wasn't too anxious to get into a fight. He noticed Sugar Bear sitting directly in front of the three Marines and taking up more room than all of them combined. "Forsythe's right. Ain't he, Sugar Bear?"

Sugar Bear nodded his head while answering with a grin, "There it is." When the Marines saw him, they turned their attention to Chaplain Hindman.

Chalice walked back to the company area alone. Confused images and phrases drove all consciousness of the present from his mind. There was no sense of surprise when he found himself standing in front of the platoon tent even before he realized he had left the chapel. It was as if he had accepted the illusion of being transported from one point to another without the necessity of moving the distance between them. He had no desire to enter the platoon tent, or to go anywhere. Something told him that he couldn't, wouldn't be allowed to remain standing there; and he accepted this as true and started walking again. Only the barbwire fence prevented him from leaving the perimeter. He could go no farther, nor did he want to turn around. Chalice suddenly realized he was standing alone and motionless. People would think this strange. They would ask him why, and he wouldn't be able to tell them. His actions were more wary than nervous as he turned his head to see if anyone was looking at him. No one was, but he knew that if he continued to stand there someone would spot him. He noticed a U-shaped stack of ammo boxes. No one would be able to see him from there. Chalice walked slowly towards them and sat down inside the base of the U. The thought 'Smoking is hazardous to your health' began repeating itself in his mind, and a smile came to his face. Soon he was laughing.

Only when this laughter stopped did he realize how strange he'd been acting — not for the past week, he had always been conscious of this, but merely for the last few hours when he'd been acting even stranger. He remembered how Pablo had looked at him while passing out the malaria tabs. At first Chalice thought about this as if he were pondering the actions of another person — "he" instead of "I" — but then he realized that this was strange in itself. "I'm fucked up!" he said aloud, and then more softly, "My mind's fucked up." He somehow sensed that this admission was necessary before he could untwist his thoughts. The mere act of saying it brought him completely back to the present — at first nervous, but then gaining control over himself and becoming calmer. His former behavior now seemed even stranger, but also somewhat amusing. He wondered why he had wanted to be alone, then told himself it was for this very purpose, to gain control over his thoughts. Feeling odd sitting between the ammo boxes, he was still confident that he could think things out. Suddenly, the surreal image that had been haunting him flashed through his mind in a tableau — the figure of a man standing before him with an expression of insane surprise, the only movement in the scene being a pattern of blood expanding on his shoulder. 'Not yet!' Chalice told himself, and by a conscious effort he was able to erase this image from his mind. Surprised that he had been able to control his thoughts, Chalice began purposefully to think, trying to arrange his thoughts logically. Intuition told him to start with something simple — the reason he was alone. It now seemed obvious. He had tried to justify the state of mental isolation by the physical state. Convinced of this idea, he sought the cause of his mental isolation. Vague reasons came to him, but they were swept away by the realization that the very method of his thinking was artificial, too structured. But he had no alternative. Besides, it seemed to be working, helping him to control himself. "They're not like me," he whispered, but then added, "They don't act like me either. . . . They must think I can't take it, that I'm crazy." His voice had gradually become louder, and the idea that he was talking to himself scared him. He continued anyway, only in a softer tone. "I'm more intelligent. . . . They don't realize. They don't understand." Again a disturbed smile appeared on his face as he thought, 'Or wander around talking to themselves.' "I am so much smarter . . . guiltier." Then a far more disturbing thought came to him — that it wasn't what had happened, but how he'd reacted or didn't react — that he was forcing himself to react and feeling guilty about having to do so.

431

Chalice touched his shirt pocket, then hesitated before taking out his 'notebook.' Write it down. Write it all down. Something permanent. He fumbled with his ball-point pen while trying to get it to write, pressing it to the notebook harder and harder until the pressure from it ripped out the page. He tried again, only more slowly, this time moving the pen in a circle. When it finally began to work, he wrote, "Madelyn Murray — atheist In God we trust." He skipped a line and wrote, "Smoking hazardous to health." He began to laugh, but calmly and while thinking, 'Who'd believe it? Who'd fucking believe it?' This thought bothered him, but he still found it amusing. He looked at the number atop the previous page. 'Fifty-six . . . it's all here. . . . Who'd believe it?'

Suddenly he was startled by Forsythe's voice. "What the hell you doing?"

Hamilton, Childs, and Forsythe stood looking down at him. As soon as he was able to put away his notebook, Chalice felt more comfortable. Now glad to see them, he answered, "Not much, just taking it easy."

"How come you wandered off after church?"

"I had to take care of some shit, do some things." He held his arms out as he said, "Join me in my humble abode." They sat down, and Chalice asked them, "What are *you* doing walking around here?"

Childs took out a pack of joints and held them up to him. "We got the time, and we're looking for the place."

"This looks like it," Hamilton suggested.

Chalice watched as Childs took out some matches. At first pleased with the thought of getting stoned, he suddenly remembered how removed from reality he had just been and was afraid to let go of it again. "Don't you guys know smoking is hazardous to your health?"

Childs had begun to inhale, but immediately burst into a fit of coughing. Finally able to catch his breath, he said while shaking his head, "Did you fucking believe that sermon?"

"It made more sense than most of them," Forsythe said in mock seriousness.

Chalice waved the joint by. "That isn't saying much."

When Childs finally exhaled, he asked Chalice, "Aren't you gonna join us?"

"Yeah, in a minute. I don't wanna get too stoned."

As Forsythe inhaled, the look on his face told those around him that he had just thought of something to say. In his impatience, he exhaled before he needed to. "That's what they ought to do — legalize it with 'Smoking is hazardous to your health' printed on the box."

"But it ain't," Hamilton objected.

432

"Whatever it does to your health, it's plenty good for your mind," Childs pointed out.

"I know that," Forsythe admitted, "but we'll compromise."

"Yeah. That's the way we'll have to do it," Chalice agreed, "just like they do in Washington."

"Do you think old LBJ will go for it?"

"Why not?" Chalice replied. "He's an honorable man. They're *all* honorable men."

"What are they doing in politics then?" Childs asked.

"Honorable men have to eat too," Forsythe pointed out.

Chalice took a long drag from the joint, then waited patiently to exhale before saying, "They do everything for our own good. Why should they legalize something if there's any chance it's as dangerous as booze, driving a car, or football? . . . They do everything they can to keep us alive. Look at the fine rifles they give us. They never jam unless you try to shoot them."

"Yeah. If it's Mattel, it's swell," Forsythe commented.

"I only wish they'd spend a little more and buy us AK-47's," Childs added.

The marijuana wasn't as strong as usual, but it began to slowly take effect. The men leaned back against the ammo boxes, remaining silent except for occasional, lethargic comments. Forsythe remembered he had a radio in his pocket, and he took it out. To their displeasure, Armed Forces Radio, the only American station, was playing its weekly two hours of polka music.

"Ain't the Marine Corps great?" Childs commented. "Music for everybody. They aren't satisfied dividing it up between Country and Western, Soul, and Rock. They try to keep the Polacks happy, too. I —"

"Even Ski couldn't stand that polka music," Hamilton interrupted. "He says his old man used to turn it up real loud before he'd beat his old lady." Hamilton had intended his remark to be humorous, but as soon as he said Ski's name he realized it wouldn't be.

A few minutes passed without a word, then Childs lit another joint. The aroma of it immediately relaxed everybody. Chalice was trying to get a long drag out of it when he suddenly heard some footsteps. His cheeks were puffed out and he didn't even have time to take the joint from his lips before he saw Kramer staring down at him. Chalice was still trying to decide what to do when he noticed the surprised look on Kramer's face as his lips mouthed, "Oh my God." Kramer turned and walked away.

Chalice immediately exhaled and asked, "What do you think he'll do?"

433

Those around him seemed less concerned, and Childs said, "What can he do, send us to Nam?"

"He might do something," Hamilton said with more concern.

"It's too late to worry about it now," Forsythe pointed out. "He ain't a bad dude — not like Lieutenant S, but he don't fuck with us."

Hamilton was almost as worried as Chalice. "Let's split."

While Chalice snuffed out the joint, Childs stood up and began walking along the edge of the perimeter. Wanting to avoid getting caught for a working party, the others followed. They wandered relaxed and aimless until it began to drizzle and they took cover in a bunker. A plank hung suspended a few inches above the dirt floor, and all except Chalice sat down upon it. He leaned across the bunker's shooting support, looking out across the quiet, green valley. The roughness of the shooting support against his forearms caused him to glance down. The once smooth wood was now carved and inked with names, initials, hometowns, and a few dates. Chalice read them to himself, trying to picture the men who had written them, wondering each time if this or that man was now dead, if nothing more than these scratches were left of him. He noticed a question mark, and tried to make out the almost obscured words before it, finally reading aloud, " 'What's the difference between the Marine Corps and the Boy Scouts?' "

"I haven't found any," Childs answered.

"I give up. What is the difference?" Forsythe asked.

Chalice read the scrawled answer. " 'The Boy Scouts have adult leadership.' " Forsythe rose to see what else was written on the shooting counter as Chalice asked, "How come nobody ever collected the bounty on Martin?"

"That was for killing him," Hamilton answered. "The sonofabitch'd sooner be a vegetable for the rest of his life than let the dude collect."

"That's what I call spite," Childs commented.

Forsythe had found some more graffiti, and he read aloud, " 'The Marine Corps is a Communist plot to take over the world,' not bad. Here's one for Childs, 'I love the fucking Marine Corps, and the Marine Corps loves fucking me.' Oh this one's beautiful: 'Lifers are like flies — they eat shit and bother people.' "

"Here's another," Chalice said, "Killing for peace is like fucking for chastity.' . . . 'God is not dead. He's just AWOL.' "

"Hope they bust the sonofabitch when they find him," Childs mumbled. He took Chalice's pen and wrote while saying aloud, "Violence must be eradicated. Kill all the violent people you know."

Chalice was trying to memorize this graffiti so he could later write it down in his notebook, when he began to wonder how much more permanent that would make it. He looked up and saw Forsythe carving something into the counter with his bayonet. "What are you writing?"

"Just my initials."

"God, sometimes I think you're twelve years old," Childs remarked.

"I wish I was."

"You could of fooled me."

"I wish I was," Forsythe repeated thoughtfully. "When I was doing a lot of acid, most of my trips were back to when I was a little kid . . . nice."

"Didn't that remind you of your father?" Chalice asked.

"You gotta expect a bum trip every once in a while. . . . No. Even then it was nice. It's all a game when you're a little kid, nothing too important, choosing a red lollipop or a yellow one. Even if you choose wrong, the worst thing that can happen is your old man slapping you around. Then you can start all over again."

"You used to get slapped around for choosing the wrong lollipop?" Childs asked.

"You know what I mean. . . . One day you realize that it isn't a game anymore, that it hasn't been for a long time. Things begin to count. You have to make choices you can't make twice. You start trying to figure things out so you don't choose wrong . . . because if you do you gotta live with it. . . . You can't get punished and start all over again."

"Like joining the Marine Corps," Childs commented.

"No . . . yeah, that's right, for you yes."

"And not you?" Chalice asked.

"No. I had to. It wasn't much of a choice."

"You could have gone to the induction physical on acid or something," Chalice pointed out.

"No chance. That's why I *had* to go into the Marine Corps. . . . At first drugs were nice, but it got so I was eating them like candy, not even knowing what they were, or caring even. It got so drugs were all there was — which ain't bad when you're on them. But when you come down, you *really* come down.

"If it was just me, I never would have realized what was happening. But then I started looking at the friends I'd made. They were so fucked-up I couldn't even stand them unless I was spaced out too. I almost went batshit when I couldn't get any more dope, but I was glad too. That was the only way I could stop. If —"

"Wait a minute," Childs cut in. "What's that got to do with joining the Marine Corps?"

"I had to join because I got arrested for drugs."

"But you just said you went off drugs."

"That's the amazing part. I —"

"Oh great. Let's hear the amazing part."

"See I was still hanging around Berkeley, but I'd been off drugs for about two weeks when I got arrested for selling grass. If I had —"

"How'd you get caught?" Chalice asked.

"That's just it. The whole thing was a frame-up."

"You got a lawyer, didn't you?"

"Hell yeah. I got one of those public defenders. He'd just graduated Berkeley — honors and everything. Man, you wouldn't believe how freaked out this dude was. I think it might have been his first case. He comes up to me all excited like I saved his life or somethin', telling me not to worry because he had it all figured out. I said, 'Great,' and started explaining how the two narcs framed me. He stops me and says: 'Don't even worry about that. I've got it all figured out.' And I said, 'But how you gonna prove it's a frame job if you don't know all the facts?' And he said, 'We're not!' And I said, 'What?' And he said, 'You're gonna plead guilty.' This really threw me. I got all excited, but he told me not to worry about it, that he had it all figured out. And I told him to figure it out again without me pleading guilty. That's when he started explaining about how the law was unconstitutional and how he was gonna file all sorts of suits and how someday my case was gonna be just as famous as Marberry vs. Madison and all those other cases in the history books. And I explained to the dude about how I wanted to get out of jail, not make history. But that didn't phase him. He kept on trying to get me to plead guilty. Just when I thought he was ready to give up, he said okay, I could plead no lo contendre or something. That means no contest, and after five minutes of legal bullshit I realized it meant guilty, only spelled differently. Boy, was —"

"When's this story gonna end?" Childs cut in.

But Chalice said, "Shut up, man. I'm interested."

"Okay, to make it short he finally gave up and let me plead innocent because it didn't make that much difference anyway — 'the principle was the same.' So when my trial came up I pleaded innocent and he had all kinds of notes and looked real confident and I figured everything was gonna be all right. Then the first narc took the stand. He starts telling all kinds of ridiculous lies, and I'm writing 'he's lying' all over this yellow pad and shoving it in front of my lawyer and he's nodding his head real confident like. But when it was his turn to cross-examine, he said, 'No questions, your honor.' I almost shit! And while the second narc is getting on the stand I'm telling my lawyer he's crazy and everything, and all he says

436

is, 'Don't worry about it. I've got it all figured out.' I told the dude I'd just about had it with the way he had everything figured out, but he said they'd never take my word against two narcs anyway. . . . Maybe he was right, but I almost went batshit when the second narc starts lying his ass off too.

"So then the judge tells the defense to call its witnesses, and of course we didn't have any, and I'm sitting there nervous as hell, all ready to get carted off to jail. But then my lawyer gets up and starts talking. I gotta hand it to that dude, it was the coolest speech I ever heard in my life — all about the rights of the individual, oppression of the state, trying to legislate morals, and something about capitalism too. Just listening to the dude calmed me down. It was like watching Perry Mason on TV, only a hundred times better. It didn't even seem like I was the one on trial. The whole rest of the trial I just leaned back in my chair and took it all in. Even when the verdict was ready, and the judge said, 'Will the defendant please rise and face the jury,' I just sat there looking around calm as can be. Then the judge said it again and my lawyer poked me in the ribs. Man, I was shocked as shit when I saw that judge staring at *me*. But it wasn't until I was standing up looking that jury foreman in the eye that it really hit me — *I was the defendant! . . . That's* when I knew it was all over.

"That fucked-up lawyer of mine was more surprised than I was when the sonofabitch said, 'Guilty.' He looked like somebody was chokin' him to death. And when I heard the jerk mumble, 'I knew we should of pleaded guilty,' I almost *did* choke him to death."

Childs cut in, "I'm gonna choke *you* to death if you don't finish this fucked-up story and tell us what it has to do with joining the Marine Corps."

"Take it easy, man. I'm getting to it."

"I'll believe it when you do."

"Well it turned out the judge wasn't such a bastard after all. Because it was my first offense, he said I could go in the service instead of going to jail. Believe it or not, that sounded pretty good at the time. I was probably about to get drafted anyway. My lawyer starts raving about how we're gonna appeal and everything, so the judge has a conference with him. I couldn't hear much of it, but I think he asked, 'What are you trying to do to this kid?' But my trusty lawyer wouldn't have any of it. He starts giving his speech all over again while I'm standing there wondering if it's all just a bad trip. The judge finally holds up his hand to shut him up, then looks at me and says, 'Jail or the service?' And *here the fuck I am.*"

"Took you a hell of a long time to get here," Childs commented.

"But why the Marine Corps?" Chalice asked.

"The Crotch was the only one that would take me. That's why a lot of guys join. There were about ten of us in my PI platoon alone. One guy had been arrested a dozen times. When you fill out the forms, the recruiters tell you to say you've never been arrested. By the time they find out you lied, you're already halfway through Parris Island. And if you haven't been in any trouble since you've been in, they usually let you stay."

"I bet you wished you *were* in jail when you got to PI."

"Naw, that place was just like home — three fathers yelling at me instead of one. . . . The fucking truth is I needed something like the Marine Corps — people ordering me around, no time to think, no *choices* to make. One thing about drugs is they fucking disorient you. You don't know whether you're up or down. They take all the fucking order out of your life — which ain't as good as it sounds. That's why the Crotch wasn't such a bad thing. I mean I didn't need *this much* fucking discipline, but I needed some of it. Besides, like Tony 5 said, I've met some of the best motherfuckers I've ever known in the Crotch, better than Berkeley. . . . They seemed cool at first, but then they started looking phonier and phonier, always screaming about revolution, calling everybody a fascist. You should of heard some of the speeches, all the same bullshit, as bad as Johnson or any of those politicians. . . . I gotta admit I've never seen so many intelligent people in one place, but they're even better at fooling themselves than a bunch of holy rollers. Berzerkley's the only place I've ever been where political fantasies are more important than sexual fantasies."

"I thought you liked the freaks," Chalice asked.

"I did . . . but they weren't real, not like the guys you meet in the Crotch."

"You call this *real?*"

"No — well yeah. I know it's like we're playing cowboys sometimes, but at least we know it. They don't."

"But they don't go around killing people," Chalice argued.

"That's what he means," Childs cut in.

Forsythe ignored Childs and said, "I'm not sure they wouldn't if they could. When they call themselves revolutionaries, they really believe it. They think the whole world is gonna change if they just keep pulling mass temper tantrums."

"But they don't go around killing people," Chalice insisted.

"No, not like us, not as many. But a lot of them don't mind getting people killed. One time we had this demonstration that turned into a riot. I did my part — knocked a cop on his ass with a brick. We trashed his ass. I'd seen those pigs do the same thing to us, so it didn't bug me a bit.

438

. . . *Then* they started shooting. . . . The guy right next to me got killed. I couldn't believe it. Two days later we had this memorial service for him. I'd never seen so many people on the same street. They started giving speeches about how the pigs were out to kill us, how he was an un-armed demonstrator. We all got real excited, yelling, 'Off the pigs! Off the pigs!' Pretty soon we had another riot going — smashing windows, beating up cops. I never felt so great. Then I saw this cop backing away from us. He was scared shitless, more scared than I was, everybody yelling, 'Off the pigs! . . .' The cops started shooting again, and another one of us got killed."

"Sounds great," Childs commented.

Forsythe ignored him and continued. "We got up another big funeral, even bigger than the first. When they started giving speeches again, blam-ing the cops and trying to start another riot, that's when I realized they wanted the same thing to happen again, to get even more people for their next riot. Sure it was the pigs that shot him, but they wanted it to happen. They didn't care how many of us got killed, screaming as if they had noth-ing to do with it. . . . Most of the freaks were all right. It was just the speechmakers. From then on I stayed away from the screamers and stuck to dope. I —"

"How do you know you won't go back to drugs when you get out of the Crotch?" Chalice asked.

"No chance, not like before. Dope can make the world a lot nicer, but too much of it makes things worse."

"What are you gonna do when you get out?" Hamilton asked.

"I want to go to Europe, see —"

Chalice cut him off by saying, "That's what I was planning! . . . But most of my friends have already gone."

"You and me, we can go together."

"Great! . . . But you get out way before I do."

"I'll wait for you."

"No shit?"

"Sure, Professor. I'll wait for you."

"That'll be cool. We can go halves on a Volkswagen camper with our separation pay."

"Yeah. . . . Maybe motorcycles 'ud be even cooler."

Hamilton said in a left-out tone, "Sounds like it'd be fun."

"You can come with us," Forsythe replied.

"*Yeah!* . . . But I'd have to check with my girl."

"I know what that means," Childs cut in.

"How about you?" Chalice asked.

"I've already been there. Europe's just as fucked up as any other place."

Still excited, Forsythe turned back to Chalice. "I knew a dude in Berzerkley, best motherfucker I met there, he used to tell me all about when he was in Europe. He had a project: to get laid in every big city on the continent. Name any city and he could tell you where the whorehouses were: Paris, start at the Eiffel Tower, go down Rue de Whatshisfuck, make a left at Rue Joan of Arc or something, then a right; Hamburg, anywhere, they're all whores; Zurich, corner of Jeckyl and Hyde; Stockholm, you —"

Excited far more by Forsythe's tone than the idea itself, Chalice cut him off. "*Great!* Maybe we can take him along."

"He OD'd."

There was hardly a day that it didn't rain; nor a patch of ground not covered by at least four inches of soft, orange mud. As soon as a man was able to put his boots on, he had to begin standing lines and going on working parties. This caused a good deal of griping, but being able to sleep in dry tents at least two nights a week did a lot to help the men to appreciate An Hoa. As soon as enough of them had recovered from their cases of immersion foot, the battalion resumed normal operations. Every platoon sent out a patrol each day and an ambush each night. Occasionally there would be platoon and company-size patrols, but they always returned to the battalion area before dusk.

The men realized that as soon as enough replacements had arrived, they would be ordered back to the bush. As always, there were just as many rumors about where they would be sent as possibilities — Phu Loc 6, Dodge City, the Phu Nons, and of course the Arizona. However, there was now one difference in these rumors, and this was the approach of the lunar new year, Tet. Everyone knew something big was going to happen, and the only speculation was about how big and where. Soon a new rumor became far more prevalent than any of the others. It involved a place very few of the men had ever head of, and was based upon facts they had read in service newspapers and head over the radio, added to by news clippings sent from home, and often greatly expanded when retold. It concerned something they could understand far better than the type of war they were now fighting. The men knew that even if only a portion of this rumor were true, it still portended the greatest single event of the war; and no one doubted that he would be involved. Ominous as it seemed, most of the men viewed this event with anxious anticipation, for this would be it, in one place and at one time, huge and devastating, the final battle — Khe Sanh.

440

It was an hour before dusk, and Second Platoon was just returning from an all day patrol. Since dawn, the rain had been coming down in a steady, unvarying drizzle. Each man's trousers were covered up to the knees with a thick coating of foamlike mud that made their legs appear encased in bright orange plaster casts. This sight would have been humorous to them if it hadn't been such a common and bothersome occurrence. The men gathered in front of the platoon tent waiting for their turn to scrape the mud off their trousers and boots with one of the sticks that was being passed around. The master sergeant stuck his head out of the office long enough to call Pablo to get the mail. This was welcome news for all the men, all except Kramer.

He entered the officers' hootch and sat down on his cot. Three times since he had returned from Da Nang, Pablo had approached him holding a letter. Each time he was sure it was the one he feared. It hadn't been. Kramer knew that every day made less likely the chance that he would receive it; but sometimes he doubted the truth of this — thinking, 'Maybe she just threw it away.' He could never really accept this thought. It seemed impossible that she would decide without letting him know.

Again Pablo walked through the door of the officers' hootch with a letter. Kramer reached out for it, thanking Pablo before he could leave. This time Kramer was sure, positive. Without looking at the envelope, he watched Pablo go out the door. Kramer had no need to look. The parchmentlike paper had a strange, foreign feel. He finally lowered his eyes and saw an ornate and unfamiliar handwriting on the envelope. The absence of a return address was more expected than surprising. There seemed little need to open the envelope or to wonder about what it contained. Instead, Kramer's mind turned back to those hours when he had been with her. This was not the first time he had tried to convince himself that they could not have happened. What were these few moments that they could take the entire remainder of his life and make it a self-destructive farce. He no longer tried to belittle the things she had said, to pass them off for their simplicity, now admitting what he had realized then — that there was truth in this simplicity. It was impossible for him to think about her except as someone within a dream. Yet he knew that she was more real than he himself, and that his only hope was to somehow be able to forget her.

Again he looked down at the letter. Opening it seemed unnecessary — nothing more than a ceremony. His fingers moved across the characters of his name. as if reading them by braille. He actually thought about burning the letter without reading it, thus preventing himself from ever really knowing. The childish, wishing nature of this thought began to seem more pathetic than embarrassing. Kramer took his bayonet and carefully

441

opened the letter. The piece of paper with his address on it was the first thing he saw, then a note.

Only now have I been able to do this. I will always remember. Some day you will understand.

                                                                    Tuyen

Kramer read these words with a sense of acceptance, telling himself no other conclusion would have been possible. Still, as he watched, it wasn't his hands that flicked open the lighter and began burning the note. While the flame did its work, Kramer remembered the Polaroid photograph in his wallet. He hesitated taking it out, and was finally prevented from doing so by footsteps upon the stairs of the hootch.

Colonel Nash entered, followed by Lieutenant Howell. They had come looking for Lieutenant Forest, the new company commander. Instead of leaving, they decided to wait for him. Kramer was glad to have something to take his mind off the letter. Solely for this reason, he asked Nash if he had any news about Khe Sanh.

"Just the same news: more mortar barrages and more men."

"What about casualties?" Kramer asked.

"More of those, too."

"Do you think we'll end up there?" Howell asked.

"They're not gonna stop the buildup now. It's just a question of who gets tapped."

"It kind of reminds you of something else," Kramer commented.

"Too much like something else."

Kramer was surprised by this answer. "You really think there's a chance it'll be the same thing?"

"No. It's *too much* like Dien Bien Phu — the concentration of troops, the artillery, even the zigzag trenches. They're too smart. It can't be that simple."

"But what if it is that simple?" Howell asked. "Can they pull it off?"

"It's not a question of that. They know we'll make them pay. It depends upon how many men they think it's worth."

"That's what I don't understand." Nash nodded to Kramer to indicate the same thing was bothering him. "It's not worth a damn thing, just a piece of ground."

"I know," Nash agreed. "They've never tried to hold anything yet."

"Our air power could level the place," Howell pointed out.

"If they can't hold it, why —"

Nash cut Kramer off. "There's only two ways you can look at it: either it's Dien Bien Phu all over again, or it isn't. If they think it is, then they'll risk everything in one shot. I can't believe they will. They've kept fighting the same type of war for twenty years. Why would they suddenly lose their patience? They must know that no matter how bad the defeat, we'll never pull out because we've lost a few square miles of jungle."

"Maybe they just want us away from their supply trails," Howell suggested.

"That's bullshit. We've got a lot less control over the area than we think we have. Besides, supply routes can be changed. It isn't worth the price they'd have to pay."

"But if they don't want Khe Sanh, what do they want?"

"The only way they'd pay the price is if they thought it would end the war; and if we know it won't, so do they."

"How else can you explain it?" Kramer asked.

"I can't. I can only guess. . . . They've done something, and we've reacted to it. They do more of the same, and so do we. We must be doing exactly what they want."

"But what *do* they want?" Howell asked.

"I don't know. I just have the feeling that whatever we're doing is wrong, and we won't have to wait any longer than Tet to find out why."

It was twelve o'clock and for the first time in a week it hadn't rained since dawn. A perfectly clear sky promised at least a few more hours of sunshine. Sugar Bear entered the platoon tent and told everyone to fall out for a company formation. First Platoon was on a patrol, and the master sergeant began speaking as soon as the remaining three platoons quieted down.

"Men, this is the first sunny day we've had in a week, so I decided we should take advantage of it —"

"They're gonna fuck with us."

"We're gonna have a parade."

"We're all gonna run around nude."

"— The master sergeant from Echo Company and I made a little bet between us —"

"How many men they can get killed."

"— I told him there wasn't anything Hotel Company couldn't do better than Echo —"

"We're gonna invade Red China."

"— So he challenged us to a basketball game. There's five cases of beer on this, and you men can help me drink the winnings —"

"I only drink with friends."

"He's a lifer. He'll never pay."

"— You can see behind you that there's about half a foot of mud on the basketball court —"

"You call that vacant lot a basketball court?"

"— That means we'll have to scrape it off first —"

"Are you shitting me?"

"Why don't we just have a swimming meet?"

"I'll bet he lost his cigarette lighter or something."

"— I've got some twelve-inch planks here that'll do the job in no time —"

"Good. Call me when you're done."

"Why don't you and Forest do it then?"

"— I know we'll be doing more work than Echo Company, but at least we'll have the home court advantage —"

"Great. I hate road games."

"You don't know what the word home means."

"— We've each got a platoon on patrol, so we'll play one platoon at a time, two out of three wins the beer, twenty point games."

"That's so none of the lifers'll run out of fingers and toes."

Though the men griped about the master sergeant's idea, they only did so because playing basketball was something they were told they had to do. Most of them were anxious to compete with another company. They had been thoroughly trained to identify with their various units. This created competitive attitudes between squads, platoons, and companies. On the company level, this competitiveness was less than good natured.

No one was too enthusiastic about clearing the mud from the basketball court, but the sloppiness of the job turned it into a joke. Three or four men handled each plank — placing it down on its edge, then slowly pushing it and the foamlike mud before it from the court. When the job was finished, there were piles of mud at the edges of the court and thick coats of it on anyone who had helped pile it there. The boards were left upright to keep the mud from sliding back. A thin layer remained; but if the ball was smashed instead of dribbled, it bounced fairly well.

Second Platoon was assigned the first game because First Platoon was still on patrol. Nobody had to tell Sugar Bear to take charge. Echo Company hadn't arrived yet, and he ordered anyone interested to get out on the court for some practice. Kramer merely watched until he saw that Sugar Bear didn't know much about basketball, then he took over. A dozen men volunteered to play. Kramer divided them into forwards and guards. There wasn't much difference in height among them. When Sugar Bear realized this, he immediately yelled for Roads who showed little enthusiasm as he stepped out on to the court.

444

The basketball was quickly coated with mud, and the backboard (the side of a large crate) was at an angle to the hoop. This made it almost impossible for Kramer to tell who was any good. He finally decided on Sugar Bear as the center because as long as he was under the basket no one else could get near it; Roads and Sinclaire as the forwards; and Hamilton, Pablo, Hemrick, and Chalice to alternate as guards.

Echo Company marched towards the court in formation, and was immediately met by derisive whistles and shouts. As soon as they broke formation, they arranged themselves along one side of the court. Those men from Hotel Company that had been standing there quickly joined the rest of the company on the opposite side. The two master sergeants shook hands and started making the rules. Both of them appeared to have had a good taste of the stakes already. Because there was no one either impartial enough or willing to act as referee, the master sergeants decided that when a player fouled he should call it on himself. The men were anxious to start, so this was the only rule agreed upon.

A platoon from Echo Company took the court to get some practice. They immediately began complaining about the mud as if it were a Hotel Company plot. The men from Second Platoon watched eagerly. They could never have been convinced that they had looked equally inept a few minutes earlier. Soon the shouts of the spectators forced the game to get under way.

Echo Company took the ball in from behind the backboard. The men on the sidelines began yelling and acting as if they'd already drunk the beer. A player from Echo Company tried to dribble in the wrong spot, and when the ball stuck in the mud he ran by it. Pablo grabbed it up and tossed it under the basket to Sugar Bear who immediately tried a shot. After missing, he got the rebound and shot again, then four more times. By the sixth try, all ten players were shoulder to shoulder underneath the basket waiting for the rebound. Roads suddenly sprang up from within this shoving, groveling mass and tipped the ball in.

The game continued in a frenzy, the players accepting without thought the reality that no one would ever call a foul on himself. This meant there were no fouls, and therefore no rules save one: If the ball went through the hoop, it was two points for the last team that touched it. This also simplified the skills required. Rarely did anyone bother to dribble except for show. While tackling was frowned upon, especially by the spectators, it nevertheless became an often-used tactic. The game had very little resemblance to basketball; but both teams were at the same disadvantage, and this satisfied the players if not the spectators.

The score was 16 to 12 in favor of Echo Company when Pablo decided

445

to drive in for a lay-up. He got within six feet of the basket before being knocked flat on his back. Only by grabbing the ball away was Kramer able to stop the game long enough for Pablo to be helped off the court, too groggy to notice the three distinct footprints on his chest. Hemrick went into the game to replace him. His first shot sailed over the backboard, enabling Echo Company to score two more points. Kramer repeatedly called time-out only to be ignored. Luckily, the next attempt at the basket went right into his hands. By holding the ball he was finally able to stop the game.

Kramer led his men to their side of the court. "All right, we've got one man who can dribble, one who can pass, and one who can shoot. This should be enough, but unfortunately it's the same man. All they need is two more points. Let's see if we can get the ball to Roads."

As the rest of Second Platoon's team dashed out onto the court, Hemrick told Chalice to go in for him. The first time Chalice got the ball, somebody jerked his head back from behind and he was barely able to pass it to Roads. While sitting in the mud, he saw Roads loft the ball through the hoop.

"Eighteen to fourteen, get serious," somebody yelled.

Hamilton intercepted the ball as it was brought in, too excited to notice that he had sent the man it was intended for sliding ten feet on his stomach. Hamilton's quick lay-up made the score 18 to 16. A basket by Roads after a pass from Hamilton tied the game. Again a man from Echo Company tried to dribble the ball. It hit his foot and Chalice retrieved it. He looked for Roads and found him lying on the ground underneath a man from Echo Company. Hearing quick, sloshing steps behind him, Chalice knew he better get rid of the ball fast. In desperation, he aimed it at the basket, and with a man from Echo Company hanging on his neck, watched it float through the hoop.

Sugar Bear yelled excitedly, "What book you read that in, Professor?"

Echo Company took the ball in, but the men on Hotel's side of the court immediately began shouting that the game was over. The yelling got so loud that the master sergeants were scared into stopping the game. They finally decided that it was necessary to win by four points. Again Hamilton intercepted the inbound pass. Unable to spot Roads, he tucked the ball under his arm and took three steps towards the basket before being tackled around the legs and falling, the ball still clutched tightly beneath his chest. A few men dived for it, and the ball disappeared. Everyone on the court joined the pile. The cursing increased until somebody lost their temper and took a swing. Sinclaire crawled away from the pile, blood gushing from his face. Within seconds, most of the men on the court were swinging

446

wildly at each other. Before Chalice could decide what to do, a fist smashed into his jaw sending him sliding backwards in the mud.

The crowds on the edges of the court stampeded towards its center at a dead run. They merged into a brawling mass of two hundred men swinging wildly at each other. Few of them had time to figure out who they were fighting, but most didn't care. Hotel Company's master sergeant tried to get to the center of the melee to stop it, and was flattened almost immediately. The brawl did more than continue, it became wilder. Men staggered and crawled away from it, blood pouring from their faces. Finally, a lieutenant fired a burst from his pistol. Most of the men dropped to the ground, thinking that someone was firing into the crowd. The officers were then able to separate the few who continued fighting.

Chalice was helped back to the platoon tent in a daze. As he came to his senses, he looked around and saw the tent was alive with excitement — men slapping each other on the back, laughing, shadowboxing, and demonstrating how they had knocked this or that person to the ground. Hamilton's chin was stained with blood and he had a gash on his lip; but this didn't prevent him from smiling as he slapped Chalice on the back and asked, "Wasn't that great?"

"If you say so."

"Sure it was. That was the most fun I've had in a long time."

"Did we win?"

"Hell yeah! I flattened three of them myself."

"I mean the game."

"Oh, the game . . . yeah . . . well, we didn't get to finish it. . . . That was a hell of a shot you made."

"Yeah . . . yeah . . . that *was* a lot of fun."

Alpha had the ambush that night. Hamilton returned to the tent with its coordinates and gathered his men together. "It ain't too long, just under a klick. We've got to set-in by the little bridge on the other side of the ville."

"Which one is that?" Forsythe asked.

"You know, the whorehouse is right next to it."

"Oh, yeah, I remember."

"Chalice, you'll walk the point."

It hadn't rained all day, but as Alpha left the platoon tent it began coming down in torrents. Chalice led his squad along the road that skirted the battalion perimeter. The heavy traffic had churned the mud into a foam, in some places almost three feet deep. Chalice couldn't see more than a few yards through the rain; and he knew the first sign of a Viet Cong ambush would be the muzzle flashes of their rifles.

He halted the column at the edge of the bridge. Hamilton walked forward to pick a site. The stream was overflowing its banks, and he had no choice but to place his men in the weeds at one end of the bridge. For an hour they sat shivering in the mud as the rain poured down upon them.

Finally, Forsythe got up and walked towards Hamilton. "This is fucking ridiculous."

"I know. We're sitting ducks down here."

"Ducks sure is the right word," Forsythe agreed.

"I wish we would of sandbagged. I'm freezing my ass off. . . . This shit is gonna last all night."

"Let's get out of here."

"To where?"

"Somewhere back in the — *the whorehouse!*"

If the rain hadn't been enough to convince Hamilton, the bravado of Forsythe's idea would have been. The whorehouse was only thirty yards away, and within minutes they were there. The four young girls inside were almost out the back door before they realized they had some paying customers. Forsythe was the first man to get his clothes off, and the prettiest girl led him to her crib. Before entering it, he turned toward the rest of his squad and recited, " 'I been *wrong*, so long,/ But *tonight*, I'm right!' "

Most of the men began arguing over the remaining three prostitutes. Hamilton quieted them by giving priority to the men with the most time in-country. Roads let it be known right away that he wasn't interested. After an hour, everyone had taken a turn. Hamilton then ordered his men to keep their clothes on.

Chalice had first watch. At nine o'clock he took the radio and stationed himself by the door. Every fifteen minutes he would hear the company giving situation reports. Someone in charge of the CP radio would say, "If all secure, click your handset twice, otherwise, three times." This same voice would then call off the various units. As Chalice pressed the button on the handset, the humorous irony of what he was doing overwhelmed him, and he felt more at ease than at any time in months. He began thinking about how having Forsythe around made being in Vietnam so much easier, and also about the affection he had for Hamilton and Childs, telling himself that as long as they were with him he could endure anything.

Hamilton didn't bother to divide the men into the normal two watches. Instead, each man had only to stand a single hour. Forsythe took over at

448

eleven o'clock. The excitement of the basketball game, the ensuing riot, and now this extraordinary ambush had combined to put him into an even lighter mood than usual. He sat holding the handset, anticipating the time when he could click it twice to let those in the rear know that the ambush was going according to plan — 'I been wrong so long,/ But tonight I'm right.' A broad smile on his face, he stared out the door and watched the rain stream down from the thatch and tin roof, thinking about how he and the rest of the men could still be shivering in the rain. Finally, it was his turn to click the situation report. He pressed the button once, then again, gaining immense satisfaction from this act. In an instant the smile left his face.

With less than horror and more than surprise, in amazed disbelief, he saw before him a soaked, astonished figure standing motionless in the doorway, the black Viet Cong uniform sticking to his skin. Frightened eyes locked upon each other, both men seeing what they had least expected; one thinking, 'Marine,' not having to remember the fear and hatred connoted by that single word; the other thinking, 'Too late.' But for Forsythe there was time; time to squeeze the handset in fear; to remember another black clad form running from him, he unable to pull the trigger of his M-16; to wonder if he would now have the same luck as that figure; to feel the weight of his M-16 resting across his lap; to know and decide without thinking or doing either that this time he would use it; time to flinch as the AK-47's muzzle flashed in his face shattering the silent tableau with a sound so deafening as to be beyond the range of hearing.

The threshold stood deserted even before Forsythe slumped forward. Hamilton dived towards it, in the same motion pointing his rifle where there was now nothing but darkness and rain. With Chalice's help, he yanked Forsythe's lifeless body away from the door. Their faces stared down in dread, not thinking, 'Is he dead?' but rather, 'He's not dead. He's not dead! *He's not dead!*' collapsing with relief as Forsythe moaned, "Stomach, in the stomach."

Stoker pulled up Forsythe's shirt and checked for an exit wound. There was none. Even before he had finished bandaging Forsythe, the other members of the platoon were ready to dash out the door. The cardboard walls offered no protection.

"To the bridge!" Hamilton ordered. "Gotta get out!"

"Hurry," Forsythe moaned as Hamilton and Roads gently placed him on a straw mat.

Chalice began running even before Hamilton finished saying, "Professor, get going."

The rain somewhat slackened as they waited nervously for the medivac chopper. Chalice and Hamilton had taken off their shirts which were now being held across the upper part of Forsythe's body to protect him from the rain.

"It burns," he said, not as if he were talking about himself, the bullet, but about a piece of plastic or wood somebody had set on fire, as if he were watching it take the flame from the match, watching the flame consume it, saying with no emotion, "It burns." His words became alternately calm and anguished. "I feel a little sick. Maybe I'm gonna . . . puke. . . . Water . . . I'd like some water. . . . Know I shouldn't drink any, not with a stomach wound. Won't ask. . . . It'd taste good though. . . . Professor."

"Yeah man, right here," Chalice not yet crying because not yet believing.

"Professor."

"Yeah. Right next to you."

"What day is it?" saying the words with great effort, in pain.

"Day is it! 'What day is it?' I never know the day. Hamilton!"

"I don't know either. Somebody, somebody, what day is it?"

Roads, softly, "Monday man. It's Monday."

"No! Number?"

"January fifteenth."

As if he were dating a letter, "You sure?"

Hamilton, excited, saying with certainty, "Yeah! He's right. I know he's right. Take it easy."

"I believe you. I believe you guys." Then drowsily, "Thirty days has September, April —"

Chalice, pleading, "Relax, Forsythe. The chopper'll be here in a minute. Just relax."

"Am relaxed. Don't worry. But it's . . . important. *Can't* get it straight. How, how many days past July eighth?"

Chalice, soaked and shuddering, "July eighth?"

"My birthday. *Hurry!* Tell me . . . how old . . . I am. Important."

Hamilton, nervously, "Hold on. We'll tell you. Just wait."

Chalice, to himself but out loud, "Monday, no, January fifteenth, *January fifteenth!*"

Roads finally saying, guessing, "One hundred and sixty days."

Chalice, thinking, How did he do it so fast?

Forsythe, calmer, "Nineteen years one hundred and sixty days. . . . I'm nineteen years one hundred and sixty days old. . . . Important. . . . Thanks. . . . Wait! What about Leap Year?"

Chalice, "Don't worry. Doesn't matter. One year is three hundred sixty-five and a quarter days. The sun, it goes around. Doesn't come out

450

even. Leap Year doesn't matter. It doesn't *matter!* The sun —" finally quieted by Roads's hand on his shoulder.

"Okay. . . . You're right — nineteen years one hundred and sixty days. Leap Year don't matter. . . . Thanks. . . . Wanted to know."

Hamilton, more calmly, "Don't worry about it. You'll be all right. The chopper'll be here any minute. I think I can hear it, maybe."

"Not worried. Just wanted to know. Nineteen years one hundred and sixty days — not a long time . . . is it?"

Hamilton, crying and shouting at the same time, "Cut it out, man. You'll *be all right!*" Chalice grabbing Hamilton's arm and shaking him, "Okay. Okay."

Chalice, "No, man, not long, but good, so many good times."

Forsythe, calmly, whispering with effort, "Yeah. . . . yeah, so many good times. . . . Still not long. . . . Twelve yet? Twelve o'clock?"

Hamilton looked at his watch, the green glow of the dials, not being able to tell time, forgetting how, nervously waiting to remember, lips moving silently, the second hand sweeping slowly, four seconds, six seconds, nine seconds — "*Eleven twenty-five!*" he almost shouts, Chalice again grabbing his shoulder, gently.

"Tell me when . . . it's twelve. Add one. You'll tell me, won't you . . . Hamilton . . . Professor?"

"Yeah. Yeah, man. *Please* take it easy."

"He's right. Please take it easy. The chopper'll be here in a minute . . . just wait."

"I believe you. . . . Can I have . . . a drink . . . of water?"

"It's twelve o'clock," Hamilton mumbled to no one. Forsythe had been dead for thirty minutes.

The rain drizzled softly upon them as they returned from their patrol. Drops of water collected along the lips of their helmets before combining and falling in front of their faces. Three days had passed since Forsythe's death. During this time the men in Alpha Squad had done very little talking amongst themselves. Chalice, Hamilton, and Childs had not spoken a word to each other unless it had been necessary, never even allowing their stares to meet, afraid of seeing their own loss in the eyes of a friend — avoiding memories that had changed in meaning. Never before had it been like this. Friends had died, but those left had been able to say to themselves, "That's the way it is. That's what it's all about. . . . Had to happen

451

to somebody," then adding, warning themselves, "Get used to it. You might be next," pretending that they could, and by this alone being able to continue. But Forsythe's death was something different — a fluke, *no!* vengeance, a trick — something that didn't have to, couldn't have, and never should have happened; something none of them could have ever conceived of happening. Even the newer men in the squad, some of them hardly having known Forsythe, respected the unspoken demands of the others. When they whispered among themselves, they did so warily, afraid of being heard, of offending.

Hamilton didn't have to tell Childs to take over Forsythe's fire team. It just happened. One man had merely replaced another. It had been understood.

Chalice still found it impossible to believe that he was here, in Vietnam, carrying a blooker he never wanted to use, the death of one friend serving to separate those left behind, himself now even more alone. Amusing and horror-filled memories clashed and fused within his mind, made it seem impossible that he could have survived without Forsythe, despoiled him of any hope he could now survive. In a few days Hamilton would leave — or be killed — then Childs. Only Roads would be left, someone far less than a stranger. Except for Rabbit, the faces of the newer members of the squad merged into a blur. He didn't, and had no desire to know any of them. They were even more different.

This time, reality did not escape him. He did not try to push it aside. For now reality seemed nothing more than death, and this was all he thought about, no longer making any effort to fit experience neatly into the conceptions of his past. It was grief that he was feeling, something that didn't involve a need for explanation. The ideas and attitudes he had once fought to retain now seemed no more than dreams. Before, while memories of the canopy and the Phantom Blooker tortured him, he had fought to erase them with these dreams that he so stubbornly refused to relinquish. 'No more,' he thought, but still wondered, 'Is that, was that the difference? Was I — are men no different than their dreams?' and though he asked, he knew.

It seemed that he had been the object of a cruel trick — someone had encouraged him, provided then fed his dreams. He hated himself for having been fooled, and his mind searched for a target to renounce, to blame. 'How long?' he asked himself. 'How long have I refused to see?' A memory came to him, now, for the first time, demanding a reaction deeper and more complex than sorrow.

The sky had been a sharp, bright blue. A crisp breeze cleansed the air and everything it touched. It was his freshman year of college. One more hour of class, a test, and he would be going home for the first time since the term had begun, taking two friends with him. Gradually, over the last few months, the world had seemed to become something he could control, hold within his hands — something he could shape. An attractive girl on the verge of tears brushed past him taking short, quick steps, fighting the urge to run. Only for a second did this change his mood, make him ask how someone could exist within his world, at this moment, and fail to share his potency.

He continued to walk, his mood restored and the girl forgotten. A dozen people were huddled together before him, staring down at something. They were too sullen. He wanted to see what insignificant thing to them seemed so important. Chalice moved closer, trying to get a glimpse of what they were looking at. He heard a rasping, metallic voice — a radio. The faces remained sullen. He wanted to know the reason so he could brush it aside. Someone looked back at him, smiling. They were the only two people smiling.

"What's going on?" Chalice asked.

The smile of the other widened to a grin, almost a laugh. "Ol' Kennedy got himself shot."

Chalice continued to return the smile, the five simple words as yet having no meaning. Even as he turned away and headed towards his class, a smile remained on his face. Only gradually did it change to a blank, questioning expression. 'He couldn't have said that. No! He was smiling.' Chalice wanted to turn back and ask again, at the same time sure of and doubting the words that he had heard. 'He was smiling? Maybe it isn't serious. . . . He can't be dying, not him.'

The classroom was only half full, everyone looking sullenly in the direction of a small, vibrating radio. Chalice sat down, hesitating to ask any questions.

A strong, calm voice came over the radio, serious and stilted. "Ladies and gentlemen, we've just received word . . . John F. Kennedy . . . thirty-fifth President of the United States . . . is dead."

The stunned faces around him seemed to share his disbelief, until a whisper came from the back of the room, saying, "I'd like to shake the guy's hand."

The instructor shuffled through the door with his usual effete, sliding gait. "Take out a piece of paper."

One of the girls gasped, "But he's dead."

The instructor glanced at her calmly, clucked his tongue, then said in his normal, effeminate tone, "Oh . . . did he die? Well let's get this test over with so we can all go home."

Chalice waited for someone to object. No one did. The tests were passed out, and he found himself reading the questions, his confused mind searching feebly for the absurd, irrelevant answers at a time when he wanted — if only for an instant — the world to stop.

Chalice now admitted that since that afternoon, those unreal hours, he had refused to see, lied to himself. It should have been so clear then, but 'I wouldn't let the myth die with him!' He now thought of himself as, not fooled, but a fool, admitted that this was the way he had wanted it, but then, finally, found it necessary to accuse. For if he had been lied to, was the guilt his alone? 'He *made* me believe — without words, just by looking at him.' Suddenly Chalice had doubts. He saw the man before him, his overwhelming sincerity. Again he wanted to believe, was willing to sacrifice everything to the myth. 'He *couldn't* have . . . He too believed it, his own *goddamn myth*,' but this thought was equally hard to accept. It seemed as if a clear choice lay before him, and he was incapable of making it. His mind backed away, but other things now seemed explained. He felt he understood why the radicals could deride things Kennedy had done and everything he represented, yet still squirm to avoid the mention of his name. They too had believed. No curses or tirades could cleanse them of the guilt they felt for having had faith in him, the product of a system they now detested, who had seemingly risen above it. All their actions strived to retain the belief he gave them while discarding him and his myth — not refusing to be lied to, but insisting on being given different lies, still living with the myth, calling it by different names, refusing not to believe, the seed of all their hatred sown by a man they can never make themselves hate, knowing without admitting, that if he failed, no one can succeed. 'There will always be someone,' Chalice told himself, 'who will refuse to believe, wait somewhere, patiently, with a rifle.'

Each day the rumors increased. Khe Sanh loomed closer, and no one doubted that it would soon be his turn to go. The men looked forward to this without fear. The inevitability of it went unquestioned, and their main desire was to live it rather than have to think of it as something in the future.

It was almost nine o'clock, and the men of Second Platoon were huddled behind the sandbags and barbwire that surrounded the battalion perimeter. The rain trickled down in a soft, rhythmic drizzle. Chalice sat shivering in the darkness. Rabbit was sitting next to him, but neither man had any desire to talk. As Chalice thought about the many times he had stood lines, he now realized the disadvantage in doing so — the bored state of mind that assumed "this night" would be as uneventful as the last — and he almost wished to see or hear something that would scare him, keep him alert.

454

Chalice tilted the air mattress lying next to him, and heard the water stream off it to the ground. He removed his poncho before lying down upon the mattress, then drew it up to his neck until it met the rain hat that covered his face. The rain gently tapped against the hat as he lay beneath its protection, thankful that An Hoa afforded him the luxury of an air mattress as opposed to a bed of mud that the bush would offer.

Chalice had the last watch that night, but he was awakened by a loud explosion before it was to begin. In fear, he dived from the air mattress to his sandbagged position. Rabbit was already there. Behind them a supply shed glowed with a mellow orange light. Two rockets swooshed over their heads trailing streams of prismlike fire, exploding within the center 'of the perimeter even before their trails had disappeared. Sugar Bear, then Pablo, dashed behind the positions to warn the men of a possible ground attack. Sinclaire and his A-gunner were set-in ten yards to Chalice's right, and Pablo stopped when he reached them to make sure they were prepared to use his old machine gun.

Chalice leaned against the sandbags, not nervous or scared, merely waiting. He could hear whispers and the sounds of men scrambling towards the line. Yet these sounds were hazy and unreal against the backdrop of a threatening silence that was finally shattered by a huge explosion from behind him.

"Satchel charge," numerous voices whispered.

Chalice knew this meant that at least some Viet Cong had made their way into the perimeter. A ground attack now seemed inevitable. Huge illumination flares burst upon the blackness like dawning stars. Each additional flare increased the eerie light that bathed the darkness without really eliminating it. Chalice scanned the barbwire before him, doing so with the knowledge that he was unprotected from any Viet Cong already within the perimeter. Nervous thoughts raced through his mind, but a glance towards Rabbit's frightened face somewhat calmed him. After a sudden flash of light, the ground around him was tremored by a deafening explosion — a mortar, then another, then two more. Explosions continued in series of two's and three's while Chalice and Rabbit cringed and flinched, knowing and experiencing their own helplessness. They no longer scanned the barbwire in front of them, but instead took quick, frightened glances above the sandbags. Mortars exploded everywhere, and it seemed just a matter of time before they or a friend would be found by one. The protection offered by the sandbags seemed insignificant as Chalice cringed against them. He felt no more than a dull sensation as the fingernails of his right hand dug into his left wrist. A quick glance above the sandbags revealed nothing, but he soon heard rifle fire thirty yards to his right. Chalice arranged some blooker rounds before him, separating the different types so that he would be able to choose in an instant. He and Rabbit alternated taking frightened glances above the sandbags. AK-47 rounds began cracking over his head. Neither he nor Rabbit dared to search out their source.

The frightened voice of Sinclaire's A-gunner yelled, "*There*, to the right."

"Not so loud," Sinclaire whispered before firing a burst from his machine gun.

Sinclaire continued firing in short bursts as his A-gunner tried to zero him in. "Up a little. . . . To the right. . . . Missed. . . . Got him. . . . Two more to the left."

Chalice took a quick glance above the sandbags and saw the body of a sapper lying within some strands of concertina wire; then two others, alive, naked except for black cloths wrapped around their groins. They were less than thirty yards away and almost directly in front of him. Seeing that Sinclaire was firing high, Chalice aimed a grenade round at the nearest sapper. It exploded by his side. He rolled over, writhing, still alive. Rabbit aimed a burst of rifle fire at him. Chalice reached for another grenade round to fire at the other sapper who was now ten yards closer. He hesitated, watching him crawl on his stomach and side through the barbwire that seemed hardly to bother him. A burst from Rabbit's M-16 hammered into the sapper's convulsing body just before an explosion came from a few yards behind him leaving a gap in the wire.

Chalice watched the wounded sapper struggling with something in his hands. In an instant, the sapper's body and the wire around it disintegrated in a deafening explosion. All along the barrier of sandbags, the firing of M-16's increased until it was almost constant. Sappers seemed to emanate from the ground itself as they continued to appear in greater numbers within the tangled strands of concertina wire. Though few of them managed to reach the sandbags, they cleared the way for other troops, both Viet Cong and NVA. Sinclaire constantly fired bursts from his machine gun, as did most of the gunners along the perimeter. But this wasn't enough. They kept coming, from nowhere.

By chance alone, Chalice saw a hand reach over the sandbags. He fumbled within his pouch for a shotgun round. Rabbit fired a burst beside his ear. With a convulsing motion, the sapper rose up from the top of the sandbags, then collapsed, the upper part of his body hanging within the perimeter. There was a loud explosion to Chalice's right. A quick glance revealed Sinclaire and his assistant gunner almost completely out of their hole and lying motionless.

"*Corpsman, up! Corpsman, up!*" Chalice screamed.

456

Within seconds, a corpsman had reached the position, found both men dead, and left them lying where they were. Hamilton ran towards the machine gun. A sapper trying to get out of the perimeter rushed madly by him and into Chalice's hole. Chalice tried to grab the frightened sapper's hands. Hamilton's rifle exploded and the sapper fell limp at Chalice's feet.

Pablo ran by and placed the machine gun at the notch in the sandbags, then yelled, "*Professor,* over here."

Chalice was in a daze, trying to make himself believe that the man at his feet was no more dead than himself. Only after Pablo yelled again did Chalice run towards him, tripping over Sinclaire's body. Even after he was next to Pablo, Chalice continued to glance at the bodies around him, feeling incapable of defending himself, no less helping Pablo with the machine gun.

Pablo searched for a target as he said, "Have another belt ready. Feed me as I fire." These words were spoken so calmly that Chalice found it hard to believe he was hearing them amidst the turmoil that surrounded him. When Pablo began firing, Chalice was still somewhat dazed, but he managed to feed the belt to the machine gun. "Sight me in," Pablo said calmly. The sound of Pablo's voice relaxed Chalice to a degree that he himself found hard to believe.

Gradually, the firing became more sporadic. Chalice scanned the bodies and what was left of the barbwire, realizing the worst had probably passed. A minute went by in silence. Then, from nowhere, an NVA soldier came charging directly at Pablo's machine gun. A short burst from it left Chalice refusing to believe what he was seeing, the NVA soldier staggering closer, still aiming his rifle, but finally collapsing, his head lying on the ground five yards in back of him.

It had been twenty minutes since the last shot or explosion. Childs sat behind his position in the rain, shivering now that he had time. Hamilton approached, calmly making the rounds of his squad's positions. "Looks like we survived another one."

"There's always tomorrow," Childs replied.

"For me there's only five more tomorrows and a wake-up. . . . You gonna see me off when I get on that beautiful green chopper?"

"I'll probably shoot you off that beautiful green chopper."

"In three weeks you'll be on one yourself."

"If they hadn't blown those satchel charges too early, I could be dead right now. . . . A lot can happen in three weeks — Khe Sanh for one."

"Tell 'em you ain't going. You got two Hearts."

"I ain't telling those bastards anything. If I knew which sonofabitch kept me in the bush, I'd blow his ass away."

"Ask around."

"As long as I don't know, I can't end up in the brig."

"You gonna miss me, motherfucker?"

Hamilton's question immediately reminded both of them of Forsythe. "I'm gonna miss a lot of people. . . . Man, I don't want to be around here anymore. Every friend I ever had is dead, gone, or leaving."

"When did you ever have a friend?" Even realizing Childs knew he was joking, Hamilton was immediately sorry he had said this. He added in a somber tone, "You had lots of friends, still have some."

"I don't know whether I can take three more weeks. The Professor's the only one worth a shit, and he's been acting fucked up for a while."

"He's all right now. . . . You were a little weird in the Arizona yourself."

Childs said with malice, "I had *good reason!*"

"It won't be so bad. You'll be the squad leader."

"I'll be *goddamned* if I will."

"It's either you or Roads. You wanna take orders from that fucking nigger?"

"He's probably got more brains that you have."

"Bullshit! What he's got is more hair up his ass. . . . Man, Alpha, the whole platoon even, is so fucking green that if the shit hits, a lotta guys are gonna get blowed away. Ask them for a job in the rear."

"I *ain't* gonna kiss their ass!"

"You don't wanna work in the rear. You don't wanna be squad leader. You got three weeks left. What the fuck *do* you want?"

"To get the fuck out of here, that's what I want!"

As Childs said this, two mortars fell less than thirty yards in back of his position. Both he and Hamilton sprawled out on the ground behind the sandbags. Within seconds, Childs was sitting up searching his pants pockets.

Hamilton grabbed his shoulder and pushed him back down. "What the fuck you doing?" he asked, as another series of mortars landed behind them.

"C-rat opener."

"What?"

"I can't find it."

"Who needs it?"

"I do!"

"For what? *Oh*, I get it. Use mine."

Another series of mortars landed, only farther behind them.

"*Quick!* Give it to me!"

"Oh, I left it in the tent."

"*You idiot!*" Childs shouted.

"You left yours too, stupid."

"No I didn't. I lost it."

"That's even stupider," Hamilton insisted.

"You got anything sharp, your bayonet?"

"I mailed it to my little brother."

Childs sat up again as he nervously rummaged through his pockets. "That's just fucking lovely."

A mortar exploded within fifteen yards of them. It was a few seconds before Hamilton was composed enough to ask, "Are you hit?"

"*Hell,* no! Haven't you got anything sharp?"

"My teeth."

"That'll never get it."

"I got it: break your glasses."

"They're my last pair."

"Who cares?"

"I do. . . . Here, I got it — my C-rat opener. It was on my dog tag chain."

"You idiot! You didn't know that?" In the glare from the illumination flares, Hamilton could see Childs hesitating to cut himself. "*C'mon!*"

"Just relax. . . . There, I did it."

"Where?"

"There."

"You pansy. You expect to get a Purple Heart for that mosquito bite?"

"It's bleeding, isn't it?"

Hamilton ripped the C-ration opener from Childs's dog tag chain and gashed his arm, at the same time yelling, "*Corpsman, up! Corpsman, up!*"

Within an hour after dawn, the men had placed their own dead in plastic bags and stacked the bodies of the Viet Cong and NVA soldiers a short distance outside of the perimeter. Most of the members of Second Platoon went back into their tent, but Ramirez and a few others stood around and watched the parade of battalion officers making their way out to the Viet Cong bodies to have their pictures taken. Some of them were wearing bush covers they had never worn before, and carrying rifles and pistols they hardly ever touched except to oil.

Pablo sat off by himself in the platoon tent examining the machine gun taken from Sinclaire's position. Thirteen months ago he had checked it out of the battalion armory. It had been new, a clear plastic bag sealed around it. Pablo remembered carefully cutting the plastic instead of tearing it, and also the smell of new metal and oil as he did this. He had slowly pulled the bolt back, then gently released it — again, and again, and again; listening to the sound of its mechanism as the metal parts slid smoothly against each other; saying to himself, 'Like a watch, like a fine watch.' With great care and even a sense of awe, he had taken it apart, spread its shiny metal parts upon a clean, white towel. They were jewel-like and of different colors. Slowly he put them back together, amazed by the way each part so neatly fit into the others. Again he began to pull the bolt back and release it, admiring the precision of its mechanism; but thinking, 'Only to kill, so precise, so beautiful, only to kill,' and then saying to himself, aloud, "But you'll keep me alive, won't you?"

His fingers now traced patterns upon the stock. Most of the scratches were old and familiar. The barrel was darker, coated with carbon. Pablo began to take the machine gun apart, cleaning it for the last time, thinking about the only other men who had ever done this, all four of them dead.

Ramirez sat down on the edge of Pablo's cot. He was careful not to disturb the array of worn parts. Ramirez remained silent, but Pablo realized there was something he wanted to talk about, so he said, "It's good when the sun comes up."

"Were you scared?" Ramirez asked.

"Till I get home, I'll be scared; and even then I'll be scared I'm really back here."

"We've been through some shit, man." Pablo nodded his head, and there was a long pause before Ramirez added, "They really come at you."

"They're hard core."

"They come right at you, and they keep coming until you kill them. . . . They ain't never gonna stop, are they, Pablo?"

"We'll never stop them."

Ramirez's voice broke slightly as he said, "I don't wanna try no more. It's their country."

"What can we do?" Pablo replied, at the same time asking himself.

"You don't have to do nothing. Two more days and you'll be out of here."

Pablo continued to assemble the machine gun as he talked. "You haven't got that much longer either."

"Seven weeks. That's a long time."

"Not that long. Just play your cards right and you'll be okay."

"I ain't playing no more cards."

"What do you mean by that?" Pablo asked, this time looking directly at Ramirez.

"I ain't killing no more of them."

"Do you think they're better than we are?"

460

"I don't know. . . . It's their country."

"We're no worse than them. The people hate them as much as they hate us."

"Not in the Arizona."

"They have the guns in the Arizona. The people are scared of them. Here they're scared of us. Do you think it makes any difference to them who takes their rice? . . . They just want to be left alone."

"But we ain't Gooks."

"No, we ain't."

"It's their country."

"It's their country."

"I ain't killing no more of them."

"You gonna let them kill you?"

"I ain't going after them no more. . . . You know how many men I've killed?" Pablo shook his head. "Eight."

"Not even half of what I've killed."

"But you don't have to kill no more."

"You think that makes a difference?" Ramirez shook his head, and Pablo held up the machine gun while saying thoughtfully, "You've seen me. Bucoo Gooks are dead because of this baby."

"But you're going home."

"And when you finish your tour, you'll go home too."

"I ain't gonna kill no more of them."

"What are you gonna do?"

"I'm telling Kramer."

"Man, you can't beat the system. They've got it all figured out."

"I'm gonna tell him."

"And he'll send you to Forest."

"I'll tell him too."

"And he'll send you to the brig."

Ramirez had hoped Pablo would make things easier, but now he was even more uneasy than before. "I don't care. I'll tell them."

"You know what they'll do? They'll try and make you look like a coward, or stupid."

"I don't care."

"You *can't* beat the system. You'll either end up in the brig or back in the bush." Pablo wasn't really sure of this, but he felt Ramirez would be better off by merely enduring his last seven weeks. Now as he looked at the sullen figure before him, Pablo realized that it was just as much a matter of pride as anything else. "You don't want them making you do something you don't want to do. Is that it?"

"That's not it."

"That's not all of it, but it's part. Isn't it?" Ramirez remained silent. "You're gonna try to beat the system, aren't you?" Ramirez nodded. "Well, if you keep your head, it won't do any harm. Kramer won't try to fuck you over."

"You think I should do it?"

"Not if you're gonna lose your head. If Forest tries to make you look stupid or chickenshit, don't let it bother you. He ain't shit compared to you." Pablo then put particular emphasis on his last few words. "You don't have to prove a thing."

"You think I should do it, then?"

"Not unless there's no other way. Remember, if you keep your head, you'll be all right. Just don't try to prove you're better than they are. Take my word for it. . . . Remember, it's you against all of them." Ramirez remained sitting on the cot, his pride preventing him from asking what he had intended all along. Pablo wasn't sure, but he guessed right. "You want me to go with you?" Ramirez nodded. "What good will that do? I'm shipping out in two days anyway."

"I trust you. You can talk to them."

"You should have someone else go with you, someone who has more time left in-country."

"Who?"

Pablo named the only person he could think of. "The Professor."

"You sure he'll do it?"

"He's been acting a lot more fucked up than you. . . . Besides, he's the Sandman. They all know *him*. . . . Let the Professor do the talking. . . . Remember, you don't have to prove a thing."

Hamilton walked into the officers' hootch and found Kramer and Sugar Bear waiting for him. "You wanted to speak to me, Lieutenant?"

"Yeah. Sit down a minute. . . . Chalice and Ramirez were just here. Do you know what they came to see me about?"

"No, sir."

"They say they aren't going to fight anymore. You know anything about it?"

"No, sir. . . . The Professor was acting a little funny a few days ago, but he seems all right now. . . . Ramirez hasn't even got two months left."

"I know, and I can't afford to lose either of them. Ramirez is supposed to take over as platoon sergeant, and the Professor'll be a fire team leader soon."

462

"He already is. He took over my old fire team as soon as Childs left."

"In any case, I can't afford to lose two experienced men. We've got too many boots as is."

"I know. If you don't have Chalice around, then Rabbit or someone from another squad will have to take over Alpha."

"What about Roads?" Sugar Bear asked.

"He says he doesn't want to be squad leader. I asked him when you told me I was taking over as platoon sergeant."

"Don't ask him. *Tell him!*" Sugar Bear said angrily.

"I got five more days left. I ain't gonna start messing with that sonofabitch. It's been bad enough having him in my squad."

In an even angrier tone, Sugar Bear said, "Well I only got two days left, but I'll fuck with him. He'll be a squad leader whether he likes it or not."

"I don't give a shit. I'm —"

Kramer cut Hamilton off. "We can settle that later. All I want to know is the story on Ramirez and Chalice."

"I don't know any more than you do, Lieutenant. Pablo might know something about Ramirez."

"If he does, he's sure keeping it to himself."

"What's going to happen to them?"

"I told them to think about it for two days. If they feel the same way then, I'll write up a report."

"The brig?"

"What do you think Forest'll do?" Kramer didn't intend this as a question, and Hamilton realized no answer was necessary.

Sugar Bear had just finished eating supper and was on his way back to the company area. He knew that Roads was walking a few yards behind him, and his rage increased as he thought about him. He'd always had a certain respect for Roads, but this was far outweighed by his hatred for him. Fists tightly clenched at his sides, Sugar Bear could hold his anger no longer. He turned. Their eyes locked, Roads having no idea what Sugar Bear was thinking, walking right past him while returning the stare.

"Just walk right by me, man," Sugar Bear said casually. Roads turned and looked blankly at him. "Just walk right by me, man," Sugar Bear repeated in a challenging tone.

Roads's stare gradually hardened as he asked, "You been drinking, man?" Sugar Bear shook his head, and Roads began to nod his. "Looks like you wanna throw some hands."

Sugar Bear also began to nod, and a confident expression came to his face. They stood only a few feet apart, Roads half a head taller yet out-weighed by thirty pounds. He started to turn and walk away, but the calm, hateful words, "Don't turn your back on me, motherfucker," caused him to freeze.

"You're fucking with the wrong man."

"I'm fucking with the right man."

"*What's* bugging you?"

"Same thing that's been bugging me the last eight months: *you*."

"I don't bug *nobody!*"

"You bug everybody, especially the Brothers. . . . I learned something right away when I got to Nam: the Gooks kill each other, the Chucks hate each other, and the Brothers stick together. You ain't never learned yet." Sugar Bear paused as they continued to glare at each other, but Roads remained silent. "You're cool, man, real cool. . . . I bet you been to college. . . . The *Chucks* might think you're cool, but the Brothers know you ain't shit — walking around like you know something nobody else does. Man, you ain't fooling the Brothers. You're the uptightest motherfucker I've ever seen, ready to explode like some wound-up junkie."

"Uptight?"

"You heard me, man. . . . I used to think if I kicked your ass, it'd teach you a lesson. Now I know there ain't no way, but I'm gonna kick it just the same."

Roads respected Sugar Bear more than anybody he'd met in Vietnam, even liked him; but he knew that it was too late, too much had been said. "I ain't going nowhere." 'Why *him* — always the wrong man?'

"You're damn right you ain't, 'cause I'm gonna kick your ass. Been here a whole tour, and ain't never seen two Brothers fight yet; but —" Sugar Bear cut himself off, realizing the purposelessness of his words and what he had already forced — 'a show for the Chucks.'

Roads broke a long silence by saying, "I can't remember the last time I had my ass kicked." 'If I keep him off me, I'll cut his face to shreds.'

"You'll remember this time, cocksucker. . . . It ain't my fault I'm the baddest motherfucker that ever lived." 'All I gotta do is get him on the ground.' Suddenly Sugar Bear swung, hoping to get Roads off balance, missing badly, himself catching a soft jab on the chin, still moving for-ward while Roads sidestepped and jabbed, neither one angered enough to really start swinging yet, feeling each other out. Roads, surprised at Sugar Bear's speed, knowing he had to take any advantage given him, dodged a right and staggered Sugar Bear with a left to the jaw, that being it — no stopping now. Roads, holding his ground, watching enraged eyes, waited for another lunge; but not long, soon fending off punches with his

464

arms, warnings that he couldn't afford to be hit anywhere else. Sugar Bear, overanxious, attempted an uppercut, regretting it as his lips squashed flat against his teeth, salt blood spurting between them, quickly drooling from the corner of his mouth. Roads watched it, too long, letting Sugar Bear get inside with three brutal punches to the stomach, feel the hard flesh and hear the thuds, knowing they had to hurt. Too surprised to fake it, Roads folded slightly as he jumped back, his stomach still feeling flat and tasting his gall, imagining it as shit, knowing it would be oozing out of his ears if he got hit like that again. Sugar Bear, still hearing those punches, missed badly with an uppercut. Roads backed away, too hurt to make him pay for it. Arms tired and knees tight, they feinted a few punches. But the taste of his own blood made Sugar Bear too anxious to draw some. Roads, still confident he could keep his distance, throwing jab after jab, pounded the blood-smeared smile off Sugar Bear's face. One eye closed, Sugar Bear slammed his fist into Roads's chest, again thinking, 'That had to hurt.' Roads saw some eager white faces. 'Watching the nigger show,' and made Sugar Bear pay for their smiles, 'Always the wrong man!' with a hard right. Overconfident, Roads stood his ground, trading a flurry to the head for one to the stomach, finally jumping back, gasping, his stomach feeling pulverized. An awkward jab brought blood gushing from Sugar Bear's nose. Desperate to catch Roads, to get him on the ground, Sugar Bear noticed a tent guy wire. Roads, now more confident, breathed easier, unaware of the wire. Sugar Bear kept circling, feinting punches not throwing them, backing Roads towards the wire, cursing as he just missed it, again stalking him towards it, now seeing the white faces and becoming angrier. Roads, knowing he could beat Sugar Bear senseless until somebody stepped between them, tiring, smashed a right into Sugar Bear's face, feeling the tissue rip from the bone. Sugar Bear, now more desperate, swung wildly, missing; but finally backing Roads into the wire. Roads, off balance, surprised, staggered to his knees while Sugar Bear dived for his neck, ignoring a flurry of punches to his head and chest. Feeling the soft flesh of Roads's throat, he held his grasp as they rolled furiously on the ground, Roads finally getting hold of Sugar Bear's throat with his right hand, pummeling his face with the left. Without relenting, Roads began to gag. Some men tried to separate them. Still on the ground, they continued to swing, often as not hitting the men trying to keep them apart. Another fight broke out, then a few more. Roads and Sugar Bear became separated in the melee. Whites began fighting blacks. More men joined in, spurred on by racial slurs. Sugar Bear and Roads staggered away as over a hundred brawling men wildly attacked each other in what was now a race riot, officers attempting to quell it with swinging rifle stocks.

465

Kramer wasn't surprised when Chalice and Ramirez gave him their decision. He had hoped for their sakes that they would have changed their minds, but it seemed far stranger that no other members of the platoon were with them. It was now Kramer's duty to inform Lieutenant Forest, and he was positive what would result. Forest's threats would make them more determined, and they'd soon find themselves involved in a court-martial. Rather than have this happen, Kramer decided to speak directly to Colonel Nash. Nash's first question was, "It's not their guts that's bothering them, is it?" After Kramer had told him that it wasn't, Nash ordered Chalice and Ramirez brought to him.

He was sitting alone in his office when they entered. Curious as to what Nash would say, Kramer entered with them. As Chalice and Ramirez stood in front of his desk, Nash shifted his hard stare from one to the other before asking coldly, "Is it true you men refuse to fight?"

There was silence as Chalice and Ramirez waited for each other to answer first. Finally, Ramirez said, "Yes, sir."

Chalice quickly repeated this answer.

"You men realize this isn't any game we're playing? You can both end up in the brig for a very long time."

"Yes, sir."

"Yes, sir."

"What are your reasons for doing this, Lance Corporal Chalice?"

"This war is wrong, sir."

"Suddenly wrong, or has it been wrong all along?"

"From the beginning, sir."

"It must have been just as wrong when you were fighting it then?"

"Yes, sir."

"Why is it wrong?"

Feeling ridiculous, Chalice hesitated answering. Once he had believed and fought anyway. Now no longer sure how he felt, he was refusing to fight. Nash continued to stare at him, and he finally said, "Politically, sir."

"I never get involved in politics myself, Lance Corporal Chalice. It's amazing you've had the time. . . . Corporal Ramirez, is politics your problem too?"

Somewhat confused by the question, Ramirez's few words were spoken nervously. "I don't want to kill them no more, sir."

"If they felt the same way, then there wouldn't be a war, would there?"

"No, sir."

"But they don't, do they?"

"No, sir."

"And there is a war."

466

"Yes, sir."

"If they shoot at you, shouldn't you be able to shoot them?"

"Yes — no, sir."

"Why not?"

"It's their country."

"Whose country?"

"The Gooks, sir."

"Which Gooks — the NVA, the Viet Cong, the people in Saigon?"

"Not the Americans," Ramirez answered without hesitation.

"Some of the Gooks want us here. That's what they tell us, isn't it?"

"Yes, sir."

"But you don't want to be here. Why?"

"I don't want to kill them no more." Nash remained silent, and after a pause Ramirez continued in a far more emotional tone. "They keep coming. We kill them, but they keep coming. We have the choppers. We have the Phantom jets, bombs, 106's, everything; but they keep coming. We kill them, but they keep coming."

Nash hadn't heard anything that surprised him, but Ramirez had stated it a little better than he'd expected. Disliking the game he had been playing, Nash abandoned it. After calling for two chairs and having Chalice and Ramirez sit down, he also abandoned the military tone he'd been using.

"You men came in here with your minds made up. Now I'm going to try and change them. I'm not going to threaten you, and all I ask is that you listen to me. Is that all right . . . Corporal Ramirez?"

"You'll try to tell me I'm wrong, but I know I'm right."

"All I ask is that you listen. . . . I'm not going to tell you what I think of this war. That isn't any more important than what you think of it. The way I see it, we're all in the Marine Corps and it's our job to follow orders. You think this war is wrong, I know that; but do you still consider yourselves Americans? I mean do you feel responsible for what your country does?"

Nash stared at Chalice. He finally answered, "Yes, sir," feeling as if he were being made to recite the Pledge to the Flag.

"And if it's doing something wrong, you both feel that you should do what you can to stop it?"

"Yes, sir."

"Yes, sir."

"Do you think that by refusing to fight you'll be doing something to stop this war?"

Chalice remained silent, but Ramirez answered, "Yes, sir."

"In what way?" Receiving no answer, Nash continued. "If every man in my battalion suddenly refused to fight, then maybe that would do something to stop this war — not because it couldn't be fought minus one battalion, but because other battalions might do the same thing. I don't think this would happen, but it's possible. But we're not talking about a whole battalion. We're talking about two men. Do you think you can have any effect on this war by refusing to fight, both of you? What do you think will happen if we shipped you back to the States?" Nash paused, but Chalice and Ramirez remained silent. "I'll tell you what would happen, the same thing that would happen if I went with you — nothing. What if I let you talk to every man in my battalion to try to convince them to do the same thing as you? I won't, but what if I did? Do you think you could convince enough of them to have any effect on this war? You, Lance Corporal Chalice, do you think so?"

"No, sir," Chalice answered in a tone indicating both hostility and agreement.

"Let me tell you something: if you could do it in this battalion, maybe people would hear about it and the same thing would happen in every battalion. Then I guarantee you we'd have to pull every Marine out of this country. But it *won't* happen, not in this battalion or any other one. If you men go to the brig, then that'll be the end of it. This goddamn war will go on just as well — or badly — as before. You'll have served no purpose but putting yourselves behind bars. . . . *Believe me*, I'd do all I could to see that you got off easy, but chances are you'd be in pretty bad shape when they got through with you.

"I've tried to convince you that what you're doing is pointless, and I hope I have. Now I'm going to try and convince you that, if you feel the way you do, the best and most honorable thing you *can do* is to continue as members of a rifle company —" Chalice winced noticeably at the word "honorable," but Nash ignored this and continued, "— I'm an American, and so are both of you. Whether you like it or not, you're Americans. I happen to like it. This is going to sound like I'm waving a flag in front of you, but listen to me anyway. When my country does something right, I'm proud of it. When it does something wrong, I'm ashamed . . . and I also feel guilty. I would hope you're the same way. But let's just think about our battalion for a minute. Every man in it has a job. Even if it's sitting behind a typewriter, we need that man to operate. If we don't have him, we'll get somebody else to replace him; but we need somebody to do that job. Let's say our battalion does something wrong, that one of our rifle squads kills some prisoners, or even civilians. I'm not gonna say the man behind the typewriter is just as responsible as the man who pulls the

468

trigger; but if it wasn't for the man behind the typewriter, there wouldn't be any man in the bush, and he wouldn't have a rifle or trigger to pull." Nash noticed a hostile look on Chalice's face. "I know what you're thinking, Chalice: if he hadn't typed out those orders, somebody else would have; but still, he did and he's partly responsible for those dead prisoners, and the people in this battalion aren't the only ones responsible. You know how that rifle got paid for? With taxes; and it was the people back home that paid those taxes — your parents and just about every goddamn person in the United States. All I'm saying is that every goddamn American whether he likes it or not, is responsible for what's going on here, maybe not to the same degree as the psychopath that blows away an unarmed prisoner, but in one way or another we're all in this together. But there's one very big difference — the difference between a clerk-typist and a rifleman. If I'm responsible for something, I want to have control over it, and I'll tell you who has more control than anybody else, the grunt, the man up to his ears in rice paddies . . . because he's the one that pulls the trigger.

"If you think you can stop this war, that you can do anything more than get yourself thrown in the brig, then the best thing for you to do is to refuse to fight. But if you think that, then you're just fooling yourself. And I'll tell you what else can happen. We've got our share of psychopaths in this battalion. You've probably seen more of them in action than I have. While your ass is rotting in the brig, maybe we'll replace you with one more psychopath. Maybe a few more prisoners or civilians will end up dead because of it. If you're in the bush, you can at least *try* to see that this doesn't happen."

Nash stared directly at Chalice before continuing. "I couldn't care less what kind of *political* speeches you give to the other men in your platoon, just as long as you're carrying your rifle and following orders. If you think this war is fucked-up, tell them what you think. It won't make any difference here, but it might — if there's enough of you — when you get home."

Nash felt that he'd said just about all he could say. He also believed that he had gotten through to them, and that it was now time to find out. He purposely looked at Ramirez while asking, "Do you think what I've said makes sense?"

Ramirez was hesitant to speak, but Nash continued to stare at him until he was forced to answer, "Yes sir, it makes sense . . . but it shouldn't."

"Why not?"

"I don't want to kill any more of them."

"Will less of them die if you don't kill any, or will that just mean that some other Marine will do the killing? . . . No, you shouldn't want to, and nobody can make you *kill* or *want* to kill. You're the one that has to pull the trigger. Since you've been here, has anyone ever ordered you to fire?"

"Yes."

"When?"

"A lot of times they've told us to open fire."

"I don't mean that. That really isn't an order. . . . Well, it would be if everybody refused, but that isn't what I mean. . . . Let's say you're advancing on a tree line, and they tell you open fire. Do they check your rifles afterwards to see if everybody fired?"

"No, sir."

"Even if they did, all you have to do is shoot up in the air. No one can make you take a bead on somebody and blow him away. All you have to do is aim over his head. I don't expect all my men to be good enough marksmen to hit a VC at three hundred yards, but I sure as hell hope they can miss him if they want to. . . . Maybe sometimes it'll be you or him, or him and a friend of yours. Then you'll have to decide and decide fast, but no one can make you kill him. It's your decision. All I ask, *demand*, is that you go out in the bush and take your rifle with you. I can't make you shoot it. That's up to you."

"But if I don't want to shoot it, why should I be there . . . sir?"

"For only two reasons. The first one doesn't sound so good. It's because if I left it up to my men where they wanted to be, all except the psychopaths would be at home. That wouldn't do anything to stop the war. All that'd happen would be that they'd replace me with some colonel that *could* keep his men in the bush. I imagine the second reason will make more sense to you: you owe it to the men in your platoon. If they're out in the bush, you should be out there helping them."

"To kill more Gooks, sir?"

"To stay alive, and there's a good chance that'll mean killing Gooks. . . . I've killed quite a few men myself. It's not the greatest feeling, but I still get my sleep at night. Maybe I should feel guiltier about it, but I don't. All I'm saying is that I'll never force you to kill, but I'll do everything I can to see that you carry your M-16 and go where your unit goes." Nash now doubted he had gotten through to either Ramirez or Chalice, so he decided to try something different. "I hope you men aren't trying to judge this whole country by the Arizona. We go in there because that's where the VC and the NVA are, and they couldn't stay without the help of the peasants. But you can't judge all the people in this country by the ones that live in the Arizona any more than you can judge all Americans by the people you might meet in some Iowa cornfield. . . . And another thing: you can't judge all Arvins by the ones we've been working with —

470

they're Popular Forces. That's like trying to judge Marines by some National Guard unit. . . . Look, all I'm asking is that you think about what I've said. Will you?"

"Yes, sir," Ramirez answered softly.

Nash turned to Chalice. "What about you, Lance Corporal?"

Chalice had to admit that what Nash had said made some sense, but not enough sense. Memories of the Phantom Blooker and the canopy refused to leave him; and he felt that what Nash was talking about wasn't something that could be argued — it was a matter of principles. "You . . . sir, you're trying to tell us that if we don't believe in something, we should keep doing it anyway."

"No. That's only part of what I'm telling you. If you feel this war is wrong, you should do everything you *can* to see that it is ended. I'm just telling you that you're choosing the wrong way. As soon as you signed your induction papers, you fell in up to your neck. The question is not what you can do, but what you can do now. Getting yourself thrown in the brig won't do anybody any good. There isn't anything stupider than the romantic notion that you can *always* do the most good by making the greatest sacrifice. That's the same thing as some idiot saying the greatest thing you can do for your country is die for it. I'd like to meet the colonel that could convince me that dead Marines are more useful than live ones.

"Your reasons for refusing to fight are emotional, Ramirez's more than yours. I'm just asking you to be practical. You're just one little person in this Marine Corps. Why fool yourself into thinking you're accomplishing something when actually you're only making things worse. It's the people back home that pull the strings. You aren't going to reach them by refusing to fight, not you alone . . . or both of you."

"What's the difference where I am? If what you say is right, then I'm only one person no matter where I am."

"Here you're a measly lance corporal. Back home you're a veteran. Maybe if enough of you come back saying the same thing, maybe somebody'll start listening. . . . I wouldn't bet on it, but maybe. In any case, the United States is the place to do your talking, not here."

"People already are talking back there." Nash's look turned colder, and Chalice added, "Sir."

"There's a few people *saying* the things you believe, but they sure as hell get drowned out by the others doing the *shouting*. Do you actually think those screaming protesters back home are any better people than the men in this battalion?"

"Yes, sir," Chalice answered, though not sure what he believed.

This reply angered Nash, far more than his tone indicated. "Well you're *dead* wrong. When they start acting like a bunch of spoiled brats and shout speakers down, do you think that does any good?" Nash's tone became gradually more emotional as he continued. "Do you think this war's gonna be stopped by burning down ROTC buildings . . . or by burning flags? You believe what you want to, but I've seen this bullshit too many times. All it takes is one idiot burning a flag, and right away you've got a hundred more idiots waving them. I —"

"They're not —" Chalice blurted out before he realized that he was cutting Nash off. Nash was embarrassed he had gotten so emotional, and he nodded for Chalice to continue. "They're not all like that, sir."

"No. You're right. I just get excited when I think about it. . . . But too many of them *are* like that, and the others get so lost in the shuffle they might as well be here. Maybe someday those selfish brats will wise up, I don't know." Nash felt mentally drained. He knew that if he hadn't made his point already, he wouldn't be able to. "We've been talking quite a while and there's not much more I can say. I certainly haven't tried to convince you that you can ever really do much about stopping this war, and I haven't tried to convince you that you shouldn't make some effort to do what your conscience tells you. If you still think you can do more in the brig than back in the States, I guess I haven't been very convincing. All I ask is that you think about what I've said. There's no need for you to decide anything until your company goes back to the bush. I hope you'll go with them; but if you don't, I'll do what I have to. . . . Will you think about it for a while before you decide?"

"Yes, sir."

"Yes, sir."

"How long have you been in-country, Chalice?"

"Six months."

"If you wanted to, I might be able to get you into a CAP unit. If you'd been to language school, it wouldn't be any problem."

"I have, sir," Chalice answered, not very enthusiastically.

"Well, then I know I can get you assigned to one within a month. You'd be working with the villagers — helping them build hootches and with their crops. It's a lot hairier than being with a rifle company — you and five other men alone in a ville — but maybe you'd be able to feel you were doing some good. You'd be surprised how many villes request CAP units, more than we can afford to supply. And you'd be surprised how many Marines owe their lives to the peasants around here, even a few in the Arizona. They might be able to tell you some stories you'd find interesting — about the times the VC have come in and started chopping heads off. . . . You don't have to decide now. . . . How long have *you* been in-country, Ramirez?"

472

"I got less than seven weeks left, sir."

"Less than *seven* weeks and you decided you wanted a court-martial? I sure hope I've convinced you. . . . That'll be all. You two can leave now." Kramer realized that Nash wanted him to stay. As soon as Chalice and Ramirez left, Nash asked him, "Why didn't you tell me one of them had only seven weeks left?"

"I guess I should have, sir."

"If he doesn't change his mind, tell him to wait while you see about getting him a job in the rear. I'll arrange something."

"What about Chalice?"

"I can get him in a CAP unit within a month if he wants. Just keep him away from me until we can work something out. I might have gotten through to them."

"I think you did, sir. What you said made sense."

"*Nothing* makes sense."

"Well, it was a good speech."

"It wasn't a speech. I believed every word of it."

"I mean I was really surprised by the way you handled it, sir. I never expected to see that."

"In the Marine Corps, you mean, and by a lifer." Kramer didn't have to answer for Nash to know that this was exactly what he had meant. "I'm one of the few," Nash said in a less serious tone, "and I haven't seen any of the others in a long time."

"Well I'm glad you talked to them, sir. I guess it would have been easier to just send them to the brig."

"I assure you it wouldn't have been. . . . What worries me about things like this is that they don't happen more often. I wonder how many of my men keep everything inside them without ever thinking it out. Sometimes I think there's only two kinds of people in the world — those that blame everything on themselves and those that blame everything on others. Ever since they were little kids, these men have been taught that the United States has always been right. We make idealists out of them, and when they find out that most of the idealism belonged to the dreamers — or liars — who wrote the history books, they can't cope with it. . . . Sometimes I think they'll either change things or destroy themselves trying . . . then I take another look around and decide they'll probably do a little of both, very little."

Chalice walked back to the company area by himself. He tried to belittle Nash by picturing him reciting the Pledge to the Flag in a Boy Scout uniform, doing so in exasperation, knowing that what Nash had said made sense. Chalice as much as admitted this by saying to himself, 'He could make shooting your grandmother seem like a patriotic duty.' Too conscious of his own attempt to avoid the logic of Nash's argument, Chalice finally forced himself to accept some of it.

What bothered him most was the way in which Nash characterized the war protesters. Chalice tried to brush this aside by comparing what they were doing to what Nash was doing; but he finally had to admit that one thing had nothing to do with the other. Bombarded by memories of events associated with the protest movement, Chalice could no longer rationalize them as mere mistakes, or excuse those responsible as ignorant of the results of their actions. Only a fool could have deluded himself into believing that some of these actions wouldn't have exactly the opposite effects as those intended, only a fool like himself. 'It was *them!* They fucked it up,' Chalice told himself, realizing that he too was one of "them." Acts that had once seemed noble, now took on an absurd and even hypocritical taint. He remembered how impossible it had seemed that those who knew the facts, who would listen long enough, could possibly fail to see the truth. It was right before them! But they had, couldn't have helped but listen. Chalice admitted this now. How absurd it was to attack everything they valued, more than absurd, hypocritical and childish, to shove things down their ignorant throats, that wasn't enough, not even trying to make these ideas, facts palatable — the hair, the clothes, the violence — not trying to convince people, but instead to show them how ignorant they were, humiliate them. He remembered himself as so caught up in ideas, the movement, that methods seemed irrelevant. Everything made sense now, but he realized that it had made sense then, and only self-deceit had prevented him from admitting it. Stopping the war hadn't been a cause, but rather a self-indulgent excuse to show everyone that he was above them, a just person. If the war had been the real issue, no methods could have proved worse than those used against it; and the root of these methods was more than childish stubbornness, it was a hypocritical lack of sincerity combined with pure, selfish arrogance. As he looked back, it seemed that only the methods had been great enough to defeat the cause. So now it was he that was having things stuffed down his throat.

Disturbing as these thoughts were, they did afford Chalice some relief. At least things were starting to make sense. Suddenly his reasoning led him further, to an excuse, a logical defense of his actions; but he found this even harder to accept than self-accusation. It involved so much more than just himself. The truth had always seemed so powerful. All that had ever been necessary to change things was to show people that they were wrong.

474

How absurd! Wanting to write a book, to put the truth before them, without the hysteria, written down, in a way impossible to deny — how absurd this now seemed — the belief that people actually wanted the truth, that they would defend and act upon it. He wondered exactly how much of his own thinking had been self-deceit, how much more important was his desire to create something indestructible, permanent — a book.

"Professor," someone called, and Chalice was glad to be taken from his thoughts. Roads walked towards him. "C'mon, we've got to help the rest of the squad unload some trucks."

"I don't feel like it," Chalice answered in a depressed tone.

"I don't feel like it either. C'mon, let's go."

"I'm not going," Chalice answered gruffly, thinking how much better it had been when Roads never talked to anyone, before he took over as squad leader.

"Both of us are going."

"Chow starts in an hour. What difference does it make?"

"If we don't help them, they'll be eating C-rations tonight. Those trucks have to be unloaded. C'mon."

"I said I wasn't going," Chalice answered testily.

Still calm, Roads said, "Oh you're going all right."

Chalice looked up at Roads, sneering childishly, on the verge of saying something. When Roads saw this, he merely smiled, disparagingly, a sense of accomplishment in his look, knowing exactly what Chalice wanted to say. Roads slowly turned and began walking. Chalice followed behind him, still thinking, 'Nigger!'

The men were gathered in the platoon tent, preparing to go on watch. Chalice was sitting on his cot when Hamilton walked over and sat down across from him. For the last few days they hadn't been avoiding each other, but neither had they sought each other out. "Cut the shit, Professor. You're depressing me. All I've got is a wake-up and I'll be on my way back to the world."

"I wish I was going with you," Chalice replied somberly.

"Sorry I can't wait, but I got here a little earlier than you did. . . . It goes by fast. You'll see."

"It's like I'm the last one here. Everyone else is either dead or home. . . . I don't even know the names of half these boots."

"You better learn them . . . just like Kovacs and Tony 5 learned your name. Besides man, the boots already know who the Professor is."

Chalice broke into a faint smile as he said, "I met some decent motherfuckers in this shit hole. If they were still here, it'd be different. . . . I'll make it though."

"You better. As soon as somebody frags Roads, you'll be squad leader."

"Roads doesn't fuck with anybody. He's all —"

"That's the trouble. He's too *good* to fuck with anybody."

"He's all right. . . . Seriously man, I'm gonna miss you — the last of the wild bunch."

"Uh-uh, you're the last. . . . We ain't done much bullshitting lately. Why don't we make up for it tonight."

"Sure. Come around to my position."

"*Hell* no! I've got some herb I wanna burn. That new boot gives you an extra man in the squad. I'll get Roads to let you off lines. I'm still platoon sergeant, you know."

"He already said we're gonna have one five-man watch."

"It's my last night — my last chance to get stoned in the bush. I'll talk to him." Chalice shrugged his shoulders, and Hamilton walked over to Roads. He came back saying, "It's okay."

"What did he say to you?"

"He never says shit. He just looked at me for a few seconds like he hated my guts, then nodded."

When the rest of the men headed to their positions, Chalice and Hamilton walked behind an ammo bunker and smoked two joints. The marijuana was strong. They sat almost immobilized until an hour after dusk. Hamilton got hungry, and he talked Chalice into stealing some ice cream from the mess hall. It was dark inside, so Chalice stayed close behind as Hamilton searched for the freezers. They finally found a three-gallon container and were on their way out with it when Hamilton heard footsteps coming towards them. He ducked behind a freezer. Chalice followed him. As they squatted in the darkness, Chalice had visions of himself going before Colonel Nash for stealing from the mess hall. The footsteps passed within a few feet of them, and when Hamilton heard a voice whisper "Quiet," he couldn't resist standing up and saying harshly, *"Stop or I'll shoot!"* Complete silence followed, but it was finally broken when Hamilton could no longer control his laughter.

An angry voice asked, "Who are you?"

"Just thieves, like you."

The voice was still somewhat angry as it said, "You scared the shit out of us."

"What are you looking for?" Chalice asked.

"Ice cream."

"We've got the last one. Do you want some?"

476

"Sure. Bring it over to our hootch. We've already swiped a big ham and some bread." On the way to their hootch, the two men told Hamilton they were from another battalion that was being sent to Khe Sanh in the morning. They had just arrived in An Hoa that night, and because they didn't have to stand lines they were celebrating.

The hootch was dark except for warm spheres of light where candles had been placed upon the floor. There were no cots, and the men sat around the flames smiling like pumpkins with candles inside as light flickered eerily on their faces. This and the constant hum of voices gave the hootch an attractively evil quality. Hamilton and Chalice made their way to one of the candles where a ham was being carved by its light. Chalice watched entranced as two greasy hands worked a bayonet into the meat, its juices beading on and dripping from the blade. Both his and Hamilton's mouths began to water as the gleaming hands placed the slice between two pieces of bread. Exchanging drugged smiles, they dropped to their knees and waited for a turn with the bayonet. When the other men heard about the ice cream, they began to wander over with spoons to dish it out of the container. Chalice watched with skulking interest as the candlelight flickered upon strange faces gleaming with ham grease and stained with ice cream.

Someone began to strum a guitar. Even before the first word was sung, Chalice staggered to his feet and wandered in the direction of the music. It was the light flickering off the guitar that he saw first. Dropping to his knees, he whispered in a disbelieving tone, "Boyd, Boyd!"

But it was Cowen that recognized him first. "Chalice!"

"Abie!"

"Hey, it's good to see you guys."

"I know what you mean. I know what you mean. . . . What happened to you? You look terrible."

Chalice stumbled over the possible answers for a few seconds, then said, "I'm all right. I just lost some weight. You don't look so good yourself, Abie."

"*Hey*, are you going to Khe Sanh with us tomorrow?" Boyd asked.

"No. I wish I was."

"I wish I wasn't. Hey, it's good to see you."

"We did that already."

"Yeah, you're right. Are you stoned too?"

A voice said, "Play the guitar, Boyd."

"Man, the whole world is stoned. . . . Play the guitar, Boyd — 'Merry Christmas, Jesus' or something."

"Boyd," a voice said pleadingly, "play the one about the cowboy."

477

Other voices seconded this request until Boyd began to sing: *"I'm a young man so you know. My age is twenty-one./ I just returned from southern Colorado./ Just out of the service and I'm lookin' for my fun./ Some day soon, goin' with her, some day soon./ Her parents cannot stand me 'cause I ride the rodeo./ Her father says that I will leave her cryin'./ She would follow me right down the toughest road I go./ Some day soon, goin' with her, some day soon."*

As Boyd sang, joints were continually passed from hand to hand, and merely breathing the air of the hootch would have been enough to stone everybody. Chalice lost all sense of place, overcome by absurd memories of Parris Island that seemed more real than anything that had happened since then. The hum of voices became gradually quieter as one by one the men fell asleep. Boyd continued to sing, watching the hootch darken as each succeeding candle burned itself to the floor. When the last flame disappeared, he placed the guitar down, knowing that he was the only man awake in the room.

"Fall out with packs on!" a harsh voice yelled. This cry was repeated again and again. Blurred, just-opened eyes slowly adjusted to the blue gray light of dawn. Men moved wearily to their feet. In minutes the hootch was empty.

As Cowen walked towards his place in the formation, he looked over at Chalice and said, "You know I had this weird dream about Parris Island last night. Green was running around choking and jumping on people, and we were all laughing . . . even some of the guys that are dead now."

"Yeah. I've heard about too many of them," Chalice said somberly.

"So have I . . . but let's save that for another time."

"Write me a letter from Khe Sanh so I'll know what it's like before I get there."

"I will."

"Don't forget."

"I won't."

As Cowen's platoon started to move out, he turned back towards Chalice and said, "Hey man, see you at Khe Sanh."

"See you at Khe Sanh."

Kramer entered Echo Company's officers' hootch. Colonel Nash, Major Lucas, and most of the battalion's platoon commanders were already seated. Kramer had heard rumors that the charges against Trippitt had been dropped for lack of evidence, and he wasn't surprised to see him there. In a few minutes everyone had arrived, and Nash began speaking:

"I guess we've all been expecting some news for a long time. We finally got it, but it's a lot different from what we expected. Practically every major city is under attack. Khe Sanh was nothing but a bloody cover-up. They just wanted to get enough of us in one place and keep us there while they tore the rest of this country apart. If we had the helicopters, we'd be out of here in two hours. As is, we'll pull out at dawn. *At dawn!* That means I want every man at the LZ before first light. We're gonna be fighting house to house, just like those World War II movies you all love so well. Things are pretty bad all over, but I think we drew the wildest card in the deck — Hue city. . . . Are there any questions?"

Hardly believing what he had heard, Kramer asked, "Sir, are they bombing it?"

This question surprised the other platoon commanders, and most of them turned towards Kramer. Nash was also surprised, but for another reason. As he answered the question, Nash wondered why Kramer had asked it. "I hope not, Lieutenant. It's the most beautiful city I've ever seen."

Kramer walked back to his company area in a daze. Luck, something he had always thought of it terms of curses, now seemed to be promising what he could never have really hoped for — too much to be doubted. It all seemed no more than a matter of time, while time rushed him towards it. The impossibility of what was happening prevented him from doubting its culmination in that final impossibility. 'I'll find her!' he thought to himself, not even considering the difficulties. It would happen. It had to happen. 'I'll find her and she won't be able to say no.'

There was little time before his men would go on watch. Kramer knew he had to tell them to get ready. "Ramirez!" he shouted, and somebody answered that they would get him. The rain had stopped. Roads lay atop some ammo boxes playing with his dog. Kramer started to walk towards Roads to tell him to leave the dog behind with somebody, knowing that this probably wasn't necessary. Suddenly he stopped short. Roads was smiling as he playfully teased the dog with a rag. He then picked up the dog and held it high above him. Kramer couldn't believe the expression on Roads's face, couldn't believe the affection he was showing for such a pathetic little mutt, and he thought to himself, 'You build a wall, shut off everything, feel safe; but then, for just a second, you let someone or something get through, and it all comes down.'

3. The Ancient City

Sheets of water cast prismed patterns against the glass. Kramer continued to stare at the helicopter window, unable to see beyond its translucence, knowing that soon it would hide the Imperial City. The helicopter landed with a settling motion upon a muddy field on the outskirts of Hue. The heavy monsoon rains and the clouds that were their source deadened the sun's light to a dull glare and hid all but a faint outline of what Kramer longed to see. He stood staring at this outline, not even bothering to arrange his platoon, saying to himself, 'I'll find her.'

Orders were being shouted, but by Ramirez. Kramer turned to see him swaggering among the men — using more words, possessing less self-assurance, but with as much pride as Tony 5 had ever displayed. Kramer glanced over his platoon. They stood with their backs towards the LZ, avoiding the stinging drops of water being whipped at them by the copter blades. They were his men. No longer did he try to belittle the sense of responsibility he felt towards them, or even the feeling of power they gave him. Now he could understand the risks men before him had taken, the desire of these men to command, to lead others in battle, so often with no other purpose than to kill and destroy, looking upon such opportunities as God-given privileges. Now, neither coveting nor shunning this privilege, Kramer understood. He stared at the hard faces of his men, again with pride; but for the first time with compassion, thinking, 'If only they had a cause . . . if not one to live for.'

The helicopters continued to arrive, leaving more and more Marines to surround the LZ. The men stood quietly in the rain, exhibiting no feelings of restlessness, faces blank and remarkably similar. If Chaplain Hindman had been there, he would have seen in these faces an unmistakable faith in God's will. General Westmoreland would have described them as evidence of the American soldier's unflinching willingness to fight for his country's honor. A politician would later have been able to stand before microphones and assure his constituents that he himself had witnessed the grim determination of their sons to protect the homes and families that

480

were constantly on their minds. If the men themselves had been asked what they were thinking, few would have been able to answer, would have been capable of expressing the confusion of their various thoughts, their sense of wonder at this awesome process that continued to sweep them along with it like so many twigs caught in a stretch of rapids — the sense of inevitability about all that had happened and would happen.

Colonel Nash ordered his men to move out as soon as the last chopper landed. He watched the battalion snake along the winding road in two columns. They were to meet up with some Arvins, a Black Panther battalion. Nash had been told by people who should know that they were the equal of any NVA battalion in South Vietnam. While continuously struggling to lift his boots from the deep layer of mud that covered the road, he became anxious to meet these Arvins; to see for himself.

Nash halted his men as soon as contact with the Arvins was made. He, Major Lucas, and a small party from Headquarters and Supply Company advanced between the two columns until they reached the edge of the city. A party of Arvins stood waiting for them. Nash had brought along Binh, one of the battalion's Kit Carson Scouts, to act as an interpreter. This proved unnecessary. The Arvin captain in charge of the party addressed the Marines in fluent English. His bearing, and also that of his men, impressed Nash. He became even more impressed as he was led to the battalion commander. The Arvins they passed along the way seemed far more disciplined and serious than any he had ever seen.

Two soldiers stood in front of the battalion commander's headquarters. Rain poured off their ponchos as they guarded five blindfolded Viet Cong prisoners who sat unprotected in the mud. As Nash entered the headquarters, an Arvin colonel greeted him in a cordial but dignified manner. He also spoke fluent English, and with the help of a map immediately began to brief Nash on what was happening within the city.

Soon another Arvin officer entered, followed by two enlisted men. The colonel explained to Nash that they were replacements. He then withdrew two rusty bayonets from a desk drawer and handed them to the officer. The colonel resumed the briefing as the two replacements were led out the door. Just as he finished, the replacements again entered — each of them holding in his outstretched hand a severed and still bleeding head. One of the heads had its eyes wide open and its mouth twisted as if caught in a scream. The face on the other head had a calm, stoic expression, this in perverse contrast to the sickened expression of the Arvin holding it by the hair. While the other replacement beamed proudly, the Arvin colonel looked coldly at the sickened replacement. Obviously embarrassed by him, he grabbed the bayonets away and ordered both men from his office.

Nash was more outraged than sickened by what he had seen. When the Arvin colonel turned to him for approval, he was met by Nash's seething glare. Only fazed for an instant, the Arvin colonel quickly returned this glare, saying neither as an apology nor an explanation, "It is better my men know what war is like before the shooting starts. They must be *hard!*"

This statement further enraged Nash, at the same time reminding him of his impotency to do anything about what had happened. Words tried to force their way between his lips, but the realization of their worthlessness caused him to do nothing more than turn his back abruptly upon the Arvin colonel and leave.

Outside, Nash saw the blood-stained trails in the mud where the two bodies had been dragged away. Now speaking for the first time, he expelled his rage on his own men, harshly ordering them to take the three remaining prisoners from the Arvins.

For seven days both the monsoon rains and the advance continued unceasingly. Through the poorer outskirts of the city, progress had been slow and costly, the fighting from house to house. Now all that had changed. In Saigon it was decided that Hue would not be recaptured by the blood of the advancing troops, but rather by the destruction of the city itself. Artillery and bombers were called in indiscriminately. The cold monsoon rains fell upon the bodies of Viet Cong soldiers and civilians that lay abandoned in the streets and beneath the rubble. The thrust northward quickened, still paid for in blood, but now mostly that of civilians who could neither flee nor find safety. The Marines no longer advanced upon a city, but instead upon its ruins.

It was a few minutes before dusk. Kramer stared cautiously out the window of what had once been a small store. Half of his platoon was across the street, as it had been all day. They could have advanced a little further; but now that his men on both sides of the street were protected from the rain, he ordered them to halt and set-in. The day, as those before it, had been long and exhausting.

Kramer looked towards the north. The buildings just ahead were little more than rubble. He could barely make out those behind them, still untouched. Kramer knew that by the time he reached these buildings, they too would be rubble. Since entering the city, his men had advanced constantly along the same street — sometimes behind the cover of tanks; more often without them. One half of the platoon at a time would dash through the ruins, then set-in and cover the advance of the other half as they passed them. Often, and not unexpectedly, a burst of machine gun

482

or rifle fire would send them sprawling for cover while dragging their dead and wounded with them. The firing would continue. If too intense, they called in artillery. If light enough, the firing would encourage them to charge and lose more men. Sometimes these charges would end with the Marines standing over the bodies of a few Viet Cong soldiers, but more often they would find nothing. In slow retreat, the Viet Cong knew when to abandon their positions. They'd set up again a few houses to the north. It was easy for the Marines to find out where. All they had to do was continue moving from building to building until another burst of rifle fire sent them sprawling to the ground.

Kramer stared out the window, trying to guess where the Viet Cong would place their first ambush of the next day. When the view before him blackened, he lay down, exhausted and hoping sleep would soon release his mind from the thoughts that now troubled him. For it was during these first few minutes of darkness that he always thought about Tuyen, realizing again the impossibility of ever finding her, wanting to look at her picture as he had done the night before they had arrived at Hue, glad he was able to keep himself from doing this. His coming to Hue, which had once seemed a chance for gaining the only thing he could ever remember wanting, had turned into an absurd joke. He wondered how he had ever deluded himself into thinking that he would find her. Hue, a city that had once seemed mystical, had now lost all of its mystery. He was there, yet Hue no longer existed. It was hard for Kramer to make himself believe that the ruins surrounding him could ever have been more than just rubble. His lips pursed into a grim smile. Hue too had become a joke. But he remembered with pain Tuyen's description of it, and finally the myth that it had arisen from the ground as a lotus flower. 'A lotus,' he thought, 'a lotus magically transformed into rubble.' With little sense of guilt, Kramer realized that he had helped transform it into rubble. The bitterness of his thoughts did not prevent him from appreciating the irony of what had happened. 'Why should Hue be any different?' he asked himself, realizing now that it was merely a city, and that no matter how beautiful it had once been, never was it anything more than the work of a destructive, brutal species that found it impossible to exist without destroying everything left behind by former generations, a species condemned to walk through the ruins of its ancestors. "The Ancient City," he repeated to himself, half laughing.

"Professor, cover that window." It was Roads's voice. From across the street, Kramer had radioed him to set-in for a while. Second Platoon was too far ahead of the rest of the battalion. They would have to wait for them to catch up. Chalice heard Roads placing his men in different parts of the house. It was very large and had once been elegant. They had found a Vietnamese family inside — a father, mother, grandmother, and three young daughters. Extremely nervous, the family had obsequiously offered the Marines what little food they had. In return, a few of the Marines had toyed with them. Roads stopped this immediately, then placed the family in one of the inner rooms for its own protection.

Supposedly watching for Viet Cong, Chalice instead stared at the body of a civilian only a few yards from the window. There was no odor, the cool monsoon rains still staving off decay. It was the body of a man, obviously having died while on his side. The corpse had somehow been turned on its back. Now both head and legs were off the ground in a grotesque attempt to roll itself into a ball. Chalice stared at the corpse as if it were an illusion. It seemed impossible that life, human life, could be reduced to something so absurd.

Finally, to avoid the sight of this corpse, Chalice raised his eyes to the rubble across the street. This too was disturbing. He wanted to explain it to himself, not as the result of some action, but rather of some process. To him, a paradox was not an explanation. Yet this was as far as his logic would take him — to the paradox of the human fear of change and the insatiability of human desires — both traits rooted in the struggle for survival, separately working towards it, yet combining to force conflict and destruction. This made sense. It explained things. But to Chalice, a paradox was a question, not an answer.

The sound of some furniture being scraped across the floor distracted him. The noise had come from the room where the Vietnamese family was being kept. At first nervous that they might be doing something, he realized from the muffled cries of one of the girls that it was they who were in danger. Chalice ran towards the room and burst through its door only to freeze, stunned beyond action. Four Marines, two of them from his own fire team, glanced back at him. While one of them kept the rest of the terrified family at gunpoint, two others held down the twelve-year-old girl, naked below the waist, for the remaining man as he tried to rape her.

"Get off!" Chalice thought he yelled, not realizing the words never passed his lips.

The men ignored Chalice as they continued trying to rape the girl. He lunged forward and smashed the stock of his blooker into the neck of the Marine on top of her. The man collapsed, but one of the others grabbed Chalice around the shoulders and threw him to the ground. Roads burst through the door and viciously kicked the man off Chalice. The

Marine Chalice had hit lay dazed on the floor while the other three dashed out of the room. Roads made no attempt to help the hysterically crying girl as she crawled over to her parents. He was too ashamed to look at anyone but Chalice.

"Professor, you all right?"

Chalice nodded his head, stunned far more by what he had seen than by what had happened to him.

Roads yelled for the man on the floor to get up. But he was still too groggy to move. Roads began kicking him until he finally managed to crawl out of the room. Chalice walked in a daze back to his window. One of the girl's attackers was casually sitting against the wall smoking a cigarette.

More in disbelief than anger, Chalice looked down at him and said, "You . . . worthless . . . sonofabitch."

"Take it easy, Sandman. She's just a Gook." In an instant, Chalice kicked him in the face. The Marine dived for Chalice's legs and pulled him to the ground. Again Roads appeared, quickly kicking the Marine senseless.

Roads walked away too enraged even to curse, while Chalice pulled himself up by the windowsill. As soon as the Marine gained his senses, he looked up at Chalice with hatred. Again Chalice saw the little girl and remembered the word "Sandman." He spit down at the Marine's face. The Marine struggled to get to his feet. Chalice pointed his blooker at him, saying calmly, "Go ahead. Give me an excuse." The Marine turned away, and Chalice again stared out the window, seeing nothing but his own thoughts, thinking about what had and could have happened, about what must be happening somewhere at that moment, about dreams and illusions and the costs of defending them.

Roads told Chalice to get his fire team ready to move out. Chalice did this immediately, glad to be leaving the house, knowing that soon he would be worrying about bullets instead of what he had just seen. Ramirez gathered his half of the platoon together. They stood watching from within the house as Kramer's half began their dash down the opposite side of the street. When Ramirez saw them finally take cover, he ordered his men to move out.

It was over fifty yards to the next standing building. As Chalice ran towards it, he, as well as the other men, felt helplessly vulnerable and longed to dive behind every piece of rubble along the way. Running breathlessly, the weight of his pack pushing him into the ground, Chalice waited for that inevitable burst of rifle fire that would send the men in the column sprawling. This time it never came.

Chalice sat with his back against the wall of the building, still trying to

485

catch his breath. The men on Kramer's side of the street were now doing the running. Chalice watched the last of them rush by. Soon it would again be his group's turn to run, to do the same thing they had been doing for over a week. The repetition did not bother them. It was good. Their fear was of the breaks in this repetition when a burst of rifle fire would catch them in the open, a burst like what they now heard as they rested.

Ramirez looked around the corner of the building and saw Kramer's men hopelessly strung out and pinned down by the continuing machine gun fire. Hearing Ramirez's description, Chalice knew exactly what would have to be done. Ramirez ordered Roads to circle his squad behind the Viet Cong machine gun.

Chalice's fire team went first, Rabbit at the point. Keeping low, the men moved quickly through the rubble, all the while hearing bursts from the Viet Cong machine gun. In a few minutes they were behind the building. Chalice looked back at Roads and was motioned towards the nearest wall. He took it upon himself to go first. The distance was a mere twenty yards, but as Chalice rushed towards the wall it seemed miles away and an inescapable burst of rifle fire a certainty. His legs refused to move fast enough. 'My pack!' he cursed to himself, suddenly realizing he'd forgotten to take it off. 'What am I *thinking. Run!* RUN!'

Finally reaching the wall, he collapsed against it, barely able to signal the rest of his fire team to join him. Chalice watched the faces of the men rushing towards him, reminded of what his own fear had been like. When his men reached the wall, they grouped dangerously close. He motioned for one of them to guard the corner and the other two to spread out. Roads's fire team had remained behind to cover them.

Chalice knew that whatever they were to do would have to be done fast. He and his men were at a disadvantage, and every second they remained where they were made their deaths more likely. Of the two windows on that side of the building, the nearest was closed and intact. The firing from inside continued in short bursts, causing Chalice and his men to flinch with each round. He motioned for the man in front of him to crawl under the open window and lob a grenade into the building. This man was the newest member of the squad and obviously nervous. Forgetting the nearest window was closed, he placed himself beneath it and pulled the pin on his grenade. Chalice scrambled frantically towards him, afraid of yelling and warning the Viet Cong inside, knowing that the grenade would probably bounce off the window, killing the Marine beneath it and himself. The man saw Chalice coming and became more nervous. Without knowing why, he handed the live grenade to Chalice who took it with both hands and an extreme sense of relief.

486

Chalice felt like waiting a few seconds just to calm himself. But a quick glance at Roads reminded him he had better hurry. He crawled cautiously towards the open window, the live grenade held tightly in his hand. He flinched each time the machine gun fired, but it was a chicom thrown from the window that he feared most. There was nowhere to run. Finally reaching the window, Chalice lay beneath it listening for sounds. Hearing none, he cautiously rose to his knees. His pack seemed trying to keep him off balance, but there was no time to remove it.

He raised the grenade, ready to release it, when he was stunned by a baby's cry from inside. So unexpected a sound left him both startled and confused. He almost rose to his feet before realizing the stupidity in doing so. Thoughts of what could have happened sickened him; but again the machine gun fired, reminding Chalice of the men pinned down by it and the urgency of what he was doing. Fearing for his own life, he raised his eye to the corner of the window, saw nothing but a bare wall. The sound of the machine gun was making him increasingly nervous. He had to do *something* . . . fast. Chalice squeezed his hand white around the grenade — it would be so easy. The arm holding the grenade dropped to his side.

Silently, he laid the barrel of his blooker upon the sill, then slowly moved his head inside the window. A group of civilians huddled in one corner stared terrified at him. Thinking about what could have happened, Chalice turned towards the other corner — but far too slowly. An exploding rifle muzzle kept him from ever seeing it. Fired from two feet away, the bullet entered just behind Chalice's ear, sending a large chunk of his forehead in the direction of the civilians. His body staggered back spastically and fell face down outside the window.

Roads ordered his men to open fire. Rabbit crawled under the window, a grenade in each hand. Roads halted the firing long enough for Rabbit to heave them inside. After throwing in two more grenades, Rabbit dived through the window. Roads fired a law through the closed window, then sprang through after it firing his rifle on automatic. Two Viet Cong lay dead beneath their machine gun. Without stopping, he rushed into the other room and found Rabbit standing over the body of another Viet Cong soldier. A child's cry caused them both to turn to the corner where some civilians lay in a pile, motionless and bleeding. The adults on top were dead, riddled with shrapnel. Beneath them lay a half-dozen children, gasping for breath but none seriously wounded. Roads called for a corpsman, and was then told what he already knew: Chalice was dead.

For some reason his men scattered when Roads walked towards the body, one of them mumbling, "I guess that's it for the Sandman."

Chalice lay face down, legs apart and arms folded awkwardly beneath him. It was Roads who took off his pack and carried him into the building — leaving behind a crude death mask in the mud.

A small arc of the sun had already inched above the horizon. Though it was still dark within the building, Roads could see a dull gray light filtering through the rain. He was tired, the only man awake because he had last watch. In a few minutes he'd have to rouse his men, knowing they hadn't gotten much sleep either. He'd heard their whispers all night, along with constant scurrying sounds. Roads was glad to know he wasn't the only man in Vietnam who hadn't got used to the rats.

Alpha Squad had spent the night inside a heavily damaged building. The walls were thick; and if Roads had been able to read the Vietnamese words above what was left of the door, he would have known the building had formerly been a bank. What remained was too small to protect half a platoon from the rain, so Ramirez and the rest of the men had spent the night in a small building behind the bank. It was Ramirez that now walked towards him, ordering the men to put on their packs. Roads watched them sit up, their drowsy expressions turning to surly scowls. Most of them began fumbling with their packs only to delay having to put them on. Realizing he'd have to put on his own pack first, Roads did so and staggered to his feet.

"C'mon, get ready to move-out."

The men gathered at the door, already hunching their shoulders and complaining about their pack straps digging into them. They stared out at the cold rain, chilled by the thought of spending another day in it. Ramirez shouted the order, and with gasps and curses the men began dashing into the street.

Roads was at first relieved by the cold sensation of the rain. It woke his senses, made him feel like running. This feeling lasted only a few seconds, long enough for his mind to admit that he was not running to avoid the rain, but only through it. The men in front of him were not moving as fast as usual. Knowing that the tactic they were using made resting a matter of distance not time, Roads felt frustrated by the slower pace. He ordered it speeded up, but without effect. Roads was no more nervous than anyone else, but the first advance of the day was always the worst, there being too much time between it and the previous dusk to sit and worry. Once the first mad dash was finished, the rest no longer took courage. The fear was still there, but repetition gave each man the illusion of proving it could be done, at least by him.

But it *wasn't* being done. The pace became even slower, begging the Viet Cong to spring an ambush. Now Ramirez also shouted for the pace
488

to be increased. This order wasn't even relayed up to Roads. He himself had to yell it to the point man. Roads could see that they were approaching the intended cover. Now fairly sure they would make it, he relaxed slightly. By the time they did reach their cover, the column was practically at a walk. His men immediately dropped down behind pieces of rubble, and Roads himself desired to do the same thing. Instead, he ran forward, eyes searching furiously for Rabbit, his point man.

Roads was somewhat calmed by the sight of Rabbit's heaving chest as he tried to catch his breath. "What the fuck's wrong with you, *boy?* We were just asking for it."

Rabbit continued to breath heavily for a few seconds before gasping nothing more than the word, "Tired."

Roads couldn't understand it. Rabbit was his best man. A quick glance told him that the rest of his men were in the same condition. He'd seen men exhausted before, enough times to make it seem like a natural state. But this was something different. These men were beaten, a condition he was seeing for the first time since arriving in Vietnam. If it were just one or two men, that would be explainable, but not an entire squad.

"Roads!" Ramirez gasped and shouted at the same time. He staggered through the rubble, his eyes shifting nervously. "Roads!" he repeated as he dropped to his knees. "What are you trying to do, get us all killed?" Relieved to see that someone else was just as baffled as himself, Roads remained silent until Ramirez asked, "Who's your point man?"

"Rabbit. Figure that out."

Though Rabbit was only a few feet away, his chest still heaving, Ramirez shouted, "You want to get us all killed, everybody? Pull that again and I'll blow you away myself."

Roads sat calmly as he watched Ramirez scramble back down the column. The excitement Ramirez had shown made everything seem more real. Again Roads looked over his men, thinking to himself, 'Not like before. These new cocksuckers are worthless. . . . Get *me* killed with them.'

"Move-out!" Ramirez ordered as soon as he saw that Kramer's men were set-in.

Roads jumped to his feet, then watched his men stagger awkwardly to theirs. While looking at Rabbit, he warned them all, "*Motherfuckers,* you *better* haul ass."

Rabbit began running down the street. Soon the entire column was rushing after him. The pace was faster than before, but still dangerously slow. Roads was just about to order it quickened when a burst of rifle fire sent the men sprawling behind any piece of rubble large enough to cast a shadow.

"I'm hit. I'm hit," Rabbit moaned.

"Corpsman, up! Corpsman, up!" was shouted down the column.

Bullets still flying, Roads dashed forward. Seeing Rabbit out in the open trying to crawl behind some debris, Roads rushed over and dragged him to safety.

"My leg. My leg."

"No shit," Roads said calmly.

"Is it bad?" The flesh of Rabbit's shin was split open, and he was losing a lot of blood.

"Relax. Not bad unless you think a ticket home is bad."

Rabbit struggled to sit up and see, but Roads held him down. "Will they have to cut it off?" he moaned.

"Hell no! Relax so I can get this bandage on."

The Viet Cong snipers saw Kramer's men trying to circle behind them, and they trained their guns in that direction. Within minutes the corpsman had finished bandaging Rabbit's leg. Roads sat patiently behind the largest piece of rubble he could find, knowing that Rabbit couldn't be evacuated until Kramer's men had taken care of the snipers.

Kramer's men finally reached the Viet Cong position only to find it abandoned. Kramer radioed Ramirez, telling him to move back a hundred yards so Rabbit could be evacuated safely. Alpha remained set-in while Ramirez and the rest of the men followed Kramer's order. Now that Roads was lying motionless, the rain seemed colder and he began to shiver. Eyeing a small building twenty yards ahead, he decided to move his men into it.

Roads noticed Rabbit's pack just as the squad began to move out. Reaching down for it without stopping, he was almost yanked to the ground before he let go of the strap. His men rushed by him as he kneeled down to see what the pack was caught on. To his amazement, it wasn't caught on anything. He finally jerked it off the ground and staggered after his men. The pack felt as if it were filled with rocks. Astounded at its weight, Roads was able to make himself believe that it wasn't really that heavy — this being impossible.

Roads finally staggered into the building and dropped to his knees. When he looked up, the eyes of his men were focused upon him. No one was talking. Exhausted as he was, Roads became excited with the feeling that in a few seconds everything was going to make sense. He hurriedly threw off his own pack and grabbed Rabbit's. It *was* that heavy. In seconds he had the pack open, seeing what he knew he couldn't be seeing. Too astounded to be enraged, Roads staggered to his feet, a glistening ingot of solid gold in his hands. His men cowered before him as he spun around glaring at them.

"*You fucking idiots!*" he screamed. "You risked your lives for *this?*

490

His own fury surprised him. "*Fools!* You'd let them kill you for *this?*" He struggled under the weight of the ingot, but refused to let it drop. It was solid, smooth. He began to enjoy holding it, never before having felt anything so substantial to his senses. Roads glanced down at his own reflection within the brilliant shine of the metal. "Idiots," he repeated, this time more softly.

Roads ordered his men to empty their packs. He became increasingly angrier as he watched each man carry his ingot to the center of the room and lay it down. Glancing at their faces, he thought, Bet it was the *niggers.* Always hustling. Fools! Must have been the niggers!

By the time all the ingots were lying in the center of the floor, Roads had finally calmed down. What had happened was too unbelievable to be really irritating. His men remained silent, almost mournful. Roads dropped to his knees. He began stacking the ingots in a neat pyramid, at first doing so to taunt his men, but soon enjoying it as a game — feeling the weight of the ingots and watching his hands and face reflected in them. The men remained silent.

Roads looked up and saw a boy, no more than ten years old, standing on the other side of the pyramid. He hadn't noticed anybody else in the room, but now he also saw the boy's parents huddled in a corner. The boy stared at the gold not Roads, and his eyes were more round than slanted. Roads lifted the top ingot off the pyramid, holding it out to the boy. Hesitant at first, the boy suddenly reached for the ingot and wrapped both his hands around its center. Roads lowered his own hands slightly. When the boy felt the weight of the ingot, he released it and backed away.

Soon there were footsteps in the street. Ramirez yelled from outside, "Roads, c'mon, we gotta move up."

The men inside scrambled to their feet, but stopped in a line just short of the door. Seeing their wistful glances directed at the gold, Roads also looked back at it.

"C'mon, haul ass!" Ramirez yelled. The men rushed out the door.

Roads again glanced back. Pointing to himself, the gold, and then the boy, he said, "Me, souvenir, you. Buy yourself a candy bar." He turned and ran out the door. His men had gotten way ahead of him, the lighter packs helping their running. Exerting himself to catch up, Roads began to laugh, admitting more than thinking, 'That took balls. It *had* to be the niggers.'

It was early afternoon, and the battalion was within two hundred yards of the River of Perfumes. The knowledge of this evoked in Kramer's mind no more than the image of a quiet river flowing between piles of rubble. Though the river itself was still hidden, he stared at the Citadel on its opposite bank. High above its massive wall, Kramer could barely make out what he knew to be a Viet Cong flag hanging limply in the rain. He watched as the Skyraiders bombed the citadel. Clouds of dust rose from within even before he'd heard the rending screeches of the diving planes.

The Marines were to set-in by the river and wait for the Arvins to take the citadel. Because they were now within the range of some Viet Cong mortars, Kramer and his men were anxious to reach the river and dig in. Hearing little sniper fire as they advanced, the men hoped that the Viet Cong had already withdrawn across the river. The sounds of exploding mortars on both sides of their platoon told them that they were lucky they weren't drawing any fire, but also that their luck might change.

The sight of the river caused them to run faster, glad that Kramer was giving them little time to rest along the way. A mere fifty yards remained to be crossed when the mortars began to home in on them. Three rounds exploded in the street, leaving large craters between the two halves of the platoon. Skyraiders continued to bomb the citadel without being able to silence the mortars. The men began to run faster, knowing that when they reached the bank they could bury themselves beneath the rubble.

As Kramer ran, he watched the point man head for the remains of a house twenty yards from the bank. He'd already decided that his platoon would dig in behind what was left of its walls. When he saw the men at the front of the column reach it and dive to the ground, safety seemed close and real. Then a series of mortars shook the ground he was running on. A man fell, and another. Kramer jerked one of them to his feet and dragged him forward, knowing he was carrying a dead man. Another series of mortars sent him diving to the ground, feeling as if the earth were cracking around him. His men rushed by, one of them helping him raise the body. A mortar exploded to his side, knocking him ten yards into the street. Stumbling forward, he was too close to stop. A terrorizing burst of machine gun fire seemed to define his silhouette, seemed to prove that he was dead. Kramer continued to run, amazed that his legs were actually carrying him the last few yards.

It was only after he dropped to the ground next to Ramirez that his dazed mind allowed him to feel the pain that he should have been aware of all the while. The flesh of his forearm was shredded by shrapnel. Ramirez bandaged his arm while Kramer called out to his squad leaders for casualty reports. Only three men had been wounded, but all of them were dead. The news left Kramer somewhat sickened, but he had heard the same thing too many times before. Remembering the mortar that had exploded only a few yards away from him, he was reminded that he too should be dead; and the fact that he wasn't still amazed him. With his uninjured hand he fumbled to get a cigarette from the pack to his lips. A few rolled down his chest before he was able to do so. He fended off the rain with his head and quickly lit the cigarette — inhaling deeply. A smile came to his face as he looked down at his chest to check for leaks. Finally exhaling, he felt as if he were floating within a dream. The smoke disappeared quickly into the rain, proving that he wasn't dead. His lips moved silently: "The motherfuckers tried to kill me, but they missed again."

A corpsman ran over and began unwrapping Kramer's bandage. "You're gonna have a nice scar, Lieutenant."

"Thanks," Kramer replied, making no effort to hide his irritation.

The corpsman remained silent until he had finished rebandaging the wound. "I guess you better get to the rear and have a doctor look at it, sir."

The idea of leaving his men behind bothered Kramer. "I'll wait till morning."

"I don't think you ought to, Lieutenant."

"I haven't got much choice."

"Maybe you *should* go now," Ramirez suggested. He then added almost apologetically, "I can handle this platoon as good as you can, Lieutenant."

"I guess you can," Kramer answered as he looked up at Ramirez. "Make sure the men are all dug in. I'll check myself in a few minutes."

Kramer called battalion to find out where he could locate a doctor. They gave him the coordinates of a supply point, and told him to wait a half hour to be sure he didn't meet any advancing Marines. Kramer checked his map and determined that the supply point was over a mile to the rear. He handed the map to Ramirez without insulting him with directions about how the platoon should be run. After checking to see that his men were all dug in, he started for the supply point.

The rain had been constant and heavy since the battalion had arrived at Hue, but it had never come down harder than now. Kramer stared at the sky, feeling as if he were gazing up at a clear day from the bottom of the ocean. He could see no farther than twenty yards, and guided himself by walking along the edge of the street. It was covered by six inches of rushing water, and only the relative absence of rubble made him sure that he was following it. The street to the supply point was two blocks to his left. He turned towards it long before he had to. Finally seeing two Marines carrying a stretcher, he knew he was going in the right direction. It was then that he realized this wound was his third, and that he would be sent back to the States immediately. The idea shocked him. He had never wanted or been able to picture himself going home. Even thoughts about what he had been through, the knowledge that nothing had changed and it had all been for nothing, even these thoughts left him less disappointed than he thought they should. His inability to get himself killed seemed ironically amusing, but he was also conscious of a pathetic degree of ineptitude in even this failure.

Kramer suddenly realized that since the second time he'd been with Tuyen, he hadn't even thought about killing himself. Watching his boots plow through the water, all he really saw was a proud, sad face. No longer did his thoughts amuse him. His survival had been his failure. He tried to convince himself that she was to blame, but finally had to admit that she was an excuse not a reason. He again thought about how he had deluded himself into believing that he would somehow find her; now with bitterness instead of disbelief. No longer was his wound something that had prevented his own suicide, but rather something that would irrevocably separate him from her. Whatever thoughts were in his mind, her sad, beautiful face remained before him and he didn't have to force himself to admit that he was still in love with her. Going home was no longer an ironic, amusing joke. It was something both final and tragic.

Despite the rain, he could see other Marines making their way to the supply point, a place he now dreaded to reach. His steps slowed and men began to pass him. Wounded helped wounded, longing to reach this place where they would be able to rest and find help. Kramer wanted to stop walking, thinking that the only dream that had ever really meant anything to him had become and would always be nothing more than a cruel joke. But it seemed only right that this should happen — no other ending being possible.

The rain beat harshly against his face. He was oblivious to it. Rain — something that had once been able to torture him, had once been an added and final torture — now had no effect on him. Then suddenly, for the first time in weeks, he became aware of it — not through his senses, but through his thoughts. He couldn't see very far. It was raining. He should be cold. He was cold. He should feel it against his face. He did. The rain was mocking him. His body, yes. Yet at the same time it was something comforting to his mind — proof of his own, of man's impotence, an argument for the meaninglessness of each step he took, an abnegation of all guilt that proved his own pathetic innocence.

Calmed without being comforted, Kramer continued walking. A whining, pain-filled voice drew his stare from the street. Three Marines were directly in front of him. The man in the middle was supported on the

494

shoulders of the other two, and he talked nervously in an attempt to relieve his mind from the pain of a wounded leg. The false bravery of his whining voice irritated Kramer. He wanted to distance himself from it. His steps quickened as he passed the three Marines. Almost out of the voice's range, he heard it say, "God! Look at that Buddha. I wish I had my camera."

Kramer continued to walk, his mind giving no significance to these words. But suddenly he froze. For a few seconds he tried to make himself begin walking again, knowing that this was impossible. Finally, he turned. Before him stood a form too huge to be obscured by the rain — a stone Buddha, facing towards the south. Kramer tried to tell himself that it must be one of hundreds within the city, at the same time hoping that it was the one Tuyen had described. His eyes searched the rain for the dragons, and it was almost with relief that he failed to see them. Still, he began to circle the Buddha, wanting to prove to himself for the last time that the dream was dead. He walked along the near side of the square and came upon nothing but rubble. Satisfied and yet thwarted, he continued to walk. Then he saw it, the severed head of a huge bronze dragon.

The dream was again alive. His steps quickened, and on the next side he saw the huge, terrifying form of another dragon. No longer could he hope to deceive himself, and he mumbled audibly, "The Square of the Four Dragons." On two corners where there had once been houses, he had seen only rubble. Kramer walked slowly to the third corner, and again he found rubble. Once more he walked along a side of the square. His eyes searched through the rain hoping to see a house, the window where she had waited for the dawn. Suddenly it was before him. A wounded Marine hobbled by as Kramer stood motionless in front of it. He began walking slowly towards the house, stepping over the remains of a stone wall. The house itself seemed almost untouched. Much of the glass remained in the windows. He approached the huge wooden door, afraid that it would soon reveal no one or a stranger.

Kramer hesitated for a few seconds, then tapped the butt of his rifle against the door. There was no answer. He knocked harder, again and again until a feeble, tear-choked voice called out, "All dead, Go away. All dead." Kramer slowly pushed the door open. The walls were pockmarked with bullet holes. In the middle of the floor sat an old woman, legs folded in front of her, rocking back and forth with her arms wrapped tightly across her chest. Her tear-reddened face looked up at him in a mute plea to be left alone. He walked towards her slowly. She turned her head away and began to cry, still rocking back and forth, pleading, "Go away. All dead. Go away." He stared down at her, wanting to leave, thinking how cruel it was that she had been allowed to live long enough to endure such grief, knowing that he was a part of this grief.

"Tuyen?" he said to her. She merely continued to sob. Kramer dropped to his knees and asked again, "Tuyen?"

"All dead. All dead."

These words sickened Kramer, though he knew she probably hadn't understood him. He kneeled helpless for a few seconds before remembering Tuyen's picture. Nervously, he took it out. The photograph was damp but unharmed.

Barely looking at it himself, he held the picture in front of her. "Tuyen?" She turned her head away while tightening the grasp of her arms around herself. Kramer forced her to take the photograph. She drew it close to her feeble eyes before looking up at him with a pathetic stare that could have meant a thousand different things. "*Dep lam,*" she said weakly.

Kramer kept repeating these words as if by doing so he would be able to understand them. "Tuyen?" he finally asked, but she refused to answer him.

Again he forced her to look at the picture. She merely repeated, "*Dep lam.*"

Kramer gently took back the photograph. Slow steps led him to the door. Without looking back, he closed it behind him. He no longer remembered or cared where the supply point was, but some Marines passed by and he followed them. Viciously forcing his boots through the ankle-deep water, he repeated, "*Dep lam. Dep lam.*" Unconsciously his steps quickened as he continued repeating these two meaningless words. He began to pass other Marines, not caring that they could hear him mumbling — wanting to run like a little boy, too drained to do so. His steps finally slowed. A Vietnamese with his arm in a sling and wearing a Marine Corps uniform passed him. Suddenly Kramer realized it was Binh, one of the battalion's Kit Carson Scouts. Kramer rushed to him. When Binh felt someone grab his arm, he jerked it away in fear. For a second the realization that it was Kramer calmed him, but then he noticed the wild look on Kramer's face as he repeated, "*Dep lam, dep lam?*" Binh tried to break away. Kramer refused to release his arm. "*Dep lam!* What does it mean? *Dep lam?*"

"*Dep lam?*" Binh repeated.

"*Dep lam!*"

With a look of confusion, Binh finally answered, "*Dep lam,* very pretty, very pretty."

496

Kramer broke into a harsh laugh as he repeated, "Very pretty, very pretty." Binh backed away a few steps, then turned and quickly walked off. Kramer continued to laugh as he followed behind, repeating, "*Dep lam*, very pretty. *Dep lam*, very pretty."

Kramer stood somberly under the eave of a house while a thin sheet of rain fell directly in front of him from its roof. He was only dully aware of the painful throbbing in his arm. A few feet away, twenty plastic bags lay side by side in the road. There hadn't been more than a dozen when he'd first arrived, and he had watched as more and more bodies were brought over and fed into these bags.

A few uncovered corpses still lay out in the rain, and he heard somebody yell, "We're out of bags."

Somebody else yelled back, "Use ponchos."

More and more bodies were brought to the supply point, often three and four at a time, carried slowly, almost in procession, the rain turning this scene into a rite, a primitive mass funeral.

A truck pulled up, and the men began to load it with the bodies. At first they did so carefully, but soon they tired and began throwing the corpses carelessly upon the truck bed as if they were sacks of fertilizer.

Someone yelled, "Did you get more bags?"

"I *told* you to use ponchos!"

"I did. Do you want them put on the truck like that?"

"Hell, yeah!"

"What about the ones we haven't even got ponchos for?"

"*For God's sake*, get them *all* out of here!"

The corpses soon covered the truck bed. Someone yelled, "All you medivacs, get on the six-by." A wry smile crossed Kramer's lips when he heard this. He walked over to the truck and saw some of the men hesitating to board it. The more seriously wounded had already been medivacked by amtrack. The remainder were now being sent by truck to a safe landing zone on the outskirts of the city. Kramer had no qualms about boarding the truck, and he was actually amused by the faces of some of the men as they climbed on.

A voice behind him said, "One of you help this guy, will you?"

Kramer turned to see a man with a bandage over his eyes. He gripped the man's arm to help him board the truck. As he was lifted up, the bandaged man placed his hand down on the bed for balance; but when he felt the uncovered face of a corpse, he quickly drew it away. A Marine already aboard helped the man towards a seat against the side of the truck. While Kramer himself boarded it, he saw the bandaged man step on one of the corpses and ask, "God, did I hurt him?"

"No, you didn't hurt him," someone answered.

Kramer sat down next to the tailgate. He felt the six-by lurch forward and watched the mud fly from its wheels. After a quick glance back, he lowered his stare to the truck bed and mumbled, "To have come so close." He had intended these words to be tragic, but a wry smile crossed his lips as he realized there was no tragedy in them. He repeated them, but this time as if they signified a victory, and they did, a kind of victory, perhaps the only possible one, and he knew it.

The truck was already outside the city. What had taken weeks and lives to gain was now left behind in minutes. Once more he glanced back at the rain-obscured outline of Hue, and he thought, 'The Ancient City.' His stare returned to the bed of the truck and the bodies it contained. Many of them had already slid from beneath their ponchos.

'At least I'm alive,' he thought, not perceiving the irony of these words, or how absurd they would have seemed a few months earlier. Only later would he realize that in a place where anguish and suffering were everywhere, a country in which human life was cheap enough to be measured in body counts, only here had he been able to place a value upon his own life.

Suddenly something strange happened. There was a glare in his eyes. The rain had stopped. For the first time in weeks the sun appeared. He looked up. The clouds were drifting towards the mountains. Almost half the sky was a deep crystalline blue, the lucent gleam of which made it seem impossible that it hadn't always been like that. Again Kramer glanced back towards the city. It had seemed so important once, promised so much. Yet something had been fulfilled. He had been there as he had dreamed — only to see its ruins. What little difference it made now, now that he could accept what he had always known. However beautiful this Ancient City once had been, it was always merely the work of man, foredoomed to ruin by and despite him, fruit of his conceit, his enchanting delusions of creation — never destined to be anything more than sand in the wind.

A patch of color caught Kramer's eye. The street was deserted except for a little girl standing by the side of the road in a bright burgundy dress. She had a smile on her face, and she waved to him — to a strange man with a gun riding in a truck filled with corpses. Kramer smiled back at her, hoping that she saw, thinking, 'It's always the children that come out first after the rain.'